RISING
STORM

ALSO BY JESSICA DRAPER & RICHARD D. DRAPER:

Seventh Seal

RISING

THE SEVENTH SEAL EPIC CONTINUES

STORM

JESSICA DRAPER
RICHARD D. DRAPER

Covenant

Covenant Communications, Inc.

Published by Covenant Communications, Inc.
American Fork, Utah

Printed in Canada
First Printing: April 2004

11 10 09 08 07 06 05 04   10 9 8 7 6 5 4 3 2 1

ISBN 1-59156-440-9

AUTHORS' NOTE

The doctrines and prophecies cited in this book are real, but the events in the story bear no intentional resemblance to any current or future persons, institutions, or events (it's a novel, not a prediction). As for reality, whatever actually happens, God is in charge, and everything will come out right.

CHARACTERS

The Callatta Family

Tony: *father, unemployed video game designer*

Carmen: *mother, friend to Merry Galen*

Giovanni: *oldest son, missionary in Chile*

Donna: *oldest daughter, seeking job*

Lucrezia (Luc): *youngest daughter, high school student*

Gianni: *youngest son, toddler*

MedaGen Pharmaceuticals

Abbott: *chief executive officer*

Zelik: *chief operations officer*

Whittier: *junior board member*

Errol Humphrey: *middle manager*

Virginia Diamante: *singer, model, celebrity spokesperson*

Julian: *Virginia's assistant*

Garza and His Men

Andrea Garza: *self-appointed general*

Johann Brindermann: *second in command*

Jorge Serrey: *Garza's thug*

Ernesto: *Serrey's partner*

Chilean Characters

Manuel Zamora: *LDS major in army, head of antiterror squad*

Michael Angel (Mercury) Zamora: *Manuel's only son, member of the Santos Soldados*

Ulloa: *captain in Zamora's squad*

Guerra: *captain in Zamora's squad*

Yazna Vasquez: *LDS forensic coroner*

Quintana: *president of Chile*

Aguilera: *vice president of Chile*

Archuleta: *major in army*

Medina: *general in army*

Erwin O'Higgins: *Aguilera's secretary*

Olivares: *director of intelligence service*

ADDITIONAL CHARACTERS

THE SANTOS SOLDADOS

Salvatore (Dove, or Hasbídí) Nakai: *leader of Santos Soldados gang*

Calvin and Perro: *Dove's friends*

LAKE CREEK SAINTS

Brother J. H. Smith: *leader of group advocating self-defense*

Rock, Porter, and Orrin: *Brother Smith's sons*

Robert Sarkesian: *software company co-owner*

Jelisaveta Sarkesian: *Robert's daughter*

Bishop Newstead: *Callattas' bishop*

Bishop Calvin: *Brother Smith's bishop*

OTHER LATTER-DAY SAINTS

Meredith (Merry) Anthony Galen: *biochemist working on cure for AllSafe*

Raul Flisfisch: *Giovanni Callatta's Chilean mission companion*

Chinedu Ojukwu: *director of Church public relations*

Chisom: *Chinedu's son, missionary in Taiwan*

President Smith: *President of the Church*

Richard Rojas: *Associate President of the Church*

Elder Molina: *Apostle in South America*

Robert Nabil: *Apostle, former doctor and medical researcher*

Jack DuPris: *Area Authority Seventy for the Illinois-Iowa Area*

CHANNEL 8 NEWS

Anne O'Neal: *religion specialist*

Leon: *Anne's cameraman*

Monk: *producer*

Kim: *Monk's assistant*

Clara Cortez: *main anchor for news*

Rosa del Torres: *Latin America specialist*

OTHER CHARACTERS

Howard W. Garlick: *corrupt senator*

Rashi Janjalani (Brother Light): *leader of the Children of Light*

Sepphira: *Brother Light's ex-wife*

Tommy Gibbs: *top TV evangelist*

Samuel Lebaron: *anti-Mormon preacher*

Cosheen Hall: *wealthy environmental extremist*

Holly Cox: *LDS senator*

Cesar Augosto: *East Coast gangster*

Travell Capshaw: *West Coast gangster*

CHAPTER 1

"Look! The sky clears, just as the Prophet foretold!"

The six men looked up to see dark clouds shredding away in a sharp wind. In recent days unprecedented amounts of rain had poured onto the rock and sand of the Sudanese desert. Now, the brilliant azure of desert sky shone between the clouds as light from the setting sun broke through the tatters of water vapor and glinted off a metal platform beside the men.

The platform's original military insignias had been painted over with wandering script; the letters had run slightly in the heavy mist, but their hymn of vengeance and ruin remained legible.

"Now the unbelievers will face the wrath of the One True God," the man continued, grinning beneath the crimson scarf that wrapped his head and covered his face, leaving only his eyes to convey the hatred he felt for those who did not bow to his master's commands.

"Shut up and finish securing the platform while I program the guidance sequence," another man said, his fingers tapping out a complicated rhythm on the missile's control panel. "The unbelievers' eyes will clear as well. But they must see only the light of the star bringing destruction, not those who sent it."

None of them used names in addressing each other; none knew the others' names. Five of the men, the ones wearing red scarves, no longer even claimed their own names, regarding them as relics of a past, unenlightened life, before they had joined the Children of Light. As martyrs to the Great Cause, they had given up their individual identities to become members of the Hand of the Prophet, a select group dedicated to bringing destruction to all who worshipped false gods. In return, they would receive their rewards in paradise.

"They'll figure out where it came from soon enough," pointed out the man standing guard farther up the slope, where the ridge gave him a clear view of the lonely road winding through the desert. He hefted his rifle, pointing it at the sky defiantly. His eyes shone beneath the scarf that hid his face. "Let them see! Let them see who sends destruction upon them! Let them send their assassins to kill us! We shall rise from our gore in glory to trample them underfoot—"

"Those are not our orders," the man at the control panel said. "We are not called upon to die yet. Hold to the plan. We strike, and we vanish, leaving the glory to the One True God."

Another hooded figure, finishing his task of securing the launch pad, simply nodded.

The sixth man, standing apart from the rest, breathed a sigh of relief and glanced up at the clearing sky, then across the rocky, barren expanse of Sudan's desert hills toward the north. Martyrdom wasn't on his list of things to do that day—or any day. He had a name too, and an activist handle—Oak—though he hadn't bothered to tell either of them to his companions; he wore sunglasses and a broad-brimmed hat, rather than their red scarves. They'd shot him suspicious glances ever since they'd met in the muddy caravansary back in Wadi Halfa, but they'd accepted the cargo loaded on the trailer behind his late-model Land Rover without hesitation. They viewed him as an unbeliever—which he definitely was—and tolerated him only because their Prophet told them to cooperate with him. He viewed them as uneducated nutcases who in the new order of the world would disappear completely, along with the overpopulated conditions that produced them.

Religious fanatics, in Oak's opinion, were unreliable, untrustworthy, and reckless—quite unlike his own organization, which took extreme action only when the leaders of wasteful, polluting governments refused to listen to reason. Too many governments had willfully closed their eyes to the lethal stupidity of throwing Nature's perfectly balanced systems out of alignment. Well, it was time for Nature to reassert herself after years, decades—no centuries!—of abuse. One of the more virulent strains of the human virus infecting the world was about to get its first dose of antidote.

"It is ready!" The man at the control panel stepped back, brushing his hands nervously together. He looked at the unbeliever and pointed to the missile. "Now, Son of the Unclean, we need your codes."

"That's what I'm here for," Oak assured them. They stepped away from the weapon as he came near. *Probably trying to avoid superstitious contamination*, he thought scornfully. The world really would be a better place once they'd eliminated the surplus population, just like his leader, Cosheen Hall, said.

Crouching beside the missile's control pad, he flicked open his PDA, connecting to headquarters through the very spy satellites they feared. "Ready, Mother," he sent. A few seconds later, a code scrolled across the tiny screen, followed by, "Mother says thank you." He tapped the code into the console, watching the row of indicator lights flicker to green one after the other. A low hum filled the silent air as the preflight warm-up sequence began.

"And she's ready to fly," he told the others as he stood up, flicking the PDA closed with a flourish. "We're taking care of two polluters with one petition here, boys. Redress a deep insult to the earth, and punish all those nasty, unbelieving heretics out there for not listening to whatever your prophet said this week—"

A bullet in the throat interrupted his sentence. A second, through his skull, interrupted whatever thoughts he might have had about it. The Hand of the Prophet left the body lying where it fell. The man who pulled the trigger scooped up the remote communicator and piled into the Land Rover with the others. He paused just before closing the door to firmly press the Send button. The purr from the missile's systems deepened as the ignition sequence began.

The Land Rover's engine purred to life as well, and the heavy vehicle careened down the steep, rocky track, its tires throwing spatters of mud against the boulders. It had reached the third bend when a soft, feminine voice requested, "Please enter security code now."

"Security code?" The driver stared at the dashboard, where amid the standard readouts a yellow light began to flash.

"Second warning. Please enter security code now," the voice repeated calmly. The light darkened to scarlet.

"Infidel dog!" the driver exclaimed. "He booby-trapped the car!"

"Glory to the Prophet!" shouted the eager martyr. "We come to paradise!" He didn't bother to try to open the door—not that he had time to do it.

The light stopped blinking and glowed steady just long enough for a signal to reach the "security system" under the hood. With a single click of a relay, the engine exploded, throwing its occupants and a flying mess of metal shards and glass crystals into the air and across the muddy desert soil.

Behind the explosion, a thin, brilliant jet of fire blossomed into a roaring inferno. The missile's engine threw it into the atmosphere, where it became a tiny star arcing across the darkening desert sky. The lethal needle shape of the missile oriented smoothly onto its programmed trajectory, data from the GPS satellites coursing through its guidance system, ruby splatters highlighting the black-painted curse it carried toward its intended target and unsuspecting victims.

* * *

"Let's read what it says here: 'And the third angel sounded, and there fell a great star from heaven, burning as it were a lamp, and it fell upon the third part of the rivers, and upon the fountains of waters; and the name of the star is called Wormwood: and the third part of the waters became wormwood; and many men died of the waters, because they were made bitter.'" Tommy Gibbs looked up from the huge, gilded Bible on his equally huge, gilded lectern to gaze charismatically into the camera broadcasting his Sunday-morning worldwide sermon to an adoring audience of millions. "That's from Revelation, brothers and sisters. Revelation 8, verses 10 and 11. Now, many people have asked me what this means. How can a star be made of wood? And what do worms have to do with it?"

The Reverend Thomas Jefferson Gibbs had caught the growing millennial fever across the Christian world, combined it with movie-star looks and a dynamic speaking style, and rocketed to the top of his field. With a true showman's instinct, he realized that people wanted reassurance that they would be safe, that their enemies would suffer, and that Jesus would save anyone who said His name with enough hallelujahs behind it, regardless of how they lived their lives—and he delivered it all in spades. His weekly broadcasts regularly broke ratings records (much to the delight of Channel 8, the channel that sponsored him), his crusades pulled in record numbers of attendees, and his massive charity organization earned more money every week than many small countries.

He smiled, turning to face the side camera, leaning comfortably against the lectern. "Well, as you already figured out, John's using a symbol to tell us what Jesus wants us to know. 'Wormwood' is actually a little plant called artemisia, a desert herb. In the Bible, it's a symbol for bitter disaster." The split screen showed a small, scrubby plant growing out of sunbaked sand. "Just a little plant, a little, inedible plant, one that grows in dry places and can make people sick if they're desperate enough to try to eat it."

Gibbs straightened, gazing forward again, his expression becoming serious. "So what John is warning us about isn't a real star, a real meteor, but something poisonous, something called wormwood. It's not literally a poisonous herb, brothers and sisters, nor even just physical pollution. It's a carelessness of the things of Jesus, the source of everlasting life, the water welling up forever to eternal life. The wormwood that devastates a third of all the waters, the wormwood that kills, is poison in our spiritual lives, the poison of carelessness, the poison of faithlessness, the poison of pride."

He gestured emphatically, pulling his virtual congregation toward him as if to save them from a literal flood of bitter water. "Oh, my dear brothers, my dear sisters, be sure you don't have that poison, that wormwood, in your veins! Drink the waters of eternal life, receive the seal of Jesus on your forehead, as John urges us so strongly—not the mark of the beast on your head and hands.

"But what is Jesus' mark? Is it a streak or pattern of paint?" The split screen flickered, showing a group of pilgrims at the Ganges, red and ochre pilgrimage marks on their foreheads, then Indian women with intricate henna patterns on their palms. "No! Is it the swirling patterns of those who paint their faces with tattoos?" The scene changed, displaying Maoris with facial tattoos, then urban toughs sporting similar markings. "No! Is it special clothing, uniforms that show a false sign?" Now the pictures displayed uniforms of faith: Catholic priests in vestments, Muslim clerics in turbans and robes,

Mormons in dark suits filing into the Independence, Missouri, Conference Center. "No, a thousand times no! His mark is the joy in your face, the light of accepting Christ as your personal Jesus!"

Tommy Gibbs hit the lectern with a closed fist, while reaching out with the other hand in warning. "Of course we know that. But remember, many out there have the false mark, they've been struck by the falling star, Wormwood; they have deadly poison already running in their veins. Even if they look all right on the outside, inside they carry that deadly poison, that infection that kills. You must remember that poison isn't visible; it doesn't always show on the outside. Sure, sometimes it's obvious." The screen darkened into a clip of revelers at a neon-and-shadow bar, laughing, raising glasses, watching scantily clad dancers writhe in the lights. "But wormwood, that fallen star, that spiritual poison, is more insidious than that. It's all around you, poisoning the waters. Look around you. Look under the surface. So many profess to love Jesus, but they preach against Him. So many let that poison in, drink great gulps of it, and try to tell you that bitter is sweet. Turn away, tell them to go away, testify of Jesus to cast out the poison, to cleanse that water from wormwood—"

Viewers at home saw the screen change again, both sides this time. The flashing logo of a Channel 8 Emergency Alert replaced Tommy Gibbs's handsome face. Kathy, Channel 8's in-studio anchor, shuffled papers urgently, gazed into the camera with all the authority her blow-dried beauty could convey, and announced, "We interrupt this program to bring you a Channel 8 Emergency Report. Terrorists have blown up the Aswan High Dam in Egypt, and the Nile is flooding. Satellite footage from the International Space Station shows that a single, long-range missile was launched from Wadi Halfa in Sudan, 150 miles from Aswan . . ."

Only minutes before, a tiny star had risen high above the desert, turning at the apex of its flight to fall, shining like a meteor, down through the darkness, flashing over the dark waters of the swollen lake behind the dam. The streak of the man-made star revealed the dreadful mistake Tommy Gibbs had made in allegorizing Wormwood; it was all too real. Extreme weather in Sudan and Ethiopia, due to an unusually strong El Niño, had filled the reservoir beyond capacity already. The High Dam had been adequately engineered for hydroelectric production and holding back the Nile's normal flow, but under strain from the unprecedented high water, it was no match for the fury coiled in the missile's payload. A brilliant flash lit the dam and the lake, and a roaring wave crashed through the rent in the dam and down the Nile's ancient watercourse.

The water hit the riverbed, blasting through the Nile's channel in a wall of foaming rage, brushing aside the older Aswan Dam like so many sticks in a flood, blasting toward the First Cataract. The ancient, original site of the Philae temple complex, underwater since the construction of the dam, rose momentarily out of the floodwaters. At its modern site downstream, the new, smaller structures of the dock toppled under the rushing waters. The flood buried the island, wiping out all traces of modern civilization; but the huge, intricately carved walls of the temples withstood the onslaught of the current, leaving the ancient gods and goddesses smiling serenely above the foam.

Aswan, Elephantine Island, and Kitchener's Island fell beneath the wave. Wooden boats with their flapping, tearing sails smashed against ancient monuments. Villages of mud brick and modern cities—Kom Ombo, Edfu, Hierakonopolis, Esna—fell under the monster inundation, as the Nile's chained strength broke its shackles and escaped to the sea. At Luxor, the floodwaters blasted into the bend in the river and jumped the traditional course, spreading out across the city, fields, and desert beyond, flooding into the temple sites of Karnak, reaching toward Cairo.

Satellite channels crackled with pictures, words, bits and pieces like a mosaic that formed the whole of the disaster.

"The scene here is utter pandemonium," a shivering reporter shouted into his microphone. Behind him, water glistened under the stars, dark debris floating on its surface. Scattered lights shone weakly. Screams and wails sounded dimly in the distance. "Refugees have escaped to higher ground, above the floodwaters, but there are so many that didn't make it to safety. There was no warning, not this close to the dam. Hundreds are reported drowned, thousands homeless, but we don't have firm reports yet. Emergency services are virtually nonexistent, and all power is gone. So is Edfu." The camera focused on a drenched child, huddled in a blanket, utterly alone in the rush and bustle around her, her eyes staring emptily across the watery devastation.

With dawn's light, the extent of the devastation became visible. Every hilltop, every ridge, teemed with refugees, like ants from the perspective of the satellite images broadcast in Channel 8's coverage. People crowded together, crying out for their missing friends and family members; all of them were wet, some frantic, some staring in shock at the destruction. The cracked hull of a small boat had come to rest on the top of two temple walls, its shivering, praying crew of two waving frantically at the passing news helicopter. The body of an ox floated by on the current, a pair of sodden chickens huddled on its motionless side.

The scene shifted, showing turbid water spreading through the streets of Cairo. Slower now, an unstoppable flood rather than a tidal wave, the water glinted and lapped beneath walls and windows. Thick muck swirled beneath the surface; silt and mud washed into every crack and cranny.

"As you can see, Kathy," a relatively dry and composed reporter intoned, "the flooding has devastated Egypt along the entire length of the Nile. The human cost has been incredible. To give you a sense of the magnitude of the disaster, the latest census reports that 3,000 to 13,000 people per square mile lived between Aswan and Luxor. Literally millions are left homeless, and the situation is dire without clean drinking water. The floods have contaminated all sources of water with sewage and toxins from every source imaginable. Even as the country's overwhelmed emergency services and government try to handle the situation, blame is already starting to fly, with claims that the flooding is due to poor irrigation, mismanagement at the High Dam, and corruption at higher levels of government."

"Thousands of feddans of agricultural land are destroyed," an Egyptian official exclaimed through an interpreter. "Millions of people are killed, homeless. We have no good water. We have no food. Disease will spread. I have no time to talk!"

"We have reports that the Hand of the Prophet, an extremist group with ties to the Children of Light, has claimed responsibility," the reporter continued. Images of red-scarfed men riding jeeps through the streets of Manila, shooting rifles into the air, and celebrating their accomplishment accompanied his statement. "They claim that the One True God is punishing Egypt for persecuting his followers. A statement sent to Channel 8 reads in part, 'The Hand of the Prophet is raised against all unbelievers. Christianity and Islam are false religions. They now feel the wrath of the One True God. Their false gods cannot protect them.'

"Unconfirmed reports also implicate the Whole Earth Alliance, an extreme environmentalist group run by multimillionaire Cosheen Hall." Footage of the celebrating Children of Light was replaced by footage of WEA's rallies, middle- and upper-class students waving pro-environmentalist placards, throwing Molotov cocktails, and breaking windows in clashes with the police. "WEA has refused to issue a statement, and Cosheen Hall, the organization's leader, was not available for comment. Speaking on condition of anonymity, one WEA member stated that the Aswan Dam has been a blight on the Nile since its creation, and that Nature, quote, 'has broken free of her chains to bless the earth with her waters and fertility once again.' Whoever is responsible, ecoterrorists or followers of the One True God, from here it looks like the dam that Khrushchev once claimed would drown capitalism has instead drowned Egypt. This is Selim Abdullah, reporting from Cairo."

"Thank you, Selim," Kathy said. "Rescue and humanitarian efforts are already underway." New images scrolled beside her, cargo planes unloading bales of supplies, volunteers rushing to fill kits of basic necessities, row upon row of containers of emergency rations. The parade of plenty disappeared, however, into empty shelves and forlornly vacant loading docks, as the anchor continued, "However, the latest crisis comes at a time when resources are stretched thin. Disasters have struck all around the world, leaving thousands dead and tens of thousands homeless and in dire need of immediate aid."

Now, the background video displayed footage from the gigantic earthquake that had struck San Francisco, the Philippines, and eastern China only months earlier; thick plumes of volcanic smoke hanging over ash-coated towns and villages; huge sandstorms burying oases in the Sahara and Gobi deserts under gritty, amber dunes; refugees trudging through snow and mud, fleeing the civil wars ripping across northern China—all followed by a flurry of pictures showing overworked rescuers, exhausted aid workers, empty ration cartons, and torn cardboard boxes that once contained medicine.

Kathy frowned, careful not to furrow her delicately plucked brows. "Unfortunately, donations to the Red Cross, UNICEF, Doctors without Borders, Worldwide Relief Agency, and other premiere charities are at all-time lows."

* * *

Dear Chisom,

It is hard to believe that you are now halfway through your mission. When you left, the two years looked very long, especially for your mother, but she was saying just the other day that she can't believe how fast the time has passed. I am glad you are enjoying being a district leader and that the work in Taiwan is progressing well. Our work with the southern Chinese delegates has also progressed well. In spite of opposition from Philippine-based Rashi Janjalani (or, as he calls himself, "Brother Light") and his followers, the Children of Light, we are close to official recognition by the new government. When that happens, then, as you and I speculated, you will probably be part of the first wave of full-time LDS missionaries into mainland China. The Church is getting ever closer to fulfilling its mission to preach the gospel to every nation, kindred, tongue, and people, a condition that must be met before the Lord comes. The word from the Brethren is, however, that we must make haste, for His coming is upon us.

This brings me to your question about John the Revelator's statement that the seventh seal opens with a period of silence from the heavens for the space of about a half hour. I was amused by your comment that some of your contacts are saying they haven't "heard" it yet, asking you if it has happened. I believe it has, but not as some people speculate. There are many who, using Peter's statement that one thousand years is a day to God, translate the period as lasting twenty-one years. They feel that it represents the period in which the Lord will remove His Spirit from the earth such that even revelation will cease.

Though I can't argue on point of logic, I can theologically and apocalyptically. The Lord has not nor will He cease to lead His people during the last days. So that notion is out. Further, Wilford Woodruff, in the late nineteenth century, told the Saints that God was then withdrawing His Spirit and would continue to do so until the world (not the Church, but the wicked) would be left without it. As we look at the idea of heavenly silence in the scriptures, we find it does not represent a period in which revelation ceases but rather the pained silence of heaven just before the wrath of God is unleashed. We are now and have been living in that period of silence for some time. In Doctrine and Covenants 38, the Lord said that "the powers of darkness prevail upon the earth, among the children of men, in the presence of all the hosts of heaven—which causeth silence to reign, and all eternity is pained, and the angels are waiting the great command to reap down the earth, to gather the tares that they may be burned; and, behold, the enemy is combined." Thus, the period of pained silence opened about the time the Church was restored, and now that the judgments have commenced in earnest, it is nearly over. Doctrine and Covenants 88 tells us that the period of silence will end with the Second Coming. Then, the scripture says, though the enemy be combined, he will fail.

As you can see, the enemy is truly combined. Look at what some of his henchmen did to the Aswan Dam. The death toll of that man-made disaster is staggering and heartbreaking. Surely the plagues John the Revelator predicted in Revelation chapter 8 have commenced. Satan moves with power, and it is our task to oppose him with all we have. Therefore, work diligently while you still have time. We are certainly doing all we can on our side.

With love,
Your father,
Chinedu

* * *

Dust spurted up from the wheels as Dove's dirt bike hit the downside of a short hill. *Floods in Egypt—nothing but cracked soil and dying shrubs here in New Mexico*, he thought. *And if it doesn't rain soon, they'll all dry up and blow away.* Dove suppressed a cough, blaming the dust for the scratch in his lungs. The Navajo shepherd who owned the grazing permit on this strip of lonely mesa had already moved his sheep to marginally greener pastures. Without sheep, nothing moved in the desert landscape except for a spiral of scavenger birds slowly wheeling against the high cirrus clouds.

Up ahead, Mercury waved and pointed, turning his dirt bike toward the incongruous shape of a sixty-foot saguaro looming out of the scrub and rock. The transmission relay tower's mock-cactus disguise looked stupid enough under normal circumstances; the addition of a cluster of metallic spikes on one arm didn't help matters. Mercury pulled up at the foot of the monstrosity; Dove pulled up beside him. The grating whine of the dirt bikes' engines died into the background noise of the desert wind and the harsh cry of the birds.

"See?" Mercury asked, gesturing at the silver spikes wired and welded onto the green surface.

Dove looked at them, then looked at the dust-covered kid pointing at them. He knew Mercury only slightly. He was one of the border rats who hung around the edges of Abuelo's gang, not old enough to really be part of the gang, but useful for sending messages and running unimportant packages. That's why Dove had tagged him with the name Mercury—the messenger to the gods—which pleased the boy to no end. Getting a nickname meant he not only had caught Dove's attention but was worth paying attention to. He'd helped spy on Slick, one of General Garza's lapdogs sent from South America, and since then had transferred his allegiance to Dove's gang, the Santos Soldados, eagerly joining their efforts to defend Amexica against Garza's thugs. When Dove gently but firmly disarmed him ("Gotta be at least seventeen to pack heat in God's army" seemed to work for the moment—though Mercury would have done anything Dove asked him to, out of sheer hero worship), Mercury found other ways to contribute to the cause. Such as spotting new spikes on a fake saguaro.

"I see," Dove agreed, shading his eyes as he looked up at the cell booster. "I just don't know what I'm looking at." He glanced around, keeping watch on the rocky landscape. They'd come a long way out of the Santos' secure territory, beyond the Mormon settlements and into the badlands. The Santos had held off Garza's banditos closer to the border towns and the expanded territory of the Navajo Reservation. But out here anybody could travel the roads—especially roving gangs and Garza's thugs, or anybody armed well enough to fight them off. Dove had a gun under his jacket and a knife in his boot, but he'd rather spot trouble before it spotted him and get out of its way. This was a reconnaissance trip, not a raid.

"It's a tap," Mercury told him, rummaging in the saddle bag of his dirt bike. "Somebody's wired into the transmission circuits so they can use the digital network to send their own encrypted messages." He pulled out a tiny computer, neatly clicking the inputs into place and slinging it over his back as he started up the line of handholds along the side of the fake cactus.

"And you don't figure it's just Desert Bell doing some upgrade or repair?" Dove asked, grinning as the kid monkeyed his way up to the pirate installation.

"No," Mercury shrugged off the simple explanation, hooking his computer into the jerry-rigged antennas. "For one, it's a hack job. For two, it's caused an echo in the normal transmission channel."

"Which you know how?" Dove asked, watching the wheeling birds. Something in the ravine had caught their attention. *Maybe a sheep that died from thirst and the heat before the shepherd moved the rest of the flock?* thought Dove. Nothing else moved.

Mercury glanced down at Dove, a guilty grin stealing over his face. "Well, I noticed the noise on the wires when I was channel surfing, listening to the chatter coming over the border. It's not much, just a little hollow—like when somebody puts you on speaker. Not normal for a digitally encrypted network."

Dove looked up at him with raised eyebrows. "You listen to other peoples' phone conversations a lot? Or just when you get bored?"

"Not a lot," Mercury said defensively, not wanting Dove to think he was a Net peeper. "I first did it just to see if I could. It was a trip, hacking into an encrypted comm channel." He grinned, remembering the thrill when the random bleeps and static clarified into two voices. Sure, they'd just been talking about what brand of chili to buy, but the fact that he could hear it was exciting enough. Randomly surfing phone channels palled after a while—and his conscience bothered him—so he'd dropped it. Until now.

"I started scanning around again when I noticed that gang of banditos we jumped around Los Marias had hot-stuff phones on them. Started wondering if Garza had set up his own comm channels." Mercury gestured at the addition to the repeater tower. "Sure enough, I started getting hints that the transmission security wasn't all that secure anymore. But when I tried to listen to their conversations, I couldn't get through the additional level of encryption."

"So you went looking for towers that somebody had messed with?" Dove asked. "Why?"

"To make sure I was right—and because if I found it, I could piggy-back on their tap. Hack the hackers." Mercury clipped two more wires into the mess and leaned back, pleased. "Voilà! We're in now. Whatever Garza has to say to his goon boys, he's going to say to us too."

"Voilà?" Dove shook his head, grinning as he watched the kid skin back down the handholds. "French, now. Where you from, Mercury boy, with your southern Spanish and your Net-head hacker ways? How did a border rat like you get into broadband ghosting?"

Mercury shrugged casually. "The accent's 'cause I was born in Chile. Can't shake it, no matter how much I want to sound like the rest of you Amexicans." He followed Dove, as the Santos' leader walked toward the ravine, drawn by the crying birds.

After a few moments of quietly brushing through cheat grass, he laughed. "Man, you got that Navajo listening thing down, you know that? Ask a question, then wait till you get the whole answer. Okay. I grew up in Santiago—not out in the country, in the city. Went to a private Mormon school, and they had a really good computer lab. I got into it; programming just comes easy. When I was ten, they even called my parents in 'cause I figured out how to get into the grading database."

He waved his hands as Dove glanced at him. "No, I didn't change anything. Just wanted to see if I could. Not that it mattered with my dad. He was mad because I'd done it at all; it wasn't an 'honorable' thing for a Zamora to do."

"Zamora," Dove said, as Mercury stopped talking, busy reliving the confrontation. "As in Manuel Zamora, one of the leaders of the March Revolution?"

"Yeah, he and a bunch of officers mutinied and threw out the president-general." Despite his tense relationship with his father, Mercury still felt a rush of pride, which Dove could hear under his casual tone. "They made sure the new elections went through too, and they cleared out the old corrupt officials. Papa even pushed for an independent investigation board, to make sure the military didn't take over the civilian government again."

"Exciting times," Dove said. He'd read about the March Revolution and the cadre of military men who had worked with civilian reformers to topple the repressive government—defying the military death squads and risking their lives for their fellow citizens. Then they'd refused high appointments and had gone back to their military assignments as an example of the way the system should work. *That was about fifteen years ago, about the time Mercury was born. So the famous Zamora had a young wife with a baby on the way through the whole thing.* He eyed Mercury with new interest. "So how'd you end up out here?"

Mercury's smile faded; he kicked a stone out of the edge of the ravine. Beyond the next bend, the noise of the birds sounded loud and harsh. "After Mama died a couple years ago—cancer, nothing anybody could do—Papa was gone a lot, chasing rumors of rebel guerillas starting camps in the mountains. When he did come home, we usually fought about something I'd done in school, or something I hadn't done at home. He'd get all stone-faced military officer on me; I'd get mad and go do something, like hacking or graffiti, to get on his nerves—it was bad around home. Maria didn't know what to do with me; the school would call her, or the cops would, and she'd wring her hands and try to get me to promise not to do it again." Telling the story to Dove, and from the wiser perspective of nearly sixteen, Mercury felt his thirteen-year-old's antics looked considerably less smart and glamorous than they had at the time.

"Maria was your babysitter?" Dove asked. Still no movement except the flash of sun on black feathers, but he felt his nerves tighten.

"My nanny," Mercury admitted. "Mama's family had some money. Tía Anabel still does. She's lived up here for years now. Papa sent me up here to live with her, to see if a change of scenery and full-time adult supervision would help me shape up. Didn't work really well. He was worried too that the rebels would come after me to get at him."

"Anabel Soros." Dove put the name together, and shot Mercury a disbelieving look. Anabel Soros was one of the wealthiest—if not the wealthiest—woman in the border towns, living on the private ranch she'd bought to pursue her artistic leanings. She had enough money to pay Pizarro to make sure nobody bothered her, and she rarely ventured out of her luxurious private world. "You live with Señora Soros, in that house, and you're sneaking out to hang with a bunch of gangsters?"

Mercury rolled his eyes. "Hanging with gangsters instead of listening to Tía Anabel go on about her nerves and artistic temperament? No contest. Okay, at first, I was sneaking out to prove that I wasn't under Papa's thumb. And school here—man, boring beyond belief! Don't they have laws here against cruel and unusual punishment? So I hit the computer lab, then the street."

"Yeah, getting messed up or killed in a gang fight would prove plenty to your papa, teach him to get on with defending his country instead of spending all his time babying you." Dove had a hard time understanding the kid's attitude. Dove hadn't known his own father, who had gotten Dove's mother pregnant and then disappeared, but his memories of his grandfather held a sacred place in his heart. And while he had given his big brother, Benny, low-level trouble occasionally, he never would have outright defied his orders. It still hurt to think of Benny, who had been shot in a gun fight with Garza's agent Slick. Dove had emotionally adopted the Begay family, who took him in after the gunfight, and he saw the Santos as a pack of brothers, but he still longed for a real family of his own. "Your papa's a good man, even if he didn't know what to do with you after your mama died. You man enough to give him the respect and help he deserves?"

That struck Mercury's conscience—a conscience that had already pushed him to the same conclusion. "Enough to respect him," he said softly. "And I'm working on helping him."

"You've done a pretty good job helping us." Dove pretended to say it grudgingly as his boots hit the bottom of the ravine. "Especially if you can listen in on the General with that contraption." He grinned at Mercury and slapped his shoulder, releasing a puff of dust.

"Garza's got no secrets from us." Mercury grinned back, his shoulders squaring, then scrambled down the side of the ravine after Dove. "You know, I think Papa's suspecting that Garza might be behind the rebels too—like he sent Slick up here. Everybody knows the guy thinks he's Caesar or something, wanting to take over the world. And if it's him, Papa's fighting the same enemy that we are. So if the General's bandits did set up the patch tap, I'm already helping him."

"Could they set up the patch tap?" Dove asked, ducking back a step as a flock of birds exploded from the bush.

"No, it was actually pretty good—looked like a professional job," Mercury said. "Maybe they bribed somebody from Desert Bell to do it. Wonder how much they paid him."

"Seventy-five cents," Dove said, bending to look under the low-hanging branches.

"What?" Mercury stared at the back of Dove's jacket, the sword-bearing angel of the Santos' logo gazing steadily back at him. "How do you know that?"

"Because that's how much a .45 bullet costs." Dove unclipped the safety strap of the holster under the jacket. Beneath the bush, the eye sockets of a dead man in a Desert Bell uniform gaped as emptily as the hole in his forehead.

Mercury looked over Dove's shoulder and swallowed hard against nausea. He'd seen death before, but death plus carrion birds looked even grimmer.

Dove stood up, scanning the horizon with narrowed eyes. The silver needles of the General's parasite communication channel gleamed in the sun. "It was Garza, all right. That's how he pays his servants. He's coming—and he'll keep coming until he finishes what Slick started."

"But now we'll know his plans when he does," Mercury said softly, hefting the control box he held.

"Maybe it's a good thing you stiffed school to hang in the computer lab. Let's get out of here and set up a listening post." Dove coughed again, shaking his head against the faintness that followed. "Stupid dust. Now, can you conjure up some rain?"

"Oh, sure, I hack the comm system, and now I can crack into God's weather controls?" Mercury laughed, hiding his concern over Dove's cough. He'd heard Calvin trying to convince Dove to get Dr. Joe to look at him, but Dove kept saying it was just dust. "Might as well ask me to rebuild the Aswan Dam while I'm doing miracles!"

* * *

"At least there's a little good news about the missionaries in China, with all these heartbreaking stories about poor little kids and their houses getting washed away in the flood," Carmen Callatta said with a sigh. The sigh turned to a growl. "What kind of evil creeps would blow up a dam?"

"Dam creeps?" Donna, her eldest daughter, suggested with a grin.

Carmen couldn't help smiling at that, but her expression sobered as she turned away from the sad accounts of the Egyptian disaster playing endlessly on the television. Her gaze fell on the yarn and crochet hook dangling from their overstuffed craft basket. "I wonder if Egyptian kids need mittens."

"I doubt it." Donna scooped up eighteen-month-old Amber Evans, a girl they tended at Carmen's in-home day care, and gently detached a toy truck from the toddler's mouth. "Can you crochet a galabia?"

"Yeah, sure, I could make an Egyptian robe—in all my spare time." Carmen grabbed Amber's brother, Andrew, as he ran by, shedding the coat she'd just put on him. She caught the coat and the kid in a single sweeping motion, borne of long practice, and started the recoating process as a talking head on the TV screen droned out a list of the dead, injured, displaced, and dispossessed. A box in the left corner flashed, promising excellent rates on group casualty programs to protect investments against just such eventualities.

The four-year-old twins, Carly and Simon, ignored the flickering images and concentrated on building yet another ziggurat of blocks to knock down. Three-year-old Gianni, Carmen's youngest (and, she assured everyone who asked—or didn't—her last), contributed more to the demolition than the building, but he did his best to help. The twins' baby sister, Sarah, bubbled happily to herself on a blanket nearby, waving a captured block in the air.

Carmen cast a quick eye over the other three kids, automatically ascertaining their current status—*Condition green: nobody choking, crying, or trying to kill anyone*—before turning her attention back to her captured quarry. "Do we have to leave that on? Don't we have enough troubles in this world, without the idiot box using earthquakes and floods to sell extra insurance?"

"It's an assignment," Donna said, somewhat less adroitly stuffing Amber's chubby limbs into her little coat. The baby babbled happily, chewing on the increasingly soggy pom-poms at the ends of the hood's drawstrings. "Brother Kensai in my institute class says these are the last days and we're seeing signs of the times all over the place. He told us to watch the news for a week and count the number of prophecies fulfilled."

"Has he told you about being prepared and not fearing? Because, my girl, if we don't have these two squirmy wormies"—Carmen paused to nuzzle Andrew's tousled hair and tickle him—"in their coats and ready to toss in Mommy April's car when she drives by, we'll really see the end of the world!"

For once, however, April Evans, one of Carmen's first customers and definitely the most ambitiously driven, wasn't in a frantic hurry to stuff her babies into their car seats and blaze off into the distance when she arrived today. Instead, the usually decisive executive stood on Carmen's worn but well-vacuumed carpet, twisting the ends of her cashmere scarf between nervous fingers and looking vaguely toward the wall displaying the collected Callatta family portraits—a photo of Carmen and Tony smiling on their sealing day, Giovanni's missionary picture, Donna's senior portrait, a nice posed shot of Lucrezia, and an out-of-date but still adorable picture of baby Gianni—all arranged around a print of the San Diego temple.

"Nice, aren't they?" Carmen asked, smiling at her babies' photographed smiles. "Tony's brother Angelo took them. He's an artist too—or wants to be, as soon as he can get his own show at a gallery. 'Course, right now he's getting most of his artistic experience painting houses to pay for his photo supplies. Tony's been helping out; he's learned a lot more than he wanted to about house painting.

You should hear him growl about crown moldings! But that's the way life goes, isn't it? You just do the best you can, take care of your family and neighbors, and that's good enough."

"Yes, they're very nice." April smiled nervously, her hands still winding the scarf's soft folds back and forth. Her gaze rested distractedly on her son, who had run over the instant she had come in the door, coat still askew.

Andrew grinned up at her, holding out the macaroni necklace he'd created. "See?" Thinking he'd momentarily captured his mother's rare attention, he began chanting, "One! Two! Three! Four! Five! Seven—"

"Yes, that's very nice too," she interrupted—or tried to.

Andrew had no intention of relinquishing the stage, or her attention, quite so easily. He simply raised his voice and continued, with the omission of eleven, to thirteen—before Carmen caught his eye and placed a finger over her lips. He reluctantly lowered the volume then leaned against his mother's legs, still whispering numbers. Carmen gave him a high-five sign.

Donna hefted Amber on her hip and smiled at April. "Don't worry about the missed numbers—we learned one through twenty today, counting each macaroni on the string, see. Andy got it right until number six broke—that's when I realized he'd been naming them 'One,' 'Two,' and all." She laughed. "Quite a kid! Then he decided to test whether uncooked pasta tasted any good, which was the end of number eleven . . ." She trailed off, looking at April's tense shoulders and set expression.

Carmen had been watching April as well, and did some rapid figuring of her own. "But that's not what you're worried about. April, what's wrong? Are you okay, honey? Can I help?"

"Oh, Carmen," April began. She swallowed hard, and the words came out in a rush. "It's not that I don't trust you personally—you've been great, you and Donna, and the kids have learned so much, and they really like coming over, and I couldn't ask for a better day care—but with all the diseases going around and all the problems, I just couldn't stand it if the kids got sick, so I can't bring them over anymore. I'm sorry." The rush ended as quickly as it began, leaving her silently twisting her scarf again, her expression a mixture of apology, embarrassment, determination, and anger.

"What?" Donna exclaimed.

"It's the AllSafe thing, isn't it?" Carmen asked, glancing at Donna.

"Yes," April told them, squeezing Andrew's shoulder defensively. "Your family hasn't been immunized, and I just can't risk having Amber and Andrew in that kind of environment."

"But April, you know that President Rojas warned everybody against taking that vaccine!" Donna waved one hand emphatically, then hugged Amber as the baby started and looked worried. She lowered her voice several notches. "That vaccine's nothing but a time bomb, even if they're not admitting it. Merry found the evidence that proves it'll make you sick if you don't get a follow-up shot within a year, and there's no cure for the cure either! Don't tell me you've fallen for that slick, marketing cr—"

"Donna," Carmen interrupted firmly. "Watch your tone."

"Mom!" Donna protested, but swallowed her hot protest as Carmen gave her the Mother Evil Eye.

"I'm really sorry to hear that, April," Carmen said, turning her attention back to April. "And, even if Donna didn't say it diplomatically, AllSafe just isn't. Safe, I mean."

April's diffident nervousness faded as impatient, defensive anger replaced it. "It passed the FDA tests, Carmen. It's certified safe, by the entire government. Just watch the news. The people who made it know what they're doing—and it's worked, even on horrible diseases like AIDS. With all the bioterrorists lurking around the world, it's just crazy not to immunize the kids! President Rojas may be a perfectly fine General Authority, but he's no doctor. What does an ex-pilot know about cutting-edge medicine? What happens if terrorists strike our water supplies—our schools, like Senator Garlick said on *Straight Talk* last week? Would you want to see Gianni get sick—die, even—because you didn't get him immunized?"

"Even if that did happen—and I figure Senator Garlick's got his own irons in the political fire—it's better to see Gianni maybe get sick because I didn't get him immunized than to see him for sure get sick because I did," Carmen said. "And President Rojas is a lot more than an ex-pilot—he's a *prophet*. You know that, April—or you're supposed to. Don't you figure he gets his information about cutting-edge medicine from a source a lot more dependable than the company that's pushing to make everybody dependent on getting their boosters?"

"Elder Nabil's a surgeon," Donna pointed out. "He's an Apostle, and he knows medicine, and he's the one who believed Merry when she brought him the evidence she found in MedaGen's databases—"

April had clearly had her fill of the whole conversation; it hadn't gone the way she'd wanted it to. They should've understood, gracefully admitted she was right, and promised to get immunized immediately. It's not like it would cost them anything—with Tony out of a job, they could certainly qualify for government health care—but instead, they tossed President Rojas at her. As much of a hassle as finding a new day care center would be, it was better than leaving the kids with a couple of—fanatics! She glared at both of them, but Carmen's concerned expression made her swallow the nasty comments she'd been thinking. She didn't want to hurt Carmen's feelings. That made her even madder, at them and herself. She snatched Amber from Donna's arms. Startled, the little girl began to cry.

"Industrial espionage isn't exactly the most credible source," April snapped, latching onto the least personal argument that came to mind. She caught Andrew with her free hand and pulled him toward the door. "I'm sorry, I know she was a friend of yours, but you've got to admit that what she did was unethical. And what you're doing is just suicidal. You do what you have to, Carmen, but I'll tell you right now that I think you're wrong, and you're really going to regret it." She came to a sharp stop, regarding the doorknob that foiled her righteous retreat.

"Nothing like a closed door and two hands full of kids to mess up a perfectly good exit line," Carmen said, her eyes sparkling as she helpfully opened the door. The joke didn't go over well. Carmen sighed and followed April down the walkway, hefting Amber's diaper bag and Andrew's little backpack. She neatly settled Andrew in his car seat, ignoring the barbed looks that April, annoyed about needing her help, shot at her during the whole process.

She gave both kids good-bye kisses on the head and snugged them in firmly. Amber, as usual, cried and reached for Carmen, who stroked her cheek reassuringly and firmly closed the car door. She patted April's arm through the open car window. "You do what you need to do, April. No hard feelings. But I'll never regret following the prophet—and you won't either."

April just sniffed, blinking back tears as she shrugged off Carmen's hand, slammed the car into reverse, and roared off down the street.

"There goes about half of our babysitting business," Donna remarked from the doorway.

"And a couple of my favorite little people in the world," Carmen sighed, sending up a silent prayer for Amber and Andrew—and for their misguided parents.

By the time Tony got home four hours later, Carmen had sent plenty more pleas heavenward—for patience, for calm, and for a really big lottery win.

"Of course, it'd help with winning if we actually entered the lottery," she sighed, snipping the last of the gum out of Gianni's hair. Where Carly had found the gum was a puzzle for the ages, but she had happily shared it with the two boys. Fortunately, only Gianni had decided to run his gum-covered fingers through his hair.

"He looks like a miniature skinhead punk," Donna observed, laughing.

"Call your little brother a punk, huh?" Carmen ruffled Donna's hair affectionately. "You want fashionable haircuts, you ask Lucrezia. With me, you get the newest army barber."

"On a really bad day," Donna agreed.

"A really bad day," Carmen agreed back. It sure had been. The sound of the door opening distracted her from the knot in her stomach.

"Anybody home?" Tony called. "The hunter returns!"

The obnoxious ring of the oven alarm punctuated his announcement. "Hey, Daddy!" Donna shouted, blowing him a kiss as she walked into the kitchen to rescue dinner.

"Ah, it's the love of my life, the light of my eyes, and the father of my children," Carmen exclaimed, tossing Gianni to his daddy. "Here, you wrestle with them for a minute. I guess you've come home hungry, have you?"

Tony caught their newly buzzed boy, set him on the floor with a big kiss on the face, and met her mock scowl with waggling eyebrows. "You know me baby—I'm *always* hungry!" The animated eyebrows and light tone couldn't hide the tension in his face, though, or the discouraged shadows in his eyes. The hunter had returned empty-handed.

"It didn't come through, did it?" she asked, as Gianni raced off to join Donna in the kitchen.

"No," Tony said simply.

"They're idiots for not snapping you up as soon as you walked in the door." She thumped into Tony and hugged him, resting her head on his shoulder. A faint smell of paint and turpentine still clung to him, despite the shower he'd taken before heading off to yet another round of interviews. She noticed his suit jacket was getting worn too. Four years in the bishopric meant a lot of wear on a suit. She closed her eyes, leaning on Tony for a minute. He rubbed her shoulder, leaning on her too.

"What happened here?" he asked quietly.

"What didn't?" she returned, managing a grin at him. "Gum in Gianni's hair—"

"That explains the marines-have-landed look. Hate to say it, but you're not getting any better with those shears, sweetie."

"Simon got a black eye from a flying block." Her smile dissolved. "And April fired us."

"What?" Tony exclaimed, looking down at her.

"April's not bringing Andrew and Amber back because we're not vaccinated," Carmen told him. "She's concerned about them catching some crazy virus and figures she's got to get them on AllSafe or it'll be disaster—"

"If that woman—and her fool of a husband—could get their priorities in order for one second," Tony exploded, "and do the right thing instead of sacrificing it all for social climbing—"

"I know, I know—and Donna told her all about it too." Carmen squeezed him hard enough to stop his usual tirade about April's financial fetishes. "Such a mouth on that girl. Reminds me of you."

"Yeah, she's a fireball, all right. But I figure she takes after her mother. Bet you didn't let her get off without a few words," he said. *April's husband could do with a good chewing out too*, he thought. He had asked to be released from the elders quorum presidency so he could focus on building his plastic-surgery practice, telling Tony they didn't need home teachers anymore. *Like so many in the ward lately.*

Anybody with even half a crack in their testimony is flaking off like old paint. He grinned at the inadvertent painting simile, squeezed Carmen back, then ran a hand down his face, wiping away the irritation, reminding himself that it didn't pay to get mad about things he couldn't fix. With all the frustration he'd felt in the last few months, though, it was getting harder and harder to calm down sometimes.

He took a deep breath. "So we're down by half. I'll get Angelo to rustle up a couple more houses for next week. There's a company buying up old row houses downtown, turning them into condos for the gene whizzes working the bio revolution. Maybe they'll need painters."

"Maybe see if you can get four more houses," Carmen suggested.

"Four more?" he asked, looking at her. "What else happened?" He looked around reflexively, trying to spot the damage. His eye traveled over the usual semicontrolled chaos—toys strewn around, posters on the walls, crayons, papers—it all looked fine.

Carmen sighed this time. "Mike's decided to move to Temple View. He's only going to need us to tend Carly, Simon, and Sarah for a couple more weeks, until he closes the deal on selling his condo."

"It's a tough housing market right now," Tony pointed out, not wishing bad luck on Mike, but really not wanting to lose the extra income. "Maybe it'll take a while."

"Doesn't really matter." Carmen half smiled. She and Tony thought a lot alike. "I asked him about it, and he says he's going anyway. His sister's there already, so he'll move in with her until he can get another place. With Cheryl's life insurance, he really doesn't need to sell his condo to buy another house. He says he wants to get the kids somewhere safe, with all this craziness going on, and with so many Church members living around the San Diego temple, it just seems like a good place to go."

"Zion's gathering," Donna informed them, reappearing from the kitchen. The rich smell of baked rigatoni wafted through the door with her. "It's just like Brother Kensai said. We're in the last days."

"Oh, and we've had that going on all day too, with the TV jabbering." Carmen waved a hand at the screen, currently playing footage of exploding volcanoes in Italy, Alaska, Japan, and Oregon. The lava fountains and flows shone like earthbound fireworks against the black of the clouds billowing from the broken cones. "It's been floods in Egypt and volcanoes in Oregon and droughts in Africa and earthquakes shaking people out of their beds—like the one we got last week. Waves so big even the surfers have given up on them out at Venice Beach, typhoons ripping through the tropics, even worse stuff coming, if you believe all the predictions about changing wind patterns they're seeing up at the International Space Station. Donna's had the set on all day today, eight hours of disasters, with ads for cars, hamburgers, weight-loss programs, politicians, and AllSafe constantly running between. It's enough to make you lose your appetite."

"Not me," Tony assured her.

"Oh, right, you're always hungry," Carmen recalled, laughing.

Tony liked hearing that rich chuckle again. He shrugged, squeezing her. "And maybe we can hope for a really big earthquake around here too. Just think: we get out, buy some nice desert land on just this side of the Sierras, we're set—it'll all be beachfront property in a couple months!"

It was an old joke, but Carmen grinned and said good-naturedly, "Good plan. That's what we'll spend our lottery winnings on. You get to work on that, or paint enough houses tomorrow to get us some investment money, and I'll call the nearest real estate agent. We'll set up our own planned community just outside of Reno's little temple, gather a bunch of Mormons for a ward, and wait for the beaches to come to us."

"Sure thing," Tony agreed. "But can it wait until after dinner?"

"Oh, well, I guess so." Carmen shrugged nonchalantly, kissing his cheek. "Take off the jacket and tie, and we'll get the salad on."

Tony caught Donna and kissed her. "Hey, big girl."

"Hey. Don't worry, Daddy. It'll all come out all right." She returned the squeeze and let him go.

"Where's my little girl?" Tony asked from the coat closet door, loosening his tie.

"Lucrezia's studying with friends," Donna said. "Her friend Lupe's bringing her home after the mob goes for pizza. I swear, I never spent that much time studying for anything."

"Which explains your grades, right?" Carmen said.

"I'm doing fine now, Mom. I'll get a few more GEs out of the way at the community college then get into the teacher-ed program at a university when I've saved enough for tuition."

"Lupe's the redhead?" Tony asked, hanging up his coat.

"No, Lupe's the really skinny brunette, the one with the butterfly tattoo on her neck," Carmen corrected, dealing portions of fresh salad onto plates. She sighed. "I wish they'd always come here for their study sessions, but I guess they can't get into too much trouble at a pizza parlor."

Donna rolled her eyes. "Why? They're loud, and Lucrezia's taste in friends is iffy at best. I admit, I was a social bug, but at least my friends weren't dustheads."

"All the more reason to have them here," Carmen said. "Where I can keep an eye on them, and love them, and smack them if they need it. They're good-hearted kids. They just don't know what they've never been taught."

"That's what I love about you, sweetie," Tony said as he poured water into their glasses. "Everybody's a good heart."

"Well, maybe not everybody," Carmen snorted, glancing at the TV set to see Kathy's "hard news" seriousness go soft and shiny as she relinquished center stage to Garrett, another of Channel 8's resident personalities, for what seemed like the day's hundredth entertainment segment. MedaGen's spokesmodel, the currently blond Virginia Diamante, swished onto the set and, with a flourish of bare thigh, arranged herself in the guest's chair beside the immaculately groomed entertainment specialist.

Carmen reached for the Off button as a bulletin, running beneath the picture of suggestive celebrity banter, announced: "Government troops, led by General Garza, have pushed back rebel forces in Ecuador, with mounting casualties on both sides . . ."

CHAPTER 2

General Garza had established his base camp outside Bogotá, close enough to the city to take advantage of its power supplies and politicians, but far enough to discourage his elite corps of troops from mingling with the civilians in the city. Like Genghis Khan, he wanted to keep his warriors "pure," hardened and hungry, not softened by the decadent pleasures of city living—or the personal entanglements that might lead them to question his orders. The tight-knit complex of olive-drab buildings formed a neat grid, its boundaries delineated by the sharp edges of razor wire and the sharper beams of invisible motion-detector lasers. In plain sight, well-equipped sentries patrolled the perimeters and guarded the two gated entrances, screening all who came to negotiate, pay tribute, deliver status reports, or curry the General's favor, which an ever-increasing number of highly placed diplomats and military men did as the General extended his iron control over South and Central America. Befitting the hub of a military machine that spanned two continents, the square compound hummed with constant, purposeful activity.

The man responsible for the precision of that machine strode from the command center, punching up the latest news reports on his PDA. Johann Brindermann, second in command to General Garza, watched the news stories streaming in: the dam disaster and resultant floods had devastated Egypt; the death toll climbed continuously, disease now increasing the initial casualty count due to the raging waters themselves. A plume of pollution had moved out into the Mediterranean as well, poisonous silt from the most horrific inundation in the Nile's ages-old history. The need for fresh water, always scarce in that dry region, had taken on a new, dire significance. Rumors spread of new unrest brewing in an area so recently brought to a semblance of peace after decades of intifada and retaliation; this time, however, the war would be over water, rather than oil or ideology, a war with no diplomatic solution, one that could plunge the entire region into conflict.

Chaos. Brindermann closed his eyes for a brief moment, visions of burning, screaming, and pleading rising from his memory. He had been only a child when age-old religious and ethnic hatred had flared into life in Eastern Europe, unleashing monsters to ravage the countryside and cities alike, monsters that took the form of neighbors with enemy uniforms and blank, hate-filled stares. With the firm hand of totalitarianism removed, freedom had meant bloodshed, fire, and confusion. Gangs had taken over when militias and armies had disappeared; crime lords replaced field captains, and the vicious cycle of killing continued. Even as a child, Brindermann had recoiled at the senselessness, the mindless waste of it all. He had resolved then to fight for order—order by any means necessary. His rise through the ranks of the slowly coalescing military constellation of the European Union had been steady, if not spectacular; he requested the most difficult postings, the knottiest problems, the most chaotic supply lines, and he resolved them all, only to go on to the next post, leaving a well-trained staff and perfectly codified processes behind. He had no wish to draw attention to himself, just to gain the skills and knowledge that appealed to his practical, diamond-edged mind. Brindermann knew he was no Napoleon, no Caesar; his talent lay in administration, not in diplomacy or demagoguery. Thus, he had waited, fulfilling his administrative assignments, watching the world inch closer to the edge of total chaos, watching for exactly the right opportunity, the right leader, the one movement or person who had the characteristics he looked for, the will, ambition, and power necessary to crush chaos with the iron fist of absolute order—with Johann Brindermann's more than able assistance, of course.

General Andrea Cesar Garza had perfectly fulfilled his requirements. The terrorist-soldier (and would-be Napoleon) had suddenly appeared in Colombia, promising his aid to the beleaguered government forces in their losing battle against the drug cartels. They had laughed at first, disdaining this adventurer with his Italian-accented Spanish, quasi-military black leathers, and cocky, arrogant manner. The sniggers rapidly changed to gasps, however, when three weeks later he strode into the president's office and tossed the severed head of one of the cartels' primary leaders onto the piles of papers covering the presidential desk. The grisly thing rolled to a stop against an ornate pen holder, staring blindly at the top government officials gathered for a high-level meeting.

"A gift," Garza had said with a smile that would become famous for its charm—and its edge of nonchalant menace. "And a challenge. Can you do better? Because now you will have to—or die when this man's friends avenge him."

"Avenge him?" the president had exclaimed. "We had nothing to do with this!"

"But the cartels know you did." Garza's smile never wavered. "They believe you hired my people to help you against them. Will you deny it and meet their onslaught alone, or make their assumption correct and line up eleven more skulls beside this one?"

The debate had been heated but short. Faced on one side with certain death from the infuriated cartels—which had paid handsomely to keep the government's troops incompetent and innocuous—and on the other with undeniable, if unpredictable, lethal competence, the president had extended a special contract and official military commission to General Garza. He signed the order with the blood-smeared pen Garza handed him and stood staring at the mess on his desk as Garza strode out as decisively as he'd come in, sweeping the top military officials off in his wake. By the time the heads of eleven other cartel leaders had joined the first, three months later, the president had committed suicide, clearing the way for a new regime. Garza modestly refused the offered nomination in his place, directing the Senate to appoint an experienced politician who could bring Colombia out of years of internal strife, and indicating exactly which man he meant, the one who could ensure that the troops outside the capital—whose ranks now swelled with a surprising number of new recruits suspiciously similar to the disbanded drug-runners—would not be forced to step in to "maintain order" after the free election.

Thus, President Benitez, a mediocre military man but astute politician who had argued for Garza's appointment—and, whispers asserted, provided the General with access to the former president's office—ascended to the top of the civilian government of Colombia. General Garza pronounced himself overjoyed to serve the new president, and set about securing Colombia's new borders with a proactive zeal that President Benitez could only admire. When Garza appeared in Guatemala, offering to assist that country's government in putting down the insurgent factions in their own military, he brought a glowing letter of recommendation from President Benitez.

He also brought Johann Brindermann, who had flown to Colombia, leaving his former commission and post to offer his own services to the General. Brindermann's ice-steady stare, command of languages, extensive administrative résumé, and iron nerve impressed Garza. Brindermann had convinced the General that what destroyed the plans of previous conquerors—Alexander, Caesar, Hannibal—came down to a lack of able administration, an absence of overarching vision and the will to accomplish it. The Catholic Church had ruled medieval Europe not because of its dynamic leadership, but because of its all-pervasive bureaucracy and administrative control. The Communists, first in the old Soviet Union and then in China, had gathered the reins of control firmly, only to let them shred away as the leadership wavered and lost its central vision in the face of outside ideas and forces.

"You, sir, inspire men to fight and die for your cause, to expand and protect the borders of the empire," Brindermann had told him. "I cannot do that. I have not the fire, the charm, nor the interest. But I can train bureaucrats, security personnel, and intelligence officers to keep the conquered lands peaceful, productive—and orderly."

Garza had laughed disdainfully at the idea of a man lobbying to become a paper-pushing drone, but he had seen the cold and immovable determination in Brindermann's eyes. Brindermann imposed precision on Garza's collection of semiorganized factions—and spread his vision of inhuman efficiency throughout Garza's ever-growing military machine. From the beginning, Brindermann felt no personal devotion to the man himself. That had not changed with closer association; if anything, the gulf between the two men had widened, as

Garza's volatile, spontaneous style contrasted, and occasionally conflicted, with Brindermann's robotic reserve and precision. Garza was a means to an end—a powerful, unpredictable, and dangerous means, but an undeniably effective one. And perhaps, when the conquering was done, the end accomplished, the means would no longer be necessary. Visionary leaders, Brindermann reflected, were often even more inspiring dead than alive . . .

General Garza stood outside the command center, where several men had gathered beside a chicken-wire enclosure to watch a dogfight. Two dogs met in midair, jaws snapping, paws scrabbling with sharpened claws against thick hides, snarls filling the air as they strove for a solid hold. Brindermann walked around the far side of the cage, ignoring the combatants. Death and destruction on a far larger scale rolled in statistics and numbers across the tiny screen in his palm. He glanced up from the screen as he came to a halt beside the General.

For a few minutes, Garza's attention remained on the growing crowd of soldiers and their canine gladiators. He watched the men more than the dogs, sizing them up as their owners sized up each others' dogs. Garza finally turned his gaze on his lieutenant. "What have you got, Johann?"

"Latest reports on the Aswan Dam attack." Brindermann offered the PDA. He watched Garza read the summary statement and observed, "Maximum effect with minimum effort, including both casualties and material damages, and there is no solid evidence that the International Terrorism Courts can use to prosecute those responsible." The lack of proof didn't mean a lack of suspects. Claims of responsibility for the Aswan Dam disaster had poured in from almost every extremist group in the world, overwhelming the media outlets. Everyone from the Christian Liberation Army to the Militant League for Spelling Reform wanted to take credit for the strike—and experts on all sides had promptly dismissed their claims. Others, primarily environmentalist and anarchist groups, hadn't claimed responsibility but had approved of the results—from a safe moral distance, of course. The most likely suspects, the Children of Light, had gone on record to express their lukewarm disapproval with a thin statement condemning "unjustified" violence. Brindermann, along with every other intelligence agency in the world, already had a copy of the report outlining the composition of the equipment and body parts found in and around the hulk of the bombed-out Land Rover, including the dead men's hoods and a shredded prayer book published by the Children of Light. All that, however, was only circumstantial evidence, enough to tell the world to fear the more radical element of the Children of Light, but not enough to give a footing to prosecutors already hamstrung by strict rules of evidence for international terrorism trials. They had put their message across very clearly indeed, without exposing themselves to legal risk.

"Excellent strategy, excellent execution," said Brindermann. "Were they some of ours?"

Garza handed back the PDA and smiled at Brindermann's blandly inquiring look. Brindermann knew that Garza's plots and power stretched beyond his South American power base but had no idea just how far. His ignorance, which frustrated him terribly, played into Garza's hands. Keeping him in the dark kept him off balance just enough to ensure his continued loyalty.

"No, not ours." He shrugged, turning to applaud as the dogfight came to a bloody end. The victor's master flushed, pleased at attracting the General's attention, and saluted. "The strategy was good, but the equipment was better. Anyone could slip into Sudan—it's a choice slice of chaos since the civil war started—but not just anyone could get a state-of-the-art missile, or program it so exactly. I have some agents tracking the source of the missile and technical skills now. Such a contact will be useful."

"Unless that contact is one of Brother Light's brainwashed devotees, seeking salvation through spilling the blood of the infidels," Brindermann suggested. "He would be unlikely to offer us the same services."

"Even religious fanatics have their price," Garza assured him. "But in this case I think we won't have to match a heavenly reward. Have you heard the rumors of an American body found at the launch site?" He nodded at his lieutenant's sharp look. That rumor hadn't made it into the official report; it must've come from one of Garza's informants in Sudan. "Makes it more interesting, doesn't it? The Children of Light have the will and spirit to conquer, but not the technology—until now. Knowing who provided the Hand with fire from the sky will prove useful later, when we need access to weapons more effective than rifles and mines."

The howl of a wounded dog and the shouts of the bettors pierced the air. Garza smiled at Brindermann. "For now, we worry less about who destroyed the Aswan Dam and why they did it than how they got the tools to do it. And in the meantime, the more independent factors causing chaos, the better."

Brindermann smiled slightly, quoting, "Where chaos reigns, evil prospers."

"Do you imply that because I profit, I am evil?" Garza laughed, appreciating the barb. "What does that make you, Johann, with your lethal lust for order? An angel?"

"Simply efficient, sir," Brindermann said. "Unlike our current supply system. With the amounts of money and matériel we are bringing in, the original channels are no longer sufficient."

Garza waved off the impending avalanche of bureaucratic details. With Ecuador about to fall, the government of Belize accepting his offer of protection, and Chile ripe for conquest, who had time to think about housekeeping and political chores? Especially when there was a kink in his growing domination up north. His forces had met surprising resistance on the Mexico-U.S. border from a group of petty thugs and canny businessmen. They had exposed a former favorite as a blundering idiot—but Garza viewed a temporary defeat as a challenge, which he would overcome shortly. He had sent another team into Amexica, with better communications and stricter orders. This time, the General's agents wouldn't be so soft on the recalcitrant border dwellers—or their hired gangs of enforcers. The United States couldn't protect its southern skirts against a determined assault, and once he had breached the border, the real war would begin.

An elite squad led by Garza's new favorite came rumbling through the camp's gates. "Take care of it, Johann. Use your usual efficient methods."

Brindermann watched Garza lope across the packed dirt road, shouting an obscene greeting to the squad leader, an arrogant but undeniably effective rebel chief. The commandos trailed after him, yelling their own comments to the returning rebels. Garza stood out in the crowd, his charismatic confidence easily dominating the boil of soldiers, inspiring them with sheer personality as much as with promises of wealth and power.

They are wolves and sheep at once, Brindermann thought. *Vicious brutes to the weak, fawning dogs to the powerful.*

The German dismissed his derisive thoughts and returned to the command center to call his appointed mayor in Buenos Aires. "Round up four more opposition leaders, del Campo," he ordered, blowing through the man's nervous compliments. "And this time, get their confessions of resistance to the government on video before killing them. Written statements are not enough. People can see even when they can't read. Release the confessions—and send pieces of the traitors to cities in the provinces. Make it clear that the General will not stand for opposition. From anyone."

Del Campo's frantic assurances blathered in Brindermann's ear as he scanned the reports of his informants. A son reporting his father's deception as a double agent caught his eye; he smiled grimly as he scribbled an order for his agents to terminate them both. He signed two more termination orders, as well as the standard payment authorizations; Garza paid informants well, using financial incentive or deadly threats to turn people against their principles, governments, and each other.

Brindermann glanced up at the monitors displaying an endless stream of images from the international news services and noticed an example of their sterling work. He smiled as he broke the connection to Buenos Aires in the middle of del Campo's timid sign-off. Argentina had been flattened under the General's, or more precisely, Brindermann's, iron fist. Brindermann watched the ex-president being paraded through the streets—tried and convicted and on his way to execution. He had proved a particularly vocal and annoying opponent, trying to hold his executive privilege long after he had lost his grip on the reins of power. Brindermann's subtle pressure and network of spies had worn away the president's support at last, removing a minor thorn from Garza's side. The president's humiliating, and deadly, fall would please Garza too. For the General, it was not enough to win—someone else must lose.

* * *

"See, it's not that Switzerland won." Elder Raul Flisfisch waved his hands to emphasize the point for his ignorant Yankee companion. "It's that Italy lost."

"Italy lost," Elder Callatta repeated, turning a dark look on the shorter missionary. Giovanni Callatta didn't follow international soccer, but he was big and broad and had excellent eyebrows for scowling. "And that's good?"

"Right. And—" Elder Flisfisch, Giovanni's native companion, hesitated as he processed all the data: *Callatta, Italian name, glower. Did I just dis my companion's home-country soccer team?* But he instantly dismissed the idea. *He's an American, duh.* He laughed, punching Giovanni's arm. "Ha, Elder Gringo, got you there. Didn't fall for that one. Yeah, Italy lost, which means Switzerland goes up in the standings, which means Chile—"

Giovanni mostly tuned out the rest of Flisfisch's Theory of Football Relativity, letting his soccer-fanatic companion rattle on as they walked. He glanced around at the neighborhood where they were tracting. Modest but neat houses gradually gave way to larger dwellings, flower box blooms bright against the walls and windows. A group of school kids ran by, a tide of white shirts and never-ending energy. "Hey, gringo!" several boys shouted.

"Hey, *naranjas!*" Elder Callatta yelled back, grinning.

Calling them oranges didn't make a lot of sense, but they laughed and waved, happy at the big American's weak grip on Castellano; he'd quickly learned that Chilenos don't speak mere Spanish. Besides, if the kids like you, he figured, their parents were more likely to listen to you. The building they poured out of looked like a true cathedral school, gray and weathered on a street of refurbished, whitewashed mansions and chic shops, all closed and quiet in the sleepy afternoon sun.

Giovanni had just transferred to Santiago, and the capital was still new enough to be interesting. This neighborhood was a bit more upscale than the one they'd visited last week, and they weren't here to stay, just passing through. Most of the areas they worked in were middle class or lower—not slums, but not exactly what Giovanni was used to in suburban San Diego either. Downtown was a different story, with wide avenues and impressive public buildings, newly renovated after the March Revolution, the coup that put the current democratic government in place. La Moneda, the presidential palace, looked like it would fit into any European city.

Chile used to be called the England of South America, Giovanni remembered, a bit of cereal-box trivia he'd picked up before he started his mission. His first impression was that the entire downtown area was surprisingly clean and modern looking. *Or maybe not surprisingly*, he reflected. For the last few years, Chile had finally gotten a stable government after decades of military dictators, socialist rebels, and ineffective puppet politicians. The economy had stabilized too, with a slow but steadily growing technology and information sector to supplement the traditional mining and industrial exports. Or so his mom, Carmen, had told him in her last letter. She'd mentioned that Tony figured the increasing population of Mormons in the area hadn't hurt either; they had helped get some moral people into government and military positions. Whatever the reason, since he'd arrived, Giovanni had seen people even in lower-class areas who had more confidence and a better education, due in large part, he knew, to the Perpetual Education Fund. He had seen a brighter outlook for the future than he'd expected, given the dire reports coming out of most South American countries. Between the drug runners, the military coups, the rebels in the jungles, the natural disasters, and General Garza, who seemed to be taking over the entire continent, it was a wonder that everything hadn't fallen completely to pieces.

Of course, it seemed like dire reports came from everywhere these days—even back home, with dust-bowl conditions in the Midwest, volcanoes erupting in the Northwest, the decay of the Rust Belt, and the deepening divide between the richest and poorest members of society. Sure, some people had struck it unbelievably rich, but for many workers—even skilled ones like his dad—the bottom had fallen out of the economy. *Hopefully, the hard times will make people more teachable*, he thought.

Up ahead, the crowd of kids parted around a man leaning against a street lamp, his eyes darting from one side of the street to the other, his aimless fidgeting redolent of paranoid anxiety—or booze mixed with cheap meth. But that idea didn't go with the beautifully tailored suit, gaudy stickpin in the tie, sparkling cuff links, or neatly trimmed mustache and hair. He looked blankly at the children flowing around him, then his restless gaze focused on the two missionaries. He blinked, despair lifting slightly as the image blossomed in his hazy brain. He straightened, pulling away from the lamppost, then suddenly startled as he got a clearer look at the two dark-suited, official-looking men. Tearing his gaze away from Giovanni and Elder Flisfisch, he tried to walk nonchalantly away, abandoning his lamppost for the mouth of an alley between the high walls of two houses.

"Hey, where you going, Elder?" Elder Flisfisch asked, as Giovanni changed to an intercept course, heading for the same alley.

"I think we ought to talk to that guy," Giovanni told him. In Giovanni's mind, the man was either in trouble or had a guilty conscience, which might make him more receptive to a message about repentance and forgiveness. Whichever, he was worth talking to.

"Some druggie? Why?" The shorter missionary shook his head. "Listen, you got us talking to enough crazy people already, with that guy trying to tell us that Brigham Young said the Virgin of Guadalupe was an alien—and that other loco, the one who asked if Mormons use peyote."

"Hey, Ignacio at least knew who Brigham Young was, and his wife's really been touched during the last two discussions," Giovanni pointed out. "Besides, this guy—what makes you think he's crazy or stoned? He may just be sad." Giovanni's long legs carried him swiftly across the street. The man had disappeared into the alley. His sharply tailored, freshly creased suit didn't fit with the initial impression of a loiterer on the street. And why had they made him so nervous?

"So we need to talk to all the sad drunks?" Elder Flisfisch waved his hands helplessly as his companion showed no signs of stopping. "He wants to talk, he'll wait for us. Come on, Callatta. We're supposed to be talking to people who want to talk to us."

Elder Callatta wasn't afraid to start a conversation with anybody, which was good; the downside was that he would start a conversation with *anybody*. Especially anybody who caught his attention because they did not want to get involved with Mormons. Elder Flisfisch gave up and closed the distance between himself and his companion to the short few steps the mission rules prescribed, but he kept up the protests. "What is it with you? If they run, you gotta follow them?"

Giovanni grinned back at him. "Yeah, something like that. I'd just like to talk to him."

They had come up to the mouth of the gloomy alley. A brilliant crimson spray of flowers spilled out of a bracketed flower box above them.

"Looks like that guy wants to talk to him too," Elder Flisfisch said, his voice suddenly much quieter.

Another man had intercepted their target, a much shabbier, leaner one, with a desperate look. He sprang out of the shadows, rasping an order to stop, though the worn leather blackjack swinging from his hand already spoke volumes. The sad man started back, staring wild-eyed at the mugger, his hands coming up defensively.

"Please, no! I didn't tell, I wasn't the one—" he pleaded. "Arturo, he said—"

"Arturo? Another viper? You better tell, tell fast—" The mugger's hissed orders stopped abruptly as he stared back, equally wide-eyed, not at his intended victim but over his tailored shoulder at the six-foot missionary bearing down on him.

"Stop!" Elder Callatta yelled.

The mugger didn't; neither did the missionary. The blackjack swung up and around, aiming at the sad man's head, and rebounded off Giovanni's shoulder. That shoulder promptly slammed into the mugger's chest, bringing him down in a sloppy football tackle. They hit the ground hard, rolling just once. When Giovanni came up on top, he stayed there; Carmen's lasagna and Tony's genes gave him plenty of mass to fight with, and he easily kept the smaller man pinned to the ground despite his writhing struggles.

"Okay, let it go, drop it, nobody has to get hurt here, including you," he said quickly, grabbing the wrist supporting the blackjack. After a token resistance, the blackjack dropped to the ground. "That's good, that's great, just calm down," Giovanni assured the mugger.

Elder Callatta glanced up at the white-faced man, who was leaning against the wall and regarding him with almost the same look of terror he'd given the original attacker. "It's okay, sir. Elder Flisfisch will be back with the police any minute. Everything will be fine."

Elder Flisfisch had indeed waited only long enough to see his companion pin the guy to the ground before shouting for the cara-bineros, tearing out of the alley to flag down the uniformed patrolman walking his slow beat through the upscale neighborhood. His frantic explanation elicited a burst of speed from the bored flatfoot, who ran up to the mouth of the alley.

"Here," Elder Flisfisch exclaimed. "That man was attacking the other—" There was Elder Callatta, still using the mugger as a cushion, but no sign of the erstwhile victim. "Where'd he go?"

"Took off," Giovanni said, as puzzled as Elder Flisfisch and the patrolman. He dragged his gaze from the empty depths of the alley and looked at them. "He stared at me like I was some kind of maniac, muttered something like, 'You're not them,' then took off. Didn't say anything else, just ran."

"A maniac," the carabinero repeated, his deadpan gaze sweeping over the rumpled missionary and flattened thief. "Can't imagine why he'd think that."

The mugger didn't have a chance to retreat as his target had; despite his dry comment, the patrolman didn't need an excuse to offer a long stay in the local jail to a shabby blackjack wielder.

"Permiso," he said to Giovanni, indicating that the big missionary could get up now.

Giovanni did, surrendering the mugger into official custody. The two missionaries watched the carabinero hustle the mugger away, ignoring the man's complaints about being tackled by an American bully. The pair turned the corner; the missionaries turned too, heading down the street in their original direction.

"Everybody says 'permiso' and 'adelante,' but nobody listens," he observed. He glanced at his companion as Elder Flisfisch fell in step with him. "So, if you said 'permiso' and hit somebody, could they get upset? After all, you asked permission, right?"

"You said nobody listens, so how would he know you'd said 'permiso'?" Elder Flisfisch sighed, then punched Giovanni's arm. "You're a real superman, eh? Laying some swat down on the bad dudes—"

"Smack," Giovanni corrected. "Laying some smack down on the bad dudes. And your accent in street English is worse than mine in Castellano."

"Whatever." Elder Flisfisch rolled his eyes. He had *that* Californianism down cold. "Callatta, we're saving souls, not wallets. How about being more careful?"

Giovanni grinned at him. "Sure thing. Superman's always careful. But we can't just let thugs go around beating people up, can we? If the good guys do nothing, the bad guys win, right?" He checked his watch. "Pick up your feet, Elder Flisfisch—we've got an appointment with Señora Llancando in fifteen minutes."

"We would have a half hour to get there if you hadn't decided to play superhero for a guy who didn't even want to be rescued," Flisfisch grumbled, as Giovanni set off at a lope.

Across the street, two more men opened the door of a restaurant (closed for business in the quiet siesta hour) whose large windows faced the street. They walked casually down the street, watching the missionaries fade into the distance. The sunlight glittered on their sunglasses and the stickpins decorating the ties perfectly coordinated with their dark, neatly tailored suits. In a bad light, you could almost mistake them for missionaries.

"One down from the Factory, and a local boy," the smaller observed.

"Bunch of interfering busybodies," the other growled.

When the missionaries turned the corner, the men strolled across the street and slipped into the alley.

A pale face peered at them from a shadowed doorway. The man Giovanni had rescued stepped out, not sure if he should feel relieved or terrified at the sight of the men. He straightened his tie, drawing himself up out of the panicked hunch that had drawn Giovanni's attention. "There you are. What took so long? For a second, I thought those boys were you—"

"Those boys are gone," Ernesto, the larger of the two, noted.

"Wouldn't it be embarrassing if you'd tried to hand it off to them? Or did you give it to that man you were talking to just now?" Serrey, the smaller one with a lazy stance, asked.

"Of course not—" their prey began defensively, but didn't get a chance to finish.

"Poor old Erwin, out all alone with nobody but missionaries to protect you from bandits," said Serrey.

"He's got us," Ernesto pointed out, putting a heavy arm around Erwin's nattily suited shoulders. "You believe we'd protect you, don't you, Erwin?"

Erwin jerked at the big thug's touch, but knew better than to pull away. He managed to inject a hint of superciliousness into his smile. "Of course I do. As long as I'm giving you what you pay for." He pulled from his pocket a disk that glittered with rainbow ripples in a stray shaft of sunlight. He thrust it at Serrey.

Serrey took the disk, turning it neatly between his fingers before it disappeared into his own jacket. "Did you get it all, Erwin?"

Erwin's smile melted like ice on a stove. "Would you two messenger boys know if I did or didn't have it all?"

"We wouldn't," Serrey admitted easily. "But we don't have to, 'cause the General will."

The mention of the General demolished Erwin's half-constructed armor of superiority. "No, I didn't get it all—but I got a lot of it." The last shreds of his arrogance boiled away under Ernesto's glower and Serrey's unwavering smile, leaving only panic in its place. He reached reflexively toward Serrey's sleeve, but flinched back at the last second, warned off by the deadness in that steady smile. His hand landed on Ernesto's arm. "Listen. Security's catching on. That wasn't a mugger. Those might not have been missionaries. I can't keep doing this. They're watching me!"

Ernesto impatiently shrugged off the man's manicured fingers. "Security." He spat, unimpressed.

"Nasty habit," Serrey observed, giving his partner a dark look. His sunny smile returned, however, as he beamed at Erwin. "But it's your lucky day."

"Yeah," Ernesto agreed, looking at Serrey sidelong. He reached into the bag he carried and brought out a paper-wrapped package and tossed it to Erwin. "It's your lucky day. The General's decided to retire you, with a bonus."

Erwin fumbled with the wire-reinforced ribbon wrapped around the packet. The sharp end of wire drove into his thumb, but greed won out over pain at the sight of four stacks of crisp new bills. A bonus, all right—double the usual fee!

"That's enough to buy a really nice black suit," Serrey noted.

Erwin gave him a sharp look. "Or anything else I want. Like a long vacation."

"At a nice resort with rules to keep out guys like us," Serrey finished Erwin's unspoken thought.

"Have a nice vacation," Ernesto growled, looming briefly over the informer before he walked slowly away.

"Aren't you going to ask me about the guy who tried to mug me?" Erwin asked, the golden glow of the money fading as the errand boys seemed to be leaving. "The carabineros have him. What if he talks? What if he gives them my name, tells them I'm passing information to the General? I told you security's after me! If he talks, if they hear about it, they'll put the pieces together. I'll get—fired!"

"Oh, don't be so pessimistic," Serrey urged, patting Erwin's shoulder lightly. "Keep looking on the bright side of life, Erwin. After all, you won't see us again. And have a nice rest of your life too."

Erwin stared after them as Ernesto paused just long enough for his partner to catch up with him. A thug and a freak, he thought, and a megalomaniac behind them. But hey, it wasn't like he was handing off state secrets; if the General wanted proof that the vice president was taking bribes on the side, let him have it, as long as the pay was good. And it was. He broke the package of bills in two, stowing one in each inside breast pocket. He pulled his phone out to make room then flicked the memory dial. "Vorhouse? Erwin. Bring the car to Las Palomas. I'm through with my meeting."

"There goes a very lucky guy," Ernesto said a quarter hour later, as the long, black sedan glided by the restaurant's windows.

"How so?" Serrey asked, gently closing the door of the pantry with a sigh. The General didn't need witnesses. Especially ones who happened to lsee Señor Erwin O'Higgins of the vice president's office meeting with a pair of the General's operatives.

"We didn't shoot him," Ernesto said, checking his pistol. Two rounds down. He replaced the clip and tucked the gun back into its holster under his arm.

"Not with bullets." Serrey opened the back door. "Not with bullets. Just a wire in a ribbon."

"So now what, Serrey?" Ernesto asked, slipping out of the restaurant and into the small, nondescript car parked in a parallel alley.

"We bring the disk to the General," Serrey reminded him, speaking slowly and carefully.

Ernesto snorted. "Now what with Erwin?" he clarified, starting the car.

Serrey leaned back in his seat, flipping the disk between his fingers, watching a flight of pigeons startled by the sudden engine noise throw themselves into the blue sky. "We watch the obituaries, chico. Just relax and watch the obituaries. There's nothing we need to do about Erwin now."

* * *

"But what can we do?" Escobedo demanded. "You come in here saying that there's a bandit crew coming in to shoot up the town, and you want us to stop them?" Escobedo, the borderlands' most successful tobacco merchant, sat at a long table in the back room of Carlito's, the town's single strip club and impromptu meeting place for the coterie of businessmen who actually ran the border towns. He glared at Dove.

"That's right," Dove said firmly, suppressing the cough. It was getting worse; so was the pain in his head. "But they're not bandits. They're General Garza's men, a reconnaissance party he's sending up here to intimidate us." His eyes swept across the faces of the other town leaders sitting around the long table. "You've all heard the news about the General taking over Central and South America. I told you myself that he'd sent Slick up here to open a hole he could attack through."

"You also said that they were parasites rather than predators, and if we stood up to them once, they'd back off," Señor Martel reminded him, his expression more speculative than challenging. Martel owned most of the Main Street businesses in the border towns, and a good half share of Sheriff Pizarro from years of bribes, political protection, and influence.

"And we did that," Pizarro pointed out, leaning his significant bulk back in a creaking chair.

"You mean the Santos did that. We," Dove corrected, gesturing at Calvin and Mercury beside him, Perro and the others at the door, "faced Slick down, and the General pulled back. For a few months. He hasn't give up though—and he doesn't believe we can stop a larger army. And he's right. We can't."

A low mutter rose from the town leaders around the table.

"But you can." Dove overrode the murmuring. "All of you, if you work together, can make this town—all of the border towns—too costly to make good targets for the General."

"And just how are we going to do that?" Escobedo sat back, folding his arms defiantly.

"The same way we did." All eyes turned to an unassuming man at the corner of the table. He stood, his quiet confidence drawing their attention. "My name is Dillon Yazzie. I've met some of you." He glanced at Pizarro, who glared back at him. "I am an officer with the Navajo Tribal Police—"

"And a Mormon," Martel said. "A bishop, I believe."

Bishop Yazzie nodded. "Right. And I've dealt with these guys in both capacities. The Mormons, as you may have heard, have a real talent for getting under the General's skin. He's sent raiders out to the Rez and to a few small towns between here and there trying to scare us." The bishop's teeth showed in a tight smile. "It hasn't worked."

"Because you got a gang protecting you," Escobedo snorted, nodding at the Santos.

"Because when they pulled up to torch our chapels, we walked out to meet them, and let them know that they didn't scare us," Bishop Yazzie corrected. "It's not a question of firepower—it's a question of not rolling over, of not being an easy target. Garza can't pull a full-on invasion yet; he's too busy with the fights in South America, and he doesn't want to draw the attention of the U.S. army. But if we let him start moving his guys in here, he'll have the foothold he needs when he does decide to invade."

"Invasions." The front legs of Pizarro's chair hit the boards. "That's all speculation and big talk, like the guys who sit in their recliners fighting the war in Ohalajishi. It has nothing to do with us."

"How's this for something to do with you?" Dove nodded at Mercury.

Mercury stepped forward, setting a recorder on the table and flicking it on. The voices of two men came clearly through the tiny speaker, trading coordinates and timeframes, speaking in a military-sounding code that did nothing to hide their intent: each party would arrive in a different town the following afternoon, and their orders were to occupy and pacify both towns quickly and completely, wreaking dire consequences to any uppity citizens.

"We picked up that phone conversation this morning," Dove informed the suddenly silent gathering. "And we've been out to see. There's a raiding party heading this way. And whether they're the first arm of an invasion or just a bunch of thugs who want you under their thumbs," he added for Pizarro's benefit, "you have to decide to fight for yourselves. I told you before that I'd stop Slick and the General, but you'd have to make sure he wouldn't be able to get back in."

"And when you did, we decided we would too." Martel stood, bringing one hand down hard on the table like a judge's gavel. "Shut up, Escobedo. Enough said. Sheriff, you will deputize all of us. Chavez, break out the guns."

Pizarro and Chavez grumbled, but knew better than to keep arguing—especially since the other men around the table stood as well, chiming in with plans and encouraging comments. Bishop Yazzie grinned across at Dove, giving him a quick nod as he moved to counsel Martel on what the Mormons at the reservation had done to push back the General's raiders.

"That's the best way to beat bandits," Perro said smugly.

"What is? An ambush?" Mercury asked, nodding toward Bishop Yazzie drawing town diagrams for Martel. He stowed the recorder in his pocket again, proud that he'd provided the warning—and the evidence that convinced them.

"No," Perro swatted the younger man's head, ruffling his hair. "Have somebody else do it!"

"I want a seat for this one though," Mercury said.

* * *

He got one. From the upper story of Carlito's, Mercury and Dove leaned their rifle barrels against the window sill as they watched six dusty jeeps roll into town, armed men bristling in every seat. The lead vehicle pulled to a stop in the square, in front of the dry fountain, the others ranged in a sloppy half circle behind it. Martel, sitting in the shade of the hotel's overhang with Bishop Yazzie and Sheriff Pizarro, watched them calmly.

One man, whose air of cocky authority marked him as commander in the absence of standard military markings, got out and walked toward the hotel's verandah. If the dead silence of the town's seemingly deserted streets made him nervous, he didn't show it. His men, less self-possessed, couldn't help glancing at the blank windows all around them.

Their leader stopped, spat on the road, and turned his sunglassed eyes on Martel. "Where's the man in charge?" he challenged. "I have something to say to him."

Martel stood, graceful and cool in a white suit. He took two steps forward, still in the verandah's shade, and said, "I'm here. Speak your piece."

"Speak my piece, huh?" The soldier looked him over, grinning nastily as he pulled out his pistol. "How's this for a piece?"

Martel looked pained. "Do you have something to say, or shall we just move to the next phase?"

"I've got this to say. This town and all of you belong to us now," the soldier growled, "and anybody who doesn't like it gets shot. There is no next phase. That a good enough piece for you?"

"I heard it," Martel shrugged, looking bored. "You've said your piece, and now I'll show you mine."

Pizarro lumbered to his feet as Garza's man sneered. "That all you've got?"

"No," Martel said calmly, nodding to Pizarro. The sheriff, with a speed surprising for his bulk, drew his sidearm, firing one warning shot that whined past the soldier's ear. Instantly, on the signal, every window on the square sprouted black gun barrels. Men stationed on rooftops stood up as well, covering the invaders from above. The doors of the shops opened, armed men spilling out of every building. They surrounded the jeeps, gun muzzles and hard glares equally unwavering. Every man in town—and several of the women as well—stood shoulder to shoulder with Dove's Santos and Mormons from the nearby towns. The soldiers stared in shock, their own aim wavering from target to target in the well-armed crowd.

"As you can see, we disagree with your statement that this town belongs to you," Martel informed the raiders' commander. "We belong to ourselves—and every citizen here will defend that freedom. Do you think you can shoot us all before you die yourselves?"

A long moment passed, ample time for Garza's men to evaluate their chances and come up with a discouraging result. They'd expected sheep; they found wolves. Would it be better to start shooting now, or go back to report their failure to the General? The leader didn't decide in time; his men made the decision for him, pulling their gun barrels down and raising their hands in surrender.

With a glare at the other soldiers, the commander retreated with as much dignity and menace as he could muster under the circumstances. "You're going to pay for this," he shouted, swinging into the jeep again.

"Perhaps," Martel conceded. "But we'll make sure that collecting the bill is very expensive. Be sure you tell your bosses that too."

The crowd opened on one side of the square, leaving one narrow corridor for the jeeps. Silence reigned until the rooster tail of dust was all that was visible of the would-be conquerors. Then the town erupted into wild cheers and a few celebratory gunshots. Martel let them cheer, but the look he traded with Bishop Yazzie showed he fully understood that this was just the beginning of a long fight.

* * *

"It was the shortest standoff in history!" Mercury informed Tía Anabel, as he acted out the entire episode in her beautifully appointed living room. "Voom—they drove out of there like the Santos were after them! We didn't even have to fire a shot."

"A shot," Anabel said faintly, waving a scented handkerchief before her face. The handkerchief, like the white eyelet dress and the girlish style of her long hair, was part of her image: the delicate artist. She watched her nephew with alarm. He looked a little like her sister, but he certainly didn't share his mother's poise and grace. No, instead, he got all of Isabel's wild-eyed revolutionary spirit, the same rebel streak that led her to marry a lowly army officer and then get involved in his dangerous fight against the government. Anabel had escaped Chile as soon as possible, leaving the violent world as far behind as possible. But now the violence had found her again—and Michael Angel, her own nephew, was part of it! As a favor for her dearly departed sister, she'd taken in Michael Angel—Michael, not Miguel, in honor of her and Isabel's American grandfather. She'd enrolled the boy in school, provided love and the computer equipment he asked for, and he'd decided to get mixed up in a gang war. The very thought made her heart flutter alarmingly.

"We've got a tap on their communications now, so we can listen in on the echo bounce," Mercury assured her. "We'll know exactly where they are and be able to stop them. All the towns around here will stick together; the bandits can't hit everywhere at once, so wherever they go, they'll find us waiting for them. And the bishops have been great too—I sure never thought of elders quorum as a militia!"

Anabel sat up, her eyes wide with alarm. "As a militia? From the Church?" She hadn't been to church in years, but she still considered herself Mormon—it was so much more exotic than being Catholic.

"Yeah." Mercury nodded. "They're getting in with the Santos, training in tactics and everything. We've set up a good practice ground out at SkateTown—"

"*We* have." Anabel held up an imperious hand. "Michael Angel, you're not yet sixteen years old. I cannot have you mixed up in a war! What would your father say?"

"That I should be careful, but that I was doing the right thing," Mercury told her. "Tia Ana, he's a soldier—and he's fighting the same enemy we are! I'll bet anything! The same rebel tactics, the same kind of nasty bioweapons, the whole thing—"

"Bioweapons?"

"Remember Dove stopped the gang that was bringing them into town?"

"Well yes, but that certainly doesn't mean you should be involved! Maybe your father should be the one responsible for your welfare," Anabel said. Her eyes filled with tears. "I'm sorry, Michael Angel, but I just can't take this. I just can't be responsible when you put yourself in danger. I know I looked the other way when you skipped school, but I thought it was just your sensitive temperament. It's just too dangerous here. You'll be much safer at home. I'll make the arrangements as soon as I can, and we'll get you back to your papa."

"But Tia Ana, listen—"

Smiling with relief that the decision was made, she kissed his forehead. "I love you, and I will miss you terribly. But you'll be happiest back home, sweetheart. Don't you worry about a thing; I'll get it all set up and arranged." With that, she disappeared in a swirl of white lace.

* * *

"I'll be safer at home. That's what she said." Mercury glumly tossed a handful of beans back into the sack. He slumped against the counter of the kitchen at Mama Rosa's, poking at the pantry supplies.

"Safer? Isn't your dad like a military guy or something?" Perro asked, looking up from the domino game laid out on the scarred table.

"Yeah, he's a major in the Chilean army—and now he's head of the special antiterror squad too," Mercury said.

"Sounds totally safe to me," Calvin muttered sarcastically, clicking down another domino. He'd challenged Perro to learn the game as a brain exercise and wasn't a bit pleased to find that Perro had a natural talent for it.

"I don't want to be safe—I want to be here!" Mercury snapped back.

"Hey, chico, watch the tone. Don't go all Skywalker on us," Perro said.

Dove stood up, snagging a tortilla from the stack Franklin, Mama Rosa's owner and chef, had left momentarily unguarded, and caught Mercury with the other hand, pulling the younger boy away from the counter. "Come on. Let's check the phone bill," he suggested.

Mercury obediently fell into step with his noble leader. Instead of staying in the small room that contained Mercury's computer listening post, after seeing that no new recordings had come in, Dove walked into the parking lot and sat on the hood of the Dogmobile, Perro's battered pride and joy. He leaned against the windshield, motioning for Mercury to settle as well, and closed his eyes.

"Hey, Dove, are you okay?" Mercury asked, concerned at the paleness under Dove's copper skin.

"You really think your dad's fighting Garza down there?" Dove ignored Mercury's question.

"Well, I think he thinks so," Mercury said. "It makes sense."

"Then he's going to run into bioweapons sooner or later," Dove said. "He'd better know that." He paused, then said softly, "I didn't know my father, but I think I'd miss him if I did. If he were worth knowing, and I wasn't with him."

"Well, sure you would. But you don't need to worry about that—you've got us, the Santos. And the Begays too; they act like you're one of theirs."

"It's not the same, though, is it?" Dove asked. "It's like me missing Benny—and my grandfather Nakai. Family's something serious. Like you missing your mama—and, even when it hurts, your papa."

"My papa." Mercury sighed. He'd been afraid that's what Dove was driving at. He bonked the back of his head against the windshield, staring at the stars in the thin desert air. "Yeah, I miss him. I don't miss fighting with him, but sometimes he'd look at me like I'd done something really great, and . . ." His father's face filled his memory, exasperated, angry, sad—and somewhere under there loving him no matter what stupid thing he'd pulled.

"Yeah," Dove agreed. He sat up, looking solemnly into Mercury's eyes. "So you go back home, and this time you straighten up and fly right. You've learned how to be a Santo Soldado, and now your papa needs you to help him fight the dark. You think you can do that?"

Hero worship and homesickness put a lump in Mercury's throat, which he ruthlessly swallowed to keep his voice from cracking as he said, "Yes, sir. I can do that." And he would too—as soon as Tía Anabel got around to making the arrangements. But he couldn't help hoping that it would take a while.

CHAPTER 3

"No, sir. The mission did not succeed." The image of the soldier's face wavered slightly, as sunspot activity interfered with the reception on the video phone.

"Why not?" General Garza asked, his eyes darkening dangerously. Before the man could answer, however, the General cut him off. "You have one more chance, Lopez. Do not disappoint me this time."

"Trouble?" Brindermann asked, watching the General pace.

"Yes, trouble." Garza stopped, a cynical smile crossing his face. "For me—but for them as well. The Mormons are becoming a hindrance in our northern campaign." Garza hadn't paid any attention to the Mormons at first; on the religion front, he'd concentrated on the traditional Catholic hierarchy of Latin America. He had rapidly learned his mistake, as Mormons seemingly sprang from the ground to oppose him.

Zamora was the worst of them, a military officer who not only refused bribes but whose men were so loyal that Garza hadn't been able to infiltrate his inner circle. Captain Ulloa, who wasn't even a Mormon himself, had nearly killed Serrey; the enforcer had made the mistake of offering a bribe for military arms too blatantly. Zamora, with his sharp sense of tactics, had come close to unmasking the rebels—and the General's guiding hand.

"Consistent of them," Brindermann said. The Mormons had been a hindrance in the southern campaign as well. They quit their jobs rather than collaborate with Brindermann's organization, and they refused to inform on each other or anyone else. Fortunately, they hadn't organized an armed resistance in South America as they apparently had in the Amexican borderlands. In fact, in the regions under Brindermann's control, they'd begun to gather into smaller communities of their own volition. That made them easier to watch—and spared him the effort of deporting them to prison camps. He flicked through the day's reports, noting that the Mormon community around the Bogotá temple had grown during the last week. As long as they stayed quiet, let them isolate themselves.

"Yes, very consistent," said Garza. "And unacceptable. What to do about the Mormons, the so-called Santos Soldados in the north—and our friend Major Zamora in Chile?"

"I may have the solution to both," said Brindermann. "His father may disregard threats to his own safety, but will he feel the same way about threats to his son?"

"You mean the one who escaped Serrey's clumsy assassination attempt—escaped all the way to the United States? Unfortunately, Zamora's Captain Ulloa found the cut brake lines on the boy's school bus before anything came of that solution."

"Yes, but I have reliable intelligence that the boy is coming back soon."

"Well then. El Jaguar now has new prey," Garza said.

"I am sure he will enjoy wounding Zamora, after the setbacks the major has dealt him," Brindermann said.

"The setbacks are over." Garza shrugged as he opened communication with El Jaguar, the guerilla commando in charge of destabilizing the Chilean government so Garza could sweep in and offer assistance. "Thanks to our new ally and the inside information he can supply, Major Zamora is about to find his winning streak coming to a sharp end."

* * *

"There's nothing we can do for him." Captain Ulloa looked up from the bloodied face of a farmer whose body lay sprawled in a mess of broken cornstalks. The captain gently laid the dead man's head down again, crossing himself reflexively as he rose to his feet again. "Maybe we should call a priest—"

"No." Major Zamora, the head of the expeditionary force, shook his head sadly as he noticed a white undershirt under the dead man's worn work denims. "He doesn't need a priest. He's taken care of the eternal side of things." *The one blessing of a temple in a war zone*, he thought. *Brother, rest in peace, until the Lord hears the blood of the Saints crying from the ground and executes His judgment against your murderers.* A less pious part of his mind added, *And I hope He uses me to do it, the sick dogs.*

Manuel Rafaelo Rivera Zamora held the rank of major in the Chilean army, first division. He was a decorated veteran of the March Revolution, which inaugurated Chile's most stable democratic government, and a month ago he had received a presidential commission to lead the antiterror forces trying to stop guerilla raids into Chilean territories. His sterling record in the March Revolution and his reputation as a loyal, intelligent, and capable officer prompted President Quintana's top general to recommend him; his complete lack of political ties cinched the appointment, which he had accepted reluctantly. He knew that the problem with being loyal and diligent was that people kept handing you messes that required even more loyalty and diligence. Thus far, his elite troops had met with less and less success. At the same time the rebels seemed much too comfortable carrying out raids this close to the capital. Zamora's team had never succeeded in capturing one of the rebels, even when they'd arrived at the scene of the attack with almost inhuman speed. Like they had at this one.

The call had come just before noon, a panicked woman crying into one of the cheap cell phones that Zamora's force had given to citizens to use in case of attack. She was now dead, along with three other women, six kids too small to go to school, and seven men who had made their living working these small fields. Zamora walked from house to house in the far end of the small farming village; the houses on the other side, closest to the road, were burning, set ablaze by the rebels to cover their retreat. His impassive face masked the sick hurt and anger welling inside him. He'd seen casualties before—the Revolution, while quick, had been anything but bloodless—but this was butchery. Every member of the small community was dead, killed as they tried to stand, run, or hide. This strike, wiping out all witnesses, hinted of an icy logic, a promise of inevitable defeat at the hands of a rational, and in Zamora's judgment, profoundly evil opponent.

There were at least four antigovernment or rebel groups claiming responsibility for the raids, spreading propaganda over the radio and Web, advocating everything from communism to unfettered capitalism to stone-age anarchy. Three of them were all electronic bluster; they took credit but didn't fire a shot. The real responsibility lay with a new group, the Chilean Liberation Movement, led by a man who styled himself El Jaguar. From Tierra Del Fuego to Antafagasta, El Jaguar's guerillas staged lightning raids aimed at isolated farming and mining communities. They burst out of the mountains, hit hard with a ruthless thoroughness, then evaporated back into the wilds of the Andes, leaving terror and blood behind them. The violence was nothing new in South America's long history of civil wars and terrorist activity, both against governments and on their behalf, but a whisper of insidious terror accompanied El Jaguar's raids: villages that refused to harbor or supply his rebel forces burned—or succumbed to a plague that wafted in from the jungle. Bullets and blades, terrible as they were, paled in comparison to this invisible, deadly enemy.

The random attacks and pervasive rumors of bioterror fed worries over economic collapse and dwindling income. A screaming mob waving Chilean flags paralyzed the downtown the month before, demanding that President Quintana do something drastic. The president, looking at an imminent call for new elections or, according to the vice president, an imminent violent overthrow, assured the nation that his administration had no intention of bowing under pressure from terrorists. He announced a dynamic, proactive response from the legitimate military, which meant commissioning a squad to track and destroy El Jaguar's guerillas, whoever they were and wherever they had come from.

Zamora had his own theories on those questions. He surveyed the ravaged cornfield, his eyes drawn to the twists of smoke rising lazily from the village beyond. "Seventeen dead, five orphans on their way back from school, and half a village burned to the ground. We arrived within fifteen minutes of the call to find bodies and burning ruins but no rebels. We've got El Jaguar suddenly springing up in areas that haven't had legitimate complaints since we tossed out Generalissimo Lopez. We've got antigovernment movements with vague agendas all over the free press and airwaves, when the government has already resolved long-standing disagreements with unions, mining interests, the Catholic Church, and the military. Right over those mountains, we've got General Garza blackmailing almost every government into giving him free rein and all the men and matériel he wants and, if the rumors are correct, using biological weapons to strike down his enemies—just like El Jaguar can seemingly do. And we've got President Quintana, who's refused General Garza's offer of assistance—twice." His gaze returned to Ulloa. "Does any of that sound suspicious to you?"

"Yes, sir," Ulloa agreed, "it pretty much all does." He fell into step behind his commanding officer.

"But here's the problem," he added a minute later. "We need proof to tie them together, someone who will tell the true story behind all the lies, but the lies are very convincing." He stopped to examine a dead man in a forest-camouflage quasi uniform. The red cat-head badge of El Jaguar's Chilean Liberation Movement had been sewn on his sleeve with crude stitches.

They knew the logo well, from graffiti scrawled across walls in blood here and in spray paint on Santiago's walls, from neatly printed letterhead in missives demanding the government's immediate abdication, and from the exclusive interview Channel 8's local representatives broadcast with El Jaguar. The interviewer, Rosa del Torres, described him as "charismatic and mysterious"; Zamora saw nothing but a romantically named figure in a black hood spouting dire threats against President Quintana's "occupying forces" and giving vague promises of safety to citizens who supported the *Liberacion*. When Rosa asked him about reports that the strikes were the work of the People's Democratic Army, a rival group spreading their own propaganda through Ecuador's war zone, El Jaguar promised that they would have proof, real proof, soon. And here it lay. This man wore a black hood along with his arm patch.

"That's a rebel guerilla, right down to the boots," Ulloa noted.

"Indeed," Zamora agreed, his voice dry. "Right down to his boots, and apparently surprised in a frontal attack by a farmer armed with nothing more than a pitchfork." The farmer in question lay close by, shot twice through the chest, presumably by the dead soldier's squad mates. "Surprising for an experienced guerilla. Especially when he and his comrades had so efficiently executed everyone else they encountered."

"Think it's a setup?" The captain glanced at his superior officer, wishing for the thousandth time that Major Zamora's famously calm expression were easier to read.

Zamora prodded the inert form with the toe of one boot. No wonder he had been surprised—how could he expect a pitchfork in the chest from someone on his own side? "Yes, but not for us."

A sudden flash lit the scene, bringing the muzzles of twelve automatic rifles to bear on a woman with a camera. Rosa del Torres lowered the camera to let it dangle from its neck strap, raised her hands dramatically, and gave the antiterror cadre a saucy smile. "Adelante, chicos. No threat here. You can put the guns away—or point them at the terrorists. How about you try protecting the citizens instead of threatening them? Or is the army playing its own game? Again?"

"Right on cue," Zamora muttered. Ulloa closed his eyes momentarily.

"Looks like you've come too late to save these innocents," Rosa noted. She looked pale, but her professional composure—aided by determined ambition—kept her voice steady as she gestured to the bodies that lay covered in shrouds, identified and documented.

"We came as soon as we got the call from a woman in the village," Ulloa informed her. The captain couldn't quite keep the defensiveness out of his voice.

"Did you?" The precision of the professional interviewer sharpened the question.

"Just as you did," Zamora said. "Who called you, Ms. del Torres?"

The reporter didn't flinch. "My sources," she shot back. "Whose identities I have the right to protect, even in the face of military threat. You and the president cannot disappear them, Major Zamora, or me. The people have the right to know the truth of what's going on out here."

"I'm sure you'll make sure there are no secrets left—excepting your own, of course." Zamora's eyes met hers steadily; after a silent duel of consciences, the reporter looked away. "You've seen what you came for, and what your informants wanted you to see. Be careful. Remember that the governments you despise—the ones who did disappear their enemies—also began as rebels who saw nothing wrong with killing civilians to make their political points."

Zamora turned to Ulloa. "Get her out of here. Gently. Find the other one too. Channel 8 never sends just one. And get copies of whatever they've got in their cameras." He raised a hand, cutting off the reporter's incipient protest with, "No secrets, Ms. del Torres. I know my rights too."

Six soldiers peeled off, tracking the second reporter by his camera light and the running commentary he recorded along with the gory images. They hustled the unauthorized investigators offsite, then began their own investigation in conjunction with the civilian specialists who promptly joined them. Dr. Vasquez and her team spilled from the two unmarked white vans that pulled up in a scatter of wet dirt. The doctor, a trim figure in a white coat, hit the ground already whispering notes to herself into her hand recorder, neatly deploying her team to cover every inch of the murder scene. Yazna Vasquez had built up an impressive reputation as a forensic coroner in Santiago's toughest police districts and now worked for Zamora's specialized military-investigation team at the major's special invitation. He knew her both from his research of top coroners and from her surprisingly touching talk at the Church's last regional conference. To her coroner's training she added an expertise in epidemiology, and she had successfully tracked the mutated cholera outbreaks a few years ago. The major was convinced that General Garza backed El Jaguar with soldiers, bullets, and even germs, and he needed credible authorities to verify the facts.

* * *

Ms. Zelik lifted a steak from the silver platter and gazed with distaste at the puddle of red juice underneath it. It was "rare" only in the sense that it had spent a few seconds over a fire, just long enough to char the outside. She had no great love for breakfast, in any case, and firmly believed that if it must exist, it should do so discreetly, with nothing more obtrusive than mild cinnamon sugar over hot oatmeal. Steak, fried eggs, and butter-swimming grits (not even polenta, just white grits!) simmered in the chafing dishes set out on the elegant sideboard in the executive conference room. With a shudder and a curl of her patrician lip, Ms. Zelik let the steak flop back into its grease. She snatched a cup of coffee from the hand of an obsequious waiter, took her place in the calfskin chair at the conference table, and turned her disgusted look to the host of the breakfast meeting.

Mr. Abbott, the newly appointed CEO of MedaGen, the world's largest pharmaceutical company, took no notice of his chief operating officer's acid stare as he sliced off a chunk of beef and chewed it with vigorous enjoyment. At the moment, however, the steak had competition for his attention.

"Santa Maria, a tiny farming village only fifty kilometers from Santiago, is the latest casualty in the war haunting Chile's mountain forests." Rosa stood in front of a representative section of that forest, gazing into the camera at Channel 8's worldwide audience. "Although the People's Democratic Army has claimed responsibility for the attack that killed the inhabitants of this community, we have exclusive proof that the attack was carried out by the Chilean Liberation Movement forces of El Jaguar." The scene shifted to a jumpy picture shot with a handheld camera. The camera caught Major Zamora's antiterror squad, who appeared as blurs of camouflage-colored movement amid the greens, browns, and fire-blacks of the devastated village. The image steadied and cleared, however, as it zoomed past the soldiers' legs to focus on a red badge glittering from the arm of a corpse. The camera panned down the body of the rebel guerilla, boots, uniform, hood, blood, and pitchfork.

Rosa reappeared. "El Jaguar, in an exclusive interview with Channel 8, promised proof that the Chilean Liberation Movement had declared war on what he calls the corrupt Quintana government. Now we have that proof. The question is, what is President Quintana doing to answer the rebels' charges?"

Still images of Zamora's antiterror squad and forensic investigators examining bodies filled the screen now. "Thus far, the army's efforts to prevent these horrible massacres have proved less than effective. Are they incompetent, or is there some truth to the rumors of collusion between the military and the rebels? Are these investigators unable to capture El Jaguar, or do they hope that the rebel attacks will weaken President Quintana's government and give the army a chance to execute another military coup? What is the real conspiracy here?

Stay tuned as our investigation continues. This is Rosa del Torres, Channel 8 News."

"Whoever they are, the government is ruing the day they allowed freedom of the press," Zelik said.

Whittier grinned around a mouthful of steak. "Ay caramba, now they've got muchachas running around poking microphones into their faces." Whittier was a junior member of the board, whose sarcastic wit, treachery in ousting his grandfather from the family company to sell it to MedaGen, and innate ability to irritate Zelik had made him one of Abbott's favorites. He was thrilled to be included in Abbott's famous breakfast meetings. They weren't official board meetings or policy roundtables; they were where the real strategic planning took place. As Whittier said, "The smoke-filled room, only with cholesterol instead of tobacco." The line pleased him so much he'd repeated it to anybody who'd listen.

The other members of the Breakfast Bunch, as Whittier termed them, discreetly glanced at Abbott and, seeing that he failed to laugh, turned their attention back to their own plates. Senator Garlick, one of the few outsiders invited to the breakfasts, snorted in general disapproval of nosy reporters.

The lack of immediate reaction to his original attempt at political humor prompted Whittier to add, "That one's a hot tamale too."

Zelik shot him a withering look. "Tamales are Mexican. She's Chilean. If you have to make dull-witted jokes, Mr. Whittier, try to keep your cultural geography straight."

"Of course, Ms. Zelik." Whittier mock bowed in her direction. "I should've said hot empanada."

"She sure is," Abbott agreed. "Wonder where Channel 8 finds them?"

"Probably the same place you do," Zelik informed him tartly, glancing at the leggy, redheaded secretary sitting behind Abbott's executive chair. "Though theirs can at least speak intelligibly when prompted."

Abbott didn't defend his secretary; he didn't even bother to learn their names. He simply laughed, and flicked off the monitor. (As alpha male, he had the remote.) "All right, boys and girls, lick up your crumbs. Now that we're fortified, let's get to business. What's our first topic of discussion? How about you, Whittier? Anything you just happen to want to share with us?"

"Why, as it happens, I do have something," Whittier said, raising his eyebrows in surprise. "How's that for a coincidence?"

Abbott, who never shared the spotlight willingly, gave him a quelling glance.

Whittier, subordinating sarcasm to professional survival, got down to business. "If you would turn the monitor to the internal network, sir, you'll see my entry in today's show-and-tell."

The monitor sprang to life again, its ebony surface suddenly filling with pink-tinged creaminess. A sinuous beat began, a rolling bass line undulating as the camera traveled over a curving, undeniably female surface. "Can't get enough," a female voice cooed, "can't get enough." Pulling away to reveal the curve of a hip, traveling up a back, then over a shoulder, the visuals moved in time to the beat, emphasizing the song's breathless lyrics. The camera followed a sudden fall of golden curls up to a bare shoulder, then to glossy, magenta lips that whispered, "Can't get enough—of me." The shot slowly widened to show Virginia's face. She licked her lips flirta- tiously, then blew the camera a kiss, throwing her head and curls back in a flowing wave that bared shoulders, collar bones—and the screen went dark, leaving only a seductive laugh behind.

At the bottom of the screen, as legally required but hidden in plain sight, a thin line of text flowed through the ad, outlining the risks and benefits, possible side effects and indications; the dense medical jargon told anyone with the training to read it that AllSafe required regular doses to maintain the medicine's effectiveness—and recommended the vaccine only for those already suffering from incur- able viral infections. The text that accompanied Virginia's wicked little giggle, however, stood out clearly in the middle of the screen: "AllSafe. Get yours—and get more." The MedaGen logo glittered from the lower corner.

Zelik's voice dropped like an ice cube into the heated mental, well, sort of mental, atmosphere of the room. "That's the best you could do? 'Get yours—and get more'?"

Whittier blinked at the unexpected attack, but he hadn't climbed to this height without a large measure of resilience. He grinned. "It works—for the demographic we targeted for that ad. So does the nonbroadcast version, without the cutaways."

"I'll bet it does." Zelik shrugged, taking a sip of her coffee as she turned her attention to Senator Garlick. "And what about the more important, much larger demographic—the ones who actually think with their heads?"

"Oh, you mean nuns? That more important, much larger demographic?" Whittier suggested, laying out the stills from Virginia's photo shoot one by one, to the intense interest of the men around the table.

"I mean," Zelik said, her voice slicing easily through the few chuckles, "what about promoting AllSafe as a necessary component of homeland security?"

Senator Garlick cleared his throat. "All in good time, Ms. Zelik. I do not have the homeland security appointment—yet. Politics is a delicate balancing act. You may be able to market your vaccine with pretty pictures, but achieving political consensus, building voting coalitions, requires more than mere product marketing—"

"Yeah—it takes a bigger budget," Whittier said. "Bribery and corruption don't come cheap."

"And neither does Virginia," Abbott reminded him. "We've—"

"Oh, no," Whittier said, high on poking a pompous politician and figuring he was on a roll now. "Being *that* cheap costs a lot of money."

No one, no matter how amusing, interrupted Abbott. Whittier realized that just a moment too late, watching the amusement fade from his boss's eyes.

"We've run into other problems with the latest campaign as well," Abbott went on, as if Whittier had never spoken. "It's not going as smoothly as we'd hoped—rather like Senator Garlick's maneuvering for the homeland security post."

"Senator Cox and her cronies can't hold up the nomination much longer," Garlick informed them, misjudging Abbott's comment as a request for information rather than a dismissive dig.

"Ah, yes, Senator Holly Cox." Abbott steepled his fingers. "She's got a distressing habit of mixing so-called moral absolutes with political necessities."

"Another one of those Mormons," Zelik snarled.

The venom in her tone drew a surprised look from Whittier. "They're just one of several groups opposing the AllSafe vaccine," he pointed out.

"But an influential one," Abbott said. "And they've proved less than cooperative on several fronts. The Church owns vast tracts of rainforest and jungle in Africa and South America, where they harvest a steady flow of the biologicals for nature-based drugs. They not only create the pharmaceuticals via privately owned R&D companies but distribute them as well, especially to poorer or disaster-struck areas." His eyes narrowed. "And, more to the point, they have resisted any offers of partnership, codevelopment, and market cooperation."

"They've also filed a friend-of-the-court brief on behalf of Meredith Anthony Galen in the industrial-espionage trial," Zelik added.

Whittier knew the story from Errol Humphrey, one of his midlevel managers. Meredith Galen had conned her way into MedaGen and found the original source codes on AllSafe and the original data from the human trials MedaGen had secretly conducted. Copies of the whole data packet had vanished with her when she escaped right from under Zelik's nose. That the case had gone to the courts, and that it appeared MedaGen's lawyers were having a very difficult time persuading the courts to disregard the old federal "whistleblower" protection laws chafed Zelik to no end. She wanted Galen prosecuted, jailed, hanged, drawn, quartered, and stuffed for her mantelpiece. From the looks of it, her hate of the woman had splashed over to cover the church Galen belonged to as well. And given the set muscles in Abbott's jaw, it looked like Zelik wasn't the only one who had problems with the Church.

"Mormons?" Whittier asked. "Are we talking about the same outfit? Temples? Big conference center in Independence? Favorite target of Tommy Gibbs and his Christian soldiers?" He laughed, disbelieving. "Come on—what can a few thousand fundamentalist nuts do?"

"A few million fundamentalist nuts, Mr. Whittier," Zelik snapped. "Twenty-seven million, to be precise, half of them in North and South America, with a tendency to rise to positions of power and influence in business, industry—and politics."

"Not numbers to take lightly," Garlick said.

"Certainly not," Abbott agreed.

"Taking them lightly is the best way to handle them," Whittier protested. "I mean, come on—Brigham Young and forty-six wives? Refusing a vaccine because they're afraid the devil's lurking in the needle? Actually insisting that people have to get married? Saying that being gay is unnatural? Who's going to take them seriously?"

"Nobody." Abbott began to laugh. They stared at him as he snorted, slapping his knees. "Nobody at all."

Zelik's stare turned speculative, then a hint of a smile played at the corner of her mouth. "Nobody at all. We step up the overt ad campaign—and the poison propaganda too."

"Exactly," Abbott said. "Senator Garlick here is an old hand at attack ads. What say you lend us a bit of expertise, in return for all the support we've thrown your way?"

"Which has been as much for your benefit as mine," Garlick reminded him, but nodded, acceding to the idea. He could show these MBAs a thing or two about political mud wrestling all right.

"And old Monk owes us plenty, for all the sponsorship dollars MedaGen pours into Channel 8's ad revenue," Zelik said.

"No problem, then." Whittier leaned back in his chair, outwardly casual as he seized credit for the idea. "We just orchestrate a media campaign to discredit the Mormons. They lose face on AllSafe and the industrial-espionage charge. Two birds with one stone. Easy as shooting fish in a barrel."

"Got your shotgun primed, Whittier?" Abbott asked.

"What?" Whittier sat up abruptly.

"You've said that you're ready for more responsibility, for something different," Abbott said. "So I'm giving you the chance. In addition to overseeing your usual marketing team, you're the point man on our new information campaign. I'll expect a full report on your progress at next week's breakfast."

Zelik smiled as the color drained from Whittier's face. The upstart climber had reached for the brass ring—and found a bear trap in its place. Her smile faded as quickly as Whittier's complexion, however, as Abbott added, "Congratulations, Ms. Zelik—Whittier's on your team now. You're his new mentor. And I'm sure you'll have all his rough edges knocked off in no time."

She forced her smile back, casting a cobra eye on her assigned protégé as she said, "Won't that be fun?"

"That's it, kiddies," Abbott announced, clapping his hands. "Everybody out—I've got a massage scheduled in ten minutes and a hostile takeover in twenty-five. No rest for the wicked, as our Mormon friends would say."

The meeting broke up amid a general rustling of napkins and clinking of cups. Abbott went to stand at the door as the Breakfast Bunch filed out. "Senator, take a few steaks for your bulldogs," he suggested genially, gesturing to the two heavily built bodyguards wearing suits in the anteroom.

"Be careful out there, Ms. Zelik. Forecast says it's an unseasonably warm week for fall—wouldn't want you to melt right away in a hot Santa Ana gust." He returned her smile, fire to ice.

"And Whittier." His large hand caught the other man's arm, holding him back as the last person left. "I understand you've been concerned about some of our R&D projects. Sure, you started in R&D, but you're moving on. You're a bright guy. You're going to go far—as long as you catch the right elevator." He smiled, easy and handsome, with a glint of steel under the affability. "It would be a shame if the door opened and you got nothing but shaft."

"Sure would. With all the workouts in the executive gym, I'm as thin as I want to be," Whittier managed, but his heart wasn't in the light reply. He left, still feeling the press of Abbott's fingers on his arm, glancing at the discreet eye of one of the omnipresent security cameras and resisting the impulse to look over his shoulder. Humphrey was right—Zelik wasn't the only one who saw everything that happened at MedaGen.

* * *

"Checking out résumés?" Humphrey asked, walking into Zelik's office. "Need my expert help in sorting the good from the bad?"

Zelik turned from the monitor and glared at him, then slowly smiled. "As it happens, I do need your expert help—but not in sorting résumés. Or in detecting frauds."

Humphrey inclined his head, acknowledging the dig. They both knew where they stood on the matter: Zelik had promoted Merry Anthony Galen and given her access to the vital data she had stolen;

Humphrey had been the traitor's direct supervisor—but he still had a copy of Zelik's letter authorizing the promotion. They hated each other, but neither would let go of a potentially useful tool. She held the key to his rise from indentured servant to free executive, and he had the weasel slickness to carry out her orders. Zelik turned the monitor toward the junior supervisor.

"Tony Callatta," Humphrey read. "A programmer, specializing in game interfaces. I don't know him. What has the poor man done to deserve your personal attention?"

"He and his wife, a stay-at-home nonentity, helped Meredith Galen get away with the AllSafe research files," Zelik said.

"Why look at his résumé?" Humphrey asked. "Why not just arrange a nasty accident for the both of them—and their little dog too?"

"There is no dog. Use your head for something besides a speaker, Humphrey. Think. The trial's still boiling along, high public interest, lots of attention. An accident now would look too suspicious. BritPharm is already sniffing around for weakness; a direct hit would give them more ammunition than they need." Zelik stood, a wintry smile crossing her face, and gazed out the floor-to-ceiling windows. "No, no accidents for the conspirators. Instead, I want you to make life difficult for them. They're already in dire financial straits. Make the water deeper. Send out the word on Tony Callatta—any firm that hires him will do no business with MedaGen or any of its subsidiaries. Any bank that offers the Callattas credit will lose our accounts. Put a lien on their home."

"Sabotage their dinner parties. I get it," Humphrey said. He almost felt sorry for the poor shlubs—and very glad that he held that promotion and permission letter; it was the one thing keeping his own head off the block Zelik designed for the Callattas. "Why kill them when we can hurt them so much they'll wish they were dead?"

"Exactly," Zelik nodded, motioning him out with one sharp gesture. Watching Humphrey's reflection in the glass, she waited until the door closed behind him to whisper, "And then I'll give them their wish, when the spotlight has disappeared and no one will notice, or care."

* * *

Twenty-five screens flickered in the darkness of the producer's booth—the cockpit from which Monk oversaw the vast media empire that was Channel 8. Every live feed Channel 8's agents opened—ground wire, satellite, and wireless transmissions—ran through this room. In the center of the liquid-crystal grid was a larger screen showing the current Channel 8 program. With the flick of a finger, Monk could send any of the live feeds—or archival footage, canned human-interest stories, backup video, public-service announcements, and endless barrages of advertisements—into millions of television sets around the world. Not that he'd flick his own finger; he had people for that.

Specifically, he had Kim for that. He looked down from the main monitor as his ever-present assistant slid the day's directives from Upstairs across the console. The bright blue pages looked like a quaint anachronism compared to modern security measures, but Channel 8's board of directors found that tried-and-true technologies, suitably enhanced, met their needs better than the latest digital tricks. Web crackers could never break into a literal envelope and sell its contents to Channel 8's two distant but hungry competitors, and none but badge-wearing, voice-printed Channel 8 employees had access to the production booth or internal mail system. As an additional security measure, the specially formulated ink would fade in a matter of hours, leaving no trace of the letters that now stood out stark black against the light blue as Monk read them. The security measures, however, weren't the reason the producer's eyebrows rose as he read the day's missives.

"Hmm, would you look at this. We got all kinds of surprises coming down from Upstairs today." Monk tossed the pages over the console to Kim, who caught them and riffled through, neatly separating out the pieces that had caught Monk's attention. Amid the usual directives about the week's sitcom debuts, ideas for infomercials, reviews of various Channel 8 on-air personalities, and recommendations for the day's programming, two items stood out to Kim's practiced eye.

The first took just one line: "Contract negotiations unsatisfactory, resignation desired," followed by an employee ID number.

"Looks like somebody asked for more money and respect than Upstairs had on the table," Monk said.

The second merited an entire paragraph. The new directive concerned "the Mormons," as the memo termed them. A new public-service campaign about the Mormons cosponsored by several prominent evangelical Christian groups—Tommy Gibbs's Crusaders for Jesus topping the list—hereby had priority play on Channel 8's ad roster. So did MedaGen's latest set of spots attacking the Mormons for the Church's stance on AllSafe. Upstairs expected to see more exposés on the Mormon Church's bizarre beliefs, monopolistic business practices, puritanical snobbery, and illicit political power.

Monk chuckled. "Looks like Salt Lake isn't playing ball with the big boys, and now the big boys have decided to go from touch to tackle. With spikes." He caught a look from Kim. "Right. Independence. Whatever. Like I have so little to do I can keep track of some cult's headquarters."

The fact that the suits Upstairs had asked him to create controversy and stir up dirt for no other reason than making a major sponsor happy didn't bother Monk. The Mormons had plenty of chances to dip into their pocketbooks to deploy their own attacks or buy insurance against MedaGen's, but they'd ignored the opportunity. More than ignored it— downright spurned it, on the grounds of principle and truth overcoming all. Everybody had dirt, everybody was hiding something; he figured that finding the skeletons in the Mormons' closet or account books wouldn't be difficult. Anne O'Neal, their religion reporter, was popular with the viewers and already had an in with the Mormons' top guys; she asked the hard questions too. Yeah, they'd turn Anne loose and see what happened next.

Monk glanced at the blue pages in front of him, then at the central monitor, rubbing his chin thoughtfully. "Round up the usual suspects, Kim—and wangle us a one-on-one with Tommy Gibbs. He's got a crusade coming up, and he's a popular one in the Southern markets. That'll put a dent in WREB's little Saturday-night gladiator games and their drag races too." He picked up the first blue paper, flicking it with a fingernail. "So will trading in our classic for a late-model coupe."

Kim glanced up at the central monitor. There, Channel 8's current and deeply dissatisfied primary anchor, Kathy Williams, bantered with Garrett de Long, the entertainment reporter and perennial gossip monger, about Virginia Diamante's latest escapades. Kim caught Monk's eye, turned one fist thumb downward, and looked inquisitive.

"Yup, Kathy's not playing ball any better than the Mormons do." Monk leaned forward as Kim sent the newscast to commercial. On cue, Kathy stood up, snarling, "Oh, shut up," at Garrett.

"Oh, what's the matter, sweetie?" The entertainment reporter stood as well. "Contract negotiations not going well, or is it just that time of the month?"

Kathy drew herself up to her full, heel-enhanced height. "I do not have to tolerate that kind of sexist comment from you," she announced. "But speaking of contract negotiations, my agent tells me it's going much better than you hope. In fact, if you want to keep working, Garrett, you'd better learn to treat me with more respect."

"Belay that order, de Long," Monk announced over the studio's speakers.

Kathy startled, looking at the camera as if her glare could burn Monk right through his monitors. "What does that mean?"

"You'd be safer telling de Long to treat you with the respect you deserve," Monk said. "And finding yourself another agent. Goodbye, Hairdo."

Her makeup suddenly looked starker as the blood drained from her face. "I will not work for less than I am worth," she announced. As a veteran newscaster, she even managed to keep her voice steady. Even Garrett's smug grin faded around the edges.

Monk gave her a round of long-distance applause as she stalked off the set. Garrett joined in, then exited stage left at high speed, his own agent on speed dial. "So, she quits, and we get a younger, more ambitious replacement," he told Kim. "Better demographics—and there's nothing like a warm chair to remind you that the trapdoor hinges are good and greased." He leaned back, unwrapping a candy bar. "And nothing like a new, fat paycheck to make it really easy to read the words on the prompter without getting snarky about it. Get the B list on dial-up."

Kim already had the secondary cast's phone numbers programmed into the console, with Anne O'Neal's number right on top.

* * *

The studio lights came up, the Channel 8 News logo lit in the background, the endless weather/stock ticker/advertisement crawl sparkled from the bottom of the screen, and the anchor chair turned around to face the desk. "Good morning. I'm Clara Cortez, taking over for Kathy Williams, who has gone on to other opportunities. We'll miss you, Kathy. Now we're back to Channel 8's continuous news coverage." She turned easily to face the second camera, her experience as a field reporter showing in the ingrained poise—and the intensity of her stare.

"Smile," Monk reminded her. "Smile. We're in the studio, not the jungle."

She didn't look startled or touch her earpiece either, Monk noted approvingly. Instead, she smiled—professional, reassuring, and impersonal, just like she'd practiced in her hotel room for hours last night—as Cal Weathers, Channel 8's too-appropriately named weather clown, joked about how overjoyed he was to have her there. She put up with his inane jokes and smiled. Her cheek muscles felt stiff, but what was a little facial soreness compared to the anchor spot at Channel 8? She had urged Kathy to hold out for more money, more respect, more camera time—and it had paid off nicely. No more jungles for Clara Cortez!

"Thanks, Cal," she responded, doing a decent job of making it sound spontaneous.

Clara gratefully dumped the happy talk for the actual news. "In the headlines today, residents of Santa Sonoma, California, are angered to see the Mormons moving in." The crawl across the bottom ran a flood of mini-ads touting the phone numbers and Web addresses of realtors in the Santa Sonoma area. Video sprang into the second frame of the screen, next to Clara's face, showing a quiet suburban neighborhood in Southern California, all tree-shaded lawns, neat houses—and furious old-timers.

"They've been moving in the last eight months like—like locusts or something!" an angry middle-aged woman informed the camera. "Our school is bursting at the seams now."

"This whole place was fields, until that Mormon temple went in, and now there's houses everywhere," an older man growled. "Urban sprawl, that's what they call this."

"Yup, pretty much nobody comes down here but Mormons anymore," a shop owner drawled, leaning against the butcher-papered windows of a small-town grocery. "They've bought out the old buildings all along Main Street there, putting in a bunch of computer businesses or something. And in another couple months, they'll open up a grocery too. Run me right out of business, after forty years."

The image of a newly built chapel replaced the run-down store, the families entering its glass doors photographed at a subtle angle and in gray tones that lent an air of menace to the scene. Clara gazed seriously from the screen beside the expertly prepared footage. "All across the United States, Mormons are gathering in small and large cities, often displacing the original residents, always forming their own tight-knit, exclusive communities. They take over local schools with their large families and replace local businesses with white-collar companies. Unfortunately, the Mormons fill the jobs themselves, widening the gap between haves and have-nots, especially in the depressed agricultural areas of the Midwest and towns in the failing Rust Belt." Now freeze-frame images clicked by in a dizzying barrage, a sequence of dried-out fields, huge grain-storage silos with Angel Moroni logos, gray-faced workers in unemployment lines, well-dressed General Authorities, tiny children in ragged clothes, well-fed members of the Mormon Tabernacle Choir.

The picture changed again, to a street scene in a busy city center. "Downtown Independence, Missouri, once a depressed area, has undergone a Mormon renaissance. But at what cost? Concerned citizens say that the Church has interfered with free-speech rights of those who don't belong to the Church, not only on Church property but throughout the city." A close-up of a No Smoking sign faded into a sequence featuring a pair of police officers hustling a shabby-looking man into an Independence PD cruiser.

"Will this alarming trend continue?" Clara asked, regaining center screen. "According to Channel 8's demographic experts, the answer may well be yes. Stay tuned for an exclusive Channel 8 in-depth report on this century's new Mormon Migration."

"And we're out to commercial," Monk announced, as the snaky bass of yet another AllSafe ad filled the airwaves. "Good job, C.C. You just might still have a job at the end of the week."

"Don't try to scare me by implying I'm on your famous blacklist." Clara leaned back in her anchor chair. "Better learn to like it, Monk, 'cause I'm here to stay."

"She'd better hope so," Monk told Kim, as he grinned into the blue dimness. He didn't bother to turn off the audio feed on his headset. "She's here until somebody pays Upstairs to do a smear job on her—or until the ratings fall. Then it's blacklist time."

* * *

"I tell you, it's like I'm on some sort of stinking blacklist!" Tony violently shoved himself back from his desk, as if trying to get as far as possible from the latest rejection letter glowing from the computer screen. The battered office chair rolled sluggishly then tumbled backward as a seasick caster edged off the mat and hit the rug. Tony's video-gamer reflexes kicked in fast enough to land him on his haunches beside the chair, but not fast enough to keep the chair from crashing into the wall, knocking over a pile of backup disks and scraps torn out of printed-out want ads. The crash brought Carmen to the scene.

"You okay, baby?" She peeked cautiously around the door. Many years of mothering and mess monitoring—in particular, the episode of Giovanni and the Flying Paint Box—had taught her a valuable rule of thumb: Always check the terrain before charging in.

"I'm a complete unemployed loser buried in a stupid pile of trash!" Tony exploded, surging to his feet in a fury. Well, almost surging to his feet. He grabbed the arm of the chair to assist his sudden rise—and the chair picked that moment to lose the gimpy caster altogether. Tony crashed to the floor, taking the rest of the pile of desk detritus with him.

"You can add klutzy in there too," Carmen said as she rushed to his side and started picking papers and disks off him. It didn't look like he was hurt, but his fall worried her.

"Klutz, huh?" he growled. His hand shot out, catching Carmen off balance. She toppled over, right onto him—and into his waiting arms. "Takes one to know one." He squeezed her tight.

They picked themselves up off the floor and started picking up the avalanche as well.

"So what happened?" Carmen asked, glancing at the computer, which was helpfully running a screen saver.

Tony's face suddenly turned red. "Ah, nothing much. Just spazzing out, falling over. Gotta get that chair fixed."

Carmen ran a hand through Tony's curly hair, dislodging a paper clip. "Tony, I'm not feeling a goose egg on your thick skull, so I know you don't have amnesia. Come on. Tell me what's up."

Behind Tony's half-grin grimace, macho ego battled the need for sympathy. Ego suffered a decisive defeat when Carmen hooked the crippled chair over, set him down onto it, and rubbed his shoulders. He sighed and punched a key, revealing the rejection letter in all its bland, bureaucratic antiglory, then leaned his head back against her. "This stupid job hunt is making me nuts, Carmen."

She read the boilerplate over his head. In an impersonal, passive-voice tone that made it even nastier than a personal diatribe would have been, it said that Tony's application for the position was rejected, his résumé would not be kept on file, and he was prohibited from posting on the employment board in the future. "Ouch," she said. "All they didn't say is, 'you and the horse you rode in on.'"

"Oh, they said that too, when I applied over at CyberClaw," Tony assured her. "They don't even bother to talk to me. Nobody—software, Web dev, games, nothing. One outfit sent this back to me." He scrabbled through the mess on the floor (Carmen steadied the chair as he leaned) and handed Carmen two halves of a disk.

"Your portfolio," she said, looking at the colorful label. "Busted right down the middle. Did that happen just now?" Her stomach sank. She knew the answer, but she had to ask anyway.

"No, they did that. Broke it in half and had it messengered over. Messengered! They paid extra just to dis me!"

He stood up, successfully this time, and paced the well-worn strip of carpet from desk to door as he'd done for hours and days.

"Something will come up," Carmen said. She ached for him, for his frustration, for the extra gray that had appeared in his hair and the spring that had disappeared from his step. It was scary enough knowing that the family was skimming the thin edge of financial disaster; watching it eat Tony from the inside out was a nightmare. "You're the best game designer in SoCal, and they know that—"

"They don't care." Tony stopped, facing the door. "They've all got reasons. I followed Jay out to his car when I finally got an interview at Gamesters—the one with the smarmy ten-year-old manager who kept telling me they were looking for 'something in a different direction'— and Jay said I've got a major strike against me."

"MedaGen," Carmen said softly.

"What?" Tony looked over his shoulder at her.

"MedaGen." Carmen said it more firmly this time. "I bet it's MedaGen. They know we helped Merry. They were even here at the house! They know who we are, Tony. You bet they do. And now they've put out the word on us. Big outfit like that, probably got tentacles in every pie in the city! Can't get to Merry, so they decide to take it out on you! Donna was right—they won't rest until they've ruined our lives. If I could get my hands on them, I'd—"

"Carmen." Tony caught her shoulders, shaking her lightly. He couldn't help grinning though at her tirade. "Hey, baby, calm down, before we're both saying words we don't want Gianni to go repeating."

She stifled the tears along with the rant. "It could be them though."

"It could be," Tony said. He had wondered about it too, but an actual MedaGen conspiracy against them seemed outlandish. Why would a multibillion-dollar company bother to squash the career of a freelance game developer? His intuitive understanding of video-game villains, while artistically exciting, didn't extend to the petty vindictiveness of real-life malefactors. "But according to Jay, it's simpler than that. They're booting me because I'm still a drawing-board developer at forty-one, instead of a manager, and I'm a Mormon."

He glowered at the computer. "And I'm not changing any of that! I may have some gray in my hair, but I'd rather be a developer than some pencil-pushing middle manager. And yeah, I'm Mormon. And I'm going to stay that way! And I'm going to keep smacking my head against this stupid wall until I break it down. They can't count me out yet. I'm 41, Carmen. Just 41! That's not dead! Am I dead? Do I look like a dead guy to you? Do I *act* like a dead guy?"

"You look plenty lively to me, baby." Carmen raised her eyebrows, glad to see the spark return to Tony's eyes. "We got a three-year-old kid, Tony—if you died, you did it in the last couple years."

He grinned back.

"I know you'll get something. You always do. That's what I told my daddy when he asked if I was sure I wanted to marry an Italian boy from Jersey: 'He'll always get us something. Even if it falls off the back of a truck.'" She kissed him.

"Hey, I'm an artist, not a stevedore." He returned her kiss.

"Okay, make that, 'Even if he has to repaint something that fell off the back of a truck.' That better?"

"Yeah, that's better." Tony ruffled her hair. "We'll beat them— MedaGen or whatever's blocking us. I'll find us something."

"We'll beat them," Carmen agreed. "Now, come on and we'll pray for some inspiration about which truck we ought to be looking under."

"I guess that's not the craziest method of job hunting I've heard of," Tony said. He'd been praying for divine assistance ever since SpielTech laid him off, but Carmen had a way of prying open the windows of heaven.

CHAPTER 4

"A little to the left, so we can get that big lady in the flowered dress." Leon checked the shot through his camera again.

"You're wearing all the flowers we need and more," Anne assured him, glancing from his psychedelic Hawaiian shirt to the rumbling protesters surrounding the hotel doors behind her. Nervous security guards watched them from behind the glass, making no move but staying alert. On the other side of the street, a few police officers loitered, the sun glinting off the beetle-black sheath of their armor.

Leon disregarded the comment on his taste in clothes. "You could've made the big time there. Anchor for Channel 8 News. Cushy office. Big ol' chunk of change waiting in your account every month. Perks for your favorite camera guy."

"My promotion means perks for you, huh?" Anne practiced her unruffled reporter smile. It was a good expression for hiding the twitch of worry the thought of Monk provoked. "He was teasing about the anchor slot anyway. You know I don't have the face-recognition numbers they need for a star anchor."

"He wasn't teasing about the second-anchor chair," Leon said. "You could've stepped into Clara's shoes and got your name above the title."

Anne shrugged off the suggestion with a faint shudder. "I think I'd rather stay a bit farther away from headquarters for now. The guys Upstairs are too intense. You didn't have to come up with an answer for Monk when he asked how 'loyal' you are to Channel 8—or to the Mormons."

"Well, that President Rojas is a mighty fine-looking man." Leon raised his eyebrows suggestively.

Anne wished she had something to throw at him. "Oh, shut up, Leon. You and Monk both. Yeah, he's handsome. He's also an interview subject—and married!"

"Hey, that's no problem—he's Mormon, remember?"

"Well, I'm not. I'm an objective, professional journalist looking at Mormons because they're where the action is. And I'm a field reporter, and I don't want to get stuck behind an anchor desk yet and sell out for a cushy set and perks for you. The real stuff is going on out here, and it's getting realer—and weirder—all the time."

"Okay, okay, you've convinced me." Leon looked more amused than convinced as he flicked on the camera light.

The crowd behind Anne shifted. Murmurs rose into exclamations. A few signs rose as well: "Are You Anti-Mormon or Anti-American?" "Church, No! Cult, Yes!" "Mormons Go Home!"

"Get ready for more weirdness. Looks like they've caught a scent," Leon observed. He zoomed in to spot a couple of quietly dressed individuals in the motley crowd. They'd be the ones with the cell phones and connections, the ones who had organized this "spontaneous" protest.

"And, go!" Leon ordered. The red light flicked on.

"Thank you, Kathy," she began.

"Clara," Leon told her. "Good thing we're not live, eh?"

Anne sighed, shook her head, and stepped up to her mark again. "Thank you, Clara. We're here at a hotel in Chicago where President Richard M. Rojas, Associate President of The Church of Jesus Christ of Latter-day Saints, is staying. The Mormons are gathering here in Chicago for a regional conference, and as you can see, protesters are gathering as well."

Leon angled the camera, catching the crowd milling around the hotel entryway and spilling into the garden area. Following Monk's instructions, Leon shot the crowd from exactly the right angle, making a group of one hundred look onscreen like an army. He lingered on the woman in the flowered dress, the old man waving a picture of Jesus, the little girl holding a flag; he avoided the pierced, rainbow-haired anarchists lurking at the far fringes and the toughs shouting obscenities.

Anne's voice continued over the images. "Protests and resistance to the Church are becoming more intense and more organized all over the United States and overseas as well. The protests aren't just fundamentalist Christians with bullhorns either. The Church has made powerful enemies as well. MedaGen and its parent companies are spending large sums of money on public-relations ads, which you've probably seen, accusing the Church of being un-American or even collaborating with terrorists, due to its opposition to the Garlick-Benyanny Health and Security Bill now under consideration in the Senate. The bill will make the AllSafe vaccine freely available to all citizens and make it mandatory for anyone who works in high-risk areas or has contact with the public."

Another rumble sounded from the crowd. Leon caught a shot of a placard with a red circle-and-slash painted over a picture of the golden angel Moroni statue that appeared on all Mormon temples.

He turned the camera back to Anne, nearly catching her blink as she read the prompts Monk sent over the portable monitor. "Other MedaGen ads use humor to undercut the Church's position on AllSafe. And prominent cultural critics, such as Dr. Sidney Anthony, noted feminist scholar and author, have revived the usual arguments against the Church, accusing the Mormons of being reactionary, puritanical, judgmental, fanatical, and intolerant."

"That's not what the prompt said, Annie," Monk growled into his headset. She was supposed to give the full quote from Sidney, not mention the ads. MedaGen hadn't bought the airtime to have a reporter pull the curtain back on the wizard. *So she's keeping it neutral instead of nasty, showing her independent streak*, Monk thought. *Probably mad we didn't chase her harder on the anchor job, and she's making a political move for later negotiations.*

Kim glanced at Monk, waiting for the word to feed a "kill" order into the prompt. Monk caught the look and shook his head. "Nah, let it go. We'll fix it up with the ads and quotes at broadcast time and see how it plays. She wants to take a gentle poke at MedaGen and company, let her. They bought the spots; they didn't buy the entire network. Besides I like Anne. The numbers go up when she's on."

"More seriously," Anne continued, back on script now that it let her talk about real journalistic concerns, "the Church is coming under fire for unpatriotic practices and for unfairly driving out local businesses in the areas where Mormons have gathered. The Mormon economic miracle, as pundits have termed it, has boosted the Church's bottom line but reduced its approval ratings among those who do not share—"

With a sudden roar that drowned the audio feed entirely, the protesters behind her surged forward as a dark sedan emerged from the hotel's underground parking garage. It moved slowly but steadily, moving the protesters aside like a reluctant bow wave. Another vehicle closely followed the lead car, this one even more nondescript than the first. Four figures were dimly visible behind the tinted windows, two men in the front seat, a man and woman in the back. Hotel security men moved forward as well, trying to deflect the shouters and sign-wavers from the driveway. Frustrated in their attempts to get to the car itself, the protesters raised the volume of their shouts.

The pair of cars kept moving, accelerating as the cordon of security men began to falter. The woman in the flowered dress broke through the thin, brass-buttoned line and rushed the second car, pounding on the trunk, screaming snatches of scripture, and accusing President Rojas of being the Antichrist. A sign thrown at his car bounced off the back door. Plastic bottles, trash, and a few bricks rattled to the street as the sedans sped away. Some of the mob ran after the car for a few feet, still shouting. The hotel's guards retired gratefully into the safe confines of the lobby.

Only then did the police move in, funneling the crowd down the street, away from the store windows. About half of the protesters backed off; they'd come to shout and throw things at the Mormons. The other half, however, had come just to shout and throw things, and the sight of the riot-suited cops moving into the street triggered the expected reaction: more bricks flew, joined by plastic bottles full of gasoline and garnished with flaming rags. The police added their own catalysts to the rapidly expanding reaction. Beanbags and tear gas blasted back at the protesters. The organizers quietly faded away, reporting a successful confrontation to their anonymous backers—and making Ms. Zelik's afternoon a little brighter.

* * *

"That was the scene in Chicago yesterday," Clara announced. "As Channel 8 has reported during the night, a full-blown riot exploded as Mormons clashed with demonstrators. The protesters had gathered to oppose the presence of the Mormon regional conference in the city yesterday. The Chicago Police Department is defending their handling of the incident, as accusations of conspiracy to provoke a civil disturbance fly against the Church itself." Leon's footage of the riot played beside Clara's concerned expression, the crawl at the bottom of the screen tallying material damages, injuries, and monetary claims in lawsuits already filed via Armstrong Associates' Insta-Suit service.

"How does the Church explain the controversy?" Clara asked. "What do the leaders of the world's second-fastest growing and most controversial group have to say to their critics? To find out, Anne O'Neal, Channel 8's religion specialist, talked to Richard Rojas, Associate President of the Church."

"I'm here with President Rojas in the Independence, Missouri, headquarters of The Church of Jesus Christ of Latter-day Saints," Anne announced, as the red light on Leon's camera glowed. This time it was a live report. "Thank you for agreeing to meet with us, President Rojas."

President Rojas smiled politely. "You're welcome, Anne."

Monk smiled also, watching the ratings spike upward. Saturation coverage of the Chicago riot, carefully spun to look like a fight between Mormons and others—along with statements from the Crusaders for Jesus and the ever-present MedaGen public-service ads—had made the Church's public-relations problems the hottest stories since the Egyptian dam disaster last month. *Bless Anne's independent little heart*, he thought. *Her streak of journalistic integrity might make things hot for MedaGen once in a while, but it guaranteed us an exclusive interview.*

"I know you don't have a lot of time, with so many pressing issues to deal with," Anne said. "The Church of Jesus Christ has undergone tremendous growth in the last few years, a pattern that doesn't show any sign of slowing."

"Which is a good thing," President Rojas interjected, his smile more sincere now.

Anne nodded noncommittally. "I think some people would disagree with you. They see you as both exclusive and ever expanding. Rumor has it that you plan to build a temple in Israel, perhaps even in Jerusalem itself."

"Rumors do get around, don't they? I'm sorry, but I can't comment on future temple plans. As you know, Anne, the Church's policy is not to discuss possible locations for temples until the land and permits have been secured."

"That's not a denial, President Rojas."

"It's not a confirmation either, Anne." President Rojas's dark eyes twinkled.

"Well, I do have confirmation that the Church is planning to dedicate a new temple in Missouri, a very unusual one. Can you tell us about that?"

"Indeed I can. It's the new temple just about to be dedicated at Adam-ondi-Ahman. In addition to the temple itself, there will be meeting halls, state-of-the-art communications facilities, and a visitors' center, all set in a landscape of gardens and working farms."

As he spoke, architects' sketches of the proposed temple complex filled the screen, showing the proposed buildings and landscaping alternating with shots of the current fields and rolling hills.

The scene returned to Anne. "An ambitious project," she said. "But you're known for ambitious projects, both here and abroad. The Church has been building temples all over the world at an amazing pace. Over three hundred now?"

"Three hundred sixteen, counting the ones currently on the drawing board," President Rojas said. "The temple at Adam-ondi-Ahman will be the three hundredth. Amazing! We feel blessed to have worked with so many good people around the world in finding sites, gaining local approval, and building the temples themselves."

"You have also seen many protests and been denied building permits in many areas. The opposition comes from the Church's policy of buying the land around the temples as well. In fact, you have made a habit of taking over or building entire towns around the temples, with hundreds of Mormon Church members moving in. In fact, many opponents of the Church say that you are in effect destroying the local communities, forcing out the original owners."

President Rojas shook his head gently. "Unfortunately, some people misunderstand what's happening—and others distort reality for their own purposes, as happened with the reports of the disturbance in Chicago. That was a protest against my presence that got out of hand, not a clash between Mormons and protesters. They ambushed us at the hotel and threw rocks at us. Not just at me, but my wife as well." A flicker of anger sparked in his eyes, but his voice remained calm. "And then they started a riot with the Chicago police. There were no Church members participating. None."

He raised a hand, gently forestalling Anne's comment. "The same kind of distortion has happened with the reports about the temple communities. Yes, the Church does buy as much land as possible around temple sites. Once we have approval from local authorities and residents, we establish planned communities, including farms, homes, hospitals, shops and other businesses. However," he smiled again, his confident charm reaching through the camera lens, "those communities aren't exclusive. Anyone is welcome to live there. In fact, I highly recommend them. These towns are great places to live—they are ecologically responsible, with convenient shops, low crime rates, safe streets, and good schools."

"Great places to live if you don't mind having Mormons as neighbors," Anne suggested. "Which some people absolutely do."

"Which is really too bad." President Rojas leaned forward, addressing the viewers. "Mormons are very good neighbors. We welcome everyone who is willing to join us in creating livable communities. Please come! We're gathering out of the world, away from the violence, greed, unfaithfulness, pornography, and dishonesty that we see growing on every side. All people of good heart, whatever their religious persuasion, are welcome." He leaned back, sober but not discouraged. "Unfortunately, many people, for whatever reason, don't understand that the Church encourages cooperation, good citizenship, and peaceful relations with everyone. Members of The Church of Jesus Christ of Latter-day Saints are loyal and true citizens, wherever they live. Despite persecutions, legal challenges, and even violence in some areas, we work within the system to resolve the problems."

"However, there are some reports, President Rojas," Anne broke in, "that some Mormons have taken matters into their own hands, rather than waiting for legal solutions. In Lake Creek, Illinois, for example, Church members are suspected of vandalizing several businesses in retaliation for vandalism of Mormon churches in the area."

"I hope those reports are untrue, Anne—and we will know shortly, because local authorities are checking those rumors. If something is happening out there, it will be resolved on the local level. As far as a general mandate for the whole Church, President Smith, myself, and the presiding officers absolutely discourage any Church members from striking back at those who oppose the Church. The Lord will protect His people. What we need to do is help each other and others who need it, keep spreading the gospel of Jesus Christ, and be prepared for the troubles to come."

"What troubles are those?" Anne asked.

"We are truly in the last days," he said calmly, his tone matter-of-fact. "We are seeing the fulfillment of scriptural prophecies on all sides. The evil forces in the world are becoming more wicked, but the good is becoming that much better. More than ever, it's vital to stand up for the right, for the eternal principles of truth and right."

"Many other people are talking about the end of the world drawing near," Anne pointed out. "Tommy Gibbs has conducted revivals preparing people for the Rapture at the end times, and others, including Christians like the Reverend Lebaron's Millennium Brotherhood, which relocated from Alabama to Illinois, and charismatic religious leaders like Brother Light, have gained a lot of attention calling brimstone and earthquakes down upon the wicked. Do you really see the horrors of the New Testament ahead of us—iron locusts, fiery hail, and huge wars? Are you worried?"

"No, I'm not worried. The Lord has assured us that those who are prepared shall not fear. Now is the time for us all to be prepared. And that doesn't apply just to Mormons. For everyone who comes to Christ, who takes upon themselves His name, who follows His teachings, the day of the Lord will be truly wonderful. Now is the time to repent. He has promised that those who trust in Him will be spared the trauma and horror that will visit the wicked."

"Tommy Gibbs promises much the same to his followers," Anne said neutrally. "That they will be swept up in the Rapture, leaving the wicked to burn behind them."

President Rojas smiled. "I have to disagree with Reverend Gibbs there. Our call is to bring the gospel to all the world, to build the beginnings of the kingdom of God on this earth. We believe that the Savior will come and establish His kingdom here once and for all."

"That will put an end to a lot of political aspirations," Anne interjected with a smile. "I'm sure that Senator Garlick is hoping you're wrong. Thank you, President Richard Rojas."

"You're welcome, Anne." He gazed at her, his eyes holding hers as the light blinked off. "And thank you, for giving us a chance to tell our side of the story."

"Just doing my job," Anne said, slightly flustered as she rose and disconnected her pin mike.

"You're doing well." President Rojas smiled, disconnecting his own and handing it to her. He caught her hand in both of his as she extended it for the usual formal handshake good-bye. "Anne, be careful out there. Manila's a troubled place these days—like so much of the world. Follow your instincts and keep your standards high, but don't push too hard or too long, and you'll be just fine."

Over the camera case he was packing, Leon watched President Rojas leave, his assistant falling into step with his long strides. They were already deep in discussion of the day's next appointments before they left the room. He glanced at Anne. "Be careful, huh? Did somebody tell him you were going to Manila?"

"No, not that I know of. We only found out this morning." The prescience, advice, and encouragement both reassured and troubled Anne. Whatever he really was, Richard Rojas had a presence that made the title "prophet" uncomfortably appropriate. What did he know about her—or Manila? His concern was so genuine that the idea that he'd run a backdoor investigation on her simply didn't fit. She shrugged off the shiver that ran down her spine and checked her watch. "Speaking of which, we better get moving too."

They headed for the Channel 8 broadcast van, where the tiny monitor glowed as Clara introduced a special companion report. They drove to the airport half listening to Channel 8's expert commentators arguing about the "millennialism" movement sweeping the nations, giving rise to charismatic preachers, self-proclaimed saviors, hopeful rapturists, disdainful atheists, hopeless suicides, wealthy psychiatrists, reassuring psychics, "spiritual manifestations," con artists of all descriptions and persuasions, and endless video commentaries on television as well.

* * *

My Dear Chisom,

We continue to delight in the Vids you attach with your e-mails. I'm sorry your district wide P-day turned out to be less fun than you intended, but then a sprained ankle will do that. I, too, am glad you did not break anything, but be aware that sometimes a sprain can be worse than a break and may even be more painful. I would caution you to go easy on it for a week or two. Push too early, and you could do some permanent damage.

Current conditions here in the States have really put pressure on me and the other members of the Church's public-relations staff. In my last letter I quoted D&C 38 where the Lord warns us that "the enemy is combined." What the Lord is telling us is that a secret combination, and probably more, will arise that will work to over-throw God's kingdom and destroy His children. Current events have shown that our enemies, at least some of them, have combined. We know who some of them are. MedaGen has put more than a million dollars into advertisements and other programs to smear and discredit the Church, and a number of television networks have taken up the banner and are twisting everything to make the Church look bad. The worst of the bunch is Channel 8, though a few of its reporters seem fair.

President Rojas is a marvel. The inspiration of President Smith to revive the office of Associate President, which hasn't functioned since the death of Joseph Smith's brother, Hyrum, is certainly clear. It has given the Church its needed spokesperson and freed President Smith to concentrate on the things of the kingdom.

I am pleased to report that all the effort and money our enemies have put into their smear campaign have done little to stop the growth of God's kingdom. As I mentioned, my PR team is really under pressure, but most of that is responding to all the enquiries we are receiving. It is true that all this bad publicity has reinforced the position of those who hate righteousness, but it has not made much of an inroad among the many goodhearted people that are out there. Many have seen through the spin and deceit and wondered why the attacks. Their curiosity has been aroused to investigate us. The result has increased missionary efforts considerably and given us a forum to tell our story.

I assure you, though harm will come out of this, the good will eclipse it. In the end, our enemies will know acute frustration. The Lord told Joseph Smith in section 121, "As well might man stretch forth his puny arm to stop the Missouri river in its decreed course, or to turn it up stream, as to hinder the Almighty."

I take comfort in something else the Lord said in the same section. He said His hand is upon our enemies "to blind their minds, that they may not understand His marvelous workings; that He may prove them also and take them in their own craftiness; also because their hearts are corrupted, and the things which they are willing to bring upon others, and love to have others suffer, may come upon themselves to the very uttermost."

You'll be happy to hear that the Church is making progress with the delegation from the newly formed states in southern China. We were successful in defusing all the problems caused by Brother Light's representatives, and we have only a few more bridges to cross before we will have permission to send in missionaries. We are also at last seeing a softening in the Near East. The war fought a decade ago has made more and more people willing to compromise and get along. I am very pleased to report that Israel has officially recognized the Church. Though we are still unable to proselyte, we are no longer forbidden from answering questions and even teaching if we are approached. The Near East and China were the last major areas where we needed to send missionaries. The Brethren are very pleased, because it means we are close to fulfilling the Church's mandate to preach the gospel to every nation, kindred, tongue, and people.

So you have personally run up against some of Brother Light's people, have you? He is aggressive and has the ability to infect his followers with a fervor that runs deep and hot. And yes, they do believe they have divine authority, or what we call priesthood. He claims his call came directly from God through multiple revelations and visions. During one of these, he says "beings of another world" bestowed upon him the authority he now gives to his followers. It is interesting how his "call" echoes the experiences of Joseph Smith, albeit without the persecutions.

I am not surprised you are disturbed with his people's claim to divine authority. If you haven't heard already, there is even more disturbing news. Mr. Janjalani claims the gifts of the Spirit and has made quite a show of them. These false spiritual gifts are fooling many.

We hear of his followers practicing glossolalia, or the speaking in tongues. Don't be concerned about this. Satan has imitated that power for centuries. If you get a chance, pay attention to what they do. You will find that they really don't speak in tongues, but rather babble. Also, there is no interpreter, and that violates the Bible's instructions. There it says, "If any man speak in an unknown tongue, let it be by two, or at most by three, and that by course [that is, in turn]; and let one interpret. But if there be no interpreter, let him keep silence in the church" (1 Cor. 14:27–28). It says further, "He that prophesieth speaketh unto men to edification, and exhortation and comfort. He that speaketh in an unknown tongue edifieth himself; but he that prophesieth edifieth the church" (1 Cor. 14:3–4).

The word translated "prophesy" means the same as bearing testimony (see Rev. 19:10). Understanding this helps us see that the Saints express the true spirit of prophecy during fast meeting services. And it is you and your companions who testify and teach in Chinese who possess the true gift of tongues.

Satan also imitates the priesthood power of healing. Here, too, the Bible gives us direction. James counseled his readers saying, "Is any sick among you? let him call for the elders of the church; and let them pray over him, anointing him with oil in the name of the Lord" (James 5:14).

According to the book of Revelation, we should not be surprised with false miracles. John tells us that there will come a master of deception. The Seer refers to him as a beast having two horns like a lamb (thus, an imitation of the Savior), but speaking through the inspiration of the great dragon, Satan. He will be able to deceive those who dwell on the earth by the means of miracles and signs and in that way seduce many to follow the ways of Babylon. Those whom he overcomes will persecute all who will not bow to Satan's will. (See Rev. 13:13–15.) There are dark days ahead.

The Lord, however, has not left us unprepared. The Bible counsels, "Believe not every spirit, but try the spirits whether they are of God: because many false prophets are gone out into the world" (1 Jn. 4:1). Jesus warned us that in the last days "there shall also arise false Christs, and false prophets, and shall show great signs and wonders, insomuch, that, if possible, they shall deceive the very elect" (JS–M 1:22). The Brethren have assured us that, though the scripture shows that most will be deceived, the elect will not be. I take great comfort in knowing that even now the elect, both within and without the Church, are seeing through the false signs and wonders. For that reason, they have the edge that will lead them to safety through righteousness. In not

*being deceived, we will be in tune with the Spirit and see
the path to follow to find security and happiness.*

*All this highlights the importance of what you and
the other missionaries are doing. The more you can bring
into the fold, the fewer Babylon will have to seduce.*

Work well, my son.

With love,

Your father,

Chinedu

* * *

"What is God?" the boy whispered under the blows of the rod
and shouts of his furious teacher.

"There is no God but Allah!"

The intricate calligraphy of the mosque's walls whirled into brilliant mandalas around them. The teacher's words submerged into
chanting mantras.

"What is God?" the boy asked again, his voice weak but still
yearning.

"There is nothing that is not God."

The mandalas melted into murals of Christian saints and sinners
glowing in the flames of the candles. The mantra bled into low-voiced
plainsong. The candles illuminated crimson trails from the boy's
bloody knees as he knelt before a black-robed priest.

"What is God?" The boy's voice, roughened and husky, rose
through the menacing chants.

"God is justice." The priest's stony face melded with alabaster and
jade visages of flower-bedecked statues. Mobs drove the boy from the
temple under the calm gaze of ochre-robed lamas.

As he escaped, a jungle canopy closed over the boy's head like the
beams of the cathedrals and temples, blood-red and snow-white
flowers in the green riot of leaves, dapples of sunlight disappearing
into the blackness between trees. Shadows moved within the blackness, glimpses of horns and twisted limbs and faces screaming hate.
The darkness grew overpowering, the roar of chaos and dissolution
rising to a crescendo.

"God is One." A single note, high, sweet, sustained, grew to a piercing volume, then faded into silence. A brilliant light filled the boy's eyes.

"God is One!" The boy's voice rang forth with the clarity of ultimate truth. In the temples, worshippers turned from stone statues to bow before him.

"God is One!" In the mosques, prayer rugs oriented to Mecca lay empty as their owners turned to the slight body of the dark-haired, dark-eyed boy.

"God is One!" Supplicants left candles burning on altars before smoke-blackened icons to run out into the sunlight and dance amid showers of flower petals. The boy, grown now to a dark-haired, dark-eyed man, smiled benevolently upon the Children of Light.

"God is One, and we are one." The man's bright eyes reflected a kaleidoscope of Asian, Arab, Islander, African, European faces. Music filled the world, harmony and counterpoint in rapturous flows of sound.

"The world is many, and division is pain." Distortion crept through the harmonies. Shouting faces distorted with rage, wealthy guests laughed at a lavish wedding, flames licked through bullet-riddled cottages, high-rise buildings glittered diamondlike above neon brilliance, thin blankets half covered the wasted limbs and ribs of starving children, bracelets jingled on the limbs of half-veiled dancers.

"Division must heal into unity." In mosques, temples, and chapels, white-robed monks swayed in sedate rapture, counting rosaries on rainbow beads. Children laughed and splashed in the fountains of a palace. Masked, robed men danced with flashing blades, their comrades shouting prayers and waving rifles. Parades of white-clad monks, blue-robed women, red-masked warriors, and laughing streams of brightly clothed children danced over streets strewn with flowers and shattered remains of material excess.

"Life and death are one, sorrow and joy two faces of the same reality." Weeping mourners walking behind a black-draped coffin faded into joyous celebrants of a new birth. The man appeared, blessing babies, touching children, smiling into the eyes of young mothers, comforting bloodstained young men, speaking to attentive audiences of distinguished elders, blessing the still form of a martyred soldier, touching the hand of an old man.

"We are one." The Children of Light marched in the streets of Manila, filled a village in Madagascar, marched in platoons across the plaza in the old Kenyan capital, danced in Singapore's central park, prayed in a Sumatran mosque, smiled in a shower of brilliant water drops and flower petals.

"God is One," Brother Light proclaimed, his voice rich and captivating. Light shone around and through his eyes, their darkness brightening into the brilliance of sunrise.

* * *

The brilliance was reflected in Anne's eyes as the film ended, leaving the flower-and-sword logo of the Children of Light glowing against a black background.

"Whew. Not bad." Leon nodded. "Looks like they actually hired some professionals for that one."

"Bradford-Matsuma," Anne supplied. "Marketing firm out of London and New York."

"How much can we use to spice the report?" the cameraman asked, checking the data transfer from the disk into his own camera.

"All of it." Anne double-checked the disclosure contract the Children of Light had supplied along with the video documentary of their leader's "revelation of the divine power and strength within him and conversion to the true order of the universe." The contract, in fact, urged her to air the documentary in its entirety, and offered translations into a long list of languages. "Looks like they want us to spread the good word for them."

Leon rolled his eyes. "Them and everybody else. Remember when religious leaders and politicians didn't want to talk to the media?"

"No." Anne shot him a grin. "I'm too young to remember the Dark Ages."

"Ha, ha." Leon grinned back, lifting the camera. "Let's get outside, catch some of the skyline for your intro bit. The hotel garden's nice, even if it looks a little staged."

Leon brought the camera to his shoulder as Anne pasted on her professional smile.

"This is Anne O'Neal, reporting from Manila. This city, so

recently torn by natural disasters, is the headquarters of the fastest-growing religious movement in the world. Led by the former Rashi Janjalani, the organization known as the Children of Light has grown exponentially in Southeast Asia, Micronesia, and the Philippines. The movement, attracting thousands of followers among people homeless, impoverished, and oppressed by governments and economic collapses, is now moving west to India and Central Asia, as well as making inroads into mainland China.

"Brother Light, as Janjalani is now known, preaches a combination of Buddhism, Islam, and Christianity, proclaiming that God is One, and all people should be one as well. According to their charismatic leader, it is time for believers to stand up for truth and unity, even in the face of persecution. And while there has been some persecution, particularly by the governments of China and India, the Children of Light have steadily overcome all opposition.

"However, it appears that as the Children of Light have grown in power and influence, they have begun their own persecutions. Brother Light declares that life and death are two faces of the same reality; the Children of Light also seem to have two faces: peaceful, protesting monks and red-masked soldiers. Reports say that these soldiers, known as the Hand of the Prophet, force conversions or kill unbelievers, especially in remote or isolated areas. Official statements from the Children of Light, however, maintain that their volunteer soldiers step in only to protect peaceful citizens from roving gangs and criminals that the civilian police are powerless to stop. Other reports, available from confidential sources, implicate the Children of Light in terrorist activities, like the assassination of a Mormon Apostle and even the destruction of the Aswan Dam—"

"Brother Light calls for you, Miss O'Neal." The camera slewed around to frame a man dressed in a hotel uniform, and a tall, red-masked figure standing behind him.

The uniformed servant gracefully faded back into the baroque halls of the hotel as three more of Brother Light's soldiers emerged from the lush greenery of the hotel's lobby and surrounded the two American journalists. With gestures but no words, they indicated that Anne and Leon should come along with them, then they led the way out of the hotel and into the street, where a military transport waited.

The driver sped wildly through the streets, forcing other vehicles to dodge out of the way. Crowds scattered, but to Anne's surprise, they threw more flowers and salutes than dirty looks and curses. The vehicle screeched to a halt in front of the intricate facade of a Catholic church—a former Catholic church, now one of the headquarters of the Children of Light.

Four "fingers" of the Hand of the Prophet neatly surrounded their charges, leaving the last—*the thumb*, Leon thought reflexively—with the logo-painted jeep. The huge, carved doors swung open noiselessly before them, revealing the long, candlelit cavern of the nave. Colorful tapestries stitched with scenes of lovely, young dancers replaced the sober depictions of the Lives of the Saints; a large portrait of Brother Light with rays of light emanating from his lambent eyes hung in place of the traditional blood-stained crucifix. The rows of pews had disappeared, leaving a rug- and pillow-strewn floor, tiled in endlessly repeating sword-and-flower patterns. Swirls of incense smoke twined in the air like scarves around the limbs of the dancers in the murals, which shined in multicolored light from the stained-glass windows.

The slender form of a woman emerged from the intricate layering of light and shadow. A discreet door closed behind her as she stopped in front of the railing that had once guarded the altar. Ruby lights glinted in her dark hair and cast deep violet dapples over her blue robe as she stood waiting. Her eyes flicked over Anne and Leon and the four tall men surrounding them, then beyond, as if someone else paced along behind them.

The tallest of the soldiers halted before the woman and made a polite gesture of greeting and said a couple of words in Tagalog.

The woman responded briefly, waving a hand as if in dismissal, but none of the soldiers moved. Her flickering eyes rested momentarily on Anne, then on Leon, and she smiled. The expression was more polite than welcoming, and strangely sad. "The reporter and the cameraman from America," she said in melodically accented but clear English. "I am Sepphira. Welcome. He is expecting you. Please come." She turned and glided away through the heavy atmosphere and opened the gilded door.

"She's the ex-wife," Leon whispered to Anne. "The one who got hit in the head with a rock back when they were just starting up."

Anne nodded; she'd done her homework for this interview. Sepphira was smaller than she'd expected, a bird-boned creature under her flowing blue robes, and also more intense.

She led them into the vestry, the small room the priest had once used to dress for Mass. It had undergone an even more dramatic transformation than the chapel. Lush hangings hid the formerly bare, stone walls; banks of candles glowed in gold-shot crystal containers; deep, velvet upholstery covered the chest benches. The small gilt door at the far end of the room swung back, giving them a glimpse of an even more luxuriously appointed suite.

The man who came through the door, however, immediately caught their attention. Though not tall or unusually handsome, and dressed plainly in unadorned white, he dominated the room the moment he entered. His presence, bearing, and confidence outshone the surroundings, his eyes shining deeper and brighter than the jewels starring the tapestries. At the moment, those eyes rested on the young woman who emerged with him. She knelt and kissed his hands, then rose and drifted out into the hazy depths of the chapel as Sepphira opened the door, pulling her blue robe into place around her.

Brother Light didn't watch her go, or see the way Sepphira's eyes followed her as she disappeared. He fixed those remarkable eyes on Anne and smiled—and suddenly she knew why multitudes gathered to listen to him. "Anne. Welcome." He extended one long-fingered hand, placing his palm lightly on her hair, then touched her chin with his fingertips. His touch tingled.

Leon felt it too, when Brother Light greeted him by name with the same touch, which made him twitch. "Thanks, Mr.—Bro—Rev—?"

Brother Light laughed, the rich sound of it filling the room. "Relax, Leon. I claim no special title. My Children call me Prophet, Father, Reverend, Lama, Mullah—all just cultural terms they learned before they came to the truth. If you must call me anything, call me Brother; I am simply here to serve the Great Cause of True Unity."

He gestured gracefully at the cushions surrounding them. "Please, sit. Make yourselves comfortable." He settled neatly on a soft pillow, drawing his bare feet up to sit tailor fashion—and in exactly the right position for the light from the candles to cast a rosy aura around him in the camera's eye, Leon noted automatically.

Anne noticed too. As she looked at him, the sudden memory of President Rojas's smile blossomed in her mind—and her cynical reporter instincts stirred as she settled on the edge of a padded chest lid. The ruby glow of Leon's camera light hardened her mental armor. She could play this game.

"Thank you. You've certainly made this a comfortable place." She smiled back, gesturing around the room before running one hand along the intricate brocade of the seat. "This is very elegant, especially in a city as badly damaged and economically depressed as this one. We've heard that the Children of Light are busily building up the material foundation for an earthly kingdom."

"Indeed, yes," Brother Light agreed easily, his voice rich, deep, and amused. "But don't let willfully dense critics lead you to an incorrect understanding. Yes, this is elegant, and it is earthly. The important thing to realize is that the earth itself will be heaven, now that the truth of Divine Unity has been revealed. Unity will result in the ultimate transformation of the earth, and the Children of Light will be the agents of that cleansing fire. They are the enlightened ones, the hands of the Divine Oneness, and they will be ever victorious."

"Victorious," Anne repeated. "That sounds as if you expect a battle."

"We do—a battle against the evil and greed that causes disunity and disparity," he said, a sudden glint of steel in his smile. "The Children of Light are both brave and determined and will do whatever is necessary to bring about that ultimate unity."

"Including engaging in armed clashes with Muslim, Hindu, and Christian militants in Sumatra and India," Anne suggested.

"Whatever is necessary," Brother Light said. "Living for the truth—or dying for it." He leaned back, pantherlike in his supple ease. "The Children of Light do not fear death, and there are thousands willing to lay down their lives if called upon to do it. After all, death is simply the reflection of life; those of my children who lay down their lives for the great cause will be reborn in a glorious resurrection."

"That's quite a promise," Anne observed, openly skeptical. "When will the valiant martyrs rise from their graves?"

"If I told you, would I have to give Channel 8 the exclusive footage of the miraculous event?" Brother Light teased, the smile lingering on his lips as he continued. "No, Anne, there will be no amazing scenes of reconstituting skeletons for your viewers' amusement. The truly valiant will be reborn without the traditional processes of karma and reincarnation; they will return to Earth immediately, in the bodies of babies in the womb." His hands flew outward, embracing the room, the chapel, and the city beyond. "Here, to a real, material heaven. Therefore, it behooves us to make sure this earth is as heavenly as possible, all rewards in place."

He glanced to the still form of the woman still standing beside the door. "Which we have begun to do, haven't we, Sepphira?" The woman nodded, but he had already returned his intense gaze to Anne. "We have worked with international relief agencies, private businesses, and governments to ensure that everyone receives basic necessities—and what few luxuries are available in this, as you say, devastated and depressed city. Unity is paramount, Anne. All property should be held in common, and any disparity in wealth is a sign of disunity."

Anne glanced at Sepphira as well, watching as the woman's wide-eyed gaze drifted past Brother Light to the bank of candles. The reporter pulled her attention from the haunted woman's face to the man whose charm seemed to wrap around her like the soft folds of a velvet boa constrictor. Instinctively, she fought against the enveloping psychic folds. "Therefore, the Children of Light tear down the homes and buildings of the wealthy for redistribution among all believers—specifically, the homes and buildings belonging to local merchants and groups, like Mormons, who don't agree with your program."

A flicker of annoyance crossed Brother Light's face, giving Anne a jag of satisfaction. She continued quickly before he could respond. "But you've also made sure that big corporations have protection and official welcome to rebuild—and keep their own profits and property. How do you reconcile that with the ideal of all property held in common?"

The annoyance disappeared into a sharp-edged smile. "All is held in common," he assured her. "Haven't you Americans always said that there's plenty to go around, if distribution were equal? Right now, we need to make sure that everyone has a chance to become comfortable with that distribution. We must bring the sheep into the fold before we can harvest their wool."

"Or shear them?" she suggested. "And what about those who aren't Children of Light? Reports and even my own observations suggest that your aid stations distribute this common wealth only to your followers. Those who aren't in the Light family, so to speak, don't get to eat."

"Was that a question, Anne?" he asked, leaning forward attentively. He was enjoying this, playing for the camera.

"No, that was more of a statement," Anne admitted. The sudden vision of how he would look on tape, the benevolent cleric tolerating a badgering reporter, itched in her head. She leaned back, crossing her legs. "How about this question: Are you distributing aid only to your followers, and persecuting others, even assassinating those who oppose you?"

Brother Light laughed, but a spark snapped in his eyes. "Nonsense. It is the Children of Light who have met with persecution at every turn. After the Revelation, when I first began preaching the Oneness of God, my first disciples and I were the victims of stoning in this very city, an attack that badly wounded Sepphira." He gestured toward her, Leon's camera instantly following the direction. Sepphira's darting eyes came to rest on the red light above the lens, and she smiled shyly, one hand rising to touch the side of her head, where a jagged scar remained from the stone that had struck her skull—and had opened her eyes to a world she could find no way to escape.

"It could have ended with me—with all of us—literally burned at the stake, Anne," Brother Light said softly. "But through me the Divine spoke commands which the mob heard as the tongue of angels, and the ropes that bound us miraculously broke, falling into the mess of broken boards at our feet. My touch healed Sepphira— and one of the men who had attacked us and had been trampled in the confusion. We extend the hand of charity, of love, of unity, despite hatred and persecution."

"I saw extended hands this morning, Brother Light," Anne said. "But they were throwing bottles and bricks. We saw your followers attempt to stone a woman and young children who were probably Mormons. Are you sure that you haven't encouraged your Children to convert everyone to this Great Unity—by whatever means necessary?"

He rose to his feet, gently stroking his chin as he gazed down at her. Leon had to shift to catch his profile. The pause was just long enough to let him seriously consider her question—but not long enough to look like hesitation to search for the right answer. "Of course I'm sure," he said, his smile unwavering. "No matter what opposition we face—and the Mormons have opposed us, as have the Catholics, the Islamic Front, and other fundamentalists—I would never encourage violence."

"Have you told your people that?" Anne drove on, aiming for the thin crack she felt in his armor. "Or told them who you really are? I've been able to recover some information about your past, Mr. Janjalani. You're from Australia, not the Philippines. In fact, weren't your parents members of an environmentalist commune? From the records Channel 8's investigators have uncovered, you grew up on a sheep station, running with a gang known for vandalizing water-pumping windmills. Local ranchers called in the law, and it seems you took off to avoid arrest—and suddenly emerged from the Philippine jungles with a new name, a new vision, and an army of red-masked soldiers. Have you just moved up a rung, from leading a juvie gang to commanding a terrorist movement?"

"A terrorist movement? Me? The Children of Light? What an imagination you have, Anne!" Brother Light's laugh rang around the room as he flung his hands out. He quieted, smiled, and suddenly reached out to touch Leon's camera. It sparked, a thin string of smoke rising from its innards, and the crimson light faded away.

He turned sharply, leaning over, nearly nose to nose with Anne. "So fragile, technology—in the face of true power. Beware. You have set yourself in opposition to the Divine and are treading on the edge of a precipice." A long finger traced her cheek, ran slowly down her throat and came to rest between her collarbones. "It would be so very easy to push you over. Remember this, Anne O'Neal—anyone who opposes me will be destroyed in the final confrontation—or before, if necessary."

Anne didn't let herself flinch at his touch. "You can't threaten me." She kept her voice steady. "If you do, I will tell everyone. Everyone in the world, everywhere Channel 8 broadcasts."

He nuzzled her hair, the chuckle in his chest vibrating through her shoulder rather than through her ears. "Who will believe you?

Your masters, the half-witted Western opinion-makers, love me because I make the Pacific Rim stable for their businesses." He pulled back, smiling into her eyes. "And my dear children will never believe you, because you are an American whore." He kissed her, mockingly.

Anne jerked her head back, shoving him away. Leon sprang forward, his usually amiable face set hard. The door opened again, and the four red-masked soldiers lumbered into the small room, surrounding the two journalists.

Brother Light stepped back, looking at the two Westerners between the soldiers' heavy shoulders. "Thank you for the interview, Anne—it's been most enlightening. Please feel free to use all the footage you have in your report later." He swept up his long, white over robe, swirling it around his shoulders as he moved to the door. He paused as Sepphira opened the glittering portal. "Oh—a word to the wise. Consider the state of your soul—and, if word leaks out that you hate the Children of Light, you may want to consider the state of your car, apartment, and mailbox as well. I do not advocate violence; I really don't have to. Have a pleasant flight back home." He swept out, Sepphira fluttering after him.

Anne was tempted to send a sharp response to his threat when the warning from Richard Rojas jabbed into her mind. She decided to follow it for now. She had caught a glimpse of what Janjalani really was, and she intended to reveal it, even if it meant facing danger.

CHAPTER 5

Emerald leaves waved as they snapped back in the wake of the swift-moving soldiers. "Assume formation and move in." The troop split neatly into three groups at the order. The two captains led their men out to the sides of Major Zamora's detachment. A reliable tip placed the area now surrounded by Zamora's squad as the location of a camp of El Jaguar's rebels.

"Ready on left." Captain Ulloa's voice crackled in Zamora's earpiece as the captain led three men through the feathery green cover of ferns. One glanced nervously at the sky, hoping the rain would hold off long enough to give them clear sight lines for the fight.

"Ready on right," said Captain Guerra.

"Quiet, quiet, thirty more yards, then hit dirt. We don't want a massacre—yet." Zamora whispered the orders into the comm-set snugged around his neck. Lightning flashed through the gray sky above the trees. Through the thick leaves, he caught sight of an answering flash from the bright scarlet jaguar badge adorning the side of an olive-drab tent, just where his informers had guessed it would be.

"Three tents," Ulloa informed the team from his advance position, peering through the vegetation and dull-painted binoculars. "No movement. Wait—we got one. Coming out of the middle tent. Three men, one in the lead." The excitement in his low voice came clearly through the open channel. "Looks like we found our jungle cat!"

"Here, kitty, kitty," Guerra whispered. A couple of soldiers chuckled under their breath.

The laughter stopped abruptly, however, as El Jaguar turned to look squarely at Ulloa's position—and smiled. The ambushers abruptly became the ambushed.

Bullets ripped through the leaves as El Jaguar's guerillas burst out of their camouflaged positions. One of them broke out from what had looked like the solid trunk of a huge, storm-blasted tree right behind Zamora's position. The major whirled, his own gun rising, as the soldier beside him jerked, gasping as perforations appeared across his chest. The bullets hit Zamora's rifle, ripping it from his hands. With no room or time to dodge, Zamora stood his ground, a half-formed prayer in his mind. He jerked his sidearm from its holster and drew bead on the guerilla in one smooth motion. The major and the rebel gazed at each other over the dulled black of their gun barrels. The sound of the wild firefight around them seemed far away, echoing like the sound of the ocean captured in a shell. A vicious grin spread over the guerilla's face as he compared his fully automatic rifle to Zamora's pistol. Both men pulled their triggers. The crack of the major's gun drowned the hollow click of the rebel's automatic rifle misfiring. He still looked surprised as he tumbled backwards to sprawl against the tree he had used for camouflage.

The pandemonium of the battle roared back into Zamora's head, cries and orders almost drowned in the deafening noise. "Pull out!" he bellowed into the open comm channel. "Ambush! Pull out! Captains, get your men out of here!"

He grabbed the young, wide-eyed soldier next to him and shoved him hard in the direction they had come from. "Get out before the noose closes. Move!"

The other members of Zamora's detachment needed no additional incentive; they fell into an orderly withdrawal pattern, laying down cover fire as they retreated back down the game trail.

Guerra shepherded his men into retreat formation and led them right through the rebels' camp in a mad, unexpected dash for safety. They tore past El Jaguar's decoy tent and disappeared into the heavy undergrowth beyond, shooting wildly behind them to keep the guerillas' heads down.

Ulloa's men, caught between the ambushers and the camp, formed a loose, fast-moving line. Zigzagging around every branch and shred of cover, they maneuvered for an opening. Zamora grabbed the rifle from the hands of the dead soldier beside him and threw himself flat on the wet ground. He held the rifle steady and fired a low, vicious stream of shots parallel to the ground. Screaming and clutching their legs, two guerillas fell into the thick bushes.

"Forward!" Ulloa shouted, guiding his men toward the opening Zamora's shots provided. As he drew even with one of the wounded rebels, Ulloa paused. They needed a live witness, someone who could confirm their suspicions of El Jaguar and his possible link to Garza. The captain glanced behind, seeing the guerillas bearing down on him. He kicked the rebel's rifle away, pulled him to his feet, and hauled him along.

Zamora lurched to his feet and ran toward Ulloa, laying down cover fire as he neared the captain and captive. The guerilla leaned heavily on Ulloa, then stumbled suddenly onto one knee. Ulloa jerked at his arm, shouting at him to get up, glaring toward the rebels tearing toward him. He never saw the flash of the knife the guerilla pulled from his boot sheath. The guerilla buried the blade deep in Ulloa's chest just as Zamora reached the pair.

Zamora watched the young captain fall. The first few splashes of heavy rain hit Ulloa's chest, water mingling with the blood, as Zamora's grief turned temporarily into fury. He caught the guerilla's hand in a punishing grip and twisted hard, breaking the wrist bones. The guerilla yelped, the knife falling from his now useless fingers as the major jerked him along toward the game trail.

Shouts behind them were suddenly matched in front. Guerra and the other men who had managed to regroup erupted out of their own hasty camouflage, laying down a withering barrage of fire to cover Zamora's escape. The major slogged through the mud, rain pounding against his head and shoulders, water running into his eyes.

A figure appeared suddenly out of the thickening rain. Another blade flashed in the glare of a lightning bolt. Zamora and El Jaguar looked at each other as Zamora struggled to shift his captured witness and bring up his own weapon—then the knife descended. The rebel winced as his leader plunged the knife into his ribs then drew it out. A bullet whined past Zamora's arm and sent the knife spinning away; El Jaguar spun as well, tearing the dead rebel from Zamora's grasp, and dived into the undergrowth as more bullets tore through the curtain of rain. Beyond the noise of the water rapidly turning the path into a small creek, the sounds of the rebels' retreat registered dimly in Zamora's ears.

"Major!" Captain Guerra shouted. "We've got the bodies of Ulloa and Santiago. Fresno and Gaete are wounded, but everyone else is ready. Do we pursue?"

Through the rain, into who knows what further ambush? Somehow, El Jaguar had known they were coming; he had hit them hard and disappeared into the rain, taking even the dead rebels with him. Following him would only expose them to more risk for no reward. El Jaguar undoubtedly had his escape plans set, just like his decoy campsite, before Zamora's men arrived.

"No. Fall back to the vehicles," Zamora said. "We won't find them in this rain. Secure the area—don't touch anything until you check it for traps. We'll report and get investigators out here." *And then I will find the words, somewhere, to tell Mrs. Santiago and Mrs. Ulloa that their husbands will come home for the last time.* He silently prayed, for the dead men's families, for the wounded, for the strength to lead his men home. The prayer was heartfelt but wordless, as the rain seemed to pound all thoughts out of his head but one: How did El Jaguar know? His informants were reliable and his information good. That meant only one thing. Someone on the inside was working for the enemy.

* * *

Thoughts fluttered through Sepphira's head as she ran two steps behind Brother Light. Always two steps behind, showing proper deference; always two steps behind, never knowing what he would do next. The members of the Hand who waited to whisk them away in the limousine didn't know either, but they didn't care, didn't worry like she did.

She startled as their group emerged from the old chapel into the hot afternoon. To her eyes, a shadow twined sinuously through the bas-relief carvings covering the facade. She saw a smoky face turn toward her, its eyes glittering with darkness blacker than reality, the suggestion of its teeth sharp as a guilty conscience. *Go away, dark spirit,* she silently commanded. *Go away. We have no need of you now.* The apparition's immaterial grin widened; she had no authority over it, and it knew that.

"Great Prophet." The leader of the Hand greeted Rashi with a deep bow, opening the glossy door of the car. His eyes followed his leader worshipfully; he didn't see Sepphira at all as she climbed into the back seat, sitting tensely across from Rashi, next to another member of the Hand who ignored her just as thoroughly. They cared nothing for women, either Sepphira or the girl who had come with the car, shyly snuggling up to Rashi. They simply waited to do their master's bidding and carry out his orders without question or thought. Rashi called them weapons, automatically guided, semi-intelligent weapons that he pointed in the right direction and launched.

Does he think that of Anne O'Neal, of her cameraman Leon? Are they new arrows for his quiver and bow? Unbelievers make dangerous weapons, unreliable, prone to misfires that wound their wielders. Why had he touched her? The question burned like acid in Sepphira's mind, trailing a parade of other questions: *Why does he touch the others? Why does a girl wait for him wherever he goes, a different girl always? Why does he turn away from me, who loves him more than life? Why does he deny himself only the love of a wife, saying that true unity denies him an exclusive pairing?* These were questions that she should not even let herself think. Rashi teased her that he could still think rings around her, still evade even her foreknowledge. And he could; the shadow spirits that haunted her mind only laughed when she dared to ask them what Rashi was thinking. It was easier to think of the first question anyway, the one she could think of strategically.

Why did he touch Anne O'Neal? Because he wanted to frighten her, to show he did not fear her, to seduce her into filing a positive report—or to anger her into denouncing him. Channel 8's broadcasts provided saturation coverage, going to every country in the world via satellite. If Anne O'Neal told the world that Brother Light brought a divine message to all the children of the world, a fashionable religion suitable for sophisticated believers, dilettante spiritualists in the United States and Europe—the self-termed First World—would embrace him. *But*—a slow smile spread across Sepphira's thin face—*if Channel 8 denounced him, Rashi would win supporters in all the war-torn, weather-beaten, poverty-stricken corners of hell in this world.*

Rashi glanced at her expression and smiled back at her, his fingers still stroking the starry-eyed girl's hair. He winked then turned his attention back to the young thing cuddling into his touch.

Why did he take other women? *Because the martyrs deserved noble reincarnations, because the Children of Light are the true children of the Divine, because love brooks no barriers, because the connection we share grows far deeper than physical expression.* The mantra of reasons and reassurances spun through her head in Rashi's warm, convincing voice. It drove the hurt deeper, sinking past her conscious mind and into her soul. Sepphira barely waited for the limousine to stop before she opened the door, stepping out into the thunderstorm of cheers and flashbulbs surrounding the huge reception center.

The crowd surged forward, throwing flower petals and wailing hymns as Brother Light made his grand arrival at the gala reception welcoming the leaders of the United Nations to Manila. The other dignitaries could only watch in envy as the white-robed man made his slow progress through the fragrant shower, glowing in the lights of a hundred cameras and a thousand adoring eyes.

Sepphira followed, two steps behind, a shadow in blue among shadows in black and red. They left the cheering and chants behind and entered the reception room. The powerful, wealthy, influential, and ambitious men and a few women—the ones who wore ornaments instead of being ornaments—gazed at them with practiced eyes, evaluating potential threat, possible advantage. Brother Light smiled back at the ones Sepphira subtly indicated—the ones who trailed darker shadows, shadows that twined around and over them with hints of glittering eyes and sinister grins.

The secretary general of the United Nations came forward to greet the leader of the world's fastest-growing religion or, as some said, insane cult or radically dangerous fundamentalist movement. The stately woman and the religious leader exchanged air kisses, a formal benediction for each cheek, in the steady glow of the invitation-only cameras.

The lights glinted off the secretary general's subdued jewelry as she stood behind the podium a few moments later, delivering a graceful speech expressing the world's sympathy for the disasters Manila and so many other cities had endured, promising international aid and support, and thanking so many organizations for their generous efforts in behalf of the victims. The light glinted from the elegant plaque an aide held up for the cameras, and in Brother Light's eyes as he gracefully approached the podium at her invitation. He smiled humbly as the secretary general proffered not only thanks but an announcement that the United Nations hereby formally extended official recognition to the Children of Light.

The representatives applauded the speech. Despite substantive reports of violence or coercion, enough countries, either long-established but resting on unsteady foundations or newly formed and dependent on the goodwill of volatile gangs, had voted to recognize and officially congratulate the Children of Light for bringing stability to the region. Other nations had gone along without protest, mostly because they knew that the Hand of the Prophet could destabilize any government that opposed them. The representatives also applauded Brother Light's eloquent thanks on behalf of all who worked to further the great purposes of the One God, and they breathed a sigh of relief when the divine messenger glided off the podium and out into the hot evening, his entourage falling in around him, Sepphira two steps behind.

She stood beside him on the platform at the mass rally, however. Devotees filled the stadium, dancing, singing, chanting, cheering as Brother Light stood in the spotlights. Sepphira gazed over the crowd. Spirits whispered in her aching head: "She misses her mother, Rosa." "He thinks he has cancer." "She is pregnant, and no one knows." "He stole from his parents' store and has given himself an ulcer over it."

Above all the voices, Rashi's beautiful voice filled the air, weaving a sonorous spell over the rapturous listeners. They called out responses, falling to their knees in ecstasies. The sermon ended with a stirring call to arms, an exhortation to guide the world toward Divine Unity under the One God, and a vivid recitation of the pleasures of an earthly heaven. Brother Light stretched out his hands, calling for those in pain, the lonely, the halt and sick. Closing his eyes, he intoned the names Sepphira whispered through his headset, calling the individuals whose weaknesses and needs made them vulnerable, made them want to believe.

Red-masked lieutenants escorted the parade of supplicants to the platform. Under Brother Light's hands, they writhed, cried, and rose up, calling out in strange tongues. He called forth visitations from deceased ancestors and holy angels. His "divine" power, the innate talent of a born manipulator—and Sepphira's soft voice—told him exactly what to say, the dark reflection of the gift of tongues.

* * *

Far beyond the borders of the stage, Anne and Leon watched the service, intensely aware of the speculative glances of the red-masked soldiers all around them. Channel 8 held one of the exclusive contracts for U.N. broadcasts, and thus Leon had recorded the secretary general's speech and Brother Light's gracious acceptance. Now, the red light of Leon's camera had no official sanction; neither did other Western journalists who hovered at the edges, catching footage from a distance. Other cameras, in the hands of Children of Light, recorded the scene for dissemination to believers—and would-be converts—all over the world. Channel 8's live broadcast drew high ratings, however, even without the favored camera angles and despite, or maybe because of, Anne's dark-toned introduction. In the rebroadcast, she had closed her brief summary of the day's events by calling Brother Light a "charismatic but megalomaniac cult leader."

That had drawn a chuckle from Monk, but he shrugged off her much more explicit account of what he had done and said after shorting out Leon's camera. "You're a pretty woman," Monk said, his voice whispering into her headset. "When you meet one of these evangelist types who doesn't make a pass at you, that'll surprise me."

President Rojas didn't, she thought, but said aloud, "I don't think we should be giving him more publicity. He's dangerous, and he's using us for his own ends."

"Like we're not using him," Monk sighed wearily, exchanging a glance with Kim, who shrugged. "What happened to objectivity, O'Neal? Everybody uses everybody, and everybody knows it. Caveat emptor. It's our job to cover whatever the people want to see when they want to see it, not make judgments about what they should see, based on our personal opinions."

"Unless somebody pays us to?" Anne shot back.

"Sure," Monk said easily. "Like I said, so long as it's not based on personal opinions. Just remember that I'm not stopping you from voicing your opinion. Go ahead and give him a bad review if you want to. But we're out to Clara in three—two—now."

"Darn it, Monk," Anne muttered, as the broadcast light on Leon's emergency backup camera went out. Brother Light's voice, amplified through distortion-free speakers, gave her the shivers; she couldn't deny his presence, his attractiveness, but even from across a stadium, she felt the weight of his fingertips on her face, the promise of menace breathed against her hair.

"You don't like this one," Leon observed. His camera remained steady, still recording the scene for archival footage.

"No," Anne agreed, glancing at the cameraman. "And neither do you. Thanks for being willing to jump in and defend my honor, by the way."

Leon grinned, somewhat abashed. "Hey, you're my meal ticket, right?" He lowered the camera and tucked it into its case. "Gotta keep the other guys off you. Can't have you putting on a blue dress and disappearing into Janjalani's harem—or Rojas's either."

"President Rojas is in a completely different league." The depth of conviction in her voice startled her, as did the momentary flicker of reassurance she felt when she thought of the Mormon leader. "I wonder if he could tell peoples' fortunes like that?"

"He might be able to." Leon zipped up the pack. "But he doesn't have to. Say what you want, at least Mormons are sensible folk—their head men don't jabber in tongues and make people roll around in fits."

"No, they're not into spiritualist tricks. But could Rojas short out a camera just by touching it?"

Leon laughed. "Sure he could, if he had the little mobile demag/EMP generator that our friend Brother Light did." He nodded at Anne's questioning look. "Yeah, little handheld thing. They're pretty common. Used for short-circuiting obnoxious peoples' PDAs and cell phones."

"So it wasn't an actual curse, huh? Sister Mary Edward at my Catholic grade school would be so disappointed—a heathen magician without any demons up his sleeve." Anne laughed at herself for feeling better about the explanation. Rationally, she didn't believe that Rashi Janjalani possessed supernatural powers, but her gut told her otherwise.

"Maybe not demons," Leon said as he picked up the backpack, leaning in close as he nodded toward the black-uniformed soldiers slowly beginning to converge on their position. "But we could do with some angelic help on our side. Let's hope St. Christopher isn't too busy to help us squeak out of here, because the crowd's looking ugly."

"It's St. Anthony who's the patron of travelers now," Anne absently reminded him, already moving.

"I'm good with whatever saint's available, so long as he gets me back to the car in one piece."

* * *

"This is Carl Jensen, science specialist for Channel 8 News. I'm at Shelton State, where several major environmental groups, including the Whole Earth Alliance, have joined with consumer-advocate organizations to protest the development of genetically engineered corn and other 'Frankenfoods.'"

The camera zoomed in past Jensen to focus on sign-waving protesters besieging the agriculture building at Shelton State. Other protesters, dressed as giant ears of corn and stalks of wheat with dramatically painted stitches and bolts, danced around the edges of the crowd. A tall, handsome man with a flowing, leonine mane and the lithe step of a born performer stepped up to the makeshift podium, raising his hands for quiet. The volume of the chants lowered, but the rhythmic rumble didn't quite die away.

"Cosheen Hall, a multimillionaire, has invested much of his wealth in establishing the Whole Earth Alliance. His organization has been successful at raising public consciousness about the perils of overpopulation and the destruction of the earth's limited resources. The WEA is not without their critics, however. Some accuse its members of using strong-arm tactics to get their way, though allegations that the WEA participated in the terrorist bombing of the Aswan Dam in Egypt have largely been dismissed." Jensen hastily finished the introduction as Cosheen began to speak.

"These companies expect us to believe that manipulations that change the very nature of a living thing will have no effect on us," said Hall. "Their biotechnicians take genetic material—the very blueprints that govern how living things grow—and arrogantly toss them into a technological blender. The miracle corn, the golden rice, and the enhanced soybeans companies sell for billions of dollars a year actually contain the genetic ingredients of not merely other plants but fungi, viruses, and bacteria!" Boos and shouts of disapproval erupted from the audience, their signs shaking vigorously.

Hall's perfectly modulated voice rose above their noise. "These mutant plants, plants that would never be found in nature, produce toxins that destroy native butterfly populations, poison birds and small animals, and crossbreed with wild plants. The bioagricultural companies say they're producing food for the world's excess population; what they're producing is a crop of superweeds that will choke out the natural plants that keep the environment healthy!"

Amid shouts of approval that verged on the hysterical screaming usually reserved for pop stars, he retired from the podium and into a waiting car covered with stickers proclaiming it a "clean fuel" vehicle. The camera left the next speaker, who liked to quote statistics— always a buzz kill on the ratings—to give the protesters their individual close-ups.

The science specialist extended his handheld microphone to a young woman with long hair covered with beads.

"The world is in trouble already," she exclaimed, tears filling her eyes. "How can we offend the Goddess even more?"

"It's all about the bucks," her buzz-cut companion growled. "They make plants that kill butterflies and deer, then get the world hooked on cheap corn and charge thousands for seeds to grow the next year's crop."

"Irradiating live foods introduces single-bit errors into the DNA!" another woman shouted, waving her "Go Organic" banner over her head. Irradiating food to preserve it wasn't directly related to the discussion at hand, but it made for a good sound bite.

"Of course, we have deep concerns about the safety of genetically modified foods," a neatly suited man assured Channel 8's science specialist. The caption introduced him as Dr. Benjamin DeWitt, president of the American Whole Foods Consortium. "Our research has shown that organically grown produce, as well as free-range, antibiotic-free meats and poultry, contain far fewer harmful chemicals than those produced by standard farms. We simply do not know enough about the environmental effects of genetically modified crops to feel comfortable with the idea of planting them out in open fields—or feeding them to consumers."

* * *

"Nah, you should feed them bug-infested apples and sick chicken carcasses instead," Ivana Mir grumbled at the tiny screen showing Channel 8's broadcast above her Doppler-radar display. Amid the dials, screens, readouts, touchpads, and multitude of controls lining the International Space Station's walls, the blue glow of the television screen stood out as a constant broadcast from the human side of home. Earth itself glowed blue outside the window, its smoothly spiraling clouds hiding the chaos, desperation, and greed that raged in their shadows.

"What?" James Hideyoshi glanced at the climate scientist, before the wildly flailing lines of the InSAR satellite system drew his attention back to the earthquake rattling the Oregon coastline. The precisely calibrated satellites could measure the ground rising or falling by fractions of inches; the high-tech system had given him (as tectonic specialist aboard the ISS) and Andre Becker (the researcher on the ground) their first subtle hint that something big was happening under the old volcanic peaks of the Three Sisters. At the moment, however, he could measure the deformations of the earth's surface around the newly named Big Sister volcano just by eyeballing the readouts from old-fashioned ground-based seismographs.

"The whole report—the whole protest too—was probably bought and paid for by that Whole Foods outfit," Mir continued. She watched the newscast religiously (it was all she did religiously), even though the fatuous science reports never failed to irritate her. "A little staged protest, then end with an ad for 'organic' food. Channel 8's just lapping up the bribe money from all sides while a bunch of tree huggers spread idiot theories and make science look like black magic, and I can't even smack some sense into them. Instead, I'm stuck in this vacuum-packed tin can with a nut who dreams about the earth moving."

"I do dream about the earth moving," Hideyoshi agreed with the part of her rant he understood—and cared to respond to. "Don't I, Becker?"

"What?" Becker, the ground-based researcher, paid more attention to his own direct observations than Hideyoshi's end of the conversation or the instruments chattering away at him. "Look at that smoke."

"Oh, for the love of Pete, don't let him mention smoke," Mir groaned. She'd finished the last of her supply of nicotine lollipops the day before, and the wait for the supply shuttle seemed interminable.

"Andre, could you not go on about smoke?" Hideyoshi dutifully relayed. He couldn't keep the grin out of his voice.

"Smoke? Rolling, boiling clouds of nice, thick, tasty smoke?" Becker asked, rising instantly to the occasion. "Whitish-gray, fluffy, curling around in the air, wisps and strings of—"

Mir hit Hideyoshi at that point, but that's not what stopped Becker. The explosion of melted rock from the volcano's growing cone did that. Becker swayed as the shockwave ran through the ground under his feet, adding his own expletives to Mir's description of both his and Hideyoshi's personalities and family histories.

"Wow, she's feeling frisky this morning," Becker said, regaining his equilibrium as the major shock rolled by. He walked easily to the well-secured instruments cabinet as the ground heaved more gently. After a year working on the emerging volcano, he'd become adept at keeping his balance through the minor quakes. Displays glowed at him, showing the waves moving through the rock, spreading like slow-motion ripples. "That's going to cause shakes all the way down the West Coast."

Hideyoshi checked his own displays, where the computer made its best guess about how the eruption would affect the rest of the fault line. A brilliant red stain spread along the Rocky Mountains, fading to orange and gold at the edges. "Sure enough. Better warn the guys downstream." He pressed the button that sent the data—and earthquake alert—to the ground-based stations all along the Rockies.

Earthquakes, ranging from tiny temblors to china-tossing rolls, had rocked the Great Basin already, and it showed no signs of stopping anytime soon.

Mir cocked an eye at her own monitors, watching the smoke plumes Becker described wrapping themselves into the weather systems. They would spawn rainstorms, block the sunlight, cool the ground and water, and play havoc with the jet stream and trade winds. A baby typhoon, still just a tropical storm with an attitude, gathered in the South Pacific, but nothing made her push a panic button—yet. The big problem was the slow swirl of wind and rain brewing over the Gulf of Mexico, moving inland, uncomfortably close to Houston. She leaned back, floating in the lack of gravity, sipping her coffee. *Coffee from a bag—there's a thought. And running low too, which is a worse one. That supply ship better get here soon, or they are going to have some very cranky people around here.*

Not Jamie, though, she thought, watching Hideyoshi floating to and fro in the cramped confines of the geo-aero lab, comparing readings, simulations, and data with Becker. *Him and his wacky Mormon dietary rules.* She didn't know how he managed to deal with life without coffee or nicotine, but he did. Just watching him made her tired.

"Nope, it's not related to the winter volcanic cycle either," Hideyoshi told Becker. "But maybe the weird weather's been affecting the water volume around the coasts. What do you think, Ivana?"

"I think you're the busiest guy I know—and the one with the biggest phone bills too, thanks to Becker. I hope you guys know that these intense long-distance relationships never work out." She grinned as he rolled his eyes at her, but pulled herself over to her readouts to check the weight of water piling up along the coastlines from winds and temperature pressures. The theory that the ocean's seasonal movements affected volcanic eruptions and earthquake activity didn't explain everything, but it sometimes helped predict the earth's sudden shifts.

Her own studies were even less predictable. Weather, by definition, was a complex, unpredictable system, but it had gotten even more chaotic lately. Charts, maps, and live imaging of the atmosphere roiling far below them showed extreme weather all over the globe. "I think things are wacky all over, Jamie. What do you want? We got it. Amazing changes in climate: tornadoes, global warming, hailstorms, loose icebergs floating around, typhoons, global cooling, floods, droughts, heat waves in January, snowstorms in June—"

"—tectonic shifts, earthquakes, seamounts exploding up, dormant fault lines grinding themselves into a frenzy," Hideyoshi finished.

"Maybe Cosheen Hall's people are right about the weather," Becker contributed. "Mother Nature's throwing a fit, trying to get rid of all of the nasty humans."

"Or something," Hideyoshi said quietly.

"They're nuts," Mir informed them with a shrug. "All we're seeing is good old global warming in action. We know humans contributed to the problem, but not as much as the eco-nuts want to believe, and now they think it's getting its revenge, attributing consciousness and purpose to weather systems. Things go along one way, then they change due to physical causes and effects. It doesn't mean they've offended the Sun God or whatever. Typical nonscientific thinking."

Hideyoshi gave her a sidelong glance. "Are you sure there's no purpose? What about—"

Mir groaned. "Oh, please. Can we not get into this supernatural weather—"

"Attention." Captain Nakima's deep voice over the intercom interrupted. "Due to weather conditions and concerns over security, the shuttle flight has been delayed again. The secondary shuttle will attempt liftoff from the Russian facility in three days. Control says sorry about the delay."

Mir groaned again as the captain clicked off the intercom, a groan many of the fifty-person crew echoed. She was really getting squirrelly stuck up in the ISS so long.

"Hey, Ivana," Becker chipped in from the ground, "if you don't like the weather, you should do something about it; you're the climate specialist."

"Oh, really?" Mir shot back. "When are you going to do something about all the tectonic shifts we're seeing?"

"Wish we could," Hideyoshi said, "but we can't stop it by ourselves."

"Like anybody could," Mir snorted.

"Humans may be a contributing factor," Hideyoshi said quietly.

"Because we're concentrated on the coasts?" Mir grinned. "What, you want everybody to get together in Iowa and jump up and down at the same time to shake things back together?"

Hideyoshi grinned at her, but his eyes were serious. "No, I want everybody to get together and straighten up and get their lives together."

"And that's going to make the volcanoes go away?" Mir asked, laughing. "And the earthquakes? I can see it now: special report from the ISS—'Repent, Because the End Is Near!'"

"Quite possibly," Hideyoshi said softly. The phrase from the Doctrine and Covenants rang in his mind: "the testimony of earthquakes." His readouts told him that earthquakes could be eloquent.

This time it was Mir's turn to roll her eyes. "Oh, please, not this. As I was going to say before, I am *not* going to sit—float—around talking about supernatural weather or earthquakes! They're natural phenomena, Jamie—that's the whole point. *Natural.*"

"Whoa, look at this!" Becker's voice caught both their attention. "Jim, take a look at the fissure that last roll shook open. Looks like we've got another live magma flow." Both tectonic specialists gazed at the combination of simulation and real-time data. Becker laughed. "The fundamentalists might get their wish to send Hollywood to hell—how about a couple of volcanoes in LA?"

"Didn't they make a movie about that?" Mir asked. She shook her head. "Maybe I'm glad I'm not down there after all. Smoke and rain are bad enough—how about some lava on the side? Bummer trip for all those surfer boys and girls. Time to break out the happy pills."

CHAPTER 6

"So, have any of you ever tried drugs?" The teenage interviewer adjusted his perfectly mussed hair with a careless head flip. He turned his pouty gaze on the audience of his peers, carefully chosen for proper racial mix, conventional good looks, and adherence to the latest adolescent fashion codes.

"Depends on what you mean by recreational pharmaceuticals," one bare-bellied girl pointed out. "I mean, like, if you're talking about crack or something, no!"

The boys and girls around her nodded, one of them making a face at the thought of using such a déclassé substance. They could all afford much better.

"It's not that it's illegal." Lucrezia looked down from the screen in Joel's Current Events classroom to whisper to her friend Lupe. "It's that it's cheap!"

Lupe giggled softly, then ducked her head as Joel's disapproving stare swung in their direction. Joel—who fancied himself far too young and hip to answer to "Mr. Shapiro" in the classroom—took the DV8 Report, Channel 8's special youth broadcasts, very seriously. At least as long as they advocated his point of view on social issues, which they usually did.

"Let's talk about legal stuff," Reporter Boy suggested on the screen. "You know, like MJ or Bliss."

"Oh, sure." Again the group nodded, not quite in sync.

"Anybody who's part of the scene knows about that kind of thing. It's like, you know, smart drinks and flavored oxygen. Makes the party better."

"Makes you feel, you know, better than normal."

"Yeah, looser, like what people think doesn't matter."

The reporter gathered a few other comments along the same lines—none of the high school students saw anything wrong with popping pills, inhaling medicinal vapors, or smoking "all natural" herbs to get high. All also strongly denied taking any illegal stimulants.

"So if we're not taking the drugs, who is?" Reporter Boy asked.

"I'll bet he's done a few," Lucrezia whispered across the aisle, under cover of her notebook.

"Good question, Skye," the adolescent anchor girl responded. "Who is taking the drugs?" The screen beside her lit up with easily read charts and graphs, the statistics for use on several classes of drugs intertwining like Technicolor snakes, but all trending upward for the last few decades.

"And where are they coming from? Drugs of all kinds, illegal as well as legal, are still flowing into the United States in larger quantities than ever." Now the illustration showed a map of the world, the snakes' colors splashed across the regions that produced the ever-shortening list of drugs still considered illegal in the United States.

"General Andrea Garza, the revolutionary military leader, has assisted South and Central American governments in stopping the decades-long trafficking in cocaine." Now images of Garza appeared, looking dashing and dramatic in his black uniform, waving from the open roof of a chromed and shining Humvee. "Johann Brindermann, General Garza's executive officer, told us at DV8 that the General has completely stopped the drug dealers."

"The American cartels are destroyed," Brindermann stated flatly, gazing calmly into the camera. To underscore his point, graphic footage of drug runners and their employers walking in chains from the court to the execution yard moved across the screen. "But that hardly puts a stop to the worldwide traffic in drugs. Wars in the Persian Gulf area are funded by profits from opium. The party drugs so many of your friends in America enjoy come from designer labs in Europe and Asia."

"Or from labs like MedaGen's right here at home." This time, Lucrezia's comment came in the dramatic pause before DV8's anchor girl wrapped up the report on illegal drugs with a neat segue into the teaser for tomorrow's in-depth look at the latest generation of mood enhancers.

Joel clicked off the screen with more force than absolutely necessary. Lucrezia's snide comments, and her confident refusal to look at him adoringly as a guru of "tolerance," rubbed his psyche like sandpaper. The fact that she made it clear she thought he was full of it was bad enough; the fact that she was one of the best students in the class made it worse. That girl needed a good dose of reality therapy to put her right back in her place. Handy for him that current circumstances gave him the perfect lever.

He didn't often get a chance to score points with his classes, since the students could smell desperation a mile off, but he'd long since mastered the high school tactic of making himself big by belittling someone else. He faced the class with a sly smile playing around his mouth. "Before we get into our class discussion about the advantages of legalizing all safe recreational drugs, let's all listen to what Ms.— oh, sorry, *Miss*—Lucrezia Callatta has been contributing to the professional news broadcast. Go ahead, Lucrezia—do you have something to say to us about drugs?"

Lucrezia swallowed, looking back at him, feeling the animosity behind his purposely mild expression. She glanced at Lupe, who ducked her head in shared embarrassment, then around at the class. Brett the Jock leaned against the wall, grinning obnoxiously; he made kissy lips at her as his friends sniggered. Muffy and Britney watched her with disdainful sneers. Even worse, in a way, the majority of the class, the ones she thought of as the "normal kids," watched her like she was some kind of alien—half ready to mock her because everyone else was, half feeling distantly sorry for her but glad that they weren't the ones on the spot. They weren't the ones who scratched "Mo Go Home" into the door of her locker; they were the ones who saw somebody else doing it and said nothing. The sneers, the "jokes," the comments, the looks had all gotten worse; the "wedding invitation" posted on the school's virtual bulletin board happily announcing her marriage to "A Hairy Old Guy with Three Wives" was kind of funny, but the guys who posted it hadn't meant it as a joke. Neither had the ones who denounced her and the few other Mormon students as bigots and homophobes in a school newspaper editorial promoting "tolerance." And they didn't run the essay she sent in response, asking why Mormons had to tolerate everybody, but nobody had to tolerate Mormons.

Anger flared in Lucrezia's eyes, heating her blood as well as tingling in a blush on her cheeks. He wanted her to mutter a denial and shut up. Well, fat chance! "Okay, here's my opinion. There's no reason to legalize drugs, because they don't help anything. All taking drugs does is let you run away from your problems for a little while. They don't help anything; they just make it even worse when the high wears off and you have to deal with it all."

"So drugs don't work, huh?" Joel neatly snipped her argument into its least sensible summary. He glanced around the class, gauging his audience, his smile growing broader. "What else do we expect from our resident Mormon?" The class laughed.

Lucrezia's ears burned. "I didn't say—"

"Let's take a look at some scientific data that disagrees with Miss Lucrezia," Joel interrupted, overcoming Lucrezia's protest by raising his voice and turning his back on her.

He flicked on the monitor again, pulling up the latest AllSafe commercial. As Virginia gyrated in the center of the kaleidoscope, images of healthy, young, beautiful people laughed and frolicked around her, while a slightly out of focus fringe of dour, old, and ugly faces watched with deep disapproval from the shadows. All the while, the names of deadly diseases flashed onto the screen and disappeared in small bursts of light when they hit the AllSafe logo. The promo ended in a sound bite from an attractive doctor (or at least a hand-some man in a lab coat) assuring the viewers that AllSafe was completely effective against nearly all viral diseases, and almost completely without adverse side effects.

The screen went dark, and Joel faced the class again. "Looks like there's at least one drug that works," he noted—then looked surprised as Lucrezia's hand shot up.

"Miss Lucrezia?" he asked warily.

"If you don't get the booster, AllSafe will kill you. MedaGen just hasn't bothered to tell people that," Lucrezia said. Before he could cut her off again, she raised her own voice and continued, "Besides, we're discussing legalizing recreational drugs, not genetically altered medi-cines. AllSafe isn't—"

This time the bell rang, unleashing a general stampede for the exit. Lucrezia caught Lupe's hand as her friend headed for the door. "Just a sec. I've got to—"

Lupe shook her head. "Meet you out there," she mumbled and fled with the rest of the herd.

"Listen, Mr. Shapiro—Joel," Lucrezia corrected herself, approaching the teacher. "I know I shouldn't make comments during the show, but I—"

"Class is over," Joel told her curtly. "And I'd appreciate it if you'd keep your intolerant opinions to yourself. Trying to undermine my authority in the classroom isn't winning you any friends."

"I'm not—" Lucrezia began, but only halfheartedly.

He dismissed her completely, turning his back on her again to focus on the essay Britney shoved at him for reevaluation.

Lucrezia growled under her breath and stomped out of the room, slipping like a minnow through the teeming throngs crowding the school's run-down halls. The metal detector between the social science and math wings didn't beep as she passed between them; she'd long since learned not to wear any metal—not even barrettes—to school. She managed a smile at Roz, the guard who didn't look at her like a freak, but her black mood didn't lighten on the trip to her locker.

It only got blacker when Ms. Locke caught her. The counselor looked harried, as usual. "Lucrezia! I've been trying to contact you, but you aren't answering your e-mail."

Lucrezia sighed. She'd gotten the notes—every one of the dozen—but didn't want to deal with them. "I'm sorry, Ms. Locke, but I—"

"Lucrezia, I don't want to get in your face or make you feel bad," the counselor barreled on, "but I really can help you. Please, come into my office and talk to me. You really need to talk to somebody, somebody who can help. I promise that everything you say will be confidential, just between us. Just tell me what's going on, and I can make sure that you've got somewhere safe to stay."

"Safe to stay?" Lucrezia stared at her. "I'm just fine, perfectly safe—"

Ms. Locke shook her head at Lucrezia's willful lack of comprehension. "Now, denying the problem won't help anything. Your parents have a duty to look after your health and welfare, and they just haven't been doing that. Their unorthodox beliefs do not give them the right to deny you basic medical treatment."

Lucrezia protested, "They're my beliefs too, and—"

"You don't need to be afraid," Ms. Locke repeated, leaning in close, glancing around the teeming hall as if looking for eavesdroppers. "I'll make sure that you are safe from any reprisals by your parents' church." The second bell rang, signaling the start of class for everyone who didn't have lunch hour. She jumped. "Oh dear, I've got a meeting. Remember, Lucrezia, make an appointment with Carlotta to come and see me, as soon as possible—my door is always open!"

Lucrezia, blinking in disbelief, watched her bustle away. Several collisions, as various bodies and backpacks clonked into her, broke her stunned bemusement. She shook her head and plowed on.

She finally reached her locker, and as she slammed its transparent door open, she asked Lupe, "Can I even get out one sentence without somebody interrupting—"

"Nope," Lupe said, then laughed as Lucrezia's eyes rolled.

"Me," Lucrezia stubbornly finished, but smiled ruefully back at her friend.

Lupe shrugged off the whole Current Events scene, checking her hair and the sparkle paint on her butterfly tattoo in the mirror stuck inside of the locker door. "Don't worry so much, Luc. Joel's a dork. Nobody likes him."

"Yeah, well, nobody likes me either." Lucrezia sighed.

"I do," Lupe protested, rummaging in her purse. She pulled out a small, prettily decorated bottle, dumped into her hand a tiny, lavender pill with a capital B embossed on it in darker blue, and washed it down with a swig from her water bottle before Lucrezia could stop her.

"Lupe!" Lucrezia protested. "What are you doing? Popping Bliss already? It's like noon!"

"Oh, like you care what time it is." Lupe applied a layer of glossy glitter to her lips then waved the applicator wand in Lucrezia's direction. "That's your problem. You're just so straight-arrow, so post-toastie, so just a little bit better than everybody. You know what's right, and you're going to shove it down everybody's throat whether they like it or not. So I need a Bliss tab to get through these stupid classes—how does that hurt you? So people want to make sure they never get AIDS or ISDS—you don't like that, so you have to say AllSafe's going to kill them? Nobody likes Mormons because you're just major buzzkills."

Lucrezia's stomach hit her shoes. Words—angry, betrayed, grieving—whirled through her head. She finally managed to blurt out, "I'm sorry you think that."

"Oh, come on, Luc." Lupe sighed as they made their way to the food court. "It's not you, not you personally. You're great. Your mom's great—so's your dad. But you've got to see that the whole Mormon thing is nuts. Even Mormons don't like it. Come on, you know Bobbie's family dumped your church because of the whole AllSafe thing, and Steve said he was getting out because they won't let his sister marry her life partner in your temple thing."

"And nobody wants to hang out with somebody who's the punch line to every comedian's new routine," Lucrezia added, gesturing toward the AllSafe poster on the school's ad wall, a Mormon-mocking image of monochrome 1920s beauty queens gazing in prudish horror at full-color Virginia Diamante and the AllSafe logo painted over her otherwise bare torso.

"Right." Lupe waved a hand dismissively as she picked up her tray and slid it along the railing of the salad bar. "It's not you, Luc. You're cool." She gave Lucrezia a sidelong look out of overbright eyes, a half smile playing on her glittered lips. "And if you'd just give up and finally sleep with your boyfriend, everybody would know you're normal."

"Glenn? Oh, please!" Lucrezia laughed. "He's not my boyfriend, he's just my friend. Besides, I know they've got a betting pool on me, and I'm not helping anybody win." She sobered slightly as she added, "I know better than that anyway."

Lupe poked at a thin slice of cucumber that had escaped from its container, then dug the salad tongs into the big bowl of randomly torn greens. "So, if you're not claiming him, can I have him?"

Their serious discussion dissolved into teasing over the ownership of the boy in question, a smart kid, borderline geek, and Mormon, then wandered into the usual high school gossip, complaints about homework, and speculations on the release date for the next Seraph CD. Underneath it all, though, Lupe's comments about Mormons echoed uncomfortably in Lucrezia's head.

* * *

The slow hum and click of the antique digital clock turning the hour—1:59 to 2:00 with the flick of a plastic tile—seemed to echo in the silence. Donna resisted the urge to run her hand through her hair or straighten the dark-blue skirt and blazer she'd bought for college admissions interviews. SpielTech's demise, MedaGen's blacklist, and the collapse of the day care business had put a hold on that particular plan; the Callattas needed an extra income a lot more than they needed a tuition bill right now, so she had not registered for another semester at community college. She had done decently in school, with plenty of activity in choir and clubs, but not well enough to win a scholarship; the only way she could get her teaching degree was to stockpile enough money to pay the tuition herself—after she very discreetly helped her mom and dad.

Good thing the suit would work just as well for job interviews. Seven of them so far, eight counting this one, all yielding compliments but no offers. Her heart fluttered, tension tightening at the base of her skull. She took a deep breath, looked at the humming clock, and concentrated on looking calm, cool, and professional for the tiny eye of the video camera in the corner of the waiting room. Or rather, the conference room to which the receptionist had shown her after she filled out the application form, provided her ID and credentials, and took the private school's specialized aptitude test. The questions, part SAT, part personality quiz, danced through her head: "Play is to learning as homework is to . . ."

The click of the door latch broke the mental quiz. A man ducked into the room, smiling nervously as he glanced from the sheaf of printouts in his hand to Donna. "Ms. Callatta?"

"Yes," Donna said brightly, standing to offer her hand. "You're Mr. Luther?" *You look more nervous than I am*, she thought.

"Indeedy," he agreed, shaking her hand in a tentative, slightly moist grip. He let her go quickly, motioning her to take a seat again and settling on the edge of the chair across the small table from her. His eyes instantly fell to the printouts again, avoiding her gaze. "Well. You've given us plenty of information here. Good grades, lots of extracurricular activities, after-school jobs. And you're working with your mother's in-home day care now?"

"Yes," Donna agreed. "I'm the primary assistant. I help arrange the activities, fix the lunches, and change diapers occasionally. It's been really fun, getting to know the kids, learning how to work with their little personalities. The child development class I took in high school was interesting, but there's nothing like real life, is there?"

"No, nothing like real life," Mr. Luther agreed. He risked a glance from the papers to her face. "So, your résumé says you're looking to go into education."

Statement or question? she wondered. Donna decided to take the tone rather than the actual sentence and answered, "I'd really like to be a teacher, especially with elementary-school kids. I like kids that age, before their bad attitudes have fossilized." She chuckled, then sobered as Mr. Luther gave her a furtive look. "Seriously, I'd like to work with kids when they're younger, when a supportive teacher can really make a difference, get them off on the right foot for the rest of their lives. This teaching-assistant position will be a great opportunity for me to get some real-life experience in a school and let me go into school with a solid foundation."

"Well, that's very nice," Mr. Luther said, clearing his throat. He glanced at her, specifically at her neckline (high) and her skirt's hemline (low). For a moment, Donna thought he was scoping her out, but his next comment disabused her of that idea. "You're a very conservative person, Ms. Callatta." He waved one of the sheets vaguely. "You scored very high on the online aptitude test."

So, my wild guesses on the stranger questions paid off. Cool. Donna smiled modestly.

Mr. Luther didn't smile back; the worry lines across his high forehead deepened.

"Is there a problem?" Donna asked.

"Well, you see, you also scored very high on the personality test." Mr. Luther hesitated, then the rest spilled out in a rush. "It's just that really high scores are suspicious. It's very sad, but there it is. Being that honest usually means a person's lying. Are you sure you never steal? Not even office supplies?"

Donna blinked. "I—well, I don't know what to say."

"You really meant this?" Mr. Luther asked, tapping the test results.

"Yes," Donna told him. She couldn't help smiling at the incongruity. "I didn't know that I was supposed to lie about being honest—by saying I was dishonest."

Mr. Luther didn't smile. "Well, that's just a psych test. There's another problem here." This time, the sheet he pulled bore the heading "Medical History." Most businesses required basic health information from prospective employees; with possibly preexisting conditions, they could apply for federal matching funds to help cover the cost of the employees' health insurance. Or offer a consulting contract instead of full-time employment, which meant no insurance benefits at all. Donna's medical history was exceptionally clean—except for one red-flagged item. "You haven't updated your shots, Ms. Callatta. Have you scheduled a vaccination?"

Donna suppressed a sigh. *Oh, please, not this!* "No, I haven't. But I'm also not in any high-risk group either—I don't take drugs, I don't sleep around—"

"I'm sorry, but we can't consider your application further." Mr. Luther swallowed hard, avoiding her eyes. He shuffled the papers together, abruptly lurching to his feet.

"Why?" Donna exclaimed, standing up herself.

"I'm sorry, but you don't have the qualifications we're looking for," Mr. Luther muttered.

Donna came around the table, half reaching for the personnel officer's sleeve. "But, Mr. Luther, I meet every qualification on your list."

Mr. Luther hesitated, his narrow shoulders slumping. For a moment, he stood there, head bowed, then turned back to face her. For the first time, he met her gaze, but his eyes flicked over to the lens of the camera. He pivoted, putting his back to the camera. "We can't hire you because you haven't got your AllSafe vaccination." His voice hovered barely above a whisper. "Our parents just wouldn't feel comfortable about that—or about a Mormon teaching their kids. I'm sorry, but that's the way it is."

"It's illegal to discriminate against me because I'm Mormon," Donna said, just as softly.

"We're a private school," Mr. Luther told her. "The board can draw its own lines. They've been sued before. It hasn't worked."

"And I'm not an oppressed minority," Donna filled in, "just a wacky cultist with no rights."

"I'm sorry," Mr. Luther whispered. His voice rose along with his tight, professional smile as he added, "Well, so sorry that we're not a good fit for you, Ms. Callatta. We wish you the best. Good luck."

"Good luck." Donna muttered. "Thanks." *Good luck finding somebody who'll hire me without the mark of the beast on my records.*

* * *

Donna rubbed the back of her hand across her eyes, clearing her vision. The brightly colored blurs through the windshield turned into crowds of students streaming out of the high school's doors.

Lucrezia stood out in the crowd. Her little sister's overlong violet and lavender scarf fluttered behind her as she raced to catch up with Lupe. After a brief conversation, however, Lucrezia's friend climbed into a low-suspension chopped car with a pair of greasy boys and a girl sporting more tattoos than shirt. All the bounce drained out of Lucrezia's step as she wandered across the lawn and sidewalk to the Callattas' beat-up car.

"Lupe doesn't need a ride?" Donna asked.

"No," Lucrezia threw her backpack into the back, then threw herself into the passenger seat. "She said she has 'things to do.'" Lucrezia slid down in the seat, planting her shoes against the dashboard.

"Hey," Donna reached over, tapping Lucrezia's knees. "I know the car's not much, but it's all we've got at the moment." She glanced sympathetically at her little sister as Lucrezia slammed her feet down onto the floor. "Kid, you look as curdled as I feel. Hard day?"

"You can say that again," Lucrezia agreed. "Mr. Shapiro was on one again, making unbelievably stupid comments about Mormons and drugs—and then Ms. Locke tells me I'm an abused child because Mom and Dad are cultists who won't get me injected with AllSafe and offers to dump me into foster care. It's the same with Glenn's family; his mom's so upset that they're thinking about moving to Temple View, even though there aren't any more apartments available out there. He says they can just bunk in with his aunt until something opens up, or the Church builds more houses. Which means there's one less good Mormon kid at school, and I'm getting lonelier every week! And now Lupe's getting all weird too, not wanting to hang out with me because people say things about Mormons, and she's got this new boyfriend who's a total freak anyway, and when I tried to talk to her about him, I thought she'd start swearing at me—" Her litany of woes, more operatic with every sentence, lasted the entire drive home.

Donna listened sympathetically, letting her little sister vent without comment beyond a few encouraging noises—"mm-hmm," "yeah," "too bad." As Lucrezia listed her grievances, however, a matching set of concerns flew through Donna's mind: nobody had threatened to put her in foster care because her parents hadn't signed her up for an AllSafe vaccination, but they wouldn't give her a job for exactly that reason. Her two closest friends from high school had disappeared as well, one to the Mormon community growing up around the Portland temple and one to San Francisco to live with her life partner. Dad couldn't get a job either, Mom's clients had flaked out or had to move, and—

The sudden appearance of a gray sedan making a wide left turn out of their street made Donna swerve. *And traffic is getting nuttier all the time too*, she thought. The configuration of the other car's taillights in the rearview mirror caught her attention as she parked in the Callattas' driveway. The red lights looked strangely familiar. *Of course they do*, she told herself. *That's a popular car, whatever it is. It's on that commercial that's so annoying, the one with the showers of money falling out of the sky.* Still, something tickled her memory. What was it about that car?

"What?" Lucrezia asked.

"What, what?" Donna blinked at her.

"What's up with you staring at the rearview like Lorenzo Seraph's standing there?" Lucrezia looked behind them, but the gray car had vanished—and there was no sign of the blond male half of Seraph,

Lucrezia's current favorite band; the other half was Maggie, Lorenzo's wife. She liked the music, and she liked the fact that they were unapologetically Mormons even better.

Donna grinned at her. "No such luck. I just had the feeling that I'd seen that car before."

"Oh, sure. On the ads, right?" Lucrezia shrugged off the automotive déjà vu and grabbed her backpack off the seat. She groaned as she hauled it onto her back and headed for the door. "Man, I can't wait to graduate and not have a ton of books and homework. Of course, then it's just college and even more books and homework—if I get a scholarship. Oh, yeah—" She pushed open the door. "How'd the job interview thing go? Did you get the TA job over at Sunshine Heritage?"

"Yeah, how did that go?" Tony asked. He was standing in the door, pulling on his suit jacket for a job interview of his own.

Donna pulled a smile onto her face and shrugged nonchalantly. "I'll just say that they did not meet my employment needs at this time."

"Well, I'll just say that they really missed out on a terrific teacher's aide," Tony informed her, catching his big girl in a tight hug. He squeezed his little girl too and kissed her head.

"Hey, no bad karma, Daddy," Lucrezia said, patting his shoulder.

"You'll do great," Donna added.

"If they try to tell me otherwise, I'll give them an earful, as your mom says." A wash of discouragement blunted the edge on his smile. "And then we might have to move to the wilds of outer Siberia—if outer Siberia has any software or gaming companies."

"Fine with me," Lucrezia growled. "I've completely had it with San Diego anyway." She stomped off, the troubles of the day crashing into her mood again.

"Hard day." Donna offered the unnecessary explanation.

"For all of us," Tony agreed. "Go tell your mom that we're going out to eat tonight. No matter what. We could all use a break."

Donna watched him go, thinking a silent prayer—for him and all of their family. Things just had to turn around soon.

"Mom?" Lucrezia's voice echoed from the kitchen.

"In here," Carmen called back.

"Here!" Gianni happily echoed. "Here, here, here!"

"So, can I have a couple of cookies before—" Lucrezia ran down the hall, catching the door frame to shorten her turning radius. She stopped, noticing the ID portrait at the top of the digital message her mother was reading. "Hey, is that Merry? Tell her she looks good on TV."

Merry had looked good, pale but composed, during the brief clip they'd seen of her leaving the courtroom after her acquittal on industrial espionage charges. The cameras hadn't followed her long—she disappeared into a car and off the media's, and MedaGen's, radar. She hadn't disappeared altogether, however; she still wrote notes to Carmen almost every day, talking about her daughter, Missy, the events in Salt Lake, and her research into finding a cure for AllSafe.

"No cookies," Donna said. "Dad says we're all going out to eat tonight."

"Eat out! Taco Joe's?" Gianni eagerly suggested.

Carmen ruffled his hair, shrugging off the momentary worry about how they could afford even Taco Joe's, and smiled. "Maybe. Or maybe somewhere even fancier."

"Gianni can't imagine anywhere fancier than Taco Joe's," Donna said. "But at three years old, I guess he can be forgiven his lack of vision."

"Go find your shoes," Carmen said to Gianni, knowing that would keep him occupied for at least a half hour, between looking for the stray shoes, running back to report on the other things he'd found, and asking Carmen where to look next. He ran off, and she punched Send on her message to Merry.

"Better get your shoes too," Carmen told Lucrezia, as the three women followed Gianni out of the office and into the kitchen. He started his shoe search in the oven drawer.

"Oh, Mother. I've got my shoes on."

"You've got those psychedelic flip-flops on. I don't call those shoes."

"But they're cute."

"And cold. Catch your death that way."

"At least she's not wearing a string halter and tattoos like Lupe," Donna interjected.

"As if," Lucrezia said, not sure whether to be grateful for the moral support or annoyed about the slam at her friend. "I want to look cute, not slutty."

"Cute is better than slutty," Carmen agreed, gently deflecting Gianni as he headed for the cupboards with further excavations in mind. "But there are more important things than looking good."

"Like what? Saving the planet?" Lucrezia asked, dumping her biology homework on the table, a text sponsored by Greenpeace.

"Like saving the people on the planet, like Merry's doing," Donna suggested.

Lucrezia rolled her eyes. "Oh, yeah, like we can all be biomedical experts."

"We can't all save the world. Some of us settle for raising good kids to do it for us," Carmen said, smiling. "Like you three, and Giovanni."

CHAPTER 7

Ilda's here, saving our bacon as usual. Giovanni paused in his letter writing to listen to Elder Flisfisch chatting with the hired housekeeper who came to get their laundry. *Having someone to cook, clean, and do the laundry is a real perk of being in Chile. She's a really nice lady—not quite like having Mom here, but she's almost as bossy as Donna. (Love you, sis!)*

Elder Flisfisch wandered back into the tiny apartment's living room, his eyes hungrily devouring the pages of yesterday's newspaper. He knew he shouldn't be reading the news, which Ilda generously provided, but he just had to check the soccer scores.

"You ought to talk to somebody about this addiction of yours," Giovanni told his companion, playfully swiping at the newspaper. "It's leading you into bad habits."

Elder Flisfisch jerked the most important pages—the sports summary—out of the way. The rest of the paper fluttered to the floor, scattering over the worn boards. "Never come between an addict and his fix!" the smaller elder warned mock-threateningly.

"Yeah, yeah, you're just lucky it's P-day and I'm in a good mood," Giovanni growled back, grinning. He didn't push it any further as his companion retreated to the comfortably sagging couch. *Elder Flisfisch really does do a good job,* he thought. *And aside from his soccer fetish, he has his mind on the work.* Instead, he knelt to gather up the scattered pages. Most of the headlines shouted the outcomes of various sports contests, opinions about the outcomes, and projections for the outcomes of future games. None of it particularly interested Giovanni; he was a football guy himself—American football, not the "football" that so excited the rest of the world—and he'd rather play a game than watch one anyway.

The ads were another problem altogether. For a supposedly straight-laced Catholic country, Chile's advertising companies didn't skimp on the skin. *What the heck did a bikini babe have to do with a big sale on auto parts, for crying out loud?* Giovanni rolled his eyes (an expression he shared with Lucrezia) and folded the page back together. Ads here were almost as bad as the ones back home.

As Giovanni grabbed the last sheet, a picture on the back page caught his eye. A middle-aged, mustachioed man wearing a smug smile and an expensive suit stood in front of La Moneda. The suit, and especially the ostentatious tie pin, caught his gaze and his memory. He'd seen the man before, fidgeting nervously on the square, then staring in shock as Giovanni tackled the guy who'd tried to mug him.

"Hey, Elder Flisfisch," Giovanni called. "Remember that guy we rescued from that mugger last month? The one who ran away, who didn't even say anything?"

Elder Flisfisch looked up, clutching his score sheet reflexively, then relaxed when he saw Giovanni's attention riveted to the page. "Yeah, I remember. Smart guy. Who *wouldn't* run away, with some crazy gringo coming down like a head tackle?"

"Nose tackle," Giovanni corrected absently. "Listen. It says the guy's name was Erwin O'Higgins, secretary to the vice president. Wow, there's a big shot for you. Right after we saw him, he got a big inheritance, quit his job, and went on vacation. Now he's died of some nasty disease that nobody's seen before, and his wife's come down with the same thing too."

"That's too bad," Elder Flisfisch said out of automatic politeness. His native fatalism reasserted itself quickly, and he shrugged. "Death wanted him, death got him. Maybe he was meant to die of being mugged, and when you saved him, he got sick instead. Can't escape fate."

"Oh, come on," Giovanni protested. "Get a grip, Elder. There're no scriptures that back up the idea of fate ruling everybody's destiny."

"No, but plenty of them say that God can make things happen when He wants to," Elder Flisfisch said. "And so can other people."

"Why would Erwin O'Higgins get picked for a divine rubout?" Giovanni asked, chuckling at the thought. His laughter faded though as he saw his companion's serious expression.

Elder Flisfisch leaned in, his voice dropping. "People say there are spies in the government—even high up in the government. And not just Señor Olivares's spies either; his spies work for the government, for the intelligence service. These guys work against it, like secret combinations. You know what's going on with Peru, all the fighting. They say the spies are working for the General, trying to make the government ask for his help with the guerillas. Maybe the vice president figured out his secretary was working for them."

"And arranged for somebody to mug him downtown?" Giovanni asked skeptically.

"Sure, why not?" Elder Flisfisch nodded. "Didn't you think it was strange that the carabinero just took the mugger away on foot, didn't ask a whole lot of questions or call a wagon or anything?"

"Well, yeah, but I don't know how carabineros work," Giovanni said. "For all I know, that's usual for around here."

"Well, it isn't."

"Well, it's not like you mentioned anything at the time."

Elder Flisfisch shrugged off the implied accusation. "I just wanted to get out of there in one piece. Doesn't do any good to get mixed up with government business."

"But it's your government." Giovanni blinked at his companion. "The carabineros are Chilean police, not a bunch of invaders. Don't you trust them?"

"Trust them?" Elder Flisfisch laughed. "Sure I trust them—I trust them to do what their commanders tell them to, and sometimes what's right. You got to understand, the government might be harmless right now, but we've had plenty of bad ones too, and the carabineros aren't always on the good guys' side. They're practically part of the army, and you can't always trust the army."

"What about that LDS guy, the one who faced down a tank to keep the communications lines open for the March Revolution?" Giovanni asked, pulling out the best story he could remember from his study of Chile before he came.

"Captain Zamora. He's army too, a major by now," Elder Flisfisch admitted. "Yeah, he's one of ours, like a bunch of other military brass and government guys. And maybe even some carabineros. That's why I said you can't always trust them, because sometimes you can, depending on who it is." He shrugged. "I'm just saying that there's a lot going on there, and the best way to keep breathing easy is not to know too much about government business. That's all I'm saying."

"Okay," Giovanni said. "I'll try not to know too much about government business."

"Good man, Elder." Elder Flisfisch thumped him on the back. "Now, finish writing to your mama so we can meet up with the other elders, and I'll teach you how to play real football."

Giovanni just rolled his eyes and settled back down at the desk, picking up the pen to finish his letter. Now, however, a vaguely threatening shadow hung over his usually sunny outlook. *Having free laundry service is great, but it's not as good as having a free country with a government we can mostly trust. The longer I'm here, the more I love the people, and the more I want to share what I have with them—a testimony of Jesus Christ, the knowledge that everything's in good hands. They could really use it, because things are getting scary around here. Everybody's worried about General Garza and the guerillas, and I was just told that some people here think their own government is going to sell them out. I wish I could reassure them, help everybody stand up for what's right. Mostly, I wish I could help them believe, like I do, that it'll all come out okay in the end. And it really will, even if it gets rough before then. I believe that with all my heart.*

* * *

"I believe that the AllSafe vaccine is our very best defense against bioterrorism. The Garlick-Benyanny Health and Security Bill signed into law today was the first important step in securing this great nation," Senator Garlick informed Clara at the Channel 8 twenty-four-hour newsroom.

"And you have other steps in mind, pending your appointment as head of homeland security?" Clara asked, smiling blandly as she wrapped up the interview.

Garlick chuckled. "Well, let's just say that such an appointment would not catch me unprepared, Clara. Of course, the decision is up to the president. All I can say is that I'm ready to serve in whatever capacity when called upon to do so. In the meantime, Senator

Inverness and I are drafting a bill that will allow the head of homeland security to implement the measures necessary to protect this great nation."

"Thank you, Senator Howard W. Garlick, front-runner for appointment as secretary of homeland security. The corruption scandal erupting over the travel practices of the current secretary, Consuela Russ, makes someone else's appointment certain. We'll have an in-depth report on that, and an interview with Senator Holly Cox, who opposes Senator Garlick's appointment, in our next hour. We turn now to the dramatic events in Central America, where Channel 8's Latin American specialist has the breaking story."

The camera panned through the streets of Lima, showing colorful banners that waved above the heads of a shouting, cheering crowd: "Justice!" "Equality!" "Garza!" The handwritten words echoed the chants of the people gathered in the streets. Armed men marched in the victory parade under a shower of flower petals and general approbation.

"Thank you, Clara. In a move that has stunned observers, the Peruvian rebel group that has posed a dire threat to the embattled government has joined forces with the dissatisfied elements of the populace." The camera pulled back to reveal the slim, dark-suited form of Rosa del Torres. She gazed at her unseen audience, her dark eyes intense and radiant. "Amid charges of corruption, widespread labor strikes, and peasant uprisings, the rebels announced that their enemy was the government, not the people. Joining with strike leaders, rebels overthrew the forces of the corrupt government in a pitched battle that left entire blocks of Lima in rubble."

Over the heads of the celebrating populace, the broken facades of burned and bombed buildings provided mute but eloquent testimony to the vicious fighting. Soldiers dressed in the stark black of Garza's forces revealed who had really swept up the reins that the outgoing military and governmental authorities had abruptly dropped.

"General Garza, who has been instrumental in bringing peace to this war-torn region, provided vital support to the people's cause." Rosa gestured, drawing the viewers' attention to the sentries, at the same time expertly telling them what to think about what she was pointing out. "The General, in a formal statement, said that he and his special forces supported the Peruvian people and their new allies 'because it's right.'" A long shot of Garza, looking confident, charismatic, and selflessly noble in profile, underscored the statement.

"The new interim government, supported by General Garza, has announced the formation of a new regime, including democratic elections as soon as the situation stabilizes." Rosa regained center stage as she wrapped up her report. "We'll keep you posted as Peru starts on the long road to stability. For Channel 8 News, this is Rosa del Torres, live from Lima. Back to you, Clara."

"Thank you, Rosa." Clara's smile betrayed nothing but professional blandness as the scene shifted back to the Channel 8 newsroom. As she slid into the next segment, the anchorwoman's expression completely covered her growing dislike of the ambitious young woman using Latin America's wars to further her journalism career.

"Lima's had a lot of rain lately, hasn't it, Cal? What's the outlook for the rest of us?"

Cal Weathers beamed affably. "Lima had a very soggy week indeed—record breaking. As a matter of fact, weather records have been falling like dominoes all over the world."

The footage that ran behind Cal overshadowed his clichéd weatherman patter. While he blathered about records for rainfall, drought, high and low temperatures, the pictures told the real, much more serious story. The long, gray fingers of tornadoes reached down from billowing clouds and stirred earth into the sky, along with the broken bits and pieces of houses, stores, schools—and lives. Hail dropped out of the sky, shredding crops and damaging property. Torrential rain churned ground into mud, sending waves of sluggish destruction down hills, taking trees, rocks, and houses with them. And in what had always been the breadbasket of the United States, the sky turned to brass and copper, only the thinnest of clouds trailing across the pitiless face of the sun—thinner and far less substantial than the choking billows of dust rising from the fields, blowing across entire states in the hot, dry winds. Heat and desperation worked into the minds and hearts of the people, just like the dust seeped into houses, crept into machinery, filled wells, and gathered in plant-smothering dunes. In many places throughout the American heartland, smoke joined dust in staining the yellow-tinged sky.

* * *

Anne watched the dust swirl lazily above the dry, dead grass lining the small parking lot. Just watching it made her back itch, as if the tiny particles had sifted through her clothes already.

"From jungle wet to desert dry in one flight," Leon commented from behind her. "This is going to ruin my lovely complexion."

"Oh, sure, concentrate on your problems. It's my skin that's our meal ticket," Anne returned lightly, appreciating Leon's attempt to lighten her apprehensive mood. The interview with Brother Light had shaken her more than she cared to admit. The climate might have changed in their trip from Manila to Springfield, Illinois, but the situation hadn't; only the details differed. Now she stood in a cluttered but comfortable office, waiting to talk to a man for whom the dust storm meant more than irritated skin.

The door opened abruptly, the muffled conversation behind it resolving instantly into crystal clarity. ". . . on the move by noon. In the meantime, get me the phone numbers of the bishopric in the Garden Ward, so I can call them personally." Jack DuPris, the Area Authority Seventy for the Illinois-Iowa Area of The Church of Jesus Christ of Latter-day Saints, strode into the office, issuing orders over his shoulder at his secretary.

He turned to face the Channel 8 reporter and her cameraman, brushing one hand through his rumpled hair. His expression didn't soften as he looked at them; no politician smile warmed the fierce expression on his strong, angular face, but he didn't look hostile either. "Okay, the Channel 8 people, here to get the official Mormon line on all the trouble we've been having. I apologize for the delay—lately I've been running. But you know that; it's the reason you're here." He gestured to the slightly worn, comfortable chairs across the desk, the years he spent as a marine officer still apparent in his abrupt manner. "Sit down, and let's talk."

"Thank you."

Anne followed DuPris' example as he settled onto a chair, at rest but poised to continue his flight as soon as the interview finished. Leon took up his position at right angles to the pair, positioning the camera to catch both Anne and the Mormon leader.

"I'm Anne O'Neal, and this is my cameraman, Leon. We appreciate your time."

DuPris glanced at the camera, grimacing slightly, then raised his eyebrows in Anne's direction. "Got to get the pictures, eh? My brother used to tell me I had a great face for radio." He shrugged and looked at Anne. "So, do I start or do you?"

"I will," Anne said. "And don't worry—we're not live. This interview will be broadcast later."

"Guess I don't rate a breaking-news announcement like President Rojas yet, do I?" DuPris smiled slightly then shrugged off the comparison. "Whenever it airs, I'm not worried. All right, what do you want to know?"

Quite a contrast with President Rojas's calm graciousness, Anne thought. DuPris was a dynamic, charismatic guy, very fierce about his responsibilities and his people. He was also in the middle of a firestorm. "Let's start right in then. Dustbowls and tornadoes have wiped out most of the farms in this area, putting the farmers out of business. The government doesn't have any more money for subsidies, the banks are collecting on debts, and the farmers who weren't prepared are going under. But many here are blaming Mormons. Members of your church have been accused of creating monopolies, undercutting businesses, using unfair farming practices, even poisoning other farmers' crops and wells—"

"They've even resurrected the old rumor that we have horns," DuPris said. "All of it is completely false. All of it! It's a classic case of scapegoating. They're blaming the Mormons, because the managers of our Church farms and co-ops planned for disasters up front and didn't get into debt in the first place."

"That's excellent planning," Anne observed. "Amazingly good, especially since the extreme weather and drought has affected even the large farming companies in the area."

"Remember that we have an advantage in that area," DuPris reminded her, a hint of smile on his face. "Divine guidance goes a long way toward smoothing out the bumps in the road."

"It is true that the Church's farms escaped the hailstorm that damaged not only orchards but barns and other buildings," Anne conceded. "But some people say that's not divine influence, but power coming from the other direction."

DuPris' expression hardened. "You don't believe that any more than I do. The Reverend Samuel Lebaron has been accusing this church of everything from heresy to devil worship, and nothing he says has a grain of truth in it. In fact, he and his group, transplanted from the South, are behind the outright persecution that's ripping apart communities around Lake Creek. One of our chapels there was vandalized. They did several thousand dollars' worth of damage, broke windows, destroyed computers, spray painted threats on the walls."

"Reverend Lebaron's arguments are persuasive, for people watching their livelihoods disappear," Anne said. "The farm failures, combined with the failure of businesses and industries around the area—"

"All means that there are a lot of angry people looking for somebody else to blame for their situation," DuPris said. "It hasn't been just weather that's caused the problem. Success comes from taking responsibility, working hard, and staying honest. That's why the members' businesses are still up and running. They've got better technology, smart financial programs, and ethical business practices. And a little divine intervention doesn't hurt either." He sat back, fire in his eyes.

As she listened, the deep contrast with President Rojas struck Anne. Despite his dynamic charisma, DuPris made her uneasy—probably because he was so very different from her expectations of a Mormon leader. "You certainly don't hesitate to give your opinion," Anne said. "That fits the reputation you earned in the Mediterranean War as a successful but somewhat reckless frontline officer. Do your current superiors have as much trouble with you as the marine brass did years ago?"

"Successful, courageous, impulsive, and reckless. That's the full list of adjectives they used to hang on me, in performance and conduct reports as well as in the press. I guess that still fits me as well as anything else." He half smiled. "I'd say that I know how to size up a situation, decide on the best course of action, and implement it with no further delay—and tell anybody exactly what I think of it too. Yeah, my blunt speaking sometimes gives the Brethren back in Independence heartburn, but I'll go with Brigham Young and call it as I see it. Like now. Members of the Church of Jesus Christ are catching a lot of resentment for their preparedness, the preservation of their farms, and the fact that they're buying up properties from defunct businesses and bankrupt farmers. Now's not the time to pussyfoot around, sugarcoating what's going on."

DuPris sat forward, his gaze driving into Anne's. "Blatant discrimination is giving way to outright violence, church burnings, carjackings, beatings. Mobs target Mormons all over the South and into the Midwest. It's everything from outright banditry to subtly freezing them out. In some places, in this area especially, the cops mostly turn a blind eye to everything but blood and fire. They just give the mobs free rein to damage property, threaten, and intimidate."

"Some Mormons have reputations for doing the same kinds of things," Anne pointed out. "In Lake Creek especially, anti-Mormon activities have met with violent retaliation from some in the Mormon community. In that situation, the police are caught in the middle."

"They've also realized that ignoring anti-Mormon crimes is profitable, because it diverts attention from corruption. Besides, grabbing Mormons' property is lucrative, especially when the local governments and law enforcement agencies are taking bribes to turn over confiscated land. The governor doesn't do anything; he's paid well by big corporate interests on one hand, and he's making political hay out of the problem on the other, emphasizing the need for keeping civil peace against troublemaking outsiders."

"Those are strong charges," Anne said.

"They're strong actions, and they provoke strong reactions," DuPris told her. "The important thing is that the word gets out about what these criminals are doing to innocent people around here." He glanced at the camera, then back at Anne. "I hope that the interview you run later will reflect that. At least the three of us know what really happened."

"Mr. DuPris, if you are concerned about my journalistic integrity—" Anne began hotly.

"Not yours, Ms. O'Neal." DuPris sighed, running his hand through his hair again. "But I don't have as much confidence in your superiors. Thank you for listening, and I hope they'll let you tell the story straight."

"I will," Anne said, "but remember that I'll tell the other side too."

"Look for the truth, and you'll find that we're in the right." DuPris looked at his watch and stood. "Time to put out another fire—and bind up a few burns. If you'll excuse me, I need to go and comfort some of those innocent people—until we finally decide to defend them."

Anne and Leon watched him leave, his secretary and his two large, grim-faced counselors trailing in his wake. The two counselors, according to Anne's research, had been under DuPris' command as sergeants in the Mediterranean War. She knew their names, former ranks, and that they had both joined the Church. Both were hand-picked by DuPris when he was called as president of the area.

"Breaks that old-guy stereotype of the Mormon leadership, doesn't he?" Leon observed. "I wouldn't want to mix it up with Jack DuPris. The people who want to run him and the Mormons out are going to have their hands full."

* * *

"But remember, my dear brothers and sisters, Jesus will sweep His people up into His bosom. Those who confess Jesus will leave this sad earth before the devastation of fiery hail, bloody seas, and iron locusts. Confess the good Lord and Savior, and you will watch from the clouds of glory the wicked burn as stubble. The Rapture awaits the Chosen People, but they must be pure to be caught up in the clouds of glory. The Rapture will happen when you have cleansed the evil from your hearts, homes, and lives." Tommy Gibbs held out his arms wide, hands spread. Above him, the gigantic screen magnified his image a hundred times, as if to embrace the huge congregation that filled the indoor stadium beyond capacity. "Come back to Jesus, brothers and sisters! Leave the wicked ways of the world! Cast out the evil from among you! Accept your Savior—and He will save you!"

Lights flared up brilliantly around the evangelist, gilding his entire body with a divine halo. The choir burst into song, swaying and clapping, their voices rolling like soul-infused thunder over the cacophonous testifying of the congregation. Tommy Gibbs smiled beneficently, then retired into the shadows of the wings. He shrugged off the heavy blue and gold robe he'd worn for the revival. An assistant sprang forward, caught the cloth before it hit the floor, then folded it reverently in his arms.

Taking a towel from another starry-eyed assistant, Gibbs wiped the perspiration and stage makeup from his face. He smiled at Michael Romanoff, his producer and primary event organizer. "I'd say that was a success, Mike. We brought thousands of souls to our Lord tonight."

"And millions of dollars to the Crusade," Mike noted, tilting the screen of his handheld computer toward his boss. The End Times Revival Tour had packed stadiums all over the Midwest, from the Bible Belt in the south to the Rust Belt in the north. Tommy Gibbs's preaching about the end times had hit willing ears—and open wallets—belonging to people desperate for hope without any price beyond a quick cash or check donation.

Gibbs tossed the towel at him. "We're doing it all for Jesus, Mike," he admonished, but he grinned back at the producer as he shrugged on the coat his assistant held for him. "Now, let's get out there and do it again. We've got to run the devil out of Tampa next."

His entourage trooped out of the staging area, following their leader to the shiny black limousines standing ready in the well-guarded loading area. The evangelist's motorcade purred out of the stadium lot, rolling easily down an empty street lined with the flashing lights of police cruisers—and his swooning, cheering flock singing the preacher's praises.

One man wasn't singing. In fact, he barely looked in the direction of the departing spiritual leader. He didn't need to look after Tommy Gibbs's motorcade; he didn't even need to hear the preacher's words. He already knew his mission in life. The flickering light of a match threw the Reverend Samuel Lebaron's craggy face into high relief. The red glow illuminated his bushy brows and met an answering spark in the deep-set eyes beneath them. A thick cloud of smoke puffed up from the pipe clenched between his teeth.

He shook out the match, glancing up at the hard-faced men clustered around him. "You heard 'im, boys. We gotta cast out the evil from among us."

The men nodded, some solemn, some with vicious grins echoing the acid look in their eyes. It was a long drive back to Lake Creek in their own motorcade—this one of battered pickups and rust-dotted sedans—but the Millennium Brotherhood were fully willing to put in long hours in service to their leader and their religion. They didn't get back to town until dawn. And that's when the fires started at the Mormon granary. Firefighters belatedly pulled the two caretakers from the vicinity and treated their injuries, but they couldn't do anything about the granary, which burned to the ground. Or the Mormon families terrified by the men who drove, whooping and screaming profanity, through their farmyards, throwing threats—and Molotov cocktails.

* * *

Dear Chisom,

I am sorry to hear that some of your investigators and a number of members have been harassed. Conditions for the Church grow worse all over the U.S. too. For the first time, we had one of our chapels vandalized in New England, and two more burned in the South. Fortunately, both state and national governments view these as illegal, dishonorable, and bigoted acts. Even so, with governmental forces trying to contain the ever-growing lawlessness in so many areas, even the best-intentioned governments cannot help us. City and state resources are simply stretched too thin. Even the federal government, due to the overseas deployment of troops to keep terrorist nations in check, has little strength to help the states.

Outside the United States, conditions are even worse. Portions of South America are in shambles. Africa is one continual round of mayhem. Europe is fragmenting. Where civil law is breaking down, the Church is really under fire. I fear the ten-horned beast of Revelation is having a field day. John prophesied that the powers that this beast symbolized would make war against the Saints and, for a time, prevail against them. Daniel saw the same thing. He used the symbol of a single but very powerful horn that successfully moved against the Saints of God until the Ancient of Days (Adam) returned. Whether a beast or a horn, the picture is not pretty. Our enemies are alive and well. The Brethren, sadly, assure us that we haven't seen the worst of it.

I think it is interesting that John's beast dominates kindreds, tongues, and nations. Nearly all the world will come to worship the beast. The reason is not out of love. It is because he intimidates them into loyalty through fear. "Who can make war with the beast?" they say. Better join than be destroyed. See Revelation 13 and Daniel 7 when you have time. Right now, brute force dominates many areas, and strong men are rising who force whole populations to buckle under. For example, we are keeping a careful eye on General Garza, of whom I have written before.

For a time, many believed that one great but secret organization controlled all that was going on. They gave it several names—the Illuminati, the Trilateral Commission, the New World Order, and so on. Supposedly, its few members drove all that happened. Their men and women, so the story went, were amassing great fortunes and power. Their wealth allowed them to have ever greater domination of the world. Some insisted that these people were the Antichrist who would oppose the Savior and His people in the last days.

Now we see the reality, and the scriptures had it right all along. Nowhere do the scriptures show the evil in the world forming a single evil order. That is not to say that certain entities will not combine. I suspect we will see a number of temporary alliances formed. What I mean is that Satan, who is the only single power, never has had a single organization through which he worked. Joseph Smith taught that the beast of Revelation with its horns represents not one system but many, all promoting Satan's ways. Through Babylon, Satan's whore, the devil has seduced many leaders—in politics, religion, and business—into doing his will. But this has not united them. Instead, they fight and quarrel and war, bringing chaos, destruction, starvation, and misery everywhere. Exactly what Satan wants.

The books of Helaman and Third and Fourth Nephi are types of the last days. Note that Nephite wickedness did not bring unity and order but disunity and chaos. Civil conditions deteriorated so badly that by the time the Lord came, no centralized state remained. All were living on a tribal level, each tribe headed by a strong man.

But do not despair, Chisom. The world situation may look hopeless, but it is not. Isn't it interesting that in spite of the persecutions and numbers that are leaving the Church, it continues to grow? The miracles and power of the Spirit you report sustaining the members in Taiwan are happening all over. Nephi's vision is being fulfilled wherein he saw "the power of the Lamb of God, that it descended upon the saints of the church of the Lamb, and upon the covenant people of the Lord, who were scattered upon all the face of the earth" (1 Ne. 14:14).

What both John and Daniel show is that events really are moving according to God's design. We are going through a tough time right now, but it is all part of the Lord's plan, and victory is not far off.

For now, understand that your job is to be a voice of warning to the nation of Taiwan. Just watch. The power of God will continue to increase among the righteous there. The Lord is with His people. May His Spirit sustain you.

With love,
Your father,
Chinedu

* * *

"In what some are claiming is an act of divine intervention—others, a freak accident—a huge dust devil has swept through a small town on the Navajo Reservation, apparently halting a raid by an outlaw gang. Channel 8 has exclusive footage of the attack—and the amazing natural disaster that stopped it."

Grainy home video lit the screen behind Clara as she turned to face it. It showed two whitewashed frame houses, a low-lying hogan, and a few weathered sheep pens before the red-brown rocks and gray-green scrub of the desert, the picture jerking as the camera shot through the cracked window of a pickup truck. Distorted voices, saying something about getting the Mormons, rumbled as the truck jolted to a halt and its passengers, including the cameraman, piled out and ran toward the houses. Glimpses of them, dressed in partial camouflage, their faces hidden by bandanas, appeared around the edges of the frame.

Other figures appeared in the center of the camera's eye, coming out of the houses, running from the sheds beside the sheep pens. One shepherd, waving his hands and shouting, tried to head off the front-runners. He went down hard as an expertly thrown rock struck his shoulder; a woman went to her knees beside him, crying his name. Another woman gathered a small group of children and ran for the battered pickup trucks parked beside the houses. Two others, a man and a boy, ran toward the sheep pens, trying to hold off the attacking gang. They backed suddenly, raising their hands, as the muffled sound of a shot came through the distortion of the video's soundtrack.

Fire flared in the attackers' hands, the camera diving in to catch a close-up of amateur but effective incendiary bombs. One of them arced across the blue sky, landing in the shed of the nearest sheep pen. Fire spread rapidly through the bales of dry fodder. The flames suddenly flattened, however, blown almost out in a gust of wind and dirt. The indistinct shouts changed from triumphant and threatening to amazed—and then frightened. The camera spun around—flaming shed, clapboard houses, desperate shepherds, masked attackers going by in a blur.

The scene stilled and cleared as the camera focused on what appeared at first to be the plume of dust from a vehicle approaching across the flat, sandy ground. As the dried-out husks of small tumble-weeds blew by in the strengthening wind, however, the plume resolved into a whirling tower of dust and debris. Growing larger as it approached, the gigantic dust devil bore down on the scene of the attack. The howling roar of the wind obliterated all other sound. The camera shook as the operator tried to hold his ground against the gale, then he tumbled to the ground as the wall of rusty ochre dust hit.

From a sideways angle, the camera recorded flailing bodies stumbling past, as the attackers retreated to the pickup. A board, ripped from the rickety fence, swatted the former cameraman's head; he crashed to the ground and rolled a few times in the force of the wind. Another masked man made a desperate grab for the camera, before the wind picked him up and threw him into the air and across the yard. He disappeared into the swirling dust, tumbling head over heels.

The dust devil disappeared as quickly as it sprang up, a few eddies of dust blowing into the lens of the camera. The blue sky reappeared over the miraculously undisturbed roofs of the houses and sheds. Another hand, framed by a ragged sleeve, picked up the camera. The scene swept across the supine bodies of the attackers, their pickup truck turned on its side, the shepherds standing over their fallen enemies. Then the camera turned off in a blizzard of digital snow.

"That was amazing," Clara said. The crawl beneath her image told viewers that they could buy their own copy of the amazing video, along with a dozen other extreme-weather events. "Channel 8 obtained the video from the sheriff's department that investigated the attack and its remarkable aftermath. And we have that sheriff, Enrique Pizarro, with us live from his headquarters. Welcome, Sheriff Pizarro. Thank you for talking to us today."

"Glad to, Clara." Pizarro flashed a gold-trimmed smile beneath his luxurious moustache. Hard desert sunlight glittered from the gold badge on his chest and glowed from the whitewashed walls of the Southwestern-style building that was Pizarro's new headquarters.

"Sheriff, I understand that you have recently been appointed as chief of state as well as head of county law enforcement in both southern Arizona and New Mexico," Clara said, as the map graphic beside her image highlighted the long stretch of Mexico–United

States borders of both states, a region dubbed "Amexica" by the pundits. "That's quite an honor—and quite a big job."

"Yes, it is, but it's one I'm ready to take on," Pizarro agreed, expanding under her praise. "But it's not an appointment, Clara. I was elected by the city and county governments—and the citizens, of course."

That was the truth, or at least good enough to pass. Law and order had collapsed in the borderlands long ago, as the increasing population who came to work in the factory towns buried law-enforcement agencies in an avalanche of thefts, murders, violence, and corruption. Federal border patrols, overworked and under-budgeted, had sold out to the highest bidder; organized and not so organized crime pervaded the system; community, stressed by poverty and lack of basic necessities, had disappeared into chaos. The corporations that ran the maquiladoras turned a blind eye to the situation, as long as the mobs of workers kept coming and the flow of finished products remained strong. The situation had spawned local strongmen who ran gangs of thugs, enforcing order through violence and extorting protection money from towns, ranchers, and anyone else in a vulnerable position.

Dove Nakai and his friends had stopped the problem and also energized the citizens to stand for themselves. They just needed a figurehead as the focus for their community-policing efforts. Pizarro hadn't run for the position; in fact, he'd heartily protested against the idea, pointing out that he had no desire to become a prime target for every gang, drug cartel, or crazy dictator who came along. Over his protests, a combined council of big men and landowners from both sides of the border had appointed Pizarro as their official protector because he already controlled most of the bent police forces and border patrols. So far, Pizarro had stayed in line.

Pizarro smoothly assured Clara that his forces had rounded up the gang who had recorded their attempted raid and worked with the Navajo Tribal Police to track and arrest other thugs. "We've got it covered," he finished, looking out of the screen with macho confidence. "And I got a message for anybody coming down to my juris-diction thinking of making trouble: better make sure you got enough savings to pay for a funeral, 'cause down here, we play for keeps."

"Thank you, Sheriff Pizarro," Clara said, as Pizarro's image disappeared. "However, law enforcement isn't the only group in Amexica that has taken a strong stand against criminal activity. All over the Southwest, especially in small towns in and around the Navajo and other reservations, local 'neighborhood watch' groups have successfully rebuffed criminal activities in their communities." Scenes of mostly clean-cut, smiling young men and a few young women walking the streets of small towns and medium-sized cities flowed across the screen. "Many of these groups seem to be affiliated with the Mormon Church." The montage ended with the image of a chapel, panning from its distinctive steeple to the lettering across the building's front: The Church of Jesus Christ of Latter-day Saints.

"Unconfirmed reports of other, more militant groups enforcing peace in communities have also surfaced," Clara said, as the pictures changed to long shots of considerably less respectable looking young men lounging against battered vehicles. One turned to flash a cocky grin at the camera, the streetlights glinting from the sword-bearing angel stitched onto the back of his leather jacket, and the silver letters spelling *Mercury* above it. One of the others noticed what he was doing and smacked him upside the head. "Known as the Santos Soldados, or Soldier Saints, rumors say they take a more aggressive role in the community-patrol efforts. Sheriff Pizarro's office will neither confirm nor deny the Santos Soldados' involvement in gun battles against anti-Mormon forces on the Navajo Reservation and in other communities, but some community leaders claim that the Mormons have created their own gang. Has the Mormon Church finally taken its militant hymns to heart?" The strains of the Tabernacle Choir swelled under the end of the report, their voices raised in the chorus of "Onward, Christian Soldiers."

CHAPTER 8

The trio of battered vehicles rumbled onward in the twilight along the twisting, rocky desert track leading into the backcountry of the Navajo Reservation, the brilliant flashes of muzzle fire blasting from every broken window. It wasn't the road they had planned to take, but when the Santos ambushed them at the isolated trading post they'd meant to raid and blocked off the way of their planned retreat, they had to improvise an escape route through unfamiliar territory. The drivers took the rough road at insane speeds, bouncing over rocks and ruts, barely staying in control. Their wild driving made them difficult targets for the gunmen perched on the roaring motorcycles pursuing them—but it also threw off their own aim. Bullets hissed through the air, ricocheted from the rocky walls of the rapidly deepening arroyo. The track bored into the dry wash; the fleeing vehicles hit larger rocks and crashed down into deep pits of sand.

"Estupido!" screamed one of the riflemen, adding several more profane words as he reached through the shattered back window and rapped hard on the driver's head. From his perch standing in the back of the last truck, he could see over the tops of the thick stand of brush at a bend in the track—and the walls of the arroyo closing in before them. "It's a trap!"

The warning came too late for the two lead vehicles; by the time they realized that the road didn't come out from between the hills, they had gone too deep into the wash to climb out. The third truck, the one with the heavier ordnance, made a sudden dart to the side, trying to break out of the dead end that the motorized pack had rapidly herded them into. With a mighty heave and a whining roar from the overstrained engine, the vehicle careened up the side of the wash. It teetered perilously on the edge of the bank, its tires spinning futilely in the air. The four men in the bed of the truck heaved themselves forward, hitting the back of the cab as hard as they could. The tires screamed against a boulder, caught, and heaved the truck out of the ditch. Four of the motorcycles roared through the cloud of dust churned up by the truck's desperately digging tires and pursued the lead vehicles into the trap; two more slewed to a halt farther up the track. When the track dead-ended at the stark wall of a mesa, the men in the first two trucks piled out, hefting their weapons and diving for cover behind rocks, trees, and trucks. The pursuers dodged out of direct line, drivers as well as passengers enthusiastically returning fire from their own makeshift cover. The noise of the firefight echoed and reechoed down the arroyo.

Meanwhile, the escapee truck spun around 180 degrees on the short margin of the bank, then thudded back into the track upright. Its unbroken headlight gleamed like the eye of a cornered animal at the two riders standing between it and freedom, their own headlights glinting through the thin foliage of the brush. The driver gunned the truck's engine, adding mechanical threat to the staccato of cover fire.

"Oh boy. And the whole ambush thing was going so good up to now," Perro said, ducking reflexively as bullets knocked a flutter of tiny leaves from the pathetic shield of the bushes. He glanced at Dove, then back at the headlight. "Feel like playing chicken with a Ram?"

"It's a Ford," Dove muttered as he looked down the arroyo; the other Santos had the lead banditos boxed in. "Looks like it's not chicken, Perro—we're playing rabbit!"

The truck roared around the brush, shots from its bed-mounted machine gun kicking up a fast-moving trail of dust. The two Santos Soldados wrenched their bikes around and blasted back down the track.

"Break left!" Dove shouted, thinking of more practical alternatives. "Toward Samson Tsossie's place!" On the good side, Tsossie's farm had overgrown irrigation ditches deep enough to stop the truck permanently. On the downside, it was five miles away—over open country.

The two bikers jumped the track, and the truck bounded up after them. Bullets whined past Dove and Perro, but neither turned to fire back; instead, they crouched low over their handlebars and concentrated on widening the distance between them and the truck while zigzagging enough to keep out of the crosshairs. The truck hit a sudden dip hard enough to send one of the guys in the backseat flying out of the truck bed.

"Don't lose 'em!" Dove ordered, as he and Perro swerved close enough to shout to each other.

"Why not?" Perro screamed back. He didn't expect an answer because he already knew it; the whole point of the ambush was to catch the raiders. These guys had tried to hit the Navajos, and Mormons, and borderlanders, but they weren't putting up with it anymore. Losing them meant leaving them free to try to burn down another trading post.

The cycles bounded up a short hill, catching air as they roared over the crest. Both made the landing, but Dove lost control momentarily as he swerved to avoid a clump of thorn bushes. Skidding through the dust almost on the bike's side, he fought to pull out of the slide. The whirling in his head closed in, a cough ripping out of his chest. The bike pulled upright just enough for the brake to catch; he hit it hard, slowing the bike before he laid it over on its side. It and Dove parted company, both rolling through the dust. The bike came to a halt and spun in a slow circle until the engine sputtered and died. Dove coughed hard, tasting blood, and felt the sting of gravel-burn ripping up his arm and the side of his face.

Perro looked back, saw Dove go down, and pulled the bike into a tight turn even before he started yelling, swearing, and praying incoherently. He reached Dove's side and pulled his friend up as the truck came over the hill, the front tires leaving the ground as it crested the rise. It roared toward them, the bandits grinning maniacally.

Their grins disappeared, however, as another set of headlights beamed over the next fold in the desert, heading toward them. Poacher lights shot through the night like steady lightning, pinning the pickup in its sharp glare.

"Freeze!" an amplified voice bellowed. "Police!"

The banditos froze—for a couple of seconds. Then the truck wheeled around, the gun spitting lead above Dove's and Perro's heads toward the lights as it dashed madly away. This time, however, an answering burst of machine-gun fire ripped toward the truck, thudding into the metal sides, shredding the back tires. The gunners held their ground until the bullets perforated the bed of the truck, then took the lesser of two evils and bailed out of the truck bed. The driver didn't get that choice; the bullets ripped up the back of the cab and through his body. A tire struck a boulder, overturning the truck. It rolled several times, bouncing across the scrubland until it came to rest in a cloud of dust.

The new arrivals screeched to a halt, and figures in the uniforms of the Navajo Tribal Police and sheriff's department jumped out. They instantly covered the ground, surrounding the former occupants of the truck, shouting orders from behind their rock-steady gun barrels. Pizarro walked over and stood looming over Dove and Perro. "Busy night, huh boys?"

"Man, never thought I'd be happy to see you, Gordo!" Perro grinned with relief.

"Gotta keep order in my jurisdiction," Pizarro growled, watching his deputies and the NTP officers cuff one of the banditos; the other needed medical attention. "Even if it means working with Mormons and Navajos—and you crazy Santos."

"You stay in line, Gordo, and we'll keep on doing your job for you," Dove assured him, all cocky confidence. The confidence lasted just long enough for Dove to get out of Pizarro's sight and join the crowd of celebrating Santos. Dove grinned at Calvin, but the head-lights blurred around his friend's head, smearing into long streaks of blinding light. Dove was almost grateful for the darkness that flowed in from the edges, dousing the glare, as he sank into the welcoming gloom.

"Dove, are you—" Calvin caught him as Dove's knees buckled.

"Blood!" Perro shouted, helping Calvin ease Dove to a sitting position against the tire of an NTP patrol car. He began frantically patting him down. "Find the blood!" All Perro could think was that Dove had been shot during the chase.

"No blood," Dove growled, smacking Perro's hands away. "I'm okay, it's just—" A deep, racking cough interrupted his protest. He muffled it against his bandana.

"There's the blood," Calvin noted softly. "Dove, you're not okay. You haven't been okay for a couple weeks now." He stood up, disregarding

Dove's half-formed rebuttal; another cough tore it to shreds anyway. The sound of it hit Calvin hard. Dove hadn't been acting normal for a while—not weak, not sick, in fact just the opposite, like hiding something under his feverish plans to organize the borderlands' neighborhood watch and beat off the bandits and General Garza's thugs. He was running as fast as he could, and Calvin feared he was running from something inside. "You stay right here."

He rose, motioning for the younger Santos to join him. "Mercury, go get a medic, and the cop who runs that car. Move!"

Mercury nodded and ran fleetly, even with battered boots instead of winged sandals. The sight of Dove down, coughing harder than ever, shook him to the core. Why did it have to get so bad right before he had to go home? Tía Anabel's secretary had delivered the long-dreaded airline tickets last night. He'd be leaving just when Dove needed him most.

"That's not a cold," Perro informed Dove. He biffed Dove lightly upside the head, hiding his sudden worry under annoyance at Dove's excuses. "Trying to fool me."

Dove managed a half grin. "Trying? Did."

A shadow falling over them saved Perro from having to come up with a reply. He looked up to see one of the EMTs following Calvin toward them, Mercury hovering behind. Dove half considered resisting, but couldn't muster the energy. He managed a smile and knowing nod at Mercury, a wordless reminder of the kid's promise that he'd help his father beat Garza's thugs in Chile—and, more important in Dove's mind, be a good son for a good man. Mercury nodded, getting the message. Dove closed his eyes. Fear flickered under the whirling lethargy he'd been fighting all day, the spreading weakness that had started in his chest and slowly expanded throughout his body. He cooperated by holding still as the paramedic searched for wounds, but found none, but flinched away when the woman shone a light into his eyes.

The move brushed his cheek against her hand; her eyes widened as she felt the heat under his skin. Her thermometer registered a fever of 103 degrees, and the cough he vainly tried to smother told her she wasn't looking at a gunshot or broken bone. She shook her head. "Go home, bundle up, drink lots of juice, and for heaven's sake, stop tearing around the sheep trails when you've got a fever." She swept up her kit and moved away to find someone who actually needed an ambulance.

Calvin and Perro watched her go, then looked down at Dove. He didn't look back; he didn't want to open his eyes. "Just the flu," he repeated for them.

Calvin's comment to that, as colorful as it was vulgar, made Perro grin. "Whoa, guess that dip you took getting baptized Mormon didn't clean out your mouth." He looked down at Dove. "Too bad, boss—nobody believes you." Then he leaned into Calvin, his smile dropping for the worried puppy-dog expression that emphasized his nickname. "What do we believe?"

"We believe we need another doctor," Calvin informed him, eyeing the police car Dove leaned against, then glancing back. "Mercury, tell the others you and Cochise are taking Dove's and Perro's bikes back. We're catching another ride to visit Dr. Joe."

Dove looked up at them, considering rebellion, but common sense asserted itself. Benny, his older brother, would've smacked some sense into him by now, if he were alive. He couldn't keep denying that there was something wrong with him. Dr. Joe had stitched him back together when he got shot in the ambush that killed Benny. He would figure out what it was and fix it, and Dove would be back defending his people against the forces of evil. Dove didn't just see the world in black-and-white; he saw it through the visor grille of Captain Moroni. So he obediently folded into the backseat of the cruiser next to Perro, who made some nervous jokes about nobody being able to make the charges stick.

The NTP officer at the wheel rolled his eyes at Perro's reflection in the rearview mirror and looked at Calvin, who slipped into the front. "So, tell me about the ambush."

Dove dozed through the bumpy drive and Calvin's recounting of their plan to ambush, herd, and contain the raiders until the legitimate forces arrived. But by the time he was sitting, shirtless and shivering slightly in Dr. Joe's examination room, he was wide awake. Dr. Joe started out talkative, teasing the guys, telling them that the saying "chicks dig scars" was a myth so they'd better take care of their hides, and warning Dove that he'd just taken the stethoscope out of the freezer. The jovial joking died away though when he pressed the silver disk against Dove's chest. He finished the examination without saying more than "Breathe deep" and "Hmm," then took four blood samples and left the room.

"Okay, that didn't make me feel better," Perro said, speaking for all three of them while he paced nervously from one side of the small room to the other. His face lit up, however, as the door opened again and he recognized the broad-shouldered man standing there. "Hey, Samuel the Lamanite!"

"Can it, Perro," said Sam Begay, the closest thing Dove had to a father. He ruffled Perro's hair, patted Calvin's back, and hugged Dove. "Hey, Hasbídí, what have you got yourself into now?"

"More like what's got into him." The four of them turned to look at Dr. Joe, who came in holding a printout. His grim expression deepened the lines on his weathered face.

"Flu," Dove guessed. "That's what the EMT chick said." Watching Dr. Joe's eyes though, he shivered with cold that had nothing to do with the fever.

"How long you been feeling bad, Hasbídí?" Dr. Joe glanced from the printout to Dove. Using the Navajo version of his name softened the no-nonsense tone, betrayed the affection the doctor felt for the crazy kid.

"Just a couple weeks," Dove tried, then revised his statement under the barrage of skeptical gazes. "Okay, four weeks, that's when the cough started. It just got worse the last couple days, when I started going dizzy. I figured it was a cold or something."

"Then it knocked him off his bike," Perro added. "Wham!"

Dr. Joe glanced at Sam, whose face went suddenly still, then back at Dove. "It's not a cold." He gestured with the printout. "You've got a virus, yes—but it's an engineered one. It looks like the same stuff the investigators found when they searched the headquarters of Garza's man, Slick."

"How'd you get a sample of that?" Sam asked. "Are you sure it's the right stuff? The FBI gives Bishop Yazzie trouble about divulging a suspect's prior arrests for drunk driving—and he's with the Navajo Tribal Police."

"I got it through the backdoor. Pizarro didn't trust the feds," Dr. Joe said. "I know it's tough. And I can't do a full analysis here, but the antigen reaction looks dead on."

"Dead on," Dove repeated, feeling the black humor of it over the fear in his gut. He waved off Dr. Joe's half-formed apology. "It's okay. But the stuff the feds found in our house—the stuff Slick tried to stick me with—it didn't work. He didn't get the needle into me before I shot him." The memory still made him sick; the sight of Slick's eyes as he died haunted his dreams. He shook his head. "I'm not saying you did it wrong, Dr. Joe, but that can't be it."

"Yeah, and it killed Sasha pretty quick," Perro pointed out. "That fight was like four months ago."

"Sometimes they don't hit all at once," Calvin said quietly.

A flicker of surprise that Calvin would know that crossed Dr. Joe's face. "It's called latency. The virus gets in, then lies low, quietly building until it hits critical mass. This one's related to the one Sasha died of, but it's a slower-acting version. Four months would be about right. You didn't get it from the syringe, Hasbídí. You got it from Slick himself. When you shot him, you got his blood all over you, and you had plenty of open wounds at the time."

Vivid memories played in Dove's mind of Sasha—the woman infected with Garza's virus as an example to anyone opposing Slick— coughing her lungs out in the small cell of a Buddhist nunnery. The cough building in his chest echoed the hacking in his head. He was dead—walking dead. The image of his brother, Benny, accompanied that thought, which was a lot less scary than he expected. He didn't fear dying; meeting Benny again, seeing his Savior, carrying on his mission on the other side all sounded intriguing. Another thought, however, chilled him to the bone. He looked at Dr. Joe, his eyes wide. "Am I contagious? Did anybody catch it from me?"

"No," Dr. Joe assured him quickly. "No, it's not contagious through touch or breathing; it's better engineered than that. So you haven't infected anybody else—unless you've shared blood with some-body."

"Nah, he's not been as klutzy as usual," Perro said, his grin crooked.

Dove relaxed slightly. "It's okay, then."

"It's not okay," Calvin growled. "Man, Dove, that stuff will kill you."

"Not if we can help it," Sam replied, looking from Dove to Dr. Joe. "What can we do? What can kill this bug? Can we stop it?"

"Yes, we can stop it," Dr. Joe said, looking at Dove. "One dose of AllSafe, a couple weeks' recovery time to heal the damage, and you'll be well again."

"No." Dove stared back, ignoring the protests that erupted from Sam, Calvin, and Perro. "No, not AllSafe. Remember what President Rojas said? The whole Church has come out against it. That's the order. I'm not taking it."

"Listen, Hasbídí." Sam took him by the shoulders, looking into his eyes. "That's a general guideline, not a commandment. The Church opposes AllSafe because it requires a booster to keep it from overstimulating your immune system. Taking the medicine that will save your life isn't a sin."

"It's too much like sinning, planning to repent later." Dove looked back steadily—until a cough broke his gaze.

Sam looked at Dr. Joe in exasperation, as Perro assured Dove that sinning wasn't all bad, and Calvin joined the fray by asking Dove who'd lead the Santos if he left.

"Can you stick him while he's not looking?" Sam asked, under cover of the argument.

Dr. Joe shook his head. "I could, but if I did, he'd never let me get close enough to give him the booster; we'd just end up killing him in a year or so instead."

"A year's more than we've got now," Sam pointed out. "I don't want to tell my wife that we let the kid die in a couple of days because he's too heaven-struck and starry-eyed to be sensible."

"We've got a bit more time than that." A speculative gleam flickered in Dr. Joe's eyes. "He's healthy, he's fought it off for this long. If we can slow the damage to his lungs, I figure we can stretch it out to a couple of months."

"And that helps us how?" Sam asked.

"It gives us enough time to get him to somebody who may be able to help him," Dr. Joe said, as he remembered the details of the message that had come through the Net discussion he'd read. "Listen, you've heard of Meredith Galen?"

"Dr. Galen? The one who busted MedaGen about AllSafe?" Calvin broke out of the argument and into the others' conversation. "The one they're trying to toss in the pen for industrial spying?"

"Right," Dr. Joe agreed, revising his estimate of Calvin upward for the second time in fifteen minutes. "She's not in the pen yet, and some wealthy benefactors—okay, with Church backing—have set her up in a lab out in Salt Lake City, working on an antidote for AllSafe—and all the other bioengineered viruses terrorists have come up with. She's looking for human guinea pigs for her research."

Silence descended as they all considered that statement.

"Going up there would help stop Garza from using this kind of poison?" Dove asked.

"It could," Dr. Joe said. "It could also keep you around longer."

"And keep me out of trouble with Renata, who doesn't want you dead," Sam added.

"Hey, you look like a guinea pig to me," Perro told Dove. "Try wiggling your nose."

* * *

The elevator eased to a stop with a soft chime as the door whooshed open, and Senator Garlick emerged out of the mahogany and glass box, followed by a man in a precisely tailored but subdued suit and a conservative haircut. The man was flanked by two body-guards dressed much flashier. More mahogany and glass greeted them, with glinting brass accents and a wide-eyed, perfectly dressed secretary who rushed to meet Garlick.

"Senator," she began, her voice fading momentarily as Cesar Augosto and his watchdogs strode into the plush confines of the senator's off-Capitol office. "Your other . . . associates have already arrived. They're waiting in the conference room."

"Thank you, Ms. Lincoln." Garlick smiled at Augosto, making a courtly gesture. "Come right this way, Cesar. I'd like to introduce our new allies."

"I love meeting new people." Augosto walked past the senator with a cool smile. The smile got cooler as the heavy, soundproofed doors of the conference room whispered apart in front of him. In fact, it absolutely froze.

"Well, look who's finally here." The man lounging back in one of the butter-soft leather chairs pulled his feet off the mirror finish of the conference table, pushing a scantily clad woman off his lap. She pouted, but joined her twin lounging on another expansive chair. "Here we thought maybe you got lost or something. And you brought some buddies too."

He stood, stretching insolently as he expertly sized up Augosto and his two bodyguards. His own pair of hard boys adjusted their stances behind their boss, folding beefy arms across their equally beefy chests. All three of them looked like exactly what they were—gangsters, in the classic "urban" mode, heavy jewelry and expensively fashionable clothes, their West Coast glam contrasting with Augosto's New York–Mafia cool.

"Senator?" Augosto looked at Garlick, raising an eyebrow. He didn't bother to hide his disdain. "I understood this was a private meeting."

"Oh, it is, it certainly is," Garlick assured him. "Cesar Augosto, Travell Capshaw. Ms. Lincoln, if you would escort these young ladies to a more comfortable room, we'll get on with it." His perfect smile lasted until the heavy doors closed behind the women. Then he turned on Capshaw, fury tightening his face. "Have you got a brain in your head? Who the blazes are those two tarts? How much do you know about them—anything?"

"Hey, they're just bunnies," Capshaw protested. "No problem."

"Just bunnies," Garlick snarled. He collected himself, slowly relaxing the hands that clutched the yielding back of a deep-cushioned chair. "We can't afford bunnies, Travell. Bunnies have eyes, ears, and tongues, even if they don't have brains to use the information for themselves. Somebody else can—and we're too close now to risk a security leak."

Capshaw shrugged. "Then the bunnies get skinned. What you call us here for, Howard? And what's with the stiffs?"

Garlick's Old Testament eyebrows drew down at the gangster's use of his first name. "Cesar is a very important ally—just as you are. And drop the inner-city syntax, Capshaw. It isn't amusing." He rubbed his hands together briskly. "And we have serious business to conduct. Sit down, gentlemen."

Capshaw and Augosto settled into the leather chairs on opposite sides of the five-sided table. Their bodyguards withdrew to stand against opposite walls—then started, half pulling their pistols, as the green light above the door flashed and the portal opened.

"So sorry I'm late." Mr. Abbott smiled as he slipped into the room, closing the secured door behind him. He took his place at the table, nodding to Garlick. "Have we started yet?"

"Just about to," Garlick informed him. The rebuke in his tone slid right off Abbott's slick self-assurance. "Just waiting for you."

"And, I imagine, watching our two new friends circling and sniffing each other warily," Abbott suggested, earning a glare from the two gang bosses. He smiled and opened his hands wide in faux apology. "Kidding, just kidding."

"Enough with the kidding. I'm surrounded by comedians." Garlick leaned forward, planting his hands on the table. "You are all here because I have something to offer you."

"Like?" Capshaw asked, bored and getting restless. He'd done a couple of lucrative jobs for Abbott before, piloting new recreational drugs on the street before MedaGen rolled them out officially. If the unofficial human trials turned out well, MedaGen made them official; if there were nasty side effects, MedaGen was never involved. He knew Abbott and MedaGen backed Garlick financially. What he didn't know was why Garlick had called him and paid his way clear out to this upscale bunker in the middle of the Virginia political boondocks.

"Like membership in an exclusive organization that will give you more power than you have ever dreamed of." The senator looked from one face to another, seeing the interest ignite in their eyes. He leaned back, touching a control in the arm of his chair. The table lit from below, a map of the United States glowing up at them, surrounded by photos of each of the men at the table. "I am organizing my own Internal Security Committee, gentlemen. It will, of course, be very secure. You'll submit to retinal scans, which will be your passport into this room and the computer system that contains all the information you'll need to extend your influence even further. Right now, each of you has a well-defined domain, turf that you have won by eliminating your rivals."

Bright markers all along the West Coast lit up under his fingers, a gleaming line tying them to Capshaw's photo. Other markers spread over the East Coast and lit a handful of cities in Nevada, all connected to Augosto's image. Another set of colored spots connected to Abbott's smiling visage marked the businesses, banks, and territory MedaGen controlled.

"Impressive, but incomplete, and not completely secure," Garlick noted. He nodded toward Augosto. "You've got the FBI on your trail, poking their noses into your businesses wherever they can. And you, Capshaw, have been losing a war against the new organization behind the drug trade in Mexico and South America. When I am secretary of homeland security, I'll have the leverage to persuade my international contacts to work with your boys, instead of against you, in ensuring a steady and extremely profitable flow of happy pills to customers all over the country." He looked back at Augosto. "And I can give the Bureau a new set of priorities—ones that have nothing to do with an upstanding businessman like yourself, whose outstanding patriotism has won him several lucrative defense contracts."

"What about him?" Capshaw asked, imitating Garlick's nod toward Abbott.

"Oh, the senator's already been very helpful with the FDA," Abbott said airily. "And the Garlick-Inverness Homeland Security Initiative—if it passes as easily as the health bill he wrote with Benyanny—tosses him the keys to the federal piggy bank."

Augosto steepled his fingers, gazing at Garlick over their perfectly manicured tips. "We join your Internal Security Committee, everybody's happy, everybody's getting something. So what do you get, Senator?"

Garlick tapped the control on the chair arm, superimposing over the map his own image, smiling against a campaign banner, raising his hands in victory. "I get your help in securing the homeland security post."

"If you're angling for more campaign contributions, I gave at the office," Augosto said, frowning.

"And you don't want my name showing up on your soft-money list, do you?" Capshaw grinned.

"No, I don't need contributions from either of you." Garlick eyed them coolly, his gaze traveling from the bosses to their pet thugs. "Mr. Abbott and my other supporters take care of that very well. I have more than enough cash to meet my needs—and secure the cooperation of politicians, lawyers, and judges. I need you, gentlemen, for your specialized talents. Money is not the object. Mayhem is."

* * *

"The mayhem ripping apart the newborn African republic of Ohalajishi has spread to neighboring states." A map behind Clara showed the area of the latest civil war. "Both sides claim to represent the will of the citizens, and both accuse the other of hate crimes, ethnic cleansing, and genocide." Images of hollow-eyed refugees, burned-out villages, soldiers clutching rifles, and photos of mass graves alternated under her words.

"And Ohalajishi is not alone in facing the horrors of war," Clara said, as the images of refugees, soldiers, and villages changed from African to Chinese. The hollow eyes were the same, as well as the devastation of homes and fields, the dead bodies, and the smirking viciousness in the faces of the soldiers; only the outward details changed. "Warlords continue their campaigns against the central government in China. Two, Lord Xi Xian and General Huang-ti, have declared themselves the founders of new dynasties and claim the mandate of heaven has turned in their favor, justifying the downfall of the current regime." Tanks flying the banners of emergent warlords rumbled through battered streets. Peasants waved smaller versions of the banners, yellow dragons on black fields or stars and sickles on red—they didn't care, as long as waving the flags meant the soldiers in the tanks would stop blasting their towns and fields and families.

"So far, the Chinese government has denied that the situation is serious and has refused the president's offer of American help. That may be a blessing, given the overextended state of the U.S. military. While the secretary of defense and the Pentagon continue to claim that we are capable of sustaining a multifront war with technologically advanced armaments and surveillance, critics say that the military is dangerously overextended. The United Nations has threatened to pass a resolution to formally censure the United States for involvement in civil strife all over the world.

"Yesterday, U.S. peacekeepers in Eastern Europe were involved in clashes between nationalist groups. Three soldiers were killed, and several groups have claimed responsibility, as well as issuing new threats of terrorist activity." A grainy scene showed a brilliant burst of fire on a busy European street and American troops running, shouting, and evacuating civilians.

Under it all, the running ticker displayed a sports-style scoreboard, ranking rebels and defenders, terrorists and American troops, on numbers of towns captured and numbers of casualties. Beside it, an ad glittered, showing the odds and point spread on Ohalajishi's embattled government and the rebels, offering easy voice betting for either side. No official TV ads offered bets for or against the American military; for that, gamblers had to go to the Web sites the casinos ran anonymously.

"The war seems to be heating up on the domestic front as well," Clara continued, over scenes of terrified crowds running through clouds of smoke billowing from a burning tenement building, investigators poking through rubble that had been a neighborhood police station, edgy National Guardsmen frisking the crowds lined up for a football game.

"Terrorist threats have come over the Internet from a wide variety of shadowy groups, among them the Whole Earth Alliance associated with millionaire activist Cosheen Hall, as well as fundamentalist religious groups both in and outside of the United States." The images stilled, focusing on wounded police officers, stricken firefighters, and a crying twelve-year-old boy bleeding from a bullet graze. The pictures faded into the background as Clara frowned solemnly. "Several police stations have been bombed, and firefights have broken out in a resurgence of inner-city gang wars. Is there any way to stop the tide of violence threatening American cities and citizens?"

"Here it comes," Monk directed, gazing intently at the monitors. "Get ready with the press conference, and make sure the national anthem comes in when the senator starts talking."

Kim finished slotting the appropriate clip into place even before Monk finished speaking. Supporters of Senator Garlick had contributed handsomely to Channel 8's recent defense against monopoly charges, sending both legal funds and amicus briefs. It was strictly coincidence that Channel 8's board of directors ordered their producer to pay close attention to the senator's campaign for the homeland security post.

"At least one prominent senator believes there is," Clara said, turning slightly as if she were watching the screen behind her along with the viewers.

"What will keep us safe from terrorism?" Senator Garlick asked rhetorically, his silver hair ruffling in the breeze that lifted the American flags above the outdoor podium. "American values will keep us safe from terrorism! Values such as freedom, power, and determination. Safety, like peace, depends on our willingness to implement measures—even drastic measures—to protect it!" The crowd filling the grassy expanse of Central Park cheered enthusiastically. "Some opponents to my proposals for increasing the safety of the American people whine about 'invasion of privacy' and say that my measures will impose a Big Brother society on you. Don't believe it. Your privacy is absolutely safe. I don't care what you good citizens say in your private conversations. I don't care how you run your legitimate businesses. I don't care what you do for fun during your nights on the town. I don't care what recreational drugs you take—as long as they're legal and don't fund terrorist activity." That earned a few laughs and catcalls. "And I certainly don't care who you sleep with." Another cheer erupted, punctuated with whistles and encouraging shouts.

Garlick waited for the applause to die down, holding his hands up and smiling. "Don't fall for the privacy argument. It's nothing but the pathetic whining of people who don't have the courage to ensure public safety. They're the ones with something to hide. They are trying to hide their subversive activities behind upstanding citizens who have no reason to fear a terrorist investigation. They are trying to gut homeland security, cripple the watchdog that keeps terrorists out of your cities, homes, and schools." The crowd booed loudly, waving fists in the air.

"Do you want to keep terrorists out of this country?" Garlick asked. The crowd cheered.

"Do you want to uncover the terrorist plots that threaten the very freedoms we cherish?" Cheers.

"Do you want to protect your homes, your schools, your friends from terror attacks?" Cheers.

"Do you want all terrorists apprehended and locked up before they can carry out their evil plots to destroy the American way of life?" The cheers got louder.

"Do you want to know that your government is protecting you from bioterror attacks, by providing immunization against viral diseases?" Shouts of "AllSafe!" sounded among the cheers.

"Do you want to protect the freedom that lets you live your life as an American citizen, free to do what you want to when you want to?" Garlick stretched his hands out, virtually pulling the whistling, stomping, applauding crowd into his embrace. "Then let your elected representatives know that you support the Garlick-Inverness Homeland Security Initiative. Help us keep you safe!"

After the perfectly scripted and choreographed news conference, the impromptu interview of the opposition in the corridors of the Senate office building looked unimpressive.

"The best way for us to keep our communities safe," a dark-suited woman informed the camera, "is to get involved ourselves, not to cede our freedoms to a government agency to do it for us." The caption identified her as Senator Holly Cox, leader of the opposition to Senator Garlick's unofficial but obvious campaign for the homeland security post. The fact that it also identified her as a Mormon had nothing to do with her argument and everything to do with the tactics of hardball politics. "Drug dealers, terrorists, and criminals don't like light, they don't like attention, and they don't like communities that pull together. The best way to fight the bad guys is to get the good guys out on the street. The Garlick-Inverness Homeland Security Initiative is full of unconstitutional and very dangerous measures that won't stop terrorists at all—they'll give the secretary of homeland security the power to control every aspect of domestic law enforcement."

"Looking good, but losing momentum," Monk muttered, checking the lighted ratings bars as Clara efficiently wrapped up the news segment and led into the teaser for the next program. "Time to pick it up. And now we go to pretty people yelling at each other."

Under Kim's efficient fingers, Senator Cox's brief moment in the limelight gave way to the brighter glow of celebrity. To the thumping beat of an urgent leitmotif, the backlit set bloomed into brilliant life, illuminating the handsome face of Channel 8's political commentator. He smiled, perfect teeth glinting in a perfectly calibrated smile. "Good evening. I'm Darren McInnes, star of *Newsroom*, Oscar-winning actor, and host of *Sunday Morning*. We're here tonight for a special report: 'Terrorism in the Heartland.' We'll investigate the secret plots of terrorist cells right here in the United States. Who are these dangerous groups? We'll investigate threats from the ecoterrorists, antiabortion activists, and religious fundamentalists who populate the Net—and our neighborhoods. And we'll discover why the current homeland security laws cannot touch them. Stay tuned while we discover the truth about terrorists in the heartland—and the secret and public collaborators who aid and abet them."

The public service announcement that Kim cued up among the ads made sure that everybody knew that the Mormons were very likely among those who aided and abetted fundamentalist psychopaths. It also urged members of the Mormon "cult" to leave, offered protection against the inevitable reprisals, and touted the growing numbers of former Mormons who had been courageous enough to break the bonds of the Church's fundamentalist brain-washing. The final shot showed a warmly inviting church with its doors open, and the motto "Come Home to Jesus." It was sponsored by the Coalition for Christian Living, which also sponsored Tommy Gibbs's latest crusade tour.

CHAPTER 9

"This kind of thing makes me just nuts," Elder Callatta growled, gently holding the new window secure while Elder Flisfisch smoothed the glazing paste into place around the frame. The muscles across Giovanni's shoulders tensed at the thought of the culprits and their cowardly attack. "It's not even like she has a lot of windows."

"Good thing," Elder Flisfisch noted. "If she had more, we'd have to replace them all too."

Señora Ulloa, in fact, had just two windows in her very modest home. Both had shattered when the stones hit them, the young thugs who threw them laughing and shouting obscene threats at her. They'd promised to come back with more stones—and worse intentions—if the elderly lady and her daughter-in-law's young family became Mormons. Elder Callatta and Elder Flisfisch had come for their appointment with the ladies, only to find a grim-faced Señora Ulloa sweeping up shattered glass while her daughter comforted the three crying children. She apologized to the two missionaries, the story of what had happened spilling out between swipes of her broom.

"They wouldn't come like this if my son were still alive," she told them, fury fighting with the tears in her eyes as she dumped glass shards into the waste bin with more force than necessary.

"He is coming back," her daughter said softly.

"Rudolfo's commanding officer, Major Zamora, visited us himself to convey his condolences." Señora Ulloa turned to the missionaries and lowered her voice. "But Luisa still believes that Rudolfo lost his way in the mountains and will be home soon." Her eyes showed her concern. "I've stopped trying to convince her of the truth. I just let her believe it. It gives her hope."

The loss of Rudolfo and the death of Señor Ulloa years earlier in the March Revolution had made her attention snap into focus when the two missionaries mentioned eternal families, life after death, and reunions with loved ones. She had invited them in out of courtesy, but the missionaries' message reached deep into her heart, kindling hope that she had thought died with her husband. She listened to their lessons, their scriptures, and their heartfelt testimonies, the clarity of their message appealing to her hardheaded practicality. Luisa listened as well. The message of love, of God speaking to His children, somehow penetrated the hazy shield of denial she'd woven around herself. The Mormons who met in the small chapel the elders brought them to had been welcoming, and the service, even with its background of baby noises, had been simple, straightforward, and uplifting, unlike the rote masses Señora Ulloa had attended all her life. She thought that she might have found the way back to her beloved husband at last.

Now, dread and shame clouded her face as she looked at the two missionaries finishing the glazing job.

"There! Good as new," Elder Callatta said. "Elder Flisfisch is more talented than he looks."

Elder Flisfisch rolled his eyes at his companion and smiled at Señora Ulloa's thanks. "You're welcome, Señora. Is there anything else we can do?"

"You can sit down," she said, waving them to seats on a pair of old but well-polished chairs, "and eat something. If you won't let me pay you for the windows, I can at least feed you. All that hard work." Bustling about, she served the two boys hot cocoa and empanadas, watching them intently as they gratefully finished the snack. She caught Louisa's questioning glance and shook her head firmly. Louisa said nothing, gathering the missionaries' cups and plates as they stood, apologizing for having to leave.

They thanked Señora Ulloa for her hospitality, and Elder Flisfisch asked, "When can we see you again? We'd love to continue our discussions."

There it was—the question she dreaded. She hesitated for a moment, doubt warring with practicality. Saving the soul was well and good, but saving the body meant more in the immediate future.

Giving in to the bullies hurt her pride, but she could not protect her daughter-in-law and grandchildren against them. What if they came next not with stones but with fire? Or guns?

"I'm sorry, but maybe you shouldn't come back for a while," she said, furious embarrassment making the words sharper than she intended.

"Señora Ulloa," Giovanni began to protest.

"Very sorry," she repeated firmly.

Elder Flisfisch caught his companion's arm, subtly pulling him back. "We understand. Please call us if you change your mind."

"Yes, please call us," Giovanni said, managing a warm smile despite his disappointment. "And keep reading the Book of Mormon. Pray about the Church and what you should do. It may take a while to get an answer, but Heavenly Father always comes through."

"Be careful," she said, tucking their scarves closer around their necks. "You don't want to crack your jaws, drinking hot cocoa before going outside." She'd grown up in Osorno, and even in Santiago's mild climate, old habits, and folk beliefs, died hard. She waved the missionaries out, watching them through the clear panes of her new windows, breathing a silent apology.

They walked in silence for long minutes, passing houses, small shops, and a few carabineros. Their fellow pedestrians glanced at the two missionaries with curiosity, frowns, and a few smiles, depending on their disposition toward the Church or the rumors they'd heard about it lately. A scattering of cars went by, an especially battered one pulling off to the side of the road beside the police station as the two missionaries passed it. The driver got out but didn't respond to Giovanni's hopeful smile. Elder Callatta let it go. *If he's not interested, the next one might be.*

"Where does that come from, that idea that our jaws will crack if we go out in the cold after drinking cocoa?" Giovanni asked. He glanced aside at Elder Flisfisch's set face, trying to lighten his companion's mood as well as his own. "Talk about nutty. I mean, did that ever really happen? Somebody takes a big swig of cocoa or whatever, walks out the door, and CRACK—half his face falls off?"

Elder Flisfisch didn't smile at Giovanni's dramatic reenactment of that historic moment. "Elder, we lost her. Because of those—those—"

"Don't say it," Elder Callatta warned, knowing his companion's talent for colorful metaphors. *Probably learned them playing soccer or something,* he thought. "We didn't lose her. She's tough. She just needs a little while to remember that. I've seen that kind of fire in my mom's eyes."

"And what if she does?" Elder Flisfisch burst out. "She gets more rocks thrown at her—or her house burned down, like Brother and Sister Vodanovic. Or loses her job, like Brother Sanhueza. We keep teaching the gospel, most people are too scared to listen, and the ones who do listen get hurt. What's the use?"

Giovanni nodded to show he heard, his face growing serious. "My dad told me that doing good isn't easy, but it's worth it." He put his hand on Elder Flisfisch's shoulder. "Listen, Elder. Life's tough. Life's especially tough when you can't count on other people being decent. But the important thing is that they know the truth. They can have the Spirit with them, get the comfort they can't get anywhere else. Brother and Sister Vodanovic got out of their house with their kids, and they're going to be all right. In the end, we're all going to be all right. You just got to take the long view."

"In the end." Elder Flisfisch sighed. "The long view. Try eternal view."

"Yeah," Giovanni agreed, a sliver of his irrepressible grin breaking through his solemnity. He couldn't stay discouraged for long; his psyche was set up for action, not brooding. He slapped Elder Flisfisch's back bracingly. "Come on. Where's that Flisfisch fighting spirit? We're at third down, and they're two goals up. We've got to make a run for it."

"Second half," Elder Flisfisch corrected. "Football doesn't have downs."

"Our football does. Okay, so sports metaphors don't translate. We just need to keep trying, keep going, and we'll win. As long as we're out slugging, we're going to find the people Heavenly Father knows we can help. Somebody will call us over and ask us for the truth. Or something."

"Or something. Elder Callatta, don't you ever ask yourself why—" Elder Flisfisch began. His latest attempt to engage Giovanni in a philosophical discussion about the place of trials in the eternal plan, however, came to an abrupt halt.

Before he could finish the question, a flash stopped them, a brilliant sear of yellow light. A sound quickly followed, like the crack of thunder right overhead—or in this case, down the street. They whirled, as the blast of air hit them—carrying dust, particles of brick, the smell of fire—and almost knocked them down. A gaping, smoking rent had replaced the front of the police station. The battered car Giovanni noticed earlier had disappeared, leaving a deep hole in the pavement and a mangled metal skeleton burning on one edge of the crater. For a second, time seemed to stop, silence ringing after the crack of the explosion. Almost in slow motion, the upper story of the station bowed, stretched, then fell in on itself, the building collapsing into a jagged ruin under another cloud of dust and smoke. The dust settled on the wreckage, the street, the scattered bodies, the horror-frozen watchers. Time snapped back into place when the screams started.

Without even a glance at each other, both missionaries raced back. Giovanni knelt beside a dust-covered, coughing woman, helping her sit up, looking at her legs, arms, the slow welling of blood from a cut across her cheekbone. "Are you okay, ma'am?" he asked urgently, then, mentally kicking himself, said it again in Spanish when she stared uncomprehendingly at him. Finally, with another cough, she managed to nod. "Let's get you out of here, away from the buildings," he suggested, gently raising her to her feet. He handed her off to two other women who had run out of a small shop down the road, then he ran across the street again.

Elder Flisfisch yelled his name, motioning frantically from farther inside the thickening cloud of smoke. The two of them grabbed a thick beam that had fallen, trapping a man under it. Giovanni shifted, taking most of the weight, as Elder Flisfisch pulled the wounded officer out from under the rubble and hauled him out of the way. Giovanni dropped the beam and took the officer's other arm, as the man's leg crumpled. The two missionaries half carried him away from the wreckage, toward another carabinero who, despite the dust-crusted blood covering the side of his head, had taken charge of the situation.

The man, a captain from his grimy badge, looked momentarily surprised as he glanced from his fellow officer to the two rescuers. A half smile flickered across his battered face. "Well, if it isn't the two heroes."

Elder Callatta grinned, recognizing the officer who had taken away the mugger they had apprehended. "We're not heroes, but we'd like to help."

The distant wail of sirens caught the captain's attention; he looked up the street, then at the ruin of the station, the flames beginning to flicker in the rubble. "Come on—we've got to find anybody trapped in there." The two missionaries followed as the captain ran toward the wreckage, working with the few remaining police and the neighboring merchants and residents who poured into the street to fight the fire, dig away rubble, find the wounded, and retrieve the battered bodies of the dead.

They were much too busy with the desperate rescue efforts to notice the brighter light of the mobile camera in the flashing visual chaos of the street, or the lovely young woman in front of the lens. She glanced behind her, making sure the flames silhouetted her dramatically without glare. Her informant hadn't led her astray; she had arrived before any other reporters. And now she had dramatic footage of the latest disaster in Chile's mounting crisis.

"The scene here in a quiet suburb of Santiago is chaos and despair as firefighters and carabineros try desperately to rescue their own. Early reports say at least a dozen officers and bystanders died in the attack as a car bomb destroyed the station on San Juan Street. A communiqué from the rebel leader known as El Jaguar claims that the responsibility for the blast lies with the 'corrupt and oppressive government,' and threatens further action against the 'minions of the state.' President Quintana has issued a statement denouncing the attack against civilian police and calling for an end to what he calls the rebels' terrorist activities. Some rumors accuse factions within the government of aiding the rebels; others implicate groups from the Mapuches to the Mormons. Whatever the truth is, with the escalating violence spreading from outlying villages to the very heart of the capital, the end is nowhere in sight. From San Juan Street in Santiago, Chile, this is Rosa del Torres for Channel 8 Global News."

* * *

Dear Chisom,

I am sorry to hear that intolerance and persecution are escalating in your area, and I am saddened to hear about the family you baptized last month. Being rejected by friends is one thing, but having them throw stones is another. I'm pleased their son was not hurt any worse than he was.

I am not surprised that you asked why the Lord is letting this happen. That is an especially good question in light of the two earthquakes that struck this past month. The quake that hit Turkey killed hundreds. The one that shook Salt Lake City and the Wasatch Front in Utah did a lot of damage, but fortunately took few lives. The earthquake, however, seems to have destroyed more than buildings. Testimonies seem to have tumbled as well.

And that brings me to your question. There are probably a number of reasons why the Lord is permitting these things to happen, but I will mention the two that seem to be the most important to the Brethren.

First, the Lord is cleansing His house. He has been warning us that He would do this, if necessary, for a long time. As early as Joseph Smith's era, the Lord warned that the day of His vengeance was coming in which there would be weeping, mourning, and lamentation. The Lord revealed that His wrath would hit the earth like a tornado. The Church would not escape. Indeed, He said, "Upon my house shall it begin, and from my house shall it go forth." It would especially hit those who "have professed to know my name and have not known me, and have blasphemed against me in the midst of my house" (take a look at D&C 112:24–26). The unrighteous among us, it would seem, have caused this problem. We cannot say the prophets have not been warning Church members that they must either repent or take the consequences.

We must not view this housecleaning, however, as a punishment. In reality, the Lord is preparing the Church for something truly marvelous for which we must be *pure. The pressure of persecution and pestilence is forcing Church members to take sides. Most of those who have been lukewarm, untrue, or hypocritical are leaving.*

It breaks my heart that some active members of the Church are now leaving. As I have talked with some of these, I've learned that they feel betrayed. As I probe, however, I see something else. It seems these Saints, though often very active, served not out of love for God or His children but for selfish reasons. Goodness was to them an insurance policy. Thus, they never paid the price to gain the Spirit and feel the full power of conversion. They believed, and some even preached, that really bad things never happen to good people. Now they know that they were wrong. Most of them can clearly see that it is often the most faithful who receive the brunt of the persecutions, and the earthquake did not spare the homes of the righteous. Their worldview is destroyed. As a result, they feel betrayed and leave.

Of course, not all of these shallow members have left the Church. Some still cling to their erroneous view, insisting, often with whispers, that those who were hurt were sinners at heart. They are rather like Job's friends, who kept insisting he was, in spite of all appearances, a very bad man. Joseph Smith warned against such a notion. In connection with the Second Coming, he said that "it is a false idea that the Saints will escape all the judgments, whilst the wicked suffer; for all flesh is subject to suffer, and 'the righteous shall hardly escape,' still many of the Saints will escape, for the just shall live by faith; yet many of the righteous shall fall a prey to disease, to pestilence, etc., by reason of the weakness of the flesh, and yet be saved in the kingdom of God. So that it is an unhallowed principle to say that such and such have transgressed because they have been preyed upon by disease or death, for all flesh is subject to death; and the Savior has said, 'Judge not, lest ye be judged.'" (That's from his Teachings on pages 162–63.)

The second reason why the Lord is letting this happen is so that the world can stand condemned. He can justly bring His judgment against the world only when it is fully ripe in iniquity. The Book of Mormon teaches us that the world must meet three conditions in order to be fully ripe.

First, the world must reject the gospel. With missions shutting down, we can say the world is rapidly meeting that condition.

Second, it must persecute the Saints. We see that happening in more places and to ever greater numbers. Not only that, but the Saints are being condemned because of their righteousness—that is, because of the stand they take against perversion and evil.

Third, the worldly must drive out the righteous from among them. We are seeing the beginnings of this final stage of iniquity. Already, in some areas, the Saints are leaving because of hatred and persecution. They gather for protection and security. The prophets are quietly counseling members in some areas to move into temple communities within their nations. This gathering will continue until the Lord comes, and it will prove the protection of the Saints. The rejection of the righteous by the wicked will prove their utter doom.

If you want to study this idea, look at the following references: 2 Nephi 28:16; Alma 37:28, 45:16; Helaman 7:5, 13:14; and 3 Nephi 20:28.

Therefore, Chisom, as the Church becomes more righteous, do not expect the persecutions to slow down. I suspect that they will, in fact, escalate.

Nevertheless, the Saints are going to be all right. The Church continues to grow, as you know, not only in spite of all the problems but, in many instances, because of them. We do have the answers, and the good-hearted are drawn to us. Move forward in faith. Strengthen your people and keep believing. God is at the helm.

With much love and respect,
Your father,
Chinedu

* * *

The match flared in the darkness, then arced gently through the air like a firefly flitting across a romantic woody glade. When it hit the floor, however, the enchanting illusion disappeared. The flare reflected for a split second in the thin film of alcohol spread over the tattered vinyl, then landed with a soft pop. A wash of blue flame rippled to life, the yellow of deeper flame rushing behind it as the fire burned through the accelerant and began to eat into the floor itself. The flames spread, licking up the walls as the first thin cloud of smoke filled the room. The two men in the doorway watched until the blue disappeared into furious orange and they heard the deep-throated roar of an inferno.

"I do love a barbecue," one said, grinning under his mask.

"The guests'll be here in a minute," the other replied. "Let's get ready to greet them." He turned from the flames, scooping up the long, black bag from the doorway as he ran from the flaring building. The pair sprinted down the steps and across the street, where another dark-windowed tenement loomed. They easily opened a door, which looked nailed shut, and ran up the interior stairs to the roof.

Above the roar of the fire, the distant wails of sirens became audible. "They're here already," the first said, cocking his head toward the sound, his hands never pausing their expert assembly of the tripod he had taken from the bag.

"Sure. Mr. Augosto owns most of this block." The second laid out a spread of ammunition on a tarp within easy reach of the two rifles. "The faster the feds get here, the better the story for the insurance guys."

"Pay back the client and get paid at the same time," the first man said, looking through his scope. The flames had spread through the building they lit—and dirty orange tongues of it licked from the three other tenements on the block. Blue, red, and white flashing lights twinkled as he turned the scope uptown. By the time the fire-fighters arrived, the entire block would be as hot as the mouth of a volcano. *Even hotter, actually*, he thought with a nasty smile.

The fire trucks skidded to a halt, their brilliant lights almost dim compared to the towering flames. Firefighters spilled out of the engines, racing to unwrap and connect hoses to hydrants, the pumper-truck crew blasting their initial supply of water into the flames. Steam erupted in billowing clouds as the stream hit the heat, blasting back at the men trying to subdue the flames. A series of distant pops began, growing louder, then resolving into explosions as the ancient supports of the tenements exploded in the molten heat. With a groan, the roof of the corner building fell in, sending a fountain of sparks into the smoke-choked air. The fire captain shouted orders into his headset, and the firefighting team pulled sharply back as the flaming rubble cascaded down to the street.

He started shouting again, more frantically, as bullets tore into the hoses that the second engine team pulled toward the fire. Another series of shots ricocheted off the hot walls, the engines, and the gratings in the street as the snipers opened fire from all around the burning buildings. Caught between the flames and the gunfire, the firefighters beat a hasty retreat, using their engines as cover while they summoned another squad of specialists to quell this very different kind of fire.

* * *

"Amazingly, this block of east Philadelphia is burning to rubble not only because of arson, but because of terrorism," Channel 8's Philadelphia correspondent reported. "Fires break out in the empty quarter of eastern Philly all the time, but this one had an important difference—when the fire trucks arrived, the shooting started. Snipers shot at the firefighters from the roofs of buildings around the block where the fire started. The engine companies pulled back, but by the time the Philadelphia police SWAT team arrived, the snipers had disappeared, leaving only this message: Death to America. Homeland security agents say they're doing everything they can to finger the terrorist organization responsible. But how many more buildings will go up in flames—and how many more firefighters and police officers will be seriously injured before the federal authorities can prevent atrocities like this one?"

"And we go to commercial," Monk ordered sarcastically.

Kim's fingers danced over the board, and Senator Garlick's handsomely disheveled face appeared on the screen. "Of course, I'm shocked by this horrible tragedy," he lied. "But I am even more shocked that those who have the charge to protect us have failed to guard the heroes who stand between us and true domestic terror—the firefighters and police of Philadelphia. The secretary of homeland security has shown that she is unwilling to take the measures necessary to stem the tide of terror that threatens to overwhelm our country."

The senator's self-promoting speech rolled on, Kim expertly embellishing his points with footage of the wounded firefighters and police officers, the burning buildings—and a single blurry zoom photo of a sniper leaping from the roof under cover of flames.

"We've got a real spike on the East Coast," Monk noted. "And we're rolling west. That'll give us a nice segue into our special report on the tragic results of terrorism all over the globe." He sucked the end of his stylus thoughtfully, one finger tapping the ratings display. "And then get the skin show ready—we don't want to lose eyeballs because people get too depressed and decide to Bliss out."

* * *

Clara Cortez looked into the camera, expertly exchanging her worried voice into a sunny smile. "Now, on a lighter note, Channel 8's entertainment specialist, Garrett de Long, has a special report of his own. What's going on in the celebrity world, Garrett?"

"We have a special guest with us tonight, Clara," Garrett purred. "And she's hot enough to make everything melt, just by walking into the room. And here she is, for an exclusive interview, Virginia Diamante!"

To the applause of an extremely enthusiastic audience, Virginia slinked out of the wings. She posed seductively, wrapping herself in the brilliant colors of a diaphanous cloak, her lush hair flowing over her shoulders and down her back. When the whistles and stomping reached a crescendo, she threw her arms wide, showing off the cloak's vivid butterfly pattern—and the skintight gown over her own perfectly sculpted body. She blew kisses to the audience before turning to take Garrett's hands and exchange air kisses with him.

He settled her on his own luxurious divan and smiled, wiping his brow dramatically. "Well, you surely do know how to party, my dear!

I wish I could've been to your last one. The concert at the Queen of Sheba certainly looked like fun," Garrett said. "But, sweetheart, if I can offer you a bit of friendly advice, you really ought to be more careful! It looked like you were eating real cheesecake!"

"Oh, it was," Virginia assured him, wide-eyed.

He looked at her in honest surprise then recovered enough to pull his smirk back onto his face. "Isn't that just deadly for one's girlish figure?"

"This figure?" Virginia leaned back against the cushions, breathing deeply. The audience moaned on cue. "Seriously, Garrett, with the new metabolic enhancer I'm using, I can eat anything I want." She ran her tongue over her glossy lips. "Anything. And I never have to worry about it."

"Really?" Garrett had regained his equilibrium. Virginia's defection from the strict model diet of cigarettes, designer water, and pills shocked him until he realized that it was all for a higher cause—marketing. And he was more than happy to play along. "Holy cheesecake! This wonderful development must be a present from your dear friends at MedaGen, right?"

"Absolutely right," Virginia purred. "I've always said that your IQ was higher than your shoe size. Yes, thanks to MedaGen, Slendrin will soon be available absolutely everywhere—and at such a reasonable price. Just think—anybody can eat anything they want without worrying."

Monk knew all about the real purpose behind Virginia's sudden publicity blitz, even if Garrett didn't. On cue, the ticker scrolled through the particulars of MedaGen's latest breakthrough, indications for use, promised results, dates of availability, and preorder information.

"Speaking of your contributions to everybody's fun, what about this AllSafe booster shot we've been hearing so much about?" Garrett cocked his head at her, all interest. "Can getting a little shot every year really protect anybody from—" He paused delicately, then finished, "Easily transmittable diseases?"

"What else?" Virginia flirted, batting her eyelashes, then grew serious. They'd warned her about the booster rumors, and her orders were to downplay them as much as possible. No denials, just change the subject to promote AllSafe. "Honey, people are going to do it anyway, so why not make sure there're no consequences?" She winked at the audience and camera.

"But what would you say to the puritan types—like Seraph, that Mormon band at the music awards," Garrett enquired, "those who say that you're corrupting the morals of the entire country?"

Virginia shrugged, a flicker of irritation beneath the calculated insouciance. "Why morals," she asked with a wink and kiss toward the camera, "when the country can have me?" Julian, Virginia's lanky assistant, stood in the wings just off the set, intently watching Virginia, mouthing the words, ready to prompt if Virginia lost the thread. She didn't. She also didn't thank Julian—or acknowledge the reporters who gathered around her as she swayed out of the studio and into the waiting limousine.

"Whew!" Virginia breathed, running a hand through her hair, then holding out the hand. Julian put her custom-made ivory compact into it. "That's done—and I didn't forget anything, after you worried so much." She poked Julian before turning her attention to the face reflected in the extra-large mirror.

"Actually, you forgot this." He handed her a flimsy length of black chiffon. "Your scarf. Which you left at Abbott's apartment. He had it sent."

Virginia glanced at her assistant and smiled smugly. "Oh, dear, sweetie—is that jealousy I'm hearing? A little green-eyed monster?" Her attention turned back to her own reflection, and she snapped her fingers. Julian handed her the beautifully embroidered backup makeup box. "What's the first rule?"

"No rules, just freedom," Julian repeated. The seductive appeal of those words had dimmed, however, over the last two years; talking about total freedom to love anybody and everybody with no commitment and no exclusive relationships sounded great when the two of them cuddled and plotted Virginia's meteoric rise to pop stardom. In practice, an empty apartment, no matter how lush, got extremely cold when Virginia decided to exercise her option to be elsewhere. The thought hurt. "Ginny, you shouldn't do that."

"What?" Virginia asked, only half listening as she checked herself in the compact mirror, then in the smooth, reflective glass of the limo's privacy window. Mirrors drew her attention like flames drew moths, sometimes with equally flaming results as she scanned the reality they revealed for any possible flaw, any crack in her perfect facade, any excuse for her deep insecurities to erupt to the surface.

"Go to his room when he wants you," he said. "Then disappear so you're gone in the morning when he wakes up. Like you're cheap."

Virginia laughed, a brittle edge to the silver tone. "Watch it, baby, or you're sleeping outside the door." She shrugged, carefully applying a slick of gloss to her perfect lips. "Besides, that's the way I like it. I don't have to toss him out of my room."

"Abbott's a big man now," Julian said. "Thanks to you, but he's taking all the credit for it with MedaGen's board of directors. They've stepped up the AllSafe campaign to the ultimate degree, and—"

"And I light my rocket off his, and fly even higher," Virginia finished.

"If you don't get overexposed and flame out. Pop-tarts come and go. Like waves on a beach. Temporary, identical, and forgotten. Don't let that happen to you." *To me—to us*, he thought. *To all the wonderfully free dreams I believed in. Still believe in.*

"I won't." The slightest hint of a frown line appeared between her sculpted brows. She sharply clicked the lip gloss wand into its holder. "All I want is his publicity contract, and then he's out just like those silly waves you're on about. I don't like him anyway; he's too self-absorbed. The guy at his last party, though, the one who came in with the senator, he looked like a promising replacement."

"Who, Johnny Mack, the gangster's bodyguard?" Julian made a face, remembering the empty-headed, lust-struck expression on his face when Virginia walked into the room.

"No, idiot—his boss." Virginia snapped the compact closed, irritated at Julian's incessant carping. "That Cesar guy."

"Not him," Julian said flatly. "He's out of your league—"

"Out of my league!" A hot rush of blood brightened the rouge on Virginia's cheeks. "Out of my league?" She grabbed the makeup case and flung it at Julian along with a stream of vicious curses.

"I meant he's a gangster," Julian said, half deflecting the missiles. "He's a gangster, Ginny, not a smarmy businessman, not a club owner or record exec or anybody we can deal with." *Like Abbott's not a gangster?*

The idea whispered insistently under the description of Augosto, but Julian didn't want to think about that. "I just want you to be careful, because I love you."

"Yeah, you do." Virginia took a deep breath, contempt icing her tone. Her expression suddenly warmed, however, as the limo rolled to a stop at the set for her new MedaGen commercial. She smoothed her face out for the photographers as the chauffeur swung the door open, and she leaned over in what looked like a sexy cuddle and softly reminded Julian, "You're just jealous. You do what I tell you to. And I'm telling you to cuddle up to Johnny Mack and get me a personal introduction to Cesar Augosto."

Waving, smiling kittenishly at the inevitable mob of paparazzi, Virginia slipped out of the limo. Julian swept up the contents of the makeup case, feeling the familiar wash of sick anger and betrayal at Virginia's vicious attack—and careless, cold dismissal. She wanted Augosto, so she fell back on offering her friends as party favors. A flash of red caught Julian's eye, a reflection of auburn in the mirror of the compact that had opened as it fell. The image in the mirror smiled wryly. "Is that what you are? Just another living carpet?"

"Honey?" Virginia's seductive, impatient voice broke Julian's bitter contemplation. "You coming?"

"I'm coming." Julian swept the makeup case and Virginia's luscious fur jacket off the seat and hurried to join her, thinking, *I gave up my entire life for you, my identity, everything I was, because I believed you. Now you've got a big career, and I've got a broken heart. And there's no cure for that.*

CHAPTER 10

"This is the place. Or maybe I should say, 'This is the right place,' to be historically accurate." Jonathan Crow smiled as he drove past the prominent statue of Brigham Young then glanced at his passenger to see if the joke worked. The young man had said almost nothing since Jonathan picked him up from the rail station; he'd been polite but not friendly. Of course, that could come from the fact that the poor guy was obviously very ill. He wouldn't be here otherwise—and Jonathan wouldn't be picking him up to escort him if he hadn't been both sick and someone who, with his surprising crusade in New Mexico and the Navajo Reservation, had caught Elder Nabil's personal attention. To Jonathan, Elder Nabil's right-hand man, the young man didn't look like a rebel leader who could marshal entire towns to successfully fight the rising tide of drug dealers and violent gangs in the border areas, but there had to be more to him than his thin, long-haired, denim-intensive, young but battered appearance suggested.

Dove looked through the windshield at the statue, the seagull-decorated arch, the darting traffic, the surprising midcity gardens, and the brilliantly reflecting glass and granite walls of the tallest buildings he'd ever seen this close. He'd driven through Phoenix before, but not into the city itself, and this place was even bigger, a solid mass of buildings that filled the wide valley from end to end. He saw little damage from the earthquake; most of the repairs had been made already. Then he looked at the driver, who was smiling hopefully at him. Dove smiled back, out of courtesy more than understanding the joke, and tried to stifle a cough.

Jonathan politely looked away, not acknowledging the weakness, and Dove was grateful.

"Look, Dove. You're going to get better. Merry Galen and her team are working very hard to find ways to stop the vaccine from doing its damage. And Elder Nabil, the member of the Twelve I work for, has a special interest in the research going on at Section 89." Jonathan paused. "Get it? Like the most health-conscious section of the Doctrine and Covenants. Anyway, it's a privately funded, state-of-the-art research facility. Some wealthy members of the Church anonymously fund the place. Before he was called to the Twelve, Dr. Robert Nabil was a star in the field of molecular medicine, specializing in cancer research. He drops in to discuss Merry's progress every time his schedule allows it—which isn't as often as either of them would like.

"Merry is really something else. Elder Nabil swept her right into the office—and more important, into the lab outside it—at Section 89 as soon as she came to him with the information about the AllSafe vaccine. We helped her get the word out right away, and he used his contacts to double-check the data she and her husband, Chris, had pulled out of MedaGen's computers."

"He's the one that got killed, right?" asked Dove, remembering this part of the story from Dr. Joe.

"Yeah, that's right. It's really tragic. She disappointed her feminist mother by leaving a prestigious research position to be a stay-at-home mommy for Missy, her three-year-old. Now, she's gone back to work but hardly under the circumstances she would have liked."

"How do you know so much about her?" asked Dove.

"My wife, Tasha, watches Missy. That is, when the little girl's not at her Grandma and Grandpa Galen's house. Merry's had a harder time than she ever imagined she would being away from Missy. She really misses her. She misses Chris too."

Over the folds of his bandana, Dove discreetly watched the young Church agent, sizing him up as he steered them onto the quieter side streets of Salt Lake City. Jonathan Crow didn't fit his name, Dove decided. He'd never met anyone so unlike a crow—no ruffled feathers, sharp eyes, or predatory instincts there. From Jonathan's neatly combed hair and perfectly pressed clothes to his shining shoes and equally scrubbed expression, he radiated an efficiency and innocence that reminded Dove of the zone-leader missionary he met back home. *Life hadn't smacked Jonathan around much*, Dove thought, *but he could probably take it if it did.*

"Okay, this is really the place." Jonathan maneuvered into a small, tree-shaded parking lot behind a long, low, pleasantly nondescript building. "Section 89. This is where they'll find the cure for AllSafe—and the new strains of genetically engineered viruses that keep cropping up in the wrong hands."

"Don't know what the right hands would be." Dove got out of the car, his eyes narrowing as he scanned the building. It looked like nothing much on first glance, but a closer look spotted the surveillance cameras. The windows had a sheen to them that suggested they were not only well insulated but probably bulletproof too. And the pleasant-faced receptionist who met them as they passed through the key-coded doors shared the comfortably elegant foyer with a large, sharp-eyed guard.

"Jonathan Crow, with Salvatore Nakai, to see Dr. Galen," Jonathan told her, offering his ID card.

"Of course, Brother Crow," she said, dutifully looking at his card, even though she knew him from several previous occasions. She smiled as she logged their visit. "How are you? And how's Tasha?"

"Just fine, Sister Levine—and she's as wonderful as ever," Jonathan said, a soft light in his eyes at the thought of his wife.

"That's good." She nodded. She turned her smile on Dove. "And welcome to Section 89, Mr. Nakai."

"Thanks." Dove pushed his own ID across the high lip surrounding the desk, wondering if she'd spot the driver's license for the fake it was. It was a good fake—Scribbler Jones had done all the IDs for Abuelo's gang, and while he charged top prices, he also delivered top-quality product. None of them had ever bothered to go through normal channels to get drivers' licenses; the folks at the DMV had inconvenient hang-ups about correct birthdates and letting fourteen-year-olds drive. Pizarro hadn't tried to crack down on the fakes either; he'd just charged Scribbler a modest "service fee" every year. "I'm not contagious," he belatedly added, as she reached for the license.

"I know. We got the folder on you from Dr. Gee yesterday. But thank you." She gave the license a hard look, glanced at Dove, then smiled as she handed it back. "Looks like you've finally caught up to your age too. Go on back—Dr. Galen's expecting you. She'll be in her office." A soft light lit above the door on her left, the latch giving a soft chime as she released the security lock.

Dove smiled back and took the license, tucking it back into his wallet as he followed Jonathan to the door. "She was a cop once?" he asked softly, as they stepped out of the warm-toned reception area into a starker, more clinical hallway.

Jonathan looked surprised. "Sister Levine? I don't think so. She worked as an emergency-room nurse when she was younger, but not as a cop." He frowned, searching his memory. "Maybe her husband is with the police, now that I think about it. I'm not sure though. Why?"

"No reason," Dove shrugged casually. "Just wondered." Another bout of coughing saved him from further explanations but left him dizzy and leaning against the blue-tiled wall for a moment.

"Come on, let's get you to the doctors." Jonathan's frown deepened, concern replacing curiosity. He considered taking Dove's arm but thought better of it. Instead, he waited for the younger man to regain his balance then led the way to another door and the examination room beyond. "Okay, if you'll stay here, I'll go get Dr. Galen. Be right back."

Dove watched him leave, then settled into one of the chairs against the wall, eyeing the examination table suspiciously. A few seconds later, he heard voices approaching. He picked out Jonathan's light tones then a woman's semiaudible reply.

The deep, accented voice that came next, however, he heard very clearly. ". . . in some ways so much like the test of the Israelites, when Moses held the brass serpent aloft and pleaded with them to have the faith to look and live."

"I wish it could be so easy this time," the woman replied.

"Easy is all a matter of perspective." Dove saw their shadows on the wall outside the door. "You are forging that brass serpent now, Merry, which is a challenge and a blessing for you and your team as you move forward in faith; I am afraid that the rest of us still face the test of actually looking at it."

Dove tried to stand, but the whirling in his head didn't let him. He settled back, hands on the arms of the chair, and gazed steadily at them as they came in.

The tall, dark, distinguished man caught his attention first, an elegant figure in a dark suit and tie. Jonathan walked a pace behind him, not so much his shadow as his right hand, ready to spring into action at his superior's command. *Which would probably come as a polite request*, Dove thought, watching the tall man's compassionate expression as he extended a hand to Dove. "Brother Nakai, welcome. I am Elder Robert Nabil."

Dove took his hand briefly, just a light touch, balancing courtesy with caution about exposing the Apostle to the virus inside him. "I know you, Elder Nabil. It is an honor, sir."

Elder Nabil smiled. "And I know you, Hasbídí—is that right?" He accepted Dove's surprised nod as an affirmation of his pronunciation and continued, "Your unorthodox—and valiant—efforts on behalf of the Church and citizens in the borderlands have made quite a splash here—and in Independence. I look forward to visiting with you at greater length, when you feel better. And, alas, when my schedule permits me such a pleasant appointment. Now, however, I fear that I must take my leave, and Brother Crow as well. We leave you in Dr. Galen's conscientious hands." He smiled again, leaning close for a moment to add in a stage whisper, "See if you can convince her to take a break now and again."

Dove smiled but didn't commit himself to any agreements. One look at Merry, whose intensely focused eyes marked her as both brilliant and probably stubborn, made him think that convincing her of anything she didn't agree with would take more patience and debating skill than he could muster. She looked nothing like Sam's wife, Renata, Dove's ideal image of a competent, compassionate, intelligent woman, but she had the same kind of light in her eyes. He nodded and half smiled at Jonathan's quick good-bye then focused all his attention on Dr. Galen.

"First, thank you for being willing to help us." Her voice betrayed her nervousness, as if she were uncertain about how to tell him what she needed to, but plunged on anyway. "We—our team here—have been trying to find a cure for the genetically engineered viruses that have appeared recently—"

"I know," Dove said, interrupting her as gently but firmly as possible. His Navajo grandfather would have disapproved of the discourtesy, but he wanted to cut through the preliminaries and get to the point; each cough that racked his aching chest told him that he didn't have much time. "Jonathan—Brother Crow told me about Section 89 on the drive here and that you work with genetic medicine to overcome genetically engineered diseases. That's probably all I'd understand anyway. You need experimental subjects who have the diseases you're working on. I've got one, thanks to one of General Garza's agents. So, Dr. Galen, what do you need me to do?"

She blinked, then seemed to relax—and got more businesslike at the same time. "Well, good. What I need you to do is read this and sign it." She offered him a clipboard containing several sheets of paper with a pen clipped to the top. "It's a release, officially giving us permission to give you our antiviral medication. It also says that we, Section 89, are responsible to take all reasonable precautions to ensure your safety and health and to provide you with treatment, care, and living arrangements at no expense to you."

"And burial costs?" Dove asked, deadpan, as he scanned the pages. Beneath the legalese, it seemed to be exactly what she described.

It took just a second for her to decide it was all right to smile at that. "Certainly," she said in the same dry tone. "Only the best spot in the crematorium for our patients, and the finest urns."

"Sounds good." He signed with a flourish and handed the clipboard back—then had to press the bandana to his face again as the cough ripped through his lungs.

"That doesn't sound a bit good," Merry said as Dove leaned back in the chair, trying to hide his shaking. She tucked the clipboard under her arm and brushed her hands together briskly. "All right, let's get to work on making it go away. First, Dr. Resnik will examine you to find out what damage has already been done. We'll have to help you heal from that as well as stopping the virus itself. So we'll give you a dose of AllSafe to knock out the virus for the moment, until we've got the antidote ready to go—" The expression on his face stopped her quick rundown. "What?"

"I won't take AllSafe," Dove said flatly.

"If you don't, you won't last long enough for us to find a better cure for the virus," Merry said, equally flatly. "And that's the whole point of bringing you here. AllSafe can't destroy the virus totally, but it can hold it in abeyance long enough to give us the time we need."

The duel, stare versus stare, was as silent as it was intense.

Finally Dove said, "Dr. Galen, the leaders of the Church—the prophet—stood up and told us not to get the immunization. Specifically. By name."

Merry sighed internally. *Ironic that the warning I worked so hard to get out now comes back to bite me,* she thought, but she kept her voice level and patient. "President Smith warned the members of the Church against taking AllSafe because of its deadly side effects if someone doesn't get a booster shot within a year. Even MedaGen isn't totally denying it; they're just trying to skirt the issue. But the point is that healthy people don't need it and shouldn't take it to prevent the vast majority of the diseases that it's advertised to cure—like AIDS and other IDDs—because there are easier ways to prevent them that don't involve selling your future to MedaGen. The one thing it can do that we can't right now is beat off genetically engineered viruses. And that's where you come in. Mr. Nakai—Salvatore—"

"Dove," he suggested, remembering Dr. Joe's derisive reaction to his theory that taking AllSafe was like sinning while intending to repent later, and knowing that he wouldn't win this argument either.

"Dove." She blinked, but didn't let the incongruity of that name on a battle-scarred border rat shake her from her train of thought. "I've got to have somebody to experiment on, somebody who's been exposed to the bioterror viruses—and then, later on, somebody who's had a dose of AllSafe so we can eradicate it too. Everybody who's getting immunized now wouldn't want me to defuse AllSafe, and I don't want to give AllSafe to some random volunteer just to test our cure."

"So I'm a kind of double-bonus guinea pig," Dove said. He couldn't come up with a decent comeback for that one, and hearing that agreeing to take AllSafe wouldn't undo his baptism was a relief. Captain Moroni used any means necessary to defeat his enemies— could Dove do less? The only question was how to capitulate and save face at the same time. So he'd follow Perro's example; if he made it a joke, he could give in without actually conceding defeat. "I ought to get twice the desserts or something."

"Definitely, if you behave yourself and cooperate." Merry didn't let her relief at his capitulation show. She was a researcher, not a practitioner, and had never felt entirely comfortable dealing directly with the patients her research eventually helped. "You can do the best for everybody by getting well. Then you can help us put a stop to AllSafe and MedaGen too. So, you can cooperate right now by letting us get you healthy enough to be a good host while that virus and our cure battle it out."

Dove shot her a skeptical glance, but couldn't totally suppress the sparkle in his eyes as he said, "Doctor lady, it's never a good idea to get caught in the middle of a gang war."

* * *

"Take that off, diphead." The biggest thug smacked the kid with the crimson scarf wrapped around his wrist, then tugged the cloth covering the boy's head. He grinned, the chips of diamond flashing from his sharpened canines as he hefted a newly stolen gun. "Terrell don't want his colors flashed on this job. We not flying with the brothers this time. Anybody see you tonight, you ain't a Ghetto Lord, you a religious extremist."

The black van pulled to a stop at the back of a parish church in Los Angeles. The men crowded into the back tensed to move, taking the last tokes on their cigarettes, cocking their guns, checking the cans of accelerants and paint.

"We ready for Freddie?" Diamond Tooth's hand hovered over the latch.

One voice came through the general growl. "But man, a church?"

"Shut up, chico," growled another gangster.

Diamond Tooth raised his pistol, the black mouth of the barrel gaping before the holdout's eyes. "You got no problem shooting up that Jew place. Saw you torch the big scroll thing yourself. So now you yellow on a church, choir boy? How much you really believe in angels?"

"Not that much, man." Choir Boy broke the twanging tension with a flick of his lighter. The flame lit the manic grin on his face.

It also lit the hangings on the overturned altar. The intricate windows exploded, shattering into gemlike shards under blows from bullets and pieces of altar furnishings. The Presence lamp shattered, as did the glass holders of the candles guttering in the small side chapels, wax and flame running free over the wooden statues. The ancient marble of the altar itself proved too hard to crack. The pews, however, burned easily, sending up a smoke that replaced incense with the sickening odor of hate and violence. The flames woke the neighborhood; cries of puzzlement came dimly through the jagged window holes.

"Evaporation time!" Diamond Tooth paused at the broken doors to survey the damage and the flames creeping through the pile of pews. He grinned, the jewels in his teeth catching the light of the fire as he ran to the van. He jumped in as the tires squealed against the rough asphalt. They careened out of the alley, sending a hailstorm of shots into the sides of the damaged building as they made their escape.

Diamond Tooth leaned out of the open doors at the back of the van, waving his gun, making sure the wide-eyed priest got a good look at the whooping, cursing passengers—and the red-checked kaffiyehs covering their heads, securely tied on over their black masks.

* * *

"In a night of ecumenical terror, Muslim extremists broke into a Jewish synagogue and a Catholic church in Los Angeles last night," Clara announced. Pictures of the broken, charred buildings alternated in quick succession with the horrified faces of the people who came to find their places of worship wrecked. "The attackers left notes that suggest the vandals are Muslim extremists, probably joined with overseas terrorist groups. The notes also hint that these attacks are, quote 'only the beginning of the punishment of the ungodly.' Later tonight, in a Channel 8 exclusive, Rabbi Ben Israel, Father Wallace O'Shaughnessy, and Senator Howard Garlick will discuss the growing threat of sectarian violence in the United States.

"Now it's time for a check on the status of the U.S. peacekeeping and security efforts. In Ohalajishi, U.S. troops clashed with rebel forces in Ojibwa. Four peacekeepers and fifty rebels were killed in the raid, with approximately a dozen civilian casualties. An Eagle troop-transport helicopter went down outside the U.S. base camp in

Kharagizstan; the Pentagon denies the claims of a group calling themselves the Hand of the Prophet shot it down."

The battle images accompanying the report faded into shots of
the equally vicious but verbal wars flaring through the Capitol.
Senator Garlick pounded the pulpit as he made a point. Senator
Holly Cox, pale but determined, leaned forward to ask a question in a
Senate hearing. "Meanwhile, heated debates on the Hill have split the
government into rival factions, as the House and Senate debate
measures that would bring our troops home—or extend U.S. involvement in even more regional conflicts. Is U.S. involvement in 'nation
building' hurting security here at home? Tune in to the Channel 8
special report, 'War or Domestic Violence?' for details."

Clara waited a beat while the advertisement for the special report
faded, then continued. "In the rest of the world, conflicts continue.
In Chile, government forces raided a suspected guerilla camp, but
were unable to capture the rebel leader El Jaguar. Meanwhile, in
China, a coalition of northern insurgents led by Lord Xi Xian have
dynamited a hydroelectric plant, badly damaging the dam and threatening hundreds of villages built along the river." The tally went on, as
she sped through a brief update on the highlights for each hot zone.
Beside her the latest information from the front scrolled along, listing
the totals for rebels, governments, and U.N. peacekeepers: territory
won, bombing raids conducted, towns taken, and casualties lost.

"Closer to home, the hostage standoff at the library in North
Dakota continues." Clara suppressed a smile, keeping her serious face
firmly in place as the split screen showed the tiny library and the
handful of local officers standing around it, looking exasperated and
sipping coffee in the cold. "The suspects, members of a tiny Christian
splinter group calling itself the Holy Army of God, are demanding
the immediate resignation of the entire United States government, the
compulsory adoption of the old 'under God' version of the Pledge of
Allegiance, and that the Pentagon nuke Hollywood immediately."

* * *

"Catching up on the news? I am disappointed, Mr. Whittier—
and Mr. Humphrey." Ms. Zelik's icy voice cut through the drawling

tones of a North Dakota sheriff explaining that old Bill Whitehead wasn't a bad guy, just a little crazy, and that he wouldn't really hurt anybody.

Whittier started, turning slowly away from the conference room's wall-sized screen to hide the flash of fear freezing his spine. Errol Humphrey, recently promoted to Whittier's division and secure in the knowledge that Zelik's hatchet would fall on his superior first, calmly leaned back in his deep leather chair and looked attentive.

"Or were you going to place a bet on that miserable war in Ohalashushi or wherever it is?" Zelik walked toward the two men, her heels clicking on the marble.

"Ohalajishi," Whittier said automatically. "Not that it's important—with the job they're doing wiping themselves out with guns and starvation, they're hardly a market for AllSafe—or Slendrin."

"Then shut it off and concentrate on doing your real job. I didn't call this meeting to give you an opportunity to waste time on useless markets," Zelik snapped. She stood straight and tense, her nails tapping the satiny wood facing of the long table.

Whittier glanced at her, then at Humphrey, who shot him a knowing look and flashed a subtle, smoothing gesture at his boss.

"Then let's get to why you did call the meeting," Whittier suggested, taking Humphrey's hint and moving the conversation onto safer ground.

"I called the meeting because I want the campaign against the Mormons stepped up," Zelik said. "Hit them hard. Work with those flyover-country religious fanatics if you have to, but I want that cult's credibility absolutely destroyed. And I don't want our name brought up."

"Countersuits against the Mormons and Meredith Galen not going well?" Whittier asked.

Zelik shot him a fierce look. "They are proceeding."

The countersuits, alleging that the Church sponsored industrial espionage against MedaGen, demanded a court order to stop them from revealing any more of MedaGen's intellectual property and requested damage awards in the billions of dollars. They were proceeding, but not as well as she would like. She'd cracked the whip on the lawyers running the civil suits; the criminal case had died under federal whistle-blower protection. The thought of Merry, vindicated as a whistle-blower in Salt Lake City, well guarded, and working in a privately funded medical research lab, brought her to a furious boil. Only adding fuel to her rage was the fact that Abbott had used Zelik's inability to retrieve Merry and the stolen information to cut Zelik out of the credit for the successful AllSafe rollout.

"The new campaign's already in process, officially under the auspices of the illustrious Tommy Gibbs," Humphrey assured her calmly. "Nobody will connect MedaGen with it."

"Contact Monk at Channel 8 when you have the new campaign ready and send me a preview. And do it by the end of the week." She glared from one to the other. "Why are you still sitting here?"

"Just making sure we've got all our directions," Whittier assured her, rising to saunter out, mainly to reassert his independence after her unexpected entrance caught him slightly off guard.

Zelik's sharp-nailed hand caught Humphrey's sleeve as he moved to follow Whittier. He looked into her eyes, and felt her gaze freeze him all the way to his feet. "Speaking of Meredith Anthony Galen, it's interesting that it took you so long to alert security when you found her downloading the research data on AllSafe."

"I called as soon as I checked what she was doing," Humphrey said. He could see that a generic excuse didn't cut any ice, and he shifted into offensive mode. Subtly. "After all, she had permission to check any files on the system, and I didn't want to bother security if she was just doing her job. In fact, I'm sure I have a copy of the memo giving her total access—the one you signed for her."

That blow chipped the ice slightly; if Abbott had proof, he would hold it over her head for the rest of her career—until he found a way to knife her permanently. The possibility hardened the threat in her low voice. "Really? That's one piece of history that had better never come to light."

"That's true. It looks like we've all got reasons to protect each other." Humphrey smiled.

"Yes," Zelik agreed. "And we've got others to punish. I have a special assignment for you, Errol. Or an expansion of the assignment you've been doing."

"From rumor mongering and reputation destroying to what?" Humphrey asked, raising an eyebrow.

"Use your imagination," Zelik said. "And remember to tell me what you have planned so I can make sure our local law enforcement know to look the other way."

Humphrey just smiled coolly and nodded once as she swept past him, her heels clicking down the hall. Law enforcement, eh? He almost felt sorry for the targets of Zelik's malice—but the Callattas had chosen to put themselves in her sights when they helped Meredith Galen disappear. Between Zelik's personal vendetta, Tommy Gibbs's well-funded campaign, and Garlick's political machinations, the Callattas, the Mormons, and anyone else who crossed MedaGen and its allies would find out just how stupid they were.

* * *

"Thar she blows." Medea sat back in her chair triumphantly, gesturing toward the wall display. The Ten Tribes logo, Medea's signature visual, glowed above it. That sign could send chills down the spines of FBI agents and homeland security cops in all fifty states, visions of broken codes, scooped passwords, and stolen corporate secrets whirling in their minds. Cursor lights danced across the screen, following the expert cracker's movements, forming contrails over the confidential financial reports of several of the biggest Net firms in the world. Her eyes reflected the glow of the screen, staring avidly at the wide-open portals to the finances, research reports, and trade secrets of multinational powerhouses from BritPharm to Pacific East Ltd.

When Johnny Mack, Augosto's tattooed bodyguard, had walked into her carefully concealed den and said he could give her a set of encryption keys that could help her open the tightest virtual safes in the world, Medea had laughed at him. But an hour of expert byte blitzing by Medea and her team proved that the lug's backers were smarter than he was and earned him a front-row seat for the fall of New Babylon.

Johnny Mack laughed. "I get it—pirate talk, because you're a cyber-pirate chick, right?"

Medea's eyes rolled. "Use your mouth for something useful, Trendy Boy, and tell me the rest of what your boss sent you here to ask me to do."

Much to her disappointment, Augosto's orders didn't entail anything that strained her abilities. She ignored the bodyguard's Luddite commentary as she led her cyber commandos on a raid that blacked out the Web sites of half a dozen of the world's most powerful companies.

In mahogany-furnished offices all over the globe, furious executives shouted into phones at frantic techs as a skull-and-lightning logo spun, cackling, on their screens. Below it, the manifesto of the Anarchist Crusaders scrolled, calling for the utter destruction of all agents of Western capitalist imperialism, beginning with eradicating the plague of corporate greed infecting North America. Their customers saw the same thing—and so did the stock analysts. Within mere hours, formerly dominant BritPharm shares promptly dropped into the economic sub-basement, leading the avalanche of stock prices that swamped a few giants and hundreds of smaller businesses. Stock tickers registered the damage as fast as the corporate techs slammed closed the doors the crackers had used. New encryption codes sealed the barn doors again—but only after the electronic horses were well and gone.

Johnny Mack watched, thoroughly impressed, as Medea's team dealt a deep wound to the major competitors of MedaGen and its conglomerate partners. MedaGen's stocks rose, catching the bounce as BritPharm hit bottom. He wasn't a financial expert by any means, but he recognized the names scrolling by on the stock ticker—Garlick got his terror attack and the publicity he wanted, while Augosto made a couple million dollars on his legitimate investments.

"Not bad, kitten. Maybe the salary we're paying you is worth it after all." He looked over the flame-maned cracker babe in the high-tech pilot's chair, impressed with her skills—but not with her wardrobe. "Too bad you doesn't dress better though." He ran a hand over her upper arm and shook his head. "Before you get a halter top, you better tighten up. All this geek stuff ain't doing your figure any good. You could use a couple hours in the gym."

Medea shrugged off his hand. "Get lost, face paint. And if your boss comes up with any more keys, toss them my way. The door's over there." She ignored his leer, half listening to the click of his fashionable boots on the metal-grate floor as she used one of her own electronic skeleton keys to trash his credit rating. Then she whirled her chair, looked around at the electronic oracle's cave she had constructed so carefully over the last six months, sighed, and said, "Okay, gentlemen and ladies, let's zip it up and de-res. This place just turned into an oven, and it's going to heat up soon. The legitimates are probably on their way already, and BritPharm's boys will be out for blood." She surged out of her chair, neatly unhooking the data pickups from her hands. Her team followed, detaching themselves from their own electronic webs, disassembling the banks of computers as their leader headed for the door and a contact who could find them a new lair. She paused at the door. "And this round, let's all make sure Caesar Augustus doesn't manage to find the real-time address for our office. Time for the Ten Tribes to get lost again."

* * *

Dear Chisom,

If the world situation keeps going the way it is, the elders and sisters being called this month may be the last group the Church will be sending out. From all appearances it looks like the "day of the Gentiles" is rapidly coming to an end. The Brethren have decided to close more missions due both to the lack of conversions and the growing persecution of both local members and missionaries in some parts of the world. Once again, it impresses me that prophecy is being fulfilled. You see, the Book of Mormon foretold this would happen. Let me explain.

The term "Gentile" technically and most exclusively refers to those who have no ancestry connecting them to Abraham or Jacob. The term "Jew" technically refers to those Israelites whose heritage reaches back to the kingdom of Judah at the time it split from the Northern Kingdom, and more particularly to those who returned from the Babylonian captivity and rebuilt the state of Judah about 530 B.C. Some scriptures, however, use these terms differently. For instance, the Book of Mormon views only those who were in Judea at the time Lehi left (and their descendents) as Jews. Thus, even members of the ten tribes in their lost condition were classified as Gentiles. Therefore, in Book of Mormon terms, members of the tribes of Ephraim and Manasseh, for example, belong to the gentile nations. Joseph Smith, we are told, was an Ephraimite, but the Book of Mormon refers to him as a Gentile.

The term "Israel" is another matter. It refers to those who are the chosen, foreordained people of God who have the blood of the ancient patriarchs flowing through their veins, or who are adopted into Abraham's family. In this light, we can see that Joseph Smith was a Gentile, an Israelite, and an Ephraimite. The gospel was restored among the Gentiles, but it was to Israel that it came, and it was mostly Israel who accepted it and promoted it.

Now, the Book of Mormon prophesies that when the missionaries have testified to the nations and they, by and large, have rejected that testimony, the Lord will take the gospel from the gentile nations and bring it to the Jews. Then the earth will see its greatest troubles ever.

These troubles are now becoming a reality. Due to sinking economies and growing lawlessness and the concurrent persecution of our members, especially of our missionaries, the Church is closing down the missions in Europe, Russia, Balkans, parts of Africa, and some of South America. We have been in these areas for decades, and in some cases, nearly two centuries. As a result, those nations have been warned, and the Lord has freed the Church from their blood and sins.

Many missionaries with less than six months left are being honorably released and sent home. The others are being reassigned to more peaceful areas, many, where possible, to their native lands. The shutting down of missions in some areas has freed the Church to concentrate its efforts on other areas. As dark as the situation is, it has turned out to be a boon for the kingdom. President Smith mentioned in passing that we may be nearing the period when the 144,000 will need to be called to take over the missionary work.

We live in interesting times, if you see what I mean. So continue to preach and prepare the Saints. I am very pleased your area has seen relatively light persecution and that the civil situation is still stable enough that you can continue to work. Do be zealous, however, for we do not have long before we will have to bring all the missionaries home. For this poor old world, I rue the day when that happens, because it will mean that it has had its chance to repent and has failed. The result will be its destruction.

With deepest love and urgency,
Your father,
Chinedu

CHAPTER 11

". . . And the cleanup in Tokyo continues after the huge earthquake that shook the Japanese islands," the straight-man DJ announced.

"That's what I call shooky-yaki!" the funny one broke in, over the cheesy, pinging "oriental" music and the sound of a giant, scaly monster roaring in the background. Guffaws from the prerecorded studio audience drowned the annoying sound effects.

The straight-man DJ laughed too, a professional chuckle that disappeared immediately as he turned to the next story. "Here at home, more shakeups in the courtrooms. A higher court has refused to overturn the decision in MedaGen's industrial-espionage lawsuit against Meredith Galen—"

Carmen's hand paused on the Scan button at the mention of Merry's name. She could hardly stand the morning DJs on Lucrezia's second-favorite station, but she left the radio on to hear the bit about Merry as she pulled out of the grocery store's parking lot. Cracks and scrubby weeds decorated the lot's asphalt, the aluminum siding on walls of the store itself dented and peeling. The buildings in the neighborhood didn't look any better, and neither did the empty-eyed loungers flopped on the porches of the battered houses along the road, but the place had the best prices Carmen could find on produce, and she needed to save all the money she could.

"The spy who loved me!" warbled the funny DJ, to the inevitable spy-movie music—and prerecorded laughter.

"She's covered under federal whistle-blower laws, but her church might not be. The circuit court will hear MedaGen's complaints

against the Moron—I mean Mormon—Church later this month."
The straight man threw in the mistake and correction with a snigger;
why let his partner get all the laughs?

"She's a hot one, isn't she? Bet they'd love to get their hands on
her down at MedaGen! And if you're listening, Dr. Galen, feel free to
turn yourself in at our studio. We'll take good care of you!" The
funny DJ panted into the mike.

"Oh, put a sock in it," Carmen growled, hitting the Scan button.
Garbled advertisements, talk shows, and ear-splitting fuzz rock blared
past. She stopped on the intricate guitar melody of Seraph on
Lucrezia's first-favorite station. The Mormon husband-wife duo had
grown on her after two months of listening to them through
Lucrezia's door.

The music couldn't distract her for long. Worry tightened her
shoulders as last night's phone call replayed in her memory. She'd
picked up the phone to hear one of MedaGen's lawyers threatening to
implicate the Callattas in the lawsuit against Merry.

Tony had taken the phone from her and told the lawyer to either
serve papers or leave them alone and slammed the hang-up button
off. He contemplated the silent phone for a moment, his hand tightening around it dangerously, but he put it down before the casing
cracked. "Don't worry, baby," he told Carmen, rubbing her shoulders.
"They won't do it. It's a long shot in any course. But you can't beat
calls like that for good harassment."

She knew he was right, but the threat added to the uneasiness that
she couldn't shake. Donna had mentioned an unfamiliar car parked in
their neighborhood; Lucrezia said she'd seen it too prowling around
the block. After seeing a pair of gardeners show up two days later in
the coveralls of furnace-repair technicians, Carmen had to face her
creeping conviction that someone was watching the house. She
stopped at a stop sign and signaled a right turn. The problem was that
she couldn't decide if MedaGen had sent them, or if they were the
case men for a ring of thieves, or if they objected to Mormons—

A sudden, hard jar shook the thought out of her head, jerking her
forward against the seat belt. "Oh, great," she exclaimed. "Rear-
ended." The first thought that crossed her mind was to make sure
Gianni was safe in his car seat, and he was, surprised but unworried.

The second involved the carton of eggs in the trunk. In the rearview mirror, she caught a glimpse of a car with heavy window tint and a rusty custom paint job much too close behind hers, the driver already pulling toward the curb despite the green light.

The door opened and the young woman in the driver's seat got out, frowning at the back of Carmen's car, then toward Carmen herself. She waved apologetically, pointed to the back of Carmen's car, and said something Carmen didn't hear through the closed window. A glint shone from the dim form in the passenger side as the young woman closed her door. Did her passenger wear as much jewelry as she did? Her face, strangely excited under its concerned expression and garish makeup, sent a vague tickle of unease through Carmen's mind.

Sighing, Carmen unhooked her seat belt, reaching for the door handle. A flash of emotion stopped her hand—not panic, not fear, but a calm certainty that she should absolutely not stop to find out who else lurked behind the darkened windows. Without hesitating, she slammed her foot down on the accelerator and sped around the corner and down the road.

The woman beside the once-fancy vehicle stared after Carmen's retreating car and its broken taillight. So did the two men who surged out of the other doors, sunlight glinting again on the pistol one of them held. He aimed it after Carmen's car, then dropped his aim, swearing. Carmen didn't hear the words, but she saw enough over her shoulder to confirm her intuition or, better, inspiration.

* * *

"It was inspiration, I tell you," Carmen declared, catching Gianni as he ran by, laughing. "Come here, baby boy! We had an adventure today, didn't we?"

"You about had an adventure. Good thing you didn't get out of that car, whether it was inspiration or just a slightly too late attack of common sense." Tony scowled; the thought of carjackers targeting his wife and youngest child froze his gut—and therefore made him angry. "I don't see why you have to go into that part of town anyway. The cops don't even drive down there anymore!"

Carmen hugged Gianni (carefully, to avoid transferring the dinner mess to her freshly arranged hair and good dress) and pinned him down to get him undressed for his bath. As usual, he'd happily decided to eat his dinner and wear it. She concentrated on gently pulling his sauce-stained shirt, trying to keep the acid out of her tone. She only partly succeeded. "They had a good sale on tomato sauce and some other things, Tony. We just didn't have any fresh vegetables in the ol' food storage—and the stash is getting thin anyway. I've had to take deals where I find them, no matter what section of town they're in."

Her answer, even delivered in a relatively neutral tone, deepened Tony's frown, set his jaw as he finished tying his polished but cracking dress shoes. Carmen didn't look up from Gianni to hide the frustrated tears in her eyes.

Donna glanced from one parent to the other, wanting to say something to dispel the aching tension but not knowing what could do it. They'd been too tight too long, a family with hot Italian tempers under pressure in a house that felt like it got smaller every day.

The front door banged open, startling them all. Lucrezia slouched in, half dragging her backpack. "This was in our mailbox with the bills. Looks like more hate mail." She tossed the envelopes and a much-folded sheet of paper onto the living room table.

Carmen looked up from untangling Gianni's shoelaces (how that boy managed to turn shoelaces into macramé simply escaped her). The sight of the anonymously printed flyer—the third one in two weeks—added extra weight to the heavy feeling in her stomach. She blinked hard and pushed away the shudder of anxiety about leaving the kids alone while she and Tony went to the stake meeting tonight. Donna could handle anything that would realistically happen; she'd even backed off those spies from MedaGen. Lucrezia—well, she had her moments, but she was a smart, good girl. She silently added a prayer that they would be all right. All of them.

"Like bills aren't bad enough. Same old thing?" Tony asked, flicking the note with a finger.

"Another mash note?" Donna rolled her eyes. "Tonya said they've been getting them too. I've talked to like ten people in the ward who say they're getting pressure from some anonymous letter writer to either drop Mormonism or leave, and the cops won't do anything about it."

"What can they do? Arrest anybody with a printer and stupid ideas about what 'Christian' means? They'd have half the city in jail." Tony shrugged into his suit jacket, pulling Carmen's nice coat out of the closet. The dark plastic button on the end of the row of shining brass ones caught his eye—and hurt him. Their money situation got worse every day; they'd just about burned through their savings. The painting jobs he and Angelo relied on for subsistence funds weren't coming often enough anymore; with everybody but top management getting laid off, fewer and fewer had money to pay for home renovations.

He hadn't sent out as many résumés in the last couple of weeks, not because he'd stopped searching, but because he'd already applied for just about every possible position. A couple of companies still hadn't outright rejected him; the educational software outfit in Illinois had even replied politely to his inquiry, saying that his portfolio had impressed them, the phone interview had gone very well, and they said they would be in touch. That thin thread of hope kept him going, but hope couldn't pay their bills. *Even if we were willing to give the anonymous Mormon bashers the satisfaction of running us out, we wouldn't have the money to leave,* he thought bitterly.

"Well, the police probably wouldn't do anything anyway. They've all been paid off." Donna picked up the note, smoothing it out to put in the folder with the others, on the off chance that an uncorrupted policeman might need them for evidence later. "I mean, look at it—all over the country, neighborhoods are segregating out. Even if you don't count the temple towns, it's like Mormon ghettos out there."

"So maybe they'll make us wear yellow Angel Moroni badges next," Lucrezia suggested, rolling her eyes at the absurdity of the thought. "And then start a bunch of programs against us."

"It's pogroms, Luc," Donna informed her, big-sister condescension dripping from her tone. "You laugh, but you haven't been out there. Nobody will hire Dad or me, because we're Mormons. It's getting bad, just like Brother Kensai said it would."

"Oh, come on, you sound like that Tommy Gibbs fanatic. Last days this, end times that," Lucrezia said, needled by Donna's superiority and wanting to strike back. "Haven't we got enough problems without worrying about the end of the world? Or is that why you want the world to end—so you don't have to keep looking for a job?"

"All right, enough!" Carmen stood up, wrapping Gianni in his hooded towel. "We've got enough enemies outside, we don't need a fight in here."

"Speaking of problems," Tony broke in, doing his bit to interrupt the impending sibling riot. Unfortunately, the water bucket he chose contained gasoline instead. "We got another call about your attitude problem in Current Events class, babykins."

Lucrezia groaned, the weight of the incredibly dense adult world weighing heavily on her fifteen-year-old shoulders. "Oh, please, Dad, don't even read them! Mr. Shapiro is such a jerk! Always picking at me, because I call him on the dumb stuff he's trying to make the class believe. He can't stand me, because I'm Mormon and I don't go along with his stupid, irresponsible, lame-brained ideas." Her hands waved wildly to illustrate her point. "He's enough to make me think Donna's crack-brained conspiracy theories about the world going to pieces might not be total bunk."

Donna growled under her breath. Carmen and Tony exchanged a look, sharing suppressed smiles.

"I don't doubt he's wrong about a lot of it." Carmen slipped her arms into the coat Tony held, then took her youngest daughter's face between her hands. "And you don't have to believe him, or even go along with them. But, sweetie, how about you try not to say that he's an idiot right to his face in front of the entire class?"

"But, Mom, you wouldn't let him spout that garbage if you were there!" Lucrezia pointed out.

Carmen considered denying it, but she'd had her share of notes from the school too. "All right, maybe not. But we're not students in the class, and we're not the ones they're complaining about, so let us deal with Mr. Shapiro. And if they ask you, we discussed it, all right?"

"All right, but I still think it's all a bunch of baloney," Lucrezia agreed, accepting her mother's good-bye kiss with poor grace.

Donna hugged both parents and picked up Gianni, who got his good-bye kisses, waved an enthusiastic bye-bye, and threw his customary fit. It lasted just long enough for the car's remaining tail-light to disappear around the corner. "Bath!" he commanded.

"All right, messy boy. Bath time." Donna shook him around, much to his delight, then shot a dark look at Lucrezia. "I bet Luc would be happy to give you a nice bath while I work on another bunch of job applications."

"Why me?" Lucrezia shot an equally dark look back. "I don't need to get soaked tonight. I'm going to Lupe's to work on that stupid Current Events portfolio. Dad said I could."

"He didn't tell me," Donna informed her tartly.

"Life's just full of surprises, isn't it?" Lucrezia picked up her backpack, irritation from a bad day at school, the hate-mail note, and the constant tension they'd all felt for the last year making her voice sharp. "Well, he did, and I'm going."

"If you go, you're walking," Donna snapped back. "We only have one car."

"Just another problem with this family!" Lucrezia glared at her sister. "No wonder I'd rather hang out with Lupe."

"Oh, sure, you like Lupe 'cause she's got a boyfriend with a car. Why you want to hang out with that druggie fashion victim in the first place—" Donna said, critically.

"It's better than hanging out with you!" Lucrezia shouted, wrenching open the door and running down the steps.

Behind her, Gianni started to cry. So did Lucrezia. She ignored Donna's furious "Get back here! Don't be stupid!" and ran on, the streetlights and porch lights blurring into trails of yellow fire in her tear-filled eyes. They didn't understand—how could they side with those horrible school people against her? Didn't they understand how hard it was, all the snide comments, the looks in the hall, people pushing her books off the desk, and Mr. Shapiro making lame jokes about her? And Donna thought she was all that, flouncing around all adult, just because she had a little college. Well, anybody could do that—retarded monkeys could do that! She was sick of being a nice girl, trying to be polite all the time and a good example. She wanted to swear, scream, punch out those sneering faces. That would show them how fun it was to harass the Mormon girl!

The musical chime of her phone sounded from the depths of her backpack. First, it startled her; when she dug it out and saw the number on it, however, it just made her even more angry. Oh, so now Donna called her! Probably going to order her home, be even more bossy and impossible. Lucrezia punched the phone off and slammed it back into her pack and ran on.

The sheer heat of fury propelled Lucrezia through the dark streets in a haze of righteous rage. By the time the tears had cooled into self-pity and her headlong rush faded to a heavy-breathing walk, she had run half a dozen blocks, out of their neighborhood and into the streets that led to Lupe's apartment. Now that she paid attention to her surroundings instead of her internal rant, the darkness between street-lights seemed blacker than before, the gleam of headlights rushing past slightly sinister, the low moan of the wind threatening. She glanced around at the dim, blue TV glow behind shuttered or barred windows, everyone locked securely away from the vague menace of the night-time streets. New stories about gangs, thieves, and worse gibbered in the back of her mind. Even as she told herself not to get paranoid, this neighborhood was as safe as hers, her pace quickened again.

At last, Lupe's apartment came into view. The surge of relief Lucrezia felt didn't last long, however, at the sight of all too familiar cars parked carelessly along the road, the low lamplight filling every window, and the dim sounds of thumping music and loud conversations filtering through the door. *Oh, great,* Lucrezia thought, *Lupe's having a party with her new friends.* For a moment, she considered turning back, but her temper flared up again at the thought of Donna's smug comments. The heat propelled her up the steps, and she hit the doorbell hard—only to have the sound disappear into the aural chaos inside the house. The second push didn't have quite as much force behind it, but it caught someone's attention.

He opened the door, leaning against the frame casually, a hand-made cigarette dangling from his mouth. Nano tattoos glittered under the skin on his chest where his shirt gaped open; he looked like a pile of fashionable laundry left on the floor for a week. She recognized him with a sinking feeling as Brett, the boy with the hot chopper car, the one Lupe talked about sleeping with but hadn't yet (at least she didn't admit it to Lucrezia). When his bleary eyes focused on her, it took him a few seconds to process who he saw, but he recognized her too. He grinned. She didn't.

"Hey, Loopy. Door," he called into the house, adding a stream of profanity directed at inspiring somebody to relay the message when she didn't instantly materialize. His gaze shifted back to Lucrezia; she stared back at his frankly appraising look with enough intensity that her disapproval finally started registering in his fume-soaked brain. "Your moron friend's here," he announced, vaguely relieved when Lupe finally made her way through the smoke and crowd.

"Mormon," she corrected, smacking his shoulder. She hit him again, equally ineffectively, as he pulled her against him and kissed her. "Not now." She pulled away, then giggled as she ruffled his scarecrow hair. "In a minute. You go get me a drink."

He muttered something uncomplimentary about pushy women and disappeared into the thick haze. Lupe edged out onto the doorsill and brought the door mostly closed behind her. "Hey, Luc." She didn't quite look Lucrezia in the eye.

"Hey, Lupe. Looks like a party."

"Yeah," Lupe agreed, shifting her weight uncomfortably.

"So, can you get away to work on Shapiro's portfolio?" Lucrezia didn't have to ask—she knew the answer with an inevitable, sick certainty—but she did anyway. "Or are you hung up here?"

"Well, see, Brett came over, and some of his friends, and since my mom's out, they decided to stay for some movies and stuff." She looked past Lucrezia at the cars parked by, on, and over the curb, her face pinched and worried. "Listen, Luc, I'd invite you in, but it's not really your scene—you know . . ."

The hot tightness in Lucrezia's chest hurt as she nodded. *Yeah, I know,* she thought. *And I want to make you say it, say that you don't want me around because I make everybody nervous, like they're doing the wrong thing.* But aloud, she merely said, "Nah, doesn't sound like it. You be careful. See you tomorrow." The words almost caught in her throat; she swallowed hard and spat them out, already halfway down the steps.

She didn't look back at Lupe, standing guiltily in the doorway. Lucrezia didn't look at much of anything, keeping her eyes ahead, blinking back tears again as the wind whipped her hair around her face. Lupe's brush-off hurt, even though she'd expected it would happen eventually. They'd gone too far on two very different roads to try to keep their old friendship; either she'd have to join Lupe, or Lupe would have to come with her, or they'd have to let go. And despite her efforts, Lupe wouldn't come with her. She'd chosen social acceptance (and drugs and drinks and that sleazeball, Brett) over Lucrezia.

Lucrezia had never felt so alone as she trudged back through the deserted streets. At first, she felt too depressed for paranoia, but the lurking shadows wormed their way into the back of her mind. The white flash of headlights and the sound of a car slowing down beside her shot a thrill of panic down her spine. It cruised slowly past her, the dim streetlights playing on its shiny paint, then turned at the corner and sped up again.

"They were only turning," she whispered to herself. "Don't panic. Just run!" She tore along the sidewalk until she reached the familiar street that led to her house. Now the thought of Donna waiting for her, worried and angry, felt reassuring. They fought sometimes, but no matter what happened, Donna would be on her side when she really needed it.

The light from the windows looked warm and safe, as she rounded the final corner, slipping through the deeper shadows of the neighbor's tree-shaded yard. The flash of a different kind of light at the side of her house didn't look safe at all, though it definitely looked warm. Lucrezia froze, her dark-adapted eyes picking out a trace of movement, the vague shadow of someone lurking in the backyard. Another flash silhouetted the figure in a halo of sharp-edged glow— the kind of glow that came from a tiny flame. It disappeared in a gust of wind.

Lucrezia grabbed her phone from its pouch on her backpack and stabbed the button without having to look. She could almost hear the phone ring from outside, a dim echo of the tone in her ear as another flash of light erupted and blew out. The ring tones cut off.

"Lucrezia, if you're dead of a mugging, I'm going to kill you," Donna's irritated voice began.

"Donna, there's somebody in the backyard with matches or a lighter," Lucrezia blurted. "He's having problems, but he's trying to burn the house down!"

"Just one?" Donna lowered her voice.

"Just one," Lucrezia confirmed, scanning the yard for any signs of movement and finding none.

"On three, it's Comanche time," Donna ordered. Lucrezia saw her move to the back door, a shadow behind the kitchen curtains. "One, two, three!"

Instantly, the backyard light came on. Donna leapt out of the door, shrieking vicious threats in pseudo-Italian. Lucrezia barreled out of the neighbor's yard at the same time, yelling like a whole troop of bloodthirsty banshees. The noise and movement triggered lights in the surrounding houses, as the neighbors left their TV screens or dinner tables to find out what had prompted the sudden outburst of pandemonium.

In the abrupt illumination, a figure in black and dark-green camouflage rose out of the cover provided by Tony's rosebushes. The hooded head turned from Donna to Lucrezia, both rapidly converging on the spot, then to the lights and opening doors of the neighbors' houses. A metallic sparkle arced through the air, distracting both Callatta girls for the split second it took for the intruder to make a break around the corner of the house. Donna and Lucrezia rounded the same corner just in time to see taillights light up across the street. The gray paint and blacked-out license plate flashed in a streetlight's yellow radiance, and then the car was gone, leaving only the fading roar of its engine and distant screech of its tires as it took a corner too fast.

"Whew!" Lucrezia gasped, leaning against the corner of the house. "Did you see that? Whoever he is, he should've gone out for track. That's right, you punk, run!" she shouted. "We catch you, we'll barbecue your sorry butt!"

"And we'll use his own lighter." Donna grinned fiercely, holding out the gold-cased lighter the prowler left behind. Then she blinked, as a memory slotted into place. "Luc, that was the car that's been hanging around, the one we keep seeing, the one that looks like the one those MedaGen people were driving, Ms. White and what's his name—"

"Donna? Lucrezia? What the Sam Hill is going on over here?" The girls turned to see a large man standing on the border between the Callattas' property and his own, his arms folded over an impressive expanse of bathrobe.

"Not sure yet, Mr. Lemmon," Donna told their neighbor, coming back around the house to the backyard again. "Somebody was creeping around our rosebushes. Luc saw him, and we ran him off."

"Well, you woke up the entire neighborhood to do it," Mr. Lemmon growled. He disapproved of the Callattas on general principles, not because they were Mormons but because he didn't like anybody.

"It's a good thing we did." The slight break in Lucrezia's voice caught even his attention. She stood a few feet away, staring at the grass beside the bushes. "Donna, look."

"Oh, boy," Donna breathed. "Good thing it's windy."

On the grass lay a pair of boards nailed into the shape of a cross—and soaked with kerosene.

* * *

"It was a lynching, that's what it was, in fine old-fashioned style!" Jack DuPris glared out the window of President Rojas's office in the new Church headquarters building. Flames danced in his mind, flames reflecting on the dull finish of a crowbar, the shinier patches of blood on the iron—and on the head of the man who had caught the vandals breaking into the chapel and tried to stop them.

"It was a senseless, deeply tragic misjudgment." President Rojas looked at the Area Authority's tense back with sympathy and shared pain. "But, Jack, they didn't mean to kill him. He surprised them, and they reacted stupidly."

Jack turned from the window, to glare at President Rojas. "That's what they told the police. That's what the police believe. I don't. You haven't been out there. You haven't seen what I have. Lebaron is organizing mobs with that Millennium Brotherhood of his, making threats—he's already got the county sheriff and Lake Creek city police under his thumb. If you think they'll stop with a few incidents of 'minor' vandalism, you need to think again."

He leaned forward, resting his hands on the desk. "We can't just let our people sit there, hoping for mercy from a bunch of barbarians!" His fist struck the glossy surface of the desk. "They're not driving us out of Illinois again. There are a lot of good men out there, smart and well organized; some of them have had combat experience overseas. If we just give them permission to dig in, to start hitting back—legally for preference, but forcibly if necessary—"

"No." President Rojas's soft but firm denial brought Jack up sharply. "We cannot start a brawl, let alone a war. I know it's hard, but we can't advocate force. You need to lead them, Jack, but not into battle."

"So we're going back to the old strategy of appeasing tyrants? Giving the forces of evil free rein?" DuPris glared at President Rojas. "You used to be a military man, President. Didn't you study enough history to know that never works?"

President Rojas sighed, meeting DuPris' eyes squarely. "We are not appeasing any tyrants. We are trying desperately to keep our people out of the tyrants' line of fire. If you'd think about it, you know that it's not the role of the Saints to fight until the Lord explicitly commands it. Until then, the Lord has promised that He will protect His own in His own way."

"Well, He hasn't been protecting them," DuPris pointed out.

"Yes, He has," President Rojas said forcefully. "And He will do what He sees as necessary when the situation demands it. Think about it tactically, Jack. If we strike back, return violence for violence, we'll be annihilated. The Saints are too few to take on the world by themselves—look at the sheer numbers of Children of Light versus Latter-day Saints in the Philippines, for instance."

DuPris didn't want to hear that. "What about Gideon's army? A pitiful band of Israelites defeated an army that vastly outnumbered them."

"No, the Lord defeated the army, to prove His point to the Israelites," President Rojas corrected. He stood, placing his hand on the other man's shoulder sympathetically. "And, just as important, He specifically called them to fight—just as He specifically called you to lead the Saints in the Illinois-Iowa Area. You have the persuasion and leadership abilities we need to shore up the people and work with the civil authorities to come to a peaceful, legal solution to the problems out there."

"Then what am I supposed to do?" Jack snarled, shrugging off the comforting hand.

President Rojas caught his gaze and held it. "Do what you can to support your peoples' testimonies, remind them to live the gospel, and wait for further instructions. You can lead them, and lead them well. You just need to be sure you're leading them in the direction God wants you to, not what you want—or think is best."

"I'm well aware of that, and I've asked for direction." Jack looked up, then turned half away, glancing out the other window, the one that faced east toward his own beleaguered territory. "What I feel is that there's so much pain out there, and I can't do anything about it! 'Turn the other cheek' doesn't work when the other guy's got a crowbar! What do you want me to tell the little girl whose daddy isn't going to come home? That it's okay that the bad guys killed her daddy, because he's happy with Jesus now?"

"Yes," President said, softly but with absolute certainty. "That's exactly what you should tell her. Because he is. That's what we believe—that's what we have testimonies of. I wish good people didn't have to suffer from the malice of evil men, Jack." He blinked hard, the glint of tears in his dark eyes. "I wish it wasn't this way too—but it's the way things have to be. We can't strike back. We just have to take care of our people the best we can."

"And if we're too late to take care of them?" Jack's eyes glinted, but not with tears. Their dark gray had taken on the hard sheen of steel.

"Then we offer comfort and reassurance that it will all work out for the best—and trust that God will take care of dispensing justice." A weary but peaceful smile crossed the president's face. "And it really will, Jack. It really will."

"Is that your final decision?" Jack looked past President Rojas's shoulder.

"Yes, and the direction comes specifically from President Smith." He paused, looking at DuPris for a moment, then adding, "Jack, prayer is always good, but sometimes we need more direct inspiration. Do you want a blessing for guidance?"

Again, silence spread between the two men, but DuPris broke it with a decisive shake of his head. "No, thank you, President. I'll stay with prayer and indirect inspiration for now. It's working just fine."

"Very well. Just remember that you're not alone in this—and don't let pride get in the way of help. You faced down a tank battalion in the Med without reinforcements, but you don't have to be out on the far flank anymore. Move toward the center, Jack. And don't hesitate to call on us if you need backup."

Jack nodded silently once, then turned crisply on his heel and stalked out of the office. His two bodyguards fell into step behind him without a word, their faces turning as grim as their superior's. Sister Nguyen, head secretary in the First Presidency's office, watched them go with a silent sigh, then looked up as President Rojas came out of his office with his own frustrated expression. She knew better than to ask about a private conversation; instead, she simply smiled sympathetically and said, "Elder Nabil is on the line. Do you have time to take the call?"

"Of course." President Rojas turned back toward his office. "I hope he's got good news for us."

* * *

"On that matter, I can offer only my sympathy and support for you—and for those poor beleaguered Saints in Illinois and all over the world." Elder Nabil looked up at Jonathan's quiet knock, then motioned him in. His frown eased as he saw Dove slip in behind his assistant, and he turned back to his phone conversation with a slightly lighter tone in his deep voice. "But I can offer a bit of good news on another front. Dr. Galen's research is proceeding well; she has succeeded in isolating two strains of man-made virus and is now working on a way to untangle their warped DNA. In fact, one of her experimental subjects just walked into my office. Salvatore Nakai, from New Mexico. Yes, he is quite healthy enough to be out." The Apostle's eyes twinkled knowingly at Dove. "In fact, I daresay it is healthier all around to have him wandering the streets rather than the lab corridors."

Dove didn't know whether to smile or look repentant; he ended up blushing and examining the toes of his boots. Though he had talked to Elder Nabil twice in the last four weeks, he still felt starstruck in the man's presence, amazed that an Apostle actually knew his name, let alone cared about him.

Jonathan smiled, looking sideways at the young man's expression. Dove acted like such a cocky bounder now that he was feeling better, into everything, wanting answers, making requests that sounded more like orders—until Elder Nabil came in, and the self-appointed commando leader suddenly looked like an eighteen-year-old kid again.

Dr. Galen could put him in his place too, when she had to, but most of the time she let him get away with drowning her in questions. Today, he'd been so restless, and relentless, that she'd given him the latest data and sent him out with Jonathan when he came by to get her status report and check on Dove.

Jonathan visited not only because Elder Nabil was interested in Dove's progress, but because Jonathan felt a kind of vague responsibility for the sick kid. Not that he'd stayed sick; he'd recovered very quickly in the last three weeks, with only a slight cough still hanging on as his lungs healed. It wasn't enough to keep him down, and certainly not enough to put a dent in his self-confidence—in fact, on the way to Elder Nabil's office, Dove had automatically run interference for Jonathan as they walked downtown, staying between him and the various protesters and panhandlers who infested the streets, as if he were Jonathan's bodyguard, or Jonathan were a naive, inexperienced kid who needed protection, but Jonathan preferred the first explanation.

Elder Nabil accepted the data disc Dove handed him, commenting on Dove's apparent good health, gently reminding him to cooperate with Merry, and asking if he'd written to his family lately. That made Dove smile as he said he had, but he didn't ask whether Perro counted as family or a pet.

"Very good." Elder Nabil flicked the disc into the air, neatly catching it again. He smiled, patting Dove's shoulder. "Very good indeed. Thank you—and convey my thanks to Dr. Galen as well. For now, best that you not overexert yourself. The cause needs healthy guinea pigs."

"Yes, sir," Dove said, accepting both the encouragement and the dismissal. He wouldn't argue with Elder Nabil in any case, but as he and Jonathan made their way through the elegant corridors, he also felt a creeping weariness that told him he wasn't back 100 percent yet. It worried him, made him want to push harder to regain the strength he'd lost—which Merry cautioned him against. Pushing too hard would just set him back further. *Catch-22*, Dove thought, feeling frustration welling up. He wanted his strength back, wanted Slick's virus and the AllSafe poison out of his system, wanted to do something to help build the kingdom. Captain Moroni hadn't pushed a broom while his comrades fought!

Dove glanced at Jonathan as they got into the car, looking for a distraction. "Trouble?"

"What?" Jonathan blinked.

"When we came in, he said something about the Saints in Illinois having trouble," Dove clarified. "What's up? Or is it confidential, that you can't tell me?"

"I might not know either," Jonathan suggested, then grinned at Dove's skeptical expression. "I'm flattered by your confidence in my vast knowledge." The grin faded into a slightly worried expression as he continued, "Well, here it's your first time at Church headquarters, and you run into a conversation about Elder DuPris. Somehow that fits—you're the kind of guy who can never avoid a hot spot."

"And Illinois is a hot spot for this Elder DuPris?" Dove asked, picking out the relevant bits of Jonathan's statement and disregarding the rest.

"Illinois is a hot spot for everybody." Jonathan's eyes narrowed against the sunlight through the windshield and against the memory of the reports he'd seen. "Jack DuPris, Elder DuPris, is the Area Authority for the Illinois-Iowa Area, and there's been a lot of trouble out there, especially around a town called Lake Creek, and a bit even reaching Nauvoo. Anti-Mormons have made a lot of noise, especially the ones going by the name of the Millennium Brotherhood, following a guy who calls himself Reverend Lebaron—they even beat up a few members. This week, it's taken a really nasty turn. A man out there, the building supervisor for a chapel, ran into a bunch of them breaking into the building with gasoline. He figured they were going to set fire to the church—two other chapels have burned down in that area—and he tried to stop them. He got hit with a crowbar in the fight, hit so hard that he died. The cops called it an accident and pretty much dropped the case."

Dove watched Jonathan spit out the last sentence, his own face becoming expressionless as he heard the story. "Bought off or siding with the raiders?"

"Could be either one," Jonathan admitted, feeling cold at either possibility. It seemed impossible to him that police in a civilized country could stand by and watch that kind of thing happen; it was worse to imagine that they approved of it. But it was happening—one look at Dove's hard-edged glare out the windshield reminded him that law and order were rare and unreliable in many parts of the country. The good cops were stretched too thin, the bad cops had nobody to rein them in. The rising tide of chaos had already swallowed the borderlands and lightly populated areas; now it licked at the hollow hearts of big cities and the borders of depressed towns.

"So what's Elder DuPris doing about it?" Dove asked.

The question jerked Jonathan out of his gloomy vision. "He wants to fight back—gather veterans and any willing volunteers in the Church out there to form a militia and go after Lebaron's men."

"Has he got a line on an arms dealer?" Dove considered the problem. "He'll need a good one, if he wants to back them off—especially if they've got the cops backing them up. And it sounds like a town fight too, not an open-field run. Urban warfare. That can be really nasty. They'd better get some heavy-duty explosives and build themselves some solid barricades."

"No, he doesn't have an arms dealer!" Jonathan exclaimed, momentarily shocked at the suggestion. Then he remembered who he was talking to—and the news footage of smoke curling into the desert sky. His tone softened slightly. "He's not supposed to have an arms dealer. He's not supposed to be fighting force with force anyway. The First Presidency has already told him to calm down twice, to concentrate on getting his people out of the really hot zones and do everything he can within the system to calm things down."

"We're fighting them off in the borderlands," Dove pointed out. "And Elder Nabil—or President Smith or President Rojas—hasn't told us to stop."

"I don't think they will either," Jonathan said. "Your people are defending their homes and lives against an organized threat, a serious invasion. And you're defending, not attacking."

"Elder DuPris wants to defend his people too," Dove pointed out.

"Different situations." Jonathan shook his head. "It's not an outright war in Illinois, not like where you came from. It's a few hotheaded idiots who blame the Church for their own failures, and a few Church members who ought to know better and are egging them on. Not all the churches that have burned in that area have been ours, and Elder Nabil's had messages about a nut calling himself Brother Smith who keeps declaring that the Mormons are going to forcibly take over the entire state of Illinois as revenge for the mobbing that happened to the early Church. If people would calm down—and follow President Smith's advice and move to the temple towns when things get violent—they would come out all right."

"Sounds bad all the way around." Dove sat back, pressing his hand to his eyes for a moment. The image of Captain Moroni appeared in the swirling colors behind his eyelids, grimly determined to win the battles forced on him by any righteous means, but not seeking a fight. Defend, not attack. *But why wait until they attack you?* The contrary voice whispered in the back of Dove's mind. *Take the initiative; finish the problem before it begins. It's been done before.* "Nephi didn't wait until he had to defend himself."

"Nephi had direct orders revealed to him." Jonathan shook his head again, decisively. "And Laban had already declared war on the family. It was when the Nephites became the aggressors, took the war to their enemies, that the Lord no longer supported them. We can't have that happen. It's the divine approval that's important, and so far Elder DuPris doesn't have it." He glanced at Dove as he pulled the car into Section 89's parking lot. "I think you know what I mean."

Dove met his eyes, a sober smile flashing across his face. "Yeah, I do. Thanks, Jonathan."

Jonathan watched him walk slowly up the walk and through the door, thinking about revelation—and dust, bullets, and blood—all the way back to Elder Nabil's Salt Lake office.

"Have you delivered our stripling warrior back to Dr. Galen's tender care?" Elder Nabil asked, smiling at Jonathan as his assistant came through the door. "How is he?"

"Yes, I did." Jonathan looked up, his open face pinched with worry. "He's getting better, but he's seen way too much for an eighteen-year-old boy."

"Too much for anyone to see," Elder Nabil agreed solemnly. "But I fear that we will all see things we wish we did not—and things so wonderful that we will hardly believe our eyes. Times are changing, Jonathan, the world is changing, and we are witnesses of the change." He smiled suddenly, brushing his hands together. "And we are agents of change as well as observers. Come with me, and we'll inspect our new domain."

Jonathan hurried to catch up with the Apostle's long strides as Elder Nabil left the office. "New domain? Are you changing offices again?"

"No, not offices this time. Assignments. I think you will find this one intriguing." He opened the stairway door, blithely clattering down the long flights with Jonathan hot on his heels. "Speaking of changes, Jonathan, I strongly advise you and Tasha to move your family into a home in Deseret Heights, as soon as possible."

"The new development around the Lakeview temple?" Jonathan asked. The Church had bought the property years ago, and had started to develop it into a walkable community, with plenty of environmentally friendly green space and an airy neo-urban design that impressed environmentalists and architects alike. It was pretty, but farther away from downtown than their current apartment—and probably out of their price range. "We've saved as much as we can for a down payment, but I don't know if we have enough to look at that neighborhood. And I don't know if Tasha would want to move out there."

"Talk with her, by all means, and listen as well. She's a wise woman," Elder Nabil said. "Which is why I believe she will feel the same way I do. Don't worry about the finances overmuch, Jonathan. Do what you need to so your family will be in the right place at the right time. As we are now."

They had reached their destination, a floor well under street level. Elder Nabil gestured to a closed door in a utilitarian hallway. The door looked utterly unremarkable—except for the state-of-the-art retinal scanner beside it and its subtle but pervasive air of impenetrability. He knocked twice briskly and stepped back.

Just as Jonathan opened his mouth, the door opened. A pair of bright eyes under a shock of unruly curls and over the loudest tie Jonathan had ever seen blinked at them through enormous glasses. The look of curious incomprehension vaguely visible around the spectacles changed immediately to a broad smile. "Hey, Elder Nabil. Come on in! This your assistant?"

"Indeed he is." Elder Nabil followed the nerdy apparition into a room filled with more electronic gear, communications equipment, and computing power than Jonathan had ever imagined, not that he imagined such things often—or ever, really. "This is Jonathan Crow."

"Great! We'll get your eyeball prints in a minute. Gotta have those, if you're gonna come down here—security's job one, you know. Or you're gonna find out!" He stuck his hand out enthusiastically. Jonathan took it, shaking it gingerly (the hand was thin, white, and warmer than he expected—with a much firmer grip). "I'm Maynard Stockton—but call me Socks. That's Juliet Faux over there. She's Fox on the Net. You know, f-a-u-x, like *fox*. Get it?"

A female figure, hunched over a flat-panel display across the room, waved vaguely at them.

"Fox . . . and Socks. Glad to meet you." Jonathan grinned and gently retrieved his hand from the technician's grip. He cast an inquiring glance at Elder Nabil, who stood surveying the room, mentally preparing for his new, but not distasteful, challenge. "This is the Church's local communications hub, isn't it? And the secondary data center, after the one in Provo?"

"It certainly is," Elder Nabil agreed. "It is also part of our new assignment. We need to become intimately familiar with the communications and technology side of the kingdom, as we will be working with people halfway across the world. Brother and Sister Cohen, to be precise, and the Hassan family."

"And what will they be doing?" Jonathan asked, excitement stirring under his calm tone.

Elder Nabil smiled, looking from Jonathan to Fox as she sat up and announced, "I've got the secure satellite link set. We're online with Jerusalem and the space station anytime you want to talk—without anybody listening in."

"Jerusalem," Jonathan said softly.

"Yes." Elder Nabil sounded almost as awestruck as Jonathan. "We are going to help oversee the construction of a temple in Jerusalem."

CHAPTER 12

"And what is the purpose of your visit, Mr. Cohen?" The customs agent looked from the passport to Benjamin Cohen, carefully comparing the holographic representation to the flesh-and-blood version. Over her shoulder, the lens of a camera did the same, mapping every line and ratio of his face and comparing the results to the record stored in the computer's extensive memory. A green light flashed on her console, signaling his positive identification as Benjamin Joseph Cohen, citizen of the United States of America, forty-five years old, architect, member and employee of The Church of Jesus Christ of Latter-day Saints, authorized to enter the state of Israel and city of Jerusalem on an extensible two-year work visa.

"We're here to build a temple," Benjamin told her, and smiled. The computer didn't react to the sheer joy in his expression, but the customs agent did; the emotion was so contagious that she found herself smiling back.

"That's 'business,' Ben." Hannah Cohen poked her husband's ribs, then turned her no-nonsense gaze on the customs agent, extending her passport. "We're here on business for The Church of Jesus Christ of Latter-day Saints, working with the Jerusalem Cooperative Council."

The computer confirmed her identity with a green light as well: Hannah Glass Cohen, forty-six years old, project manager, likewise a member and employee of the Church and authorized to enter the state of Israel and city of Jerusalem on an extensible two-year work visa. Her expression held none of the dreamy happiness of her husband's; as he floated through the airport in a reverie, she kept her attention firmly down to earth, towing him along.

"It's better you don't go telling everybody why we're here, not at first," she advised, her voice low but firm as she leaned into his arm. "Elder Nabil told us to keep a low profile, remember?"

"I remember the last time I was here." Benjamin's eyes roved through the long corridors, taking in the orderly crowds, uniformed airport security personnel—and armed soldiers in fatigues standing apart from the crowds. They came in pairs, their armbands showing blue stars of David on white and white crescent moons on green, a cooperative effort between the two wings of the government in assuring peace and stability. The original idea involved setting the watchmen to watch each other, but it had provided an unexpected side benefit: working together every day might make one more likely to want to shoot the other, but less likely to actually do it. On duty, identical uniform caps replaced the guards' traditional kaffiyehs and yarmulkes as they watched over the travelers coming and going in fashionable Western clothes, flowing robes, turbans and beards, black hats and side locks.

"That—" Benjamin nodded toward two young recruits. "That we would never have seen all those years ago, before the peace accords finally worked."

In the bright sunlight of a peaceful afternoon, the tension of those weeks seemed both immediate and immeasurably long ago; the endless waits for updated news reports as he and Hannah paced the floor with their firstborn; the fragile, desperate hope slowly blooming into possibility, then certainty. The new leaders had listened to each other then, Israelis and Palestinians alike desperately seeking a way out of the bloody maelstrom of war into which extremists on both sides had plunged their people. Those people had finally risen against the warmongers, refusing to allow the terrorists and militants to speak and act for them. The nonmilitant leaders had the weight of the people behind them, which at last broke the grip of the violent minority; they invited representatives from both camps to come together, calling in international facilitators to smooth the negotia-tions. At long last, the cycle of hatred broke, as good-hearted people stood for their true beliefs and worked out solutions that did not involve machine guns and suicide bombers.

Hannah followed his gaze. "No. And in those years we never thought we would either. But He will intervene, in His own time."

She glanced at her watch. "Speaking of which, time slips away. Come on, pick up your feet. We must meet Mr. Hassan soon."

"Brother Hassan," Benjamin corrected gently. As a child, Hannah had lived in the war-torn neighborhoods of Tel Aviv, before her parents had moved the family to the safety of the United States, and while she had accepted both the gospel and the peace, old worries still lurked under the surface of her practical, diamond-sharp mind.

Rather like the new aquifers bubbling to life under the once-barren deserts of Palestine, he thought. The weather, wilder and less predictable every year, and the earthquakes that brought so much destruction in other lands had proved a boon to Jordan's and Judea's arid hills and plains. Data from the exquisitely calibrated monitors on the ground and on the International Space Station drew maps of new lakes filling underground, pure water available for the pumping to turn the waste-land into a garden. The Church had provided the expertise and initial funding to bring that water to both Palestinian and Israeli farmers and families, all under the direction of Mohammed Hassan, the newly appointed chief superintendent for the long-hoped-for Jerusalem temple that was now becoming a reality.

Benjamin touched the case slung over his shoulder for the thou-sandth time since Elder Nabil had seen the Cohens off on their mission. The Apostle had called it a mission indeed, a vital calling that would help to bring salvation to countless souls, a dramatic mile-post in the gathering of Israel. Now the plans for the temple hung from his shoulder, the fruit of months of labor, consultation, prayer, and inspiration embodied in digital diagrams and paper sketches, waiting to be born in crystal and stone, iron and wood, into the light of day.

"Brother Hassan," Hannah said.

For a moment, Benjamin thought she simply repeated the words to show she understood, then snapped out of his reverie when a deeper voice answered, "Sister Cohen. And Brother Cohen. It is good you have come. Did you have a pleasant flight?"

Mohammed Hassan offered the architect and project manager a polite smile.

"What can we say? Hurtling through the air in a steel tube all through the night, with only a stopover in Paris—it was as pleasant as could be expected." Hannah's rare but beautiful smile softened her face as she added, "But we are here safely, and it is good of you to greet us."

"My pleasure as well as my duty," Hassan assured her, meeting her eyes with a gaze that shared understanding. "As is working with you both." His smile broadened. "Two Jews and a Palestinian, all Mormons. We will turn some heads, even in this time."

Benjamin smiled back, seeing the humor in the situation. President Smith, with his background in psychology and astute judgment of interpersonal relations, as well as a healthy dose of revelation, had selected the personnel for the temple project with exquisite care: Brother Hassan to marshal the labor force and skilled craftsmen, still overwhelmingly Palestinian; Sister Cohen to bring order and schedule to the huge project; and Brother Cohen to work with the Israeli engineers and technical experts. They each had a part to play, and all were determined to do it well.

"We received the preliminary plans over the secure satellite link," Hassan told them, gently taking the handle to the heavy rolling bag from Hannah's hand. "They look very good. Our team has already begun the initial preparations on the site, readying the present building and hillside for further construction. We have the permits we need for the first phase and preliminary agreements for the rest. We can work for about three months on what we have now. After that—"

"After that, you discover why I am here," Hannah told him. "If you will give me the information on the final permits we need and the people who control them, I will do the rest."

"She will," Benjamin assured Hassan, who didn't look skeptical so much as slightly amused.

"I believe you," he assured them both. "I could almost feel pity for those bureaucrats who try to halt our progress." He looked ahead, outside the glass doors, and his expression hardened. "Unfortunately, stubborn bureaucrats may be the least of our worries."

Benjamin and Hannah followed his gaze. Two knots of grim-faced men stood beyond the portal, just out of range of the airport security curtain, keeping scrupulously apart from each other even as they jointly stared through the glass. Under the kaffiyehs and black hats of their fundamentalist uniforms, the expressions on their faces were identical. So were the underlying messages of the words they shouted at Hassan and the Cohens when the Mormons emerged from the airport terminal building. The Mormons should return to their hell-spawned country immediately, remove their blasphemous presence and influence on the pure believers in Allah or the Torah. They did no more than shout, however, under the narrowed eyes of the security detail.

"What, they don't dare throw stones?" Hannah snorted as Hassan led them quickly down to a lower parking level.

"A custom that, fortunately, is disappearing," Hassan said. "No, instead they protest, shout, and march with their followers. Groups of them haunt the construction site, trying to deafen us with their accusations and cries. They can do no more than that; we have the protection of the authorities. It does not stop them from trying to deafen us, however. There, the blue car is mine."

"And whose is that?" Benjamin asked, nodding toward the long, glossy black vehicle pulled negligently across two parking spaces.

Hassan's face darkened. "It belongs to a new group here to challenge the authority of the mullahs and rabbis. For all the good things the new agreement has brought, I sometimes think that too much religious freedom has hurt us as well as helped. These come from a new cult trying to gain a foothold among the disaffected."

The limousine's door opened, revealing a driver clothed all in black but for a crimson scarf around his face. He unfolded himself to an impressive height, then bowed as he opened the passenger door. Another figure, this one a smooth-looking, middle-aged man in loose-fitting white clothes, emerged to gaze impassively at the three walking toward him.

He waited until they drew even with the limousine, then stepped forward, radiating arrogance and thinly veiled hostility. "Mr. and Mrs. Cohen. I bring you a message from Brother Light: the One God refuses your entry into this holy land which he claims eternally for his own. Unless you become one with the Great Unity, you have no place here. Go now in peace; if you stay, you and all your people will be smitten and driven out."

Hassan growled, Hannah opened her mouth for a scathing retort, but Benjamin stepped forward before either of them could answer.

"We will stay, to do the work of God here in this holy land with no regard to threats from any adversary. Every kindred, tongue, and nation will hear His word, including this one. You are welcome to listen—or to get out of the way."

With that, Benjamin walked past the limousine, Hannah and Hassan following without a backward glance. They quickly loaded their bags into Hassan's car and drove away, leaving Brother Light's emissary to glare impotently after them.

* * *

Dear Chisom,

Yes, I am glad to report the rumors going around your mission are true. Parts of China are now officially open to missionary work. The Church is preparing its first group of elders and sisters for the adventure. As a zone leader, you will likely be one of those asked to lead the way. If that happens, I will be anxious to hear your firsthand reports on how it goes.

With the opening of China, we are now recognized in nearly every nation on the earth. There are still a few holdouts, but not many. It is true that there are quite a number of areas where we do not have full-time missionaries, but in most of those places we have members who are carrying forward the work. This situation is true in a number of African nations and some of the Balkan States where we can no longer send elders and sisters. So we are rather rapidly reaching the point where the gospel will be preached to every nation, kindred, tongue, and people. Once we do that, then the end can come. As I say so often, we are certainly living in the day when signs are being fulfilled. In fact, we are finding that quite a few people here in the States have joined the Church because they see the fulfillment of prophecy.

Speaking of the fulfillment of prophecy, I suppose you have heard that the Caribbean, Mexico, and the U.S. have experienced the worst hurricane season in history.

Nine have hit land, of which five were category three or above. Two category-five storms slammed into the Caribbean and then into the Southern states. Damage has been terrible. Just last week, after the hurricane season should have been over, the East Coast was brutalized by a category four that had slowed only to a category two by the time it hit Nova Scotia and finally faded away. In addition, some areas have been savaged by tornadoes. One area was hit by a hailstorm with some stones as big as softballs. It is of note that areas where the Saints are strong have been mostly spared.

Add to that the damage caused by looters. I can't believe how many people are engaged in that. It shows just how low some segments of our society really are. Mob rule grows in some areas, but others, especially some of the big cities, are controlled by the Mafia and gangs. With the police overwhelmed, people in some areas have formed protection groups and are taking on the gangs. Nothing short of civil war has broken out due to turf battles. We are seeing people flee the inner cities in hopes of finding places of safety outside. This movement is causing additional problems for there is nowhere to house them. People are truly in turmoil. With the economy so depressed, I don't know where the funds will come to repair the damage, fight the gangs, and bring order out of chaos. Bloodshed is endemic in some areas. Fortunately, many of the smaller cities are coping, and much of the heartland (with the exception of Illinois) and the Intermountain West are stable.

Thus far, the Church has been able to take care of its own. That's because so many of the Saints were prepared. In fact, we have been in the news lately because the Midwest and especially Missouri have been spared the worst of the problems that have hit elsewhere. The report noted that the Church continues to thrive and its farms and other holdings are doing very well for the most part. The reporters continue to emphasize how rich the Church is without noting that much of what they count is in temples and meetinghouses. They do have it partially correct. The Church really is doing well. What the reporters can't see is why. The Saints that have remained true are being faithful in paying their tithes and offerings. As a result, even in these financially hard times, the windows of heaven are open, and the Church is greatly blessed. Therefore, we can help our own, keep building our chapels and temples, and keep our missionary work going. And because most of the Saints are self-sufficient, the resources of the Church are available to assist those in the hard-hit areas. Of course the Church has its detractors. No matter what we do, there are those who put a bad face on it.

Our biggest critics are those who were once members and have now abandoned the Church. Some continue to wail and cry because they feel the Church has not come into the twenty-first century on moral and social issues. Our stand against situation ethics, moral perversion, and the renewed and very aggressive feminist movement has sent them into apoplexy. Critics on the other side feel the Church has compromised far too much with the world. They dislike the quiet and balanced position the Church takes on social, civil, and environmental issues. They are especially incensed that the leaders have not ordered the Church to arms. They feel that it should form its own militia and insist that the day for a Captain Moroni has come. They chafe that Presidents Smith and Rojas are so passive. So they have sought leaders elsewhere.

Some feel that the Brethren do not know what is happening. They are very wrong. Reports are coming in all the time, and we have a very clear view of what is happening worldwide. Much is ugly, but the Lord's kingdom is moving ahead. The Lord knows what He is doing and is communicating His will to His servants. President Smith is only having us follow the will of the Lord. We must have faith and remain at peace. That's the role the Lord is assigning His people. I know it tries the patience of the Saints, it certainly does mine, but we will follow the Lord, right?

I am impressed with the advantages Satan has. We must keep everyone in the middle of the spiritual bridge, moving forward in a united front. He can push them off either side. What is interesting is that he does not care which side of the bridge they fall off, just as long as they fall. The more zeal and self-righteousness he can convince them of, the quicker they fall off and the more they hate the Church.

Just remember, Chisom, the Lord will never let the prophet lead the Church astray. You tell your people to keep an eye on President Smith and what comes under the signature of the First Presidency. These men will never take us off the right road.

Well, this letter has not been as positive as I would have liked. Still, I feel it is good for you to know what is going on so that you can see the big picture. Despite the problems and challenges, the Lord's kingdom, as you well know, is moving forward. And just think, we get to be a part of it!

In the meantime, continue to work and let me know from your view what happens in China, and I'll let you know from ours.

With love,
Your father,
Chinedu

* * *

"The governors of New York, Massachusetts, and Rhode Island have joined the eleven states requesting federal disaster aid in cleaning up the damage from the once-in-a-century storm that hit the coastal areas," Clara said, as the screen showed an aerial view of flooded highways and smashed docks. "The president's spokeswoman says that the administration is sympathetic to the plight of the many who lost property and possessions in the storms, but adds that there's simply not enough emergency-management money to go around. Reports of violence and looting are coming out of many of the hardest-hit areas. According to some accounts, mobs have broken into homes and stores, often accusing the owners of hoarding supplies—"

"Glenn told me about that," Lucrezia said, looking up from her calculus book at her mother, who came in hauling yet another basket of clean clothes out of the utility room. "And, I read on the Net that there are mobs all over the Midwest and South, out looking for Mormons to burn down their houses and steal everything they can."

"Don't believe everything you read on the Net, honey." Carmen thumped the laundry basket down on the kitchen floor. Due to the deepening water shortages, their neighborhood had been assigned Tuesday as their heavy water-use day, which meant that Carmen spent all of Tuesday doing laundry. "And how about you turn off the TV while you're doing homework?"

"I'm supposed to watch the news. It's for Current Events, and you told me to be more cooperative with Mr. Shapiro," Lucrezia pointed out in her reasonable voice.

Carmen rolled her eyes. "I'd tell you not to be a smarty, but I'm glad you're a smart girl." She ruffled Lucrezia's hair then pulled Gianni out of the clothes basket. He loved burying himself in the warm folds of fresh laundry. "All right, fine. So while you're doing Current Events homework, you can put down that pencil and help fold clothes."

Lucrezia sighed dramatically, greatly put upon but secretly glad to leave the world of vectors and transformations for the simpler folds of socks and T-shirts. "Still, I bet that's who tried to burn down our house," Lucrezia persisted. "All those letters we get—it's the anti-Mormon mob."

"It wasn't a mob, it was a single guy," Donna said, flopping onto the floor by another basket, this one mostly jeans. "Mobs are, by definition, more than one person." She softened the correction with a smile; their successful rout of the would-be cross burner had done a lot to repair the sisters' stress-fractured relationship.

"Okay, so it was one person," Lucrezia acceded the point. "But he was still working for a mob—or kind of a mob. Don't they call organized crime 'the Mob'? You ask me, that's what's going on here, but it's not the Mafia behind it this time—it's those MedaGen goons. That car he jumped into didn't have a license plate, but it sure looked like the one that's been hanging around, and the same one that Ms. White and her goon buddy drove when they came after us looking for Merry."

Donna looked sideways at their mother, Carmen's hands busy sorting and folding pairs of socks, her expression neutral. That meant she didn't want to worry them. "They're out to get us because we helped Merry," Donna said, "and since they can't do anything to punish us legally, they're trying to scare us and starve us. Mom, even you and Dad were talking about—"

A shake deep in the foundations of the house, followed by a slow roll that rocked the walls, interrupted her. Gianni squealed, delighted with the "ground ride," as he called the temblors that had become increasingly common throughout Southern California. His mother and sisters rode it out as well; Lucrezia caught her glass as it threatened to tip juice all over her homework; Carmen watched the ceiling, looking for the cracks that Tony assured her wouldn't happen; Donna just sat still, hands flat on the floor, feeling the earth stir beneath them like a giant animal beginning to wake. The initial shaking passed, leaving a small trail of minor aftershocks behind it.

"Wow!" Lucrezia grinned triumphantly. "I didn't sleep through that one!"

"Ah, that wasn't even a four-pointer," Donna said.

"Oh, come on, four-two at least," Lucrezia said.

A few seconds later, the crawl at the bottom of the Channel 8 News told them that the quake had measured 3.9 and centered on the fault line east of San Diego. These days, a minor quake like that didn't even make the main screen. Carmen declared both girls right and directed her laundry slaves to keep folding.

"We can't stay here, Tony," Carmen said later that night. "We can't stay here, and we can't keep our kids here." She said it softly, as she and Tony knelt beside their bed after prayer. "Between the earthquakes and the schools and the jobs and MedaGen, I've just had it."

"What are we going to do, Carmen?" Tony asked, sympathetic but frustrated. "You want to follow Mike out to Temple View? We don't have the money for a down payment on one of those condos."

"We could really follow Mike's example and bunk in with somebody until we scraped up the cash. Reiko Inouye and I were in the Relief Society presidency together when I was secretary—she and her husband, Roland, have moved to Temple View," Carmen suggested, but her heart wasn't in it.

"No." Tony said it for both of them. "When the prophet tells us to gather, we'll go, but it's not time yet. Come on, baby. We'll get something. We've been fasting, praying, and digging like mad. We've got a son on a mission. There are still a couple of doors open, even if they look as small as mouse holes from here. Softlearn hasn't broken my portfolio in half and sent it to back to me yet. And maybe StudentWare will decide they'll take a chance on a Mormon with an attitude. We'll get out of this spot." He squeezed her hand, bumped her shoulder with his, the echo of his old, sly grin creeping onto his face. "This is one for the books, eh—me telling you to have faith?"

Carmen leaned into his shoulder, squeezing her eyes shut to keep the tears in, but smiling in spite of the knot in her stomach. "One for the books, all right. I love you, Tony."

"I love you, Carmen." He held her close.

"This would be a bad time to tell you I'm pregnant, huh?" she asked, her voice slightly muffled.

"What?" Tony looked at her wide-eyed then groaned as she grinned back. "Carmen!"

"I'm not," she admitted, "but I was just thinking, with our luck, we'd get a new baby just when we couldn't afford one."

Tony shook her affectionately, his hands creeping to her ribs to tickle her into giggles. "Much as I love our kids, I think we've done our duty at four! What would Giovanni think, coming home from his mission to a new baby brother or sister?"

"Maybe we'd actually find out, if he was home." Carmen wiggled aside enough to reach Tony's ribs too. "We wouldn't have to depend on the scamp writing us letters from Chile!"

* * *

"We are surrounded. Chile is the last holdout, sir." Major Zamora stood before his superior officer's desk, the fire in his eyes belying his semirelaxed stance. "This caudillo who calls himself General Garza has taken control of every country to the north and east of us."

"*General* Garza has offered his valuable assistance in suppressing rebel forces and terrorists." Major Archuleta stressed the title, glaring at Zamora. "No matter what your Mormon peasant informers tell you. And after defeating the insurgents, he has stood by to assist as each country elected its own government. That is hardly taking control."

Zamora gazed back at his fellow officer—fellow in name only. Archuleta was Vice President Aguilera's lapdog, utterly opposed to Zamora's special antiterrorist assignment as a waste of money, time, and lives. Archuleta made no secret of his opinion that Chile should follow the example of other South American countries and accept General Garza's assistance in stopping El Jaguar's depredations. President Quintana, thus far, had refused to accept that suggestion, but with every attack Zamora's squad failed to stop, every week that El Jaguar remained at large, the president's position became more unstable. The people, frightened and furious, demanded that someone do something to stop the guerillas who spread destruction, death, and terror even in the capital itself. What they could not see, and what Zamora strongly believed, was that El Jaguar was himself an agent of General Garza's, sent to harass the Chileans into opening their arms to the General's primary forces.

"You've seen the intelligence reports that describe the 'free' governments. Garza oversees the execution or imprisonment of the former government, then appoints his own men and collaborators as *mayores* to rule the people, funneling money and matériel to his base camp in Colombia. That is not taking control?" Zamora said it not so much to remind Archuleta as to remind General Medina of the reality behind Archuleta's—and the vice president's—urgent arguments. The general sat silently behind his desk, watching the two officers over steepled fingers.

Zamora addressed the general alone, ignoring Archuleta's attempts to interrupt. "They are nothing but puppets dancing on Garza's strings. Just like these alleged rebels. The mountains have guarded us from eastern attacks, but with Peru and Ecuador falling under Garza's hand, his operatives have a clearer road. They are finding ways through the mountains as well."

"So, El Jaguar is not merely the leader of a vicious band of terrorists supported by disaffected *campos* and the Mapuches—he is the spearhead of a subtle, irresistible invasion!" Archuleta exclaimed scornfully. "You have not lost men and battles against a terrorist, but against a modern Napoleon. A convenient excuse from a man who cannot do the duty assigned him."

"I make no excuses," Zamora said quietly, the cold steel in his tone cutting through the other's emotional heat. "El Jaguar and his men take their orders from Garza—and they have help, information, from agents who know our strategies and locations."

A flush rose on Archuleta's cheekbones. "Do you accuse—"

"I have heard no accusations but one," General Medina cut him off. "And that is against Garza." He leaned back, regarding Zamora expressionlessly. The major was an excellent officer—and a hero of the March Revolution—whose consistent failures to apprehend El Jaguar or any of his men both surprised and worried Medina. The president demanded results, the vice president openly derided Medina's decision to create an antiterror group under Zamora's command, and El Jaguar grew bolder every week. And yet, he could not dismiss the conviction in Zamora's steady eyes.

Medina met those eyes. "What you say sounds logical." He held up a hand, stopping Archuleta's protest. "But you have no solid evidence. Find that evidence, Major, and stop El Jaguar, whoever he reports to. The president cannot justify continuing to rely on your efforts in the face of consistent failure, when so many of his opponents point to Garza's consistent success. The people want to feel safe in their homes and streets. If we cannot provide that, they will turn to someone who can."

"Yes, sir." Zamora saluted.

"Dismissed, Major." Medina stood, returning the salute. "Find El Jaguar—or at least find proof that Garza is behind him. Otherwise, we may have no choice."

* * *

The conversation played in Zamora's mind as he paced the tight confines of a camouflage command tent well hidden in the lush vegetation outside a small mountain village near the northernmost border. Over the jagged horizon lay Peru—and the advance guard of General Garza's forces, poised to sweep across the border and into Chile the moment Vice President Aguilera finally convinced President Quintana to ask for the mercenary leader's help in defeating El Jaguar.

Rain poured down outside the tent, dripping inside, running in small streams to join larger ones, gathering like the clues the antiterror squad followed today. Rumors, hints, and whispers from carefully cultivated intelligence sources, refugees, and the few but faithful members of the Church who were still sprinkled throughout the ravaged counties to the north reported that El Jaguar used the pass as his road from Chile to Peru. He traveled it himself occasionally, but more often Garza used it to send reinforcements, weapons, and supplies into Chile. Some of the supplies came from the General's depots in the occupied countries around them; others, however, the rebels extorted or stole from villages along their routes, using the threat of terror or promises of rich rewards to persuade farmers to hand over their own scanty provisions. Some of those farmers had other reasons to cooperate; a few of the most courageous Mormon farmers and merchants had agreed to join Zamora's network of eyes and ears all over the mountains, heartened by their own love of country and encouraged by Elder Molina, the Apostle assigned to oversee the Church in South America.

Zamora's network, which he had painstakingly built over the last few months, provided the clues that had warned Zamora's team of two of El Jaguar's planned strikes; they had prevented another bombing, this one at a train station, and had frightened the rebels away from a village raid. Each time, however, El Jaguar's men had melted away at the last moment, as if they had been warned as well. Zamora had no doubt that someone was feeding information to the rebels and had a growing suspicion that the leak didn't simply come from local malcontents. If someone with access was manipulating the situation, Señor Olivares, the director of the intelligence service, would be his best ally in finding the inside informant. He occasionally wondered exactly whose side Olivares was on, but the man had previously proved himself adept at uncovering antigovernment plots in both the military and civilian circles. Zamora felt he could be trusted. The leak had to be coming from somewhere else.

The sound of running broke Zamora's grim reverie. He reached the tent flap at the same moment as Captain Guerra. "Sir! We have a trace on them!" the young captain exclaimed. "The locator we gave the informant at Santa Teresa just clicked on. We've got a few minutes before they detect it—if they do."

"Yes, Brother Neruda!" Zamora's face lit. He clicked on the all-call channel and commanded, "Target acquired. Intercept formation. Move out!"

The antiterror force, well honed after months of intensive preparation, leapt into action. Light, efficient transports bumped over the rough, muddy trail, following the blinking light of the tracker glowing from their screens. Above their heads, a helicopter thudded through the air, braving the vicious crosswinds of the rainy canyon to spot the exact location of the rebels' camp. Zamora leaned forward, wishing he could wipe the rain away from his side of the windshield, looking out and down over the storm-tossed trees for any sign of El Jaguar's butchers.

"Nothing yet," the comm officer said, glancing at the electronic readout, "but we're coming up on the tracker. They should be in visual range in three minutes."

"Keep it low," Zamora reminded the pilot.

The man didn't need the reminder. An experienced member of the antiterror force and a battle-seasoned veteran of the wars against the drug cartels, he expertly guided the ungainly metal dragonfly through the wind and rain, splitting the difference between the wild sky and the sea of trees below.

The right curve of the smuggler's road came into view at the same moment that a series of sharp sounds came dimly to the men's ears through the noise of the helicopter's rotors.

"We have visual," the comm officer needlessly announced; the ragged line of heavy-duty vehicles halted along the roadside were visible through the mist. One hand pressed against the ear of his headset, he glanced up at Zamora with wide eyes. "And we've got gunfire—maybe a couple of grenades!"

A sudden blossom of fire against the greens and browns of the ground confirmed his suspicion; one of the trucks burst into flame.

The noise of the explosion reached them a second later. Swooping down through the gray air, the helicopter's passengers caught glimpses of camouflage-clad men bursting out of the forest on the sides of the road to fire on the convoy. Other men, the red flash of a rebel arm badge occasionally visible, huddled around the trucks, desperately fighting the ambushers.

"They're not ours," the pilot said. "Who are they?"

"Let's get down there and find out," Zamora ordered, feeling a sinking in his stomach that had nothing to do with the sudden descent and wide turn as the pilot banked low over the convoy, then lifted toward the clouds again. A swarm of whining lead hornets accompanied them. Zamora clicked on the comm, shouting, "Captain Guerra, full speed—you're running into a firefight, and I want you to put an end to it. And if you can't stop it, cover them and get down. I don't want them leaving!"

"Who are they?" Captain Guerra asked, after shouting the order for more speed through the dripping, wind-whipped greenery. Zamora had only one theory, which he didn't bother to broadcast over the open radio channel.

Guerra got his answer—and Zamora got his suspicion confirmed—when the captain and the rest of Zamora's men burst onto the scene, taking a high position up the hill from the battle to cover both sides. By that time, however, the shooting had stopped. The wind shredded the columns of thick, oily smoke rising from the burned-out hulks of the trucks in El Jaguar's convoy. Men in camouflage and rain slickers slipped from wreck to wreck, bending over the figures sprawled in splashes of rain-diluted crimson around and inside of the charred trucks. Occasionally, a flash of silver caught what little light came through the clouds, or an isolated gunshot competed with the retreating thunder.

They were aware that Guerra's men were staring through the sights of machine guns and one rocket launcher, which explained their caution to keep out of the direct line of fire. They didn't shoot up the hill, but they also absolutely disregarded Captain Guerra's amplified orders to drop their weapons and come forward with their hands up.

The captain growled, snapping to the flankers, "Show these monkeys we aren't kidding!"

"Belay that," Zamora interrupted. The helicopter landed in the road beyond the convoy, no cloud of dust, thanks to the rain, as the antiterror squad pulled their aim. He joined Guerra as the younger man agilely scuffed down the slope and finished the statement in person. "It's over already. No use getting one of our boys shot over nothing."

"Nothing?" Guerra snorted, then remembered who he was talking to and straightened his shoulders. "Sir. We arrived after the firefight ended, and took observation position as ordered."

Zamora looked around, noting that a trio of men had detached themselves from the cover of the mangled convoy to walk a few meters along the road toward them. "And what did you observe, Captain?"

Guerra's already dark eyes darkened further. "It looked like they were finishing off the guys in the convoy, sir. Sir, they kept out of our sights and disregarded orders to disarm and advance."

"No wonder. Basic training, Captain, not to walk into the line of fire." A wry smile flickered across Zamora's face, then disappeared into weariness. "It appears that they're willing to talk now, however."

"Major Zamora!" The three came to a stop within speaking distance. Their leader, one of Garza's recently promoted favorites, Marcelo, stood with his hands behind his back, smiling thinly as he surveyed the Chilean leaders and the helicopter behind them. "I have heard a lot about you—and your troop, of course."

Zamora's gaze traveled from the black uniform jacket, with its stylized dragon insignia and captain's bars, to the hot spark in the man's eyes. "And I have heard much about your troop, Captain—and your leader as well. What brings one of General Garza's crack assassination squads to Chilean territory?"

"Assassination squad? We prefer 'security' detail," Marcelo said.

"What brings one of General Garza's crack security details over the border into Chile?" Zamora said.

"So sorry about that, but General Garza figured you'd appreciate the help. We're just cleaning up some trash spilling over the Peruvian border. With the General's compliments," Marcelo said casually, gesturing toward the human carrion littering the road in front of them.

"We can do our own garbage collection," Zamora said coldly. "Without help from Garza's sanitation specialists or the master trashman himself."

Marcelo's ironic smile melted into a sneer, his hackles rising at the major's dismissive tone.

"Secure the scene for the forensics team," Zamora instructed Guerra, disregarding the cause of the mess. He didn't bother to ask Garza's agent his name; at this point, he didn't care. Intelligence could undoubtedly run an identification on the man. What mattered now was salvaging as much as possible. Whatever Garza wanted cleaned up was worth prying into. He turned to the pilot. "Get Dr. Vasquez on the line, and tell her to bring a double team—with a year's supply of body bags."

"You can't—" Marcelo growled, stepping forward. He stopped as Guerra, the pilot, and the comm officer all pulled guns; behind him, his two thugs did the same. All over the hillside and road, men behind the black bores of rifles glared at each other through the misty air.

Zamora stepped forward as well, nearly chest-to-chest with Marcelo, completely ignoring the imminent death all around them. "I can, and I will. You silenced them; you won that round. But you did it in my country, on my mud, and if you push us, you'll end up as dead as they are. Do you want to push?"

"Hot pursuit crosses borders. We caught them on the other side and followed them here, and we'll do what we want with them." Marcelo stared back, reading the cold certainty in the major's steady eyes. For a moment, everything seemed to stop as the two faced each other, like two dogs just entering the cage. The awareness of Zamora's men, and their superior position up the hill, weighed on the guerilla leader's mind. He could shoot Zamora, and then Zamora's men would kill him and everybody in his squad. The calculations weren't difficult.

Marcelo broke the tableau, stepping back and throwing his hands up with a sharp laugh. "Who gives a peso? You want to play with dead things, Major Zamora? That how you get your kicks? Have your fun then. Me and my boys, we'll drink a round to you during our victory party tonight."

"You do that." Zamora watched Marcelo's troops re-form and march away to their own carefully concealed vehicles. The moment they were gone, he ran to the nearest of the smoldering trucks and looked inside. Crates marked with the address of Brother Neruda's shipping business smoked inside. Crimson streams oozed across the logo; the guard riding in the back of the truck had died of multiple gunshot wounds, with a slit throat just to make sure. Every one of the rebels had met a similar fate. Zamora ordered the squad to thoroughly investigate the convoy but to touch nothing until Dr. Vasquez arrived.

"They're dead three times over—each," muttered one of the soldiers, coming back from his investigation of part of the convoy. He looked slightly green around the gills from the stink of burned blood and sight of butchered men.

Captain Guerra nodded. "Looks like they completed their orders. Dead men can't tell us how Garza set up El Jaguar."

"They won again." The soldier's shoulder drooped.

Zamora, silently joining them, patted the disappointed soldier's shoulder. That startled the young man; he relaxed when he realized who it was, then straightened to attention when he really realized who stood next to him. "Only halfway, chico." Bending toward the dead guerilla at their feet, he touched the jaguar patch on the bloodied jacket sleeve. "Dead men can say a lot more than you'd think, if you know the right questions—and have the right lady to ask them. Every shred of evidence adds to our picture. There's much more than a shred here. With all this to analyze, our Dr. Vasquez," he said, gesturing toward the clouds, the sound of the chopper's blades slicing through the heavy air, "may be able to tell us whose army these boys enlisted in originally."

CHAPTER 13

"News from God's army at last!" Carmen burst into the office, waving an envelope. Gianni ran after her, happily waving a piece of junk mail.

Tony turned slowly from the screen as Carmen read through the letter, liberally inserting editorial comments and affectionate complaints about Giovanni's spelling and grammar into the body of the altogether too brief missive. "So he's doing fine, he's running out of socks, he's heard that missionaries are being pulled out of Peru and Ecuador but not Chile, he's loving all his investigators, he's not quite brawling with the anti-Mormons, and he's learning too much about soccer from his companion," she summed up.

She didn't add any summary or editorial comments, however, as she read the official letter from the mission president included with Giovanni's note. "The political situation here in Chile is unstable, and we have received word from the First Presidency that no foreign missionaries will be joining our mission for the foreseeable future. We are fortunate to have a high percentage of native missionaries and faithful members to shoulder the burden and move the work forward. When we talked, Elder Giovanni Callatta indicated his willingness to serve out the remaining months of his mission in this area, and I have accepted his service. Your son has served valiantly and faithfully, bringing the great gospel and love of the Lord to the people of his mission. I am grateful to have his service still. He is making a very fine zone leader. We thank you for your prayers on our behalf and ask that you continue to support us in faith. Sincerely, President Reyes," she finished.

After silently contemplating "unstable" and remembering the news reports of government forces clashing with El Jaguar's rebels, she said, "So Giovanni's not moving."

"But we are," Tony said.

"What?" She blinked, seeing the stunned expression on Tony's face gradually melting into incredulous triumph.

He stood up, grabbed Carmen, and lifted her feet right off the ground as he kissed her. "You're in the strong and capable arms of Softlearn's newest interface designer!"

Carmen's whoop ended abruptly as she kissed Tony back.

"Me too!" Gianni demanded, raising his arms.

Tony laughed, letting go of Carmen momentarily to sweep Gianni up and over his head, then hugging him. Carmen hugged both of them, then detached Gianni, co-opting Tony's chair to look at the screen. "Come on, let's find out about Daddy's new job."

"New job!" Gianni beamed.

"Yup, new job," Tony said, as Carmen, with Gianni's eager help, investigated the message offering Tony a position helping design the interface for educational software providing online courses for elementary through university students. Softlearn, according to its official Web site, offered accredited courseware as an alternative to the hit-or-miss curriculum most home-schooling organizations offered, as well as a rigorous, challenging learning experience that underfunded public schools could not provide. The samples of their material looked thorough, well organized—and dull.

"Sounds like it could be interesting," Carmen said, "but not the way they've got it here."

"Exactly." Tony pointed to a few more pages, showing examples of more in-depth, valuable information wrapped in a sleep-inducing electronic package. "That's why they need me. My background in game design and visual applications caught their attention. They've got good content, but their presentation, in a word, bites. The best part is that one of the partners who started the company is a member of the Church, so our being members doesn't bother them. And they're small enough and independent enough that MedaGen's interdict hasn't gotten to them." He pointed to the specific clauses of the contract they offered. "It's not huge, but it'll give me a stake in the company as well as a salary. And they'll pay our moving expenses as part of the standard contract package."

"Good, nice." Carmen scanned the agreement. "So where do they plan to move us to?"

"It's in Illinois, pretty close to Nauvoo, but it's not a temple community." Tony scanned through the information. "Ah ha, here we go, Lake Creek, Illinois. I got a note from Rob Sarkesian too. He's the Mormon co-owner. He says a lot of Mormon families have moved in, gathering around the new core of Net businesses growing in the city."

"It also looks like a lot of other families have moved out," Carmen noted, pulling up the Web site for Lake Creek itself. Even through the glowing chamber of commerce report, signs of hard times showed. Lake Creek had started as a manufacturing town in a rural area, prospering until the end of the last century, when the factories had closed. The current economic slump had hit it hard too; the site dressed up empty buildings and a thinning population as "investment opportunities" in a "buyer's real estate market." But signs of an economic renaissance appeared as well, with Lake Creek's recent growth of online-support businesses, fueled by information-infrastructure improvements that Softlearn had invested in. That led to eager plans for downtown beautification projects and glowing reports of the ongoing "urban renaissance."

"Code for Mormons have moved in, the roughnecks have moved out, and people can walk the streets at night without having to fight off hookers or muggers," Tony summarized. He turned to Carmen. "So, what do you think? Shall we pack the wagons for the trek to Illinois?"

"Lake Creek." The name tickled in her mind, then clicked. "That's one of the places that made the news, isn't it, with somebody burning a chapel?"

"Probably, but that's not exactly rare anymore." Tony shrugged. "At least we'd have Mormon neighbors, which will cut down on the love letters in the mailbox."

"Might as well go; what else can go wrong?" Carmen smiled, rueful at first, then more happily. "Or right. What else can go right? Looks like we asked for a way out, and we got it." She squeezed Tony.

Tony hugged her back, looking at the invitation glowing on the screen. "Hey, we're Callattas—we can take anything, as long as we're together. And who knows—we might find out that hopping out of the frying pan lands us on the stove top instead of the fire."

* * *

"Man, talk about from bad to worse! I only like guns when I'm carrying one." Mercury glanced around the Chilean airport terminal, hitching his bag up on his shoulder. Soldiers in airports weren't unusual, but in the Albuquerque airport they hadn't held machine guns at waist level and watched the passengers as if they were potential targets in a shooting gallery. Home, sweet home.

"Sh," hissed Señora Colón, the woman who had sat in the next seat on the bumpy flight. She'd worried about sitting next to a rough-looking teenage boy, but he'd been surprisingly friendly. They'd had plenty to talk about too when he asked her about Mormons and she told him she was one. She was quite surprised to find out he was one too. After a few minutes talking to her newly devout seatmate, she mused that first appearances don't always tell the truth. What both thought was a potential missionary discussion turned into a lively conversation about the state of the Church in Chile—and in the borderlands. "You're not in America now, chico. Here, the army can shoot you if you look at them."

"They don't shoot you," Mercury muttered, thinking of his father's stern honor but looking away from the sentries just in case. "They send you up north to live with your aunt."

He took a deep breath and straightened his shoulders under the Santos jacket, remembering Dove's orders. *I'm here to help Papa fight the General,* he reminded himself. *So suck it up and stop feeling like a scared kid.* Fighting the feeling wasn't as easy as he would like—especially when he didn't see any sign of Major Zamora in the terminal. Stifling an internal groan, he mentally shook Tía Anabel. *I'll bet she didn't tell Papa,* he thought, *to save herself further psychic dissonance. And I didn't think to call either. Dumb. Better start thinking more strategically, chico.*

Shrugging off the momentary panic and sending a silent prayer for guidance to find his ever-busy father, he picked up Señora Colón's heavier suitcase and carried it out to the battered but serviceable van waiting at the curb. Her husband swept her up in a passionate embrace, and nearly did the same to Mercury, but the junior Santo politely avoided the hug by handing Señor Colón the suitcase. He did accept their offer of a ride into Santiago (*one obstacle down—thanks, Heavenly Father*) and settled in the backseat then watched the city flowing past the windows, half listening to the Colóns' conversation. White walls, bright window-box flowers, wide streets, smartly uniformed carabineros—exactly as he remembered them.

The snarling-cat graffiti, rubble from a bomb blast, and nervous soldiers posted in the squares, however, were new and disquieting. *Garza*, he thought. *Moving down from Peru, like Dove said he would. That reporter, Rosa, got it all wrong, making Garza out to be some kind of hero, sucking up to that scumbag El Jaguar guy—putting down Papa as corrupt and incompetent.* That hurt, which surprised Mercury. *Guess blood really is thicker than water*, he thought. *Even if you don't get along.*

A flash of white on the sidewalk caught his attention—two young men walking along in white shirts, ties, slacks, and name tags. Mercury leaned forward, lightly tapping Señor Colón's shoulder. "Could you drop me here, please? Gracias, lots."

Grabbing his bag, he jumped out of the van, waving additional thanks at the Colóns (who looked at each other, smiled, and shrugged), and ran across the street. "Hey! Elders!"

Giovanni turned to see what might be a junior gang member bearing down on them, blinked, and amiably deflected a hearty slap on the shoulder. "Hey, uh," he looked at the back of the kid's jacket. "Angel," he guessed.

Mercury looked at him, surprised, then grinned. "Ain't heard that from anybody but Tía Anabel for a couple years. How'd you know? You got revelation going already, ese?"

"No, you've got an angel on your jacket," Giovanni told him, returning the grin. "What's the writing? Santos something?"

"Santos Soldados." Mercury turned slightly to show the emblem. "Up in Amexica."

"That's the Mexican–United States border, isn't it? You sound like a Mexican," Elder Flisfisch said.

"And they told me I sounded southern. You sound like a city boy," Mercury shot back, then shrugged. "I've been gone awhile—up to New Mexico for school and some other stuff. Family stuff that pretty much has to get over with now, or there'll be real fireworks." The concern in his face lightened as he shrugged off the thought of what his father was going to say when he suddenly appeared on the doorstep, unannounced. He forced the old heat down; it was going to be better this time. He'd make sure it was. "Listen, you need somebody to go on splits with? Let me know, right?"

"Sure thing," Elder Callatta said. "You give us your name, and if you're in our area, let your bishop know you're interested, and we'll do it."

"Know a barber? And do you own a suit coat that used to be a plant instead of an animal?" Elder Flisfisch looked skeptically at Mercury's hair and leather jacket.

"I feel like we've made a real connection already," Mercury informed him. "Antipathy at first sight isn't all that common, you know. It usually takes longer than that for two people to detest each other. But since we're in the same corps, that's no problem. You got a piece of paper, Super Elder?"

"I hope that kid lives way out of our area," Elder Flisfisch said, watching him go.

"Pass that over." Giovanni examined the writing on the back of the pass-along card, surprisingly neat for a border-rat gangster boy. The name was surprising as well. He shook his head. "Sorry, Elder. He's on the edge, but he's in our territory."

"Out on the barrio edge," Elder Flisfisch guessed with an eye roll, imitating the kid's accent.

"Nope, on the other side." Giovanni tapped the card, handing it back to Elder Flisfisch. "Check the name."

Elder Flisfisch's eyebrows rose. "Not that one."

"Know any others?" Giovanni asked. "In that neighborhood?"

"Santa Maria, he wasn't kidding about family problems, was he?" The address on the back of the card indicated a house in the upper-class neighborhood at the far end of their area. The name was Michael Angel Freeman Zamora.

* * *

"Michael Angel Freeman Zamora." Major Zamora leaned against the door frame, arms folded, as he gazed down at his son sitting at the computer. The major's distant, cool expression hid the weariness of pursuing the rebels and escorting the carrion wagon to the morgue—as well as the sense of aching disconnection and helplessness that rose in his heart.

This tall, rough-edged, long-haired punk was his baby boy? He'd found a long, semicoherent message from his sister-in-law, Anabel, waiting on his voice mail at the office; she fluttered on about all the wild and wicked events surrounding her lovely hideaway and hinted that his son had played a significant part in them. The third time through, he'd finally picked out that she'd bought airline tickets to send Mercury home where it was "safer." The thought made him cringe—more like sending a lamb into a lion's den! The message sent him rushing to the house, already making contingency plans, hoping against rationality that Michael Angel had made it home safely. Fortunately, Anabel's scattered spontaneity in making the arrangements at the last minute had prevented El Jaguar from setting up a surprise attack—as well as preventing Zamora from being there to meet his son.

Mercury clicked Send on the "safe arrival" message to Dove and looked up from the screen at his father. "Major Manuel Rafaelo Rivera Zamora," he said, standing up, awkward under the air of casual bravado. *Don't do it,* he told himself, as the brat in him automatically reacted. *You're a Santo and a man now—or nearly a man, anyway. Act like it!*

"Papa," Zamora suggested.

"Mercury," Mercury returned the recommendation. "That's what my friends call me now."

"Your borderland gang friends," Zamora growled.

Mercury groaned and flopped back into the chair. "We going to do this already? Couldn't you at least pretend to be glad to see me, just for an hour or so?"

"I am glad to see you," Zamora said softly, forcing his voice not to rise. "I am concerned, however, about the chicos you ran with in New Mexico. Your Aunt Anabel told me about them—and about what you did while you stayed with her, ditching school and running with thugs." He held up a hand to ward off Mercury's hot retort. "I know,

Anabel's not the most reliable witness. Far from it, in fact. But I sent you up there to instill some discipline in you, to get you into a new environment, to give you the opportunity for a better education than you could get here."

"And to get me and my bad attitude out of the house," Mercury pointed out, his honesty and new willingness to reform pulling the confession out of him. He'd heard it from the school counselor, but with Dove's authority behind it, it made sense. "I don't blame you; I was a stupid adolescent reacting badly to Mama's absence, at a time when you were grieving yourself, under the additional emotional stress of coping in a society steeped in machismo—"

"Michael Angel." Zamora's warning tone brought the pop-psychoanalyzing, and attempt at changing the subject, to a halt.

"Okay. Sorry. I did ditch school—but school wasn't all that we hoped either. Some stupid private high school, charging sky-high tuition for basic classes taught by uncertified teachers? Forget that! I learned a whole lot more on my own—especially about computers."

"Playing computer games," Zamora corrected.

"And programming them," Mercury said. "Didn't Tía Anabel tell you about that? Real, serious programming—and communications, and strategy, and tactics, and current events."

"And vocabulary lessons—in Spanglish and street cant." Zamora sighed and finally eased himself onto the sofa.

"You're the second person today who said I sound like a Mexican. Good thing I take that as a compliment, even if I don't believe it." Mercury leaned forward. "I know Tía Anabel told you about what's going on up there. Sure, Dove's guys started as thugs, but they're so much cooler than that now. They're fighting the same guy you are." His hands flew, gestures illustrating the story, as he told his father about the situation up north—Dove Nakai, the Santos, Pizarro having to keep things straight, the Church members on and off the Navajo Reservation banding together with the town councils to keep out the drug dealers, Garza moving into the borderlands with bioweapons and drugs.

By the time Mercury sat back, Zamora had leaned forward, his dark eyes intent. "How do you know that Garza is using bioweapons and running drugs?"

"We've been fighting the dealers. Dove's got Sheriff Pizarro and the town councils in on it too. Last year, the General sent a guy named Slick up to take over all the borderland gangs, kill anybody who wouldn't go along. And he killed them with bullets or viruses, whichever worked better. Dove carried a package over the border for Slick, and the guys who got it ended up dead of something the FBI and CDC couldn't figure out until they sent it up to the big lab for analysis. Then, in the big showdown, Dove killed Slick, but he got Slick's blood on him and got deadly sick. He had to move up to a secret lab the Church runs in Salt Lake City—you've heard of Dr. Galen, right?—to get treated for it."

"Slick was Garza's man and infected with a genetically engineered virus," Zamora said, filing away the information with connections to the secretary in the vice president's office killed by a sudden illness and to the villagers on the periphery of Garza's territories who had died of a mystery disease. Rumors said Garza used bioweapons against the drug cartels but had problems keeping his own men free of infection and had to keep them supplied with temporary cures. The dead faces in the morgue wagon stared blankly in his memory. Did their cold blood contain the clue that would prove the connection between El Jaguar and the General?

"What are you thinking?" Mercury asked, watching his father's expression.

Zamora snapped back from the bloody jungle into the quiet, lonely living room. The house hadn't felt like home since Isabel died, since he had buried himself in training his soldiers to defend the delicate democracy that he and Isabel had worked so hard to build, since he had sent Michael Angel away—a vulnerable, rebellious child who in two years had turned into a young man with dark experiences and brilliant conviction in his eyes. "I'm thinking that you need to stay out of trouble here, because things have become very serious."

"I know. I also know what's really important now." Mercury nodded, then hugged his father tight.

Surprised, a vulnerable warmth as well as tightness in his chest, Zamora hugged his son back, wanting to hold on to him forever. He patted the kid's long hair, then gently let him go.

Mercury looked at the carpet for a moment, his own machismo forcing him to hide the bright tears in his eyes, then grinned. "So, what do you have to eat in this place? Or are we going out?"

"We're going out. As soon as you're cleaned up. You're lucky you got through airport security in that getup."

That earned a laugh. "You're the second person who's objected to my wardrobe today. I got through security on the apron strings of a nice, matronly lady. And I don't look that bad. Come on, let's go. If you'll spot me some cash, I'll even buy a suit tomorrow. Got to clean up anyway, if I'm going on splits with the missionaries."

"Splits?" Zamora looked at his son, pleased but puzzled. After Isabel died, Mercury had refused to have anything to do with the Church at all, totally rejecting his papa's assurances that God still loved them even though He'd let the cancer take her away and that the Church gave them the knowledge they needed to rejoin her forever. "With the missionaries. I'm pleased, but why?"

Mercury shrugged on his elaborately painted jacket and smiled. "I'm interested in joining God's army—even if I'm not disciplined enough to be a good recruit for yours."

"I think you'd do better than most, with this new attitude," Zamora said. "I just hope you don't have to."

* * *

Sinking into the luxurious leather cushions of a long, black limousine, Brother Light rubbed his eyes wearily. Sepphira reached over, gently rubbing his shoulders. He leaned into it for a moment, then shrugged her off when his crimson-masked bodyguard extended a blinking phone. "We hear you." A slow smile spread over his face as the voice spoke from thousands of miles away.

"You have chosen wisely," he said at last. "The One God will reward you richly with more wisdom." With a chuckle at the response to that statement, he clicked off the connection. "It seems that our friends at MedaGen feel they do not stand in need of wisdom—only of assured profits from their medical research facility. Which they have decided not to pull out of Manila, as they threatened to do."

Sepphira risked a smile, because Rashi was smiling too. It was good news; without the major multinationals' support, the economy in the Empire of Light would quickly unravel, taking its leader's aura of omniscient invulnerability with it. So far, Brother Light had proved exceptionally adept at prophesying the effects of the flow of money and greed through the international markets, and his expertise, combined with the incentives he could provide as god-emperor of a quarter of the globe, had quickly convinced the boards of those companies to throw their support behind the new regime, fascist theocracy or not.

"I told them I received stock tips from an angel, and they urged me to pray all the harder," Brother Light noted, a cynical light in his eyes, an ironic smile on his lips. He casually reached across to take Sepphira's hand in his. "So, my dearest sister in the Great Unity, what do our angels say tonight?"

Through the flush of pleasure at the good news, and at his pleasure in it, a slow chill spread from its dark burrow inside Sepphira's soul. She closed her eyes in pain. She knew what the CFOs and financial analysts believed, the rational explanation they used to explain Brother Light's uncanny ability to manipulate markets; they told each other that Brother Light's assistant Sepphira was a financial genius, talented at reinvigorating wobbly investments and assuring foreign stock-holding companies that the economy would only get better. Some of them had tried to contact her directly, to sway her from Rashi's side with promises of high salaries. Their attempts had failed, even the ones that got through the tight security net that the Hand of the Prophet drew closely around her; she would never leave Rashi. But even more, she could never tell them that her abilities to predict the vagaries of the stock market came directly from unseen but constant companions, the smoky figures that whispered to her from the dark corners.

Those ethereal creatures filled her with dread; she prayed every day that the One God would banish them, but without faith. She hated them, knew they hated her, wished them gone as much as they wished to tear at her—but she needed them, as much as they needed her. Without them, without their whispered advice, Rashi wouldn't need her anymore. She opened her eyes and turned to look into the far corner of the huge car.

"Choose MedaGen over BritPharm and open negotiations with WorldChem. Declare all religious property in the Philippines government assets, especially the Church farms and factories." Sepphira's voice sounded dead, all animation drained out of it as she relayed the message from the shadows. The spirits could be wrong, and occasionally lied, but in financial matters they rarely failed. They were nearly infallible in predicting—and influencing—the flow of money, which involved all the emotions they knew and used best: avarice, envy, anger, and fear.

Brother Light waited until she had finished to fire another question. "What about formally moving into the United States? Is it time yet?"

Sepphira shivered again, as the spirit laughed soundlessly, showing the emptiness behind its human-shaped facade. "Not yet. They only laugh. Not yet."

"They laugh." Anger flared in his eyes, then died away. He believed in the shadows who whispered to Sepphira, knew them as the opposition of the One God who had revealed itself to him—and believed that he could use them until they no longer provided an advantage, then dispose of them. He would have been surprised to know that they thought exactly the same about him. "How convenient that they're in a good mood. That should prove amusing for tonight's show, if they pick out the more entertaining victims—I mean spiritual seekers."

In that, at least, the shadows didn't disappoint him. Sepphira whispered tales of adultery, treachery, cheating, and hypocrisy to Rashi, as he called trembling, worshipful people out of the audience to reveal the messages that the One God had for each and every one of them. Thousands of miles away, ratings bars flickered; all over the world, Brother Light's reputation spread and grew along with the hopeful belief of the spiritually lost. And so did his power, his reach—and his ability to command not only the hearts but the minds and hands of an ever-growing army of followers.

* * *

"Despite the official doctrines of peace and unity that are at the heart of the Children of Light organization, its fundamentalist followers have stepped up their campaign of suicide bombings and shootings in northern China, India, and Australia. Statements from the bombers say that they are giving themselves to martyrdom to bring the Great Unity into countries that persecute true believers. Government sources in the affected areas believe that the upper echelon of the Children of Light are directing the members of the Hand of the Prophet on their bloody missions." Behind Clara rolled footage from an interview with Brother Light, highlighting the preacher's elegant self-assurance and accentuating his brilliant eyes. "The prophet of the movement, Rashi Janjalani, or Brother Light, denies official involvement."

"The One God is a god of peace, of truth and light," Brother Light explained. "That truth will eventually spread to all the world, overcoming all struggle. I can only say that I believe that justice will prevail because the Great Unity wills it, beyond the efforts of evil men to stop it—or the efforts of courageous spirits to spread the great Word."

"Neither an admission nor a denial from the leader of the Children of Light," Clara noted. "In other news, floods have devastated the southern Florida watershed, washing miles of wetlands into the ocean, while the Midwest still bakes under the worst drought since the dust bowl of the 1930s. Cal Weathers will have a full report on the nation's weather outlook in twenty minutes. Now, stay tuned for a Channel 8 special report on a threat potentially more devastating than drought or flood: 'Terrorism in the Heartland.'"

To the urgent drumbeat and discordant notes of Channel 8's "Domestic Terrorism Theme" rolled grainy, security-camera footage of the supposed terrorists: shadowy figures carrying bombs into subway tunnels, sniping at firefighters from tenement roofs, carrying suspicious packages into shopping malls, wearing painter's masks on trains.

"In the last two months, federal agencies all over the United States, from the FBI to the CIA to the office of homeland security, have been absolutely blanketed with electronic messages promising further violent attacks against 'soft targets.' And what have they done?" Senator Garlick glared at the reporters gathered behind the camera, glaring into the camera itself on behalf of all his frightened constituents. "Heightened the announced threat level? Yes, and that's all. They've brushed off the subway bombings, the church burnings, the violent attacks on legitimate shipping companies, the assassination attempts on our brave firefighters and police. This goes far beyond mere sloppiness or incompetence—bad enough in the best of times—this is criminal negligence that cannot be allowed to continue!"

Senator Cox's weary, patient face replaced Garlick's furious one. "Accusing the secretary of homeland security of criminal negligence for failing to stop any and all terrorist attacks is simply not realistic. How can any of us know what psychopaths are planning?" She spoke as she walked, the footage not from a formal press conference but from an impromptu interview in between Senate debates on further funding for the troops embroiled in the Ohalajishi conflict. The playback cut off abruptly, leaving the impression that she had given up even trying to defend innocent citizens against terrorist operations. It also didn't include her concern about Garlick's ever-broadening definition of "terrorism"; he applied the term to everything from terrorist-credited bombings to the increasing gang violence in cities all over the U.S.—which gave the secretary of homeland security wider powers than any branch of the government to investigate, prosecute, and even legislate. Her popular support, as recorded in the poll numbers running along the bottom of the screen in a neck-and-neck heat with Senator Garlick's, predictably fell.

And Garlick's rose as the Breaking News banner cut across the special report on terrorism—to report more terrorism. A renovated old hotel in a fashionably gentrified Chicago neighborhood had imploded during a conference on world trade, killing at least forty delegates and hotel workers, wounding at least as many more. As scenes of weeping, dust-covered civilians, shattered windows, and cracked masonry flashed by in a montage of pain and destruction, the inevitable claims of responsibility poured in—many of them directly to Channel 8.

* * *

"Anarchist Coalition Against World Monopolies?" Johnny Mack groaned, watching the updates scroll across the TV screen as Clara updated the initial reports with additional, equally overheated and inaccurate, information. "Man, that is so dumb!"

Augosto looked up from his PDA screen, wondering if his body-guard had actually picked up on the irony inherent in a coalition of anarchists, then sighed as Johnny Mack went into a profane rant about the media's gullibility in believing that a bunch of black-masked pansies could have used members of the Maintenance and Housekeeping Union to smuggle the implosion charges into the hotel. If Johnny had less talent as a bodyguard and hadn't been a nephew by marriage, he would have earned forcible retirement months ago.

"Agreed," Augosto wrote across the screen with a flourish, wrap-ping up the electronic negotiation with Travell Capshaw on trading laundered money, jewels, and gold for a shipment of weapons and explosives. Augosto had the money, but needed the armaments; Capshaw had money too, but could always use more, and he had ready access to weapons thanks to his thriving gun-running trade.

Beginning but not ending with the other West Coast gang lords, Capshaw was also extending his turf as far as he could, under cover of Garlick's command to create as much mayhem as possible. The mosque, synagogue, and church strikes that Capshaw's men carried out, along with an intensifying campaign of carjackings, barrio riots, and cop killings, increased support for Garlick's strong rhetoric condemning the current homeland security administration. Thanks to the intelligence Garlick's efficient secretary funneled to him, as she did to Augosto, Capshaw knew about law-enforcement efforts to apprehend him and his boys. Still, there were holes, and unless he was careful, he could fall in one. Until he became secretary of homeland security, Garlick didn't have full access to all intelligence reports. He assured Capshaw that his appointment drew closer every day; in fact, the old man had said that in another week, he would sweep into office on a wave of popular support, thanks in large part to the reign of terror Capshaw's and Augosto's private armies had so enthusiasti-cally implemented.

* * *

"And we've got a solid line." Hideyoshi grinned, waving at the tiny lens of the camera mounted above the banks of blinking lights in the secondary communications center of the International Space Station. Under the camera, a steady oscillation tracked the new, permanent, and encrypted transmission channel that connected the station to the Church's satellite network.

"What are you doing?" Mir poked her head into the doorway, incongruently upside down to Hideyoshi's present axis of orientation.

"Hooking up another land connection," Hideyoshi said shortly. He'd hoped to avoid hearing Ivana's opinion of this particular project, but fate (or karma or the universe's perverse sense of humor) went against him.

"Why's that your monkey? Wong usually takes care of the comm hookups—it's his job." The climatologist gave him a narrow-eyed look. "You're doing it because it's Mormon business."

Hideyoshi looked at Mir and sighed. "Yes, it's Mormon business, but it's station business too. I got Captain Nakima's permission to tie into the Church's satellite network, to send specific humanitarian-aid information to them about the floods and problems. The system is completely self-sufficient, encrypted, and fully backed up—and they'll let us use the network as a fall-back if our own communications fail."

"Like that would happen," Mir snorted.

"You're the climatologist. Think about the way the weather's going," Hideyoshi said, making the final adjustments. "And then think about what Wong was saying about the sunspot activity heating up. Even when you wear a belt, having a pair of suspenders handy is a good idea."

"In zero-g, you're talking about needing a belt. That makes exactly no sense." A speculative look replaced the scornful expression on her face. "But it got you comm access."

"Yes, it did," Hideyoshi agreed. "But—"

"But nothing." Mir grinned. "The captain gives you comm access, he can give me comm access."

"For what?" He shook his head. "Just because I've got it?"

She shrugged. "Oh, no particular reason—just in case I need it. You never know when a private line might come in handy. And if the captain gives me static about it, I'll say I talked to you about it. The last thing he needs is trouble about playing favorites, with all the stress around here."

Hideyoshi watched her glide smoothly away, wishing, not for the first time, that Ivana let her more pleasant personality traits out to play more often. She wasn't kidding about the rising stress levels on the station, with the insane weather and natural disasters back home delaying the last two shuttle flights, but some of the tension came from the emotional abrasion of psyches rubbing against each other too often for too long—and hers had more sharp edges than most. He sighed, silently wishing the captain luck in the imminent confrontation, then turned back to the camera, clicking on the Send/Receive switch. A flurry of static crossed the screen, then the glass panel treated him to a close-up view of the Church's chief communications technician, his blue-lit face distorted by the retro-chic fish-eye lens on the land side. "Hello, Salt Lake! How's the weather down there?"

"Hello, Spaceman!" Socks exclaimed. "Good morning, Dave— Jim. Captain, darling. Ground Control to Major Tom and all that." Hideyoshi's question bubbled to the surface of his attention, through the fog of ancient pop-culture nostalgia. "Weather?" the tech asked, blinking. "Just a sec, I'll check." Leaning over to eyeball another monitor, he announced, "Partly sunny and breezy. Why?"

"You're actually down there, and you have to check the readout on the screen to know that the wind's blowing?" Hideyoshi shook his head. The almost subliminal hum of the station's air-circulation fans grew suddenly louder in his ears as he thought longingly of a cool breeze rushing out of a sky full of patchwork clouds, a breeze that tasted of rain, dust, and plants instead of chemicals, plastics, and the rest of the crew. "Weather, like youth, is wasted on the young—and on young computer geeks."

"Sorry, gramps." Socks shrugged. "I've just got more to do down here than topside. Weather's not my thing." He patted the monitor affectionately. "This is. Woo hoo! The whole world in a box!"

"Brother Hideyoshi can see the whole world from a window," Socks mused after the transmission ended. Then, reaching for his keyboard with enthusiasm, he said, "But I do the same thing with just a few strokes of these keys."

Across the room, Fox rolled her eyes at her colleague's geeky enthusiasm—but she didn't exactly disagree. While she worked on her degree in computer science and information systems at MIT, she never thought she'd end up working at the old Church Office Building after grad school. She'd always envisioned herself working for a top-flight company, expertly running a multinational network. Interviewing for the positions available to a recent graduate with her sterling qualifications and reputation for implementing innovative solutions, however, had proved disillusioning, between the dismissive comments about Mormons and concerns about her willingness to engage in industrial espionage—not that they phrased it so bluntly. Her mother had sent the subtle job posting, hoping to bring her daughter back to the family stomping grounds. The prospect of working for the Church grew much brighter when an initial interview showed her that the Church had a lot more technology behind its gray-granite walls than most people, including her, would have dreamed. A full suite of satellites, providing communications coverage and data transmissions all over the world, independently powered and secured with an encryption system only slightly less sophisticated than the one Fox had created for her graduate project.

Now, she surfed the bits and photons for the Church, helping super-geek Socks secure a steady connection between the International Space Station and the Church's satellite network and figuring out how to filter sunspot interference out of global transmissions. "We're totally connected," she informed Socks. "Anything happens in the world now, we'll know about it."

* * *

"Does anyone know you're there?" Abbott leaned back in his soft leather chair, examining the perfectly polished points of the tooled cowboy boots he'd bought on MedaGen's credit card as a souvenir of his trip. If he had to spend a week in Boondock, Texas, for an international medical convention, the company could provide fashionable footwear—a bonus for running his own errands.

"Everybody does. We also appear on the venue surveillance tapes, as figures wearing distinctive jackets and hovering on the edges of the crowd entering the stadium." The answer came clearly through the secure private line even though the man on the other end spoke softly. "But only one old man saw us come out of the maintenance closet—the same one who heard us speaking some 'crazy foreign lingo.' Ready on your signal, sir."

Abbott smiled. For all Zelik's personal faults and professional ambitions, she knew how to recruit operatives for special corporate assignments. He half wondered who these guys were—ex-military, disillusioned by the lack of veterans' benefits coming from a nearly bankrupt government? Slick middle managers looking for a shortcut on their climb up the company ladder? Wanna-be commandos too psychotic to get past the psychological screening program for the special forces? He shrugged off the speculation; he'd never know, and it was just as well he didn't, just like he didn't know their names, faces, or, after a tiny tweak of MedaGen's phone records, their contact information. He didn't have to know—Zelik handled the hiring, and she'd take care of the payoff details. Glancing out the window at the sprawl of Dallas stretching away into the blank dusty expanse of Texas desert, he said, "Let's make our political friend a happy man. Start the party."

"Yes sir." The man in the orange-and-black striped jacket and matching face paint clicked off the connection and tucked the tiny phone back into his inside pocket. As he slipped out of the bathroom stall, the blank, bright-eyed expression on his face altered instantly to one of feverish excitement. He roared and thumped chests with another overexcited football fan as he charged out of the rest room, grabbed another overpriced, watered-down beer from the vendor, and ran back to his bleacher seat, as if he were eager not to miss any of the action. He hit his seat and high-fived his tiger-striped companion as the Alamo High School Tigers scored another amazing touchdown in the well-attended preseason exhibition game against their hated rivals, the Juarez Javelins.

As their hands came together, the tiny transmitters built into their souvenir Alamo High rings caught each other's signal, then broadcast the combined key to the third transmitter waiting with infinite electronic patience in the stadium's secondary maintenance room. The signal ran down two wires and started a tiny motor. The nozzle on the front of the box attached to the transmitter—and to the stadium humidifier equipment—turned on full. A nasty variant of a common pneumonia virus, engineered in MedaGen's labs to test the effectiveness of the AllSafe vaccine, sprayed into the pipes, mingling with the high-pressure combination of air and water pumping out to keep the fans cool in the unusually hot Texas weather. It poured invisibly over the endless stream of football addicts crowding into the concession area. It drifted down over the throngs making their way out of the stadium after the game ended, jubilantly cheering in orange and black or growling imprecations in royal blue.

Channel 8's first report on the big game featured footage of their local sports stringer standing in front of the overturned truck burning in the parking lot, a casualty of the brawl that erupted between two groups of well-lubricated fans, then spread through the streets around the stadium. It played as a sidelight of the weekly sports wrap-up. The second report on the aftermath of the game aired in prime news time and featured their much better-known medical specialist, Robert Silverman, standing in front of the regional hospital, breathlessly alerting viewers to the outbreak of a previously unknown, bioengineered strain of pneumonia.

By the time the first victim died—an elderly woman who had come to see her grandson's team play and whose already weak immune system succumbed to the viral attack within two days— claims of responsibility had already reached the police, the media, and the homeland security officers investigating the case. The rebel forces in Ohalajishi issued a statement condemning American military interference in the war ripping through the country and warned that further American action would result in further American casualties: "You kill our people, we kill yours."

You didn't need to have Monk's keen instinct for selling the news to know the story had legs, but it helped. He played it well, coming back to the spreading outbreak just enough to keep his viewers watching, but not enough to saturate their attention with so much detail that they turned the channel. Several of his competitors weren't so astute and either over- or underplayed the story—which was why Channel 8 consistently came out on top of the ratings heap.

"Twenty people have died in Middleton, Texas, in the first four days after the latest and worst bioterror attack in the United States. Two agents of rebel forces in the African nation of Ohalajishi were found dead in a motel some thirty miles away from Middleton, apparently killed by the very virus they unleashed on the unsuspecting football fans, according to reports from forensic specialists. The two men were identified as the terrorists directly responsible for the attack from surveillance footage and eyewitness testimony from a Mr. Beau Duffy, who saw them emerge from the maintenance closet. FBI investigators found a small device in that closet, which the terrorists used to spread the aerosolized virus through the stadium's air-conditioning system." Silverman summarized the current state of affairs for anyone who'd been in a coma for the last week. The story itself hadn't changed, except for the casualty numbers and the increasingly shrill denunciations of the authorities who had let such a thing happen.

"How do things look now, Robert?" Clara asked.

"Fifty-three more people have been hospitalized with symptoms including fever, dizziness, and severe respiratory distress." He looked casually rumpled, his hair slightly mussed to show the emotional and physical strain of attending the bedsides of the tragically ill during the intense media coverage of the tragedy. "Health authorities expect that number to rise, as the virus overcomes the natural defenses of other infected people."

"In all this bad news, there is a bright spot, isn't there?" Clara prompted.

"Fortunately, there is," Silverman agreed, neatly picking up his cue. "Attendees at the football game who had already been vaccinated with AllSafe have escaped infection. It appears that AllSafe has had its first major test, and it passed with flying colors."

"It certainly has. Thank you, Robert." Clara turned to the audience. "It looks like once-controversial public support for AllSafe has passed with flying colors as well. We'll be talking with Senator Howard Garlick, cosponsor of the Garlick-Benyanny Health and Security Bill that made AllSafe available to everyone in the country to prevent exactly this kind of tragedy. The political repercussions from this indefensible terrorist attack are likely to be as widespread as the medical ones."

Or even more so. The harried secretary of homeland security appeared in a news conference to confirm previous leaks about the origin of the virus—and the fact that both men appeared in their database (after the attack, anyway) as potential suspects. Speculation on the airwaves and Web sites and in offices and factories—to that point blaming CIA, South American commandos, even Mormons—changed to looking for holes in the official explanations coming from the Department of Homeland Security. No one thought to question the coroner's report; the fact that MedaGen's specialists did the diagnosis didn't even come up. Nor did the amazing incompetence of the team in finding a pneumonia virus to be the cause of death for the two major suspects when the immediate cause was extreme neck trauma. By the end of the week, common consensus laid the blame squarely on the secretary of homeland security, who couldn't even keep a high school football game safe from known international terrorists.

"Thank you," Senator Garlick said, as the microphone-wearing flunky appeared to tell him his interview would begin in five minutes. He adjusted his tie in the greenroom mirror, practicing his patriarchal frown and reassuring smile. They would ask him how it felt to have been absolutely right about the necessity of getting all citizens vaccinated with AllSafe; he would say that he only wished it were legally mandatory, to save even the few who died. They would ask him about the incompetence of the homeland security operation, missing a pair of known agents. He would argue against placing the blame on the overworked, well-intentioned homeland security agents and argue for combining all law enforcement, intelligence, and civilian defense under one agency to reduce the opportunities for potentially fatal confusion. They would ask whether that would be enough to guard against such attacks in the future. He would subtly shift blame to the current secretary of homeland security and declare again his willingness to shoulder the responsibility. And, on the swell of public support bursting from massive media coverage of a minor incident in flyover country, and a massive public-relations coup growing from a small event involving a handful of eminently expendable casualties, he would sweep into the office from which he would make himself the most powerful man in the nation.

"Careful, now, Howard," he reminded himself, quelling the swell of exhilaration he felt. "You haven't got the appointment yet." But he would soon; only a few hurdles still loomed in his path. Just before the flunky returned to lead him to the sitting-room set for the interview, his phone rang. He listened, smiling, as the vice president congratulated him and agreed to support his nomination, in return for Garlick's understanding in the matter of the vice president's rumored—and only marginally helpful, according to Augosto—ties to organized crime. Garlick heard him out, then simply said, "Thank you, sir. It is a pleasure to work with you." He hung up without answering the man's unspoken but burning question about where he'd found the evidence of Mob ties. One hurdle down.

Another fell dramatically, during Garlick's on-air interview, as the president fired the secretary of homeland security. Shortly thereafter, Garlick graciously accepted the nomination to replace the disgraced official.

The last hurdle thudded to the ground by the end of the week. Senator Holly Cox, the head of the Judiciary Committee and long-time opponent of Garlick's proposals, formally opposed his nomination, but she had no proof of her suspicions that he had engineered the nomination with methods even more underhanded than the usual political maneuverings, and she was too astute a politician herself to lay out unsubstantiated accusations. Thus, she based her objection on the ethical questions springing from Garlick's ties to MedaGen and his subsequent promotion of their AllSafe vaccine, as well as his stated intention to expand the office far beyond prudent or necessary bounds.

"While the senator is theoretically correct that a person with nothing to hide has nothing to fear from loss of privacy," she pointed out during a roundtable interview hosted by Channel 8's Darren McInnes, "the degree of actual damage depends on who has access to that private information. I don't think that's a difficult concept, and I'm sure nobody would argue that we need some protections. After all, none of us wants a thief to be able to look up our credit card numbers."

"Are you comparing the office of homeland security—and the federal government of the United States—to a thief?" Garlick asked, photogenically shocked and appalled at such a suggestion.

"More to a den of thieves," Senator Cox quipped, to the amusement of the spectator gallery.

Humor and solid arguments couldn't overcome Garlick's well-orchestrated cultivation (or blackmail or bribery, as appropriate) of the other members of the Washington pack, however. Garlick and his supporters met Cox's objections with tolerant smiles and lawyerly responses in the hearing chamber—and a barrage of personal attacks outside it. She never had the chance to directly respond to the accusations floating through the Senate chambers and over the airwaves that her opposition to Garlick's nomination and the AllSafe vaccine was based on direct orders from the Mormon cult leader, President Smith—or his foreign-born second in command, President Rojas.

Senator Garlick launched his career as the new secretary of homeland security with a speech promoting his homeland security initiative, which would give the secretary expanded powers of observation, authorization for registration programs, and control of state militias and national guards. To a nation of sheep terrified by the coyotes circling their pen, letting a wolf inside to protect them seemed like a good idea.

CHAPTER 14

Dear Chisom,

I am pleased to hear that you are preparing to go into mainland China, and I'm not a bit surprised that you are getting careful instructions on how to proceed. The Brethren feel we will have great success there. We have learned sad lessons from the way we did missionary work in the Philippines and South America a couple of decades ago. We know the lack of success that comes from baptizing large numbers before the people are converted. We also know the importance of having leadership in place. The sad lack of retention of new members we've seen before will not happen in China. I am glad, therefore, that your instructions stress conversion, not baptism, as your main goal. That way, President Smith feels, the Church will balance growth with leadership. Initially, a large number of the current Seventy will take up residence there to train and guide. Eventually, China will come into its own.

I am sorry to hear of the persecutions some of our Taiwanese Saints are suffering. You asked how long the Church must take the persecutions before we fight back. We have a number of members, some in important positions, who say the time is now. The mob that hit the ward in Spartanburg three Sundays ago proved what we feared—that we can be targets. It also shows how much some people hate us. Fortunately, no one was killed, but with seven of the Saints hospitalized and two in critical condition, we can't rejoice. This event elevated the cry of our more militant members. We hear that in some areas, groups are forming and arming themselves. The Brethren are doing all they can to stop such activity and with good reason. We can't win, for the Lord has not commanded us to move. Until He does, He will not sustain us.

God showed John the Revelator that the Saints would be in for a rough time for a bit. He notes that those who receive the mark of the beast (that is, play by Satan's rules) and worship his image (acute materialism) "have no rest day nor night." Their greed, avarice, desire for power, and, most of all, their pride, continually drives them. Because the Church stands in their way, we will bear the brunt of much of their nervous energy. It is in this context that John says, "Here is the patience of the saints: here are they that keep the commandments of God, and the faith of Jesus" (Rev. 14:11–12). In other words, this is the time we must do as the Lord commands through His prophets no matter how hard that will be. It will demand great patience to do so, but that is our calling.

The scriptures are very clear on the role of the Saints in the last days, and it is, indeed, primarily passive. We are not to fight but to have faith in God. The Apostle John put it this way: "He that leadeth into captivity shall go into captivity; he that killeth with the sword must be killed with the sword. Here is the patience and the faith of the saints" (Rev. 13:10). The Seer's point is clear. There will be a brief time when God will not protect every righteous soul, when He will permit the dragon to have his moment at the expense at of the Saints. During that time, God's people are forbidden to launch an aggressive war or one that could be interpreted as aggressive. The Lord will not help those who do so. The Saints' greatest trial during this period is having to practice restraint and to wait for the Lord to move. Yes, that waiting is taking, and will continue to take, a lot of faith and patience, even, unfortunately, a few lives, but that is what the Lord expects. That is not to say that the Lord will not help at all. We have numerous reports of miraculous events occurring to protect the Saints in various areas. For example: lightning hit a mob leader and the mob scattered, members hiding in a barn were unseen by thugs sent to roust them out, firebombs hit a house and none exploded. And the list goes on. I'll share others with you when you get home.

Let me assure you, Chisom, the Lord knows what He is doing. As surprising as it may seem, evil is supposed to have its day. We are now in the period of the beasts of Revelation whose rule is for 1,260 days—that's three and a half lunar years. I take the number symbolically and look at its implications. It is half of seven, suggesting that which is interrupted in its course to perfection, an excellent symbol of Satan and the period in which he rules. This condition squares well with Daniel, who notes that the opposition to God's people will continue for "times, time, and a half time," or, in other words, Revelation's three and a half years. It would seem that we are now in the period when evil has control and is essentially unopposed. What you must get clear is that wickedness is supposed to have the upper hand, to do its work almost unhindered, at least for the time being.

John shows us that the task of the Church is neither to heal Babylon nor to actively fight against her. She is to grow fat and sassy, to become ever more arrogant and strong, to remain ignorant that the day of her destruction rapidly approaches. The task of Church members is to flee Babylon, preach the gospel in all the world, assist in perfecting the Saints, continue the work for the dead, and move toward that purity that will bring again Zion.

In Revelation, neither the 144,000 nor the remainder of the Saints take any part in any opposition to Babylon, the dragon, the beast, or the false prophet.

The Saints are absent from all battlefields. The 144,000 are engaged only in gathering out those who will come to the Church of the Firstborn. The only task Revelation assigns to the Saints is to worship God (not the beast), to endure in faith and patience, to withstand persecution, and to preach the gospel.

Evil really is to have its day. Therefore, the Church, for the present, is concerned mainly with its own internal interests, strengthening its doctrinal foundations and theological ramparts, bringing into its fold all those who will come, and leaving the world to build that hell in which it will all too soon perish.

All of that is not to say that the Saints cannot defend themselves and their property. They certainly can and should. In some instances the difference between protection and aggression may blur, but local inspiration and counsel from headquarters should clear things up. If push comes to shove, the Saints are free to act, but must never be the aggressors. The same is true for the general Church. We will wait for the Lord. The Church may have to protect itself, but, let me stress, it will not be the aggressor.

Let me say again that the Lord knows what He is doing. He is aware of His faithful children, and He has prepared a way for their escape. In the meantime, as I noted above, we must wait in faith and patience.

President Smith tells us that your area will be spared all this for a while so that the Lord can get a foothold for His Church before the end comes. So work hard, love the people, and enjoy what peace you will have.

With love,
Your father,
Chinedu

* * *

"It's about time we escaped this mess." Lucrezia thumped a box of towels onto the growing stack of boxes in the back of the small rental trailer, furiously expressing her views to the only person who hadn't told her to suck it up and be brave today—herself. "But dragging a trailer behind the van? All the way across the country for days and days of watching Gianni's video collection? Ugh! Stupid Garlick and stupid airports and stupid-idiot terrorists."

The Callattas found out a week before that they'd have to drive to Illinois. The airline clerk gave them the bad news—the Callatta family wasn't eligible to fly, due to homeland security restrictions on "biological risks." Since Senator Garlick's appointment and the strict enforcement of the Garlick-Benyanny Health and Security Bill, that classification now included anyone not vaccinated with AllSafe. Never mind that the Callattas posed no real risk to those who had received the vaccine. The Callattas weren't flying anywhere, and Lucrezia was taking it personally.

Turning to stomp back into the house, she nearly tripped over Gianni, who had set up a toy-car freeway on the short metal ramp into the trailer. "Gianni, how do you make messes so fast? Mom!" she yelled. "Can we please pack up Gianni's stupid trucks before he breaks my neck?"

"And add a screaming Sunbeam to the rest of the chaos around here?" Donna shot back, scooping up Gianni and his traffic jam, and taking the lot back into the house, where she settled him down in a box-sheltered corner. Lucrezia followed, growling under her breath as she picked up another box.

Tony didn't bother to keep his growl under his breath. He nearly ran down Lucrezia as he barreled into the house. They traded a bared-teeth glare and continued on their separate ways. "Carmen!"

"In here," Carmen called from the kitchen. She sighed, stacking silverware into a box and wiping out the drawers as she talked to the Relief Society president on the phone. "No, we've got it all—well, I was going to say under control, but I better say 'underway' instead. And the moving company will come to pick up what we've packed. If you could just let them in on Tuesday, that'd be great." A glance at the flush on Tony's face as he came to a fuming halt in the kitchen doorway, and she finished the conversation in a hurry. "I know—I'll miss you too, Soon Yi, but we've got to go where the jobs are. Thanks so much for watching the house until it sells."

"She won't have to," Tony said flatly—then slammed his fist into the wall.

"Gotta go. I'll let you know." Carmen clicked off the phone and dropped the rest of the knives back in the drawer as she rose to face Tony. "What? And be careful—you've put a dent in the wall! We're trying to sell the house, not demolish it."

Tony looked at the dent, smiled, and hit the spot again. This time, his fist cracked the sheetrock.

"Are you nuts? What are you doing?" Carmen lunged forward and caught his hand, checking it for damage and then holding onto it. She felt the tension in him, muscles tense under the skin. "What happened? Tony, why doesn't she need to watch the house?" Her own eyes darkened, but she tried for a light tone. "It's not going to sell, is it? 'Cause we're Mormons who've infected the place with the plague, and no reputable real estate agent is going to bring any poor lambs in here?"

"No." Tony's shoulders slumped; he didn't smile at Carmen's hyperbole. "No, we're not selling it. MedaGen slapped a lien on our house." He held up a registered letter. "We can't sell it, this letter says, unless we come up with fifty thousand dollars to pay off the lien. That means we have to hire a lawyer to kill it for us—and persuade a judge that the complainant doesn't have a legitimate case against us, if we can find a judge who'll listen. MedaGen's trying to keep us here where they can get at us more easily."

Lucrezia and Donna, who had run to the kitchen when they heard the thuds, stood there wide-eyed, watching their parents. Even Gianni came, sensing something was wrong and leaning against his sisters' legs.

Along with everybody else, Carmen felt her stomach sink. Fifty thousand dollars—impossible. They'd scraped, saved, and pushed to pay off their first home, and they'd burned through their reserves in the last year. This meant starting over in Illinois with no equity from this house. She summoned up her stubborn determination. Surf it or drown, baby, as her daddy used to say. And after a life full of sudden reversals, she hung ten like a pro.

"That's it!" She tossed the cleaning rag into an empty drawer. "We're not doing any more cleaning."

Donna and Lucrezia looked at each other. Another rag poofed up between them. They looked down at Gianni, who laughed like a loon. Donna shrugged, grinned, and tossed her own cleaning rag. It caught on the ceiling fan. Lucrezia looked disbelieving.

So did Tony, until the pleading look in Carmen's eyes broke through the emotional hurricane roaring through him. He grinned, looked around at the half-packed kitchen, and jumped out of the waves and onto the surfboard. "Well, if you don't give this disaster area your white-glove treatment, we can get out by one. I'll get the pizza."

Carmen grinned and thumped a box into his chest. "Lucrezia can get the pizza. You can start carrying the heavy stuff out to that trailer. And stack it tight, 'cause anything that doesn't fit stays here for the moving guys to pick up. That's one advantage of working for Softlearn—we just have to haul the essentials ourselves."

That suggestion brightened Lucrezia's day, even if Donna did have to go with her as she drove to the cheap take-out place, just in case a cop stopped them and Lucrezia had to flash her learner's permit.

The border-patrol agent who stopped the Callatta family car and its mini-trailer at the California-Nevada checkpoint wasn't interested in a learner's permit. He looked at Tony's ID, checked the car for produce and drugs, made Tony open the trailer door—then backed off, intimidated by the scientific packing job that rivaled the stonework of the Incas. He couldn't have slipped a piece of paper between those boxes.

He sneered and tossed the paperwork back at Tony. "That your food storage, Mo? Gonna take over Missouri with the rest of your buddies?" He leaned over as Tony got into the car. "Not that we care where you go, long as you're taking your germs with you."

His partner in the glass booth sniggered. Both their sniggers turned to growls as the van pulled away and Lucrezia leaned out of the back window to yell, "Last Mo leaves, the barbecue's gonna start. You're gonna sizzle, pork chops!"

Gianni sang a random song about pork chops until he fell asleep in his car seat.

* * *

"Do you have difficulty falling asleep? Do you feel tired all the time?" the radio announcer asked in the bored sing-song of yet another ad during the news. "Both of these are symptoms of depression. If you have these symptoms and are between the ages of eighteen and forty, you may be eligible to join a nationwide clinical trial for a new drug to combat depression. Check MedaGen's Web site for details."

"Seems like everybody out there's got the deep blue somethings—and if they don't get a lift from MedaGen, they're hitting the doobies," the DJ observed. "Bet they're raking it in down at MedaGen."

"They are, judging by the record levels of antidepressant prescriptions," the announcer responded. "At home and abroad, hopelessness seems to be growing, and a syndrome that some psychologists have dubbed 'industrial malaise' has cost corporations and governments tens of millions of dollars in medical insurance payments, lost work, and suicide—which has gone up steeply in the last few years. Suicide shops are open twenty-four hours a day in Scandinavia and do a brisk business."

"So, what do you wear to one of those places?" the DJ asked. An edge had crept into his voice. "I mean, you can really decide what you'd be caught dead in, right?"

The announcer ignored him, letting the prerecorded laugh track react to the stupid jokes. "Japanese authorities report rising suicide rates as well, attributed to growing despair among lonely people as the traditional family disintegrates."

"Who writes that stuff for you? You're sounding, like, poetic or something." The DJ shuffled papers, sounding as if he'd snatched the script from his straight-man partner. The papers hit the wall and dropped, and he dropped the fake-droll radio voice. "Let's dump the poetry and talk about something real for people around here. People don't have to kill themselves; other people will do it for them. Everywhere you look, things are getting tougher: inner city, countryside, suburbs—all have roving gangs. Wars all over the world have burned out cops and toasted armies. There's even mobs of nutball farmers burning other farmers' houses out in the Midwest. So, let's get into it. Toss the script. Should the U.S. bring the troops home to keep peace in Illinois?"

Tony turned off the radio, looking through the bug-splattered windshield at the quiet plains around them. "Looks peaceful enough to me." He glanced at the rearview mirror. Donna had sacked out with her book in her lap, Lucrezia leaned against the seat belt, lost in the world inside her headphones, and Gianni fiddled with the chest strap on his car seat, trying to unbuckle it. They all looked as sick of this eternal van ride as he was.

Carmen smiled at him. "Sure does. Downright boring, even. Illinois looks a little different than Kansas, but not all that much. At least it's a little greener. All that dead corn got hard to take."

"Hey! Look!" Lucrezia suddenly came back to Earth, pointing excitedly at the green highway sign. "Lake Creek, five miles. We're nearly there!"

"Good timing too," Tony observed, checking the gas gauge. The battery looked good, but the internal-combustion side of the hybrid engine needed more fuel. According to the map Bishop Newstead sent—along with a warm welcome, a list of apartments to check, and the address of the church—two freeway exits led to Lake Creek. It was pretty easy to decide which to take; at the first one, the brilliant red and blue of a gas station sign showed through the green of the trees.

Lucrezia disdainfully said that the service station itself looked like something out of an old movie—a bad one with a lot of roughs in it. She had a point, starting with the name of the place: Beauregard's Pit Stop. A collection of neon beer signs glowed in the windows and behind the register, complimenting the antique cigarette and chewing-tobacco ads. Jerky, candy, overpriced groceries, a small selection of sporting goods, and various rural sundries crowded the shelves. The smell of overdone hot dogs rolling on hot metal treads competed with the pervading odor of old coffee, dust, and motor oil. Two overall-clad men, owners of a pair of pickup trucks parked outside, leaned over the counter and chatted with the proprietor, while a couple of younger, long-haired men in grubby baseball caps (Raiders and Buccaneers) poked through the selection of magazines, leering over the pictures of Virginia Diamante and her fellow pop stars that filled half of the rack.

"Coming in from out of state." The counterman didn't ask, just stated the obvious, surveying the Callattas with expressionless disapproval.

"Sure enough," Tony agreed, counting out cash for gas—and slushies for the kids and Carmen, who had headed to the back of the store in pursuit of Gianni.

"Staying or moving on?" the old-timer on the left asked, blowing a thin stream of pipe smoke toward Tony's wallet and California driver's license.

"Staying," Tony said, his cheerful tone belying the cold glint in his eyes. "We're heading for Lake Creek, just down the road there."

That caught the attention of all five of the locals, bringing the scruffy pair of football billboards around the magazine racks. The other old-timer glanced through the window at the license plate on the grubby van. "California, huh? What you want 'round here?"

"I've got a job over at Softlearn. It's the educational software outfit in town." Tony glanced from one hard face to the next, then caught Carmen's eye and gave her a subtle "come here" signal.

She nodded, passing the look to the girls, who obediently and casually, without the least bit of sidling, moved to where Carmen was standing, keeping the shelves of high-intensity sugar and fat between them and the suddenly threatening locals looming around the counter. Gianni, however, had other ideas. Unwilling to relinquish his freedom quite yet, he took a good grip on his slushie cup and ran for it, giggling mischievously. Carmen grabbed for him, and just missed the back of his coveralls as he cornered around a display of ball caps. She caught up on the straightaway though, snatching Gianni up and swinging him around.

The swing—and the laughing remonstrance that accompanied it—came to a sudden halt as Carmen came up short to avoid smacking into one of the greasy, long-haired men. She backed a couple of steps, giving the Raiders fan a glare that had backed off salesmen, Great Danes, and more than one principal. It didn't work this time. The guy's leering gaze traveled from her face to the front of her white shirt, tight against her chest due to her hold on Gianni. The leer got even nastier when he saw the outlines of her garment top through the light fabric. "Well, lookee here. We got ourselves a little bunch of Mormons."

Carmen moved to avoid his hand. "You've got yourself nothing, bubba," she growled.

"We don't need no more Mormons around here." The other long-hair, the Buccaneer, matched her growl. "Screwing up the place for the rest of us, sucking up all the money in the county. Reverend Lebaron's got it right." He stepped forward menacingly and grabbed for Carmen. "Gonna show you what we do to you—"

Tony's fist cracking into his face interrupted the incipient stream of profanity and started a general pile-on. Carmen ducked out of the way and ran for the door, but not before she'd kicked the feet out from under the idiot who'd tried to grab her. Donna held back Lucrezia, preventing her from charging in. Tony staggered under the weight of one of the old-timers who'd jumped on his back, but managed to whirl heavily around and use the man as a shield as the Buccaneer aimed a roundhouse blow at his face. The Raider, threshing on the floor, lashed out with a foot and tripped Tony. The four of them crashed into a writhing heap on the grubby floor.

The store manager pulled a shotgun from under the counter, waving it threateningly and shouting profane threats and warnings. He bellowed even less coherently as Lucrezia's slushie cup bounced off his shoulder, the cap popping off to drench him in fluorescent-green ice. Donna grabbed her little sister and hauled her out of the way, up against the glass cooler doors. Carmen ran over to join her girls. Gianni began to wail.

Tony planted a palm against the nose of the Raider and wrenched his leg away from the pugnacious old-timer. He got two steps toward the door when Carmen shouted a warning. He had just time to half turn and tumble to the floor again, taking a display of beer cans with him, barely avoiding the baseball bat that the Buccaneer had liberated from the sporting-goods bin. The second blow connected, however, thunking into Tony's shoulder even as he rolled. Tony yelped, grabbing a can of beer and slamming it into the Raider's head. Foam burst out, soaking all of them. The Buccaneer slipped, then recovered, showing his teeth in a triumphant grimace as he swung the bat up again with a curse.

With a roar, the slushie machine behind his head exploded, sending a geyser of Day-Glo frozen juice splattering over the combatants, the ceiling, and the mess of merchandise—and nearly braining the bat-wielding tough as the heavy spinner arm spun free. The proprietor stared at his gun for a second, but he hadn't taken the safety off.

Across the store, a curl of gun smoke rose from the barrel of another shotgun. Three figures stepped through the doorway. One of them grinned, blowing the smoke away, then leveling the shotgun again with the ease of long practice. "One shot down, five to go. So, who's next?"

The dogpile on the floor broke up abruptly, the ex-brawlers scattering for cover in the short aisles. Tony didn't bother with hiding; he launched himself toward his family at the back of the store, throwing over a pastry case as he went. Carmen caught his arm, pulling him to the display-case door as Donna tossed the last rack aside and stepped into the large cooler behind it. Carmen handed Gianni through and stepped in herself. Tony grabbed Lucrezia, who had frozen in place, staring at their trio of tall, blond rescuers.

"Hey, Rock, why don't you shoot a pirate?" suggested one of his companions, showing his teeth and bouncing eagerly on his toes.

"Darn it, Rock, if you—" the shopkeeper bellowed.

"If I what?" Rock yelled back, swinging the barrel of the gun around and blowing another rack to pieces right over the Buccaneer's head. Particles of plastic and potato chips drifted down.

"You want to play with some Mormons?" his wide-eyed sidekick shouted. "Come play!"

"Come this way," another voice called. Donna whirled, to see the third boy motioning through the open delivery door at the back of the cooler. "They'll realize it's just Rock and Orrin in a minute—time to get out while they're still scared, huh?"

"Right." Tony shoved Lucrezia toward the door. When she saw the boy standing there, she put on her own burst of speed.

The Callattas ran into the parking lot, piled into the van, along with the blond-haired boy, who Lucrezia had firmly by the hand, and blasted out of the drive as quickly as the van and trailer could go. A few seconds later, the other two bounded out of the store, Rock shooting over his shoulder. The plate-glass window on the front of the store erupted into billions of glittering fragments that fell as the boys' truck roared after the van. Both vehicles bounced along the ragged-edged rural road, then the truck gunned past the trailer and paced Tony on the driver's side.

Orrin leaned out of the truck's window, yelling, "Follow us—we'll take you right on home!"

Rock pulled ahead, leading the way, signaling well in advance before taking a sharp left onto another, even smaller and much more discreet road.

"How soon until the sheriff's on our tails?" Tony asked, glancing at the blond boy sitting next to Lucrezia in the middle seat.

The kid smiled, the sad cynicism of the expression out of place on a face that young. "Oh, he won't be chasing us. Old Beauregard won't even call the sheriff; this is between the locals and the Mormons. Sheriff isn't going to get in the middle of it." He glanced at Lucrezia, then Carmen, a hint of worry replacing the smile. "Nah, anybody chases us, it'll be the Perry boys—the ones in the baseball caps. They're Beau's nephews. They came up here from Alabama years ago, along with most of Lebaron's followers transplanted from the South. Bishop Newstead should'a told you not to get off that first exit—and about the problems around here. But he, well, he doesn't agree with Daddy about how serious things are."

"Things sure looked serious back there," Lucrezia said, starry-eyed. "What's your name?"

"Oh, sorry—I'm Porter. Porter Smith." He nodded to them all, managing to include Donna and Gianni in the back, Tony and Carmen in the front, and especially Lucrezia next to him. "Good to meet you all. We heard the Callattas were coming in today. Glad to have you."

"Glad you expected us. Enough to come in loaded for bear." Tony glanced back at Porter, overtly skeptical but impressed underneath it.

Carmen was more worried than impressed—yes, the Smith boys' sudden appearance had probably saved their bacon, but the ease with which Rock shot up the store, and Orrin's wild enthusiasm, made her uneasy. So did the intent, under-the-lashes stare Lucrezia turned on Porter. "How did you know we were coming?" Carmen asked. "And how did you get there so quickly?"

* * *

"I sent them." Brother J. H. Smith smiled warmly, rubbing Rock's shoulder with paternal pride as he expanded on Porter's brief answer to Carmen's question. "Had 'em watching the gas station just in case things got out of hand. The lions of Israel bounding to the rescue of a sweet family of lambs."

He gazed happily at the Callattas, seated around the long, scrubbed trestle table in the Smith family's large and very crowded farmhouse. He, his wife, the three boys, and three more girls had welcomed them with open arms and an extremely insistent invitation to lunch. Brother Smith presided at the head of the table with Rock and Porter to either side, while Sister Smith and the girls served an abundant, down-home lunch to the Callattas, the men of the house, and a half-dozen members of their ward who'd gathered to welcome the newcomers.

Tony's fork paused halfway to his mouth at Brother Smith's livestock comparison, but good manners won out. "It's lucky your lion cubs turned up when they did."

"Luck had nothing to do with it," Brother Smith assured him. "The good Lord saw fit to inspire me, and I acted on that inspiration to snatch you from the clutches of those corrupt Gentiles."

Donna shared a glance with Carmen, silently agreeing that the boys' miraculous arrival had more to do with knowing that strangers would be most likely to take the first exit, unaware of the rifts splitting the local communities down religious, or maybe cultural, lines. Lucrezia didn't get in on the skeptical telepathy; she was too busy playing eyeball tag with Porter across the table. The rules were simple and required no explanation; they came naturally to teenagers with crushes. Lucrezia gazed at Porter until Porter looked back, whereupon she instantly looked away and Porter looked at her, until she looked at him—they looked like spectators at a tennis match played in extreme slow motion.

"Good thing too," growled Brother Hunt. "Those Perry boys are Gadiantons through and through. We ought to run them out of the county for good, and that criminal Beauregard with them!"

"Now, now," Brother Smith cautioned, his tone remonstrative but his expression approving. "We'll cleanse this county of evil in the Lord's good time." He looked solemnly at Tony and Carmen. "I'm sorry to say that you've landed in a very hot spot here."

With Brother Hunt and Rock chiming in with details and furious editorial comments, Brother Smith laid out the situation around—

and increasingly inside—the town of Lake Creek. Crop failures from the drought and the drawn-out death of the manufacturing plant, which had been Lake Creek's largest employer and original reason for being, provided the fuel for an explosive situation. The influx of Mormons, drawn by Lake Creek's proximity to Nauvoo and the burgeoning information industry, added the spark that set the tinder alight. News reports of church fires and hate-crime vandalism only partially captured the situation, as hotheaded members of the Millennium Brotherhood, including the Perry family, and equally stubborn, Revelation-quoting Mormons—Brother Smith's boys and associates first among them—took potshots at each other in the farms, fields, and woods around town.

The most extreme hotheads, despite their Inquisition-level rhetoric, kept their activities mostly confined to the cover of darkness and the rural back roads, erupting out of the darkness to torch each other's hayricks and outbuildings or deliver a nasty beating to anyone on the opposite side stupid enough to wander out alone. Brother Hunt had converted to the Smiths' brand of apocalyptic vigilantism after the Perry boys blew up his barn. Others had drifted or leapt into Brother Smith's orbit through hostile encounters like the Callattas' unpleasant introduction to the area at Beauregard's; many of the younger guys sneaked out to join Rock Smith in raids to "punish the Amulonites." Occasionally, the running battle flared up in town as well, especially between the radical teenage and twenty-something members of both sides, but the sheer population pressure of more straight-arrow (or, as Brother Smith termed them, "lukewarm") Mormons, plus the presence of a large number of law-abiding Gentiles and truly Christians souls, kept the outright brawling to a minimum inside city limits.

The sheriff, as the ranking law-enforcement official in the area outside Lake Creek, had unofficially declared himself neutral, keeping out of the conflict for political reasons. If he defended the Mormons and arrested the Gentiles, he'd lose the support, and votes, of the non-Mormon citizens; if he arrested the Mormons, he'd lose their votes, an important consideration, as more of them poured into the older areas of Lake Creek to work at Softlearn and the other high-tech outfits they started. Plus, he'd face Elder Jack DuPris, who had already hinted to both the sheriff and the mayor that any blatant discrimination against Mormons would result in a well-financed, high-powered legal battle, and rumor had it that he'd been courting the governor of Illinois too. Given all the ramifications, the sheriff and the Lake Creek police chief, who had faced the same concerns, had both decided that as long as they kept the conflict to property damage and minor assaults, discretion truly was the better part of valor. They sat out the conflict, issuing periodic general warnings about vigilantism and watching the situation uneasily, hoping that the Mormons would give up in the face of constant harassment and leave on their own. So far, it hadn't happened. In fact, more kept coming.

"And that's going to save us," Brother Smith declared. "More faithful soldiers marching to build up the shining walls of Zion."

"Bishop Newstead mentioned that there was some tension between members and nonmembers here, but no worse than it is anywhere else," Tony said.

"That's because Bishop Newstead, who I fully sustain as a judge in Israel and respect as a well-meaning man of God, doesn't have the faintest idea about what's going on out here in the lands on the borders of the Lamanites. Unlike our bishop, Bishop Calvin, who is a man of peace but understands the need for war. He has had several conversations with Bishop Newstead, attempting to make him realize the truth of the situation, but to no avail. The man lives in downtown Lake Creek, where the Gadiantons haven't clamped down the iron fist of persecution. He's not seen the vision yet, but he will. Just wait, until Lebaron sends his forces against those pretty little townhomes. Then he shall see the error of his ways, understand his blindness, and lament the wounded and dead of his people. Oh, woe to those who say all is well in Zion!"

That statement earned a round of fervent agreement from the rest of the group.

Brother Smith bowed his head then picked up the thread again. "Our Area Authority, Elder Jack DuPris, now, he's more tuned in to the sad reality around here. And when he calls us, as faithful elders, part of the 144,000 pure priesthood holders enlisted in the army of the Lord, we'll be there to answer his call! We will be the tools He uses to work His miracle of protection."

Brother Hunt enthusiastically agreed, chiming in with an "Amen!" as the others nodded.

Brother Smith smiled benignly at his acolytes. "Momma," he added, the heat in his voice disappearing as he sat back and bestowed an approving smile on his wife, "you've worked a miracle of your own on these biscuits."

Carmen agreed that the biscuits deserved the heavenly description, but she took the rest of the conversation with a grain of salt. A large grain. Brother Smith humbly mentioned that he was named after both Joseph and Hyrum Smith, as well as being a cousin to the current President Smith. He didn't bother to say he was a distant cousin—or that he believed the gift of revelation, if not the hereditary right to high ecclesiastical office, ran in the family. He poetically expressed full confidence not only that these were indeed the last days, but that he had a vital part to play in gathering and defending Zion from the ravages of the beast, the dragon, and the corrupt gentile government. He proclaimed it all calmly, occasionally raising a gentle, chuckling objection when Brother Hunt's heated comments of support got too hot, but clearly basking in the adoration of his family and followers.

"That guy is beyond nutty," Carmen told Tony through a polite smile, as they pulled out of the Smiths' long driveway, waving back at the Smith family. "Absolutely certifiable."

"Mom!" Lucrezia exclaimed. "How can you say that? He sent Porter—and the other boys—to save us from those creeps!"

"Saved!" Gianni chimed in.

"Oh, please!" Donna said. "Just because you've got a huge crush on Porter doesn't mean you have to defend his maniac father."

Carmen nodded, looking back at Lucrezia, preempting her chance to argue. "Honey, that guy has some seriously bent ideas—and sending his boys out to tangle with psychotic rednecks is proof of it."

Tony grinned, but the smile had a sharp edge that matched the dull ache burning in his shoulder. He agreed with the girls' assessment of Brother Smith's probable mental state, but the thought of Brother Smith's posse wreaking violent havoc on Beauregard and his sleazebag buddies appealed to his wounded pride, hurt shoulder, and lingering fear for his family's safety. The combination prompted him to play devil's advocate. "Is he a maniac because he claims to get revelations? This from a woman who says she's experienced inspirations and outright divine intervention? Is it his ideas that got under your skin, or the way he treats his wife?"

"Ugh!" Donna said. "Both! What a total Cro-Magnon."

"Both," Carmen agreed. "But more that he's upset at this Reverend Lebaron person for inciting riots while he's doing exactly the same thing. More important, his language sounds a lot more aggressive than defensive."

"He probably takes things too far," Tony said. "But you can see where he's coming from on fighting back. Things are pretty tense around here, with that Reverend Lebaron preaching death to all Mormons and the sheriff refusing to uphold the peace. Those Perrys weren't kidding, Carmen. Seems to me that Brother Smith and his friends have got plenty of reasons to take a militant stand."

"Led by a guy who's claiming to receive revelations about Armageddon happening right here in Illinois?" Carmen shook her head.

"And calls his wife Momma?" Donna added.

"Let's get into town fast, Tony. Bishop Newstead seemed like a reasonable person, and it's way too hot out here." Carmen suppressed a shudder, rubbing Tony's shoulder, remembering the bat cracking down. *Oh, please, Heavenly Father*, she prayed silently, *please keep us safe, help us that this move will work out all right*. A flicker of reassurance warmed the chill in her stomach but didn't banish the deep worry and foreboding lurking in there.

"Town it is," Tony agreed. "And the first thing I'm going to do is buy a gun, just in case."

"First thing?" Carmen asked.

"Third thing," Tony said, after a moment's thought. "First thing, get you all settled in one of these apartments Bishop Newstead found for us. Second, get a license to carry. Third, get a gun."

"Does Illinois still let citizens have guns?" Donna asked.

"Orrin has a gun," Lucrezia said. "I bet he could tell us where to get one if they don't."

"Dad's not going to ask Orrin Smith where to get an illegal gun," Donna said.

Carmen tuned out the sisterly argument that followed, watching the road from the Smiths' farm into downtown Lake Creek for any signs of pickup trucks, baseball caps, and shotguns. Fortunately, none appeared, but she noticed that Tony didn't second Donna's denial. Beneath the inevitable Callatta family banter, they were all shaken by the confrontation at the gas station—and by not only Brother Smith's apocalyptic attitude, but the fact that at least four other men, besides the vocal Brother Hunt, either believed him or felt threatened enough to join his crusade against the Gentiles in spite of—or because of—his prophecies.

The sight of a traffic light on a real intersection made them all feel better; for confirmed urbanites, having solid pavement under their wheels and brick buildings passing by the windows felt like waking from a hayseed-intensive nightmare. The sight of Bishop Newstead, the tall, slightly stooped, bespectacled CFO for Softlearn who warmly welcomed them into his home, reassured them too.

"Yes. Brother Smith." The bishop sighed, rubbing a long hand over his face after Tony and Carmen told him about their adventure at the gas station—and their rescuers. "I believe he means well, but he simply won't see that when you try to fight fire with fire, everybody gets burned. We're far better off working with the rest of the citizens of the community to stand against toughs like the Perry boys and Samuel Lebaron than polarizing everybody even more by burning churches ourselves. It's gone clear up to the Area Authority level, and probably past that to the Brethren, but all we can do is take care and follow the Lord's instructions. There are a lot of good people here in Lake Creek, in and out of the Church, but unfortunately, there's a lot of tension too."

"Where isn't there tension these days?" Sister Newstead asked, quirking her eyebrows. She reminded Carmen strongly of one of her aunts, all soft upholstery covering a solid iron frame.

"Only too true." Bishop Newstead rose from the couch and kissed his wife's cheek. "Sitting here lamenting the current situation isn't getting you any closer to settling in though. Come on—I'll take you out to look at those apartments."

"And you're staying here until you find a permanent place," Sister Newstead said firmly. She'd won Gianni's heart with a big hug and box of animal crackers, and his parents' with her sensible, friendly welcome. "Don't even think of arguing. Since my daughter and her family moved to Nauvoo, I haven't had a chance to do any real cooking. You just can't do much for two people. Come on, you two good girls can help me peel potatoes for dinner and watch that darling baby while your parents traipse all over town looking at apartments. And don't any of you worry—things always work out." She swept into the kitchen, taking Donna and Lucrezia with her.

"Yes, they do," Bishop Newstead said softly. He glanced at Tony and Carmen, a hint of apology on his gentle face. "And they will. Talk about out of the frying pan into the fire for you though. Here you've escaped the anti-Mormon tide in California only to get mixed up in a family feud between a bunch of irate farmers and hot-tempered Mormons."

* * *

"Mormons." Brindermann said the word flatly, as if he had tired of its taste.

"What about them?" General Garza looked up from his satisfied contemplation of the electronic battle map that dominated the central room of his command installation.

The map told the story of Garza's latest victory in phosphorescent pixels. A film of triumphant blue now stretched from the southern border of Mexico to Rio de Janeiro, from the mouth of the Amazon to the Pacific coast of Peru. Only Chile and Uruguay still showed the red tint of unconquered territories, and Uruguay would soon fall, thanks to the General's insistent offers of assistance against the forces of chaos hiding in the forests and mountains—and a handful of perfectly timed, discreetly executed assassinations of citizens who vocally opposed permitting Garza's forces to cross their borders. The map shone like the bright visions of the future behind Garza's eyes. Its glow also illuminated both men's faces, enhancing Brindermann's grim expression.

"The Mormons may prove to be more of a problem than anticipated," Brindermann said. "Given their relatively small numbers, we had expected no organized resistance."

"And they are mounting organized resistance?" Garza asked, surprised—and slightly impressed. He understood political maneuvering and demagoguery and used them with a skill rarely matched, but for the General, power always came down to bravery, bullets, and blood. Therefore, in his mind, any truly effective, potentially threatening resistance had to come down to armed resistance. "Where do they get their weapons? You have disarmed the citizens, haven't you?"

"I have disarmed them—sometimes literally, to drive the point home," Brindermann said dryly. "The Mormons do not fire on our troops or violently oppose the *mayores*. They quietly go about their business, conform to curfews, obey orders for domestic security—and find ways to communicate with each other, spread rumors and intelligence, subtly resist intimidation campaigns, and build morale among the others in their communities."

"A litter of morale builders, passive resisters, busy bees with busy tongues." Garza chuckled, taking the cigar from his mouth to gesture carelessly with it. "A terrible enemy indeed, Johann. How shall we protect ourselves against such a menace?"

"By exterminating them."

"Another 'final solution,' is it?" Garza shook his head. "No. The Mormons have built up and educated their numbers in South America for decades. If we kill the Mormons, we lose the practical layer of most domestic industries. What good is a factory without a technician to keep its machinery running? We need them to keep things humming along for us awhile longer."

"Until when?" Brindermann asked.

"Until we no longer need the supplies of matériel they provide."

"They may not work for us. In fact, they work against us. Major Zamora, the thorn in Marcelo's side, the primary threat to our operations in Chile, uses Mormons to gather intelligence on rebel operations—and on us."

"And he is one himself," Garza added sharply. "Yes, I am aware of that. Of him. Of the fact that Marcelo let him spirit away a dozen bodies from the convoy they ambushed. Of President Quintana's suspicions that we are backing El Jaguar, despite Vice President Aguilera's assurances to the contrary. Of Zamora vowing to find irrefutable proof of that connection to destroy the possibility of the government inviting us in of their own free will. Yes, I am aware of all of those things."

Brindermann noted Garza's fury with a surge of satisfaction that never reached his face. "And you are aware that Mormons do not take bribes and that they do not fear dying?"

Garza took a deep drag on the cigar, regaining his usual half smile. "Everyone fears dying—if not for themselves, then for someone else." He cocked his head, listening to the sound of heavy engines in the air, thick tires on the gravel roads of his encampment. "Ah, here is our Marcelo returning, covered not in glory but in blood and embarrassment at his incompetence."

Marcelo hid his embarrassment with bravado, jumping from the passenger side of the muddy jeep even before it stopped, landing lightly to stand facing Garza as the two commanders emerged from the headquarters. "Sir," he said, saluting. "We ambushed the compromised rebel convoy as you ordered, preventing the Chileans from taking them prisoner."

"Yes, you did," Garza agreed. In one smooth motion, he pulled his sidearm and shot Marcelo through the forehead. Blood-spattered and wide-eyed, the four men who had accompanied Marcelo stared from their fallen captain to the General. They flinched as the gun swung again and slipped back into its holster.

"But you did not prevent the Chileans from removing the bodies. A serious mistake. I am disappointed. After such a promising start, I expected better of you." Garza shrugged, admitting his error in judgment and letting it go in one graceful gesture. He turned his gaze on the most promising of Marcelo's lieutenants—and smiled. "Consider yourself promoted, Carlos," he announced, slapping the new commando leader's back. "I expect great things of you. Go get cleaned up—have your men take that trash to the furnace—and I'll see you in the officer's mess tonight."

"And so you secure the allegiance of simple men." Brindermann didn't bother to hide his contempt. "By remembering their names and giving them a chance to please you, tossing them bones from your table. Fit rewards for loyal dogs."

"Yes," Garza agreed. "Pity that securing the allegiance of complicated men isn't so easy. And when you do promise them what they want, and even provide it, their loyalty is so often doubtful." He glanced sidelong at the German, a hint of cynical smile playing around his mouth. "Speaking of complicated men, Johann, it is time for you to have a vacation from your hard work here. Go north. Visit the sunny shores of California. Take some pictures of the Lincoln Memorial. Bring me home some nice souvenirs."

CHAPTER 15

"This is what you bring us from your big medical conference in Texas?" Zelik snarled, stalking into the plush office and throwing a pile of daily news printouts onto Abbott's desk. The headlines screamed, "When MedaGen Knew!" and "Booster Busters—Double Dipping Scandal" and "AllSafe—For Now—What about Later?" The stories below the headlines made accusations, based on the information Meredith Galen had stolen and publicly released, that MedaGen knew from the beginning that AllSafe would require yearly booster shots and pressed for FDA approval anyway.

Abbott moved his new boots off the polished desktop and sat forward to leaf through the gaudy pages before looking up at MedaGen's COO with a mild, inquiring expression. "Why, no. Looks like you got these for yourself. Don't have anything to do now that the Callattas got away?" he needled.

"I printed these for myself," Zelik corrected, momentarily distracted by his mention of the Callattas. She was tempted to answer that they could not go far enough, but quickly returned her attention to the subject at hand—and the sheet with the most restrained headline and most believable article. The story featured a picture of Abbott, smiling genially while brushing aside the camera. "The point is that you dodged the reporter from *Modern Times*. It's the hottest magazine out there right now, and the hungriest for stories, and you handed them one on a silver platter. To these people, 'no comment' means 'print whatever you want.' So they're doing exactly that, implying that MedaGen hasn't denied the charges because we can't."

She leaned forward, tapping the sheets with one glittering nail. "And that makes the stockholders—not to mention the board—very nervous. They want it cleared up, and cleared up now. I know you've got their memos already, Mr. CEO Abbott. So what are you going to do about it?" The question hung in the air between them, double-edged with fear (if the truth that she had known about the initial results came to light, the scandal would mortally wound Zelik's career) and hunger (she would like nothing more than to see him go down in flames, leaving her path to the top wide open).

He returned her stare, hot arrogance against icy hauteur. He hated her, but at the same time, she inspired him to greater heights than he could have achieved without her. Easing his shoulders against the butter-soft leather, he gave the smile full play. "Why, I'm going to ask what you've got up your sleeve to combat it, of course. After all, you're in this up to your neck too. I have full confidence that you've thought of something to keep the noose from tightening."

If that blatant guilt-reflection tactic caught her off guard, she didn't show it. "Fortunately, I have become accustomed to saving your tail." With a flick of her wrist, she activated the screen built into the office wall. "I had Whittier put these together. The shouts are getting louder out there, so we can't keep trying to soft-pedal the issue, hoping it will go away."

New ads scrolled across the screen, images of Virginia in ever more seductive poses, from innocent sensuality to decadent lascivi-ousness. Music, words, and pictures all combined in a seductive miasma of subtle promises and reassurances, advocating eternal youth and freedom from responsibilities while emphasizing individual bene-fits of AllSafe in visuals and winking slogans. The first few included small print about the need for a booster, but as the campaign went on, the booster transformed from an acknowledged sidelight to a primary feature, ending with an outright promotion of consistent inoculation updates: "With AllSafe, you're safe—for life!"

Zelik watched them critically, but she had to admit Whittier's team impressed her. They'd neatly taken a potential flaw and made it into a selling point.

The campaign impressed Abbott too, though the thought wandered across his mind that familiarity with Virginia dulled the shock of her shameless sexual appeal. He made a mental note: start the audition process. They'd need a new spokesmodel next year. Maybe two—younger, more exotic and outrageous . . .

"So I've loosened the noose," Zelik said, clicking off the display and snapping Abbott's attention back to the present. "What are you going to do about getting us off the scaffold?"

"I'm going to go public with why I had to brush off the lovely *Modern Times* reporter—because my exclusive face-off with Channel 8's Darren McInnes prevented me from saying anything to anyone else." Abbot waved a hand casually toward another printout on his desk.

Zelik picked it up and read a list of questions for McInnes to ask.

"You'll come with me, of course, and we'll both be shocked, just shocked, to find out that AllSafe isn't safe!" Abbot's smug smile disappeared as he practiced his sincere expression. He dropped it quickly, shrugging his shoulders casually. "Right after that, as duly designated representatives of MedaGen—and therefore the board—we will appear before a federal hearing on the matter, which our dear friend Senator Garlick has arranged."

"And we'll get off easy, thanks to his blaming the FDA and our blaming the project team." Zelik finished the scenario without waiting for Abbott to lay it out. "And then we'll point out that we have provided a solution to the problem already and are promising to make the booster available on the same generous terms as AllSafe itself."

"I always believed that buying a senator would prove worth the investment." Abbott tilted his head, catching a flash of movement in the outer office, and moving to focus on the tall, red-headed man who strode past the discreet one-way mirrors. A moment later, his secretary's husky voice announced, "Your eleven o'clock is here, Mr. Abbott."

"Prompt as ever," Abbott observed. He rose to his feet and looked at Zelik. "So, are you going to march out yourself, or give me the pleasure of dismissing you?"

She favored him with a wintry smile. "I would go to great lengths to avoid giving you any pleasure at all." With that, she stalked out of the office, noting every detail of the visitor's appearance without giving him so much as a direct glance. Hard face, confident stance, European feel, military bearing inside civilian clothes. She keyed up the footage from the surveillance cameras and ordered the identification search to start the moment she got back to her office. Whoever he was, Abbott wanted to speak to him alone—which made discerning his identity worth her time.

* * *

Abbott welcomed his visitor into his office, offering a plush chair and a glass of brandy with casual affability, making small talk about the flight from Colombia, the strangely hot but windy weather in San Diego, and suggestions of sights worth seeing in the area. He smiled and leaned back in his chair, waving a hand carelessly. "Well, Johann—I may call you Johann?"

"You may call me Brindermann," the German said coolly.

"All right," Abbott shrugged. "If you feel more comfortable with Old World formality, I have no objections. So, Brindermann, I'll play along. What brings the organizational brain behind the infamous General Garza all the way to MedaGen's headquarters?"

"Business," Brindermann said shortly. He set the brandy glass down, untasted, and flicked a PDA across the glassy surface of Abbott's desk.

Abbott stopped the little device from sliding off the edge of the desk and glanced at its tiny readout. With a smile, he pushed the intercom button on the desk's control panel. "Kitty, hold my calls."

The secretary at the desk beyond the door replied, "Certainly, sir." Her name was actually Carole, but Abbott had taken to calling all his secretaries "Kitty."

Her response simply provided camouflage for the actual effect of his code words. At that command, the automated security system swung into action. The door closed with a barely perceptible click, electronically sealing itself until Abbott gave the counterorder. The windows darkened slightly as well, a current of electromagnetic interference curtaining the glass against eavesdropping. At the same moment, the sound-masking broadcast hissing from the intercom deepened into an equally effective sound blocker. The tiny red light above the single, discreet security camera flicked to green.

"There. The NSA couldn't hear us now. So, tell me what's so sensitive that you want me to turn on the privacy curtain?" Abbott clicked the PDA down on the desk, its screen still reading, "Secure to talk?"

Brindermann nodded acknowledgement, raising a hand to prevent Abbott from returning the device. "Bring up the memory file." He watched the businessman scan the data that scrolled across the lighted window. "You may have heard that we protect embattled governments against rebels and drug dealers."

"We don't sell weapons," Abbott said softly, his eyes riveted to the screen.

"No, of course you don't," Brindermann said, irony feathering his tone. "You sell cutting-edge drugs. We are fighting a war in a jungle full of disease—and rebel guerillas disguising themselves as harmless campesinos. We need medicine for our troops. Tactical medicine."

"Tactical medicine," Abbott repeated, handing back the tiny machine.

Brindermann's statement was absolutely true—as far as it went. According to the message Brindermann was erasing from the handheld computer, Garza did want MedaGen to supply medicine for his troops. Specifically, he wanted antiviral inoculations, perfectly targeted and calibrated to protect his soldiers from a single easily transmittable, invariably deadly disease. And he wanted the engineered virus from which the vaccine would protect them. Half-recollected news stories rose in Abbott's mind, tales of bioterror, of inhabitants of entire villages in South and Central America mysteriously dying of previously unknown strains of jungle fever. It had happened in Mexico too—actually, in New Mexico. A bunch of drifters out in the desert, then the family in an isolated farmhouse near the campsite keeled over from something the FBI hushed up. The news reports, at least, had stopped way too quickly for it to have faded away on its own. The scene slowly came clear in Abbott's mind: Garza wanted to use bioweapons against the guerillas he was fighting, but he didn't have a good way to keep his own guys from dying of the same disease.

His mind whirled through the possibilities, risks, consequences, profits. The risk loomed huge: if word leaked out that Abbott had supplied a designer virus for a purpose easily construed as bioterror, his career would come to a crashing halt—and so would his status as a free citizen. But if it didn't—if it didn't . . . the number at the end of the file glowed in his mind. A number that more than made up for the potential dip in his personal wealth if the AllSafe booster campaign failed to counteract the damage Meredith Galen's revelations could do.

Brindermann read the glitter growing in Abbott's eyes and veiled the satisfaction in his own. "Of course, the General appreciates the costs involved in developing effective inoculations. Especially inoculations without the side effects—unfortunate or serendipitous—that sometimes happen." He saw the dig hit home. "So of course, the General is willing to grant funding to the research team."

"It is a very expensive process, research." Abbott frowned skeptically, trying to give the impression that the hook hadn't sunk deep into his jaw. "And the General is a fighting man, not a venture capitalist. Can he finance a medical lab through a long-term project?"

"Fighting can be a very profitable business," Brindermann assured him. "He has resources not only to fund the research but to provide a handsome reward if the research yields usable results in the next six months."

"Six months?" Abbott blinked. A top research team, pulled from a couple of other projects—like that diabetes treatment—could probably meet that deadline. Child's play, really, compared to creating a universal vaccine like AllSafe. In fact, half the research was already done, with the viruses they'd created to test the original Corinth program. Too bad they'd lost Dr. Christoff over it, but Dr. Twilley could easily step in. After the excellent work he'd done with the human trials for the vaccine, and cleaning up both the data and the evidence afterward, the man deserved a transfer from the Philippines to corporate headquarters.

"Six months to a six-figure payment," said Brindermann. "Surely a tempting offer? The sooner the project is done, the less chance of word leaking out. You wouldn't want your competitors catching wind of it. And remember, where there are great rewards, there are great penalties."

He smiled, offering his hand. "Large rewards and large penalties just add spice to the challenge. Glad to be in business with you."

Brindermann regarded his hand, then placed the PDA in it. "Indeed. Your signature goes there. One fourth of the payment will be deposited—anonymously—in the account you specify."

"All right." Abbott smiled, flourishing the stylus over the screen in his signature—and his private bank account number. He handed it back, waited for Brindermann to countersign it, then checked his account balance on his own PDA. When the numbers updated with the first installment of the exorbitant fee, he nodded, smiled, and clicked the intercom button again. "I'm back in the office, Kitty."

As the office reverted to its usual, merely high security state, he rose and with a courtly gesture showed his new sponsor to the door. "If you have time, Mr. Brindermann, I'd love to introduce you to the head of the project team and show you our excellent lab facilities—and explain the state-of-the art equipment we'll need to order to do justice to your project."

"I would expect nothing less," Brindermann said dryly, following Abbott out of the office.

* * *

"It's what you expected, sir," Captain Guerra whispered, saluting as his commanding officer approached the ornate doors of the president's private conference room. The captain had arrived early, ostensibly to make sure that the materials for Major Zamora's report were ready to go, but also to keep his ears open as the top-level officials gathered to talk about El Jaguar and the antiterror squad's efforts to stop him. He'd set up Zamora's presentation on the console, and discreetly sneaked a preview of the others as well. "Aguilera's going to hit us for not bringing in El Jaguar—and somehow he's got pictures from the raid on the convoy—" Guerra fell silent, his eyes focusing over Zamora's shoulder.

"Major! Good to see you." President Quintana smiled, offering his hand.

"Good to see you too, sir." Zamora took his hand, then gestured for the younger man to step forward. "May I present Captain Guerra, my second in command."

As Quintana bestowed presidential benevolence on Guerra, Zamora noted the fine lines of stress around Quintana's eyes, the tightness of his jaw behind the politician's smile. The usually garrulous president didn't spend more than a couple of sentences on the young soldier before gently but firmly dismissing him. Guerra waited for Zamora's subtle nod, saluted, and strode out.

"You've got good men under your command," Quintana said, surveying the room rather than looking at the major. General Medina stood with a nondescript man in equally nondescript clothes—Señor Olivares, the head of the intelligence service. Beyond them, a secretary put the finishing touches on the elegant buffet of refreshments. The smell of sweet pastry clashed with the tension in the air; only two or three nervous attendees took advantage of the president's hospitality. "I'm sorry about the ones you've lost, the other captain—what was his name?"

"Ulloa." Zamora supplied the missing name, feeling the empty ache for all six of the men he had led, however unintentionally, to their deaths.

"Ulloa. Yes. A pity—ah, here's Aguilera." Quintana's voice rose as the vice president slipped in, with Major Archuleta in tow. "Now that we are all here, let's get this meeting started." He took his place at the head of the table, motioning them all to sit down as the military guards closed the doors. "Gentlemen, we have a grave matter to discuss concerning our national security. I had a personal call this morning from General Andrea Cesar Garza."

As the president outlined the content of their conversation, Zamora sat still, his face as impassive as ever. Even without Guerra's warning, the president's official announcement wouldn't have surprised him. It was always only a matter of time, and now General Garza had made a definite offer to President Quintana. If President Quintana accepted his help, Garza promised that El Jaguar would be brought to the scaffold in short order.

"Finally!" Aguilera's exclamation as he slapped his hand down on the table didn't surprise Zamora either. "Of course we will accept—with our own terms and conditions, naturally."

"Of course we will accept?" General Medina glared from under his formidable eyebrows at the vice president. "Accept an armed force crossing our borders to deal with a rabble of mountain terrorists? We are fully capable of neutralizing that threat ourselves."

Aguilera shot him a skeptical look. "As you have done thus far? Bombings in the middle of Santiago, villages burned, campesinos terrorized, and El Jaguar disappearing into the mist without so much as a scratch. That hardly speaks to your ability to neutralize the threat."

"We have scratched him, sir," Zamora said, the cool assurance in his tone countering the sarcasm in the vice president's. "Thanks to local informants, we have closed three of the routes he used to bring troops and supplies across the Peruvian border, as well as destroying two of his headquarters camps. We also have the bodies of twenty-three rebels—"

"Which General Garza's men are responsible for killing," Major Archuleta said sharply. "Your men arrived only in time to clean up after the actual battle."

"But we did arrive, sir," Zamora reminded him—and more important, President Quintana. "Even if it was too late to achieve our objective. We were tracking the supply convoy, both to trace its route for future operations and to take prisoners who could supply vital intelligence about El Jaguar's movements—and even more vital information about how he has managed to elude us so consistently. It's as if he had access to the same information we do."

Aguilera flicked a hand, waving away that insignificant point. "Of course he does, Major—he knows where his paths and camps are!"

"And where our paths and camps are," Zamora said. "But, because General Garza's overzealous squad leader crossed our borders without permission and shot the rebels first, we have no chance to ask them questions later."

"I don't see that you need to." Aguilera shrugged off Zamora's criticism.

"General Garza apologized to me on that score," President Quintana said. "He assured me that his squad leader has been disciplined to teach him the importance of respecting national borders."

"Can you teach a dead man anything?" The soft voice belonged to Olivares. As a civilian, he stood apart from the military command system; since the March Revolution, the intelligence service existed not only to gather information outside Chile's borders but to keep a watchful eye on its military as well, to guard against the corruption that had overcome so many regimes before.

"What?" Aguilera stared at him, not bothering to disguise his dislike. He had to work with the spymaster; they shared information often, each man for his own reasons, but neither trusted the other. Spies played games, and Aguilera always suspected Olivares of playing both sides.

Olivares met the stare levelly. "According to reports, General Garza executed the squad leader, an Ecuadorian named Marcelo Perez, when he returned to the General's Bogotá headquarters."

"According to reports," Aguilera repeated. A faint flicker of nervousness rippled under his skin, then disappeared. He smiled nastily, looking from Medina to Zamora. "Well, whether it is true or not, some of us are very lucky that General Medina doesn't exercise such strict penalties for incompetence."

President Quintana frowned warningly. "The question is not one of incompetence, but of information and resources."

"Which General Garza has in abundance," Aguilera replied quickly, but he did soften his tone. "It only makes sense to accept his offer of assistance. He and his men have utterly routed rebels and cartels in a half dozen countries. Certainly he can provide the expertise we need—especially since with every success, El Jaguar only encourages other insurgents—bandits in the mountains eastward, malcontents among the Mapuches to the south, not to mention the rabble pouring across our northern border from Peru."

"Pouring across our border to escape General Garza's iron-fisted control." Zamora leaned forward. "Which is exactly why we cannot accept his offer. If we let him in, he will never leave. Look at what's happened in Central America and Brazil—and in Peru and Ecuador. The man's hand stretches all the way to the borderlands in the United States. He is much more than an efficient mercenary—he is a dangerous, charismatic megalomaniac, like Napoleon or Hitler."

"Calling the man names because he has done what you have consistently proved unable to do does not reflect favorably on you, Major," said Aguilera.

Zamora's eyes never wavered from Aguilera's. Señor Olivares watched with his usual slight smile. General Medina cleared his throat with a growl, pricked to the core at Aguilera's slight against his military competence and that of his men.

The clear tone of a bell interrupted the incipient shouting match. President Quintana held up his hands. "I must go to meet with the envoy from the United States. Leave your presentations here—I will review them later. And I will take our discussion under consideration." He stood, refusing to give Aguilera an opening for more arguments as he moved them all toward the door. Olivares caught Aguilera's arm, quietly requesting a private conversation. General Medina glared at Major Archuleta, promising much more than a private conversation with his insubordinate subordinate. Zamora fell in behind them.

Just before Zamora passed through the doorway, however, Quintana caught his arm. "A moment, Major." He leaned in close, smiling as if sharing a joke. His words, however, were deadly serious. "I have seen Garza's mode of operation—and I have grave reservations about accepting any offer he makes. But I may not be able to stop it. Political opposition can be as fierce as any battlefield enemy. Listen—from the hints Olivares has gathered, and from the word of other, more confidential sources, it seems wise to suspect that Aguilera has a hand in some aspect of what's going on. I know you are trustworthy, and I don't think that Medina is involved in any conspiracy or political maneuvering. Find out for me, Major. Find out what's going on, and who we can trust. And watch both of our backs."

* * *

"We've got your back!" exclaimed the slogan splashed over a stars-and-stripes background, above airbrushed images of American military troops, police, and smiling civilians (especially children, of course). "Brought to you by the Office of Homeland Security, sponsored by MedaGen. AllSafe is made in the USA," read the fine print. Channel 8 played that ad as a banner on its Web sites as well as a fade-out image during its broadcasts; others like it splashed over the public video screens in every bus, subway, airport, and train station across the country.

Senator Garlick, filling his new position as secretary of homeland security to its fullest possible extent, not only put teeth in the enforcement of the health and security bill but also stepped up the AllSafe campaign, labeling everyone who hadn't taken the shot as anti-American at best, vectors of disease and terrorists at worst.

Buttons and ribbons decorated lapels all over the country, the Tigers' black and orange combined—incongruously, given their long history of interschool rivalry—with the Javelins' royal blue in sentimental, politically useful memory of the tragedy. A vote against Garlick's homeland security measures, the party line went, meant a vote against the heart of the country, against grandparents mercilessly cut down while supporting their dear grandchildren at that most American of activities, a high school football game. Surely, in the face of a threat like that, how could anyone oppose mandatory AllSafe vaccinations—or the homeland security initiative that promised to give the secretary expanded powers of observation, authorization for registration programs, and control of state militias and national guards to prevent just such a tragedy in the future?

Lawsuits, brought by a series of organizations, the majority of them sponsored by MedaGen or anonymously financed by Augosto, challenged the mandatory AllSafe vaccinations and increased homeland security powers in state and federal courts, playing devil's advocate to push the regulations to their limits, setting precedents upholding decisions in court after court to give Garlick's office emergency powers to override individual health-care liberties. Sharp lawyers, working backward from their supposed objective of representing anti-AllSafe groups, brought up point after point that strengthened rather than weakened the government's case. Judges, well aware of the political, and occasionally life-threatening implications of the situation, passed the hot potato along, recusing themselves or rubber-stamping an appeal or decision on its way to a higher court.

Not everyone rolled over and played dead as the Garlick-MedaGen juggernaut bore down on them. Senator Holly Cox and a few of her braver, or more attention-hungry, colleagues vocally opposed the measure in legislative hearings, news conferences, and even on a few talk shows. Their adversarial stance brought them increased publicity—and roaring denunciations from Senator Garlick, Senator Benyanny, and the majority leaders of both congressional houses, as well as the derision of the media establishment. Inevitably, the opposition brought up Senator Cox's Mormon beliefs, accusing her of subservience to the patriarchy, blind fanaticism, and simple-minded stupidity.

"We didn't back you for this!" a high-level party operative shouted at her over the phone. "You're a moderate. You're a woman. You're supposed to appeal to the women's vote and represent modern, enlightened ideas of government. You aren't supposed to oppose—"

"A megalomaniac trying to pin every citizen of the United States under his thumb?" Senator Cox shot back. "Of course I'm opposed! I appreciate your backing—and I have upheld all the decent ideals and legislation for this party. That's why I joined in the first place, not to give you a public-relations edge because of my gender. But don't for even a second let this skirt fool you. You wanted it to look like you had an independent woman on the team—well, it turns out you do!"

* * *

"Independence," Virginia breathed, "means doing anything you want." She ran her tongue over her glossy lips, painted to match the scarlet on her stars-and-stripes scarf.

"Nice," the cameraman approved. "Let's try it again."

MedaGen had hired this crew to shoot the next series of Virginia's AllSafe ads, and Virginia was currently trading on all of her appeal. All the new songs Virginia recorded for the new campaign continued the sexy themes, songs all about "freedom"—"Leave her, love me, leave him, love me, leave it all, we'll be free . . ." So did her personal appearances, making Garrett giggle and audiences stare as she tossed her hair away from her skimpy blouse and announced that of course she'd get the AllSafe vaccine from MedaGen—she wanted to be free to love anybody who caught her eye, and if that kind of freedom came at a price, "Well, freedom always does, doesn't it?"

Underneath the seductive smile, however, lurked a thread of withdrawing calculation. She'd thrown herself into the AllSafe booster campaign with renewed enthusiasm—because she knew that her position as MedaGen's spokeswoman was rapidly approaching its expiration date. Sure, MedaGen had given her a hand up, from the somewhat limited notoriety of the art-porn music scene to international celebrity, but she couldn't stay a pitchwoman forever. Time to reinvent herself again, take the next step toward conquering the entire world, and leave MedaGen far behind. Her plans didn't show in her actions; she used the campaign to advance her never-ending quest for self-promotion. The coverage never ended either. Virginia's face and body saturated the news, advertisements, entertainment shows, selling sex, irresponsibility—and AllSafe, but increasingly as a distant third.

"That'll blow their minds," she said smugly, touching up her somewhat more restrained daytime makeup as she joined Julian in the elevator outside MedaGen's headquarters video studio.

"Sure it will," Julian agreed, glancing at the mirrored ceiling of the elevator. The sheer prevalence of tiny camera lenses in the place made it feel like something out of a horror movie—one where the monster hiding in the closet turned out to be a corporate enforcer with somebody's video-camera picture in his pocket.

"Sure it will, or it sure will?" Virginia snapped, glaring at her assistant and oldest friend and most loyal lover, though she didn't think of him that way anymore.

"Is there a difference?" he asked, bored and hostile after a long day of watching Virginia flirt with everyone else in the room.

"Of course there's a difference!" She automatically checked her own reflection in the mirrored ceiling. Her eyes instantly flashed down again as the door opened—to reveal the back of a tall, European-looking man standing with Abbott in the plush front office. Virginia left the elevator at model warp speed and positioned herself just perfectly behind Abbott's visitor with a cheerful, "Well, hello, darling!"

Brindermann turned—and found himself face-to-face with Virginia. "And hello to you too," she breathed.

He gazed into her eyes for a moment, then stepped back, utterly unaffected.

Abbott smiled. "May I introduce Virginia Diamante, pop-star diva and MedaGen's glamorous spokesmodel for AllSafe?"

"No," Brindermann said flatly. "I am in no need of a whore, and in the unimaginable event that I were, I would not be formally introduced. Good day, Mr. Abbott." He neatly stepped around Virginia and into the elevator just as the doors closed behind him.

"A business associate," Abbott said casually, his smile never wavering. "How are you, honey?"

Seeing that Abbott had no intention of apologizing for Brindermann's rudeness, Julian immediately pressed the elevator button.

"Fine." Virginia matched Abbott's smile, though she seethed inside. She looked around, bright-eyed. "So where's your nicer associate, Mr. Augosto?"

"He's more Senator Garlick's associate than mine," Abbott told her, glancing pointedly at his watch. "Is there something I can help you with? I'm running a little late here."

Virginia matched his smile. "Oh, darling, there's nothing you can do for me. You have fun at your appointment. I know I'll have fun at mine." She swept into the elevator with a flirtatious flick of her hair.

"Don't worry about—" Julian began, stroking Virginia's shoulder, hurting for her.

"I'll worry when I worry!" Virginia exclaimed, shrugging off the touch. Her confidence peeled off like one of her stage costumes, the deep insecurity at her core bubbling to the brightly painted surface. "I'm burning out. I'm burning out, and Abbott's going to drop me—MedaGen's going to drop me!"

"You'll drop them first," Julian reminded her. "Just like we planned. Kamasutra Entertainment upped their offer. Three more months, and you can pay Abbott back by leaving him cold."

Virginia twirled her hair, confidence beginning to bounce back. "Oh, I'll pay him back—just wait until I dictate to you the chapter about him in my autobiography. He's going to come out very small. Very small. Anyway, I bet Cesar Augosto is a lot richer."

Julian stifled a groan. "Oh, please, can we not talk about Cesar Augosto again?"

"Now, now, jealousy isn't pretty," Virginia remonstrated, frowning but obviously pleased. "We don't believe in that kind of thing. Besides, I don't bother you about your flirtations, do I?"

Julian shrugged off the implied reprimand. "You know I don't love anybody but you."

The elevator door chimed, and she swayed out, glancing over her shoulder with a charming smile. "That's good—because I'm a jealous goddess myself."

CHAPTER 16

"So, tell me a little more about you." The school secretary smiled at Carmen as she handed over the registration forms. They'd come to register Lucrezia for school in the middle of the day; Carmen had taken pity on her daughter and decided to register Monday and let Lucrezia actually start on Tuesday.

Lucrezia glanced over, then went back to studying the school's front hall. It was a lot smaller than her high school back home, but the overall feeling was the same: emphasis on sports teams and Spirit Week, inane student-government campaign posters, institutional decor, and a general sense of uneasy boredom. They didn't have full-time security guards to man the metal detectors at the doors though, and she couldn't see any surveillance cameras. Small town, she decided. Well, comparatively small. Too big for everybody to know everybody, Porter had said, but too small to blend into the crowd either. He'd dropped by the Callattas' new apartment with Rock and Orrin to help unload the trailer. Lucrezia hadn't paid a lot of attention to anyone but Porter, but the other members who came to help seemed nice enough. They'd all worried about the Callattas a little. Sister Newstead had taken Carmen aside to give her a list of the stores, streets, and neighborhoods that were "safe." Porter had warned Lucrezia about the school, but before she could get any more details than, "I don't think it's such a great idea, you going down there instead of coming to school with us," Carmen interrupted to say that the pizza arrived. After emptying about a pizza box each, the Smiths left to answer a call from Brother Hunt.

Carmen had appreciated the help but took the talk about the religion-based tensions as nothing the Callattas couldn't handle, telling Lucrezia that she sympathized with her nervousness about starting at a new school, but it wouldn't be any worse than the San Diego high school—and might even be better. "Give it a chance, honey." It wasn't a suggestion so much as an order. The blessing Tony had given her the night before simply advised that she listen to the Spirit and do what she knew was right, and she would find the strength to do what she needed to do.

Now, she half watched as Carmen smiled, taking the forms and beginning to fill them out. "Well, where to start? We're just in from California—San Diego area. My husband, Tony, just got a job at Softlearn."

"My, that's a long drive," the secretary clucked. "But you're well out of there. Heavens, all the earthquakes! I'd just be scared all the time that some disaster was ready to come shake my house down. It's bad enough just hearing about it. I still get teary when I see those poor Egyptian babies on the news, with their poor homes and families washed right away. What's this world coming to?"

Lucrezia tuned out this edition of the usual adult "the world's going to hell in a handbasket" conversation. She'd heard it all before, with and without Donna's "last days" spin.

The office aide flicked her long hair back, the motion catching Lucrezia's attention. The girl leaned over the counter. "So, are you one of us, or one of them?"

Lucrezia looked from her face to the gold cross pendant dangling from her neck, and didn't have to ask the next question. "Us or them what?"

"Us, Christians, or them, Mormons," the girl explained. Her expression said that she didn't really have to ask either, but did it for form's sake.

"Mormons are Christians." Lucrezia fired the first volley. The battle lines were already drawn.

The office aide sneered, Lucrezia now confirmed as an enemy. "Mormons are a cult, and every last one of you is going to burn with the rest of the trash pretty soon, while we watch and laugh."

Lucrezia leaned on the counter too, her eyes right on level with the other girl's. "Let me guess—you're a Tommy Gibbs fan, and stupid enough to believe that Rapture baloney he's always spouting. I heard all about that in my old school, and it was just as stupid then. The sooner you wake up and realize that nobody's going to appear to whisk you away into the sky on a flaming chariot, the better off you'll be."

"The sooner you take your tail off to that hayseed 'school' you Mormons started, the happier we'll all be," the aide announced as she leaned back, reluctantly ceding the counter space to Lucrezia. Her voice rose slightly as she said, "We don't like your kind around here."

"Now, now, Shanna, don't be unfriendly to the new girl," the secretary broke in, before Lucrezia could deliver her devastating riposte—"Oh, really? I hadn't noticed." The secretary cast a warning look on Shanna, holding out a sheaf of papers. "You're here on probation, miss. Office duty is a privilege. Now, go copy these for me." She watched Shanna stalk off, then smiled apologetically at Carmen. "These kids and their cliques. You know how it is."

Carmen looked at her pleasant, slightly clueless face, then at Shanna, who met her gaze with an insolent raise of the eyebrows, and said, "Oh, yes, I know how it is." She didn't add that she was glad there seemed to be a number of good people who, like the secretary, were seeking fairness and tolerance. Instead, she took the schedule slip and handed it to Lucrezia. "There's the damages, kiddo. Want to take a look around?"

"Oh, you're welcome to," the secretary assured them, offering a hot-pink visitor's pass. "Just come back here and make sure you check out with me before you go. Got to keep things safe."

"Sure will." Carmen took the laminated card and thanked her before she and Lucrezia headed off on their scholastic scouting expedition. For a few minutes they walked the hallways, ignoring the stares from students and surveying the school logos painted on every wall and posters advertising clubs—"Christian Student Association" prominent among the others for chess club, gay-straight alliance, birth-control information, and school dances. Carmen rubbed Lucrezia's back. "It doesn't look too bad."

Lucrezia shrugged irritably. "All school is too bad. By definition. And here it's going to be worse. Shanna and her stupid 'us and them' routine. Look at these guys, geeking out the doors at us like they'd never seen humans before. What a bunch of hicks!"

"Gee, honey, don't hold back. Tell us what you really think!" Carmen suppressed a laugh. She sympathized with Lucrezia's misgivings and nervousness, especially after the encounter with the obnoxious girl at the office, but still, it wasn't the end of the world—or even the ends of the earth. Had she been this moody and angst-ridden when she was fifteen? "Take a breath and calm down. You can—"

"Oh, Mama, please," Lucrezia rolled her eyes. "Do *not* tell me to pray if I feel bad. That worked when I was in kindergarten. I'm a lot older than that now. I know that Jesus is my very best friend in the world. You know, the best friend you call every day, and who never says anything back?"

Carmen's eyebrows rose, then slammed back down. "That's enough of that! If you don't want to take advantage of the power of prayer, that's your call. But you watch your mouth about getting cynical like that. You're just cutting yourself off from the help you need, and it's nobody's fault but yours."

Lucrezia, knowing she'd crossed the line, limited her response to an eloquent sigh.

Her adolescent angst didn't prevent her from thinking a silent prayer the next day, however, as she walked into the school—and Shanna's waiting glare. The office aide lounged on the bench across from the front doors, in the midst of a few large boys with "jock" written all over them, plus a bevy of girls wearing crosses and superior expressions. The position of the crew, ranged along the hall frontage so that all the other students had to walk in front of them to get to the classroom halls, and their casual attitudes told Lucrezia all she needed to know about the hierarchy of her new school. The Christian Students' Association, the football team, and the cheerleading squad were "us." She was definitely "them." And outnumbered.

"Why look, it's the new girl," Shanna announced.

"Hey, new girl," a boy drawled. He grinned, looking her over suggestively. "Looking good."

"Back off, Bret," Shanna ordered, smacking his shoulder playfully. "You don't want any of that—it's infected. You know how Mormons are."

"Ooh, keep it away from me!" one of her cronies shrieked, much to the amusement of the rest.

The laughter roared in Lucrezia's ears. Fury roared just as loudly in her head, but no good comeback came with it.

"Hey, there you are! Come on!" Someone caught Lucrezia's arm, pulling her along the row and out of range.

By the time they reached the comparatively safer confines of the locker hall, Lucrezia had overcome her surprise enough to take her arm back and stare at her rescuer.

"Whew! What a welcome, huh?" The girl who'd swept her away from Shanna's gang smiled brightly, sweeping one of her unruly curls away from her eyes. "Don't worry about them—don't let them catch you alone, but don't worry about them. Bunch of rhinos, glaring around but nearsighted, so you can get away if you're fast enough to start running before they build up steam. They're like any kind of bullies, mainly petty tyrants, cowards, and go-alongers, dangerous if they think you're alone, but not going to attack if they know you've got a good backup team. Which you do. Oh, but you don't know that yet—I mean, you do now, but . . ." She took a breath, shook her head, and laughed. "Okay, let's start over." She stuck out her hand. "Hi. I'm Jelisaveta Sarkesian. Mormon. One of the resident pariahs."

"Lucrezia Callatta," Lucrezia said, looking at the extended, paint-spattered hand, the nails of random lengths. The ridiculousness of a formal introduction in the middle of a school hallway made her laugh. She took Jelisaveta's hand and shook it heartily. "Luc, 'cause it's easier. Glad to meet you—obviously."

Jelisaveta looked at her hand too, grimaced good-naturedly, and scrubbed it on her jeans. "Nope, it's dried on—good thing, since it didn't get all over you. Yeah, I'm an art geek. Sounds like we both got stuck with Old World names. Lucrezia—like Lucrezia Borgia, right? Did you know that they tried to canonize her after she died? Saint Lucrezia. That'd surprise all those people who think she's practically a vampire in a Renaissance costume, thanks to her nasty brother and father. The pope, yet! Goes to show that reputations depend on anything but how you really are, huh? Do you have poetic parents, or did they just go with a family name? My mom decided that if we've got a last name like Sarkesian, we might as well all get tagged with Hungarian first names too—or at least Eastern European, Carpathia, whatever—to go with her side of the family. That's what you get for having a family history fanatic for a mother. So I got Jelisaveta—that's like Hungarian or Romanian for Elizabeth, see—and my older brother's Imre—try to get anybody to spell that the first time they hear it! Looks like we're here—welcome to your own little slice of security. Not privacy, though. And my little sister's Magda. Oh, and there's April. Hey, April!"

"That doesn't sound Hungarian," Lucrezia blinked, coming up for mental air during a pause in the verbal flood. Jelisaveta had pulled her smartly along during her stream-of-consciousness discourse, and now she realized that they'd arrived at the locker matching the number on Lucrezia's assignment slip.

Another group of kids, as large in numbers as Shanna's pack, if not as big individually, quickly collected around them as Lucrezia figured out the combination on the new lock. Jelisaveta introduced the baker's dozen of them, including her much quieter brother Imre. Her cataract-style conversation had calmed to a mere fountain now that the immediate crisis and stress of meeting someone new had passed.

April, a girl with an elegant bearing and sweet smile, and not related to Jelisaveta, leaned in to say softly, "It's a little overwhelming, isn't it? Don't worry about remembering everybody's name right now. You'll get to know us all pretty quickly, hanging out with us all the time."

By the end of lunch, Lucrezia found that April's prediction had a lot of practical proof behind it. She would indeed be hanging out with the Saint Squad, as they called themselves—both because she quite liked them, and because it was the safest thing to do. Rock and Porter had told her about the anti-Mormons at the local public school as an argument for her coming to the home-school sessions Brother Smith had set up for his and Brother Hunt's kids. They hadn't told her that there were nearly as many Mormons as not at the school, which evened the odds considerably. They also hadn't mentioned Jelisaveta Sarkesian, whose dad owned Softlearn, or that the Mormon kids, most of whose parents had come to work at Softlearn or the other tech companies, had banded together inside the school for mutual support and protection, along with a number of non-Mormon but also non-rabid kids who liked having friends who didn't smoke, get blasted at parties, or beat up anybody they thought was going to hell. There were some truly Christian born-again Christians;

Reverend Teresa Burns of Unity Lutheran consistently preached understanding and cooperation, and several kids at school belonged to her congregation. In all, a tolerance predominated the halls keeping the Rhinos—Jelisaveta's term for them had stuck—in check most of the time.

The whole group watched each other's backs, traveling in smaller packs, avoiding dust-ups with the Rhinos. When a confrontation did blow up, a peacemaking strike team would cover a decisive retreat for the immediate target of the Rhinos' persecution. That tactic let the Rhinos think they'd won, while removing the Saint Squad member from the firing line without starting a fight—and attracting official attention and reprimand. The teachers and staff mostly looked the other way and the principal would not tolerate outright anarchy, and this kept at least a veneer of civilized behavior over the simmering conflict. Thus, the Mormons and their associates could for the most part avoid sectarian trouble during school.

The real problems started after school, when the combatants poured onto the streets of Lake Creek. Not only did the veneer crack, but the Rhinos met a Mormon opposition that didn't adhere to the "rescue and run" rule.

"Oh, no," Jelisaveta breathed, interrupting her scattered, English-inspired discourse on dangling participles, as she and a group of girls left the building on Friday afternoon. They headed for the city bus stop, heavily laden with homework assignments, sharing opinions on the week's events, and planning a "welcome lunch or something" for Lucrezia the next day.

"What?" Lucrezia followed her new friends' stares toward the bus stop, then to the lot behind it.

The demolished block, with its stark cement foundations and yawning cellars, had been halted in its reconstruction when the economy bottomed out. The same thing had happened in several areas of Lake Creek: original residents hanging on to crumbling tenements or evicted in favor of new development that never came. Overall, the whole thing gave the effect of a city divided in half, with the Mormon neighborhoods on one side and the gentile neighborhoods on the other, the empty or demolished buildings forming a strange kind of moat between them.

Lucrezia finally saw what had worried Jelisaveta. The foundations currently provided ledges and benches for a double handful of boys leaning or sitting casually on the battered cement footings.

"That's Porter!" Lucrezia exclaimed, instantly recognizing him as he leaned against a rusty beam.

"And Rock," April said, sounding worried.

"And Orrin," Jelisaveta added. "Oh, they are so not supposed to be doing this!"

"Doing what?" Lucrezia asked. A pretty good idea of their intent quickly formed in her mind, however, as the Rhinos sauntered out of the school and toward the invisible border that separated the school's legal authority from the freedom of the street.

Sure enough, the growing crowd around the bus stop started sorting itself out, combatants, noncombatants, onlookers, and avoiders all taking up their positions for the next act. Jelisaveta, April, and the other girls, solidly in the avoider camp, began their retreat.

"Come on, we'll catch the stop up on Ash," April said, as Lucrezia hesitated.

Love—or at least infatuation—won out over caution. "You go ahead," she said, neatly avoiding Jelisaveta's belated grab for her hand as she began walking quickly toward the bus stop. She glanced over her shoulder, giving them a smile. "I'll see you guys tomorrow."

"Oh, rats." For once, Jelisaveta's logorrhea failed her, watching Lucrezia reach the edge of the rubble and hesitate momentarily, gazing across the broken concrete at Porter.

Bret and the large, male members of the Rhinos' club came to a stop in front of the vacant lot, in the center of the excited but wary ring of onlookers. He didn't bother to look around at his audience; instead, his gaze fastened on Rock. "Well, look—it's the Morons, visiting from their special school. You coming to a real school to get smarter?" The expected sniggers followed. Shanna and her girlfriends clustered behind the line of boys, ready to cheer them on in this fight just as they did on the football field or basketball court.

"Nah." Rock smiled, uncoiling himself from his seat. "We figured we'd come down to teach you a few things they ain't teaching you in that school for sinners."

They didn't need to say any more. Orrin, who had jumped to his feet the moment Bret appeared and stood shifting from foot to foot (not anxious, but eager for action), let out a rebel yell, charged forward, and tackled the nearest Rhino. The move was as effective as it was ungraceful; Orrin's shoulder drove into the larger boy's midsection, bearing him down to the ground in a tangle of flailing, punching, kicking limbs. They barely hit the ground when the rest of the brawl erupted. Rock took on Bret, the two of them exchanging more practiced but even more vicious punches and blocks.

Rock shouted orders, marshaling his troops between blows. "Hurt the Amulonites, but don't kill them!"

Orrin whirled like a dervish, laughing as he crashed into one opponent after another, aiming primarily for faces, leaving bloody noses and swelling eyes in his wake. The blows he received in return hardly daunted him, and the Rhinos knew better than to try to close with him; the new recruit who did grab Orrin found himself trying to hold a Tasmanian devil. Orrin head-butted his opponent, then leapt atop him as he fell, punching his face repeatedly.

Porter plunged through the fray, straight-arming a Rhino who tried to stop him, ducking under the roundhouse blows two more boys exchanged, and skidding to a halt beside his brother—and his brother's victim. "Orrin!" he exclaimed, grabbing the younger boy's arm on the upswing. Porter pulled hard, half lifting his brother from the prone body. "Orrin! He's down! Let him go!"

Orrin growled, glaring at Porter, psychotic light in his eyes. Porter held his ground and the stare, until Orrin looked away with a giggle. He bounded away, tripping another Rhino and kicking him heavily in the ribs. Porter glanced at the moaning, crying form at his feet, then whirled, delivering a snap punch to the jaw of the letter-jacketed Rhino who'd come up behind him. He followed it with a kick that sent the boy crashing to the rubble-strewn ground, nearly into the gaping hole of the cellar. The Rhino lurched to his knees, trying to get to his feet, when Orrin skidded to a halt beside his brother and shoved hard to send the off-balance enemy into the gaping cavity behind him. For a moment, the boy teetered on the edge, his jacket flaring around him, then fell. One wildly flailing hand caught a length of rebar jutting out from the cement. The other hand scrabbled frantically in the rubble on the edge of the broken cellar wall, trying to get a grip to keep from crashing into the mess of mud, rocks, and iron scraps at the bottom.

Orrin's boot descended toward the straining fingers—until Porter knocked him away. Orrin raked his older brother with a contemptuous eye, spitting, "Better that one man should die—"

"Shut up!" Porter shouted, pushing Orrin away again.

The rest of their argument drowned in the howl of sirens and shouts of the crowd. Shanna screamed at Bret, motioning frantically for him to break away. Rock delivered one more blow to his retreating adversary, then roared an order to his own forces to disappear. Combatants and onlookers alike broke and ran, leaping rubble, pilling into vehicles, tearing down the street away from the flashing lights of a pair of squad cars swiftly bearing down on them.

April, huddling with Jelisaveta and the other girls, clicked her phone closed. She'd called the police, not because she hoped they would rescue the Mormon kids—with their prejudice, they were more likely to arrest the Smith boys and their friends—but because the sudden appearance of flashing lights would break up the fight. The Saint Squad prepared to run as well, aiming toward the relative safety of the school grounds.

Porter hesitated, then knelt, grabbing the Rhino's wrist. He heaved, snarling at the other boy to pull. Another pair of hands wrapped around the Rhino's other wrist; Porter looked at Lucrezia kneeling in the dirt and rocks beside him, managed a quick smile, then looked at the frantic letterman below and said, "On three. One, two—three!"

Under their combined efforts, the Rhino lurched up over the lip of the drop. Lucrezia tumbled backward, landing heavily in the dirt. The Rhino, still looking surprised at the help, shoved passed Porter and ran. Porter scrambled to his feet again, holding a hand out to Lucrezia. She didn't even glance toward Jelisaveta, who was yelling for her to come quickly; she gazed up at Porter with wide eyes and took his hand. He pulled her up, and the two of them ran to the truck that Rock started with a coughing roar. Porter tossed Lucrezia into the bed and leapt up himself as the tires sprayed gravel and dirt behind them.

She sat up, seeing the flashing lights brought to a stop in the confusion of high school students' fleeing vehicles, and felt a surge of excitement. Orrin howled another rebel yell, which the other Mormons echoed. Even Lucrezia joined in, wind in her hair and fire in her eyes. Running from confrontations, deflecting barbs with jokes, trying to fly under the Rhinos' radar, it all grated against her pride and temper. Fighting back exhilarated her. She gazed, starry-eyed, at Porter, his strong hand on her arm, holding her as the truck jolted across the vacant lot and onto a side street.

By the time they reached the Smith farm, on the far outskirts of Lake Creek, however, the rising tide of worry had dampened Lucrezia's initial excitement. The other boys jumped from the truck as they drove down the country road, running, and, more often than not, limping, back to their own homes, shouting encouragement to each other, reveling in their successful raid on the Amulonites. Rock, their noble general, saw them off with encouragement to remember their families, their liberties, and their God. He pulled into the long, dusty driveway still quoting Captain Moroni. Orrin, flexing his bloody fingers, had begun twitching with nervous energy again.

Watching them get out of the cab of the truck, the misgivings in the back of Lucrezia's mind grew.

"Whew. That's an exciting finish for a Friday, eh?" Porter leaned against the truck, gently rubbing his battered knuckles and giving Lucrezia his gentle smile.

"So it's Rock as Captain Moroni, huh?" she asked, her temper flaring as the rush of adrenaline went cold. "And who's Orrin supposed to be? Psychopath boy?"

"He says he's Teancum, mostly," Porter said softly, brushing a strand of Lucrezia's windblown hair away from her face with two fingers. "Or sometimes Gideon."

The touch distracted her for a moment, but the blood on his knuckles brought her sharply back to reality. She took his hand, worried about the damage, thrilled at the feeling of his hand in hers. "You really should be more careful. I've heard about you guys—going around provoking face-offs with the 'Christians' every time you can, like a bunch of loons. No," she laid a finger across his lips, shivering slightly but determined not to be distracted. "I've heard that you do try to hold Rock and Orrin back a bit, and you're right to do so, but do you think your actions are smart? Do you think that's a good thing to do? You're acting like a bunch of psychopaths. Mom says you are the aggressors, and you're going to bring the entire county down around our ears, even though the rest of us haven't done anything!"

Porter kissed her finger, reversing the hold so that he held her hands. "Lucrezia. Lucrezia, listen. We're doing the right thing." He shook her gently, stopping her rising voice, his own tone taking on some heat. "The Saints can't let evil ride over them. The Second Coming is about to happen, and we have to be ready. We have to show that we're brave, that we believe. 'If ye are prepared, ye shall not fear.' And we're showing we're prepared."

Lucrezia's stubborn Callatta skepticism managed to surface through the dizzy bliss of having Porter so close. "But, Porter, that's just crazy. How can you know that? The prophet hasn't said anything about it—either of them!"

"There's only one real prophet—President Smith. Rojas is just a second, an administrator," Porter said. "President Smith would have told us all, but the bureaucracy is keeping it quiet. Dad says there's some at Church headquarters who don't understand, but President Smith is sending word out secretly. Also, my father has had revelations that confirm the prophet's wishes. Dad's like Lehi receiving inspiration to guide his family. We believe in prophets, Lucrezia. Lehi, Nephi, Moroni—they all did things that looked extreme, but they did it because God told them to. He needed them to do His work, and they did."

"And you've had revelations too, like Nephi? Have you heard the Spirit telling you to kill somebody?" Lucrezia asked. "Why did you stop Orrin from knocking Curtis into the cellar, even when Orrin quoted scripture."

"Orrin gets a little overexcited," Porter sighed. "And Rock does take himself way too seriously sometimes, but we're not killing anybody. Curtis wouldn't have died anyway—just broken a leg, if he wasn't lucky. Come on, I'd better get you home; your parents are going to worry if they heard what happened and you didn't come home."

* * *

"Worried? Try frantic!" Carmen hugged Lucrezia, shook her, and hugged her again—then handed her off to Tony for the same sequence. "Hearing that there was a riot at school so bad the police had to break it up, and you've vanished off the face of the earth? How did you think we'd feel?"

"I'll kill that Smith kid if he comes around you again—if he doesn't get himself killed first!" Tony growled. "What in Hades were he and his idiot brothers thinking, putting you in danger like that?"

"They weren't thinking, that's what." Carmen waved her hands. "Just like that berserk father of theirs. Picking a fight with a bunch of rabid jocks."

"Mom, Dad!" Lucrezia protested, when she could get a word in. "It's not like that! Porter and their friends were just waiting at the bus stop, and the Rhinos started ragging on them—"

"Oh, sure, they just happened to be at the bus stop right when school got out," Donna said. She'd just come in, edging behind Tony in the small living room to hang up her suit jacket. "The whole lot of them, looking for trouble."

"It wasn't like that!" Lucrezia shouted, lying to herself as much as to her family. She couldn't quite pull it off, however. "The Rhinos have been trying to beat us up—you know that. The whole Saint Squad is scared to death of them," she exaggerated. "Our whole strategy is to run like squirrels if anybody stomps in our direction. Porter and Rock actually dare to stand up to these 'Christians' who act like anything but Christians. They're—they're like Amulonites, just like Rock said." She waved her hands even wider than Carmen had, flinging her arms out. "If we don't fight back, they'll burn us out. They hate us! We have to fight back, or it'll be Church history all over again—as in the Church will be history. The beast is coming, and we need to prove we're worthy to be God's people!"

Donna stared at her. "Worthy? So now you've bought into the last days stuff Brother Smith's been spouting? You're the one who rolled her eyes when I told you about Brother Kensai saying we've hit the last days, and you thought he was crackpot crazy!"

"Anybody can be wrong once," Lucrezia snapped, her eyes filling with tears. "Oh, leave me alone!"

Tony, Carmen, and Donna watched her storm off down the short, narrow hallway, the second bedroom's door slamming hard behind her. Gianni watched too, tears flooding down his little face in sympathy. He ran down the hall and slipped into the bedroom. Carmen half held her breath, but no explosion followed. She breathed a silent prayer of thanks for their "caboose baby," the unexpected addition who loved his sometimes prickly big sisters and brother.

"Well, I'm not going in there anytime soon," Donna announced. She ran her hands through her hair, dislodging the pins that had struggled to hold it in place all day.

Carmen decided that their younger daughter could wait through some cool-down time; it looked like their older one could use some attention.

Tony agreed; he'd had too many days like the one he suspected Donna had just gone through. "No luck?" he asked sympathetically.

"Au contraire." Donna managed a twist of smile. "Tons of luck—all of it bad."

Carmen rubbed her shoulders. "Sit down and tell us about it."

"I'd rather help set the table," Donna said. She poked Tony for giving her an exaggerated look of worry as he moved the stack of breakable plates out of her reach. "Seriously. It would help to keep my hands busy, since it looks like I'm not going to be employed anytime soon." As she dealt place mats onto the small table in their combination living room/kitchen, she said, "I know it'll surprise you, but it turns out that there are a few people around here who don't like Mormons—and a lot of them work in HR departments. I'm going through the employment list like the Nile through Aswan." The black humor of the simile earned a sympathetic laugh from Carmen—and a cynical one from Tony.

* * *

"And another one down," Donna muttered the next day, crossing out an entry on her Help Wanted list with a red marker. The scarlet scribble blurred in her eyes; she stopped on the sidewalk, pressing her palms against her eyelids until the tightness in her chest eased. Crying wouldn't help anything—especially not while she was standing on the street in her skirt and suit jacket, trying to project confidence and professionalism. Admittedly, it hadn't helped so far. Since they arrived in Lake Creek, she'd applied for a series of jobs. She'd started with the

Mormon-owned businesses, but they were already fully staffed, in most cases overstaffed, with newcomers. At the Gentile-run places, the human resources people turned her down flat every time when she admitted she was Mormon.

The buildings lining the downtown street around Donna seemed to close in, suffocating and threatening. No job meant no income, no income meant no savings, no savings meant no money for school to further her goals of becoming a teacher—and no extra income to help her mom and dad. They'd gone from a fairly nice, if modest, house to a cramped, two-bedroom apartment, from the security of having savings and some equity in their property to living on the thin edge of each of Tony's paychecks, decent, but not as much as he used to earn. Financially, they had little security at all. They'd managed to meet Giovanni's mission payments. Carmen said little miracles happened every month, attributing their financial solvency to tithing, faith, and missionary work, and they hadn't defaulted on any bills, but the feeling of skating on financial thin ice never left them.

Donna felt it, like a weight on her back, as she filled out yet another application in yet another nondescript, industrial-carpeted room. Her pen, as if greased, slid right past the "Denomination" box recently added to the application form. And when the harried midlevel functionary in the equally nondescript interview room reached the empty box, tiredly complained that she'd missed it, and asked her about what she should've put there, she heard herself saying, "Oh—sorry. I'm a Christian."

Watching him check the box and stamp the "Trainee" label onto it without another word, her conscience bothered her slightly. She was a Christian, but in context, saying that did count as deliberate deception. She was, as her mother had occasion to remark, a very good liar. And after facing down the spies from MedaGen, lying to one gray human resources drone felt like slumming in the shallow end, hardly a challenge to her ability to keep a straight face.

As he told her she could start in the online marketing division and shoved the contract across for her signature, she rationalized that she didn't outright lie about it, and this way she got a job she desperately needed. She followed the trainer through the bare corridors of the direct-marketing firm along with several other newbies. Direct marketing was pretty much the bottom of the barrel, just above the taco-folding shifts. After all, posing as a disinterested bystander in online chat rooms to talk up whatever product the firm got paid to push that week wasn't exactly glamorous or exciting work—which is why the company had enough openings to give her a job in the first place. The marketing firms and the Net-psychic outfit that rented space in the partially renovated Main Street building had piggybacked on the technical upgrades that new firms like Softlearn brought to Lake Creek.

"This is it," the trainer announced, gesturing to a small row of worn cubicles huddled against the wall farthest from the windows. Her company-mandated smile, tenuous to begin with, showed definite signs of drooping away altogether as she rattled through the required spiel. "Read the Employee Handbook thoroughly—you will be held responsible for everything in it. Drinking, smoking, and tripping are all prohibited on the job. Tardiness will result in reprimands, pay reduction, and dismissal after the third time. Damage to the equipment and furnishings will also come out of your paycheck. Your online sessions will be monitored at all times, as well as video surveillance on the work area. You have two fifteen-minute breaks and a half hour for lunch, as specified in the schedule. If you do not take a break during your scheduled time, you cannot take it later without specific permission from your supervisor. If you have to miss work for any reason, you must report your absence to your supervisor before your shift begins."

"Excuse me?" A timid girl beside Donna raised her hand. "Who is our supervisor? Are you?"

"Oh no! I'm the trainer, which means I only have to talk to you once." For the first time, the trainer's face showed a trace of emotion—distaste—but it vanished as she went back to the monotone of the official orientation script. "You'll find your supervisor's name and contact information in the Employee Handbook. If you have any questions, contact your supervisor. We're all glad to have you here. Remember that here at Best Friends Advice, we reward commitment and always promote from within. Welcome to the team." A plastic, mannequin smile appeared on her face, remained there exactly as long as the corporate rules mandated as she delivered the pep-talk part of her memorized speech, then disappeared. So did she, striding away to her own office, her interrupted personal calls, and her perusal of the job boards.

"Promotion from within," Donna mused aloud, as she sat on the squeaky chair and looked at the multiple cross-outs and write-ins on the directory listing tacked to the fraying fabric of the cubicle wall. Apparently, supervisors came and went more quickly than they updated the employee directory. "I guess that means if you survive a couple of weeks, they promote you to supervisor."

The red light above the console winked on. "We don't pay you to chat with your neighbors, Callatta," a tinny voice announced from the speakers. "Read your assignment and get moving."

Donna raised her eyebrows, but put on the headset obediently. "Roger and wilco. I take it you're my supervisor?" She scanned the list. "Allen?"

"Allen's gone. I'm Warren. And I run a tight team." Warren's face appeared in the upper corner of her screen, pinched and chinless—the perfect look for the tight, mosquito-buzzing voice. "So get to work."

Donna glanced at the video camera in the corner. "Yes, sir."

Two hours later, the Break light flashed across her monitor, releasing her from a wandering conversation with the regular users of the Galactic Empire Web site, to whom her employers wanted her to sell digitally enhanced T-shirts by posting comments about how sexy she thought they were. Her online persona, a bombshell blond with a suspicious resemblance to Virginia Diamante, came from the company along with the script she spouted—both perfectly tailored to appeal to the kind of adolescent techno-geek who would want to be able to program messages and graphics onto his T-shirt.

Donna rose and stretched, popping her back twice, then staggered away from the cubicle, leaving the online personas of the geeks babbling aimlessly on the screen without the participation of her bombshell blond. She wandered almost as aimlessly, glancing at the drab confines of the building that housed Best Friends Advice, Inc. The brightest thing about the whole place was a row of vending machines in the middle corridor—though the coppery hair of the woman smacking the glass of one of the machines ran a close second.

"Darn thing—come on! I paid for it already." She thumped the machine again.

"Here—the doors on the ones in my high school used to stick like that sometimes," Donna said, coming up beside her, expertly tapping the tiny plastic slider. "You just tickle them here, and they let go." The door popped open, and she pulled the package of air, partially hydrogenated fat, and concentrated sugar out of its prison, offering it to the copper-haired woman with a smile.

"Why, thanks so much! I know I shouldn't eat these, but sometimes I just can't help myself," she exclaimed in a soft Southern accent, taking the packaged cake.

"Good thing the junk-food companies fought off the health Nazis and their lawsuits, isn't it? The power of corporate America, defending us from enforced healthiness," Donna commented.

"And here you are, defending me from a thieving vending machine." The snack-cake addict smiled brightly at Donna. "I just knew, the minute I saw you, that you had a kind spirit."

"Really?" Donna blinked. "That's not usually the first thing people think when they see me."

"Well, I've got a special help on that score. I'm Sally Mae—and yes, before you ask, my mama got her first house through a special government loan and liked the name so much she gave it to me." She offered the hand not holding the liberated cream-filled sponge cake.

"I'm Donna." With a mischievous smile, Donna added, "But if you knew I was going to ask about your name, you probably knew mine already. You're one of the psychics?"

"Oh, honey, you're pretty much psychic yourself!" Sally Mae laughed. "I've just had people ask me or look at me funny so often I don't need any psychic powers to know that. Matter of fact, I do work for Celestial Angels, but I think the good Lord is the one who tells me how to help my ladies and gentlemen."

"He'd know," Donna guessed, not knowing what else to say. She knew that psychic hotlines were popular, but she'd never talked to a professional phone psychic. Let alone one who felt she received divine inspiration.

"He sure does," Sally Mae agreed, looking up at Donna hopefully. "You sound like you believe in Jesus—have you been saved?"

Good heavens, I'm being tracted out by a missionary Christian in the break room! Donna thought, trying not to laugh. *Good thing she doesn't know I'm a heathen Mormon, or she'd pull out the big guns.* Still, Sally Mae had a sweet, open face, and genuinely seemed well-meaning. With a glance at the surveillance camera above the door, she ignored her screaming conscience and simply said, "I do believe in Jesus."

Sally Mae brightened even further at this evidence that Donna was her kind of person. "Oh, I thought so! You got the early lunch shift?"

"I think so—eleven thirty to noon. If there's an earlier one, I feel sorry for the poor critters on that shift." Donna shuddered, thinking about working graveyards in the online social scene.

"I'm on the early one too!" Sally Mae exclaimed. "If you'd like you could bring your lunch down to the cafeteria, and we'll talk tomorrow. Some of us do a Bible study Tuesdays and Thursdays over lunch. Nothing heavy, just a few good words to keep us going. You're welcome to come if you're interested. Do you have a Bible? If you don't, I'll share mine."

"Got it covered," Donna assured her, smiling at the thought of having a Bible-study session with a bunch of self-proclaimed clairvoyants—and apparently clairvoyants with fervent evangelical tendencies at that. She'd have to try it once, just to see what it was like.

"It's so nice to have another friend—and a good Christian girl too! It's getting harder to find people like you in this town, with all the—well, strange people moving in. You know, these Mormons, taking over everything. But don't you worry about that; we don't have any of them working around here. Nice people like us, I'm sure we'll get along just great!" Sally Mae beamed, then checked her watch. "Oh, I've got to run. Missus Cornell always calls right at two thirty. See you tomorrow!"

"See you tomorrow." Donna left as well, hustling to get to her cubicle before her fifteen-minute break expired. *A good Christian girl among all the "strange people"? Oh, Sally Mae, if you only knew!* She hit her chair, deciding she'd show Sally Mae just how nice she was, just to prove that Mormons weren't that strange after all. It might not make any difference, but maybe it would convince one copper-haired phone psychic that the Church wasn't some wacky cult and that Mormons actually deserved a chance.

CHAPTER 17

"No mercy, no quarter, no victory for enemies of the One God."
The chant rumbled through the open square, as the Children of Light
waved red scarves. Brother Light stood on the steps of his converted
cathedral, his arms raised, calling down blessings on the faithful. His
own voice, flowing hypnotically through the tiny, powerful speakers
mounted all around the square, rose in the final thrilling cadence of
the prayer, coinciding perfectly with the beat of the chant. He swept
his hands down and forward, delivering the final admonition: "Go,
and cleanse the infidels from among the pure!"

With a roar, the black-suited, red-masked legion at the center of the
crowd charged out of the square, white-robed acolytes parting to make
way for the ebony and crimson flood. All over the city, the colors of
smoke and flames reflected the uniforms of the Hand of the Prophet
soldiers. Other fires spread throughout the Philippines, Indonesia,
Southeast Asia, Australia, and India, even the war-torn provinces of
northern China, as Brother Light urged his followers to conduct
massive "cleansing" campaigns against the disunity and disobedience in
their own hearts—and even more enthusiastically against the infidels,
the impure and intolerant unbelievers who fought against the Unity of
the One God. He specified some limits on their fury, ordering them to
spare the offices of corporations who displayed the symbol of the
Children of Light in their glittering windows—and paid generous
contributions to Brother Light's organization. He prohibited violence
against the property of governments that officially recognized the
Children of Light, cautioning his beloved disciples against turning the
hand of correction against those who sinned of ignorance, not malice.

Official statements—always for specially chosen media representatives and usually in English or French—predictably carried very
little weight against the fiery sermons he gave against the heretics who
oppressed and abused the humble followers of the One God. At first,
agents of the Great Cleansing focused primarily on members and
leaders of The Church of Jesus Christ of Latter-day Saints and the
Catholic Church, the most obvious intolerant unbelievers who
opposed the One God and Brother Light as his prophet. Once
unleashed, though, its agents didn't confine themselves to strictly religious targets, as they smashed, beat, and plundered through cities and
farmlands. As the movement grew, all who did not accept Brother
Light as the greatest and final messiah and swear to follow the One
God through his commands came under condemnation, making
them free game for driving, burning, and killing.

The archbishop of Manila, in a desperate effort to mobilize international outrage and support to stem the tide of destruction, issued a
caustic denunciation of the Children of Light as "servants of evil and
persecutors of the body of Christ," calling on the pope, the United
Nations, and "the civilized, God-fearing inhabitants of the earth" to
aid the Catholic Church and rescue its beleaguered believers. The
images that accompanied his distraught appeal caught viewers all
over the world in horrified fascination: houses and shops burning,
churches bombed into desecrated shells, priests crucified against
sanctuary doors, men shot in the streets, women crushed under the
weight of thrown stones and bricks, children thrown into the fires
destroying their homes—all to the cheers of wild-eyed, chanting
fanatics waving banners emblazoned with the symbol of the
Children of Light. The images played over and over again, as
pundits, philosophers, and politicians all over the world debated the
merits of charitable or military intervention in sectarian strife,
emerging religions, nativist political movements, and, inevitably, the
Catholic Church's own long history of bloody crusades and persecutions of unbelievers.

"How can an institution that presided over the torture and
murder of millions of Jews, Muslims, Native Americans, Indians, and
Africans point fingers at the oppressed masses of the Philippines?" a
calm, disdainful professor asked, from the heights of her media-wired

ivory tower and her conviction of her own European, atheistic, rational superiority.

"Nice," Monk observed, glancing from the screen to his ratings board. "We've got both sides furious, the Catholics and the atheists. Kim, cue Darren to get another statement from that fireball priest they've got down there." The soft chime of an incoming transmission drew his attention; his eyes widened as he caught a glimpse of the urgent report coming down the wires. "Whoa! Speaking of which— never mind. Cue Darren for an emergency interruption, Kim. We've got breaking news going on."

The urgent, drum-pounding leitmotif of a Channel 8 special report faded. A pale-faced Anne O'Neal appeared, replacing the debating panel. "This is Anne O'Neal reporting live from Manila, where the war between the Children of Light and the Catholic Church has taken another deadly turn. I recorded this footage only two hours ago, when a prayer demonstration turned into a deadly confrontation."

Her image disappeared into the sight and sound of the rhythmic pounding of hundreds of feet and hands. Anne's voice began again, this time on the recording, as she stepped into camera range. "We're reporting from Manila, where a huge mob of the Children of Light have surrounded the cathedral and archbishop's palace here in the heart of the city. Sources inform us that the archbishop's recent report on anti-Catholic violence has infuriated the Philippine followers of Brother Light, the self-proclaimed prophet of the One God. A prayer protest held just blocks from the archbishop's palace has turned into a near riot since the Children of Light arrived at the cathedral. They have torn down the doors and pulled out the furnishings, protesting what a spokesman calls Catholic lies accusing the Children of Light of anti-Catholic atrocities."

Behind her, a roar went up. She turned, as Leon's camera zoomed in to catch a close-up shot of the weakly struggling form that a cluster of black-robed, crimson-masked men carried aloft over the heads of the crowd. Hands reached from the sides, snatching and tearing at the violet robes fluttering around the captive.

"Now the mob has stormed the archbishop's palace," Anne continued, the confusion in her voice rapidly giving way to certainty.

"It looks like one Hand of the Prophet soldier has captured Archbishop Corazon. The Hand of the Prophet, the enforcement arm of the Children of Light, has been blamed for most of the atrocities committed against Catholics." She automatically gave the background as her reporter training took over. The camera shook and Anne stumbled as the press surged forward. The chanting grew louder and faster with rage. A series of sharp pops sounded in the distance.

"The guards at the palace are shooting into the crowd in what looks like a last-ditch effort to rescue the archbishop, but the crowd is surging over them." The camera caught the guards' last, desperate effort—and their sudden disappearance under a wave of bodies.

It also tracked the progress of the Hand of the Prophet soldiers and their captive through the chanting throng to the center of the square and the piled wreckage of the cathedral's wooden doors, pews, and furnishings. A lone pole jutted from the middle of the pile, leaning slightly. At a signal from their leader, the soldiers threw the archbishop to the ground. The leader drew a long knife from his belt, raising it high so that it glittered in the tropical sun, and as shouts of approval joined the thunderous chant, he bent down to cut away the last shreds of the archbishop's tattered vestments. He pulled the prelate up, displaying his trophy to the crowd, before two more of the Hand caught the archbishop's arms and pulled him to the top of the mound of wreckage. They lashed the frail priest to the jutting timber while their leader flourished another weapon aloft—this one a flaming torch.

"Oh, please, no!" Anne cried, her reporter's reserve cracking in a reflexive prayer as the black-robed man tossed the torch into the makeshift wooden pyre. Soaked with lamp oil and gasoline, it flared up immediately. In the heart of the blaze, Archbishop Corazon echoed Anne's exclamation, crying out as the heat erupted around him. The scene abruptly went black.

It switched back on to show Anne again, her eyes dark in her pale face, as Clara, hastily summoned from dinner at a luxury hotel downtown to preside at the anchor desk, asked, "Anne, what is the situation there now?"

"The archbishop is dead, and the cathedral is still burning. We couldn't get more footage, due to the threat of violence from the mob," Anne answered. "From the last we saw, the Children of Light were preventing the city's firefighters from approaching the building."

"A sad day for Manila," Clara observed.

"Not to mention for Archbishop Corazon," Monk added from the producer's booth. He waved a hand at Kim as Clara questioned Anne through a summary of the events in the square. "Has anybody got a statement from this Brother Light character? Don't tell me he's missing an opportunity for publicity on this one."

Kim listened to her headset for a moment, nodded, and queued up the next feed for Monk's approval. He sat back with a grin. "Okay, perfect. Run the crawl—statement from Brother Light in ten minutes. Keep running it, and put it out on the Web site too. We want to catch some eyeballs."

They did; by the time Brother Light's remarkable eyes shone from the screen, Monk's ratings charts soared. Even though the actual broadcast came through Channel 8's international affiliate in India rather than from an exclusive interview with Anne O'Neal, the numbers warmed Monk's cold calculator of a heart.

"Of course, we are all saddened by the disharmony in the world," Brother Light said, in response to the reporter's request for his reaction to the dramatic events in Manila, "especially when the refusal to accept peace leads to violence. The glory of the One God is unity, love, understanding, and peace."

"Unfortunately, it appears that the One God's followers aren't as peaceful as we could hope," said the reporter, who showed more skepticism than Monk expected. Perhaps living in an area being rapidly overrun with Children of Light made this reporter less susceptible to Brother Light's charm. "Our offices received this video just moments ago, with a message saying that it was from the Disciples of the One God, an especially devout branch of the Children of Light."

"What have they got?" Monk demanded. "Nobody told me about a video!"

The interior of a bamboo-walled room appeared, grainy and dark in the shaky, handheld image. Two bodies lay against the wall, slumped and stained with blood that looked black in the low light. In the center of the room, a disheveled man sat tied to a chair, his face bruised but calm.

A voice snarled a question from off camera; the hastily assembled subtitle read, "Do you believe your false God will rescue you?"

The man replied in the same language, "God will do what He will. I can only testify that I know He lives and loves His children, offering salvation through Jesus Christ to all who will lay aside their sins and errors to accept His Atonement. That is our ultimate rescue."

A hand holding a dully black gun jutted into the camera's view, pressing the muzzle of the weapon against the prisoner's head. "Renounce your false beliefs and swear allegiance to the One God, or you will die, just as your companions did."

The man looked up, smiled sadly, as if sorry for his captors, and said, "I cannot. I know He lives, and I will testify to that as long as I live."

The gun fired, and he slumped against the ropes, but the serenity of his expression never changed. In a flurry of static, the scene dissolved.

"We have identified the executed prisoner as Thomas J. Stacey, an American citizen and Apostle of The Church of Jesus Christ of Latter-day Saints," the reporter said, his own calm showing a few microscopic cracks around the edges of his journalistic mask at the casual cruelty of the scene. "And the Disciples of the One God are known to be one of the first groups in the Philippines to convert to the religious movement. They profess to be absolutely devoted to the One God—and to you, as his messenger. What is your response to those who have executed two religious leaders in your name?"

"Way to hit him with the hard questions! Get a copy of that recording," Monk ordered Kim. "And I want the head of the affiliate producer for keeping that little scoop under their hats instead of sending it to the home office."

Brother Light's expressive face practically glowed with noble sorrow. "I grieve for both of those men, for their misplaced faith in incomplete religions, in gods who had no power to save them. And of course, the Children of Light deplore such uncivilized, unloving actions. It pains me to know that some of our brothers felt they had to resort to such harsh measures, and I extend condolences to the friends and loved ones of all those whom disharmony has touched."

"You do not advocate violence, then?" the reporter pressed. "You claim that you do not preach against Catholics or other religious groups?"

"I advocate eternal truth and enlightenment," Brother Light assured him. "And I preach only the word of the One God against lasciviousness, greed, materialism, and arrogance."

The ratings didn't drop for several minutes, as Brother Light did indeed preach an eloquent, poetic, and simple sermon on the evils that kept unenlightened minds from the warmth and security of the One God. He easily overrode the reporter's efforts to cut him off for several minutes, long enough to catch American and European eyes, ears, and minds through Channel 8's broadcast.

By the time he rose, graciously thanking the reporter for his attention, most of the Western world had the impression that Brother Light had called the interview specifically to disown the harsh violence of a few misguided men among the peaceful congregation of the Children of Light.

Later as he settled into the back of his limousine, he spared a smile and compliment for Sepphira. "Excellent advice as always." He didn't know whether the idea to record Elder Stacey's death had come from Sepphira or the shadows that talked to her, but it had served its purpose excellently. The dead Apostle and archbishop proved that God had abandoned the Christians, that their religions had no power to save their lives. And by ordering the archbishop's death and releasing the recording while he himself stayed far away, in the midst of a goodwill tour, he distanced himself from Western blame and secured ample opportunities for free airtime. Modern religion-building, he had realized early on, relied on image-building, branding, and publicity as much as any corporate marketing campaign—and he had mastered them all for approximately one quarter of the globe, a comparatively small market. Now, he needed to broaden his reach.

Almost satisfied, he stretched his legs and tapped an exclusive number into his phone. When the voice on the other end answered, he said, "I do not want to see either of those recordings on Western broadcasts after tomorrow. They can play in Eastern markets as often as you like. If I am happy, you will receive the bonus we discussed. If I am not—let's simply say that you won't need a recording to show the damage the Children of Light can do to their enemies."

Monk received the kill order on the assassination footage even before Brother Light had made his next connection. This time, the video screen built into the limousine's console lit as well, showing the white and gray of the International Space Station's stark interior and Ivana Mir's lazy smile.

"Well, if it isn't my favorite preacher," she purred teasingly. "When are you going to talk a couple of angels into flying you up here for a personal visit?"

He smiled, effortlessly turning on the seductive charm he'd used when he first approached her through the open e-mail channel to the ISS that the International Space Administration maintained for their own publicity purposes. "I've tried to convince them to—but they're intimidated by the thought of comparisons to your overwhelming celestial beauty."

"Is there a school where they teach all of you religious types to throw rubbish like that?" Mir asked, shrugging off the flirting for more practical conversation. He was attractive, but he also knew it, and he was literally thousands of miles away. She'd never been into long-distance relationships; she was more interested in a business proposition than a personal one.

"No, it's a talent." Brother Light matched her businesslike tone. "Like business acumen. You were right about the expense of setting up my own satellites."

"Of course I was," Mir accepted his admission easily; she'd expected it. "Makes my fee look downright reasonable by comparison, doesn't it?"

"It does—if you can guarantee access when I want it," he returned.

She smiled. "You transfer the sugar into my account, and I'll hook you into the worldwide satellite network with one button. I've already cleared it with the captain. When you're ready to go, we're green."

"That's a hefty phone bill to pay for spiritual advice," Hideyoshi observed, glancing at the climatologist as she clicked off the connection. He'd come in just in time to see Brother Light's face on the screen but hadn't heard the conversation.

"Spiritual advice is always worth it," Mir informed him. "I'd expect you to agree there, Jamie."

"Oh, I do," Hideyoshi said, wondering about the mercurial Mir's sudden good mood. "Still, I'm not sure I'd be looking for spiritual advice from Brother Light. I've heard some very scary things about him."

"You'll probably hear more," Mir said, not bothering to tell him about the news broadcast she'd watched. Why upset him? He'd find out eventually about the wackos semiassociated with Brother Light. "But we can all do with friends in high places, right? Besides, it's not everyday a girl gets to talk to a god."

"It could be," Hideyoshi pointed out—one more attempt in his fruitless struggle to inject a little religion into Mir's determinedly secular life. "A prayer's all it takes."

* * *

"Pray every day for divine inspiration and help to find those souls who are desperately looking for peace and understanding in these troubled days," Elder Molina urged, looking over the audience of the regional conference in Santiago. "Then go about the Lord's work with a light heart and peaceful mind. Trust in Him and His love as you bring the truth of the gospel to our sisters and brothers. President Smith sends his own love to us here in Chile, as does President Rojas. I testify that they are truly prophets of the Lord, called to lead us in these very last of the latter days. Follow their lead, follow Christ, and all will be well. In His beloved, holy name, amen."

"Amen," the congregation echoed, a deep sound that filled the conference center. Zamora joined the heartfelt response—and felt a rush of pride, joy, and, he had to admit, relief that Michael Angel— Mercury—did as well. He glanced at his son, neatly suited and combed, putting away his PDA after taking careful notes through the Apostle's address, then sent his own silent but heartfelt prayer of thanksgiving heavenward. He still felt uneasy about this Dove Nakai whom Mercury almost worshipped, and he disliked the thought of his son participating in armed raids against bandits in the American deserts, but after two decades of training men in combat maneuvers, discipline, and honor, he knew the signs of a committed, capable soldier—and this boy, while still young, showed many of them.

Mercury slipped the PDA into his jacket pocket, smiling as he met his father's eyes. He was rather surprised himself at how good it felt to be home. Yes, that meant following his father's strict rules instead of running mostly wild among the Santos, and losing a little of his freedom did chafe slightly, but only slightly; seeing the glimmer of trust in his father's eyes, and knowing that he merited that trust, made it worth the pinch of having to report on where he was going and when he would be back.

"Pretty good speech, huh?" Mercury asked, as they rose after the prayer. "Missionary work's where it's at now, gathering the good guys. Oh—I'm going out on splits with Elder Callatta and Elder Flisfisch next week. Is that cool?"

"Cool is hardly the word for it," Zamora told him, amused at the English slang and amazed at the request. "Yes, by all means, go. It may keep you out of trouble."

"Ah, I haven't been in any trouble!" Mercury protested. "I just got into a little discussion with Father Pepito, that's all. Just showing him the error of his interpretation of—"

"Permiso." The soft request made both Zamoras turn, to see an efficient-looking man standing beside them in the clearing aisle. "Would you come with me, please, Major Zamora? Elder Molina would very much like to talk with you."

"Whoa," Mercury breathed. He'd heard that the Church security forces were good, but their spotting his father amid the thousands of people attending the conference truly impressed him.

Zamora nodded crisply in consent, falling into step with the man as they wove their way through the slowly departing crowd. Mercury followed closely behind.

"Major Zamora." Elder Molina smiled, extending his hand as the three slipped through the discreet door into the loading area behind the conference center. "Thank you for coming. This is my wife. And this must be your son."

"Yes, sir," Zamora agreed, shaking the Apostle's hand, then Sister Molina's. "An honor to meet you, Señora. May I present Michael Angel Freeman Zamora?"

"Good to meet you," Elder Molina said, shaking Mercury's hand as well. So did Sister Molina, smiling sweetly. Elder Molina said, "I could make a comment now about what fine parents you have, or how you are a fine lad who will grow up to equal or surpass his father's impressive accomplishments, but instead I will settle for simply saying that I have no doubt that you will prove an asset to the kingdom."

"Thank you, sir." Mercury returned his smile, a glint of shared mischief in both their eyes.

"Unfortunately, because we must leave shortly for the rededication of the temple in Osorno, I have no time for the leisurely visit I would prefer," Elder Molina said gracefully. "I took the opportunity to catch you now because the situation is growing more urgent. President Quintana has expressed confidence in you and your antiterror operation—and in your personal judgment and observations about General Garza."

"President Quintana?" Mercury blushed when he realized he'd exclaimed aloud.

Elder Molina smiled, raising a hand to forestall Zamora's reprimand. "Yes. The president called a meeting—confidential, so please keep it that way—with several ecclesiastical leaders, Archbishop Pravil and me among them. I had the opportunity to give the president information that I received from Church headquarters. And that information strongly supports your contention, Major, that allowing General Garza to gain a foothold in Chile would be a very bad idea indeed. According to trustworthy sources, Garza has funded and directed drug runners and other raiders who have used both conventional and bioweapons. You will receive a sealed letter tomorrow with the details. I have already shared that information with President Quintana, and he advised that I put it into your hands as well."

"Thank you, sir." The revelation didn't surprise Zamora. President Quintana's allusion to "more confidential sources" giving him information about Garza had made him wonder if Elder Molina might be involved.

They took their leave as the Molinas' security crew passed along the word that they had completed their arrangements for his departure. Señora Molina graciously took her leave, smiling at both Zamoras; Elder Molina left them with a strong handshake each, and a swift but sincere wish for their continued success and good health. Mercury glanced at his father as they walked quickly out of the conference center, saw the intent expression in his dark eyes, and contented himself with feeling a flush of pleasure at being right.

Pieces of the puzzle spun through Zamora's head on the drive home: Garza's promise of protection coinciding with the sudden outbreak of terrorism and violence, El Jaguar's supernaturally elusive rebels seeming to know Zamora's men were coming almost before they themselves did, uncooperative villagers in Peru and now Chile suddenly succumbing to a mystery illness, the extreme precautions Garza's lieutenant had taken to keep Zamora from taking any of the rebels prisoner—in Zamora's mind, they all pointed directly at Garza. The General had accomplished his meteoric rise by arranging not only protection but the stealthy rebel and bioterror attacks that made protection necessary, maneuvering governments into falling to his forces without firing a shot. If Elder Molina's intelligence from the Church gave him the end of the rope that would tie Garza to El Jaguar, Zamora could give President Quintana the ammunition he needed to stave off the political pressure and Vice President Aguilera's increasingly insistent arguments to call the General to defeat the rebels. And perhaps he could expose Garza to the rest of the world as the ambitious, bloodthirsty caudillo he was. It could very well depend on what the Apostle's contacts at Church headquarters had to say.

* * *

"What does it say?" Mercury asked eagerly, bounding down the stairs the next morning, as his father checked the messages waiting in the secure electronic mailbox displayed on the living room console. "Did they really send it?"

"Yes, they really did," Zamora said, smiling at his son's wide-eyed enthusiasm. He flicked another button, hiding the contents of the other message before Mercury saw it.

Not only one but two virtual letters had arrived for them last night—the one Elder Molina had promised and one anonymous, advising him in blandly threatening words to back off his pursuit of El Jaguar or suffer unspecified but clearly dire consequences. He'd received the personal attention of the rebels before: a grenade tossed at his car (it bounced off the hood before it went off), electronic attacks on his personal accounts and credit, threats both virtual and on paper, not to mention numerous bullets fired in his direction. This message, however, felt different, less heated, more professional— perhaps from the source inside President Quintana's administration that fed plans and data to El Jaguar? Zamora disregarded the threat but took the message itself seriously, isolating it and sending it on, virtually bagging it up for his investigators to check out. He hopped that there was a chance that they could tie it to Garza's agents.

The other letter merited much closer attention, and the encoded data inside the package made his heart beat faster. Graphs, charts, colored simulations, pages of tables and text filled the screen; words jumped out at him: *AllSafe, contagious, vectors, DNA, genetic manipulation, antidote*—and *Garza*.

"What is it?" Mercury asked, leaning forward to peer over his father's shoulder as he knotted a tie around his neck.

"The information Elder Molina promised us," Zamora replied, quickly saving the data onto a tiny, glittering disc.

"What does it mean?" Mercury watched his father tuck the disc into his uniform pocket.

"I don't know." Zamora stood, straightening his son's collar. "But I know who will. Be careful today, Michael. Stay right with the elders and come straight home when you're through, okay?"

"Things are going to get exciting, aren't they?" Mercury's eyes sparkled at the thought.

"Yes," Zamora said softly. "Things are going to get exciting. Maybe too exciting. So I need you right home."

"I'll be here," Mercury promised. He felt good knowing his papa knew he could count on him.

* * *

"What's going on here?" Dr. Vasquez muttered under her breath, as she bent over the eyepiece of the scanning microscope near the far wall of her laboratory. She nudged the focus knobs to refine the already amazingly fine calibration of the instrument. The screen beside her replayed the scene in the eyepieces: the round, dimpled shapes of blood cells grew exponentially from tiny dots to plump cushions tumbling against one another. Floating beside and between them, the sharper, thinner shapes of T cells glowed like moonlit ghosts, guards waiting eagerly to attack any microscopic enemies that might show themselves. But on the smooth flanks of the white guardians themselves, tiny shapes appeared, irregular, almost crystalline, but strangely alive at the same time.

Humming tunelessly to herself, the sound of a mental engine purring rather than an actual tune, Dr. Vasquez clicked the button that caught the microscopic scene, freezing it in virtual amber deep in the lab's server. She glanced out the single tinted window on the lab's far wall, but no ominous black vans lurked in the parking lot—yet. With another click, she retrieved another gem of data, putting them side by side on the larger screen on the console in the center of the wall above her desk. Captions beneath the biological postcards proclaimed them extreme close-ups of Diego Valera, former farmer outside Orsorno, victim of the unforeseen epidemic that left his fellow citizens dead out in the jungle, and Señor Erwin O'Higgins, formerly of Vice President Aguilera's office, victim of a sudden illness that killed both him and his wife while on vacation, the poison traced by the vice president's own investigative team to a shipment of contaminated caviar. In both black frames, the same scene burst into emerald light. Red blood cells, their T-cell companions—and the glittering, sharp edges of a viral invader.

Vasquez leaned back in her battered, stained chair and regarded the images with eyes narrowed over her steepled fingers. "There she blows—or he grows. How did you catch a rich man's virus, Diego? Did you sneak a taste of some high-priced, oversalted fish eggs when nobody was looking?" She rose, retrieved minute samples of the two dead men and several others from Diego's small village, and fed them from their hermetically sealed tubes into a small DNA sequencer.

Zamora tapped quietly on the lab door before opening it. Seeing her lab-coated back and haphazardly pinned up hair as she bent over the analyzer, he realized that the forensic expert hadn't heard him knock or come in. He walked over to stand behind her. "Dr. Vasquez," he said, lightly touching her shoulder, ready to step back nonthreateningly if she startled or yelped at the touch.

She might look like a cat, with her wide green eyes and dark hair, but she certainly didn't display a feline's nervousness. Instead of jumping, she waved a hand irritably behind her. "What? I'm working. Leave it on the table."

After a reflexive glance at the table in question, piled to over-flowing with papers, rolls of film, metal instruments, glass containers, a ridiculously lush potted plant whose tendrils trailed over the whole mess, and more data discs than he had seen outside a computer-equipment store, Zamora tapped her shoulder again. When she stood, irritated, to tell whoever bothered her exactly how much she disliked anyone interrupting her at work, he raised his own disk and said, "This is what."

"Major," she said, recognizing him; her tone offered as much apology as he knew he could expect. She took the disk, glancing at it curiously, noting the lack of identifying label. "What is it?"

"It contains data that Elder Molina received from the Section 89 clinic in Salt Lake City," he said quietly. "From what I could tell, information about viruses, genetic engineering, and General Garza. It may be proof that ties General Garza's men with El Jaguar's rebels."

"Elder Molina and Section 89," Vasquez repeated, the connections clicking in her mind. A slow, sharp-edged smile spread across her face. "The mysterious diseases in Amexica, eh? I wonder if they share the protein-sheath composition of the caviar virus that killed Erwin O'Higgins—and Diego."

"Maybe. What I want to know is whether you find the same kind of virus in the blood of El Jaguar's rebels. The virus, and an antidote for it. Check the bodies of those rebels we brought back. I want to know if they've taken the same 'loyalty' serum that the General gave his agents in New Mexico."

Reflected light from the window flashed across their faces. Turning hurriedly, Vasquez saw the black vans pull into the parking lot, uniformed figures spilling out of them along with white-suited orderlies. "They're here!" She whirled on Zamora, practically shoving him toward the door.

"Who are they?" he demanded, his jaw setting.

"Aguilera's security detail," she answered. When she realized he had no idea what she was talking about, her own jaw tightened. "Did they not tell you? They said they had." Rummaging among the scientific chaos on her desk, she extracted a crumpled piece of heavy paper.

The vice president's seal glinted in gold ink at the top. "They sent this yesterday—an order for us to release the remains of the rebels into their careful hands. It had your name on it, so I thought you'd authorized it."

Sure enough, the elegant scrawl that Zamora used as his signature appeared in bold, black ink at the bottom of the order, countersigning the primary authorization in Major Archuleta's jagged handwriting. "The lying dog," he said. "You get the samples you need, and hide them. I'll delay them as long as I can."

"Oh, no!" She caught his arm as he turned to stalk furiously out. "You get out the back door. If they see you, they'll get their macho on, and it'll turn into a nasty brawl right in my lab. I'll take care of absconding with enough samples to let me find those little crystal viruses; don't worry about that." Her eyes sparkled suddenly; her hand on his shoulder half patted, half pushed him. "This means we're getting closer. They're afraid."

A wolfish grin broke his impassive expression. "Yes. And they'd better be. Good luck, Doctor. Be very careful."

"I will." Pulling herself up to her not extremely impressive height, she absolutely radiated cold, scientific hauteur. "Me, worry about a troupe of mere security monkeys? I could handle them with one microscope tied behind my back."

"Especially if it were a heavy one," Zamora observed, looking at the impressive bulk of the scanning microscope against the wall. Sharing a triumphant smile with the forensic specialist, he, finally, took her advice and disappeared out the lab door, turning left toward the back entrance.

Vasquez clicked on the intercom, watching the vice president's security team assemble themselves into position for storming the lab, figuratively, at this point, but their weapons hinted that they could make it literal if pushed. "This is Vasquez. Delay them as long as you can—paperwork and forms, bureaucratic nonsense. Don't push them too far though. Be careful." After the front desk acknowledged her orders, she snatched up a small camera and a box of needled sample bulbs and strode out, turning right toward the labs. From the direction of the front door, she heard the uproar as Aguilera's extraction team ran into the immovable rock of her ex-sergeant receptionist.

The storage room where the bodies of El Jaguar's murdered minions lay was cool, quiet, and dim. Working quickly, she rolled out the first of the long drawers, snapping photos of the ID tag on the cold body within before stabbing the sample needles in deep and filling each bulb with coagulated blood and tissue—not ideal material for blood work, but better than nothing. Marking the first bulb with a bit of bright yellow tape, she dropped it into her lab-coat pocket. Rolling the drawer back into place, she pulled another, snapped the picture, and filled another sample bulb. As she clamped the morgue drawer shut, she heard the brisk click of hard shoes on the hallway tiles. With no time to label the second one, she capped the needle and pocketed it before practically sprinting across the room to the drawer containing Diego's sadly decayed remains (the villagers had been dead a few days before Zamora's men heard about the attack and retrieved them). The bulbs in her lab pocket bounced against her thigh, clinking softly. On impulse, she snatched them out of her right lab pocket and put them in her left one.

"Dr. Vasquez." The surprisingly soft voice accompanied the sudden cessation of the noise of the footsteps. "What's a nice girl like you doing in a place like this?"

Vasquez turned, her eyebrows already raised in disdain at the ancient line, and the carelessly disrespectful tone that accompanied them. "I am working to defeat El Jaguar and his rebels," she announced, raking an irritated glance across the young man standing in the doorway. "What is a civilian like you doing in a place like this?"

He was a civilian, wearing a dark, perfectly tailored suit instead of a uniform. Even standing upright, he gave the impression of casually leaning, and as he approached her, he seemed to drift more than walk. Another man in civilian clothes, bigger than the first, stayed by the door, watching all of them, soldiers and scientist alike, with the low-browed contempt of a street thug. He had snorted at the joke. White-uniformed orderlies crowded into the research morgue after the smaller man, with camouflage-clad security guards looming in the hallway behind them all. One of the uniformed men glared at the young man, clearly feeling that the civilian agent had usurped his rightful authority; she recognized him as Major Archuleta, the vice president's lapdog, the one who fancied himself Zamora's rival.

"We've come on Vice President Aguilera's behalf to take the rebel trash off your hands," he said, offering her the authorization chit with a slow smile that seemed to glitter coldly from his dark eyes as well as his white teeth. "So sorry the garbage collection's been late." Again, the big man at the door sniggered.

The chit identified him as Jorge A. G. Serrey, special agent in Vice President Aguilera's security force. It didn't identify the big man behind him, whom he didn't bother to introduce. *Thug One and the smart criminal*, she thought, *the one who makes jokes and the one who laughs at them before smashing something.* Thinking about the gleam in Serrey's eyes, however, she revised her first impression of which was more physically dangerous. The big one would smash things, but the smaller would probably cut them to pieces. For just a second, she considered stalling, giving them trouble, but decided she wanted them out of there more than she wanted a face-off with Aguilera's men.

"Coming this late, you've lost your tip," she informed them. With a contemptuous gesture toward the drawers, she added, "About time someone came to claim them. I need the space for other cases. Nothing mysterious about how they died."

"Sure isn't," Serrey agreed. "Help the lady clean her closets, boys."

Vasquez turned as the orderlies began transferring the dead rebels into body bags, walking to the door, past Serrey.

He stopped her with a hand on her right hip, the too-familiar touch more unsettling because of the flat shine in his eyes so close to hers. "You don't want to watch, Señora Doctor?"

"I have work to do," she snapped at him, removing his hand forcefully. "You can come to my lab when you're finished, and I will sign the chit for you." Stalking past him, she felt the sample bulbs shift in her left lab coat pocket. Still feeling the touch of his hand on her right pocket over her hip, she was glad for the inspiration.

Inside her lab, she closed the door with one hand and fished out the sample bulbs with the other. Straining her ears for the sound of approaching footsteps, she prepared tiny fractions of each sample for analysis, moistening, cooling, treating them with the photoreactive dye the scanner used. She worked slowly but surely, making certain she didn't rush or make any mistakes. At last, the deep hum of the scanner purred into life, the emerald lines flowing across the screen, forming interpreted visual images. Red-blood cells, sadly deflated and withered, appeared, then the empty sacs of the long-dead T cells. And finally, as she whispered a prayer for all of them, the scanner filled in the crystalline shape of a virus attacking the immune-system guardians. "Thank you, Father," she whispered.

Whirling away from the screen to her computer console, she brought up the data Zamora had brought, focusing on the scanned visuals of the diminutive but deadly invader. Elder Molina's message contained the basic data the Salt Lake City lab had compiled on the New Mexico genetically engineered viruses, and the antidote that held them temporarily at bay. And it appeared that Meredith Galen's digital graphics matched the scene on the scanner's screen—visually, at least.

Another analyzer began to chatter, as it shredded DNA out of the dead cells, discarding the human DNA, isolating the unknowns. Vasquez watched the readout, tweaking the filters to focus on viral proteins. After long minutes, it printed a strip of film with black streaks and spots strewn across it, shorthand for the long chains of proteins that made up the blueprint for everything from viruses to blue whales. Once again, the Rorschach pattern on her screen looked like it matched the one in her hand. She would have to culture the viruses, subject them to harsher scrutiny, but for now, it looked close enough to make a battlefield diagnosis. Unless she had made an uncharacteristic mistake, she could safely say that a high probability existed that Diego and his fellow villagers had died of a man-made plague, and that the bodies of El Jaguar's rebels had taken a temporary, crude vaccine against that disease, one that looked just like the one the local coroner in Amexica had found in the General's men.

Proof. And they had to keep the proof safe until they could show President Quintana. The console inscribed the images and data from the dead rebels, Señor O'Higgins, and Diego onto the disk Zamora brought from Elder Molina. She dialed Zamora's number while she looked around the lab for somewhere to stash the disc.

"Zamora here." The major's voice sounded crisp and close through the phone.

"Vasquez here," she responded, keeping her tone careless, her words opaque. You never knew when someone might be listening in.

On the other hand, it seemed certain that someone named Serrey would shortly appear to demand the contents of her digital files on Aguilera's orders. She didn't dare send the data over the open phone connection with Zamora; it would take too long to download. So she had to hide it until she could get it to Zamora herself. So, what would they not confiscate? The console, for sure, but she had dumped the dangerous files from it onto the gleaming disc in her hand. One of the leaves of her domesticated jungle liana brushed her other hand as she paced past the table. She smiled, inserting the disc and sample vials deep into the potting soil around its base as she said, "I have an answer to your question, sir—we have a qualified yes. It's 80 percent certain."

The sound of the door opening crashed like thunder into her ears, drowning Zamora's tightly elated answer. Clicking the phone closed, she turned to see Serrey enter the lab, coming to a halt beside her research-piled table. He moved like a panther, she noted; lazy pauses giving way unexpectedly to swift movement. The smile that flicked across his face was a panther's as well, sharp around the edges, hungry instead of welcoming. His hands roamed the pile, picking up and discarding a pen here, a disc there, a sample tube somewhere else, as if they led curious-animal lives of their own.

His large comrade followed him into the crowded space, light on his feet for such a big man, but powerful instead of graceful. "You're the big scientist Zamora's hired to handle his stiffs?"

"I am Dr. Vasquez," she informed him coldly, "the head of the forensic research team assigned to Major Zamora's antiterror division."

"Call me Ernesto," the thug suggested. He moved forward, between the table and equally piled shelves lining the wall. She moved as well, trying to keep the table between them without letting it turn into a chase. "This is your chance to trade up, chiquitita."

"That might not be a bad idea," Serrey said thoughtfully, gazing at Vasquez with half-closed eyes as Ernesto maneuvered her closer to his partner. "It's a good time to reevaluate your relationship with a certain major who's been poking his nose in where in doesn't belong. He just might end up with his nose shortened because of it."

Vasquez stopped moving halfway between them, refusing to let them manipulate her further, and folded her arms. "I assume that you have come into my lab for a reason other than making vague threats."

"Oh, yes." Serrey lazily reached into his breast pocket, extracting a sheet of parchment and an electronic pad. "We need your signature on the release of the rebels' mortal remains, Doctor. And your permission to review all of the data you have collected in relation to them, of course."

Ernesto moved to the door, whistling sharply. Two of the orderlies obediently trotted into the lab, carrying boxes. Major Archuleta and another member of Aguilera's personal security squad watched over them as they began tossing the contents of the table into the boxes.

Vasquez leapt forward, saving her potted plant from tumbling to the floor as they dislodged the ancient strata supporting it. "Reviewing data does not mean taking all my files!" she exclaimed, glaring at Serrey. "Most of that doesn't have anything to do with that lot of dead rebels you've commandeered."

"Reviewing data means whatever the vice president says it means," Archuleta snapped at her. "If you interfere, Dr. Vasquez, it can mean the removal of all of this expensive and probably unnecessary hardware. It could even mean personal interrogation to retrieve the data in your head."

Vasquez stifled her first response to that—let him try to move the scanners! Some of them weighed nearly a ton, and all were securely bolted to the floor. As for interrogating her, she knew they wouldn't dare harm her—yet. Major Zamora still had the confidence of President Quintana, so severe political repercussions would follow if they blatantly hurt the antiterror division's chief forensic officer. Instead of pointing out the futility of either course (logic would probably drive a martinet like Archuleta to order the scanners confiscated or broken just to prove his macho manhood), she let her eyes drop, as if his threat intimidated her. That pleased him, and effectively hid the contempt and smug satisfaction in her eyes. She stood aside as they worked, hugging her potted plant to her chest and emitting periodic objections to indicate semi-cowed displeasure as they haphazardly packed the filed detritus of failed searches, disconnected the console's memory drive, and piled physical files into their boxes. A line of Archuleta's men, looking like large, camouflage-dressed ants, ferried the boxes out the door, down the hall, and into one of the black vans.

"Don't worry, Doctor. Everything unrelated to the rebels will be returned to you. Eventually." Archuleta flipped her a sarcastic salute and followed the last of his men out of the lab.

Ernesto looked at Serrey, saw a dismissive flick of the smaller man's fingers, and obediently followed the major out. Serrey peeled himself off the wall where he had leaned through the confiscation process as if the weight of gravity oppressed him. He drifted past Vasquez, stopping suddenly to catch her gaze in his. His voice was as mild as his expression, but he addressed the plant as much as he did her. "Unfortunate turn of events, isn't this? Be sure to tell Major Zamora, would you? Tell him that this time it was inconvenient, if not painful. Next time, it will hurt—if he wants it that way."

"I'm sure it will," she responded, keeping her voice as level as his. "The question, Señor Serrey, is whom it will hurt."

He nodded approvingly, appreciating the bravado. "Buenos dias, Doctor."

"It is now." She shrugged, looking around the significantly denuded lab. "Since I have nothing to work on, I'm going home early." With that, she hefted the heavy pot farther up against her hip and strode past him. She didn't stop until she got to her car, climbed in, and drove two blocks from the lab; then she pulled to the curb, her hands shaking as she dialed Zamora's number once more. "They've taken it all," she said, before he could ask. "And had me sign a release giving them access to my files, digital and physical. But don't worry—they didn't take everything. I still have my lab coat—and my plant."

"What?" Zamora blinked. "Your plant?"

"Yes." Relief—and a touch of superior smugness—washed through her. They had confiscated everything but the evidence they'd come to destroy. That meant Zamora was getting close. "You remember, my liana. I'll show it to you. Meet me for lunch, will you, Manuel? And be careful—the neighbors are watching you, hoping for a scandal." Clicking the connection off, she pulled away from the roadside again, wondering how the major would react when she told him that Serrey suspected him enough—and felt confident enough—to make poorly veiled threats.

CHAPTER 18

Dear Chisom,

I was delighted to hear that your transfer to the Chinese mainland went well. We did miss your Vids while it took place, but it was worth the wait. I was most interested to hear that there were members of the Church already in your assigned area, and I will be interested to hear how they found the gospel. This is not the first time we have found a prepared people before we officially entered an area. We saw a lot of it in India and Africa. These circumstances have shown us that God is doing His part to get the word out. We have Him moving ahead of us in several ways. He is using the Book of Mormon. We have been surprised how many people have enquired after the Church because they happened upon a copy, read it, and were touched. He is also using radio, television, and the Net. By these means, a significant number of people have become aware of us and what we stand for. The Net, for all the evil purposes to which some put it, has proved very valuable. And the Lord is using angels. Joseph Smith taught the early Church that God would do that. The Prophet admonished the Saints not to be over-whelmed by God's assignment to take the gospel to the entire world. He told them it would be spread by men and angels. We have truly seen angels out preparing people in a number of areas. That makes me wonder how many pockets of unbaptized Saints there are out there who are quietly doing the Lord's work and waiting for His kingdom to reach them. We may be closer to teaching every nation, kindred, and tongue than most people imagine.

We certainly support your decision to extend your mission for another few months. Though we are anxious to see you, we can wait another half year. We too feel it is important to have as many missionaries as possible to help open up that great country to the gospel. The prophet is not calling many young elders and sisters now, however; the end of their time is coming to a close, and another era is about to begin.

I agree that right now China presents quite a contrast with peace in the south and continued civil war in the north. I understand some of the battles even rage into Mongolia and Tibet. Hundreds of thousands have been killed. It's terrible. Knowing how unsettled conditions are in the north, I was initially surprised that President Smith continued to work with the southern Chinese governments. He feels strongly, I've since learned, that all will be well and the missionaries will be safe provided they obey all mission rules. So be sure you do.

With you, we were just sick when Brother Light's people released the video of Elder Stacey's assassination. We were also appalled that Channel 8 would show it and the death of that honorable Catholic priest. It is interesting but also pleasing that these gruesome scenes did not show long in the States. Even so, the Brethren have told us what is at play here. For all its faults, the U.S. is still one of the more righteous places on the planet, and such scenes could hurt Janjalani's reputation with our citizens. He may have ordered it not to show.

All I can say is how arrogant, sick, and utterly satanic the members of the Hand of the Prophet are. President Smith has told us exactly what Janjalani's motives are. He is using this incident to show the world that the Mormon and Catholic god is no god. The prophet has shown us that Brother Light will perish in his pride and foolishness. Mark my words on that one, son.

And that brings me to the question you raised in response to my last letter to you. What possible good would it serve for God to give evil a free hand, even if it were for a relatively short time? Frankly, it is to teach the inhabitants of the cosmos graphically and unforgettably two important lessons, ones this world is perfectly suited to teach.

You see, this world is unique in a number of ways. One is that it is the most wicked of all God's creations. At least that's how I interpret God's statement to Enoch that, "among all the workmanship of mine hands there has not been so great wickedness as among thy brethren" (Moses 7:36). Since we now seem to have surpassed even that level of wickedness, we must still be at the bottom. As a result, sin flourishes here as nowhere else. And what do we see as the result? Civilization-destroying chaos. Small- and medium-sized wars are being waged all over this planet and promise to escalate into world destroyers. By the wicked, the wicked are being punished, even brutalized. If this keeps up, and it looks like it will, by the time the Lord gets here, there will be very little evil He will have to put an end to personally. That's the first lesson God wants people to learn—evil is self-destroying.

Understand this, however. God cannot allow the self-destructive nature of wickedness to act as an impersonal nemesis, an independent, self-operating moral law sweeping away all in its path. To do so would be to allow the powers of evil to carry all the inhabitants of the earth down with them to utter ruin. God would be left with a hollow, Pyrrhic victory—one that would resemble defeat far more than victory. Since God's victory must also be our victory, it must be won through righteous human agents exercising faith in God. Evil must be allowed to combine its nefarious forces against the Saints and then be forced back in utter defeat through our faith, trust,

*and loyalty to the Lord. That's the second lesson—the
Saints win by trusting God and doing as He requires.*

*Right now He is allowing evil to have its moment.
He is also requiring us not to yield to it. Even harder, He
is asking us not to take up arms against it. Most of all,
He is asking us to trust and to exercise great patience.*

*I will be most anxious to hear how the work goes in
your area. I'll keep you informed about what we at
Church headquarters see.*

With love,
Your father,
Chinedu

* * *

"What do you see?" Samuel Lebaron roared the question to the
Millennium Brotherhood, dramatically pointing ahead of them.

His acolytes, gathered around him, shouted the expected answer:
"The devil's minions!" In this case, the "devil's minions" lived in a row
of inexpensive but well-kept townhouses, nondescript cars parked in
the short driveways, trash cans sitting demurely on the curb waiting
for the morning's pickup, and yellow lights still glowing into the
night from a few windows. The Mormons abided by a self-imposed
curfew that brought everyone safely indoors at nightfall, away from
the hostile eyes that watched them downtown, the suspicious police
who waited to pull over vehicles with known Mormon occupants for
minor traffic violations, the gangs of teenagers who made a game of
pelting "Mos" with profanity and worse. So they pulled closer
together, forming a tight-knit community along the clean streets,
inside neatly restored apartment blocks in what had once been the
city's poorest areas.

The pleasant domesticity of it all didn't make a dent in the hard
armor of hate that gleamed from Reverend Lebaron's eyes—or the
despairing anger that choked the hearts of many of his followers. The
reverend made no secret that he had been duped by the Mormons in
his youth. He'd been baptized and had been ordained a priest, so he
had lived the religion himself, he told others. The reality was he'd

never really tried, so it chaffed his soul until he finally decided it wasn't true. Once he saw the light, he devoted all the considerable energies of his cracked soul to eradicating the source of the error. The men who crowded around him on the dry grass of the neglected city park on the edge of Mormon territory, beneath the thinly leaved branches of the heat-withered trees, had lost farms and jobs to the drought, initiative to their sense of entitlement, and vast quantities of self-esteem to cheap booze and learned helplessness. And they wanted nothing more than someone, anyone, to blame for their desperate situation. This quiet neighborhood, with its modest prosperity, drew their ire, envy, and blame. The Mormons had poured into Lake Creek like an unstoppable tide spilling over from Nauvoo, creating jobs where none had existed, supporting each other, renovating streets that had fallen into decay, sending their children to local schools, even running for city offices. Why, that Sarkesian fellow was buying up half the town and wanted to be mayor! And just last week, the Mormon punks had beat up the star members of the high school football team. Worst of all, however, the Mormons found jobs, they had a strong work ethic, and they made everyone else look and feel bad in comparison. For that, they deserved all the punishment Reverend Lebaron promised to rain down on their heads.

Thus, the crowd under the trees watched their leader hungrily, some stone sober in their rage, some well lubricated with alcohol for the night's work, some jittering and paranoid with the effects of a more stimulating form of chemical courage. Tweaking on methamphetamines, after all, could count as patriotism—it was the only drug trade that the squids across the border hadn't taken over.

"You know your duty," Lebaron intoned, his voice falling to a menacing growl as he raised both hands over his head. "In the name of the Sweet Lord Jesus, we will cast the devils out! Illinois was free of their stain once, and she shall be again!" His hand came down, pointing ahead.

With battle cries and the revving of gravelly engines, the convoy roared to life, the trucks' studded tires digging long gashes in the sad turf of the park, propelling them between the two condemned but still standing brownstones that marked the entrance to Mormon territory. Pandemonium replaced the serenity of the quiet streets beyond as the convoy and its load of would-be exorcists howled through the neighborhood. The trash cans were the first casualties, bounding across the pavement as the front grilles hit them, crashing and rolling, spreading their contents across the asphalt. Bricks, stones, and bottles came next, flying from eager hands into the windows of the townhouses. The brilliant flare of Molotov cocktails joined the rain of missiles, landing in splashes of liquid fire on the lawns and porches, against the walls of the townhouses themselves—and into shattered windows.

One of the flaming bottles crashed through the front window of the Callattas' apartment, rolling across the floor. The fire reflected in Carmen's wide eyes for just a moment, before Tony lurched out of the chair, dropping his scriptures to the floor as he dived for the makeshift incendiary device. Snatching it up, he hurled it back through the window, taking out more glass. A second later, the last remnants of the abused pane joined its mates on the ground outside, as Tony followed the gasoline-filled bottle out of the first-story window. Shouting imprecations as vicious as they were incoherent, he snatched up a half brick from the mess on the lawn, throwing it at the taillights of the last truck in the convoy. One of the red eyes blinked out, the sound of its demise inaudible in the fading roar of engines and growing hubbub of residents spilling out of their vandalized homes.

"Help!" The cry went out farther up the street, where flames spread quickly through the dry branches of a once-prized row of rosebushes. Instantly, a dozen men and older boys raced to the scene, pausing only to snatch up buckets, shovels, anything that looked helpful to battle the blaze. The lady of the house raced outside in her nightgown and fuzzy slippers, hauled out the hose, and turned its small stream against the flames. It produced steam, but didn't do much to dampen the blaze.

"Find the fire hydrant!" someone shouted.

"We don't have the hose!" Tony yelled back. He dug his shovel into the hard dirt a few feet from the growing flames, tossed one shovelful onto the rapidly charring bushes—then hit something metallic on the next gouge. A thin, metal pipe gleamed dully from the dry soil. "Turn on the sprinklers!"

"We have sprinklers?" The owner of the home looked surprised—his family had moved in only a week ago.

"The pipes are here. The question is whether they still work," Tony shouted back. "Find the access cover—it'll be in the ground somewhere. And find the key—a big, iron pole with a claw on one end and a T handle on the other." He caught one of the junior would-be firefighters and deflected him toward the tiny shed at the back of the house. "Try in there—and hurry!"

"Here it is." Bishop Newstead appeared through the thickening smoke, brandishing the black iron cross. Cool-headed and calm even in an emergency, he'd run to get it when he saw the fire catch hold in the bushes. "This whole row of townhouses has the same sprinkler system—we turned it off to conserve water. Just a sec." He ran by, aiming for the far corner of the property.

Tony didn't bother to watch him go; he turned his attention back to digging for fire-smothering material. In another second, the dirt began to turn to mud under his feet as the sprinklers came on all down the street. They sputtered, coughed, then rose to their full height, blossoms of water erupting into the night air. The fire hissed and crackled its defiance, but the weight of water overcame it; the tongues of flame sank to glowing embers, then died, black charcoal. The amateur fire brigade didn't waste time congratulating each other, however, before scattering again to help their wives and mothers in rendering first aid and comfort; the sprinklers put out the remaining fires, but they did nothing for the gashes from broken glass, bruises from flying rocks, or shocked panic from the violence of the unforeseen attack.

The water did feel cool on Tony's hand, which suddenly began to sting. Or rather, he noticed it stinging for the first time. Carmen waded out into the artificial rainstorm, caught his arm as he stood gazing blankly at his burned hand, and pulled him to the relative safety of their porch. He stayed only long enough to get a chemical cold pack on it, then bounded off again, to help put up boards in the yawning holes once filled with window panes. Working on the repairs kept him from choking on the swear words he didn't let himself say, thinking about all the ways he'd like to barbecue Lebaron's entire congregation—with Brother Smith as a side dish. He wanted to gather up the rest of the men and go after the cowards, corner them, and pound the fight out of them, make them realize that they never wanted to harass Mormons again, especially not Callattas.

Carmen, Donna, and Lucrezia followed him, wielding brooms, mutual reassurances, and defiant smiles. In less than an hour, and in a perfect display of one of the characteristics that so infuriated Lebaron's adherents, other families joined them, as ward members poured in from unmolested streets, bringing blankets, boards, hammers, nails, and commiseration. Brother Smith arrived with his clan and followers as well, pitching in with the cleanup efforts—and not so subtly telling everyone "we told you so" while freely giving recommendations about securing the neighborhood as well as making retaliatory strikes. Several smoke-stained people glared at him, but no one could deny that the Smith boys' strength and energy came in handy, or that Sister Smith's freely distributed biscuits provided excellent fuel to keep them going through the long night. Neither the police nor the fire department made an appearance, though several frantic people called them; the record of the calls simply disappeared when the captains conferred and decided that nobody paid them enough to intervene in a religious war.

By the time the sun peeked above the horizon and Bishop Newstead gathered the shaken neighbors together in the center of the block, most of the mess from the attack (broken glass, trash, rocks, bricks) had vanished back into the sadly dented but once again upright garbage cans. Planks and cardboard shielded the shattered windows. Several young women, Donna chief among them, had rounded up the smaller children, keeping them corralled, reassured, and entertained in the Callattas' living room.

The adults, meanwhile, had split into two camps—not opposing each other, but advocating distinctly different remedies for the situation. The general consensus in one group—the one Brother Smith stood closest to, looking on approvingly—came down to: "Let's give them a taste of their own medicine." The exact flavor of the medicine was still up for debate; some wanted to throw a few bricks through Lebaron's windows; others wanted to unleash a plague of lawyers on them. That suggestion caused a ripple of black-humored laughter when Carmen said it seemed too severe a punishment even for a bunch of ignorant vandals.

Bishop Newstead, however, came down firmly on the side of the peacemakers, gently leading the vengeance advocates aside to caution them against incendiary language. "I think we've had enough fires started for one night, don't you?" Then he addressed everyone. "Thank you all so much for your love and willingness to come to the aid of your brothers and sisters." He paused, swallowing hard against the tears that threatened to drown his voice. "It's that kind of pure charity that will get us through any trial."

"That and a 30-30 with plenty of ammo," Rock shouted the suggestion from the edge of the crowd. A few affirmative growls followed, Tony's among them.

"Returning violence for violence?" Bishop Newstead shook his head. "Let's turn the other cheek and thank Heavenly Father that no one was seriously hurt or killed and the property damage was not great. Though they threw eight Molotov cocktails, no houses were set afire. The Lord was with us, and He will continue to watch over us."

"But what do we do about the Millennium Brotherhood, Lebaron's crazies?" Tony asked the question in many of their minds.

"We pray for them to come to their senses," the bishop told him, a wry smile on his own face. "And we exercise the patience of the Saints until higher and inspired authorities tell us to do otherwise."

* * *

"We will be patient no more!" Brother Smith declared, emotion deepening but not blurring his voice.

Brother Hunter and the others who had come to Brother Smith's "militia" meeting, a somewhat larger number after the vandal attack than previously, murmured agreements and amens.

"There is a time for peace, but there is also a time for war. The Gentiles have not repented; now the children of Israel will go among them as a lion among goats, to kill and tear them asunder, and none shall escape their righteous wrath. The lovers of Babylon will drink their own blood as wine, and the smoke of the burning of sinners will ascend to the throne of the Most High as the sweet smell of frankincense and myrrh. He comes again not to bring peace, but a sword, striking the evildoers with the sharp sword of His mouth, cutting them off from eternal life. He comes swiftly, to wither the earth at His coming, and we will be ready, as angels lifted from the dark vales of the earth to join the angelic hosts of heaven for the final great battle." Brother Smith's voice flowed on, building to a righteous crescendo as he invoked his version of Isaiah, Jeremiah, Moroni, and John the Beloved in a tapestry of scriptural violence and vengeance.

The words, the images, the emotion, the darkness surrounding the candlelit circle of Brother Smith's Christian soldiers, exerted a hypnotic effect, pulling the men gathered in the Smiths' oak-beamed dining room further into a world of mighty heroes, avenging angels, and swift retribution for evildoers. In their own minds, they grew from frightened, insecure men to true foot soldiers in the army of Helaman, faithful, steadfast, and utterly impervious to any wicked force earth or hell could muster. Brother Smith's grand vision seized their imaginations, soothed their nightmares, co-opted their fondest wishes, but even Brother Hunt had caught only hints and glimpses of Smith's ultimate prophecy and plan: none knew the day or hour of His coming, but righteous Saints, led by Brother Smith, could bring about the Second Coming by precipitating Armageddon at the New Jerusalem, initiating the destruction of the wicked even if it came on a wave of blood—wicked for preference, but righteous if necessary—and he stood ready to spill his own to bring about the divine plan.

Only his sons knew the full scope of their father's apocalyptic vision; he had told even his wife and daughters merely parts of the vision that opened before his eyes after that fateful day when he fell from his tractor to the ground in a stupor and the world had blurred into chaos. The doctors had called it a seizure brought on by a mini-stroke; he knew it for the revelation it was. Like Paul, like Alma, he had been struck down in his wickedness, to be raised to the greatest heights to which mortal man could aspire. He had received revelation, not merely for himself but for all those who came into the circle of his stewardship—and that stewardship widened every day. Eventually, he knew, the whole Church would embrace it.

The only bump on the road to eternal perfection was doubt, and Brother Smith could not abide doubt. So when Porter approached him, troubled by his discussion with Lucrezia Callatta, spouting foolish questions about the rightness and righteousness of their actions, expressing concern and asking how he could receive confirmation of his father's revelations for himself, Brother Smith had regretfully but firmly taken the strap to the boy. Once Porter had taken his stripes, his father tenderly bathed his bleeding back, showing forth "an increase of love," and told him not to bother God with his foolish worries.

"Trust in your elders, lean on my faith as your brothers do, and I will lead you aright, just as Moses lead the Israelites through the wilderness," he advised.

So Porter sat wrestling with his doubts in the shadows at the back of the militia gathering, watching Rock standing tall behind his father, and Orrin fidgeting eagerly at the far side of the circle. His mother appeared, with his sisters, bearing tiny glasses of deep violet liquid, the pressed juice of the blackberry bushes that lined the Smiths' fences as sharp-edged but fruitful barricades.

"My friends," Brother Smith announced, taking a glass and raising it high. "Now is the time to put patience aside and take up the sword! The devils in the form of men who call themselves the Millennium Brotherhood and follow the self-appointed Reverend Samuel Lebaron have been divinely marked for destruction. They will lie moldering on the fair green hills of Illinois, their blood payment for the blood of the holy martyrs Joseph and Hyrum, just as W. W. Phelps predicted in verse. All who consecrate their lives to His glorious cause, let this cup represent the blood we freely spill in His service!"

Most of the gathered men followed Brother Smith's example, draining their glasses in pledge. One, however, more bold, if not more critically minded, rose to his feet, still holding the full glass as he asked, "Brother Smith, what does Elder DuPris say about this? Does President Smith believe we should take the fight to the anti-Mormons, actively fight Lebaron's mob? All I've heard in official statements is missionary work and patience."

"As you know, I am related to our beloved prophet, close in his heart even as we are separated by distance." Brother Smith smiled benignly at the man, the candlelight masking the iron coldness in his eyes as he leaned forward confidentially. His audience leaned forward as well, almost holding their breaths. "I have been in contact with President Smith" he said. "He completely backs our initiative, but can't come out and say so, due to President Rojas's opposition. The so-called Associate President has pushed himself into the highest councils, backed by a small conspiracy of those who would steady the ark. President Smith deeply distrusts Rojas. He's a foreigner, you know, and a Lamanite on top of that. Those who would prevent the Church from hearing the true will of the Lord are destined for the fire, even as King Noah!" His voice, which had grown more intense through his denunciation, rose to a near shout. Taking a breath, pressing a hand to his chest, Brother Smith composed himself, whispering a prayer for serenity and strength. Brother Hunt and the core of the militia added their amen.

"President Smith is counting on us, my friends," Brother Smith said at last, calm and confident. "We must do what he cannot—drive the Gentiles out of the land of Zion to hasten the Great and Terrible Day of the Lord. The evildoers cannot stand against us, though they summon the corrupt police, the black-hearted governor's National Guard, or the forces of hell itself. On to victory!"

The cheers shook the heavy beams of the roof.

* * *

"Onward, Christian soldiers, marching off to war, with the cross of Jesus going on before." A huge swell of organ music rattled the walls of the run-down church on the "Christian" side of Lake Creek, brought a thin drift of dust from the rafters, and almost drowned out the semimusical but wholly enthusiastic hymn.

Reverend Lebaron took the floor again to resume his sermon, pounding the creaking pulpit on the small stage to drive home the point of this miniature revival. "My brothers and sisters, we have a menace among us, a plague that has blighted our fair land, our fair families! Just as the Philistines of old, the Mormons seek to drive the children of Israel from the promised land, by sword and fire—"

Perfectly on cue, the already cracked window at the back of the church splintered into shards of glittering ice, and a flaming Molotov cocktail smashed against the floor. Screams rose with the smoke, panic spreading through the congregation as more bombs crashed through the chapel's narrow windows. Women seized their children and ran for the back exits. Men charged for the front exits, some grabbing buckets and yelling orders. The more committed, or more rabid, elements of the congregation, the true Millennium Brotherhood, led by the Perry boys and Reverend Lebaron himself, abandoned the building to the hungry flames as they raced for their trucks, a half dozen of the vehicles spewing gravel as they shot away from the burning church, pursuing the taillights of the Smiths' battered pickup. Their passengers leaned out of the windows to aim an occasional rifle shot, inaccurate in the jouncing, lurching pursuit, but possibly lucky enough to hit one of the boys.

Tires screeching around darkened corners as bullets whizzed past, the running battle thundered down semideserted streets. Inside the battered tenements, residents cowered in fear or turned up the TV to let Virginia's cooing voice drown the grim reality outside their walls. The chase came to a momentary stop as the Smith boys plunged into the vast parking lot of a shuttered major-chain store—and the asphalt lit with the brilliance of a dozen pairs of headlights. Abruptly, the hounds became foxes, as Lebaron's men assessed the odds and decided that retreat was the best option. Another chase ensued, both sides whooping, howling, and shooting. Axles groaned and tires slid as they maneuvered to push each other off the narrow urban roads into the buildings, lots, and yawning pits of uncovered cellars. One of Lebaron's trucks, misjudging distance, hit a light pole and wrapped around it. The light itself described a graceful, luminous arc, going dark as the lamp shattered against the ground. The rest of the lights winked out as the power interruption caught them, spreading into the few inhabited apartments and shops behind the lights. The rest roared on, passing from the devastated slums to the brighter lights of the downtown area as Lebaron's men sought the safety of crowded and prosperous neighborhoods.

The chase continued until the distant wail of sirens penetrated the hot fog in the combatants' brains. The police could ignore a running pickup-truck-mounted battle in the rundown areas, but the prominent citizens of Lake Creek paid handsomely for their freedom from redneck annoyances. Handsomely enough to earn the appearance of three cruisers full of police in full riot gear, who pursued a couple of the offending vehicles a few blocks before sheering off to reassure their employers with the appearance of a strong "deterrent" presence.

The firefighters took the same philosophic view of the fire in a relatively isolated block far from the homes and churches of their real customers. Thus, when Brother Smith's elated militia, high on their victory over the hated Evangelicals, re-formed to celebrate, they had a bonfire already flaming. Beside the flaming ruin of the church, Brother Smith stretched out his arms in blessing as the fire outlined him in a hellish halo. "We have struck the first blow in the final battle! The dragon's forces cannot stand against us, because the Lord is on our side—and soon we will have the earthly support of His chosen representatives, as He sends prophets to bless our cause!"

Not that Brother Smith intended to wait for the Lord to direct a prophet their way; he strongly believed that God helps those who help themselves. Thus, at the close of a well-attended regional conference at which Jack DuPris had made an impassioned plea for faithfulness, courage, and steadfastness in adversity, he found himself face-to-face with Brother Smith, Rock, Porter, and Brother Hunt. His security team looked even more surprised than the Area Authority Seventy; they thought they'd covered every entrance, exit, and contingency associated with holding such a large conference in an increasingly hostile atmosphere. They hadn't counted on the volunteers acting as additional ushers at the Nauvoo auditorium coming from Brother Smith's private, religious militia.

Brother Smith promptly seized the initiative, smiling benignly and extending his hand to Elder DuPris with just the right mix of confidence and deference to be flattering without seeming slick. "Elder, may I thank you sincerely for the inspiring—and I do not doubt, inspired—words and message you shared with us this day?"

DuPris smiled, his sharp sense of humor bubbling up. "You certainly may. When do you intend to do it?"

After a millisecond pause, Brother Smith laughed appreciatively. After a longer pause, Brother Hunt and Rock laughed too. Porter echoed the General Authority's smile, but the flip answer—and the hint of anger behind it—worried more than amused him.

"You've earned your reputation for quick wit, all right," Brother Smith observed. "So I'll offer my thanks right now. We need to hear more about the need for courage, for the faith to stand for our Faith, for steadfastness in the face of the enemy's threats and imprecations."

"You're welcome," DuPris said, his smile fading slightly into a formal, slightly glassy expression of a polite celebrity giving a standard answer to yet another enthusiastically pushy fan. "I'm sincerely glad that my words touched you."

When DuPris stepped forward with his entourage of watchful guards to go around Brother Smith's small group, however, Brother Smith neatly maneuvered to stay in front of the Seventy. Rock and Brother Hunt spread out to either side, all but body blocking the two security men. Porter stayed back, watching alertly for any signs of sudden reinforcements from the direction of the car waiting to whisk Elder DuPris away.

"Please, Elder DuPris," Brother Smith said, his voice still pleasant and respectful, but with a flash of steel insistence in its depths, "if we could have just a few more moments of your time. I promise that what we have to say will interest you. You may have had inspiration to prepare you already—I know that I have."

A faint chill rippled down the back of DuPris' neck. *Oh, great—a crazy. Worse, a crazy with three other crazies.* Tensing, he turned a warning glare on Brother Smith. "I'm sorry, but we have another appointment that we cannot miss. Please step aside."

"Oh, I understand that your schedule is very tight, but I truly think that you will see the value of giving us a few moments of your time." Brother Smith smiled again, this time reassuringly, holding his arms out from his sides, his hands flat, fingers outstretched, showing that he was unarmed and his intentions were peaceful. "Have no fear, Elder DuPris. We have not come to threaten you—far from it! We have come to offer you the assistance you have prayed for, the way to save the Saints from the vicious mobs oppressing, persecuting, wounding, and pillaging their families and homes. We are your soldiers in the Lord, at your command as the armies of Helaman of old."

"We are all soldiers in the army of Helaman," he said, not warily so much as flatly, discouraging further exploration of that topic. He just didn't have time for another endless conversation with a romantic zealot who wanted to re-form Zion's Camp. But did that description fit this situation? He looked narrowly at the man before him—noting the confident bearing, strong face, flashing eyes—and sighed internally as he recognized the man. After all the letters, phone calls, and Net messages he'd received, he knew that he wasn't in any danger—except, possibly, that of experiencing death by persistent persuasion. He made a subtle "step down" gesture to his bodyguards.

The man had become famous in Church circles, as much for the staunch defense his bishop, Ronald Calvin, mounted for him as for the reasons he needed defending. Word of it had reached the Area level, but DuPris felt strongly that stake presidents and bishops needed to handle local matters locally. He had refused to become involved, instructing the stake president to convene a disciplinary council if necessary but to leave the ultimate decision with Bishop Calvin. The last he had heard, Bishop Calvin had opted to continue working with the man, urging restraint but not recommending a disciplinary council.

So, now it appeared that Brother Smith himself had taken his campaign for official sanction to the next level, contacting him personally. Curiosity—and a hint of sympathy—softened DuPris' tone as he said, "Now I recognize you. You're Brother Joseph H. Smith, aren't you? After so much correspondence, it took me a few minutes to put the voice with the face. Are you still in one of the bishoprics out in Lake Creek?"

The pleasure at DuPris' recognition visibly bolstered Brother Smith's already impressive self-confidence, but his voice held the barest hint of bitterness as he corrected, "No longer, unfortunately. Bishop Calvin, though a well-meaning and good-hearted man in most ways, felt he had to extend a premature release. He hasn't the faith to hear the true voice of the Holy Spirit in these last and most trying days."

"But you can." DuPris' response was a statement, not a question. This must be the man he'd heard about, the one who'd decided to take the battle to Reverend Samuel Lebaron and the Millennium Brotherhood, the chief example of the kind of vigilante action that President Rojas had asked him to bring under control, despite, or perhaps because of, his own sympathy with their cause. Even with his orders to the contrary, however, he couldn't completely dismiss the famous, or infamous, Brother J. H. Smith; of all the big talkers, hand-wringers, and bleeding hearts who worried endlessly and loudly about the Saints, this man at least did something about it.

"Yes, I can," Brother Smith stated simply. He didn't miss the recognition, suspicion, and flash of interest in the Seventy's expression. "And I know as sure as I know the Lord lives that He has commanded me to offer my services—my sword, if you will—to you, as the commander who will lead the Saints to the victory they did not earn before in the battle for Illinois. We stand ready to move at your command, sir, a small but daily growing and committed militia of righteous men willing to fight for their lives, liberty, church, lands, and families."

"We're not in a war, Brother Smith." DuPris issued the standard caution, not believing it himself.

"Aren't we? Elder DuPris, the last battle has begun in earnest. The Lamb slain for the sins of the world stands in the arena against the false lamb as the whore of Babylon laughs from the stands." Once again, Brother Smith expertly touched DuPris' already twanging nerves. "The Lord will raise up His prophets in that day to lead His people to Zion and safety, loosing them as young lions to rend their enemies asunder. We lions are ready."

DuPris looked from Brother Smith, fiery as an Old Testament prophet, to the steady bulk of Brother Hunt and the fanatic gleam in his eyes, to Rock's barely bridled energy and military bearing. They were off the deep end, and their leader was quite possibly mentally unbalanced, but he could see their point. Skepticism battled with admiration for their determination and frustration at his own impotence to stop the pain his people were going through. Looking at Porter, and the bruise that marred the side of the boy's face, the product of paternal correction, not mob violence, but dramatic enough, tipped the scale.

He leaned forward, taking Brother Smith's outstretched hand. "I have no need of soldiers right now, Brother Smith, but thank you for your offer. The First Presidency has assured us that now is not the time for the Church to make a military stand against her persecutors." His own frustration and hotheaded impatience prompted him to add, "But nothing in the scriptures or modern-day revelation forbids you from defending your homes and families." Releasing Brother Smith's hand, he patted Rock's shoulder (the kid's name fit— he was built like a stone wall), smiled at Brother Hunt and Porter, and strode forward, his bodyguards lagging slightly behind, ready to prevent Brother Smith's team from another sudden rush.

"Thank you, Elder," Brother Smith called after him. "I look forward to the day we ride into battle together to wield the mighty cleansing blade of the Lord's will as He avenges the blood of His faithful servants."

"I'll look forward to that too," DuPris said over his shoulder, as he at last left the echoing concrete confines of the stadium's loading area and settled into his secure vehicle and drove away. Yes, the actions of Brother Smith's "righteous militia" probably did contribute to the escalation of hostilities in the area, but DuPris now found it easier to see even him in the light of victim striking back at his tormentors. Even if he didn't accept Brother Smith's offer to march into battle under his standard, he felt a hot-tempered sympathy for the man—and a rush of irritation that Brother Smith's little adventure with Lebaron's followers had made the local news, which Independence surely monitored. Oh, yes, President Rojas would have plenty to say to him tomorrow when he reported to Independence for another interview/micromanagement session.

* * *

Major Zamora hung up the phone. The news from his lieutenant was not good. Serrey had come back to Dr. Vasquez's lab and set Archuleta's private security force looking for unspecified "additional information," President Quintana had to delay his return home due to diplomatic developments in the United States, Vice President Aguilera had issued a formal memo demanding that President Quintana set a deadline for Zamora's force to bring in El Jaguar or admit defeat and disband, and Mr. Olivares had dropped by the antiterror squad's headquarters asking casual but uncomfortably precise questions about "other methods of tracking El Jaguar—with science, rather than swords." Further, the office had received a threatening letter as cold and calculating as the one Zamora had gotten at home a couple of days before, but this one threatened harm not just to Zamora, but to all that was most dear to him unless he backed off. All that gave Zamora too much to worry about and too much time to worry about it.

He decided to handle it in his usual way, by working off the energy trying to prevent every possible danger or ambush, military or diplomatic, that his battle-scarred and intrigue-inspired imagination could conjure up.

That included concerns for his son. He decided that he had best take no chances in that direction. He climbed the stairs to Mercury's room and coming in found his son studying the Book of Mormon.

"Your reading a very good book there," he complimented.

"Just getting the ammo so I'm ready for God's army," his son rejoined with a smile. "I really liked going out with the elders, but it taught me I have a lot to prepare for. So I'm working on it. I think I'll be a little more prepared when we go out today."

"That's very good, but I'm afraid you are going to have to save the ammo for a while. I think it best that you don't go on splits today. In fact," he said, raising a hand to hold off his son's objections, "it might be a while before you can go. Remember I told you things could get exciting?"

"Yes," Mercury said, watching his father's expression.

"Well, I believe its going to happen sooner than I thought, and I need to know you're safe," Zamora confided. "Thanks to Elder Molina's evidence disc, it looks like we've found the proof we needed to connect El Jaguar to Garza. But we must keep it quiet for a few more days until President Quintana gets back from the United States. There are those who would do anything to stop this." The major was careful not to give more than a hint about any danger, his fatherly instincts not wanting to frighten his son unduly.

"I'm sure I'd be all right with the elders," Mercury protested.

"You best stay home, Michael," Zamora affirmed. "You have plenty to do here. I need you here to . . ." His personal pager went off. He glanced at the screen and said, "I have to go. It looks like we have a lead on El Jaguar. Stay home, son."

"I'll come with you," Mercury half asked, half suggested.

"No, not this time," his father countered. "Just be here when I get back." With that he turned and raced down the stairs. Shortly thereafter he took off for headquarters with Captain Guerra, hoping the hint that came though the spy network might lead his troops to the jungle lair of El Jaguar. Had he not been preoccupied, he may have noticed the car with dark tinted windows parked not far from his house.

* * *

Dear Chisom,

I am very pleased with your work and your report on the progress of the gospel in China. President Smith was working on arrangements to come over there with one of his counselors. That is one of the nice things about having the office of Associate President functioning. It frees the prophet to go where he is needed most and stay as long as he must. He will not, however, be able to come, at least for the foreseeable future. We have a very serious situation developing over here.

A few weeks ago I responded to your question asking when the Saints were going to start fighting back. I noted that the Brethren have encouraged the Saints to protect themselves and one another, but they have never said it was all right for us to move against the enemy. The Lord, in the scriptures, has promised us that He will protect us and the First Presidency has emphasized those same promises.

We have, however, a group of Saints who will not listen to the prophet. Among these are some ranking brethren, and perhaps even a General Authority. These deluded souls feel that they have taken enough and that God will justify them in taking the war to the enemy. They are using the books of Joshua, Judges, Revelation, and selected passages from the Doctrine and Covenants and the Book of Mormon as justification, but as is so often the case with this kind of people, they are picking and choosing what they want. They don't seem to have learned the biblical lesson that God chooses when His people should and shouldn't fight, and when He does He tells His prophets. These mavericks certainly have not seen the underlying message in Mormon's work. When the Nephites became the aggressors, he shows us, the Lord removed His Spirit from them and their enemies destroyed them.

The acts of these renegades, I fear, will lead to grave problems for the Church. Up to this point, we have been at least verbally defended by the national and state governments. Few of the civil leaders, however, will understand that these renegade Mormons do not represent the position of the Church of Jesus Christ. You can bet our enemies will do all they can to ignite the fires of hatred and malice and fan them into a Church-destroying blaze. The result could be legally organized and federally funded forces moving against the Church. Unless we can stop our people, the institution of the Church, rather than being protected by the governments, could come into their crosshairs. Though the Brethren know the institution of the Church is going to come through this mess somehow, they are fearful that any aggressive fighting will cause greater anguish than need be for the North American Saints. Times are not good here.

What amazes me is the relative calm I sense among the First Presidency and members of the Quorum of the Twelve. Don't get me wrong. They are well aware of the situation and putting full efforts into trying to put a stop to what is going on. Even so, the Spirit of the Lord whispers, and the still, small voice guides, and the Holy Ghost brings comfort and assurance. Somehow, the Lord is going to get us through this. As of now, no one seems sure just how, but they know that this turn of events has not caught the Lord off guard. In the end, all will be well. I feel their confidence, but I wish I knew what the Lord had in mind. Until He tips His hand, faith will be our strength.

And we will need that strength, as the forces of evil gather their own power. All over the world, we see the tentacles of Babylon extended, warmongers spreading death and destruction, combinations secret and not so secret pledging to destroy others for their own purposes. Don't just think only of governments; the groups contributing to the troubles in America and all over the world include corrupt businessmen, gangs, organized crime, drug lords, and anyone who sells life for profit. Moroni told his modern-day readers that secret combinations contributed directly to the destruction of both the Jaredite and Nephite nations. He went on to warn latter-day people that all nations that uphold these secret combinations "to get power and gain, until they shall spread over the nation, . . . shall be destroyed." He warned the gentile nations further to repent "and suffer not that these murderous combinations shall get above you, which are built up to get power and gain—and the work, yea, even the work of destruction come upon you, yea, even the sword of the justice of the Eternal God shall fall upon you, to your overthrow and destruction if ye shall suffer these things to be" (Ether 8:20–23). Even so, Zion will escape if she obeys the Lord, and right now the Lord is saying patience. For those who do not heed this direction, I fear their fate.

My son, I am so pleased that you are showing that kind of patience and carrying the work forward. I am delighted that faith is your strength. May you enjoy your service as you push forth God's work for the last time on the earth.

With love,
Your father,
Chinedu

CHAPTER 19

"Thanks, Clara. I hope that Sacramento shapes up in the finals too. Here, however, the closing bell has rung on another round in the ongoing grudge match between Mormons and Christians in Lake Creek, Illinois. And in this round, Beauregard's Pit Stop is the latest casualty." Anne O'Neal stood in the knee-deep grass of the roadside, hoping her long pants and hiking boots would discourage the chiggers. Behind her, the occasional curl of smoke still rose lazily from the jagged, charred ruins of a minimart gas station. The viewers wouldn't have known it was a gas station without Anne's introduction; the fire had reached the pumps before the fire department could drain them, and the entire front of the building had collapsed in the blast. A half-melted snack-cake wrapper fluttered forlornly from the battered sign. "Reports of what happened vary."

"It was them Mormon vandals, that's what it was," Beauregard himself growled. He carried his Southern upbringing like a badge. His slicked-down hair fit him as badly as the ancient suit he'd dug out of the back of the closet for his TV appearance. He was sweating in the hot wool from temper as much as temperature as he faced Leon's camera and Anne's questions. "Just tryin' to put me outta business. Been tryin' for years, shovin' us respectable businessmen out. Tryin' to put a full nelson on the gas business 'round here. They already tried takin' my distributors away, offerin' better prices if they didn't deliver no Sweet Cakes over here no more."

"Me'n my brother, Lou, we was goin' down the road, goin' fishin', pulled into there for a fill-up and a six pack," Boudreaux Perry mumbled, pulling his Buccaneers cap more firmly over his mullet.

"Not doin' nothin', and them Smith boys, plus about a hundred other of them Mormon guys, just comes tearin' up, yellin' like savages, and start shootin' at us."

"That's the story from one side." Anne reappeared, gesturing over her shoulder to the west. "Others have quite a different take on matters."

"The Gentiles in Lake Creek always say we Mormons don't buy from them, so my brothers and I decided to go fill up at Beauregard's, as an openhanded peacemaking gesture," Rock Smith said, projecting country-boy charm and harmlessness (the fact that he couldn't help flexing his admittedly impressive shoulders for Anne undercut the attempt at seeming innocuous, but his tone stayed mild).

Behind him, Orrin leaned against the truck in question, grinning, flashing a victory sign behind Rock's back. Porter had disappeared as soon as the TV truck appeared outside the gate, not wanting Lucrezia to know that he'd been involved in the brawl that destroyed Beauregard's; she'd scold him hotly enough without that direct proof. It wasn't that she disapproved of defending against the Perrys and Lebaron's other goons; she just didn't feel good about Porter and his brothers starting fights. Porter tended to completely avoid the question on the few occasions when he managed to shake his brothers long enough to meet Lucrezia for an hour or two after school. He'd rather spend this rare time with her listening to her laugh, not growl at him.

Rock, troubled by no such romantically related qualms, and unaware of Orrin's unrepentant gestures, continued the story. "We drove up, began to fill the truck, when Bou and Lou Perry began taking the name of the Lord in vain. When we asked them to desist, they attempted to inflict harm upon us. We resisted, and when they realized that they could not overcome us, they commenced shooting at us. If Brother Hunt and our father had not appeared as inspiration guided them, we may have sealed our testimonies with our own blood."

"The older members of the attacking force—or rescue party," Anne added, in an attempt at journalistic impartiality, "declined to give a direct statement, as did the Reverend Lebaron, but Jack DuPris, the Mormon Church's presiding authority for Lake Creek, had his own comments on the situation in central Illinois."

In a clip from the interview with DuPris that she'd recorded earlier, the Area Authority, animated and restless, shook his head decisively. "I don't care what kind of 'provocation' went on. The simple fact is that a band of bigots calling themselves Christians has turned their prejudice and hostility against the members of the Church in Lake Creek. It's happening all over the world. I'm just disappointed that in America, where we supposedly believe in the rule of law, that the civil authorities have decided to turn a blind eye to blatant discrimination—and even outright abuse and assault—against people who want nothing more than to live their lives and worship Jesus Christ!"

"There have been reports that not all the Mormons in the area have such peaceful intentions," Anne pointed out in the clip. "In fact, according to some eyewitness accounts, some of the Mormons have started the confrontations."

DuPris waved his hand, dismissing the eyewitnesses and their reports. "You'll find, Ms. O'Neal, that truth is one of the first casualties in any guerilla war—right after supposedly common decency. Reverend Lebaron and his followers alter the truth to justify their own actions. But the truth is going to catch up with them—one way or another."

Anne hadn't been successful in her efforts to get DuPris to specify exactly what he meant by the truth catching up to them; he merely hinted that he meant more than either the Final Judgment or the kind of courtroom shenanigans that filled the lawyer shows on Channel 8's entertainment streams. She also hadn't put up much of a fuss about Monk's dramatic spin on the story, which had puzzled Leon.

"What, no big defense of the Mormons against Monk's—what did you call it when he wanted to make Rojas look like a nineteenth-century loon? Oh, yeah, biased, self-serving propaganda?" he asked, listening to the interview clip through his headphones, waiting to turn the live video feed back to Anne. "Or is it that you don't like Brother DuPris for some reason?"

"It's Elder DuPris, or President DuPris," Anne corrected automatically. Truth to tell, Jack DuPris struck her as arrogant, high-handed, authoritarian, and volatile. What also added to her decision to highlight the contributing misdeeds of Brother Smith and his "righteous militia," however, came down to a feeling of betrayal. She respected President Rojas, and from what she had seen, most Mormons were good-hearted, generous people. It almost hurt to find that her "Mormon equals good guy" theory didn't apply in all cases.

"He's no President Rojas," Leon agreed, waggling his eyebrows at her. Anne didn't have a chance to refute the implication. The interview clip ended, and she took command of the live feed again. "Whatever the truth is in this case, the Lake Creek police department referred us to the county sheriff's department, which issued this statement: 'The investigation into the alleged incident is continuing. Residents are advised to exercise caution and remain calm.' Calm may be in short supply here in rural Illinois, however, as the fires, the clashes, and the simmering resentments could burst into full-scale urban warfare.

"Or at least suburban warfare," Leon whispered, unable to resist skewering the dramatic tone Monk told Anne to take. "Or maybe semirural, since we're way out on the outskirts of town."

Maintaining her straight face and refraining from throwing something at him, Anne signed off. "From Lake Creek, Illinois, this is Anne O'Neal."

"Thank you, Anne." Clara appeared on camera, her smile as perfect, and as vaguely artificial, as her coiffure. "Stay tuned for Channel 8's continuing coverage of the tension between religion and society all over the United States. And speaking of society, here's our entertainment reporter Garrett de Long, with a brawl of his own to report. What's this about Paula Almond challenging Virginia Diamante on the charts and on the stage, Garrett?"

* * *

The screen went dark, Garrett's smarmy grin disappearing. President Rojas's usually affable expression had disappeared several minutes before as he listened to the news report; he wasn't about to subject himself to Channel 8's entertainment coverage. He pressed his fingers to his temples.

"Jack DuPris is here," Sister Nguyen announced quietly, looking around the heavy office door.

President Rojas straightened in his chair, smiling at his secretary. "Thank you. Please send him in."

DuPris walked into the office, consciously trying not to stalk, smoothing his face into blandness. He couldn't quite manage a smile; coming to Independence frustrated him. Behind him, his two loyal counselors, who showed support for their former commanding officer by accompanying him on this trip, settled onto the comfortable couches in Sister Nguyen's office. Onto, not into; even in Church headquarters, they acted as if they expected imminent attack. So did their boss.

"Good to see you, Jack," President Rojas rose, extending his hand.

"Is it?" DuPris took his hand. "What am I here to talk about? Getting a summons to a personal conference with you or President Smith usually means I'm in trouble again."

"Do you deserve to be?" President Rojas held his gaze for a long moment, not challenging so much as giving DuPris time to consult his conscience on the matter.

DuPris didn't take the opportunity; he'd listened to his frustration, compassion, pride, and anger battling his conscience so long that the conflict had become part of the endless background noise in his head. Instead, he pulled a tight smile over his lips and simply waited.

With a sigh, the Associate President motioned for him to sit in one of the two armchairs and settled into the other himself. "Jack, you have got to rein in your people out in Illinois—and rein in your own outrage. We have enough loose cannons going off, especially in Lake Creek, and your dramatic appearances as a guest on *Scream Back, America* have only given the hotheads more encouragement. It was bad enough when they threw firebombs into a church during a revival meeting; add this gas-station incident, and they are giving the Church a serious black eye out there. You must put a stop to Brother Smith and his movement, even if it means Church discipline."

"Lebaron's Millennium Brotherhood has burned six barns, four fields, and two cars, plus committing robbery, assault, and indecent exposure. In addition, they attacked a quiet neighborhood throwing firebombs and causing a lot of destruction. It's not like they haven't asked for it," DuPris pointed out, stubbornly. "Besides, nobody's gone to court, and none of the anti-Mormons have legally tight proof of their allegations." He had no doubt at all that the lack of proof was due completely to the local police removing themselves from the conflict, but he wouldn't admit that in this situation.

"No matter what the provocation, nothing is worth our members' breaking the law! I don't doubt that there's plenty of proof—yes, on both sides—if anyone decided to seriously look for it, which right now, they aren't. The local cops may have backed off," President Rojas agreed with DuPris' unspoken caveat, "but the feud—more like a running battle— has attracted enough press attention that even the most reluctant civil authorities will have to act sooner than later. And if our people have started acting like outlaws in response to outlaws, it's extremely likely that the police, judges, and courts will overlook the fact that the Mormons were the victims all along. All extremists like this Brother Smith are doing is giving the prosecution more ammunition. It's time for the Church members to back off, drop their torches, and stop shooting. When they do, it'll become obvious who the true culprits are. Let the authorities take care of Lebaron and his gang, Jack."

"The authorities will take care of it by letting Lebaron beat and burn out every member of the Church in Illinois!" DuPris exclaimed. "You don't understand what it's like out there!"

President Rojas's eyes flashed. "I know what it's like in Lake Creek—and I know what it's like in the rest of the United States, where members of the Church are mocked, shunned, and barred from airports and public transport because they refuse AllSafe vaccinations. I know what it's like in Paris, where we no longer dare send missionaries out openly, and where the government is seriously considering a bill to make Mormonism illegal, an offense against the state. I know what it's like in Manila, where members of the Church have lost not only their homes but their loved ones to the violence of the Children of Light. I know what it's like in Brazil, where the new government has ordered the Saints confined to camps as suspected rebel collaborators. I know what it's like in northern China, where the mere accusation of Mormonism leads to arrests and disappearances. I know what it's like in Johannesburg, where a stake president was killed by mercenaries last week. I know more than I ever wanted to of suffering and evil!"

Taking a deep breath, he closed his eyes, keeping the tears in; when he opened them again, his voice lowered. "I weep, ache, and forever pray for my brothers and sisters all over the world. But returning violence for violence, hate for hate, vengeance for vengeance—Jack, how can we be the followers of Christ if we use the tools of the antichrists?"

"How can we be followers of Christ if we are so afraid of mobs that we can only cower in our homes, praying futilely that our enemies won't set fire to the roof over our heads?" DuPris asked.

"We are not cowering," President Rojas reminded him. "Individuals and the Church as a whole are working within the system to bring the violence under control—as you have been doing with Governor Kerr."

DuPris rose to his feet, pacing to the window. It showed the bustling city of Independence; in his mind he saw the ornate governor's mansion in Illinois, the smooth-faced, noncommittal man sitting in its luxurious dining room. "Governor Kerr is a politician up for reelection. He'll do nothing unless he has the poll numbers to prove it. I sit across from him, and I can see him weighing everything I say against his political advisers' latest strategy. He's going to help us only when Mormons are the majority voters in the entire state of Illinois—and not a day before!"

"So pessimistic? You're a persuasive fellow, you know," President Rojas responded with a wry smile. He stood as well, moving to join DuPris at the window. "Keep trying. The governor has to listen to reason, and if he won't, God will take care of it. You do still believe that, don't you?"

DuPris said nothing, merely issuing a noncommittal grunt.

"Jack." President Rojas's tone forced the Seventy to look at him. Rojas's voice, always deep, took on a commanding tone. "I ask you, on my own behalf and on the behalf of President Smith, to reconsider your course and attitudes. You have so much to give the people of the Central Area; you were called of God to lead them in His ways. Do not abuse that trust by guiding them astray, for their sakes and your own."

The command reverberated in the silence that followed. Unheard but present in a way more real than a physical voice, the Spirit echoed both the charge and the reassuring confidence. Inside Jack DuPris, the hot fire of fury and pride flared up, its dark shadow competing with the cool, calm light of inspiration. The battle surged, one way, and then another, before stabilizing again, half white and half black, as DuPris neither rejected nor wholly accepted either side, holding his own judgment equal to President Rojas's—and God's. What he did not feel, as he told himself that he had reestablished a rational balance between the president's well-intentioned but naive advice and his own firsthand knowledge of the situation, was the soft sigh as the Holy Ghost withdrew one more step, forced beyond another thick wall of "rational" armor.

DuPris looked at President Rojas and smiled tightly. "Heard and understood, President. I wish we all had your patience. Thank you for your time." He extended his hand.

President Rojas took his hand, seemed about to say something more, then merely smiled. "Thank you for coming, Jack. You have a mighty charge; remember that you do not have to bear it alone. Pray often. Travel safely. Please give my appreciation to your counselors and my love to your wife—and do not hesitate to call upon us if you need us." He walked with DuPris into the outer office.

The two counselors came to their feet attentively, falling in beside DuPris. He nodded once, taking his leave of President Rojas, and the trio swept out.

Rojas watched them go, a hint of sadness in his eyes, then turned to the tall, dark man who had come in during the interview and stood chatting with Sister Nguyen under the suspicious eye of DuPris' counselors. He pulled a smile onto his face. "Ah, Brother Ojukwu. Have you come to ask me difficult questions, as usual? And how is your son? Has he made a splash in southern China?"

Chinedu Ojukwu, the head of the Church's public-relations team, shook President Rojas's hand. "I have, and he has as well. I will tell you about his adventures, President—as soon as you tell me the official statement about the latest development in the AllSafe controversy."

"You are a merciless taskmaster." President Rojas smiled more easily. "Come in, then, and help me decide how to tell the world that the Church's position on medical research is much more positive than has been reported. How shall we make them understand that we approve of ethical medical research while deeply objecting to MedaGen's panacea because it is more dangerous than the diseases it purports to cure?"

"We will do it persuasively," Chinedu said, smiling. He didn't vocalize the "of course."

* * *

"You do know how to put together a persuasive package." Senator Garlick eyed his visitor suspiciously. "Your message got you this far, because I'm a curious man, and I don't overlook opportunities. But how do you intend to convince me to accept a proposal when you refuse to tell me the specifics?"

"The generous donation attached to my message got me this far," Johann Brindermann corrected. "I imagine that a million dollars piqued more than your curiosity."

The German sat upright on the visitor chair across from the senator's desk, radiating cool, military confidence—and the slightest edge of sardonic disdain, which chafed against the senator's ego. Garlick frowned to hide his satisfaction at getting back a bit of his own. "As a matter of fact, it did. I did some checking on you, Mr. Brindermann, and on your boss, General Garza, as well." He smiled smugly. "And as secretary of homeland security, there's nothing I can't find out. In fact, I found out that Andrea Cesar Garza, besides having a girl's first name, is also the boss behind the new drug trade coming out of South America."

Actually, Garlick had begun researching that information even before Brindermann's carefully worded and richly accompanied message arrived, mostly to assuage Travell Capshaw's continuing complaints over his lack of progress in taking over the drug smuggling and distribution business. Capshaw had tried to mine the identity of his anonymous and powerful rival by breaking drug-runners' bones, among less savory methods, without striking pay dirt, but he didn't have the full resources of the DEA, and a couple of corrupt officials, on his side.

"True." Brindermann's expression didn't change. "Where did you think the contribution came from?"

The man's easy admission deflated Garlick's triumph slightly; he'd wanted the German agent to look surprised, try to lie, or otherwise acknowledge that he'd been outmaneuvered. What Garlick didn't know is that Garza owned the corrupt DEA officials who had given the tip to him in the first place—and had given them permission to do so. He drew himself up, bristling. "I cannot accept drug money! Or the attempted bribery of a foreign national attempting to suborn the government of the United States!"

This time, a sharp sliver of smile crossed Brindermann's face. "Of course you can—you already have. Sit down, Senator." He leaned forward as Garlick cautiously lowered himself back into his chair. "You have arranged your ascent to secretary of homeland security both ably and discreetly. A little pressure here, a few thousand dollars there, a cunning commercial to dupe the gullible, a minor outbreak of enhanced pneumonia to stampede the masses." The offhand thrust had its intended effect; Garlick's high color whitened momentarily when he realized that the German had guessed about the true origins of the football tragedy. In reality, Brindermann hadn't guessed at all; Abbott had been only too happy to supply broad hints and carelessly unsecured documentation in return for an extra bonus.

Garlick recovered quickly; he hadn't survived eighteen years in the Senate by letting surprises throw him off stride. He sat back, casually devoting all his attention to lighting an expensive cigar. After the tip glowed a satisfying cherry red, he looked through the smoke at Brindermann. "All sound, tried-and-true political techniques—at least the ones you could prove. Seems we both know a few things about each other. Guess that makes us friends, doesn't it. And friends do things for each other. So what do you want?"

"A deal, as my message said," Brindermann returned, just as calmly. "You are secretary of homeland security for the United States of America, working under the direction of the president to secure your borders and domestic tranquility. I see myself as a secretary of homeland security as well—for the newly united states of South America. But where you battle primarily external threats and only occasional domestic disturbances, I must bring order to a vast territory riddled with pockets of internal dissenters. And while you have the entire resources of the United States military at your disposal, I have only a relative handful of devotedly loyal troops." That comment was a tactical exaggeration; with so many American troops committed to peacekeeping and antiterror operations all over the globe, Garlick primarily had the National Guard.

"You want American troops down there?" Garlick's eyes narrowed.

"No," Brindermann cut him off before he could voice the objections queuing up in his mind. "The key to effective modern warfare is not bodies in camouflage, as you know. Victory relies on technology—cutting-edge surveillance equipment and equally advanced weapons. And in that race, Senator, your United States leads the field. We ask only for a chance to turn North American know-how into peace and order for millions of Latin Americans." He extracted a PDA from his pocket and slid it across the table to Garlick.

Garlick picked up the tiny device, reading General Garza's wish list from its backlit screen. Names, acronyms, descriptions, and specifications scrolled past his eyes. Garza wanted everything the Pentagon had. Topping the list were the latest generation of UCAVs (Unmanned Combat Air Vehicles), pilotless fighter planes with independent computers and navigation systems. Updated JDAMs appeared next, precision-guided armaments to fill the UCAVs' weapons bays and rain destruction down on the rebels hidden in South America's mountains and forests. Currently, the UCAVs were fitted with safety controls that prevented the planes from dropping the bombs without human judgment and permission, but Garza intended to dismantle that weak-minded safeguard. Equally advanced, if slightly less independent, military hardware filled out the tally, with biosensors, GPS trackers, satellite uplinks, laser-guided mini-missiles, atmospheric surveillance drones, and wireless cameras all listed.

"What, no tanks or helicopters?" Garlick asked, eyebrows raised. "You're asking for everything but the kitchen sink here. Why not the mass manpower movers?"

"We have enough for our needs," Brindermann said. Garza didn't need tanks in the heavy terrain of mountains and jungles; he had all the helicopters he needed from absorbing the air forces of every country that called him in to defend it. "As I said, manpower is not the point. Accuracy and automation are."

"Accuracy and automation are important," Garlick agreed. "But I don't really care what your General Garza needs. What I want to know is why I should care."

"Because if General Garza can concentrate on suppressing the antidemocratic forces in the countries that have asked for his help, he will not feel the need to expand the drug business already infiltrating your southern borders. Drug runners, as your own publicity reveals, are intimately tied to the worst kinds of terrorist activities—activities which the citizens of this country depend on their homeland security secretary to combat successfully," Brindermann replied, the threat as calm as it was ominous.

Garlick snorted. "So I play nice with you, or you play havoc with my political career?"

Brindermann nodded. "You are not the only one, Senator, who can employ 'sound, tried-and-true political techniques' when needed. After you worked so hard for this draught of power, could you give it up?"

The senator didn't even have to pause to consider that. He'd schemed, maneuvered, lied, even killed to get where he was; he had no intention of letting it go for any reason this side of sudden death. The idea of selling out his country didn't bother him either. Politics, after all, existed in a universe of wheels within wheels, and nothing had to be what it appeared from the outside.

"I want money—one hundred times the down payment for this meeting," Garlick announced. "And I want one hundred hours of good press for helping South America finally win the war on drugs without having to commit already overcommitted United States troops to the effort. I want prices on the street higher, and I want a percentage of the profits at the end of each month. I want arrests every six months, big busts with greasy-looking perps to parade in front of the press. Finally, I want nobody to know about this agreement outside of you, General Garza, and me. This is going to play as a huge victory for the red, white, and blue, with credit to homeland security."

"General Garza is always glad to help beleaguered governments fight the forces opposing them," Brindermann said, not bothering to hide the contempt in his eyes. "You will get your arrests—but you will have to provide your own publicity. Given your history, I cannot imagine that is beyond your abilities. Delivering on your promises may be, however. How do you plan to uphold your side of the bargain?"

The senator shrugged, looking speculatively at the ceiling. "Most of this is no problem—a few crates go missing, a few accounts get mixed up, happens all the time. The UCAVs and smart bombs are a different ball of wax though. Selling them to you directly is out. The boys at the Pentagon don't owe me that much. But the chairman of the Defense Appropriations Committee does, if he wants to keep his position—and his lucrative little side business in aerospace contracting." Garlick considered, tapping the PDA against his knuckles, then nodded. "Tell you what, Johann. I could 'rent' the UCAVs, with full armament, to you for testing purposes."

"For testing purposes," Brindermann repeated, then mimicked Garlick's nod. "Field tests to prove the design and capabilities without risking those precious American troops."

"Exactly. Do we have a deal?" Garlick asked, knowing that his people (or rather, the techs at the Pentagon, but Garlick viewed the entire government as "his") had the backdoor codes that could disable the UCAVs even from global distances.

"We do," Brindermann answered, knowing that Garza's techs (or computer geniuses conscripted into duty from any nation under Garza's control) could hack the backdoor codes for the UCAVs and lock the Americans out of their own systems—then replicate the weapons as quickly as newly built factories could turn them out. "Is there anything you need to put your rental program into operation? Anyone who may need convincing?"

"Nothing I can't get," Garlick assured him. "The director of the FBI may object, but don't worry. A man with skeletons in his closet is easily threatened into silence and put in his place. That's why I appointed him." The senator raised his eyebrows at Garza's lieutenant. "You need anything to get your guys in gear?"

"No," Brindermann said, standing and brushing his jacket as if to remove the taint of Garlick's guest chair from the leather. "We will be ready when you are—we too have a few people to put into their places."

"There's always the mavericks who just won't cooperate, aren't there?" Garlick asked.

Brindermann rejected the sympathy in the senator's tone. "Not for long."

* * *

"Sorry about that—been waiting long?" Mercury ran up to join Elders Flisfisch and Callatta, with Juanito from the local ward, adjusting his jacket as he came.

"Just long enough to decide you'd ditched us and feel a surge of relief about not having you around to mess up another door approach," Giovanni told him, grinning.

Mercury grinned back and gave him one of the many borderlands hand gestures to retaliate for a verbal dissing—which earned him a playful smack upside the head from Elder Callatta.

The young men's good-natured ragging expanded to include a half-dozen other teenage boys kicking around a battered soccer ball and throwing amateur martial-arts punches at each other. Giovanni told them they wouldn't even qualify as karate-chopping amphibians in a San Diego dojo. Grinning, the most vocal, and therefore the leader, of the crowd pointed out, "Gringo, you got nothing to say about the way we pass our time—we're not a bunch of guys walking around together all dressed up in pretty suits."

"No," Giovanni shot back while Elder Flisfisch rolled his eyes, "you're a bunch of guys practicing putting headlocks on each other."

The good-natured joshing went on, Giovanni taking the conversation from self-defense to defending self and family to standing up for what's right. Mercury listened, impressed; the big Californian missionary really had the gift of gab when it came to young punks— like him, come to think of it. He wasn't quite as good as Dove at grabbing street punks' loyalties, but he didn't need to lead them into a firefight, just to get through their macho defenses enough to get them interested in the gospel. Elder Flisfisch didn't have the same easy manner, but after Giovanni hooked them into talking about deeper subjects than martial arts, he could pull scripture quotes into any conversation without making it feel weird or off tone. Juanito mainly stood there and watched, trying to soak up missionary vibes before he started his own tour of duty in God's army in a few months. Mercury had a few years to go yet, but he enjoyed hanging with the hermanos; if he couldn't be on the front lines with the Santos, he could still get his licks in on the spiritual war front.

He glanced down the street at that thought, then shook off the touch of paranoia that made him scan the few passing cars suspiciously.

He'd sneaked out of the house to meet them; that morning, his father had told him to stay in because of some phone call he got—from headquarters, Mercury guessed, from tapping the callback button on the phone. Whoever it was, it had made Zamora nervous enough to tell his son to alter his plans.

Mercury asked to go with him, expecting his father to deny the request—as he did. He wasn't daunted; it never hurt to try, right? So, active participation in nailing the General's hide to the wall denied him, and feeling that saving souls took priority over sitting home slaving over a pile of the homework he'd missed during his Amexican adventures, he decided to give himself a furlough to commit some good behavior. He got around his father's prohibition by telling himself that he would be home by the time the major returned. Besides, his father still saw him as a child who couldn't take care of himself, not the savvy Santo messenger who'd helped Dove's crew defeat the General's henchmen in Amexica. He had slipped out past the soldier guarding the door by jumping from his window to the light pole on the street outside. He'd skinned down the pole, landed on the pavement, and raced to meet the missionaries. He didn't see the car with the tinted windows pull away from the curb or the man inside dialing up a number on his cell phone.

Still, he had grown up with a father deeply steeped in life-saving caution, and the fact that Major Zamora took the precaution of confining him to the house, or trying to, did worry him. Not enough to keep him in the house, but enough to prick his ears at the sound of a couple of low engines approaching. He turned, to see a pair of men on motorcycles roar up the street, heading toward them—straight for them, jumping the curb onto the sidewalk.

Mercury shouted, "Incoming!" and shoved Juanito into one of the soccer-playing would-be ninjas.

Giovanni then reacted, pushing Elder Flisfisch out of the way, as he and Mercury dived aside—in the same direction.

A flash of light shone into Mercury's eye as he hit the deck; a thrown knife clanged against the wall behind him then slithered like a silverfish across the cobbles as the first rider roared past. The shouts of the other boys dimmed in his ears, overpowered by the rough throb of the second engine and the pounding blood in his head, as he watched from his prone position on the cobbles the glittering spokes of the front wheel screaming toward him.

Giovanni, whose evasive maneuver had taken him farther sideways but left him standing, saw the second motorcyclist aiming right for Mercury and reacted without thinking. The big elder lunged forward and grabbed the nearest of the bike's handlebars, wrenching it hard to the side. Its front wheel suddenly perpendicular to the back one, the bike went spectacularly out of control, spinning out on its side, striking sparks from the stones of the street.

The rider, cannily abandoning his stricken mechanical steed before it lay down against the square, surged up quickly, but not before Giovanni grabbed one of his arms. The masked rider, a big man with heavy shoulders, tried to push Giovanni out of the way with one hand. With the other he dug beneath the badly scuffed leather jacket and came up with a matte-finished pistol, which he aimed at Mercury with single-minded accuracy. Giovanni didn't try to grab the weapon or knock the guy's arm down; he went for the direct approach and punched him in the mask. His fist cracked into the guy's nose, sending him down like a large sack of rocks.

"Should've worn a helmet," Giovanni muttered, shaking out the pain in his hand.

The comment was barely audible over the roar of the first motorcycle returning at full speed. Mercury rolled to his knees and scrambled across the cobbles to a six-foot pole, one of the martial artists' makeshift weapons. His fingers closed on the wooden length just as the bike closed the distance between them; he jerked his legs out of the way, spinning himself halfway around, and slammed the stick into the bike's spokes. The stick smacked against the wheel struts—and the wheel stopped dead, popping the bike into the air and halfway through a somersault. It crashed to the street, random parts spraying around the impact site. The rider hit a second later and lay motionless.

"Don't talk—move!" Mercury advised Giovanni, grabbing the big elder's suit coat. They exchanged a pair of giddy, relieved grins, then turned to run. They got about three steps before Mercury gasped and stumbled, clutching reflexively at the handle of a knife that protruded from his calf. He crumpled sideways, slamming into Giovanni, who caught him before he hit the cobbles.

Behind them, the first rider rose from the ground, wrenching off his blood-soaked mask to reveal a crimson-stained, snarling face and badly broken nose. Even damaged though, his face touched a chord in Mercury's memory. He flung the mask behind him and pulled another knife out of the leather bandolier across his chest.

For a split second, Giovanni considered picking Mercury up, but strong as he was, he knew he couldn't outrun a thrown knife—so he didn't. Instead, he hit the big man in a low tackle, the two of them crashing to the street. Giovanni wasn't trained in hand-to-hand combat, but he had a pain tolerance heightened by three years of varsity football, and the single-mindedness that came with it. He also had surprise on his side. Ignoring a nasty kick to his upper leg, he grabbed the man's knife hand, squeezing the wrist bones until they ground together. The knife fell, ringing on the hard street.

Giovanni, realizing that he'd inadvertently closed with a militarily trained guerilla, went into full reverse mode, pushing himself away from the rider. The rider rubbed the back of his hand across his bloody face, then spat a crimson stream onto the road beside Giovanni's feet. His teeth showed ruby as he grinned. Giovanni didn't grin so much as bare his own teeth back.

"Stop! Raise your hands!" The carabinero who charged up after Elder Flisfisch's summons came to a halt, feet apart, gun up and pointing at the combatants.

"Yes, sir!" Giovanni obediently put up his hands.

So did the bloody rider—but one of his held a black-matte pistol. He aimed it at the carabinero, then slewed it around at Mercury, who had forced himself up to a wobbly stand. Giovanni dropped his surrender stance to catch Mercury around his waist. They hit the street again, as the bullet whined above them. The carabinero opened fire, as did the other two who arrived via another street on the square. A bullet slammed into the biker, who roared, shooting at Mercury again. Another bullet hit his arm, throwing off his aim; his shot went wide, forming a tiny crater in a cobble, sending shards of rock flying. The biker went flying too, tumbling over as the third bullet hit him.

"Come on," Mercury whispered, pulling at Giovanni. "Let's get out of the way."

"Yeah," Giovanni grunted, staring at the fallen rider before turning away to help Mercury to his feet.

The warning shout from the carabinero made Giovanni look over—in time to see the wounded rider roll painfully to his knees, spit another gout of blood and a vile curse at Mormons, and bring the gun up again. Giovanni didn't have time to do more than shove Mercury over again, before the man emptied the last three bullets into the big missionary's chest.

Mercury caught Giovanni as he fell, awkwardly holding him as he crumpled. "Elder Callatta—Elder, come back!" Mercury cried, spattered with blood.

Giovanni opened his eyes, half smiled, and said, "They need me home. Tell Mama it's all right." His eyes glazed over, and his body went limp in Mercury's arms.

* * *

When Major Zamora arrived, with a squad of soldiers, they found Mercury still kneeling there, cradling Elder Callatta's body, staring blindly ahead of him, tears dripping off his chin. A few paces closer, the bikers sprawled on the pavement as well. Zamora skirted one out-flung hand, glancing at the dead man's face.

"It's Ernesto." Mercury's voice sounded faint, as if it came from a long way off. "The Ernesto in your folder, the muscle boy for Aguilera's security chief."

"We couldn't move him," a medic said apologetically, catching up to Zamora and gesturing discreetly at Mercury. "Please, sir, can you do something? He's been hurt."

"Get Vasquez down here," Zamora ordered Captain Guerra, who nodded crisply.

Zamora looked down at his son, then at the note in his hand. It had come to his office just two hours before, a warning telling him to tender his resignation of the antiterror force to General Medina by noon, or face the consequences. He hadn't; instead, he'd alerted Captain Guerra and come home—to an empty house. He didn't need to read the neat, printed lettering spelling out the rest of the message; it burned from the back of his eyes. "Don't get above yourself, Major, or those close to you will pay for your mistakes." And someone had, but not someone close to him—someone close to Mercury. He looked over at Mercury's bowed head, the dark-red stain under his wounded leg, the still form of the missionary beside him.

Mercury barely heard his father walk over to stand beside him; misery and guilt filled his head and heart. He had killed Giovanni by disregarding his father's orders to stay in the house today, just as surely as if he'd pulled the trigger himself.

"He's gone, and you can't take that back by passing out from blood loss, especially when he died trying to protect you," Zamora said softly, gently stroking his son's dark hair. The long strands of it wrapped around his fingers. He knelt, his hand on the boy's shaking shoulder, and leaned his forehead against the long hair. He suddenly wished Isabel were here; he always felt lost, hesitant trying to express the emotions he felt so deeply. *Please, Heavenly Father, help us both.*

"Michael." His name seemed to echo in Mercury's head, the echo faint and feminine, both voices full of love. "Michael Angel. You know he's not gone forever; he is still fighting the war, just from another battlefield. And we have work to do on this one." He felt the misery loosen its paralyzing grip at last; he leaned against Zamora's shoulder, finally letting go of Giovanni's hand.

Zamora lifted Mercury up and carried him to the ambulance, nodding sympathetically at the white-faced, shaken mission president standing beside a tear-stained young elder. He motioned for Captain Guerra to let the mission president take custody of the fallen missionary. On the way to the hospital, the military ambulance jarring through the streets, he comforted Mercury as much as he could, furious and shaking, tears in his eyes as he silently prayed for the American boy who died for his son—and for the father and mother who would never make the long trip to the emergency room. Above them, the siren screamed like a banshee mourning all the innocent victims in the war between good and evil.

CHAPTER 20

"There's no way they got so ticked off because of our new math-literacy program." Tony ducked as a brick flew over the ornamental half wall between the front door and the Softlearn employee parking lot, then raised his head cautiously again to look at the milling, shouting crowd. He and the other Softlearn employees leaving the building that evening had taken dubious cover behind the short barrier when the rock-throwing started.

Picketers, protesters, and hecklers outside Softlearn weren't unusual; in fact, they'd shown up outside the educational software company's headquarters in downtown Lake Creek every day since before he started work there. Their complaints about the company ranged from employing nonunion workers (a truly anachronistic complaint in the modern days of companies treating any and all workers as independent contractors) to edging out "native" businesses (which included absolutely no software companies before Rob Sarkesian started his in a refurbished Main Street storefront). Fervent evangelical missionaries joined the throng, trying to score points by converting the "heathens" to the love of Jesus, as well as protestors spouting more venomous but diffuse hatred of Mormons in general and Lake Creek Mormons in particular. The health and security bill that made AllSafe all but mandatory for employment and travel only gave them ammunition for the ideological guns they'd already assembled from general-purpose prejudices and resentments.

This time, though, the crowd had a few new faces in it—new to the protest anyway. The Perry boys and their friends were altogether too familiar sights on the outskirts of town, but the raid on

Beauregard's had finally pushed them into once forbidden territory. They slipped in under cover of the eternal protest, intending to find out how far they could push their feud, how much they could punish their Mormon enemies. Timing the reconnaissance assault for closing time, they waited for Softlearn's employees to come out of the doors—and promptly supplemented the rising protest chants with makeshift missiles. Initial success had encouraged them, but the barrage had taken the rest of the demonstrators by surprise, and several looked uncomfortable with actual physical, instead of merely verbal, violence.

"Maybe they believe the rumor that the story problem program automatically teaches kids to subtract tithing from what people earn," Bishop Newstead said dryly. He'd worked at Softlearn since its inception, when Rob brought him in as chief financial officer.

"Is there a rumor like that?" Tony asked. He'd spotted the Perrys, risking a blow from a half-empty beer can. His temper rose with every obscene shout, every noise of another piece of trash hitting the wall. After all the trouble they'd had in San Diego, with everybody from the local school to MedaGen harassing them, employers refusing to even look at his portfolio, having to scrape up every last penny to finance Giovanni's mission, and finally not even being able to sell their house for any kind of profit, facing outright persecution—not just rock-throwing idiots outside the office, but those same idiots attacking their home with Molotov cocktails, no less!—made Tony so angry that he could barely see straight. He thought of the pistol at home in his drawer, the one he had bought, not from Porter but from a legitimate dealer (well, a pawnshop owner), and which he'd actually gotten good at using. The memory of the perforated, man-shaped target did sober him slightly; maybe it was a good thing he didn't have his pistol with him, after all.

"Not that I know of." The bishop looked toward the front doors. "I wonder if Rob's been able to convince the LCPD that Softlearn pays enough taxes to merit some defense from the civil authorities."

"The civil authorities can go jump," Tony growled. "I'm sick of this. It's been a long day, I'm tired, I'm hungry, and I want to go home *now*. These idiots think they can keep us bottled in the office? They're nothing but sign-waving, chaw-spitting, greasy-skulled, drunk bullies.

Most of them can't even throw. Come on—there's thirty of us, and about twenty of them—just six, really, since the Perrys and their buddies are the only ones who might fight back. We could take them."

"Take them where?" Bishop Newstead affected an innocent misunderstanding, but the other Softlearn engineers around them expressed various reactions to Tony's proposal—the majority agreeing.

Tony looked around at his fellow employees. "Anybody play football in high school?" A general laugh met that question—they were engineers, for crying out loud, not jocks. "Okay, forget that. Video games, then. Everybody's done Normandy Beach, right? Full assault mode, guys."

"Do you seriously think starting a brawl will further the cause?" Bishop Newstead asked, distress etching a deep frown on his gentle face.

"Why not? At the very least, it'll land them in the hospital for a while. Broken noses might even improve their looks. Breaking a few faces would sure improve my mood!" Tony said it with a lot of heat, then reluctantly relented as Bishop Newstead solemnly regarded him. "We're not starting a brawl. It's Friday afternoon, and we're going to our cars so we can go home. It's just coincidence that some nasty hard boys and a bunch of sign-waving hypocrites got in the way. Okay, no hitting. We'll just go right through the line—at high speed, if we have to. Ready? Get your pocket protectors pumped."

A couple of the less pugnacious Softlearn employees yelped protests, but several agreed, some growling at the nonviolence clause, some laughing at the entire idea. When Tony yelled, "Charge!" a dozen of them vaulted the wall and thundered down Softearn's flower-bordered front walkway toward the protesters.

Ordinarily, the sight of software engineers and designers doesn't strike fear into the hearts of protesters—let alone hardened barroom brawlers like the Perrys—but software engineers don't ordinarily erupt from behind ornamental walls yelling "Charge!" with grim-faced hostility either. This unexpected feistiness from normally patient Softlearn employees was unnerving enough for the majority of the usual anti-Mormon demonstrators—and the distant wail of police sirens completed the rout. The fact that the particularly rabid fans of Reverend Lebaron had started their drinking a little early that Friday and gone beyond basic public protest to minor assault and property damage only increased the others' speed. The flashing lights convinced even the semipro thugs that time had come to pack up the rocks and beer bottles for the day. They hadn't come to get arrested, just to see if the police would turn out when the Mormons called them (and they did, but the long delay was significant). By the time the LCPD cruiser rolled up, only a vague wash of crowd detritus— cigarette butts, wrappers, beer bottles, dropped placards, a forgotten shoe—testified to the recent presence of the protesters and their violent comrades.

That and the star-shaped cracks in several windshields in the parking lot behind Softlearn, complete with matching dents, dings, and scratches on the bodies of the cars. Tony stood looking at his sadly abused van, fury rising in his tight chest. The expressions on the faces of the other Softlearn employees reflected Tony's anger or expressed varying stages of panic, sorrow, and resignation. A few managed to call good-byes or words of advice on where to find the best deals on glass and body repair. Tony simply waved, acknowledging Bishop Newstead's concerned farewell without saying anything. On the drive home, he glared out the damaged windshield, thinking that Brother Smith might be crazy, but Jack DuPris got it right when he told that *Scream Back, America* DJ and the Channel 8 reporter that in his personal opinion, and all due respect to the Brethren, it was time for the Mormons to fight back.

* * *

"The death toll continues to rise, as groups all around the world have seemingly declared open season on members of the clergy." Anne O'Neal's voice, perfectly modulated between sympathy and journalistic objectivity, narrated a segment of the Channel 8 special report "Religion and Revolution." "And as these atrocities continue, there seems to be no way for these persecuted religious minorities to effectively defend themselves." Images succeeded each other in nauseating succession: an archbishop burning in Manila, an Apostle dying in a shabby hut, the brutally beaten bodies of a pair of nuns lying beside the altar they tried to save from desecration.

Carmen came into the living room, to see Lucrezia staring, horrified, at the screen. "Lucrezia," she began, trying to pull her younger daughter away from the nightmares playing out on the television. Her next words died in her throat as pictures of other terrors replaced those in the Philippines.

"Long-established and relatively new religions have become targets in Central and South America as well," Anne continued, "and in many areas, religious and political animosity combine to form an even more corrosive acid eating at the social fabric of countries on the edge of anarchy or fascism." Cheering crowds threw flowers and ribbons over a triumphant column of General Garza's soldiers. Other cheering crowds surrounded a chapel—its outline as familiar to Carmen and Lucrezia as their own small church in Lake Creek—as a bulldozer tore into its walls, scattering bricks, splintered wood, and broken glass over the rutted lawn.

"The Church of Jesus Christ of Latter-day Saints, once welcomed in many South American countries as a force for education and civil stability, has found itself under fire, and that fire has become increasingly literal—"

Anne's voice cut suddenly, not quite at the end of a thought, and Clara reappeared, gazing solemnly into the camera. "Thank you, Anne. We'll continue with Anne's report next hour. Right now, we have breaking news coming out of Santiago, Chile, where a local rebel group has claimed responsibility for an attack that killed an American and wounded a Chilean just a few blocks from La Moneda itself. Channel 8's Rosa del Torres is on the scene. What's happening, Rosa?"

The white buildings and red roofs of a tidy suburb in Santiago, Chile, glowed out of the screen. So did Rosa, her hair blowing perfectly in the slight breeze. Her expression was a little less perfect, too much excited glitter in her eyes, not quite enough institutional mournfulness around her mouth. "I'm here in Plaza del Mundo, in the center of Santiago, where a dramatic attack occurred at noon today. Two men on motorcycles targeted a small group of Mormon missionaries, including at least one American, wounding one and killing another. The guerilla group lead by charismatic rebel leader El Jaguar has claimed responsibility, issuing a statement that decried, quote, 'northern interference in the spiritual and political self-determination of the free people of Chile' and demanding—"

"What the Hades gives them the right to demand anything?" Tony's enraged bellow drove through the television's morbid spell, startling Carmen and Lucrezia out of their horrified fascination as Rosa's cameraman focused, closer and closer, on a wide, rusty stain covering a patch of cobblestones. They hadn't heard him come home, opening the door and standing behind them in time to hear Rosa's breathless report.

Carmen tore her gaze away, looking at Tony with pleading in her dark eyes. "Tony, they said—she said they hurt a missionary, maybe killed a missionary—an American missionary—" She couldn't go on, say the sickening thought out loud; her voice gave out, and she swallowed convulsively.

The phone rang. Like a woman in a dream, Carmen saw herself from the outside, watching a stranger walk to the table, pick up the receiver, click it on, answer in a voice that seemed to come from an unfathomable distance. The man on the other end of the line, however, sounded more real, more painfully clear, than anything in the room. He identified himself as President Reyes, mission president in Santiago, and asked to speak to Sister or Brother Callatta. She said that she was Sister Callatta and listened to the man tell her that Elder Giovanni Callatta, her son, had died just a few hours earlier, the victim of a politically motivated assassination attempt as he valiantly saved the life of a younger boy who was the apparent target of the attack. Steady, precise, and inexorable, she asked for details, refused to let President Reyes gloss over the harsh reality of it. She needed to hear it, and at first reluctantly, then in a rush, President Reyes poured out the story, his own emotion and tears rising: Giovanni had died almost instantly, from three gunshots to the chest; his last thought had been of her; he had the faith to know that God needed him, had a mission that only he could do. He had been a valiant missionary and was much loved by all who knew him. His mission stood as a true testimony to the goodness of the Lord and the truth of the work. The boy he had saved was Michael Angel Freeman Zamora, the son of a prominent military officer who fought the rebel terrorists; Giovanni had simply been in the wrong place at the wrong time but did not hesitate to come to the aid of a friend. And "greater love hath no man than this, that he lay down his life for his friends . . ."

Carmen whispered, "Thank you, President," and offered the phone to Tony.

He took it, heard President Reyes's softly accented account of Giovanni's life and last moments, and made arrangements for the return of Giovanni's body as if he had switched to autopilot. His own voice betrayed no trace of the tears that ran down his face. A salty splash starred the polished wood of the table beside the phone as he set it down. Dimly surprised, he touched his cheek, regarding his wet fingertips as if through a fog.

"Baby?" Carmen's voice shook. "Lucrezia, it was Giovanni."

Tony looked at Carmen, looked at Lucrezia's white face, and became utterly still. His family was hurt beyond mending, vulnerable and terrified, living in a place where they did not dare leave the house after dark; murderers had cut down his son, a missionary doing God's work, like a rabid dog in the street; even an Apostle died for no more reason than telling the truth. How could you reason with a world like that? How could you hope for anything but hate? How could Bishop Newstead—anyone—expect him to forgive, forget, and let evil beat them down, again and again? What about Giovanni, the gentle giant who offered nothing but love? Guilt slammed into him, as heavy as it was irrational. He had failed. He'd failed his family, the one failure that nothing else could make up for. He stood, frozen, staring unseeing at the far wall.

The movement as Lucrezia ran into her mother's arms broke the mental chains that held him motionless. Looking at Lucrezia, at Carmen, holding onto each other, too stunned yet even to cry, the full boil of Tony's temper blew the icy despair into rage so white-hot that when he spoke, his voice was calm and low. "That's enough. It stops right now. No more turning the other cheek. The next slimeball who raises his hand against us is going to lose it."

Carmen gazed at him, tears welling up in her eyes. Fear of losing Tony to the hate in his eyes added its dreadful weight to the numbness of realizing that Giovanni wouldn't call, wouldn't write, wouldn't come home. She flinched, gasping frantic denial, as Lucrezia pulled away, furiously declaring, "Not just lose it—eat it! Porter's right—if we don't fight, nobody will fight for us!"

Even the mention of Porter, of whom Tony deeply disapproved, on principle as well as out of the instinctive dislike any father feels toward a boy who catches the interest of his daughter, failed to crack Tony's hard shell of pride and fury.

"What about Heavenly Father? He'll fight for us. He said He would. He's got to," Carmen choked out, but her words held little conviction, even in her own mind. She held Lucrezia's hand desperately, reaching for Tony with the other.

"God helps those who help themselves," Tony rasped, but the pain in Carmen's face made him step forward, catching up both women in his arms. It didn't make the hurt less, but combining three into one at least made it momentarily more bearable—and when Donna came in from the small park that the townhouses shared, laughing with Gianni, three in one became five in one.

Bishop and Sister Newstead arrived first the next morning, as a brief news blurb on the LDS Web site spread the real news of the tragedy in Chile. Channel 8 had already forgotten it. The bishop stumbled over his words as his gentle face expressed his care and concern; his wife bustled in to sweep up the cried-out Gianni and administer warm doses of brisk love to his stunned family. Others, ward members and coworkers, neighbors and friends, came, whispered words of comfort and support, and sat for a few moments, all they could do for the time. Carmen was especially touched when Teresa Burns, the Lutheran minister, and two members of her congregation stopped by to express sympathy and offer prayer.

Tony faced the outpouring of concern with thanks and brief explanations; telling the story of what had happened to his son made it more real, but also made it more comprehensible, made it something he could understand and own and, deep in the dark of his bleeding, guilt-ridden heart, vow to avenge.

Lucrezia clutched the details of it, repeating the fact that Giovanni was a hero, showing the message that had arrived shortly after President Reyes called, an official letter of thanks and commendation from Major Rafaelo Rivera Zamora, a major in the Chilean army who called Giovanni a true soldier of God's army.

Donna circulated slowly between answering the door, snuggling puzzled and tearful Gianni, and reassuring the more emotional visitors.

Every time she tried to think of Giovanni dead, to picture those bright eyes forever closed, her mind threw out the image, refused to even entertain the idea. Her big brother's going away, not coming home, lay in her rational mind only; it couldn't sink in all the way. That was almost comforting—if only she didn't know that it would hit later, and hit hard.

Carmen seemed to move through the day as if it were a dream; she smiled faintly and nodded when the others talked to her, dabbing at her face and the endless flow of tears, making Gianni the peanut-butter sandwich he begged for but eventually stuffed behind the couch cushions for visitors to inadvertently find. Carmen showed her characteristic animation only twice, once when Merry Galen called. Their conversation was short, heartfelt, and, for all the miles that separated them, more immediate than the room around Carmen.

"Carmen," Merry whispered through her own tears, "remember what you told me when Chris died? You've got a forever family, Carmen. Giovanni is yours, he'll be yours forever, and he'll always love you."

The words touched a place in Carmen that sang hope for a moment, the part of her that truly believed in a Heavenly Father who loved His children, the part that had always borne reversals and stumbling blocks and trouble with a determined faith that everything would work out just fine. She held to that feeling, but gently, as if it were a delicate butterfly between her hands, its wings tattered but perhaps unbroken. Guarding that tiny flame took all of her emotional effort through the long day and evening, keeping her quiet and still—until Brother Smith came in, his wife following at the customary three paces behind, already bearing a covered dish of the inevitable cheese, cream, and cornflake-covered funeral potatoes.

Brother Smith took the patriarch's position on the Callattas' couch, disregarding Bishop Newstead and leaning forward to pontificate on the glorious rewards of those who died in the service of the gospel. Scriptures rolled off his tongue, mixed and matched, mingled meanings and occasionally mangled syntax, as he assured Carmen and Tony that Giovanni had lost his life because he didn't seek it, that those who lived by the sword that struck him down would die by it, that Giovanni had laid down his own life just as the Anti-Nephi-Lehies, dying as he refused to fight.

"Oh, he fought," Tony contradicted, the ice in his tone frosting the reproof with sharp edges. He had spent the night pacing between the walls, mentally constructing alternative scenarios that let Giovanni defend himself with deadly force, walk down a different street, miss his appointment with the boy who drew the assassins to him—or where he never went to South America at all, but stayed home to help defend his mother, sisters, and little brother against the darkness crowding in around them. "One of those dogs didn't come off the ground, and the other would've been plenty hurt if the cops hadn't finished him off. Giovanni only lost because the other guy pulled a gun."

Brother Smith took that in stride. "Even the righteous fall, and their blood will cry from the ground to the Lord for vengeance in this great and terrible day—which is at hand, even at the door. Brother Callatta, your son has sealed his testimony with his blood, a true martyr to the great cause of Zion. His glorious life and death will inspire countless others. I'll proudly add Giovanni Callatta's name and the details of his death to the Martyrs' Memorial page on my Web site, so that our fellow soldiers under the Title of Liberty will know of his great deeds and deep testimony."

Tony's twisted, cynical half smile (he didn't believe in the magic power of martyrs any more than he believed in Web sites advocating militant Mormonism) utterly failed to penetrate Brother Smith's self-satisfied plans. Carmen suddenly leaving her chair to rise to her full height, eyes blazing, however, did catch his attention.

"You dare come in here and act like you're doing us a favor by exploiting our son's murder?" she demanded, her voice rising not in hysteria but in rage. "Giovanni lived, worked, and died serving the Church, the gospel, and God. You'd have to kill me too before I'd let a sanctimonious, psychopathic blowhard like you abuse his memory by making him a poster boy for a bunch of hotheaded, short-sighted fools! Giovanni went to Chile to serve the Lord, not your politics!"

"Sister Callatta," Brother Smith began, in a voice that richly hinted that she'd succumbed to the hysteria to which females were so sadly prone.

"Don't call me sister—I'm no sister of yours! Get out of my house before I wreak some vengeance on you, you hypocritical warmonger!"

Carmen glared at him as she delivered the order, pointing emphatically to the door. When he opened his mouth again, she pointed at him with the other hand as if to exorcise an invading demon. The tone of her voice matched the molten fire in her eyes, the heat penetrating even Brother Smith's nigh-invulnerable psychological armor. "I said get out!" She watched him go, Rock, Orrin, and his acolytes following him, before collapsing back into her chair, tears drowning all but the spark at the heart of the fire.

Shock and hurt piled on that spark like ashes, ashes that filled her heart and mind, made her feel dull and sleepy through the three days that followed. She forced herself to keep moving, kissing Tony goodbye when he insisted on going to work; his jaw set hard as he informed her that they couldn't keep him from providing for his family, even if they—another "they," which included Bishop Newstead—wouldn't let him protect them. She reassured Donna, who had finally realized that Giovanni was truly out of touch, but seemed to accept it, if not more easily, then more calmly, than anyone else.

Lucrezia didn't take it calmly; the morning after they got the news, she refused to get out of bed at all, but by noon had got up to stalk around the house, crying as if her heart would break between top-of-her-lungs rants against the eternal unfairness of the universe. When Jelisaveta and April came, offering sympathy on behalf of the entire Saint Squad, treading softly as they offered heartfelt support, Lucrezia challenged both of them to tell her why Giovanni had to die while both the Perry boys still breathed—and used their ill-gotten breath to brag about offing a Mormon missionary, as if they'd done it themselves! Jelisaveta, taken by surprise with Lucrezia's furious demands for answers, cast madly around for any good explanation, but her stream-of-consciousness, semi-incoherent response only infuriated Lucrezia more.

"What would you know about it?" she finally shouted. "You know nothing at all—with you, it's all run, retreat, give up and go away! Giovanni stood up for that boy, stood up and fought and would've won if they hadn't shot him! You and all the rest of you at school, ducking and running like a bunch of—of ducks! I mean chickens!"

What her cry lacked in eloquence, however, it more than made up for in emotional violence. She threw herself facedown on her bed, sobs racking through her, but when April tried to rub her shoulder, Lucrezia violently shrugged away from the touch. Donna gently caught them both, pulling them out of the room, thanking them for coming and for caring, not quite apologizing for Lucrezia's outburst. She graciously accepted the condolences they offered, thanking them and giving them the opportunity to make a graceful exit, which they gratefully took. A half hour later, Lucrezia's sobs had calmed to occasional gasps and hiccups. She curled up in the single rocking chair they had brought from their "real home" in San Diego and called Porter, who didn't need to say much over the open connection; she just needed to know he was there. He'd stayed with her, in the kitchen, that first evening, ignoring his father's command to come when Carmen threw them out. Disobedience earned him a beating and, more important, yet another gold star in Lucrezia's book. He couldn't listen to her all the time, of course, between chores, his father's disapproval, and Tony's stated, probably hyperbolic, but heartfelt, intention to skin him alive and send the pieces back to the Smith farm if he showed his face at the house again.

As usual, Carmen did most of the grunt work of emotional support, gently pulling Lucrezia's wild mood swings back toward the stable center, putting on a brave face for both her girls. She also had her hands full taking care of Gianni, who alternated between tears, wild laughter, and stubborn rebellion in his confusion and sadness. He knew that something bad had happened to Giovanni, that sad people kept coming, that Mama and Daddy and his sisters were acting strange; he simply didn't know how to deal with it.

"Is Giovanni okay?" Gianni asked, over and over again—from first thing in the morning to the last thing after prayers at bedtime.

"Yes, sweetie, he's okay, he's gone to be with Jesus," Carmen responded, over and over again. Finally, she cracked, snapping, "Gianni, I already told you! Giovanni is okay. He's with Jesus. Why do you keep asking me?"

"Don't believe it," Gianni said softly, his eyes filling with tears at his mother's sharp tone.

The sorrow on his little face cut through the ashes. She dropped the dish she was washing back into the soapy water and knelt down in front of him, taking his wet face in her wet hands. "You don't believe that Giovanni's with Jesus? Why don't you believe it, sweetie?"

"Not me, Mama," Gianni said, "you. Why don't you believe in Jesus?"

Carmen couldn't find anything to say; she hugged Gianni tight, her own eyes filling with tears. Though she distracted him with potato chips (a three-year-old can go from deep theological questions to zooming potato-chip spaceships around a table in mere seconds), she couldn't distract herself.

His question played and replayed in her head—and so did the answer. Did she believe that Giovanni was in heaven with Jesus? Did she believe he was okay? Did she believe they would be okay? Did she believe that Jesus loved Giovanni—and the rest of them, the ones left behind in a dark world? Rocking slowly, back and forth as she sat on her bed, her knees pulled up to her chest, watching the light dim in the windows, waiting for Tony to come home, she knew that all those questions had only one answer: faith. Did she have faith? Did she trust God enough to believe Him?

She'd never really had to answer that question before. Of course she trusted God. She always had, since He'd helped her find her lost CTR ring when she was six years old. He'd always been there, listening, inspiring, occasionally taking an active hand in things, as He'd done helping her get Merry out of San Diego, and again saving them from MedaGen's thugs, and helping Tony apply to Softlearn, and a thousand other incidents, small and large, that she attributed to divine intervention. Minor intervention, yes, but she'd never demanded big miracles or dramatic revelations. Financial problems hadn't daunted her; facing the disdain and hostility of people who considered her an idiot fanatic didn't put a dent in her confidence; when Chris Galen died, she'd reassured Merry with the promises of eternal covenants and glorious resurrections. Why was it suddenly so hard to believe that God knew what He was doing, that He must need her Giovanni for something really important? Why did everything that sounded so right when she said it to someone else ring so hollow when she said it to herself?

"So now it's different, because it's me—and Giovanni?" she asked aloud. Yes, it is different, she realized, as memory painted images of him on the dark wall in front of her: smiling in a football uniform, standing so proudly in a slightly too-big suit as he passed the sacrament for the first time, wiping away tears with the back of his hand after his first big breakup with a girlfriend, gazing up at the stars while he told her about his plans for his future and eventual family, apologizing to his father after losing his temper yet again, waving at the airport security checkpoint before the plane whisked him away to bring the gospel to sisters and brothers he'd never met. Each memory brought both pain and comfort, loneliness and the slightest hint of a slow-growing reassurance.

Faith. Trust. How did they relate to death, to separation and loss? For the first time in a long time she reached for her scriptures, not just to make the kids read their verses or struggle through the assigned Sunday School reading, but with a real, burning question. She opened to page after page, verse after verse: faith in things hoped for, trust in God, if you can do no more than want to believe, endure to the end, losing life to find it, blessed are they that die in the Lord, the righteous dead carry the gospel to the souls in prison. Warmth began to rise from the pages, through her shaking fingers, through her aching head. The words seemed to lift from the paper in a swelling tide, promising calm and peace, if not easy acceptance, flowing from her eyes to her heart as she heard Giovanni's young voice reading the scripture under her finger, sleepy but determined to pronounce the archaic phrases of Revelation 14:13 correctly: "Blessed are the dead which die in the Lord from henceforth: Yea, saith the Spirit, that they may rest from their labours, and their works do follow them."

Tony came home from his aimless, painful drive around the dark streets of Lake Creek to find Carmen tipped over on the bed, the blanket half over her, the scriptures cradled like a baby against her chest. She didn't stir when he opened the door; he looked at her tear-stained face, gently pulled the blanket around her, and let her sleep while he paced. Trying to outrun his pain in the confines of the small bedroom didn't work any better than trying to outrun it in the battered van, with Donna's softball bat resting against his knee. He'd half hoped to run into the Perry boys, or any of Lebaron's outfit, as if a confrontation with them would help him feel better, give him something to hit, a target for his sick feelings of inadequacy and helplessness. Fortunately, he'd realized the stupidity of what he was doing before he took the road leading out of town, into the woods and fields where Brother Smith and Reverend Lebaron waged the hottest battles of their private war. Getting himself badly hurt—or even killed—wouldn't protect his family any better, despite the self-pitying thought that it wouldn't protect them any worse either.

The same flicker of common sense or conscience that turned him back home kept trying to point out that Giovanni's death wasn't his fault, that he had done the best he could to provide for his family, that he'd been able to protect them from the firebombing raid, and that—most important but also hardest to accept—he couldn't take it all on by himself anyway. He had to trust God to handle everything he couldn't surrender the burning core of enraged pride and surrender to the ultimate plan. As hard as he thought about it though, as much as he knew intellectually what he should do, he just couldn't force himself to honestly say, "Thy will, not mine be done," to give up thoughts of vengeance and violent self-defense—which, of course, only made him feel worse, more angry, and more stubbornly determined to find his own way. After all, the cynical side of him pointed out, he'd trusted Heavenly Father to take care of Giovanni, and look what had happened. He eventually fell into bed, exhausted, envying Carmen the peace in her face, but not enough to pay the price to get it himself.

That peace followed her to the airport the next day, a thin gauze between her and the hurt, not a heavenly shield from pain but the gift of courage to accept the loss and keep moving, an ineffable confidence that the loss would be only temporary in the end. Seeing Giovanni's face when they delivered the coffin to the small funeral home, peaceful, almost smiling, deepened both the pain and the reassurance.

For Donna, seeing her brother truly dead broke the dam that had kept back her tears; beyond all reason, she had half expected him to walk off the plane. She suddenly connected the tally of three days, three days since he died to the coffin's arrival, with the three days before the resurrection. Every night, she had seen him in her dreams, heard his voice, felt his presence, and not really believed he wouldn't come home.

"Yes, he will," Carmen whispered into her hair, holding her weeping eldest daughter. "Yes, honey, Giovanni will come home. It's just that his mission got extended a lot longer than we expected."

"From Santiago to the spirit world?" Donna asked, laughing suddenly at the thought of it. The relief of seeing a touch of humor in the situation made her cry again, but it helped loosen the hard knot in her stomach too. "They must really need Spanish-speakers if they recruited Giovanni. He's still shaky on future tense—and that's all they've got up there: just what will happen next."

Lucrezia, living proof that adolescent obnoxiousness is one of the most powerful forces on Earth, managed an exasperated eye roll at that, but she didn't shrug off Carmen's one-arm hug—even though her mother laughed at the lame joke. Gianni laughed too and went back to plotting how to abscond with one of the large, white flowers in the vase temptingly set on the floor within his reach.

"Giovanni's okay with Jesus?" Gianni asked, as they filed into the packed chapel, past ward members there to show support and past strangers there to catch a glimpse of a tragedy in action. He pointed heavenward with his captured flower.

"Giovanni's okay with Jesus," Carmen told him softly, ruffling his hair. This time, they both believed it.

Tony rubbed his son's shoulder. His only son now, the thought rose out of the roar of the frustrated anger that filled his tight chest, or at least the only one he could touch, provide for, protect. Unless he failed in that too.

The funeral service was well attended. The stake president, due to a hospitalizing illness that would lay him up for weeks, and his first counselor, out of town on an extended business trip, were the only conspicuous absences. Tony, of course, spoke at the funeral service, delivering a beautiful talk about Giovanni's aspirations to be a missionary, missionary work, and the sustaining power of the gospel, but the words failed to bring any peace or comfort to calm the emotional vortex inside him.

Elder Jack DuPris took the podium after Tony finished. He had come not because he knew Giovanni or the Callattas but because losing a missionary still sent ripples through the Church as a whole. His short, ardent message invoked the death of Abinadi, a messenger of God whose killers met the same fiery fate they had visited on him. "The Lord must let evil have its day, allow it to show its true colors, give those who would choose darkness over light their opportunity to exercise their free agency," DuPris said, his eyes as fiery as the long-ago pyre. "But that is not where the story ends, brothers and sisters. Those who do evil will get the reward they deserve—and the Lord's people will not always hold back, patiently accepting afflictions. Remember Captain Moroni, Helaman, Ammon, King Mosiah—they triumphed over their enemies in defense of their homes, their families, and their God. When the right time comes, the Saints will rise up against their oppressors, and they will conquer, though they face armies tens of thousands strong!"

Listening to him, Tony felt the first flash of light, a lift in his heavy heart—not peace or comfort, but a teeth-gritting, fist-clenching surge of agreement and excitement. It blended with the sullen heat under his breastbone, the perfect compliment to the guilt and anger that he held in a death grip. As long as he could hold that defense, he could believe that he had a chance of controlling what happened to him—and to his family. Thus, Tony said amen to Bishop Newstead's gentle but heartfelt reassurances of the constant love of God and hope in the Atonement and the wisdom of trusting the Creator of all to watch over His creation, but the words bounced off the hard shell of sorrow, guilt, and anger. He said amen to the prayers too, at the funeral and at the graveside, but he couldn't find the words to pray himself, either at the funeral or when the family came home, exhausted but more at peace, leaving the most desperate sorrow at the graveside and coming away with at least somewhat lighter hearts. Well, at least Carmen, Donna, and Gianni felt more at peace; Tony and Lucrezia brought their own gray emotional shrouds of anger and wounded pride with them.

Tony firmly deflected Carmen's explanation of her reassuring experience of the night before; she quoted Revelation, trying to reassure him, trying to share the thin veil of peace that surrounded her aching but not mortally wounded heart. He didn't want to hear more about trusting in the Lord, surrendering to God's will; he smiled wryly as he reminded her that she'd always had enough inspiration for both of them. When Donna reminded him that they should have family prayer that night, he asked her to say it for them. Later, as he knelt beside Carmen, hearing her pour out her sorrow and hope to heaven, he said amen again, but even as he said it, for Carmen's sake, he felt the words of his own short prayer bounce off the wall inside his head.

Instead, still on his knees beside Carmen, he found himself wondering how much it would take, how many missionaries would have to die, how many other Mormon families would have to lose their homes and jobs and even lives, before the Brethren listened to Elder DuPris and realized that the Church needed to get organized to defend itself. Donna's teacher, Brother Kensai may have hit the nail on the head—the last days had come, and it was time for Zion to come together, beautiful, unstoppable, terrible as an army with banners. Somehow, the thought of mild-mannered Mormons as ravening lions didn't sound as goofy now as when he'd heard Brother Smith say the same thing a month ago. A lot had changed since then.

"Baby?" Carmen's soft question brought him out of dark contemplation. She leaned over, her shoulder against his. "Tony, it'll be all right." After a moment's silence, she added with a hint of her normal bossy sparkle, "Come on, Tony. Remember how this goes? Now you tell me the same thing, and we both feel better."

Taking a deep breath, forcing down a surge of irrational, defensive irritation, he put his arms around her and said, "Carmen, it'll be all right."

She looked at him, the shadow smile on her face dimming slightly before she caught it and kept it in place. *Oh, Tony, I know you're hurting. I am too. But please, believe it really will be all right, for all of us. Please, really believe it!*

* * *

"Yes, I believe it." General Medina glared across the elegantly set table at Olivares.

The intelligence chief had interrupted the general at breakfast, not so much barging as unstoppably insinuating himself past the junior officers and guards to sit, straight and gray as ever, in the general's private dining room. He'd waited until the general had swallowed a sip of coffee, then mildly observed, "Undoubtedly, Major Zamora believes it implicates General Garza with El Jaguar and his attacks. Do you believe his theory, General—or, more important, his evidence?"

Zamora had indeed contacted General Medina, the attack on Mercury—and Giovanni Callatta—pushing him to trust a copy of Vasquez's smuggled files to his superior officer, just in case he didn't survive to present it to President Quintana himself. The general had confirmed Zamora's hesitance to try to broadcast the information electronically, telling the major that the president himself had warned against sending sensitive information to him in the United States; he didn't trust the Americans, and he didn't trust his own security forces either. Now, the general's hot reaction to Olivares's question, and implied criticism of Zamora, and therefore Medina himself, confirmed the spymaster's suspicion that Zamora had unearthed vital data, which triggered the attack on his son.

"You find it persuasive." Olivares nodded thoughtfully, but his expression betrayed none of those suspicions. "The next question is whether President Quintana will believe it. I assume that you haven't been so foolish as to try to send more than a general message yet? Our communications are not as secure as one would wish."

The heat of Medina's glare deepened several degrees. "I assume that you'd know if I had—since it's your wiretaps that make our communications leaky as a shot gut."

"Charming image." Olivares raised a hand in a calming gesture, as his eyes swept the generous spread of dishes. "Please, General. Temper in the morning is bad for the digestion."

"Talking with spies is bad for the digestion anytime," Medina growled.

"But talking with spies can be very good for one's general health," Olivares returned. "General, pursuing El Jaguar and his allies—whoever they may be—is becoming very dangerous indeed. I urge you to use all possible security measures, take all possible precautions against a preemptive strike."

Medina stood, wiping his mouth with a linen napkin, looming over the smaller man. "I have taken all the precautions I feel are necessary." He suspected the spy chief of complicity in the plots that seemed to threaten his commander-in-chief from every side, and neither his words nor his tone left any doubt of his opinion of Olivares. "And you can take this back to your masters: President Quintana may not have the details yet, but we do, and he knows that

Zamora has nailed El Jaguar's hide to the wall. It is only a matter of time—very short time. And you can tell them that your threats don't frighten me, Olivares. I've never been scared of ghosts, and you're walking dead men." He dropped the napkin on Olivares's shoulder and stalked out, crisply acknowledging the salute of the guard at the door.

Olivares stood, removing the napkin with a precise gesture, gazing at the grease mark on the snowy cloth. He stood thoughtfully for just a moment, his dark eyes moving to the remains of Medina's breakfast. As commotion erupted outside the dining room, he nodded to himself and neatly swept the remains of the general's empanada from the china plate into the napkin. As an orderly ran past, calling for the guards to call for a medic, the security chief walked to the double doors. Down the long hallway, a large man sprawled on the floor, only his uniformed legs visible in the press of frantic guards and officers. Olivares, tucking the napkin packet into his jacket pocket, came to a stop beside one young man in the uniform of a captain, standing wide-eyed at the intersection of two corridors, a dispatch envelope in his hands. "Captain Guerra, isn't it?"

Guerra blinked, looking at the quiet gray man, began to salute the intelligence chief, then stopped when he remembered the man was a civilian. Confused, he decided to do nothing but answer—and try to find out as much as he could. "Yes, sir. What happened here, sir?"

"I fear that General Medina has taken ill," Olivares replied, indicating the dispatch with a casual wave of his hand. "From Major Zamora, no doubt. May I take that for you?"

"No," Guerra said quickly, then added, "No, sir. Thank you. General's eyes only."

"Indeed." Olivares began walking again, glancing over his shoulder. "Please tell your superior officer that I add my warning to those he has undoubtedly already received. And go immediately to the kitchens with a squad of soldiers you trust, erupting through the doors in that inimitable style of yours. Apprehend anyone who runs."

Guerra swept the intelligence chief with a hard stare, then got the implication and moved off, declaring, "I will. And here's a warning for you—get in our way, and you're going down too."

"I would have it no other way," Olivares said quietly and walked down the corridor without looking back. Behind him, Guerra left at a dead run toward the kitchen, shouting for his two junior officers to follow him. As they came bursting through the door, one of the cook's assistants left the kitchen at an even more desperate run, crashing to the ground when Guerra shot him in the leg. Far behind them, General Medina left in the hastily summoned ambulance— already dead of an archaic but extremely effective frog-extract poison.

Guerra found the rest of the poison, along with a red-cat bandana, in the pocket of the writhing, cursing dish boy. And then, in a move that justified Zamora's faith in him, he knocked out the prisoner with one hard blow and immediately pulled his sidearm, shouting for his two comrades to do the same as they pulled the unconscious man back into the scullery door. He peered around the door frame, then ducked back as plaster exploded from a bullet strike. He'd seen what he suspected: a black-masked sniper waiting on the opposite roof to eliminate the cook's assistant. He and his men fired back, popping out from the door unpredictably to get off a shot and dive for cover again, keeping the gunman busy. The sniper held his position until a squad of the general's own guards joined Guerra's small team, the heavy fire cratering the plastered wall around his position. He finally broke and ran, Medina's furious, and ineffective, security troop howling after him.

Guerra watched them go, wishing them luck but knowing they were probably on a goose chase through backstreets where the rebels had surely planned escape routes. Let them chase the sniper; he had the more important prey bagged. He returned to the pantry door, where his own men stood guard over the groggily stirring rebel agent who had been the sniper's intended target. He bent down, catching the man's head by the hair to look into his face. "You picked the wrong side, chico. Turns out that jaguars eat their own kind."

* * *

"A little treachery with your croissant?" Zelik slapped a slick-finished document folder down on the glossy surface of the table beside the remains of Abbott's late breakfast.

He smiled up at her. "Why, sure, Ms. Zelik. Thank you for offering. You're usually so subtle about it."

Whittier stifled a snigger to show loyalty to Zelik—but only halfway, to show support for Abbott too. He knew it was always best to cover your, um, bases.

"And you were so subtle about this," Zelik said, tapping one long fingernail on the folder. "Mr. Whittier here brought me some very interesting reading yesterday."

"It showed up on our R&D list with your name on it, sir, and I noticed that you'd pulled resources from other teams to speed it up. So I figured we'd need to get a marketing campaign up to speed as soon as possible—always staying on top of things—and then I couldn't get full specs on it to help us decide what Virginia should be wearing—I mean, not wearing—for the ads," Whittier explained, adopting an aw-shucks attitude. "Since it has your personal stamp on it, Humphrey couldn't give me any more details, so I asked Ms. Zelik to help me out."

Abbott looked from Whittier to Zelik and leaned back in his chair, taking another bite of croissant. "Well, well. The girl detective and her faithful dog, hot on the scent. So, what did you discover, Nancy?"

"I found out why we've had a German mercenary prowling around here," Zelik said. "I found out what he wants. And I found out how you're going to give it to him."

They watched each other warily, waiting for the next step in their never-ending sword dance. Zelik, unlike Whittier, had both the high-level data access and the background to understand the information in the top-secret corporate files. She knew all about the Corinth project that produced AllSafe (and its failed variants)—and she knew how to read Dr. Twilley's coded development notes. Their cold-blooded, efficient medical researcher wasn't just developing a cure for a jungle virus; he was looking for a disease that could pass for a jungle virus, deadly to its victims, harmless to those who had already taken the cure.

"Pacifica. Such an appropriate name," Zelik continued. "The question is, who is it meant to pacify? Let's see. Johann Brindermann commissioned the project, and he works for whom? Why, General Andrea Garza, who has a reputation for using all kinds of interesting methods to eliminate his enemies."

"It's a vaccine," Whittier said, looking slightly lost, a hint of worry creeping into his cocky attitude. "How would it pacify anybody?"

"Oh, the vaccine won't pacify anyone. The mother virus of the vaccine will," Abbott said, interested to see how the brash marketer would react to a dose of the truth. "The vaccine will protect the people who handle the virus, prevent them from catching it themselves."

"Who's going to handle the virus?" Whittier asked, cold apprehension finally driving out his joker attitude. A picture had begun to form in his mind, and the outlines looked uglier as they got clearer. "We're not just talking about Dr. Twilley's team, are we?"

"No. We're talking about selling bioweapons to a megalomaniac mercenary so he can eliminate the last few pockets of resistance in South America. Chile, probably, and maybe Argentina." Zelik's icy sliver of a smile chilled Whittier even more, but he wasn't the target of her attention—or venom. "I wonder how much they paid you to create a genetically modified virus and its antidote." She ran a fingernail idly along the shiny surface of the folder, giving it a tap at the end as she said, "And I especially wonder what Senator Garlick would have to say about you selling bioweapons to foreign nationals. Somehow I don't think he'd approve."

"No, he very likely wouldn't," Abbott agreed. "Do you?"

Zelik regarded him from under lowered lashes. "That depends on how much my approval means to you."

Abbott considered, hiding his irritation at her inconvenient discovery—and Whittier's surprising initiative in selling him to her. *Not bad, really; if the kid had what it took, he might prove a valuable ally for him, and possibly a replacement for Zelik.* Coming to a decision, he smiled, waving with the croissant. "All right, touché, congratulations. I'd feel disappointed if you didn't catch me being so careless. Too much haste, not enough security. Luckily, Mr. Brindermann left me with plenty of jelly to cover everybody's toast."

"I've never liked jelly," Zelik informed him, knowing that any capitulation from Abbott came with as many caveats as advantages. He'd tried to pin the AllSafe vaccine fiasco on her; she had no intention of leaving the reins in his hands this time. "And I don't want a bribe. I want control."

To her slight surprise, Abbott nodded easily. "Perfect. You take over as project manager on this one; I'm a big-picture kind of guy. With you on the details, we won't have any more security slips."

"Indeed we won't," Zelik agreed. "Will we, Mr. Whittier?"

Suddenly, Whittier realized he had become the target of two equally dangerous, predatory stares. His mind still reeling at the idea of MedaGen—no, Abbott—selling bioweapons, he could only blink back, trying not to stare longingly at the door. The meaning of Zelik's question penetrated the fog like a lightning bolt. They were offering him an opportunity to buy in, testing him. This could be the break he'd waited for, his ticket from Mahogany Row to the Corner Offices. Swallowing his shock and instant revulsion at the idea of creating a disease as a weapon, he manufactured a smile that still held a shadow of its old cockiness. "We sure won't."

"Welcome to the big league, Mr. Whittier." The smile Abbott turned on his former protégé looked as warm as ever. Warmer, even, with a hint of the vicious, implacable temper underneath. "Congratulations—you've got what you've always wanted. Your own personal stake in the real power play." He stood up, brushing croissant crumbs off the napkin tucked into his collar, checking his watch as he pulled the napkin off. "And with your usual impeccable timing, Ms. Zelik, you have staged your little coup at exactly the right moment. In two hours, Mr. Brindermann will meet us in Dr. Twilley's lab for a status report and a demonstration. I shall expect to see both of you there, of course."

"Of course," Zelik agreed, still looking at Whittier.

"Of course," Whittier echoed. Nerves and ingrained sarcasm made him add, "With bells on."

The only bells in evidence two hours later, however, chimed softly as the security lights lining the lab door switched from red to green. Abbott and Brindermann stepped through, Zelik right behind them. Whittier followed, the whirl of conflicting emotions making him feel almost giddy. Brindermann had accepted their presence coolly, but his sharp eyes seemed to engrave each of their faces on a mental list for later reference—or target practice.

Dr. Twilley met them, a hatchet-faced cipher in a long, white lab coat. He nodded in response to Abbott's hearty, "Heard you've had some success, Twilley," motioning them along the corridor of the secured lab.

"I have. Come this way, and I will demonstrate."

"I" in this case turned out to be Twilley's silently efficient lab assistants. As the VIPs stood in front of an observation window, the masked and bio-suited workers displayed a series of cages: rats, rabbits, monkeys, dogs, each paired in a set of two, sharing the same cage. In every case, one lay limply on its side, its ribs lurching up and down with each straining breath. The other breathed easily, sitting upright or scampering in the cage.

"The subjects on the left side of each cage were exposed to a version of the Pacifica virus formulated for the subject's genome. These subjects did not receive an initial vaccination," Dr. Twilley explained. "The subjects on the right were inoculated with the vaccination, then put into the same cages as the infected animals. As you see, the vaccinated subjects have suffered no ill effects, while the unvaccinated subjects rapidly succumbed to the effects of the virus."

"How long did it take?" Brindermann asked, watching the healthy monkey tentatively reach out to stroke the fur of the sick monkey's shoulder.

"Three days," Twilley said, indicating the charts on the walls of the lab room. "One day of incubation followed by two of days of escalating symptoms. In another day, the unvaccinated subjects will succumb. The others will show no ill effects."

Brindermann nodded; the virus worked as quickly as they'd hoped, and it appeared that the vaccine worked as well. "Animals are not humans," he said flatly.

"The concept is valid," Twilley responded, before Abbott could jump in with soothing words for the client. Questioning his competence or scientific judgment always provoked the doctor. "We have the data to prove it and will proceed to the final stage of the project as soon as we receive authorization. I am confident that we will see comparable results with the version engineered for humans."

The thin sound of Whittier swallowing disappeared into the soft hum of the air scrubbers.

"Consider it authorized," Zelik told Twilley. "At high-level security."

"Of course," Twilley snapped, irritated at the implied insult.

"You will use the experimental facilities we have prepared at our headquarters outside Bogotá," Brindermann said in a voice that promised a fast end to any attempt at debating the point. "Have your team and equipment ready to move tomorrow afternoon." He turned to Abbott and Zelik. "I trust that we will not find you have made the same lucrative mistake with this project as you did with AllSafe."

"Certainly not," Abbott assured him easily. "The marketing opportunities simply don't exist in this case. Right, Whittier?"

The three of them turned to look at the junior executive.

He was still staring through the glass at the dying animals, the harsh light of the experiment room reflecting in his eyes. The question—and all that it implied—rang in his ears, blending into a nightmare noise with the animals' labored breathing. Reality had come crashing down on his head in the last two hours, from the meeting in Abbott's office to the cool acknowledgment of producing viruses specifically designed to let Garza's forces destroy their enemies without dying themselves, to the gasping animals and the impending doom of the human subjects waiting in a camp outside of Bogotá. Sitting in his own office, waiting for the appointed meeting in the lab, far from Zelik's glittering eyes and Abbott's hyena smile, visions of a Senate inquiry rose in his mind, federal charges of espionage and treason, Senator Garlick authorizing the prosecution to ask for the death penalty. In a panic, he had cast around for a way out, ending up back where it all started, in Humphrey's office. The visit hadn't pulled him out of the morass; when he subtly, then more blatantly asked Humphrey to back him in a whistle-blowing move, the middle manager blew him off. "I'd rather keep breathing, thank you. And if you're smart, you'll save your breath too. You're going to need it, with the deep water you're in."

Save his breath. Breath. The ragged gasps sounded even louder in his ears. Death stood on the other side of that glass—not bankruptcy, not loss of face, not demotion, not a failed marketing campaign. Death. Under that black shadow, a corner office lost its appeal. His conscience, buried so long that it had wasted away to a mere thread, caught his weight as he plunged into the abyss—and, miraculously, held fast. As if it came from a long way off, he heard his own voice: "No. No, it's not right. It's absolutely wrong."

"This is your last chance, Whittier." Zelik's diamond-hard voice sawed against the thin resolve.

"No," Whittier said again, tearing his eyes away from the suffering beyond the glass. He looked from Zelik's hard face to Abbott's neutral expression. He didn't dare look at Brindermann. "Don't you see? They're going to use this to kill people! You can't sell something like this, let them use it on people—"

"Get hold of yourself, Whittier. We can," Abbott corrected, as if he were reprimanding Whittier for a miscalculated joke in the board-room. "And we will. What you need to decide is what you're going to do about it: make your fortune or seal your fate."

Whittier looked at him, unbelieving. "You're all insane."

"Are you going to say that we'll never get away with it?" Abbott asked, smiling again.

"No." Whittier turned away, walking toward the red-lit lab door.

A splatter of crimson darkened the red glow of the indicator light as a sharp explosion blasted through the quiet hum of the lab. Whittier hit the door a split second later, slowly sliding to his knees before falling backward against the gray floor.

"Soundproofing?" Zelik asked against the ringing in her ears.

"Rock-star grade," Abbott answered, buffing the barrel of his pocket pistol on his sleeve. He glanced at Twilley; the doctor stood beside the observation window, watching Whittier's corpse with clinical detachment. "Take care of that when you clean up the rest of the lab, Dr. Twilley. Mr. Brindermann, sorry about the little domestic disturbance here. I'm even more disappointed in young Mr. Whittier than you are."

"My employer commonly expresses his disappointment in the same way," Brindermann said dryly. He carefully stepped around the mess to the door without getting any evidence of it on his clothes or shoes.

"That was stupid," Zelik told Abbott. "It took guts I didn't think you had, but it was stupid."

He looked at her, surprised. "We couldn't let him go. He'd pull a Meredith Galen on us."

"Oh, I don't mean killing him," Zelik corrected, her voice not quite as cold as usual. His instant action had impressed her—both in

dealing with Whittier and in the implications for their own relationship. She would have to implement additional security measures. "I
mean killing him here. Now, we have to create a storyline to explain
his abrupt departure—more difficult when he disappears from his
office without explanation."

"I'm sure you'll think of something." Abbott reached to pat her
shoulder, but withdrew his hand as her stare reached absolute zero.
He substituted a smug smile instead. "That's what you're here for."

* * *

Dear Chisom,

*For some time now, weather conditions here have
been getting worse and in some instances have interfered
with our transmissions. Now the sun is getting into the
act. Sunspots are erupting all over its surface with
unusual, if not record-breaking, size and power. The poor
guys in the International Space Station are really having
difficulties. As a result of the bad weather and increased
solar radiation, the reception of your last two Vids was
very poor. We are waiting to have them repeated so we
can get a better idea of what you were telling us.*

*I hope this transmission to you comes over clearly,
because something marvelous has happened here that I
want to share with you. The Lord, in spite of all our
suffering, is with His Church. President Smith alluded to
this in his talk at the area conference last week and he
will speak more directly about it in general conference
next month. I'm sure you will find it wonderful. But, to
give you a sneak preview, in his area conference address
he reminded the Saints of a scripture Moroni quoted to
Joseph Smith from the third chapter of Malachi. The first
verse of that chapter says, "Behold, I will send my
messenger, and he shall prepare the way before me: and
the Lord, whom ye seek, shall suddenly come to His
temple, even the messenger of the covenant, whom ye
delight in." He then told the Saints that the "messenger of*

the covenant" has come to prepare His people to see His face. He went on to quote the words of the angel found in Revelation 14:7, "Fear God, and give glory to him; for the hour of his judgment is come." He then rehearsed the parable of the ten virgins, noting that he had received the message, "The Bridegroom cometh; go ye out to meet him." The time, he told the Saints, presses upon us. Now, he stressed, we must hold to the faith, fill our lamps with the oil of the Spirit, and be pure more as never before.

Chisom, the Lord has indeed come to His temple and has given the Brethren instructions on how to prepare the Church for what is coming next. I have never felt the power of the Spirit more strongly than over these last few weeks. Everything seems to be electrified because of it. Under the Lord's direction, the Brethren are preparing the stage for what is to come. This next conference will be one to be remembered, I can assure you.

With all the joy we have experienced around here, I am troubled that now, right when we have heard the cry, right when we have been promised that the time is very short, many are giving up the faith and leaving the Church. Babylon is more alluring than ever and continues to seduce many. Persecutions are becoming so severe and widespread that some can't take it any more. I fear that just as the moment of safety comes, they are trusting in themselves and thus putting themselves in harm's way. For the rest, the Lord has strengthened us and continues to do so.

As President Smith noted, we truly are living in the period predicted in the parable of the ten virgins and in Acts 3:22–23, the latter quoted by Moroni to Joseph Smith. Both warn of the separation that the Church will experience. We are seeing it now. President Rojas, at the area conference, reinforced something you already know but about which many are confused. He told the Saints that the virgins do not represent the people of the world in general. Those souls do not respond to the Lord's invitation *to come to the wedding. They stay home. No, these ladies represent those who respond to the invitation. These are the ones who have accepted the name of the Lord, made covenants with Him, and come into the Church. In other words, they are the ones who gathered to wait for the Bridegroom's coming. For a long time, the Church has been at peace, and we have enjoyed a period of rest, symbolized by the nap the virgins took. Now, however, the cry has gone out to get ready, for the Bridegroom comes. And what has been the response? Many are leaving! And why? Because they have not the light of Christ and can no longer see through the spiritual darkness that has gathered so thick around them. These are the lazy, the half-hearted, the lukewarm, and the social Saints. They have not kept the Spirit in their lives (the extra oil needed for the night) and are therefore going off hunting for the oil elsewhere. While they are gone, the Bridegroom will come and leave them behind.*

It is of note that a separation is not occurring just on the Church level. Many good people are leaving areas of wickedness to band together in more righteous communities. Many areas of big cities have been abandoned by good-hearted souls. It is interesting to see what's happening to the areas where there are large concentrations of Saints. In some places in California, the Rocky Mountain states, in Illinois, and here in Missouri, people who are not members of the Church are gathering. The same is true in some places in South America and Europe. They gather not because they want to be Saints but because they like our lifestyle, our purity, our ethics. As a result, our communities are burgeoning with good-hearted souls. Of course, many are not gathering near us. There are other communities, some even advertising, where the good-hearted are moving for strength and security. It pleases me to see this.

I am excited about living during this time. Yes, it is hard, but also most interesting and filled with portent. I am pleased that the work in China is going well. I also find it interesting that as people are converted, you are asking them to gather into more secure areas. The light of the Lord is shining even in the darkness. You are the bearer of the message of the Light. Continue to work with diligence.

With love,
Your father,
Chinedu

CHAPTER 21

"We can only pray that these poor souls, these fellow brothers and sisters in the Lord Jesus, will now be able to see the light, to wrap themselves in His outstretched arms so they can finally, at long last, come Home to the true Light that awaits them." Tommy Gibbs smiled benignly, giving his personal reaction to the news that the Catholic Church had split.

Anne, "live" from Channel 8's New York newsroom, summarized the report as the images of grim-faced cardinals, sign-waving protesters, women in priests' collars, and the tall spires of cathedrals on both sides of the Atlantic filled the screen. "In the most dramatic break of a long-running dispute, the Catholic Council of the United States has split with the Vatican, formally rejecting the rulings of the Roman pontiff on several controversial issues ranging from abortion to female priests. The repercussions will be felt throughout the Christian world—and may provide Protestant churches with an opportunity for growth, a wave of potentially disaffected ex-Catholics to swell the congregations and coffers of Tommy Gibbs and other evangelical leaders."

"Thank you, Anne." Clara turned to the right-hand camera. A ruined hillside appeared beside her, scarred with a long trail of wet sludge and boulders ending at a heap of uprooted trees, splintered beams, and mangled metal reinforcement bars. "In Vermont today, ecoterrorists have claimed responsibility for triggering an off-season mudslide and avalanche that destroyed an exclusive ski lodge. Cosheen Hall's Whole Earth Alliance issued a statement saying that the eastern United States is badly polluted, overcrowded, and abused.

In their words, 'It's time for those who love Mother Earth to use drastic measures to stem the tide of human abuse and misuse.' The ski lodge operators have filed civil as well as criminal charges, pending the discovery of the identities of the individuals responsible."

Switching cameras again, Clara turned to Cal Weathers, who stood ready beside the huge, glowing weather map. "I guess we don't have to ask about the ski report there, do we?"

Cal grinned, putting on his goofy weatherman face. "We sure don't. In fact, the ski industry has really suffered in the last four years. Due to global warming, the temperature all over the world is going up. Time to get out that sunscreen, folks!"

The canned patter couldn't disguise a real and deepening problem, however. As the weather grew less and less predictable, more wild and fierce, droughts and floods alternated over not just the eastern United States but the entire globe. Human-caused pollution and consumption vied with the devastating effects of years of climate change in producing a slow but steadily worsening water shortage. Supplies of drinkable water declined everywhere, with increasing salinity and heavy contamination killing lakes, rivers, and even ocean shores, making the water uninhabitable by anything but hardy blooms of algae. Cal's human-interest story, focusing on a small village in central Africa that had literally dried up and blown away when the last well ran out, was just one example in a world where 80 percent of the population lived without a dependable supply of potable water. While he talked over a succession of grim pictures showing starving children and parched animals, advertisements for the latest fashionable brand of designer water flashed across the bottom of the screen.

* * *

"Water, water everywhere, and not a drop to drink," Hideyoshi sang under his breath.

The tight confines of the ISS made for some odd acoustics, and for some reason the tiny bubble of a room containing the Earth-monitoring equipment sounded like a shower stall—perfect for turning off-key warbling into a full aria through the magic of making it sound not quite so bad to the singer's own ears. Mir had retreated, complaining that her ears just couldn't take it anymore, even after Hideyoshi switched from hymns to archaic drinking songs for her benefit. Some people just lacked gratitude. The thought made him smile as he checked the various blinking lights, dials, and sensors on the array of information-gathering and tracking machines that barely left enough room for two of them to squeeze into the space between the racks. Between Hideyoshi's own InSAR radar monitors and seismographic modelers, Mir's climate trackers, the high-bandwidth data feeds from stations like Becker's on the ground, and the constantly chattering video pickup dumping Channel 8's latest infotainment product into their minds, the small compartment held more state-of-the-art electronics than most military headquarters could assemble.

More than a few militaries would have loved to co-opt the equipment too, which is why stringent international laws mandated strict neutrality on the part of every crew member. The same agreements specified a country-by-country rotation for the responsibility for refueling and restocking the station, as well as ferrying crew members to and from their tours of scientific duty. The rotation had run into a severe bump lately, with the revolution in China preventing one scheduled flight, nasty weather and security fears scrubbing the American turn, and the Russians barely managing to get their backup ship off the ground. The tension level in the station continued to creep upward with each delay, each report of bad weather, each glitch in the communication or control systems. Static from huge sunspots regularly snowed out communications, sudden breakdowns plagued the station, and while the supplies of drinkable water hadn't dipped into dangerous territory, indicators showed them steadily depleting.

Right now, however, the static had cleared, as it did so often on Church-related projects, enough to become a superstitious joke among the personnel. The dry, brown expanse of the eastern Mediterranean coast filled the tectonic specialist's thoughts and the bank of monitors in front of him. The pictures showed a broad view, the typical cloud-banded blueness of a photo from orbit, then a closer view from mere thousands of feet, right down to the main monitor which brought Hideyoshi almost into touching distance of a specific patch of rocky, dusty mountainside in the wastelands surrounding the Dead Sea.

"Are you sure about this?"

Andre Becker's voice came clearly through the speakers, along with a thin, keening sound that Hideyoshi recognized, after a moment's puzzlement, as wind blowing past the geologist's research tent. *Wind! How good would that feel?*

According to Becker, it didn't feel good at all. "It's almighty hot down here, and the sand gets everywhere—and I mean everywhere. Why I let you talk me into coming out here, leaving nice, green Oregon for this hole, I'll never know."

"How about the chance to be in on the discovery of the century?" Hideyoshi suggested, delicately adjusting the InSAR display. He brought the deep-ground scanner online next, sucking data from Becker's sonar soundings of the desert terrain into the blindingly fast modeler inside the nondescript silver box. A picture began to form, the blocky bulk of the mountain, the irregular patterns of the rock shelves and upthrusts that lay hidden beneath the dust plaguing Becker. "Or how about the very nice commission the Church is paying for your help? This little job will net you enough cash to keep the Big Sister camp going for a year. You were just complaining that the cuts in government funding dried up most of your research grant. So consider a little dust chafing the price you pay to keep studying your pet volcano."

"I notice you don't mention that he's doing the poor, dusty citizens of that desert a huge favor," Mir noted, returning to the monitoring station now that Hideyoshi had stopped singing—and it looked like the excitement was about to begin.

"I just know what appeals to our friend Andre," Hideyoshi teased, grinning. "And it's not the sincere thanks of a grateful nation. Geologists are mercenary by nature."

"This geologist is getting his brains baked," Becker informed them. "And the incessant niceness of all these students your church provided as expedition assistants and this architect guy who's helping build your big canal is nearly as bad as the dust. At least his wife's got a temper on her." Becker shaded his eyes, looking into the distance where the Cohens supervised a group of students and a flock of contractors putting the finishing touches on the loopiest thing he'd ever seen: the glittering white sides of a gigantic sluice channel, starting in the middle of sun-struck nowhere, leading down the long slope of the mountains toward the Dead Sea.

If he hadn't run the numbers himself and seen the resulting sonar patterns, he would've tagged the whole thing a colossal waste of energy, money, fuel, and time—though, he had to admit, it hadn't taken as long as he'd feared. The Mormons sent the Cohens and Hassan into the desert with the geologists because they'd proved they could elicit both speed and precision from the local contractors. The contractors had come too, on the promise of double wages. Thus, under the relentless direction of Mrs. Cohen and Hassan, the crew working on the Mormon temple had temporarily left that assignment for a stint digging in the blistering desert. The project had attracted attention, not from curious locals (there weren't any in this area), but from a couple of junior members of the press drawn by yet another example of the inscrutable ways of the Mormons, hoping for an exclusive story, not caring much whether they saw success or failure, so long as they saw *something* worth reporting.

Now, Becker just hoped the whole insane idea would actually work, or they'd look like idiots. He tapped the uplink to the station and the man he'd grown to consider a friend, despite the fact that they'd never met face-to-face. "Do you have what you need yet? I really need a drink!"

"Everybody down there needs a drink," Hideyoshi said, sobering. "Do one more sounding, Andre, the big thumper over on the north-east corner of the B5 grid. That should give me the last piece of the puzzle. Then everybody can have a drink."

They needed dinner to go with that drink too, and the prices on the menu were rapidly climbing. By even the most conservative estimates, many Middle Eastern and North African countries teetered on the edge of starvation. The causes included all the usual culprits, graft and corruption in governments, business interests draining oil and money out of the region, internecine warfare, plus the destruction of the High Dam at Aswan. The weather hadn't helped either; sure, the dramatic changes in climate that Mir tracked had brought more rain to the usually dry regions, but without the infrastructure to capture and use the water, it only contributed to the suffering of the people. Band after band of clouds poured rain into the deserts, only to run over the hard ground in flash floods, wiping out anything in their way before disappearing into the desperately thirsty ground, working its way into buried streams that became rivers that grew into lakes hidden deep beneath the bones of the mountains. The caves had lain empty, as dry as underground could get, for centuries, if not millennia, until at last the heavens sent rain to fill them again. However, underground water didn't do the equally thirsty inhabitants of the region any good—or it once didn't.

Boom. The bone-shaking thunder of Becker's seismic wave generator, essentially a large cannon pointed at the ground, sent vibrations through the rock so the sonar sensors could map the composition of the ground. The sound came dimly through the speakers on the space station. Immediately, a new wash of data flowed over the monitors, the digital brain behind them integrating the new information with the old map. It now formed pictures of the deep structures of the earth made from the images of sound waves. The picture quickly developing before Hideyoshi's eyes was transmitted down to the tiny monitor in the thin shade of Becker's expedition tent. The bulk of the rock shelf under the worn hills appeared, extending downward like the superstructure of a land-bound iceberg, its geometric shape rent and split with fissures large and small, the deep pools of subterranean aquifers embedded in the rock glittering like living things as the waves of the sonar pulse passed through them. A brilliant line slashed through the ghostly shapes of rock and water, forking like lightning, ending in four distinct points on the mountain's crumbling flanks.

"We've got them!" Hideyoshi shouted, hitting the console in his excitement and sending himself into a spin in the weightless environment of the station.

"Okay, so tell me so I can tell Cohen and Hassan, and we can see if these perky students are smart enough to obey directions without blowing themselves up," Becker suggested dryly, but he couldn't hide the excitement in his own voice.

By the time the lower edge of the sun touched the rocky horizon, everything was in place. The equipment and camp had disappeared, neatly packed and stowed in the beds of trucks that now waited on the mountain ridge to the west. The students, excited and intent, strung out in a thin line along the ridge, intermingled with Israeli and

Palestinian construction workers, who leaned casually against their earth movers, took drags on cigarettes, and made wagers about the outcome of the Mormons' gamble. Word had spread beyond the camp too, and now several more cameras had joined the original media stringers.

"Charges in place," reported the construction company's burly, mustached demolitions expert.

"Computer model looks good," Becker relayed, checking the data from Hideyoshi's broadcast.

"Everyone's out of the way," Mrs. Cohen added, reflexively checking to make sure her husband was still on the ridge with the students.

Hassan nodded. He had the headset, and as the superintendent of the project, he had the authority to give the go-ahead. Much to the surprise of those unfamiliar with the ways of Mormons, instead of giving the order, he called for silence. Dropping to his knees, along with the students, the Cohens, and many of the workers, who did not believe as he did but nevertheless believed, he bowed his head and said a heartfelt prayer. "Please, God our beloved Father, we ask Thee to place Thy sheltering hand over those gathered here, and over those in so desperate need. We ask Thee to guide the water and rock as Thou hast guided us to find this spot. If it is Thy will, do for us as Thou once did for Moses, that we might strike the rock in Thy Son's name to release a fountain of pure water. In the name of Thy perfect and loving Son, Jesus Christ, amen."

The chorus of amens faded into the expectant silence as cooling shadows from clouds above them flowed over the ground. Hassan gave the signal. With a nearly subsonic rumble of subterranean thunder, eight heavy charges went off deep in the faults of the mountain. As if the earth had burst chains holding her down, mighty columns of dust and rock flew skyward—followed by higher columns whose tops rose high enough to glitter in the last fading rays of the sun, before pouring down like the rain that lifted Noah's ark, crashing down into the guiding mouth of the hastily constructed canal. The cement could not contain the vast flood, but it wasn't meant to; it held just long enough to let the first rush of the water grind deep into the ground, gouging out a path through the mountains that grew deeper by the second as the canal's man-made walls washed away. Amid wild cheers from the onlookers, the sound drowned in the head-filling rumble of the water, the released underground ocean blasted its way out of the mountains, into the Dead Sea—and, through another canal drilled through dryer mountains—to the sea, a new river pulled from underground and falling from the clouds above, bringing water and life to a once-barren desert. And far above, at the head of the stream, stood the foundations of the Lord's temple.

* * *

A sheet of water soaked Lucrezia as soon as she left the shelter of the eaves' slight overhang. Far off in the soggy darkness, a sheet of lightning illuminated the scene. She was glad of the baseball cap pulled tight over her head but wished that she had a cowboy hat instead. Then again, in a rain like this, even the broadest brim wouldn't matter; the downpour soaked her to the skin in seconds. She ran across the backyard, jumping to the top of the short storage shed, then scrambling over the board fence. A sudden burst of light illuminated her as she rose to her feet on the muddy verge of the access road behind the townhouses.

"Come on!" Porter's voice came from behind the headlights, the rumble of the truck's engine vying with the roll of thunder.

With a flutter of anticipation in her stomach, she ran around to the passenger door that he kicked open, climbing into the cab. She sat back, pushing the wet curls off her face, and stole a glance at Porter as he spun the wheel, leaving the back alley in a spray of water and mud.

"Glad you decided to come. Didn't think you would." He smiled shyly at her. "Didn't know if you'd got the message I sent. I asked Mama, and she said she'd be happy to have you wait at the house for us, especially if you don't mind helping lay out the table."

"I'm not laying out any tables. I'm coming with you." Holding up a hand toward him, she said, "And don't try to talk me out of it either. Those people tried to burn down my house—and they laughed—they *laughed*—when they heard about Giovanni. I want to hit them back!"

Porter considered arguing but decided to leave it alone for the moment, as he turned off the smaller street that ran behind the Callattas' house, watching the empty lots and dark windows of the strip of ghost town that surrounded the Mormon neighborhood. Rock would set her straight. Porter had never intended for her to come on the raid; he'd thought she'd stay with the mothers and sisters of tonight's raiding parties to prepare a celebration—which always meant food in Sister Smith's mind—and wait for their victorious warriors to return.

Lucrezia had formed quite a different picture when she got Porter's message, saying that the Smith clan and the rest of their gang planned a coordinated series of raids for that night to get back at Lebaron's forces and give them an intimidating show of strength. The brief, text-only electronic message didn't make clear what exactly they intended to wreak vengeance on Lebaron's people for; by this point in the feud, they hardly needed a specific reason. In Lucrezia's tear-filled eyes, however, Giovanni's name glowed between the lines; the crude jokes from the Rhinos at school about Chilean "pest control" rang in her ears. Jelisaveta, April, and Imre had tried to shield her from the worst of it, but their best efforts hadn't stopped Shanna from sliding a red-ink drawing into her locker. She didn't know what it said, because Jelisaveta had grabbed it right over her shoulder, but she didn't need to. Shanna, the Rhinos, the Amulonites—they all stood accused, tried, and convicted of complicity in Giovanni's death. It didn't matter that Samuel Lebaron had no ties whatsoever to rebel assassins in Chile—Lucrezia, like her father, ached to avenge Giovanni, and Lebaron's boys were the closest, and only, target she could reach. That hot, sick knot in her stomach was half of the purpose that had sent her out into the rain tonight.

The other half was much simpler and had to do with being fifteen and in love, or at least what she considered love. Carmen and Tony had a fit after she came home from school with a torn shirt and scratched face from jumping into a brawl the Smith boys started. She'd seen Shanna swing a baseball bat at Porter when he tackled Bret, and she sprang to his defense—and promptly found herself in a catfight with Shanna. She won, but first Carmen then Tony had told her in no uncertain terms that they didn't approve of her behavior and didn't want her associating with the Smiths or their friends.

In the truck, on the way to show them all, including her parents and Donna, she rubbed her wet face against her equally wet sweatshirt sleeve, a flush of excitement warming her cheeks under a fresh flow of tears. Nobody could see either the flush or the tears, however, when she pulled a dark, wet bandana over her face.

Rock recognized her even through the cloth when Porter pulled up to the muddy field where the rest of their raiding party waited. The other trucks, containing their elders and led by Brother Smith prophesying fiery destruction to the Amulonites, had already driven off on their own missions of mayhem, leaving Rock impatiently waiting for his tardy younger brother. "Porter, are you crazy? This is a raid, serious business. We march into battle, little brother. You can't bring a girl!"

"I thought she could stay with the truck, as the getaway driver," Porter hastily explained. He'd snatched the opportunity to see Lucrezia again, but he had no intention of actually putting her in danger.

That earned him glares from both Rock and Lucrezia. Before either of them could argue, Orrin stepped up, playing with a jack handle. "Hey, she lost a brother to the Gentiles. She has a right to slam some Amulonite tail anytime she's got the guts up." He grinned at Lucrezia, his teeth and eyes glinting in another distant lightning strike. "Let's give the sister her chance."

He tossed the jack handle, caught it, and twirled the slim length of metal like a baton, pointing its flattened end toward the road—and the distant lights of Lake Creek.

The jack handle was the first thing that went through the window of a small, Amulonite-owned hardware store on the far end of Lake Creek's Main Street. Orrin followed, jumping through the sharp-edged gap in the plate glass to land, grinning psychopathically, in the scree of shards. Rock and the other six boys burst in—through the door rather than the window—with bloodcurdling whoops, and ran through the store, pulling over displays, smashing racks, and generally reducing the orderly aisles to mangled, scattered chaos.

Lucrezia, slipping in behind the boys, felt a rush of relief that they hadn't targeted a church this time; she didn't know if she could go so far as burning a chapel; even if it belonged to Reverend Lebaron's mob, a church still had at least the idea of sanctity associated with it. Fortunately for her, Brother Smith had changed the battle plan, under the theory that hitting the Amulonites in the pocketbook would hurt more than torching their churches. "For their treasure is on this earth, where moth doth corrupt, and thieves break through and steal," Rock quoted his father, explaining the night's mission. That made the Hunt brothers laugh nastily, but Porter looked like he didn't appreciate being lumped in with moths—or thieves. Lucrezia didn't really like the idea of thieving either and told herself that wasn't the point of the raid. It was a sidelight, part of the punishment the Amulonites deserved. She shoved away the thought that the "real" purpose of the raid—general vandalism and terror—wasn't exactly noble.

A sudden attack of conscience made her stop, standing on the glass-covered floor, but then she caught sight of the professionally printed "No Mormons or Dogs" sign that had adorned the window. That killed the last gasp of hesitation. She grabbed a tall, rotating stand full of nails, screws, and bolts and pulled hard. With a tortured creak, the central pole leaned, then fell, sending tiny bits of sharp and round metal bits skittering across the dirty tile floor.

Shouts from the back of the store heralded the arrival of the owner and two employees. One, coming face-to-face with Rock in the plumbing area, took one hard blow to the face and ran for the back door; if resisting robbers wasn't worth his life, resisting religion-crazed Visigoths wasn't either. The other went down swinging, under the weight of three masked vandals, and found himself wrapped like a large, green-rubber mummy in lengths of garden hose. The owner was made of sterner stuff—he straight-armed the sixth barbarian and ran for the main counter, diving behind it to get to the phone.

Snatching up a shovel from the wall rack, Orrin brought it down on the counter, smashing through the glass and into the display of ammunition beneath. He brought the shovel up, pointing threateningly at the owner's throat, effectively pinning him in place, away from the phone. "Don't do it," Orrin advised, "and we might let you live."

From the front of the store, Porter called for assistance. Lucrezia ran through the litter of small components to help him as he pushed hard on the first of the head-high shelves. It contained the gardening supplies, pots, trowels, bags of potting soil, and large bank of dusty artificial flowers that the owner put up front to entice female clientele into the oil- and polyvinyl-smelling interior. Two more boys, probably Brother Hunt's sons, though Lucrezia couldn't tell through their bandanas, joined them, adding their weight. Gradually, the long wood-and-metal shelf leaned, reached its balance point, and tumbled, sending trowels and pots smashing to the floor. It crashed into the next one back, which groaned and tipped, spilling its shelves and smacking into the next aisle. In a cascade of heavily laden dominoes, the shelves defining all eight aisles fell one by one. Dust rose in a choking cloud above the devastation.

A muffled cry came from somewhere in the tangled mess, loud in the sudden silence. Lucrezia looked toward the sound, and saw a leg protruding from under a pile of bicycle tires and parts. Green hose wrapped around it, the green marked with a wash of thick red. Suddenly, the thrill of destruction flamed out, leaving her cold. "Porter!" she choked, pointing.

"Blast," he muttered. "They couldn't drag him off to the side?"

The crashing started again, Rock leading his disciples in tearing down the last few displays. Porter and Lucrezia tore into the pile on top of the mummified hardware man, tossing aside the avalanche of bicycle components. Tires bounced away, a stack of spokes clattered like metal pickup sticks, and the rest of the man came into view. The blood came from a deep gash in his leg, slashed by the edge of a metal shelf on its way to the floor. Porter whipped the bandana off his head and pressed it to the wound, sopping up the blood so they could see how bad it was. The man stared at him over the lengths of hose and the duct-tape gag wrapped around his mouth. Lifting the soaked cloth, Porter examined the damage. Fortunately, it wasn't particularly deep, and definitely not life-threatening, but the dull, iron-and-salt smell of blood combined with a rush of guilt made Lucrezia queasy. "Let's go!" Rock's retreat call rose above the last few crashes, the distant but quickly approaching wail of sirens becoming audible.

The owner hadn't managed to dial the police—he'd kept more than busy dodging Orrin's shovel, as the wild-eyed boy got bored with keeping him still and started stabbing it toward him. Orrin gave him plenty of time to get out of the way while keeping him corralled behind the battered counter, laughing as he shattered the cabinet of lures on one side, then brought down a rack of unloaded and new rifles on the other. He glowered, resisting Rock's order, not wanting to leave while the terrorizing was still fun. Rock smacked his shoulder, reaching past him to forcibly pop the cash drawer on the register. He dumped the contents into a bag he slung over his shoulder and ran for the door.

Porter looked toward his older brother, but didn't rise from his knees. "Grab a couple of those," he directed Lucrezia, jutting his chin at a display of bandanas lying like fallen battle flags as he dragged the moaning, thoroughly immobilized clerk into a clear spot by the wall. She handed them to him, watching anxiously as he hurriedly wrapped them around the man's leg, keeping the blood contained, if not stopped.

"*Now!*" Rock roared from the doorway.

"Go get the truck started," Porter told Lucrezia, bumping his shoulder against hers to get her moving. She ran, leaping through the broken front window, as he finished tying up the wounded leg.

Orrin growled at the store owner as he threw the shovel as hard as he could. The blade drove into the wall beside the white-faced man, its handle quivering. A sudden grin replaced the scowl on Orrin's face; he reached into the broken counter case and extracted four boxes of bullets. "We'll return these later." He whirled away with a wicked laugh, pausing just long enough to pull the fire alarm, which set off a blistering scream—and a deluge as the sprinklers kicked on, filling the battered store with water, completing the ruin.

A shotgun blast followed him out the window, as the owner raced forward, slamming another shell into the barrel of the gun he'd snatched from his own display. His curses blasted at them with more fire, if less actual lead, than the buckshot, as Lucrezia drove wildly away, Porter and Rock lunging into the cab with her, the other four raiders piled in the bed. Orrin rose, brandishing his retrieved jack handle and whooping, until one of the other boys yanked him down—just in time, as the blue and red strobes of a pair of police cars bore down on them. The hardware owner furiously motioned them on, his shouts lost in the blare of sirens.

A loud bang and the sudden spider web of cracks spreading over the windshield startled Lucrezia; it took her a second to figure out that the cold pellets that sprayed the back and side of her head and shoulder were cubes of safety glass from the truck's shattered back window. A bullet, she realized—somebody had shot at them, and the bullet had gone through the back window, right past her head, and then through the windshield. She froze, hands stiff on the steering wheel, feet numb against the pedals.

"Lucrezia!" Porter shouted, as the truck jerked and slowed. "Lucrezia, keep going!"

"Never trust a woman in a fight!" Rock slammed his fist into the cracked dashboard, then aimed a blow past Porter at Lucrezia.

That comment penetrated Lucrezia's panic enough to make her slam the gas pedal to the floor of the truck, throwing off Rock's aim and throwing Orrin to the bed of the truck again.

Porter caught Rock's fist, throwing it back at him, then grabbed Lucrezia, one hand on her near arm, the other slipping behind her to rest on her far ribs. "Luc, you keep hold of the wheel—keep steering!—I'm going to move you over and drive. Ready?" He didn't wait for her answer; pulling and lifting at once, he moved her over his lap, sliding himself into the driver's seat.

Lucrezia landed on the seat again and belatedly let go of the wheel, slamming into Porter as he hit the gas and turned hard to the right at the same time. Under other circumstances, the whole procedure would've thrilled her (actual physical contact!); at the moment, she had no mental energy left for anything but clutching Porter's belt loop for stability and casting a wild glance behind at the police cars closing the distance behind them.

Taking fearless right over the line to reckless, Porter blasted right through one of Lake Creek's many rubble-strewn empty lots. They jounced off the far curb, spinning tires spraying a vast sheet of mud, only to see another pair of lights gleaming through the rain haze as yet another car barreled toward them from a side street, screeching around a turn to roll directly toward them. Off to the left, the two original pursuers rounded the corner of the lot.

"Stop!" the voice, amplified through the cruiser's speakers, bellowed at them. The black barrel of a gun protruded from the passenger-side window, drawing bead on the truck.

From the bed of the truck, Orrin howled defiance, the other boys echoed him more or less shakily; all but one had taken cover, lying flat in the truck bed. Lucrezia clutched Porter's belt loop, trying not to get in his way or slide toward Rock. Porter glanced at Rock, looking for direction. Rock, his face lit with the same fanatic ecstasy that so often marked his father's, pointed through the cracked windshield. A crack of lightning lit his face as he shouted, "The Lord will sustain us. Forward!"

His jaw clenching, Porter slammed down on the accelerator again, aiming the battered grille right for the flashing lights. Another shot increased the complexity of the webbed cracks on the windshield; others banged and whined off the truck's metal shell and skeleton. Lucrezia, unblinking, watched numbly as the lights filled her whirling head with red and blue glare.

At the last moment, the police car's driver realized that the maniacs in the truck had no intention of stopping. He frantically pulled the wheel, lurching to the side of the road, then spinning hard into the mud as the back of the truck clipped his car. His partner got off a shot that missed Orrin, who was waving and shouting incoherent insults at them.

All three police cars fell into pursuit, spreading out across the road, gaining rapidly. Porter made another turn onto the highway leading out of town, the truck's wheels skidding through a deep puddle.

"Straightaway." Lucrezia managed to find her voice, sensation slamming back into her with the feel of the rain on her face, the warmth of Porter's side through his wet shirt, the pain in her knees where they'd hit the dashboard. "After this curve, it's a straightaway. Porter, they'll catch us on a straightaway."

"It's the way home," he said simply, sending a quick, sweet smile her way as the truck lunged, engine screaming, down the thin strip of blacktop between the thrashing lines of storm-whipped trees and around that last protecting corner.

The black-and-whites, like predators sensing their prey tiring, leapt forward, one only a couple of truck lengths away as they came out of the curve.

The darkness ahead of them suddenly bloomed with hot, white lights. Eyes half shut in the glare, Lucrezia thought she counted three sets of headlights, at least that many bands of poacher lights adding to the blinding illumination. Behind the lights, more of Brother Smith's raiders opened fire, not so much aiming as sending a vicious hail of hot lead in the direction of the police cruisers as they accelerated forward. The wall of metal bearing down on them parted, and Porter guided the truck through, coming to a sloppy halt at the side of the road. All three of the cab's occupants turned around, watching the scene through the jewel-framed hole where the truck's back window had been.

Behind them, the police rapidly realized that they were outnumbered and outgunned—and technically out of their jurisdiction, into the county sheriff's territory. With a squeal of protesting tires, they wallowed through the mud on the sides of the road in wide turns, and fled back to Lake Creek.

A cheer rose from the "righteous militia," along with a few defiant rifle shots into the air. Only Orrin sounded disappointed that they didn't immediately take up the chase, fox turning on the hounds. Rock slammed the door open, jumping out into the rain and his father's proud embrace. Porter looked at Lucrezia, laughing with reaction and relief, caught her face between his hands, and kissed her.

* * *

"I love you, Porter," Lucrezia whispered, gazing deeply into his brilliant eyes.

"I love—" he began, then coughed. Bright blood ran over his lip, staining his chin, dripping in a spreading stain over his shirt, her hands, warm and sticky and—

Gasping, Lucrezia lurched upright in her bed, tears flooding down her cheeks, her heart pounding painfully. The darkness of her room closed in on her, making the horrible image in her head more vivid. It didn't matter that Porter was safe at the Smiths' farmhouse, probably asleep in his own bed after the celebration of the successful raid; fear and grief overwhelmed her. "Luc?" Donna whispered from across the small room. "Are you okay?"

Gianni stirred in his little bed as well, hearing Lucrezia's sobs through his own dreams. Donna got up, hugged Lucrezia, and said, "Luc, go tell Mom and Dad." Watching her little sister stumble out, she rubbed Gianni's back until he fell asleep again. As soon as his breathing settled, she slipped out to stand in her parents' bedroom door frame.

Carmen managed to comfort Lucrezia enough to stop her stifled, gasping sobs. Tony wisely swallowed his frantic questions about what was wrong as soon as he determined that she wasn't physically hurt. In her mother's arms, Lucrezia managed to collect herself again, overcoming the irrational but very real terror of the nightmare, which brought the hard realization that while the raid had been thrilling while it happened, it left her frightened, shaken, and deeply guilty. Her memory replayed flashes of the broken window, scattered nails, and blood, mingled with the scream of sirens and crack of a bullet striking windshield glass.

"What happened, honey? Bad dream?" Carmen asked softly. "You want to talk about it?"

"No," Lucrezia mumbled, against the shoulder of Carmen's fuzzy robe. She pulled away, wiping her hands across her face. "But I have to." Without looking at them, she plunged on, telling the entire story: getting Porter's message about the raid, sneaking out into the rain, the attack on the hardware store, Rock stealing the money, the wounded clerk, the chase in the truck, the bullets, the sirens, the appearance of the men on the road, the strangely giddy and savage party at the Smith farm, finally asking Porter to bring her home, where she wriggled through the bathroom window and out of her wet clothes before collapsing in her bed.

Her parents listened as she spoke, her voice speeding along with barely a pause for breath to keep them from interrupting. When the flow stopped at last, Lucrezia didn't dare look at either of them.

"Are you finished?" Carmen asked, her voice low.

"Yes," Lucrezia said quietly.

"Good," Carmen's voice didn't rise so much as deepen, fury adding a husky rasp as she fought not to shout. "Because now I can start. I never thought that one of my children would do such a stupid, thoughtless, violent, dishonest, completely awful thing! How could you possibly do that? Even stealing from a store would be bad enough, but to help a bunch of creeps destroy a man's livelihood— and hurt him too? What were you thinking?"

Lucrezia ducked as if Carmen had struck her, tears flooding her eyes again. Her temper tried to rise, but even her famous bull-headedness couldn't deny the justice of Carmen's reprimand.

"She wasn't thinking." The calm in Tony's voice made both of them look at him in surprise. He reached over to shake Lucrezia's shoulder, not roughly but firmly, as if to reassure himself that she really had come home without any bullet holes. "She wasn't thinking about anything but how bad it feels to have people hate you because you know the truth."

"So we should hate those who hate us? Where's the truth there?" Carmen snapped. "You get dressed, young lady, and we're going to sort this out!"

"In the middle of the night?" Tony asked.

"The police station never closes," Carmen informed him, rising.

Tony caught her shoulders this time, stopping her. "Carmen. No."

"No!?" Carmen stared at him in disbelief. "Tony, you heard what they did—what she helped them do! That's not accidentally breaking a window, that's serious. If she goes in now, confesses, and explains, maybe we'll be able to convince the authorities to give her probation and community service instead of packing her up and tossing her into juvenile detention."

"Or shooting her?" Tony met Carmen's eyes, his face utterly serious.

"Shooting her?" Carmen repeated, her voice breaking.

"We're not living under the rule of law anymore, Carmen," Tony said. "How do you think they'll treat her—and us—if we appear down at the courthouse admitting that she helped Smith's goons wreck a hardware store? These are the same people who didn't send the fire trucks when Lebaron tried to set our neighborhood on fire. The same ones who fined Rob Sarkesian for filing a frivolous lawsuit when he tried to get an injunction against the protesters vandalizing his business. Do you think they'd be fair to Lucrezia—or to us?"

"No." Carmen shuddered, suddenly hugging Lucrezia as if to defend her of the dire possibilities.

Lucrezia hugged back, feeling both better for not having to face the police and worse for realizing that for the first time in her life, the police had become the enemy. Her world shook to its foundations, leaving only the stability of her family between her and complete disintegration. The guilt rose again, telling her that somehow the entire bad situation was somehow her fault. "I'm sorry," she whispered.

"So am I, sweetie." Carmen rocked her slowly, comforting them both. She didn't have to tell Lucrezia not to do it again; Lucrezia already felt bad enough about it, and she'd decided she had experienced enough violence to last for the rest of her life. No more raids for her. Or for Porter? A slow roll of worry made her queasy, remembering him dying in her arms.

"We have to get out of here," Donna said from the doorway, breaking her long silence.

"Where would we go?" Carmen asked, holding out her hand to her eldest daughter.

Donna walked over, took her mother's hand, squeezed it, but didn't join Lucrezia in a general hug. "I don't know. Somewhere safe, somewhere there are a lot of Mormons. Nauvoo, maybe, near the temple?"

"No," Tony said, pulling Donna over to sit on the bed next to him.

"It'd be safer," Carmen pointed out.

"They're having problems in Nauvoo too," Tony said. "Not in the city, since it's pretty much all Mormons or supporters, but they've had outlying farms burned and that silicon-chip factory bombed." He shook his head, leaning forward to rub Carmen's shoulder. "It's bad all over. You heard the news. Elder DuPris hasn't been able to get any support from the governor. We're on our own. Our best bet is to hold out, keep what's ours, and defend ourselves as well as we can. Nobody's going to stand up for Mormons. They never have, and they never will."

Carmen frowned, opening her mouth to argue—and they all jumped when the phone rang.

"Callattas'," Tony said warily. Outside, the first hint of dawn began to lighten the wept-out sky.

Bishop Newstead's gentle voice sounded stressed as he said, "Tony, are you and Carmen okay? The kids okay? Is everybody there?"

"We're good," Tony said, after only a moment's hesitation, glancing at Lucrezia's pale face.

"Glad to hear it." The bishop really did sound glad, as if the positive response took an infinitesimal fraction of weight off his shoulders. He didn't explain the question.

"Why? What's happened?" Tony asked, unnecessarily. He had the sinking suspicion that he already knew what the bishop would say—and why he'd called the Callattas. Everybody knew that Lucrezia had more to do with Porter Smith than anyone outside the Smiths' tight circle.

"Brother Smith's taken matters into his own hands. They trashed four stores earlier tonight and got into a running gun battle with the police. Now they've holed up on three farms, including the Smiths' spread, and are shooting any official vehicle that comes along the lane." Bishop Newstead sounded weary, angry, but not defeated. "Rob Sarkesian and I have talked to both the sheriff and the chief of police; they know that the rest of us didn't have anything to do with it. But others won't bother to make the distinction. There are already at least thirty people at city hall demanding reprisals against the Mormons, and someone's shot out the windows at Softlearn. It looks like Brother Smith's finally decided it's time to start his own personal Armageddon. We're getting the word out—calling the elders, telling them to call their home teaching families, take a roll call, and make sure everybody's all right. Ask everyone to be prepared to take others in if necessary."

"I'll get the word out to my families," Tony said.

"Do it quickly." A hard resolve came into the bishop's voice. "Let's get our people safe, tell them to be careful, and get them praying. All hell's about to break loose out there."

* * *

"You couldn't really blame them for thinking the end is near," Leon said, stowing his camera gear after finishing a filler shot of Anne standing outside the massive Mormon conference center in Independence. They'd come from Lake Creek, shooting commentary in front of a quartet of devastated mom-and-pop shops, getting close-ups of the bullet holes in the city's four police cruisers, and getting long shots—very long shots—of the deceptively peaceful fields and outbuildings of the increasingly infamous Smith farm.

The online polls showed that the public's estimation of Mormons had taken another dive, not only in the Midwestern states but generally, which would hurt their chances of winning support from the governors of the embattled states. Though the First Presidency issued a statement condemning vandalism and violence of any kind directed at anyone, Jack DuPris had refused to comment, promising his reaction at a press conference in Lake Creek the next day.

Anne and Leon had come to Independence hoping to leverage their "personal friendship," as Leon put it, to catch President Rojas for a more direct response, and to ask him if a schism in the Church was imminent. Anne's persistent inquiries had finally borne fruit: the far-flying Associate President was in town at Church headquarters for a mass leadership meeting. Unlike most large Mormon gatherings, this leadership conference had been remarkably low key. From what Anne could gather, all invitations had gone out quietly and personally, either by phone or via satellite communications all over the globe, rather than the usual general announcement. Hotels in Independence were booked to the rafters with Mormon leaders coming from the four corners of the world for the dedication of the Jackson County temples, with a "leadership meeting" tacked on a few days before. All the big shots, plus what looked almost like a representative sample of the smaller fish—like some of the lay bishops. Even getting that much, however, had strained her formidable investigating skills to their limits.

"Maybe they're just tired out, fingers bleeding from typing press releases about that big dedication hoo-hah they're throwing for the whole temple complex," Leon suggested, when Anne wondered aloud why she hadn't been able to unearth more information about the planned meeting in Independence. "They're just bringing people in to smile on the bleachers when they pull out the white handkerchiefs next week. Besides, nobody cares about some internal administration meeting or one of their priesthood things, unless they're going to start sacrificing live goats. They want us all to focus on Joseph Smith's big vision for a whole block full of temple buildings and how great it is. Too bad for them. All of us press vultures know that the big story's what's happening in Lake Creek."

"Jack DuPris isn't coming to the leadership meeting," Anne noted, tucking a windblown strand of hair behind her ear. Anne had that right, though she didn't really know the reason why, or that he had decided that preparing for his next meeting with the governor took precedence over yet another leadership meeting with a leadership who didn't understand the situation on the ground or recognize his own capability to handle it in his own way.

"He's the only one who isn't," Leon noted, stowing the gear in the back of their well-used Channel 8 van. "From what I overheard in the men's room, they've got the full slate here." He paused, looking thoughtfully toward the big building and the soberly dressed crowds converging on it. Unusually for most Mormon gatherings, none of the couples had children with them. They also seemed more quiet and intense than usual, not angry or worried, but Leon's well-honed news antennae quivered every once in a while, picking up a rolling undercurrent of excitement.

"That's unusual." Anne glanced at the bulk of the building, then climbed into the passenger seat as Leon started the engine. She reached back for her bag, rummaging through its capacious interior until she found what she was looking for. Settling back into the correct position, she began leafing through the copy of the Book of Mormon that President Rojas had given her on their second meeting.

"What are you looking for?" Leon asked. She wasn't just reading, she was flipping around, back and front, checking the table of contents and index.

"It seems like I read somewhere something about not getting all the leaders in the same place at once," she muttered. "Or maybe it's just their Apostles."

Leon chuckled. "If they do have something like that down as scripture, it wouldn't be in there. Try their Doctrine and Covenants. That's got the modern stuff—or as modern as the nineteenth century."

Anne smiled at him. "Well, look at you, the Mormon expert."

"I've been reading up too. And hanging out with you, I'm learning more about religion than I ever thought I would. The creepy ones and the innocuous ones. And the innocuous ones always have the wackiest ideas."

"I assume you're including the Mormons as innocuous. So which of their ideas are the 'wackiest'? You've got a bunch to choose from."

Leon shot her a grin. "Okay. How about them believing that not only is Jesus going to come back—the big Second Coming thing from the Bible—but that He's going to come visit them beforehand?"

"Really?"

"And that He's not just coming Himself, but He's bringing everybody from Adam to Moses to—oh, I don't know, probably Brigham Young—along for the ride?"

"That would be a story," Anne laughed. Despite how crazy it sounded, her eyes lit at the thought of being there to cover it—even as they drove away from the scoop of the century, if not all time.

Neither she nor Leon understood the sudden lightening of heart they felt as they neared Lake Creek that evening, but for the worried families huddled in their homes, the last hour of daylight brought a fleeting but powerful feeling of peace, a sense of hope and serenity as wide and deep as the sunset.

* * *

Dear Chisom,

Your mother and I rejoiced over your last Vid. We were not a bit surprised that your mission had the profound spiritual experience you shared. What you don't know is that it was the fulfillment of a promise made by President Smith. By now I'm sure your mission president has shared with you the events that took place here, triggering the overflowing of the Spirit there. The truth is, the same thing took place in every mission and stake throughout the world. The source emanated, as he told you, from Adam-Ondi-Ahman and the outpouring of the Spirit that happened there. Your mother and I were blessed to be a part of nearly every event.

Oh, Chisom, how I wish you could have been with us at those great meetings! President Smith and President Rojas considered the idea of bringing the missionaries in from the field, but in the end, they decided that they needed you with the Saints so that those who could not come would not feel abandoned. With you there, they would know that it was all right for them to be there as well. Also, the Brethren felt that the movement of so many missionaries would cause too much curiosity by the news media and others. The news crews are used to Church officials coming to headquarters for this or that, but not missionaries. Our leaders wanted to draw as little attention to this gathering as possible. President Smith promised us, however, that you and the faithful Saints who were deprived of the privilege and blessing of being here would not be left out of the endowment of the Spirit. I'm so pleased you were not.

Now let me tell you about what happened. First, I must emphasize that no words could ever capture the feeling, the power, and the love we felt flowing from the Lord the last few weeks. You see, some time ago, President Smith informed us that the Savior Himself appeared to the First Presidency and those of the Twelve that are here at the temple and told them it was time to prepare the Saints for His coming to Adam-ondi-Ahman. The world was not to know about this, so everything had to be done quietly and carefully so as to arouse as little attention as possible. Over a two-week period, the prophet gathered the people. The weather, so chaotic over the past year, has cooperated, allowing for the quick ingathering, and fortunately, international airline regulations are not so fussy about AllSafe. Those who came in first were the General Authorities from their various assignments, then the mission and stake presidents, then other leaders, and then selected people from the general membership. Many of these were directed to go directly to Adam-ondi-Ahman, where the main meetings would be held. We were successful at keeping attention low, though a few media types did show up, mostly scouting locations for the big stories on the dedication of the new Jackson County temples and paying little attention to what was happening out in the country. There was nothing for their cameras to see even in Independence, however, since they were not permitted into the conference center.

In those walls, a series of meetings were held over which the Savior Himself presided. To have the Lord personally walking among His Saints, ministering to and with them, was truly awe-inspiring. Compounding that, imagine having all the great prophets, prophetesses, saints, disciples, and apostles of past ages here, including the great parents of the race, Adam and Eve. They are spectacular and so full of love and care toward us, who are their posterity! They really do act like wise, loving, kindly grandparents—who, interestingly, look about thirty years old. Nonetheless, power and authority radiates from them. It is easy to see why Lucifer fears Adam, and why Daniel's "horn" will not prevail now that the Ancient of Days has sat (see Dan. 7:9 and D&C 116:1). I assure you, the Saints no longer have anything to fear.

The Lord's purpose in calling these meetings was to gather in the priesthood keys. All who have had or do hold keys reported to their superiors and turned over their keys. These, in turn, reported to Adam. It is easy to see that Adam truly is Michael, the archangel, he who is like God. As head of the race and father of us all, he left a mighty priesthood blessing upon us. At Adam-ondi-Ahman, Adam surrendered all keys to the Lord. All then sustained the Lord as King of Kings and Priest of Priests. At that moment, my son, the Savior began His personal reign upon this earth. It was thrilling.

Chisom, what was so wonderful was the love that permeated all that went on. The last meeting, fittingly, was the crescendo. Can you imagine a sacrament service during which the Lord Himself offered the prayers on both the bread and wine (new wine, mind you, made fresh). Here was the Lord, with the wounds of our wounding still visible in His hands, breaking the bread and blessing the wine. And the power of the Spirit was almost overwhelming. There were moments I wondered if I could stand any more. I felt as though my bones were on fire, so powerfully did His Spirit burn within me as I partook of the emblems of His sacrifice for me.

His love poured over us like a warm liquid in which I felt I could almost float. I tell you, son, I wanted that moment to never end. I now know how the Nephites felt when the Lord visited them. Mormon was right. No pen can capture the joy of standing in the presence of our Lord and God. I could ache at His absence if it were not for the fact that He will return again shortly, and then we will all see His face and feel once again that overpowering love.

This is a most significant moment, my son, for the Lord has now gathered in all the keys, and He has personally taken charge. Oh, don't get me wrong. He is not here all the time, and He still ministers through the First Presidency and Twelve, but He is now personally calling the shots. Though the world does not know it, Jesus has begun His formal reign upon this earth. It will not be long, however, before He lets everyone know it through the power of His Second Coming.

Know this, my son, now is truly the last hour. Work hard to make all hear who will hear. You are the voice of the angel crying to China, "Prepare, for the Bridegroom truly cometh."

With love,
Your father,
Chinedu

CHAPTER 22

President Quintana put the paper back in its envelope. "So you work for more than the vice president. Tell your general he will never rule Chile." President Quintana glared from his full height down on Jorge Serrey, and pushed the formal offer of assistance from General Garza across the desk with one disdainful finger. The seal and ribbons glinted in the light from the wide, frosted windows. "Take this offer and yourself out of this room and out of the country. You and your master are not welcome here."

Serrey's lazy, half-amused expression didn't change. "May I know the reason for my banishment—and the deep insult to General Garza, who has extended nothing but a generous hand?"

"While hiding the hand with a knife in it," Quintana finished.

"Perhaps you would tell us all, sir." Vice President Aguilera smiled slickly, a wave of his hand indicating the other men standing in the president's elegant office.

Many of them were members of the vice president's coterie, from the two junior officers at the door to the newly commissioned General Archuleta—the vice president's protégé who had replaced the late General Medina. Major Zamora stood beside the president's desk, watching his opposite number warily. The president's own body-guards stood in front of the windows, impassive but with their hands on their sidearms. Only Archbishop Pravil, seated in one of the beautiful, antique chairs on the deep-pile rug beside the president's desk, looked surprised at Quintana's declaration.

"Very well, I will show you what Major Zamora showed me." Quintana smiled grimly. He tapped the desk again, bringing a glowing display to life. A chain of DNA twined and spun beside a clicking column of data. "Here we have a virus found in the blood of one of General Garza's operatives in the state of New Mexico, a Colombian man nicknamed Slick." Another DNA strand appeared beside the first, its own data stream racing, slowing, and finally stopping, as light bars showed matches in both molecular fingerprints. "And here is an identical virus harvested from the body of a dead rebel—one of El Jaguar's men guarding a convoy of supplies bound for the rebels. The same men who were killed by General Garza's men before Major Zamora could apprehend them. The same men whose bodies you, Señor Serrey, removed from the forensics lab and disposed of."

Serrey shrugged carelessly. "It appears that Major Zamora is late and incompetent, and that many men from South America suffer from disease. Perhaps I am dull, but I still fail to see how these things would make you rudely reject General Garza's friendship."

Zamora gave him no reaction, meeting his insolent gaze steadily.

Quintana smiled grimly. "You are not dull, Serrey, you are lying. The virus is genetically engineered, as is the antidote that both men had taken to keep the effects in check."

"Is that all?" Serrey's sleepy eyes darkened. "Two men used the same medicine, and this means that El Jaguar answers to General Garza?"

"More like takes his orders from him." The president leaned against his desk, folding his arms. "I have nothing to tie them more firmly than that, but it is enough for me. You have taken advantage of Vice President Aguilera's trusting nature to insinuate yourself into his security force. You and your general will not find the same opportunity to come into this country as long as my eyes are on you."

Serrey sighed, shrugging, and stuffed his hands into his pockets.

Immediately, Garza's slender, young agent found himself the target of seven gun muzzles, as Archuleta, the two junior officers, Zamora, and both bodyguards drew their weapons. Archbishop Pravil startled, then rubbed his face wearily, watching the standoff from the middle of it.

"I would tell you not to move," Quintana said, smiling grimly, "but I think you figured that out for yourself." He leaned forward, twitching aside Serrey's suit jacket and withdrawing the security specialist's own gun with two fingers. He laid it on the desk. "I almost wish you could tell Olivares about the failure of his plan, but he'll have to figure that out for himself."

This time, Zamora blinked, though he didn't drop his aim. It suddenly registered that the spymaster was unusually absent. "Olivares, sir?"

"Yes, Olivares," Quintana looked disappointed, and suddenly older than he had before. "He was working with Garza, supplying the information that kept El Jaguar's men one step ahead of your task force, Major Zamora. I believe he is the same one who helped Señor Serrey here into Vice President Aguilera's security force and arranged the assassination by disease of Mr. O'Higgins from his office. He also used a biotoxin to kill General Medina. Poisoned the man's breakfast."

"Where is Olivares?" Aguilera asked. He looked not so much disappointed as surprised, Zamora noted, but a strange glint rapidly replaced the surprise in his eyes.

"I had him arrested this morning, for conspiring with General Garza to topple the government of Chile," Quintana answered. "He is in custody now. Just as you are," he added to Serrey.

Serrey glanced at Aguilera, then looked back at the president and smiled. "I think he will stay in custody much longer than I will."

"What?" Quintana blinked, staring at Aguilera as the vice president stepped forward to catch Serrey's shoulder and pull him backward.

"You're right on every point, Hector," Aguilera said softly. "Except that it wasn't Olivares who made a deal with General Garza."

Zamora leapt forward, but once again he moved too late to stop the vice president's plot. He saw Aguilera's snarl and the muzzle flash of Archuleta's gun before a heavy fist slammed into his shoulder, throwing him backward behind the desk. Four bullets slammed into President Quintana, laying him out over the gleaming surface of his desk. Papers flew into the air, dislodged by the president's last, flailing motions. The two bodyguards fired back, bringing down one of Archuleta's junior officers, but the bulletproof vests under their uniforms couldn't save them from the two neat head shots Serrey delivered with the gun he kept in his boot holster.

In the silence that followed the thunder of gunshots, Serrey's cool, mocking voice drifted through the blue haze of powder smoke. "Are you dead, Major Zamora? I do hope not. Both General Garza and El Jaguar would be disappointed if they could not make your acquaintance personally."

Archbishop Pravil, who had begun to raise himself from the brass-scattered carpet where he had thrown himself at the first shot, flattened again, praying that his deal with the devil (as he viewed General Garza) to preserve the church in Chile would not result in his own martyrdom. He saw Serrey's shining boots go past at eye level, to come to a light-footed stop beside his shoulder. Zamora dead was disappointing; Zamora alive behind a half ton of mahogany was dangerous.

Zamora watched them as well, beneath the president's desk. A drop of blood fell from where the president had slumped over on the desktop, landing on the carpet beside an obsidian paperweight that had struck Zamora when it fell. The dull ache above his ear hardly registered. From the sluggish pain he felt when he tried to bend his elbow he knew the bullet had broken the bone. He flexed his left hand around the butt of his gun as he sorted his options. Meeting El Jaguar and General Garza was not one of them. Was getting out of the office? If he wanted to keep Garza from overrunning his country and setting up Aguilera as his puppet, it was the only option he could take.

"No answer, Major?" Serrey called softly. "I knew Mormons were untrustworthy. I did not know they were rude as well." The hammer of his pistol clicked loudly as he raised the gun to point at the empty chair behind the desk—but not loud enough to drown the soft sound of two more men walking carefully around either side of the desk.

With a quick, silent prayer, Zamora rolled onto his good side, laid the gun on the carpet, and snatched up the paperweight. It arced through the air as he hurled it up and over the desk—startling Archuleta, who fired frantically at the movement, as Zamora knew he would. The bullets smashed into the tall windows behind the desk, shattering them in a burst of frosted crystal. Zamora picked up his gun and rose to his feet in one smooth motion. For a split second, his and Serrey's eyes locked, then Serrey smiled. Both men brought their guns up, but at the last moment Zamora spun to the side, shooting not at Garza's operative but at Archuleta. Aguilera's lapdog went down, howling and clutching his wounded leg.

Serrey's first shot merely grazed Zamora's back, but the assassin immediately corrected his aim. The second would have gone through Zamora's throat, if he had behaved rationally and ducked behind the cover of the desk again. Instead he threw himself out of the window. He had just time enough for an extremely quick and heartfelt prayer before he crashed into the tall flowering bushes beneath. The boughs held, then broke, dropping him from level to level until he finally hit the spongy ground of the flower bed and rolled to a halt on the thick grass.

A handful of that grass erupted skyward, the crack of the shot following a split second later. He didn't have any more time for the thanks than he had for the request as he scrambled to his feet. The long expanse of garden stretched in front of him, an impossible expanse of emerald shooting range for the president's security forces stationed all along the perimeter. Lurching to his feet, gritting his teeth against the pain, he began the long run toward the secondary checkpoint, hoping, vainly, as it turned out, that no one had alerted the guards.

More grass shredded, tossed into the air by a line of machine-gun fire that followed him as he ran. A black car burst through the small checkpoint gate and roared toward him from the front. The two trajectories met in the middle, the car's back door flying open. Zamora leapt into the offered shelter, as bullets slammed across the car's reinforced roof. The car skidded into a wide turn, digging deep grooves in the grass, crashing through the gate that a pair of frantic guards tried to close, and nearly tumbling the major off the seat. Hands grabbed his jacket, keeping him more or less upright—and sending a wave of fire down his arm and over his shoulder. He looked through the red haze to see Mercury, who smiled reassuringly. He smiled back—but the smile faded into wary surprise when he saw the quiet, gray man sitting beside his son.

Señor Olivares nodded calmly. "No, Major Zamora, I am obviously not enjoying Vice President Aguilera's dubious hospitality. I suspected Aguilera of treachery while General Medina suspected me. The evidence I was able to gather after he was poisoned only confirmed my suspicions. So I disappeared. However, I fully intend to reappear, and to do that I require allies. I picked up your son as a promise and incentive to you—after persuading Captain Guerra that

I intended no harm. And I thought that you would appreciate help in refusing the vice president's invitation as well."

"I do." Zamora eased his arm, leaning forward to look out the windshield. Captain Guerra looked back at him from the seat beside the driver, giving him a quick high sign—and very obviously putting away the pistol he'd held unwaveringly aimed at the spy chief through the wild ride through the capital and the tense wait outside the gates.

Zamora smiled tightly at his captain, appreciating Guerra's loyalty and good sense, then looked back at Olivares. "Where are we going?"

"Somewhere safe and discreet," the spymaster said. "As you have undoubtedly deduced, anyone who opposed General Garza or supported the late President Quintana will shortly be persona non grata in the eyes of the new regime." The ghost of a smile flickered across Olivares's face. "Though I am sure they will be most eager to welcome us into the fold."

"Like sheep to be sheared," Zamora agreed dryly.

* * *

"Like a lamb to the slaughter," Aguilera intoned, "President Quintana died never suspecting that El Jaguar had corrupted the man he most trusted—the chief of the antiterror task force, the same man who gunned down the president in cold blood—Major Rafaelo Rivera Zamora!"

On cue, footage of Zamora's spectacular leap from the broken windows of the president's office filled the screen, with his dash across La Moneda's grounds and escape in the low, black car.

"So the president died in an attempted military coup?" Rosa del Torres asked, basking in the glow of the story that would finally lift her from a mere stringer to a Channel 8 star. Her source, the voice on the phone that proved so helpful in telling her when and where El Jaguar would deal yet another humiliating defeat on the military task force, had earned every commission she'd paid him with the tip to have a camera set up across the street from La Moneda. She had—and she had recorded the military assassin's dramatic escape. Now, she had the first, exclusive interview with the new president—and she made sure that the camera showed her as well as Aguilera during the entire exchange.

Aguilera not only confirmed the truth of her question, but went on to detail the network of conspiracy that stretched from El Jaguar's guerillas lurking in the mountains to the headquarters of the ironically named antiterror squad to the corridors of the national intelligence agency—and finally to the supposedly hallowed halls of the Mormon Church. He implicated Major Zamora, Señor Olivares, and Elder Molina, bringing in a sweating Archbishop Pravil to testify to the perfidy of the leaders of the so-called Church of Jesus Christ.

"Surrounded by threats on all sides and within, it is only appropriate that I, as acting president until we can hold interim elections, announce the immediate commencement of martial law." Aguilera gazed commandingly into the camera. "And we hereby warn El Jaguar, the rebel terrorist, that we will fulfill President Quintana's dying wish and accept the offer of assistance from General Garza in ridding our country of terrorist rebels—and all other threats to our national security."

Behind him, Serrey smiled as he whispered a single word into his phone: "Go."

Public outcry spontaneously burst out all over Santiago. Well-organized mobs materialized out of quiet streets, targeting well-known military and civic leaders who did not support Aguilera—and any prominent Mormon they could reach. All the high-ranking Saints in the largest cities—such as mission presidents, the administrators of the Perpetual Education Fund, stake presidents, the Area Authority—appeared on Serrey's list of targets. When their would-be captors spread out to round them up, however, they realized that those whom Serrey had marked for personal attention had disappeared. Mobs led by undercover security agents burst into homes both well-off and humble to find only empty spaces and a few scattered scraps of possessions. On the back roads and mountain paths, nondescript cars rolled toward the calm, green precincts of the temple grounds. Aguilera's security forces quickly realized that their prey had flown, reporting to Serrey that the Mormon leaders had slipped out of their reach in Santiago and Orsorno.

Aguilera choked on his mouthful of celebratory Scotch, spraying the fine amber droplets over the now spotlessly clean surface of the presidential desk. "What? Where did they go?"

"To their temples, apparently. They seem to do that, gathering themselves into ghettos of their own free will. It's actually rather convenient, really. But for now, it hardly matters," Serrey assured him, calm and lazy as ever, only the hard glitter in his sleepy eyes betraying the reptilian viciousness behind the smooth facade. "General Garza will take care of them when the time comes and root the rest of them out of their nests in smaller towns and villages. For now, they are no threat to us."

"No threat," Aguilera growled, suddenly raising his eyes to glare at General Archuleta. "A snake is only not a threat without its head. I want the snake's head—Molina, that Apostle of theirs. Take him alive if you can, and if you can't, bring me proof he's dead. He's the one who told the rest of the birds to fly. I want Zamora's liver and lungs too. Make me believe you're more competent than your sorry performance today implies. Move!"

Archuleta saluted, flushing hot at the insult, and limped out of the room (Aguilera's scorn hurt only slightly less than the hastily bandaged graze across his thigh). He gathered his lackeys as he went, ordering a strike team to assemble. The parade of sleek, black military vehicles roared down the streets, passing patrols enforcing a "security curfew" and the embers of buildings burned in the sweep to cleanse nests of conspirators. When they reached the Mormons' Santiago conference center, the first flames had just begun to flare up in the trees lining the street outside.

"They're still inside," the ranking officer of the security force announced, saluting as General Archuleta emerged from the lead car. "We have the place surrounded."

"Are you sure?" Archuleta snapped.

"Yes, sir," the officer said, gesturing toward a small cluster of carabineros who stood apart from the regular military forces. "The locals showed us all entrances and exits. They said they locked it down as soon as they got word; the traitors are trapped inside. The Apostle stayed until the last minute, transmitting warnings to the rest of the Mormons."

"Such a pity he didn't take his own warning soon enough." Archuleta smiled sharply, hefting his pistol. "Let's go get them."

The security squad set off at a run, past the flaming trees and into the huge double doors and six side entrances, guns at the ready.

"You need us anymore?" the carabineros' captain asked the security officer.

The chief guard swept them with a contemptuous glance—civilian police, not tough or smart enough to make regular military. *Look at that one—old enough to be a grandfather! And the other—short, dumpy, with his oversized hat pulled nearly to his ears. Pathetic.* "No. Clear off—and stay out of the way of the real army. We'll handle enforcing the law now."

The grizzled carabinero captain shrugged, turning away. "Let's go home, boys. The real army's here to handle things now."

A few sniggers met that announcement, but none of the carabineros lingered. Especially not the tall, gray-haired man in the ill-fitting uniform, or the short, chubby one beside him. They climbed into the battered patrol car along with the carabinero captain. As the car pulled away, the captain glanced into the rearview mirror and tapped the brim of his cap. "Compliments of Señor Olivares. And us too—we met a couple of your missionaries a little while ago, Señor Molina. They impressed us."

The carabinero at the wheel snorted, remembering the tall, burly American bearing down on him as he tried to flatten that traitor O'Higgins. He'd been impressed, all right. Impressed right into the roadway—an unexpected event for one of Olivares's undercover officers on the police force. Still, it was too bad that the big gringo kid had been killed; he'd been a good one.

"Our missionaries are impressive young people—and Señor Olivares certainly has his good points as well," Elder Molina said, hugging his wife.

She pushed the hat off her hair and smiled at him. "I can't say the same for this uniform."

The patrol car wove between the military transports, until it disappeared into the underground garage beneath a small neighborhood police station—and then deeper underground, into the newborn but rapidly growing Resistance.

* * *

"Are you threatening me with some kind of armed insurrection?" Governor Kerr glared at Jack DuPris. Underneath the governor's cold stare and outward composure, doubt, fear, frustration, self-interest, and a vestige of public spirit writhed and warred. He'd never been pliable or indecisive, and he hated difficult situations. Nuance and negotiation, diplomacy and seeing all sides, only went so far. After a good-faith effort at politics, he felt, it was time to choose a position and defend it against all comers.

DuPris met his glare point for point. He intended to protect his Saints, even if it meant defying a gentile governor, or even short-sighted General Authorities. "All I am saying, Governor Kerr, is that these people have the right to defend themselves and their property against vicious, bigoted attacks."

Kerr stood suddenly. "Watch your tone, DuPris. That maniac Smith—and the rest of the fanatics you represent—don't have the right to rob, loot, and burn the businesses of law-abiding citizens."

"They did not burn the businesses, as you know." DuPris stood as well, shorter than Kerr but matching the governor's presence and command point for point. "While I do not condone the overreaction that led some people to do things that they would never contemplate if they did not feel driven to desperate acts, I cannot wholly condemn them either. Brother Smith is an extremist, but he's gaining credibility because the ones who try to protect themselves through peaceful means find themselves completely helpless in the face of Samuel Lebaron's lynch mobs."

He motioned out the window, pointing south toward Lake Creek. "Right out there, Governor, a band of howling savages set fire to houses while families inside slept! Even prominent employers like Softlearn are under attack every day, while the authorities do nothing. If we could trust the police, the fire department, the sheriff to defend us, we would not feel compelled to do it ourselves. Everywhere in Illinois, blatant discrimination runs rampant, property is confiscated, individuals are denied employment, with not a word of censure from the courts. Hate crimes against members of the Church of Jesus Christ go unpunished, as the government—from city councils to this office—look the other way." He brought his hand down on a stack of petitions, shoving them across the desk. A few other papers fluttered to the floor, among them an equally thick petition gathered by Reverend Lebaron's followers to decry Mormon atrocities against them and theirs. "You have thousands of signatures attesting to everything I've said, and you have done nothing about it. So now, it appears that someone else will have to take up the slack."

"That someone being your paranoid religious militia?" Inside Kerr's head, the battlefield abruptly jerked into focus, his trenches here, DuPris' there, no-man's-land between. He leaned forward and swept DuPris' petitions off the surface in a sideways geyser of paper. "If you think you can come in here to intimidate me—to intimidate the great state of Illinois—with threats of petty domestic terrorism, you are about to find out just how wrong you are. I can't do anything about people expressing their constitutionally protected right to free speech and free association. If they don't want to hire Mormons or associate with Mormons or send their children to school with Mormons, that's their right. And if the Mormons don't want to associate with Baptists or hire them, that too is a right. There's nothing I can—or will—do about that. And any pig-headed fools who want to start a brawl over it had better keep it to themselves."

"So you're saying that there's nothing you can do to preserve order in your own state, to defend innocents from mobs intent on doing them harm." DuPris said it flatly, calculating the perfect tone of cold contempt. "Shall I bring a bowl of water, so you can wash your hands of us?"

"Are you comparing me to Pontius Pilate or yourself to Jesus Christ?" Kerr's impressive voice, famous for overriding the bedlam babble of a state congress in hot debate, rose to full volume. "Get out of this office! And if you keep this up, I will do something about the fight between Mormon extremists and Lebaron's fanatics—something that you and your antigovernment militia will never forget!"

DuPris left the office on a tide of righteous rage, feeling himself utterly vindicated. He had tried, he fulfilled President Rojas's orders in bringing their case to the civil authorities of the land, and Caesar had refused to hear their petition. So be it, then. Once before, Illinois had turned away the Saints' pleas. This time, however, the blood and fire would descend on the Gentiles' heads. His two bodyguards falling in beside him, the Area Authority swept out of the capitol, into the waiting limousine, toward Lake Creek, his press conference, and divine destiny.

Word of what happened spread before the limousine's black door closed behind him. "He's been thrown out," an excited man half whispered into a phone, keeping his voice down in the echoing marble halls as the governor's voice echoed down the corridors of power.

"Kerr refused the Mormons' petition—threatened to call the National Guard on them!" another exclaimed, down the light-speed electronic grapevine.

"It's open season on Mormons," gloated yet another. "Not even the FBI will step in now."

"It is open season on those who defy the good grace of Christ," Reverend Lebaron said. A thin smile crossed his weathered face. "It is our Christian duty to show the heathens the error of their ways and save them from the eternal fires of hell. By any means necessary." Raising his hands high over the bowing heads of his congregation of armed and angry men, he intoned, "Oh, Lord, we go to do Thy work in holy war. May the blood spilled be to Thy glory. May Thy grace attend Thine avenging angels!"

With a roar more appropriate to a football stadium—or perhaps a Roman amphitheater—the mob poured out of the smoke-darkened church and into the drought-blasted fields beyond.

* * *

"They're coming!" Porter shouted down from the lookout post built into the Smiths' water-pump windmill. Through his binoculars, the haze of dust on the poorly graded road revealed the glint of metal and glass from the heavily occupied vehicles bearing down on them.

"As revelation told us they must," Brother Smith answered for the benefit of the hard-faced, nervous men around him. "Brethren, the Amulonites know that the corrupt governor has withdrawn even the shadow of his protection. They come now to enslave and kill us, to take our lives, property, women, and children into subjugation." On cue, Rock raised a pole, on the end of which an artfully tattered flag fluttered, artfully embroidered with characters as close to Hebrew as Brother Smith could puzzle out and Sister Smith's daughters could stitch. He pointed to his homemade Title of Liberty. "By this standard,

I call you to fight in the strength of the Lord against the wicked host. His will prevail!"

Hardly lowering his voice, he shouted over the cheers, "Mother, you will stay with the girls and children out in the chapel. Don't let anybody in—and if they try to break the doors down, remember that in the last extremity, even the women and children of the Nephites took up swords against their enemies."

The righteous militia swung into action, implementing a plan laid years ago, when Brother Smith first received the revelations that assured him of his place as a latter-day prophet, a Jeremiah to the world, called to prophesy the final fall of Babylon. They were fully armed this time, though Orrin still kept the jack handle thrust through his belt, just in case he got a chance for some up-close fighting. The Smiths and their followers piled into their own four-wheel-drive armored personnel carriers and thundered out of the Smiths' farmyard. From the Hunts' farm and two others, smaller but no less heavily equipped columns swung out as well, spreading down the truck paths concealed—or half concealed—in the fields of drought-stunted corn to encircle the encroaching Amulonites.

Halfway to the confrontation point, three vans peeled off the main column, coming to a halt in the graded but unpaved parking lot of the unfinished chapel Brother Smith's followers had used since the wards split. Two years before, Brother Smith had persuasively argued to the stake president that it made sense to begin using the chapel as soon as possible, to save the Saints in outlying areas the long drive into town. He had agreed, especially when Brother Hunt and two other men volunteered their services as subcontractors, getting the small church house operational in only a few months.

Bishop Calvin of the Lake County Ward had registered a cautionary objection but hadn't pushed the issue; he had still hoped to find a way to bring Brother Smith back into the mainstream of the Church. He still did, despite all the mounting evidence to the contrary, persuading himself that the rumors about Brother Smith and his boys were overblown, exaggerated by the anti-Mormons who followed Reverend Lebaron. Bishop Newstead, even the stake president, simply did not understand what kinds of pressures the Saints in Lake County labored under. At the stake president's encouragement, Bishop Calvin had released Brother Smith from the bishopric, hoping to reduce his influence (vainly, as it turned out), but with an attack of ill health, a heart attack and follow-up angioplasty, and the press of other duties, he had done nothing more. Thus, Brother Smith secured his family behind the strong doors of the chapel he had built himself, fastening its strong inside lock and then, curiously, the outside lock as well before he rode out to meet Lebaron's forces.

* * *

"Eyewitness accounts are conflicting, and official statements are vague," Anne said, shielding her eyes against the lowering sun and the haze of smoke that still hung low and choking over the scorched stand of small trees surrounding the blackened remains of a church. "But it appears that a confrontation between the Mormons and members of Reverend Lebaron's Millennium Brotherhood has tragically resulted in the first deaths of this long-running conflict."

She pointed toward the jagged, charred building skeleton behind her. "It appears that members of the Millennium Brotherhood, led by Reverend Samuel Lebaron, and a group of Mormons under the command of J. H. Smith—Brother Smith, as he calls himself—met three miles from here, near an old quarry. According to a confidential source, a meeting between Governor Kerr and Mormon authority Jack DuPris sparked the confrontation. The Mormons appear to have ambushed Reverend Lebaron's Millennium Brotherhood in the quarry. Shots were fired, wounding several men on both sides of the fight." Scenes of the quarry itself underscored her commentary.

"A running battle followed, with at least seven trucks involved. In the confusion, or trying to escape, two of the trucks carrying Lebaron's forces came up this road, toward a Mormon church." The road, now crowded with the trucks used by the county's volunteer fire department, a patrol car from the sheriff's office, the Channel 8 van, and a few other scattered cars, including two from Channel 8's distant competitors, lay dusty in the evening light as Anne indicated the trucks' approach. "Here, they found several Mormons who had barricaded themselves into the church."

She swallowed against the smell in the air, keeping her voice smooth despite the smoke. "Reports about what happened next are confused. Reverend Lebaron, in an official statement, claims that the Mormons accidentally started a fire inside the building, trying to launch a homemade bomb out the window. He says that his men broke the windows in an attempt to rescue the occupants of the building, because the doors were locked. However, eyewitnesses among the Mormons who pursued Lebaron's forces to the spot say that the Millennium Brotherhood started the fire, either to drive the Mormons out of the building or to kill them. Investigations into the cause of the fire are proceeding now. Whoever started it, however, the fire killed four women and six children, including the wife and daughters of J. H. Smith, the leader of the Mormons in this area."

Brother Smith's smoke-streaked, frozen face appeared, his pain and rage almost palpable through the screen. "The evil have always burned the innocent, consigning women and children to the flames," he said, his voice rough with smoke and emotion but steady and clear. "The pure souls escape their cruelty to inherit a crown of glory on high. And as the wicked men have caused the innocent to suffer, so will they meet their fate. The blood of these beloved children will cry from the ground for vengeance. The Lord will repay His debts in full." Caught on the edge of the frame, the face of Brother Smith's eldest son, Rockwell, echoed his father's righteous fury. Orrin stared into the still-licking flames as if fascinated. Only Porter had turned away, giving in to tears that had nothing to do with the stinging smoke.

"When the county's volunteer firefighters arrived, the building was fully engulfed," Anne explained, over footage of the last of the fight against the fire. "Paramedics treated five children and two adults for smoke inhalation and burns. Two are still in Lake County Hospital, in serious but stable condition. One, a ten-year-old girl, is badly burned, and in critical condition. Her future, like the future of this embattled community, remains unclear."

Though she laid out the facts dispassionately, Anne felt sick when she finished her report and signed off, turning the electronic stage over to Clara for the inevitable pundits' analysis and argument. She knew, even before Monk confirmed it to her and Leon, that the report itself was a stunning success. All of the Smiths had disappeared by the time the rest of the media vehicles arrived; only Anne had footage of them, or of Samuel Lebaron's forces driving away. She had arrived even before the first wave, after an anonymous phone call whispered word of the attack and fire; the rest of the reporters waiting for Jack DuPris' press conference had followed a little too late to catch anything but the aftermath. Monk was pleased; Channel 8 had scooped its competitors—again. Anne wasn't so pleased; while she could not swear to it, the voice on the phone had sounded unnervingly like that of Brother Smith himself. Could the man have used his own wife's death to justify his private war?

Whether Brother Smith had placed the call or not, the tragedy finally achieved the official endorsement he had sought for so long. Jack DuPris, taking the podium late that night for his delayed press conference, issued a short, passionate statement, his eyes fiery with resolve and tears: "Because the state of Illinois will do nothing to defend innocent citizens from the brutality of murdering gangs, they must defend themselves. This is a formal warning to all those bigots who hate and target others because of their religious beliefs: we will not stand for it anymore." He said nothing else, leaving the podium and shouted questions without looking back.

* * *

Jason Adams, President Rojas's chief assistant, stood in the prophet's outer office chatting quietly with Sister Nguyen, waiting for President Rojas to finish his phone call. After the Channel 8 broadcast last night, he expected fireworks—and sure enough, the grapevine said that President Smith had called a meeting of the First Presidency that morning. That explained the message from President Rojas telling Jason to come to the office right after lunch.

Jason could see the strain on the Associate President's face as he beckoned the assistant into the office and gestured for him to take a seat.

"Jason, President Smith and I have an unpleasant but urgent assignment for you," President Rojas said gravely, handing the younger man three envelopes. "Take Rex with you, and get out to Iowa. Find Elder DuPris and his counselors, and personally deliver these letters to them."

"I saw Elder DuPris' news conference last night," Jason said, accepting the letters. They felt heavy in his hand, though each contained only one sheet of paper. "I thought he'd stepped way over the line."

"Yes," President Rojas confirmed, shooting his assistant a quelling glance. Jason had zeal down pat; what he needed was tact. "And he won't take our calls—neither will his counselors. It's pretty clear that they are deliberately ignoring us." He ran one hand through his hair, anger and weariness chasing across his face. "But they made their choice when they disregarded our counsel. President Smith asked me to convene the Brethren for a disciplinary council. Jack's going to have to face the consequences. The meeting is set for three days from now, but we have to put a stop to this immediately. Be sure Jack knows that and tell him that President Smith expects him and his counselors to be there."

"I'll do it, President," Jason said crisply, standing up.

"Thank you, my friend," President Rojas said as he walked the younger man to the door. "Be careful out there. Come back in one piece."

* * *

"I think they should all pack right up and leave." Sally Mae stabbed a long, intricately painted fingernail through the cellophane on her customary lunchtime packet of snack cakes. Extracting one with her equally customary sigh of resignation at her lack of resolve in dieting matters, she waved it for emphasis. "No more violence, no more troubles, just people staying on their own land, out of each other's way. I just think we'd all be better off if certain people didn't mix."

"The wicked will get their just rewards, just like they did yesterday. You mark my words," said another of the Bible Bunch with great satisfaction.

"Just rewards?" Donna looked up from her own meager, brown-bag lunch. She'd barely picked at the peanut-butter sandwich; listening to her coworkers heatedly or humorously discuss yesterday's church burning, the fight that caused it, and the deaths that resulted had knotted her stomach so hard it felt like the knot had tangled up her lungs too. She'd said nothing, concentrating on holding back her tears.

The "born-again" women Sally Mae met for lunch twice a week to read the Bible spewed the nastiest rumors and allegations as if they came with the "gospel truth" stamp, from rumors of President Rojas's harem to Mormons sacrificing sheep, or, as some implied, children, in the altars inside their secret temples.

Donna mostly ignored it, or began reading aloud from the Bible, always passages about loving others, avoiding gossip, and forgiveness, or threw in a few jokes of her own (Martians made excellent targets for ethnic humor). Occasionally, especially when she and Sally Mae met for lunch without the rest of Sally Mae's Bible group, Donna tried to even out the field, quoting bits and pieces she'd read about the Church's even-handed humanitarian efforts, or pointing out that Softlearn's educational products had won a couple of international awards. Sally Mae, on her own, reluctantly admitted that she'd never really known any Mormons, but the ones she'd seen seemed normal enough—but then, "So did the New Andromedans, honey, and look what happened to them, all wrapped up in those blue sheets and frozen to death on the tundra, waiting for the mother ship." When Donna pushed the point, Sally Mae got nervous, asking, "Those missionaries of theirs got their hooks in you, honey? Betty's got a good preacher—he can exorcise those evil spirits right out for you, no trouble." Donna usually gave up at that point.

"You bet, just rewards," snorted the woman. "Heathens, spreading their diabolical lies—and diseases too, trying to get us all sick. Reverend Lebaron may not be everybody's cup of tea, but he's got the right idea about Mormons. It'd be a better place around here if more folks took after him."

Money abruptly faded into insignificance. Donna's conscience, squashed into a corset of economic necessity and proud independence, expanded with a roar. No job was worth this—she could ignore jokes, brush off wild rumors, but she couldn't even look like she condoned what the woman was saying. The slow nods from the other four made her almost physically ill. Omitting facts about herself to keep this crummy job was one thing; sitting silent while an ignorant, hateful woman advocated murder was intolerable for any amount of money. She looked up, her eyes shining with angry tears. "Took after him by burning churches, with women and little children inside? Is that what you mean?"

The heat in her voice surprised them all, their eyes growing wide as she plunged on. "Do you have any idea what it's like to burn to death? Or choke to death on hot smoke, desperately trying to save your babies but afraid to run out of the building because there are men out there who would shoot you if they saw you? Does anybody deserve that?"

"Well, not that exactly," Sally Mae began, trying to smooth away the emotional outburst.

"Not exactly?" Donna looked at Sally Mae, catching the phone psychic's gaze and holding it with the intensity of her own. She ignored the other four, trying desperately to drive her point home past the walls of prejudice into the soft heart beyond. "You must know they didn't deserve that. Even Brother Smith doesn't deserve that, though he does deserve to be arrested and locked up for vandalism and battery. But by far most Mormons aren't like him. They're normal people, loving their families, working hard, helping others—praying, praying every day to the same Jesus you say you love so much. Well, He loves you back, and He loves them too. Mormons are good people!"

"Good people?" The most vocal opponent leaned forward, scowling. "What's good about them? And how do you know anything about them anyway, a girl from California who's not even lived around here to see what goes on?"

Swallowing hard, Donna blew away every last shred of the cover she'd so carefully constructed. "Because I *am* one."

They gasped, as if she'd declared she came from another planet. One woman actually leapt to her feet, knocking over the cheap lunch-room chair with a clatter. Partially hydrogenated cream filling spurted all over Sally Mae's intricate manicure as her hand unconsciously tightened around the cake she held.

Before they could say anything, Donna stood as well. "Yes, I am a member of The Church of Jesus Christ of Latter-day Saints. I have been since I was baptized at eight years old—but I think I've only just been converted now. I didn't say anything—no, I *lied* to get this job! I lied because we need the money so much, because my father lost his job because he wouldn't lie about the Church himself and MedaGen blackballed him and put a lien on our house because my mother helped Meredith Galen warn all of you about AllSafe. I lied about it because I interviewed for every midnight-janitor, fry-cook job in this entire town when nobody would hire me as a teaching assistant or receptionist or meter maid because I'm a Mormon!"

Her voice, rising steadily as she poured out her fury and frustration, drew stares from the other telephone drones at tables all over the lunchroom, stares that rapidly turned from curious to hostile. "Well, I'm not lying anymore! If I have to starve to death—or get *burned* to death because of it, I will!"

Whirling to face one of the omnipresent cameras, she added, "I know I'm already fired. You don't have to tell me. I'm leaving right now, so you don't even have to send security to escort me out."

"You're going to need security to carry you out." The low-voiced threat came from one of a trio of men at a nearby table, one rising ominously from his seat. "You dirty, lying Mo."

"Go ahead and add the 'ron' to the end of that," Donna advised him, giddy with anger and adrenaline, "so we all know the right word for your intellectual level."

"Now, y'all just hold it right there!" All eyes turned to Sally Mae, who rose from the table. Somehow, the snap in her voice sounded commanding, even from a woman with a handful of junk-food goop. "Whatever happened, and whatever anybody said or didn't say, we are Christian people. If dear Lord Jesus could forgive them as they put nails in His hands and feet, and heal the soldier that came to take Him away, are we going to not forgive somebody who just lied to us? I'll take care of this." With her clean hand, she grabbed Donna's arm and hustled the surprised girl out of the lunchroom and right out the back service doors without another word.

Behind them, an explosion of discussion and denunciation burst into full volume. It cut off suddenly as the heavy outside doors swung shut.

Donna breathed deeply, feeling her bones shake from her knees to her neck. "Thank you so much, Sally Mae. They—I really think they would've hurt me."

"You really hurt me, Donna." The soft, Southern-accented rebuke made Donna turn, to see Sally Mae regarding her with tears in her own eyes. "How could you say those horrible things to my friends?"

"Horrible things?" Donna blinked. "But Sally Mae, it's true—those women and children didn't deserve to be burned to death!"

"So you have to go claiming to be a Mormon to make your point?" Sally Mae asked.

Donna's shoulders slumped, then drew back as she stood straighter. "I wasn't lying about that. I really am a Mormon. I'm just very sorry I didn't stand up for us—for the truth—sooner."

Sally Mae looked as if her world had taken a half twist past reality and she couldn't quite adjust to the new angle. "But, Donna, you're such a nice girl. And you understood the Bible so well, what it all meant, what Jesus said . . ."

"Of course I do," Donna said softly. "Sally Mae, I love Jesus as much as you do, and I really do try to keep His commandments. I want to live with Him someday, just like you do. I've studied and prayed and even taken classes to understand the scriptures. We're not that different—we just have different pieces of the whole gospel."

"You mean you have the truth and mine's wrong," Sally Mae corrected, a sharp sting in her voice.

"I mean you have a lot of the truth, and you just need a little more," Donna corrected, as gently as she could. "But you don't have to take my word for it. Here." She extracted a somewhat dog-eared copy of the Book of Mormon from her large bag of a purse. "I meant to give this to you—I've been carrying it around practically since the day we met, but I was too scared. It'll tell you the rest of the truth, or a bunch of it. You don't have to do anything—just read it, even just a little bit of it, and pray about it. Ask Jesus what He wants you to do."

Sally Mae took the book gingerly, as if it were a live creature with a sting in its tail. The blacker the picture one paints of a monster, after all, the more the temptation grows to look at it. She didn't look at Donna.

"Thank you for being my friend." Donna squeezed the little psychic's shoulder.

Sally Mae looked from the gold lettering on the book's cover to Donna's face. "I'm sorry, Donna, but I can't be your friend anymore. And if you know what's best, you won't come back here—nor show your face around this part of town. I just hope you find Jesus before you go to hell for all time—for being a Mormon, not just for lying about it." With that, she turned on her heel and marched back into the dark corridors of the office. But she took the book with her, tucking it deep under her sweater to hide it from the security cameras' unblinking eyes.

CHAPTER 23

The late afternoon sun shone off the well-blacked gun barrel as DuPris hefted it out of its box. He sighted down the barrel of the automatic rifle, looking beyond the metal notch into the even darker future. Fire guttered around the edges of his vision, fire from the past and fire yet to come. "Nice," the Area Authority said, lowering the gun to look at Brother Smith. He gestured around the barn, at the unpainted wooden cases revealed by a dozen or so removed hay bales. "Are all these guns like this?"

Brother Smith smiled like a wolverine, sharp and hungry. "Most certainly. The Lamanites are only too pleased to supply me with weapons and ammunition; the same guns that herd the South American Saints into prison camps will help us preserve the Saints in the land of the New Jerusalem."

"How did you pay for them?" DuPris asked, not because the methods worried him, but because he couldn't picture Brother Smith with the cash to pay gun runners for that many crates of rifles.

"We turned the snakes' venom against them," Brother Smith said smugly, running a hand over the rough top of the open crate. "The Lord provides—and the Amulonites' ill-gotten wealth supplies the Saints with the means to drive the Gentiles from Illinois and redeem Zion. We consecrated those funds to the redeeming of the Lord's chosen people, just as we consecrated these weapons to the noble crusade of wreaking the Lord's vengeance on the Millennium Brotherhood, avenging the blood of the innocents crying from the dust against them."

He didn't bother with a clearer explanation: that in addition to using the money they robbed from the Gentiles in and around Lake

Creek, he and his followers had also made lucrative arrangements with gun runners and meth dealers to provide safe storage space and agricultural cover for shipments flowing north, border guards weren't eager to poke through a truckload of manure for drugs or weapons. Brother Smith, seeing both drug addiction and crime as plagues on the Gentiles, gladly seized the opportunity to add to their sickness and his hoard of armaments.

Behind him, Orrin practiced "quick-draw" with a pair of pistols from another box, whipping them up to point at Porter, who didn't notice. He still looked stunned, a numbness that he couldn't shake lying just under his skin. At the coded reference to his mother's death, Porter visibly flinched.

DuPris didn't, though his eyes rolled slightly. He had come to the well-defended farm compound not to join Brother Smith's band of revelation groupies, but to leverage a ready supply of determined, impressionable—and, to his surprise and satisfaction—well-armed soldiers. One question still lingered, however, as he and Brother Smith directed the men loading the trucks and covering the boxes with tarps and a few straw bales. "Why did you wait so long?" he asked. "You have the firepower. Why didn't you start shooting to kill a long time ago, instead of messing around in redneck truck chases and half-cocked church burnings?"

"Because I needed a second prophet to confirm my revelation and sacred calling, Brother DuPris. Because the Lord's good truth comes always from the mouths of two witnesses." Brother Smith's eyes seemed to glow with an inner fire. "We are those two witnesses—and we will see the Lord's mighty work done this night and give ourselves as tools in His hands for Him to use as He burns the wicked as stubble."

A faint misgiving flared under DuPris' angry determination, but he pushed it away as weakness. He had the keys and authority over these people, and with the power came the responsibility to help them protect themselves from those who would destroy them—and if he must use unorthodox methods to do it, the Lord's chosen servants had always taken the opportunities divinely provided. Nephi and Teancum had shown no mercy to the villains the Lord put in their way. With a flick of his finger, he connected to one of his counselors, waiting outside a bar on the outskirts of Lake Creek, an establishment that the Millennium Brotherhood frequented. When his agent answered, DuPris said simply, "Sound the alarm."

Tucking his phone back into his pocket, DuPris smiled tightly at Brother Smith, who didn't ask what the phone call meant. He didn't need to; he knew that the Lord had at last persuaded a recognized prophet of the truth and of their divine calling and destiny. "I think you've got it right, Brother Smith. Let's go collect the rest of the toolbox. They're waiting for us."

More to the point, they were waiting for Elder DuPris, the Area Authority, who had called a special priesthood meeting at the Lake Creek chapel. The men standing and sitting tensely turned when the double doors opened, revealing Elder DuPris—and Brother Smith. A low murmur ran through the crowd as the two prophets, as Brother Smith thought of them, walked up the aisle. Brother Smith took a seat in the bishop's customary place, Brother Hunt beside him.

"Thank you for coming, brethren." DuPris stood at the podium, leaning straight-armed against it as he surveyed the wary, wondering audience. "I wish I called you together to heal your souls with words of reassurance and hope, but instead I come to summon you to a hard but necessary duty. As He called brave men in times of old, today the Lord calls you to defend your families, your homes, and your freedom from those who seek to destroy His people. The time has come for the righteous to go among the wicked like young lions, and none shall escape nor defend against you."

The heat in his voice, persuasive beyond the mere words he spoke, quoting violent scriptural promises and the prophecies of Brigham Young concerning the fate of those mobbers who had raised their hands against the early Saints, caught the ears and hearts of the frightened, angry, desperate men gathered in the quiet church.

As Tony listened to the Area Authority, he thought of Donna's tears as she told him and Carmen that she'd not lost but thrown away her job, Lucrezia's horrified yelp when April called to report that Jelisaveta Sarkesian had suffered a concussion when a thrown brick crashed through their front window, Gianni's little body huddled between him and Carmen because night terrors wouldn't let him sleep in his own bed, the dark shadows under Carmen's eyes from constant worrying. Everything DuPris said reached deep into Tony and inflamed his need to strike back at the enemies who made their lives miserable. Surely, the Lord had directed Elder DuPris to lead them in rescuing their families—and in keeping the lands that Joseph Smith himself had called Zion!

Seizing the hopes and fears of Tony and the others, DuPris added, "In the rush of events, the Church has issued no formal statement beyond extending condolences to those who lost loved ones in the massacre at the Lake County Ward chapel. Do not doubt that President Smith is aware of us—and of the evil men who conspire against the Saints."

"Yes, he is aware of us and them, but I haven't heard you say that you're speaking for him." Bishop Newstead rose from the front bench, his gentle face determined. "All we have heard from the Brethren—from the First Presidency—is to be patient, to follow their lead, to minimize our families' exposure to risk and trouble. I have yet to hear them say that we should meet violence with violence." Many of the listeners nodded, backing off slightly from DuPris' fiery rhetoric.

"You haven't heard from President Smith on the matter." Brother Smith rose to come to the railing and glare down at Bishop Newstead. "All you've heard is President Rojas telling you to let your families burn—not from the prophet but from a mere Associate President, a foreigner and a Lamanite as well!"

"Trust me," DuPris said, shooting Brother Smith a quelling look. His second counselor discreetly caught the older man's arm, pulling him back. A dose of Brother Smith would hurt the argument and atmosphere he was so carefully building. He'd expected resistance, and he'd prepared for it. "Of course we have heard nothing of the sort— remember, the Gentiles monitor all the Church's broadcasts. How could President Smith risk a general announcement that the Saints were to take up arms at last? He must protect us—and the other Saints around the world—which he cannot do if our enemies know our plans. A general announcement might trigger mass public retaliation against the Saints, which he cannot risk. This is why I bring the message personally; every area must take the initiative to put out its own fires. We must be ready, because the forces against us—"

The sharp tone of Bishop Calvin's phone going on emergency alert jolted across everyone's ragged nerves. The older man snatched it up in embarrassment; as they watched, the red flush on his face drained away, leaving him pale and sick. He looked up, his hoarse whisper easily audible in the waiting silence. "That was Teresa Burns, the minister of Unity Lutheran. She and many of her congregation are worried about the Saints. She says that Lebaron's armed his men, and they're coming to burn us out of Lake Creek. Softlearn's already on fire, with the Millennial Brotherhood collecting in front of the building for their attack."

Rob Sarkesian choked, lurching to his feet. "That means they're only a couple of miles away!"

Tony leapt up just as quickly, along with most of the other men, instantly ready to rush to defend their families and neighborhood. Only Bishop Newstead and a handful of others still hesitated, torn between fear, anger, and duty.

DuPris put a heavy thumb on the scale. "The Lord gives us permission to defend ourselves, brethren. We have no time to waste. Follow me, and trust in His strong arm!"

The chapel emptied in seconds, the parking lot in only a few seconds more, as the defenders roared back to their neighborhood—where, according to confidential reports that had reached Reverend Samuel Lebaron just an hour before, Brother Smith's men had gathered to launch an offensive strike against the Millennium Brotherhood, and were even now heading toward Lebaron's church, the one they'd tried to burn before. And, as DuPris had anticipated when he sent his counselors to plant the rumor of the Mormon offensive, a piece of disinformation DuPris hoped would lure the Brotherhood into a trap, Reverend Lebaron had acted just the way he wanted.

* * *

Tony ran down the darkening street, slipping into the deeper shadows beside the broken walls of a half-demolished building on the street outside the Mormons' isolated neighborhood. Off in the distance, the dim sound of thin, late-night traffic, the glow of streetlights, seemed surreal. Around him, other men also scattered into the ruins, each heading for the post assigned him on Elder DuPris' battle map. Some, including DuPris' two counselors, climbed up into the brownstones at the entrance to the main road; others scattered out through the vacant lots and ruins for an ambush; still others slipped down the manhole in the street beyond and into the sewer and utility tunnels beneath the street. The former marine officer had put his wartime experience to good use, arranging his forces in a horseshoe ambush, the curve of the horseshoe focusing on the two tall, abandoned apartment buildings that marked the entrance to the main street through the neighborhood—the same street Lebaron's goons had rampaged down on their last raid into what Brother Smith persistently called "the Stakes of Zion."

Tony took cover in his assigned place, looking out from between two rough-edged remains of reinforced concrete pillars, holding the rifle Rock had tossed him out of a stack of crates that looked like something out of a military supply clerk's back-office stash. Once in place, he flashed a quick laser signal to Bishop Newstead on his left, Rob Sarkesian on his right, and got their signals in return. The same signals flashed down the opposite side of the horseshoe, where Brother Smith's followers had taken their positions. He breathed deeply, resting the rifle against the fallen cement slab, pointing down the road toward the park where Brother Smith's spies said Lebaron's men were gathering. Extra, loaded clips pulled his jacket pockets. Beneath the jacket, he felt the lighter but more reassuring weight of his own pistol resting against his ribs.

Tony heard Lebaron's approaching convoy even as the laser-pointer signal flickered down both sides of the horseshoe from DuPris' position in the center. Headlights momentarily struck hard-edged shadows from the cement ruins, light and shadow chasing each other like phantoms across the broken walls and rough ground. Tony almost felt the light flash across his face; he reflexively closed his eyes to keep them from shining back at the oncoming trucks. The lights abruptly disappeared, as Lebaron's forces turned them off. Darkness fell, the only illumination coming from the warm lights of the Saints' homes, visible at the end of the deserted street. The noise of the attackers' approach sounded suddenly louder in the defenders' ears as sight disappeared, a rumble born of badly tuned engines and mud-digging tires. Lebaron's forces passed the far ends of the horseshoe, driving toward the center and the seemingly unsuspecting houses beyond.

Light bloomed, illuminating the center of the street just in front of the sentinel tenements. Jack DuPris stood there, in front of a single car whose headlights outlined him, his arms folded, looking as if he could stop the masses of metal bearing down on him with the power of his will alone.

The lead truck did screech to a halt a few yards from the edge of the light. The others came to a ragged stop behind it, ranged across both lanes of the narrow, residential road. Reverend Samuel Lebaron squinted through the windshield at this unexpected obstruction, irritated at the headlights keeping him from identifying the idiot standing in his way. He flicked on his own lights, then smiled wolfishly when he recognized the man. Kicking the door open, he left his vehicle to walk a few paces into his own beams of light. Behind him, others dismounted from their trucks, stalking forward with tire irons, chains, and shotguns at the ready.

"Well, Jack DuPris himself. It'll be almost an honor to hang your scalp right next to Joe Hyrum's on my trophy wall." Behind him, the Perry boys sniggered. "I don't need any more preaching from Joe; I heard all he's got to say. So you gonna tell me to go away, Jack? The governor's given you up. It's open season, and the hunt's starting now."

DuPris smiled back, his teeth glinting in the sharp light. "I'm going to tell you that you and your bully boys have one last chance to repent of your evil ways, Samuel. Throw down your weapons, promise never to bother the Saints again, and you may survive the night—and maybe save your rotten soul."

"You'd know a thing or two about rotten souls." Lebaron's voice transformed into a snarl. "We drove the Mos out once, and we fully intend to do it again—even if it means adding another false prophet to their list of martyrs," he shot back—literally.

DuPris had already started moving as the reverend's shotgun came up, leaving the expanding flock of lead shot to tear through empty air. His own hand swung up, pointing skyward, as he shot a flare toward the stars. Cold, green light burst into life, casting an eerie glow over the street—and signaling the start of the firefight. Instantly, the silence broken by Lebaron's blast shattered under the assault of a dozen rifles. The chest-thumping noise of the shot hit Tony as hard as the recoil, the rifle coming to life in his hands. He shot again and again, aiming for the tires of the trucks, the front grilles, the heavy blocks of iron in the axles—aiming to frighten the men away, to make them break and run, as DuPris had suggested to counter the objections Bishop Newstead had raised about actually shooting humans. Not that accidents wouldn't happen in a hot firefight, of course. A yowl rose over the pounding guns as a ricocheting bullet struck one of Lebaron's men in the foot, throwing him to the ground. Another bullet penetrated the gas tank of a low-slung car, starting a fire that cast its orange light over the scene.

The shock of the ambush had left many of the Millennium Brotherhood standing in the open; they ran for the cover of the big, metal vehicles, but quickly realized that the only safe direction lay behind them. They shot a few rounds back, but it quickly penetrated even their thick skulls that tire irons, shotguns, a few rifles, and methamphetamine paranoia were no match for serious battle tactics, heavy-duty military weaponry, and the fierceness of men defending their homes. One of the trucks in the line roared to life, wheeling frantically around in the narrow confines of the street, attempting to escape back down the road. After a second, another followed, spewing smoke and lurching, but leaving. Tony felt a surge of fierce relief—it was actually working!—and blasted the headlight out of Lebaron's truck, the bullet sizzling past the man's ducked head.

At the same moment, Lebaron realized that even if the Mos were the worst shots in the history of the world, they couldn't have missed that much. "Get 'em! Find 'em and kill 'em!" he roared. "The cowards aren't shooting at you!"

"You got that one right, Sam." Brother Smith appeared from the truck whose headlights had illuminated DuPris, Rock appearing on the other side as Orrin's face, and its manic grin, appeared over the top of the cab, rifle at ready. "They ain't shooting at you—but we are!"

This time, Lebaron took a dive—behind Lou Perry, who jerked as three bullets tore into him. Bou went down next, by a round DuPris' counselor fired from the top floor of the tenements looming above the green-lit battle scene. Another mobber pitched forward as Brother Hunt whooped triumphantly. Behind the riddled convoy, a manhole cover slid aside, disgorging another knot of fighters, who dropped to their bellies on the street to send another line of lead through vehicles and men alike.

Tony stopped shooting and watched in horror as the men on the left side of the horseshoe targeted not the trucks but their drivers and passengers. Bishop Newstead rose from cover, waving his arms frantically, shouting cease-fire orders that drowned in the bedlam of screams and gunshots. Tony burst out of hiding himself, to run hunched through the rubble he'd hidden in to push Bishop Newstead to the ground, out of harm's way. Rob Sarkesian quickly joined them, the ambush on the right side of the horseshoe mostly collapsing as the less hardened defenders left the fight to Brother Smith's bloodthirsty disciples.

Lebaron, dodging expertly through the carnage and chaos, roared orders for his men to retreat. As many as could follow the order converged on the few still-running vehicles. In the much-reduced hail of bullets, several of the Millennium Brotherhood rose from the ground to run.

"Don't let them get away!" shouted Brother Smith.

Tony launched himself out from behind the bullet-scarred cement barrier. He brought down a man carrying a tire iron in a low tackle—and promptly found himself in a nasty fight with an experienced brawler. Swinging his rifle as hard as he could, he managed to knock the tire iron out of the other man's hold, but the impact ripped the rifle from his own grip. He twisted, trying to break away enough to snatch the rifle back while preventing his opponent from doing the same, but instead of reaching for the gun, the man's hands closed around his throat. Dark stars swam before his eyes, the pressure on his chest and windpipe cutting off the air from his lungs. The snarling face of the man above him filled his fading vision.

Abruptly, the pressure disappeared, Bishop Newstead's long, gentle face replacing the Millennium Brother's. Tony sat up gasping and took Bishop Newstead's offered hand to stand. He looked at the sprawled body of his former wrestling partner, then looked at the bishop, who hefted the tire iron. "Knocked him out."

They both joined the unconscious mobber on the ground as another volley of bullets hummed past. The noise disappeared into the violent backfiring of a covered truck as its frantic driver urged the damaged engine into action, rolling backward on shredded tires. It bashed the burning car out of the way, carrying the last of Lebaron's men out of the immediate battlefield.

"Let none escape!" Brother Smith roared, as his own vehicles rolled out of their hideaways in the rubble, his followers jumping into them as they gathered speed.

The running battle flowed down the street, Lebaron's retreating forces shooting behind them to slow the pursuit and do as much damage as they could, but concentrating primarily on escaping. They thought that if they could just reach the gentile side of Lake Creek, they would be safe, they could regroup, count their losses—and plan their retaliation for the unexpected viciousness of the Mormons' defense. They thought wrong.

As the line of heavily armed vehicles rolled onto the railroad tracks that marked yet another boundary in the small town, Brother Smith, stood with Rock and Orrin in the open back of his truck. Porter was in the front seat at the wheel, pointed forward. "As the children of Israel left no heathen alive, we will leave no Amulonite in Lake Creek to trouble the sons of God!"

To the dismay of the ragged remnants of the Millennium Brotherhood, the Smiths and their small army not only failed to turn at the border but turned their attention and weaponry on the buildings to either side of the road as they sped into gentile territory. A heavy thud and low whistling announced that Brother Smith had obtained more than small arms from the South American gun runners. A hole appeared in the side of Lebaron's damaged church, a burst of flame shooting out of it a split second later, as the incendiary grenade from the truck-mounted launcher exploded. The battered hardware store came next, then the pawnshop beside it, as Orrin targeted any store or building owned by members of the Millennium Brotherhood or anyone else he suspected of joining the mob against the Mormons—which included everyone who didn't live in the farm compounds or Mormon neighborhood.

A few hardy souls tried to resist the onslaught, but rapidly realized that they had become civilians in a war zone. People poured out of their homes as word spread of a Mormon uprising. The reports of killing were somewhat exaggerated, after the last of Lebaron's forces went to ground; Brother Smith, a glimmer of rationality peering through the prophetic cloud filling his head, ordered his forces to spare the Amulonites for the moment, to drive them away but not annihilate them. By morning, most of Main Street on the gentile side had been reduced to charred, smoking, and in some cases still burning rubble, the houses beyond lay empty—and an infuriated, scorched, and slightly wounded Reverend Samuel Lebaron sped toward the closest National Guard post, calling Governor Kerr as he went. Behind him, Brother Smith led general rejoicing among his disciples, preaching to the converted that the victory of the Lord had begun.

* * *

At a meeting the next morning, Elder DuPris had acknowledged that the fight had become more deadly than he'd intended, and that Brother Smith's actions overstepped the bounds of the original plan. However, he assured the horrified defenders that they had done the right thing. When Rob pointed out that what they'd done was make themselves outlaws and targets for law-enforcement retaliation, DuPris met his eyes steadily, then looked around the circle of frightened people, his gaze sweeping them with cool confidence. "Don't lose faith. We're defending ourselves, and the Lord will sustain His people as long as they have faith in Him. I know this is the right thing to do, and that as unfortunate as it is, it is what must happen."

"You mean you know because you had a revelation?" The sudden question drew all eyes to Carmen. "Or you mean you figure every war has casualties, so it has to happen that way?"

DuPris' expression never wavered. "Sister Callatta, I can assure you that as Area Authority, charged with the spiritual and temporal welfare of the Saints in the Midwest, I am leading you right. That's why I'm here, personally, and why I will stay until the Lord reveals His mighty hand. You have heard President Smith say that these are truly the last days. Now is the time when the wicked will suffer, while the prepared shall not fear."

"And we're prepared," Bishop Calvin said, more confidently than he felt, but trying to reassure his people in their time of distress.

"We'll get more prepared too," DuPris added. He'd announced sentry posts and order for securing a perimeter, allowing no more questions. In the aftermath of the battle, most people wanted to hear a confident voice giving them something to hold on to, something they understood. And they understood taking inventory of their stored food and water, organizing the kids into activities, helping build barricades of rubble across all streets, and mounting a watch for enemies. Pointing to each man, he named the first, second, and third sentry rotations, then called on the Relief Society to organize food for everyone. Still giving orders, he moved on, finding something useful, or at least time-consuming, for everyone.

"Tony, this is all wrong," Carmen said, catching his arm.

Tony caught her face between his hands, looking into her dark eyes. "I know, baby. But it's going to get right. Elder DuPris says so, and we've got to believe it."

Carmen pressed her hands against his, keeping her voice calm despite the whirl of near panic welling up in her chest. "He might've got a revelation, but I didn't. I think he's up a tree, and he's going to hang us all from its branches." Her voice dropped to a whisper. "Bishop Newstead thinks so too—they said he's calling Independence, because President DuPris has gone off the rails."

"Tony! Step up. We're on duty," called one of DuPris' sentries.

"Then he'll tell us what to do as soon as he gets through—and if Jack DuPris is wrong, he'll admit it. I don't think he is though, and Bishop Newstead will find that out." Pulling Carmen in for a quick, tight hug, Tony said, "Stay busy, and you'll feel better."

She watched him lope off to join the other men, the rifle slung across his back, and swallowed hard. "Please, Heavenly Father, make it come out okay," she whispered. It didn't reduce the hot, sick feeling in the pit of her stomach. Neither did picking up Gianni, catching Donna and Lucrezia, and offering their services to Sister Newstead.

In the midst of all the methodical activity, a weary and troubled Bishop Newstead finally received a call back as he supervised the gathering of the dead and wounded. His call, urgent as it was, had traveled with unusual speed up the hierarchy of receptionists and secretaries who guarded the Brethren's time, but it still had to travel. He left the side of a wide-eyed, bloody mobber whose shot and broken leg he'd helped another ward member set. Sister Shaw, April's mother, was a registered—and at the moment, nearly overwhelmed— nurse. She couldn't quite hear his side of the conversation, but saw a sudden wash of tears flow across Bishop Newstead's face.

"What's happened?" she asked softly, unable to imagine anything could be worse than what they were dealing with now. Brother Smith's fanatics, along with quite a few men she'd thought would be more sensible, had taken positions all around their self-proclaimed Zion, ready to defend it against all comers. In the circumstances, no ambulance service would come near them, and she had four men who desperately needed medical care.

Bishop Newstead looked at her, wiping a hand across his face. "The Lord has spoken, Sister Shaw, and so has the prophet. Just a few hours too late for the man who should have listened a long time ago. We need to gather everyone who will listen—we'll all hear in an hour."

Word quickly spread through the shell-shocked neighborhood that an announcement would come over the Church's satellite channel at the end of the hour. Lucrezia, wild with tension and impatience and desperate for something to do that didn't involve tending kids or dealing with nervous, crying women, and wondering where Porter had got to, left Donna to herd Gianni and his nursery classmates while she ran from house to house, telling everyone to turn on their televisions to the Church's encrypted channel. Some did, some preferred the constant news feed that occasionally mentioned their plight to the world as a minor item of "breaking news." Her rounds took her out to the perimeter as well, where she found a tense, grim-faced Tony standing sentry duty with one of Brother Hunt's teenage sons. He hugged her, but didn't look away from the street leading out of town. The Hunt boy didn't even acknowledge her presence as he paced in a tight circle, staring toward the enemy massing out of sight past the jagged horizon.

Beyond the ruins that defined the boundary between their neighborhood and the rest of Lake Creek, noncombatants had abandoned their own houses and businesses to the growing tide of anti-Mormons pouring in to answer Lebaron's call for reinforcements. Confused reports on the radio news painted their numbers anywhere from fifty to five hundred, snatching sound bites from angry men promising mayhem and more when the Reverend gave the order to attack. From his position, Tony couldn't see the constant stream of heavily armed traffic pouring into the other side of town, but DuPris' counselors had reconnaissance duty and powerful binoculars. The reports had all the men on high alert, tightening their discussions about, as Rob Sarkesian said with sarcastic but heartfelt emphasis, "what the *heck* we're doing here." Distance and worry kept the men on sentry duty from conferring, but the feeling slowly grew among them that they had arrived at a crossroads—unfortunately, both turnings looked equally dark, with snarling barbarians waiting down either road.

The ex-sergeant reported that the news van had arrived too; the Channel 8 religion reporter stood outside it with the camera recording her from the battle zone. They could hear what she said over the portable radio Rob had brought along; from the sound of it, she believed that the Mormons in this town had finally flipped out, completely lost their minds to fanaticism.

". . . like so many misguided religious cults whose members follow a charismatic leader to suicide. Only this time, they've started a war instead. Jack DuPris, who seems to be leading the Mormons in this fight, has issued a statement warning the press to stay outside the perimeter he has established. He has also refused to negotiate with anyone but the governor." Anne spoke calmly and clearly, her voice giving no hint of the deep disappointment she felt.

"In a written statement, President Richard Rojas of The Church of Jesus Christ of Latter-day Saints has disowned DuPris' actions; he says that the Church's policy has always been peaceful coexistence with all their neighbors, and in no way do they promote violence between their members and others. Inside sources reveal that the Mormon leadership's efforts to contact DuPris have failed. In the meantime, other leaders have issued their own statements."

Another voice replaced Anne's, Tommy Gibbs taking the opportunity to comment on the harrowing events from his revival meeting in Springville. "I can only say that I am deeply disappointed with any group that commits atrocities in the name of religion—and especially in the name of dear Lord Jesus. Those who live by the sword will perish by it, condemning themselves to endless hell and damnation." In response to a shouted question about whether he supported the anti-Mormon militia rapidly growing in Lake Creek, he said, "I don't advocate violence—Jesus is the Prince of Peace—but in these perilous times, everyone who is not for Him is against Him. And the actions of these Mormons prove that they are no more Christian than the so-called Children of Light. Each person needs to listen to his or her own conscience and act as the angels direct."

"While Reverend Gibbs did not directly condemn the Mormons, Reverend Samuel Lebaron, whose fellow church members were viciously ambushed by a band of Mormons led by Jack DuPris and Joseph Hyrum Smith, is calling for all 'true soldiers of Christ' to gather to drive the Mormons out of their neighborhood and the entire town. Is this the beginning of the end for the Mormons here? Is Jack DuPris another David Koresh or Om Barishi? Only time will tell. Reporting live from Lake Creek, this is Anne O'Neal."

"Bishop Newstead says the Brethren are going to make an announcement over the satellite channel," Lucrezia informed Tony, after the voices on the radio went back to other news. "Come on, Dad."

"I'm on sentry duty, honey. I can't go now." Tony ruffled her hair, trying to sound calm and confident. "Tell you what—you go back and watch with Mom, then come tell me what they have to say."

She hesitated. "Dad, is it true that Elder DuPris isn't listening to President Rojas? Are we sure he hasn't lost his mind, like Anne O'Neal says?"

"Channel 8 never has anything good to say about the Church."

"No, but Mom doesn't have anything good to say about Elder DuPris either," Lucrezia said, lowering her voice instinctively. "She says if he's getting revelations, they're coming from the wrong place. Sister Hunt got really mad at her, but she didn't back down. Everybody's kind of splitting in two groups down there—the ones who go with Elder DuPris and the ones who think Bishop Newstead's right. Bishop Newstead's trying to keep everything calm, but you can tell Brother Smith's getting ticked off. I think the bishop's worried he might start shooting people for being traitors or something." She gave her father a searching look. "Dad, which side are you on?"

"I'm on your side, Luc—and your mama's, and your sister's and brother's. I'm out here because I believe we're defending our homes and families. Now, I want you to get back there and help your Mom—and try to help her and Donna not make everybody mad." Tony kissed her head and gave her a gentle but firm push back toward her mother and what he was determined to make sure was safety.

Tony watched her go. In the wait and silence that followed and for the first time, doubt began to gnaw at his pride and fierce determination. It was not like Carmen to be wrong about spiritual things. He had learned to rely on her solid and unshakable faith long ago. Well, he'd wait and see what the Brethren said.

Lucrezia went, deeply worried by Tony's noncommittal answer, trailing through the unbelievable scene of the neighborhood turned into something out of a war zone in Kharagizstan. A sense of doom and panic and determination hung over everything. Jelisaveta, wearing a bandage on her head, called to her, motioning from a yard where everyone was using a tap to fill up buckets of water, just in case. She waved back, but kept moving.

A moan caught her attention. She traced the sound to the tent set up outside the Shaws' house, a makeshift field hospital containing eight still-living victims of last night's fight. Under the canopy, Sister Shaw was on the phone, arguing with yet another ambulance service, promising safe passage if they would simply come to get the wounded men. Frustrated, she hung up.

"What's wrong?" Lucrezia asked, dragging her eyes away from the bandaged, bedraggled, and dangerous-looking men lying on blanket pallets.

Sister Shaw sighed, running her hands through her hair. She couldn't quite manage a smile, even for April's friend. "These guys are hurt, four of them badly, and I can't get anybody to take them to a hospital. The people I just talked to said they'd come get them—outside the perimeter."

"So we drive them out beyond the perimeter," Lucrezia said.

"I wish we could—I've asked, but Elder DuPris won't let anybody out, because it's a security risk. Anybody who steps out there might get arrested—or might get caught by the other side, which would be worse. And I really think that Brother Smith or Brother Hunt would actually shoot anybody who tried it." Sister Shaw shook her head again, muttering, "Why am I still calling them brother, for heaven's sake?"

Lucrezia smiled suddenly. "There's one person they won't shoot— and he's got a truck! You make the call and tell them where the wounded will be."

It took her a few minutes to find Porter, relegated to loading and cleaning weapons for the next assault—or what Orrin confidently predicted would be the next assault. He looked up eagerly when he heard Lucrezia's voice, only too happy to get away from Orrin, Rock, bullets, and his father's increasingly messianic pronouncements to everyone who'd listen, and more were, their faces strained and their eyes dark, grasping for any straw in the deep water in which they found themselves suddenly immersed. He hesitated when she laid out her plan—how could he disobey orders, especially to help the Amulonites? *Yes, they were Amulonites*, the logical voice inside his head pointed out, the one that got him in trouble with his father so often. *Wasn't that all the more reason to get them out of Zion? If nothing unclean could enter the presence of God, weren't they a source of contamination? Killing them in battle was one thing; letting them die on the Shaws' lawn was another question entirely, wasn't it?*

In the end, Lucrezia's big eyes, her appeal to his better nature, and his simmering resentment of his father won the internal argument. In only a few minutes more, he'd helped Sister Shaw load the worst of the casualties into the back of the truck, covering them with a canvas tarp, and headed out on a back road leading to the fields beyond Lake Creek. The road hadn't been blocked yet; the mines that Brother Smith had ordered buried in the hard-packed dirt had discouraged the single sheriff who'd tried to approach from the direction of the Smith farm. In that direction, though, several thick columns of smoke marked the end of the farm buildings, as Lebaron's men—and reinforcements—put them to the torch.

Delivering the first two wounded men to the waiting ambulance went smoothly. Brother Hunt's sentry detail gave Lucrezia and Porter a hard look, warned them against fornication, much to Lucrezia's embarrassment, but finally accepted Porter's explanation of going on an errand for Brother Smith.

On the second trip, however, things went wrong. Lucrezia, waiting in the truck with the low-hanging sun behind her, saw a glint rapidly closing down the road. It resolved itself into an all-terrain buggy, avoiding the booby-trapped road by driving over the rougher ground of the verge. A flash of gold from its hood marked it as a sheriff's specialized transport, coming on a tip from the ambulance service. "Porter!" she shouted out the window of the truck, instantly starting the engine. "Cops!"

Porter dropped the man he'd half carried to the ambulance, leaving the attending paramedic to catch him, then shoved aside the other paramedic, who tried rather ineffectually to stop him, and leapt into the driver's seat as Lucrezia swiftly vacated it. Pulling the truck around in a tight, dust-spewing circle, he laid it flat out toward the perimeter, the sentries, and safety. The sheriff's buggy accelerated as well, its bullhorn-amplified orders to halt reaching their ears muffled and distorted by speed and engine noise. The buggy skidded to a halt, however, as a line of warning shots kicked up tiny sprays of gravel in front of it.

Porter kicked up a spray of gravel too, as his father hit him hard enough to send him sprawling, roaring biblical curses at his treacherous son. Lucrezia tried to intervene, but Orrin deflected her, grinning as he pushed her toward Rock, who shoved her out of the way, telling her sharply, "Behave like a proper lady. If you can. A righteous woman might be more precious than rubies, but one who steps out of her place to defy properly constituted priesthood authority is nothing but a—"

"I'm sorry, truly I'm sorry, I repent and submit!"

Lucrezia looked at Porter as his declaration of repentance saved Rock from getting a feminine fist in the nose—or at least having to block a heartfelt swing. Brother Smith's middle son had scrambled to his feet again, standing with his head down in front of his father, the picture of repentant dejection. The look he flashed her under his lowered lashes, however, included a very slight smile.

She opened her mouth again, but this time he shook his head and she got the hint. Her walk, defiantly measured until she got out of their sight, turned into a lope, then a run. Tears half blinded her. Her headlong rush didn't slow until she reached her own home at the far end of the road from Brother Smith's commandeered headquarters, crowded with the wives and kids of many of the pro-bishop families—and nearly ran her mother down.

Carmen caught her, shook her, hugged her fiercely, then held her off at arm's length to level her with a maternal glare. "Don't you ever sneak off like that without telling me again! You could've been killed—or caught, which could be just as bad!" She paused to squeeze Lucrezia again, then smoothed her daughter's windblown hair. "But good for you—and for Porter too. Sister Shaw told me what you did. That was as brave and kind as it was dumb. You and your dad and Giovanni—my reckless heroes." For a second, tears threatened to flood Carmen's defenses. She swallowed them back. No time to break down now—not when so much was happening. "At least you came back in one piece."

"Porter's dad's really mad," Lucrezia said quietly. "Hit him. Hard."

Carmen's expression hardened. "That man should never have been allowed to have children."

"Mom!" Lucrezia looked half shocked and half approving. She hugged Carmen back. Whatever happened, her mother wasn't falling for any more lies from either Brother Smith or Elder DuPris. Now, if only her father could do the same!

"Mom!" Donna echoed her exclamation from inside the house, but more urgently. "It's starting!"

As Carmen and Lucrezia got to the door, looking over the heads of a dozen women and triple that number of children, the gentle, strong face of President Smith appeared on the screen, beamed into Latter-day Saint homes all over the world through the Church's secure satellite network. "Brothers and sisters, I have called you together through the Church's satellite network to relay a revelation for all members of the Church. The time has come to gather to Zion. We are recalling all missionaries currently in the field, and we are extending a call to all members of the Church as well: now is the time to literally gather out of the world. Please gather to the temples and other Church-owned properties to which your leaders direct you. Sell your property if you can, bring what supplies and possessions you can, but gather out of the world."

President Smith paused, letting the momentous news sink in. Even Gianni and the rest of the babies were quiet, watching the screen with wide eyes. With an expression of deep concern and compassion, the prophet continued, "We also ask that all members leave hotly contested areas rather than fight; go to the temple communities where you will be safe. As you gather, please follow legitimate procedures and legal means wherever possible. Always remember that you are members of The Church of Jesus Christ of Latter-day Saints, and conduct yourselves appropriately." With a smile as joyful and peaceful as it was warm and reassuring, he concluded, "The Lord is aware of His people, and His hand is extended over them. Come home, let Him gather you under His wings. Prepare for the great and wonderful day of the Lord. We will soon call additional brave souls as missionaries, the 144,000 chosen messengers, to carry the word of His final coming to all the world. My sisters and brothers, as much as you can, spread that great and glorious word yourselves. I testify that your Savior is truly mindful of you, and if you are faithful to His commandments, you will have joy and peace. In the holy name of the Son, amen."

The silence lasted for a few seconds, filled with the mellow tones of the conference center organ playing the bars of a hymn. Carmen broke it, clapping her hands together decisively. "That's it—we're packing up." She turned to Sister Shaw. "May, could you spread the word? Quietly at first, to the women, then have them get their husbands off that stupid perimeter and down here to help us. Donna, organize the older kids—we're going to need mules. Bring the bare necessities— clothes, emergency kits, family pictures. Seventy-two-hour kits for those who have them. And everybody get your cars ready."

"But Carmen," one of the younger women raised her hand timidly. "How can we get out? My husband said that we're surrounded by the Millennium Brotherhood."

Carmen looked into her frightened face, then around at the other women. *What do you believe, Carmen?* Giovanni's face flashed across her memory, peaceful even in death. She took a deep breath and said, "God said He'd protect us if we do what He commands—and we just heard His command. We're leaving for Nauvoo and the temple. He'll take care of the rest."

"Amen to that!" Sister Newstead rose from her chair, swinging up two of her grandchildren. "Let's go, ladies. Spread the word to your visiting teaching sisters, and I'll contact Sister Calvin and both Relief Society presidents. Women have always been more sensible about these things. We can just hope our husbands can get over their testosterone and see it the same way."

That got more of a laugh than it deserved, temporarily breaking the tension. They scattered, each back to her home, pausing only to inform each woman they met of the plan. Several found that groups watching the broadcast in other houses had come to the same conclusion; Sister Newstead didn't tell the Relief Society presidents so much as reconfirm their decisions. Others, too frightened or angry or caught up in DuPris' rhetoric or Brother Smith's grand vision, weren't convinced so easily.

* * *

Jason Adams didn't feel particularly convinced that his mission would succeed, despite the psychological and spiritual weight of the three letters in his pocket. When he and Rex Neil had left Independence to carry President Rojas's summons to Jack DuPris and his counselors, they'd thought they'd find the rebels in the area office in Iowa. But the news reports blaring through every Channel 8 station disabused them of that notion as soon as they set out. Not only was Elder DuPris still in Illinois, but he was busy organizing armed resistance in Lake Creek. Both men suspected that the reality behind the newscasters' breathless reports would prove disastrous for President Rojas's hope that an emergency disciplinary council would avert catastrophe in Illinois. His doubts didn't keep him from blasting toward Lake Creek as fast as the Church car could go.

"You think these letters will make a difference?" Rex's question came through the chatter on the radio.

"I don't know," Jason said. "I know that President Rojas called him in for interviews a few times."

"From Sister Nguyen?" Rex asked, grinning despite his worry. Jason should've been an intelligence operative, he kept such an attentive finger on the rumor pulse at headquarters.

Jason didn't grin back, just nodded and went on. "The interviews didn't make any difference. DuPris is ex-military, and it looks like he's gone loose cannon. He's got help too, with his two junior-officer counselors and the local fanatic cavalry that Joseph Hyrum Smith's brought in."

"Which leaves us what?" Rex looked out the windshield. Warning lights flashed in the distance.

"Which leaves us delivering the letters to DuPris and hoping that if he and his boys don't see the light, some of the Saints in Lake Creek will." Jason's eyes narrowed as he checked the lights down the road—looked like a roadblock.

Rex sighed. "It's just too bad, is all. Just when we've got God literally on our side, DuPris decides he knows better than President Rojas or President Smith—or the Lord Himself."

"He keeps going this way, he's going to hurt himself—and a lot of other people." Jason brought the car to a stop in front of the highway patrol trooper gesturing them to halt in front of the makeshift barrier.

"Unless we can talk some sense into people," Rex said.

Jason nodded agreement and rolled down the window, smiling at the trooper much more confidently than he felt. "Good afternoon, Officer. What's going on?"

The young officer blinked, giving the two men an incredulous look. "Haven't you been listening to the news? There's practically a war on. You're going to have to turn around, guys. Nobody gets in without official clearance."

"We've got official clearance," Jason assured him. "President Richard Rojas sent us to defuse the situation. We're delivering a message to Jack DuPris."

"Mormons." The word came out flat rather than hostile, but it didn't sound positive either. "Should've known from that Missouri plate. 'Official' means state of Illinois. Church messengers don't count."

"Look," Rex pleaded, leaning forward to speak around Jason, "we have some vital information here—it'll really help cool things down. We really need to get in there to talk to DuPris."

"No, you look," the officer said, fixing them both with a hard stare. "I believe you think you could do some good—but fact is, you can't. Things are totally out of control out there. Nobody's listening to anybody anymore." His expression softened slightly. "I'm not one of those crazy anti-Mormons—I knew some of you guys growing up, and you're not bad people. But you do not want to go past here with those license plates, or you'll get a bad case of lead poisoning." He backed a step, gesturing again, forcefully for them to turn around.

"He's not sticking around to let us argue," Rex noted, as Jason swung the sedan into a wide curve. "Maybe we could try a different road."

"No," Jason said. A feeling of calm slowly replaced his disappointment, a spiritual sense of understanding and assurance. "It's too late. The Saints in there have the prophet's word. Those who will hear, will hear. We did our best. They're in the Lord's hands now. Let's head home."

Rex slowly nodded as the same feeling filled his worried mind. Jason sighed, tucking the letters more firmly into his jacket pocket and squinting as he turned the car toward the setting sun.

CHAPTER 24

Tony, released at last from sentry duty as the sun sank in the west, ran back home through the haze, coughing in the smoke from the fires that the much-augmented Millennium Brotherhood had set to the houses in the outlying areas beyond DuPris' tightly defended perimeter. Every member of the Church in the Lake Creek stake had poured into the safety of DuPris' urban foxhole; most had come when he called the original meeting, and others had trickled in during the day, led through the woods to either side of the booby-trapped road. While initially only the homes of the retreating Mormons were burned, the pyromania, like the looting, quickly spread from there. In the no-man's-land between the two sides, and even beyond in the gentile section of town, the blazes multiplied as their ostensible targets watched from behind their thickening defenses. More and heavier armament had appeared from Brother Smith's mobile armories—full machine guns, rocket-propelled grenade launchers, tiny heat-seeking smart bombs, laser targeting systems for the rifles.

As twilight fell, DuPris made the rounds of the defenses again and again, gathering reports in person that he could easily have received remotely, but taking time to touch a shoulder here, share a smile there, bracing his troops. He answered some questions, telling them that he had received a call from President Smith, through Brother Smith's much-vaunted blood relationship to the "real" prophet, and that the news reports, as always, had it utterly wrong. He also made sure that the less rabid sentries stayed focused, quelling any talk of abandoning their posts, through force of personality, charisma, and the cold eyes of his two sergeant counselors. Occasionally, he culled this one or that one out of the ranks, starkly reprimanding him for weakness and sending him back to the women and children with a hard condescension that played on the others' macho pride, making it harder for anyone to voluntarily leave his post. Brother Smith made the rounds as well, using Porter to ferry additional ammunition and armaments to his own followers in the forward batteries. Tony appreciated Elder DuPris' rallying support, and told himself that the uneasiness he felt came from having to work with a fanatic who constantly spewed fractured scripture and prophesied a glorious, bloody future for all of them. Despite Elder DuPris' spin on the situation and his own need to believe he could do something to defend his nearest and dearest, however, Tony had quickly realized that neither DuPris nor Brother Smith had succeeded in convincing all of the stake members of the righteousness of their mission.

Tension crackled through the air around Tony as he neared his own house; women, children, and a few men eddied warily around each other, some standing grimly on their own lawns to glare at others, who carried bags and bundles out to stow in a variety of cars. He wondered about it momentarily, until he saw Bishop Newstead directing the efforts of an entire team in packing another ward member's big RV camper with all the supplies that different families brought out of their own storage. Brother Hunt, called in from outside sentry duty to internal peacekeeping, watched with a glower as heavy as the gathering clouds. Tony kept moving through it all, exchanging a carefully neutral nod with Bishop Newstead to hide the misgivings hanging heavy in his chest. He told himself it was no more than the natural resistance any civilian had to wartime necessity, and pushed through the deepening stiffness and chill under his ribs. The sight that met his eyes when he came through the door, however, stopped him cold.

"There you are, finally!" Carmen looked up from her spot on the floor, kneeling between two boxes as she rapidly sorted Gianni's clothes into a "keep" and "discard" pile. She motioned Tony over. "Come on—get off your feet, rest up, and take over dividing these up. Anything ripped, badly stained, or too small goes in the box we're leaving here. There's no way I'm having another baby at my age, so we won't need them. Knock on wood—or cardboard, as the case may be."

She suited action to words, holding up her hand for assistance in rising to her feet.

Tony caught her hand to pull her up, then retained her hand. "Carmen, what are you doing?"

"I'm packing everything in this house that we can't do without and can fit in the van," Carmen told him. "Let's get us out of the hot zone right now."

"I'm not leaving!" The force of the exclamation startled both of them, but Tony carried it to the logical conclusion. "We've already lost one house to people that hate us for believing in keeping the commandments; I'm not giving up another!"

Carmen moved past him to the table, gathering a multicolored pile of tiny socks and dropping them into the open packing box. "Yes, we are," she said, her voice hard as granite.

"What?" Tony sputtered—then the light dawned as he looked around the room, catching sight of the disconnected video screen. "You've been listening to the news, Carmen. They're never right, you know that—not even about today's weather, let alone any longer forecast. They're just as wrong about Elder DuPris. He said that he'd heard from President Smith that every gathering of the Saints is in effect holy ground, a temple, and worthy of the benefits of divine protections."

"How nice for him," Carmen snapped, her temper frayed to twine. "If you believe it. Me, I figure that President Smith meant what he said when he told us to get to actual temples and communities, and for us, that's Nauvoo. Tony, if God meant us to stay, wouldn't He have told us?"

"He did," Tony pointed out, his own temper rising. He extracted a pile of Gianni's clothes from the box, reaching to deposit it back in the laundry basket. "If God wasn't with us, we wouldn't have won last night, right? And Elder DuPris is the Area Authority, which means we need to follow his lead."

"What about the prophet's message?" Carmen shot back, taking the handful of soft clothes from him and smacking them right back down in their little packing container.

"Well, that's for generally everybody, not necessarily for us—and aren't we in a Church community already?" Tony caught her hands this time, wishing he could shake the stubbornness out of her, make her see what he believed, or at least, desperately needed to believe. "Doesn't it make more sense to finish the problem here and now, with the Lord behind us? You heard the second part of President Smith's announcement about missionaries, didn't you? Jack says that we, the ones who have the faith to stand against terrible odds to defend our homes and families, are numbered with the 144,000 valiant priesthood holders who'll fight the devil and save Zion."

"Oh, so now he's an angel?" Carmen snapped, but she didn't remove her hands from his, and her eyes had more water than fire in their depths. "Tony, Jack can't appoint the 144,000 because he's not appointed himself; he's got delusions of grandeur that even a sharp slap upside the head can't solve." Seeing the resistance in his face, she thumped his chest impatiently with one open hand. "The Lord isn't behind us—we got lucky because Lebaron wasn't expecting Jack's tactics. And Jack's gone clear off the deep end, along with Brother Smith." After the near whisper against the self-appointed leaders of the small Mormon neighborhood, her voice rose. "We need to get out, and they need to get out now!"

Tony didn't want to hear that; it struck too close to the uneasiness he'd tried to talk himself out of ever since he answered DuPris' call to meet at the stake center, the meeting that started the boil-over of this long-simmering confrontation. His own face felt stiff as he ground out, "Carmen, you're wrong. You don't understand the whole situation. You don't know what they're threatening to do—what they have done already."

"I know that they've learned from getting ambushed that they shouldn't trust a one-sided frontal assault, and I know that Elder DuPris is a slick operator in tying your manhood up with his little war." She gave Tony one of those no-nonsense stares that used to reduce him to stammering and laid her hand against his cheek. "Tony, I love you, and I love your guts—your full-speed-ahead courage. If I didn't like a little bull-headed macho, I wouldn't have married a New Jersey barrio boy. But," she slapped his cheek lightly, as if to wake him from a deep sleep, "it's time you started thinking straight."

She almost got through the thick fog of fear, pride, and self-delusion with that, puncturing the armor he'd built against the little voice inside telling him not to do this, but at exactly the wrong moment, his phone rang. Holding up one finger to her, as if it would keep her from speaking instead of just annoying her, he listened intently to the voice on the other end of the connection. What he heard drew the blood away from his face and fanned his anger to white heat.

"What?" Carmen asked, fearing she knew the answer already, but willing to take a chance.

"They're moving forward," he said tightly. "Lookouts put them only two blocks away, pushing along three streets and maybe four."

"Including the country road?" she breathed, her own face going pale.

Tony frowned at her. "No—if they come that way, we'll blow them off the road with the mines and the RPGs. They're using the buildings as cover. It's urban warfare, Carmen."

"Yes!" Her exclamation startled him. She smiled, color rushing back into her face. "I knew it! We've got a back door, and He'll make sure we have a way out. We're leaving, Tony, in a half hour, when it gets dark, right down the country road, onto the freeway, and to Nauvoo like flying monkeys are after us!"

"No," he said flatly, turning toward the door. "You're staying right here, where it's safest, and I'm going to go with the force Elder DuPris is leading to cut off the Brotherhood's approach. They ran once, they'll run again—and this time, we'll push them right out of the whole Lake Creek area."

She caught him at the door, putting herself between him and the knob. "Tony, we're leaving."

"I'm leaving—you're gathering the kids and staying right here where it'll be safe. Get the car ready if you need to, but we'll be back after we kick Lebaron's tail once and for all." He moved her gently but firmly aside. "Now, how about a kiss for luck?"

A kiss for luck? When he'd disregarded everything she'd said, let his stupid pride blind him from simple common sense? "If you leave us now, Anthony Giovanni Callatta, you might as well not come back!" Carmen's hot, bright eyes matched the fury in her voice.

Answering fury rose in Tony's chest. "I'll come back, and we'll have a long talk about who presides in this household!" He stormed out, too angry at first to think straight, but as he drew farther from home the fire cooled, and he suddenly realized he had essentially quoted Brother Smith. *What am I doing?* he questioned. Still, he had to see this through.

Carmen watched him go, running to the curb to jump into the back of one of the pickup trucks gathering the brave, stupid fools who'd decided to back Elder DuPris in his preemptive attack on the Millennium Brotherhood. She didn't see him flick a wave back at her; the taillights wavered into streaks of bloody red light that filled her tear-smeared vision. The tears rolled, unheeded, down her cheeks, as she flicked out her own phone, calling Donna to bring Gianni and Lucrezia back home; she needed help carrying boxes to the van more than others needed their babysitting skills if they were going to be ready in time to leave with the convoy Bishop Newstead had organized under DuPris' radar. What she heard next froze like ice inside her chest.

"Lucrezia?" Donna sounded puzzled, then worried. "I thought she was with you."

She wasn't—in fact, she wasn't actually with anybody at the moment, even though she dodged and pushed her way through the frightened, determined crowd gathered in the dimming light at the end of the main street. Men filled the middle of the road, armed and grim looking; women and a very few children stood on the sidewalks, some of them crying. In the center of the concentric rings, Elder DuPris and Brother Smith stood facing Bishop Newstead and Rob Sarkesian. Brother Hunt, the veteran members of Smith's army of Helaman, and more than half of the men from the Lake Creek wards stood behind and around them. Lucrezia, panting from the long run to the meeting place, wormed her way around the fringes, looking anxiously for Porter. She finally spotted him, banished to the back of the Smith side in disgrace; Orrin and Rock, the faithful sons, stood at either side of their father and slightly behind, at the center of attention.

Brother Smith stepped forward, the evening breeze blowing his halo of white hair around his head, emphasizing the Old Testament qualities of his face as he glared at Bishop Newstead. "You are called as a judge in Israel, and as such you have a voice here, and we will listen. But remember that Captain Moroni found occasion to chastise the judges when they proved themselves unfaithful to the Lord's commands to defend His people."

DuPris remained where he was, his arms behind his back, standing at parade rest. The two sergeants flanked him, watching the crowd with cold, alert eyes. His voice, lower than Brother Smith's declamation, carried clearly in the nerve-ringing silence. "What did you come to say, Bishop Newstead? We're listening."

"You've heard the message from President Smith, or heard of it, since you didn't watch it yourself," Bishop Newstead answered, his own voice shaking slightly with determination—and the grief he knew would come. "He's called us to leave peacefully. We are going to Nauvoo."

"Who's 'we'?" Brother Hunt called out. "Who's coward enough to let Lebaron take their homes, turn tail and run?"

"You going to leave your wives and children behind for the Amulonites and their Lamanite allies to capture, like the treacherous men of Ammonihah did?" Rock added.

Orrin had started grinning as tempers rose, shifting lightly from foot to foot, eager for action.

"No one will be left behind but those who choose to be," Bishop Newstead answered, his voice steadying. "Elder DuPris, please—call President Rojas for direction."

DuPris shook his head. "I don't need to call President Rojas for direction. I have all the direction I need from higher sources. I know this is what we must do, defend our homes and families. The Lord helps those who help themselves, those willing to strive for Him."

"Rojas is a Lamanite by birth," Brother Smith interjected. DuPris shot him a quelling look.

Bishop Newstead knew his argument probably wouldn't get through; he hadn't got through to Brother Smith in three years, but he had to try. "You must know that Governor Kerr has called the National Guard out. If we let them know that we intend no further violence, they may stand between us and the Millennium Brotherhood's mob. We have the opportunity now to leave without further bloodshed—"

"Without bloodshed?" Brother Smith interrupted. "Blood has already been shed. The blood of our own wives and children cry out against the Amulonites and their leader, and this time the Lord will bare His mighty arm. Neither Amulonites nor the corrupt soldiers of an apostate government can defeat the army of Helaman or destroy the New Jerusalem here in this place. The Second Coming is at hand, when Christ will come to cut down the wicked with the sword of His wrath—the time has passed for peace!"

A ripple passed through the crowd as the two sides debated, a subtle shift beginning to take place as people moved to one side or the other. DuPris' side grew slowly but noticeably, leaving fewer hovering undecided between the two camps. Tony, holding his rifle against his hip, held his position halfway between the two groups, watching the confrontation. He liked Bishop Newstead, but he trusted DuPris—or at least thought he did, though the doubts that began earlier now grew in his mind with every sentence. He wanted to believe that he could defend his family, that he didn't have to retreat, that evil wouldn't always win. His chest felt increasingly hollow though, and Brother Smith made him uneasy, still setting off the mental alarm bells he'd been trying to ignore.

"Yes, the time has passed right by, and is passing while we stand here jabbering," Rob Sarkesian agreed, a practical businessman impatient with the delay and Brother Smith's preaching. "It's time for the Saints to go to Zion and let Christ take care of defeating the bad guys. We're leaving in half an hour, with everybody who's smart enough to come." He turned to leave, catching the eye of several of his employees and friends. A few turned their heads away, refusing to meet his gaze, but more began to move back to join him.

"Those who are not with us are against us," Brother Smith intoned.

"Those who are not with you will mourn your stubbornness and its consequences," Bishop Newstead said, looking pleadingly at Bishop Calvin, who still stood behind Jack DuPris. The older man, sunk deep in internal misery, didn't seem to see anything around him. Bishop Newstead looked around the circle of faces, holding his hands out as he picked out individuals from the mob. "Please, let the Spirit speak to you. Listen to it! Bob—Amal—John—Pedro—Evan. Think of your families! Come with us! Don't stay here to die!"

"Maybe you'd better shut up or die right here yourself." Orrin's voice, lazy but sharp edged, cut across the bishop's personal pleas. Orrin's eyes looked as flat and shining as the barrel of the rifle he held aimed at Bishop Newstead's heart.

Bishop Newstead, as gentle as ever but firm as the ground under his feet, ignored Orrin and the gun completely. Focusing on the Area Authority, he said clearly, "We will follow the prophet's voice, Jack, and gather to the temple. You can try to stop us if you must, but I warn you now that nothing you do will keep us from obeying the Lord's commandment."

"Trying for a battlefield commission to General Authority, Bishop Newstead?" DuPris asked with a hard smile. He looked past the bishop to the men standing behind him, the group walking away with Rob. "Fine." He shrugged, dismissing the dissenters as if they hardly mattered, and caught the barrel of Orrin's rifle, shoving it up to point at the threatening and ominous sky. "Go if you must. We don't need cowards in our ranks. The Lord demands soldiers made of iron, not plastic."

That struck home, as he'd intended it to; a few men who'd begun to move toward Bishop Newstead's side of the circle stopped. The others, ranged behind DuPris, shifted where they stood, a rumble of derisive comments seconding their leader's comment.

Bishop Newstead, realizing he had lost, simply said, "I'm sorry—for all of you." He turned and walked away, his head up and step firm, but a few tears slipping down his gentle face.

"Faithless, gutless, and heartless," Brother Smith summarized, provoking a few nasty laughs from his followers. He turned to face his faithful with a triumphant expression. "Those who will not follow the Lord will inherit eternal punishment. They will burn in an endless lake of fire and brimstone, or gnash their teeth and wail in the freezing fastness of outer darkness. And we, the faithful and constant, will look down from our heavenly mansions on the suffering of the sinners below us, and know that it is just!"

DuPris stepped forward at last, taking the stage from Brother Smith. "Before we get to those heavenly mansions, we'll send Lebaron's Millennium Brotherhood to start roasting in hell. You have the guns and guts to make this happen. The deserters are right— Governor Kerr's called out the National Guard. He also thinks that worries us, that we are cowering behind weak defenses hoping we can talk our way out of this—which we have no intention of doing. We have the perfect opportunity for a surprise attack; if we move now, attack when they don't expect it, we can skin Lebaron's animals before the professional soldiers get here." He paused, in mock forgetfulness. "Did I say professional? I meant part-time. These guys are stock boys and file clerks in real life; they can't hold a candle to a real marine—or a real Mormon. I can tell you this, which I know as I know God's orders for you: you are the lions, the eagles, the dragons who will eat them alive! Get ready to move out—dinner's ready!"

Brother Hunt started the cheers. Orrin laughed, firing his rifle into the sky as if defying heaven to contradict DuPris' pronouncement. Several others followed.

Hellfire and damnation, treachery and deceit, violence and death. Tony hadn't moved, now at the edge of the shouting pack—a pack of wolves, if wolves could hate other wolves that much. Their shouting, snarling faces filled his eyes, his own fury, doubt, and fear filled his heart—and suddenly Giovanni's smiling face filled his head. Giovanni, beaming in his new mission suit, proud and a little embarrassed at the fuss Carmen made over how handsome he was; Giovanni in the Vid he sent on Tony's birthday, grinning and showing off his name tag, then sobering as he told them about the gangs who beat up a couple of his investigators. He'd helped put in windows, clean paint off walls, repair fences, and replant burned lawns after attacks by anti-Mormon vandals. He'd also visited members and investigators in the hospital or in their homes when the vandals damaged the people as well as their property; he'd cried, he'd growled about the gangs, but he'd never hated them or anyone else. Even dying at the hands of murderers, his last words had been a message of comfort, not condemnation. The contrast—love versus hate, faith versus pride, good versus evil—hit his conscience hard.

For just a moment, his pride reared up, snarling at the Spirit's sharp rebuke, but this time Tony slapped it down himself. Blood rushed into his face, his hot anger at himself opening his eyes—and, being a Callatta, his mouth. "Stop!" he bellowed, grabbing two men beside him and shaking them hard before plunging forward into the crowd, using his weight and momentum to plow his way through them. Breaking through the ring, drawing several glares, he came to a stop where Bishop Newstead had made his last stand. Waving his arms, he yelled, "Are you all crazy? Do you know what you're doing?"

"We do," DuPris informed him in a voice like hot iron. "But you don't. Disappear now, Callatta, if you're scared, but don't insult us with more little-girl whining."

"Like this little girl?" Rock shouted, suddenly pulling Lucrezia out of the horde.

Tony stared at her, too stunned to say anything.

Porter lunged after her, trying to pull her out of his elder brother's grip. Rock let go of her with one hand to lash out at Porter, who deflected the blow and caught Rock's wrist.

Glaring at Rock, Lucrezia pulled away, then stared defiantly at the ring of hostile faces. She, unlike her father, because she didn't quite realize the danger she was in, was neither stunned nor speechless. "This girl's smart enough to know her daddy's right—and if you're smart, you will too. If you think you can beat the National Guard, you're just all nuts! Come on, Porter, let's get out of here—let them commit suicide if they want to!"

"Sounds like little-girl whining worth listening to." Shaking off his momentary paralysis and any fear of the once-familiar strangers around them, Tony took Lucrezia's hand and clasped her to his side. His other hand dropped to the pistol under his arm, the gesture echoing the warning glare he swept over the crowd around them. His eyes narrowed at the men standing in their way; they reluctantly moved to either side. Stalking through the opening in the wall of bodies, he shot one last command over his shoulder. "Come on, Porter."

Brother Smith let out a harsh laugh, catching Porter's arm in a punishing grip. "No son of mine will follow a harlot away from the Lord's service."

"Let it go," Lucrezia said quickly, grabbing her father's arm, looking back at the boy she'd come for. "It doesn't matter what he says. Porter, please come!"

Porter hesitated, but lifelong conditioning won. "You go on," he said. "I'll call you when we win."

Brother Smith slapped him hard on the back. "Go on, Isabel," he advised Lucrezia, his face a study of triumphant tyranny. "And take your henpecked father with you."

Lucrezia didn't have to catch Tony this time; he just grinned back at the mocking comments—everybody knew Carmen—as he and

Lucrezia left. He knew her too, but he still felt a hint of trepidation as he ran up the walk to steady a heavy box that threatened to topple his wife off the front steps. Carmen's dark eyes appeared over the large cans of pineapple, pears, and other food-storage fruits in the box; she hung on to it, resisting his help.

"Hey, lady, could you use a hand?" he asked.

"Depends," she shot back, "on whether the hand's owner will listen to good advice."

"He will from now on," Tony promised. "Yours and his Father's."

Carmen let go of the box, staggering Tony slightly. He recovered, fit the box into the back of the already mostly full van—and staggered again, this time as Carmen thumped into him, wrapping her arms around his middle and squeezing hard. He hugged her in return, burying his face in her hair, his tears of relief dampening her wild curls. "I love you," Tony whispered.

"I love you too." Carmen sniffed, her face against his shoulder. "And tomorrow, after I really bawl you out, I'm going to remember some reasons why."

"You two can get a room later," Donna advised, grinning broadly as she stood on the porch holding her little brother and his backpack. "We're supposed to be making a dramatic escape, remember?"

"Scape!" Gianni exclaimed, flinging his arms out, making Donna duck to avoid getting slapped in the ear. She nosed him in mock retaliation.

"Right," Tony saluted with one hand, the other arm still around Carmen. He slipped the other around Lucrezia, kissing the top of her head. "Let's get out of here."

Two convoys rolled out of the besieged Mormon neighborhood ten minutes later, after two very different prayers for protection and success. One convoy heavily laden, headed out into the countryside toward the haven beyond the burning; the other heavily armed, plunged into the ruins of the no-man's-land and a self-deluded holy war. One stayed together, following each other along the open road; the other split into three columns, advancing through the broken maze of devastated city streets and into the darkness.

"Stop where you are!" commanded a voice of thunder from the sky.

DuPris looked up at the observation helicopter coming into view over the jagged top of an abandoned and half-burned apartment building, and showed his teeth in a feral smile. "Engage!" he ordered. The instruction rippled down the three lines, relayed electronically to the team leads in each vehicle. Even before the last strike team got the word, two heat-seeking bombs arced toward the dark clouds hiding the sunset sky; the two small lights converged, then combined into a huge burst of fire where the helicopter had been. Amid a rain of bits of molten metal, a whoop of victory roared up.

It turned into a battle cry, as the two flanking columns burst into the wide square facing the burned-out shell of the Softlearn building—and ran full on into Reverend Lebaron's massing forces from either side, laying down a withering hail of gunfire. Caught only partially by surprise, thanks to the warning from the helicopter pilot's last, frantic message, the much-augmented Millennium Brotherhood shot back, diving for cover—and running for the open doors of the buildings around the square, trying to get the advantage of an elevated position above the battlefield.

Running wildly into the dark hallways of another recently abandoned but not yet burned office building, Lebaron's hand-picked special teams headed at top speed for the stairs. Cursing the treacherous Mormons for attacking under a flag of negotiation before they could do the same, they mounted the first-floor landings, opened the doors—and had just enough time to see the guns leveled at them before the shots sent them sprawling and rolling back down the stairs. DuPris' third column had slipped through the block, infiltrating the buildings and lining the last street out of the square that the other two columns hadn't filled with exploding destruction. Leaving sentries to guard the street entrances, DuPris' hand-picked sergeants led teams into the upper stories, using the advantage to fire down into the melee below, picking Lebaron's men off as they ducked behind the lines of cement barriers they had set up as cover.

Under the unremitting hail of lead, the Millennium Brotherhood went down like grass under a lawnmower—or, as Brother Smith would have it, like stubble before the refiner's fire. Samuel Lebaron himself, shocked at the Mormon's firepower, but slightly more secure in his headquarters inside the charred lobby of the Softlearn building, spat furious curses at DuPris, Smith, God, and himself. "Get out!" he finally roared, reluctantly forced to give up his hopes of a dramatic victory. "Fall back to Oak and Walnut!"

His order didn't flow quite as efficiently as DuPris' through the wild chaos of the battle; he hadn't divided his men into strike teams, nor made sure they all had wireless communications, but he hardly needed to. Men who hadn't got the official word began to break and run, followed immediately by those who did. Most held onto their weapons, laying down a ragged cover fire behind them as they retreated; others dropped their guns and just ran for any safety they could find. They were the lucky ones.

The self-proclaimed righteous militia roared forward, blazing in pursuit of the retreating Amulonites, with Brother Smith urging them to leave no apostate still breathing. All three columns re-formed, running down parallel streets toward Lebaron's fall-back position between Oak and Walnut streets. The constant tattoo of gunfire accompanied them, the deeper roars of RPGs crashing into buildings where the Millennium Brotherhood took cover, the collapse of masonry adding a bass rumble to the symphony of pandemonium. Fireballs and flashes lit the streets, their light glistening from shards of glass, tangled metal, and pools of blood.

As the battle surged into Oak Street, the number of explosions doubled. Streaks of fire flew toward DuPris' forces as well as away from them. A line of tracer fire like glowing scarlet Morse code lanced out, targeting the lead truck in DuPris' left flanking line. A missile followed the coded instructions, screaming out of the darkness to bury itself deep into the iron engine. The engine shattered into millions of shards of half-melted metal, gasoline oxidizing explosively into a mushroom column of fire, its passengers, including one of DuPris' counselors, thrown violently from the wreckage.

Behind the bombs, fully armed, fully backed National Guard troops charged forward. The Millennium Brotherhood's hopeful cheer changed instantly into terrified screams, as they found themselves caught between two grindstones—and targeted by both sides. Governor Kerr, out of patience with any brand of religious fanatic and wanting to put an end to the conflict once and for all, had ordered his commanders to shoot anyone with a gun, and to take the rest into custody as domestic terrorists under the authority of homeland security. He made it quite clear, however, that he expected far more casualties than prisoners. Very clear.

It became quite clear to Lebaron as well; abandoning his bolt hole and the remains of his force, he slipped away, using the cover of Oak Street's neighborhood yards to hide from the National Guard—and the few Mormons still left standing, and more important, shooting.

DuPris had prepared his men well for a battle against thugs armed with civilian-issue firearms and Molotov cocktails. But their off-brand, smuggled military hardware and limited-force military tactics were no match for the actual military. The National Guard cut through the panicked ranks of the Millennium Brotherhood easily, barely pausing in their forward charge. The wave crashed into DuPris' heavier lines and slowed slightly—but only slightly. Brother Hunt and his sons, confident of divine protection, drove their truck forward in a blatant frontal attack on the armed personnel carrier in front of them. Lightning, in the form of a smaller, more efficient heat-seeking bomb, found not the personnel carrier but the pickup truck. The blast lifted the remains of the truck streetlamp high, sending it crashing and rolling back into the vehicles behind it. Another explosion brought the wall of a building down in a masonry avalanche, burying the last car in the left flank line and cutting off retreat in that direction.

"Hold your ground!" DuPris shouted into his comm, refusing to believe the testimony of his own eyes as he saw his divinely given forces cut to pieces. This couldn't happen—he had led them against an enemy to defend their homes, their families, their religion. He had used all his skill, all his experience, all his will to force the world to bend to God's will. Climbing out of his truck, numb with shock and disbelief, he stared upward, into the dark sky above the fireballs. A streak of light appeared, flying across the black vault of heaven. *A sign.* The whisper rose unbidden from the depths of his mind, the part that had once made him a potentially great Church leader. *A sign of my arrogance.* The thought hit DuPris with the force of a bullet— and so did an actual bullet, driving deep into his back, throwing him to the ground.

In the howling chaos, Brother Smith turned in time to see DuPris fall. He shouted for Porter to drive forward, to rescue their fallen leader. The truck rumbled forward on flapping shreds of tires, Orrin laughing wildly in the bed of it as Rock swung the mounted machine gun around, clearing the way. The scream of another incoming missile grabbed their attention. Shouting a warning, both dived out of the truck bed; Porter and Brother Smith abandoned the cab at the same moment. Right behind them, a fireball engulfed the vehicle.

Brother Smith rose to his knees, scrambling forward to DuPris' side. DuPris lay still, but drew a ragged, sucking breath when Brother Smith rolled him over. Flames reflected in his eyes, the wide pupils showing Brother Smith's face wreathed in fire. "We were wrong," he whispered.

Brother Smith heard the words, but they never reached his mind, let alone his heart; he refused to believe it. Even the impenetrable armor of his delusional confidence, however, could not shield him from the sights all around where he knelt beside the mortally wounded man.

"Father, they are coming," Rock warned, staring wildly around, realizing that the National Guard troops had them completely surrounded. For the first time, doubt crept into his voice.

Orrin fired again and again, until the hammer of his rifle clicked on an empty chamber. Automatically reaching for a clip, his hand encountered nothing hanging from his belt. "I'm out," he announced, surprised. He looked lost, with the certainty of a loaded gun gone.

"We were wrong," Porter repeated, DuPris' words ringing and echoing in his head, dimming even the sounds of screams and explosions all around him.

"No." Brother Smith surged to his feet, the demon voices inside his head howling defiance as he raised his arms. "No! Do not lose faith! You will not fall into the hands of the agents of the destroyer. The Lord will come to his New Jerusalem, and the infidels will burn as stubble! Wait in paradise for the glorious resurrection!" He brought his hands down, then the right one swept out in a graceful arc, punctuated by three sharp jerks as he pulled the trigger on his own pistol.

Rock went down first, the bullet that hit him freezing the doubt in his blue eyes. The next ripped through Orrin, who went to his knees, then rolled to the broken pavement. Porter watched the gun turn on him, too fast to dodge, and felt the last shot burrow into his breastbone, completing the ruin of his broken heart.

Tears flowed down Brother Smith's face as he turned to face the National Guardsman who rose from behind the smoldering remains of the truck. He smiled. "Behold, we are the two prophets who give our lives as testament to His truth. Our bodies will lie in these streets for three days, before we rise again to glorious triumph!" With that, he shot DuPris, stilling the labored breathing, then pointed the pistol to this own head and pulled the trigger. He fell, still straight, to lie full-length beside the fallen Area Authority. The heavy transports rumbled past a few minutes later in pursuit of the retreating Mormons, their passage covering the still forms with smoke and dust.

* * *

Dust rose from the back roads in a long, hazy trail, illuminated white from many headlights. Inside the dust cloud, a line of motley vehicles rolled forward—"like a wagon train on steroids," in Jelisaveta Sarkesian's words. The Newsteads' sedan, packed to the roof with supplies and children whose mothers had, in defiance of their husbands' orders, begged the bishop to take away. Similar refugees rode in nearly every car or truck in the train, along with the owners' families and as many necessities as fit between the live bodies. Far behind them, explosions rumbled, the first distant thunder of a storm that would sweep the entire earth.

Lucrezia, lying flat atop a pad of blankets covering the stack of boxes that reached nearly to the van's ceiling, looked beyond the middle seat and between Carmen's and Tony's shoulders at the thin wedge of windshield she could see. Headlights reflected from ghostly swirls of dust and the back of the Shaws' van in front of them. If she could have turned enough to see out the back window, she would have seen another set of headlights, and beyond that one more; they'd taken a place nearly at the tail of the automotive snake. She'd begged to be allowed to drive another of the cars in the convoy, but her argument that state laws shouldn't apply to them anymore because they'd obviously become outlaws hadn't convinced Carmen. Thus, she'd wiggled into the high perch, overlooking Gianni and four other children, envying Donna's driver's license and place as a driver in the Newsteads' second car. Carmen had told her it would be too dangerous to let her drive, because they might have to resort to evasive maneuvers, but so far, the hour-long trip had been boring, steady, and slightly nauseating, progress over country but mostly paved back roads. Bishop Newstead chose these even though it would take longer to get to Nauvoo, because they wanted to avoid attracting attention.

The only dangerous bit had been the mile or so that Brother Smith had said they'd strewn with land mines—and that had gone by without incident. Though the battered police car lying on its side halfway up a tree was eloquent testimony to the mines' reality, no explosions interrupted their progress. Carmen said it was a miracle, because they had to have rolled right over several of them—and, for once, Tony hadn't argued that credit for their escape should go to Bishop Newstead's cautious guidance.

With a sigh, Lucrezia closed her eyes. Who would've thought that a dramatic escape would be so boring? A shudder replaced the sigh, as she thought of the women and children who hadn't come, who were waiting back in the broken neighborhood for their husbands and fathers to come back. Porter didn't have anybody waiting for him. That thought produced a hard knot in her throat. *Oh, please, Heavenly Father, make sure Porter's safe.*

The jingle of her phone startled her out of her fervent prayer. Contorting to reach her backpack without being able to bend correctly, she hit her head on the side of the van. Rubbing the bump, she answered, "Hello, Lucrezia here."

"Lucrezia." The word came through faintly, a whisper in a cloud of what she thought was sunspot static—before a distant boom obliterated the messy background noise.

"Porter!" she exclaimed. "Porter, where are you? Are you all right?"

"They're coming." His voice grew stronger, but it sounded bubbly. "They're coming after you—to kill you all. Run fast."

"Are you hurt?" she barely registered his words, concentrating so hard on his painful breaths.

"Lucrezia . . . he knew. He said we were wrong. We were. I'm sorry," he said, then coughed horribly. His voice cleared again. "I think I loved you."

"Loved me? No, you love me, Porter!" she exclaimed.

Another voice came through the distant roar of the mopping-up operation. "Hey! Looks like this one's still alive. Better shoot the—" A gunshot obliterated the last filthy word.

"No!" Lucrezia shrieked.

Tony started, the van lurching as he whirled in his seat to look back into the depths. Gianni and another baby started crying. Carmen tried to move, but couldn't reach her daughter. She muttered her disapproval, then, over their wails, called, "Lucrezia—what's wrong, honey?"

"Porter," Lucrezia began, then had to stop to collect herself. He'd called, he'd used the last words he ever said, to warn them. "Mom, Porter called—they're coming after us. I think he meant the National Guard, not just the Millennium Brotherhood. He said they were going to kill us." Her voice broke, but she forced out the words. "And then they shot him."

Carmen closed her eyes tight, sick at the thought. "Lucrezia, can you call Bishop Newstead and let him know?"

Lucrezia swallowed again, calling the bishop's car at the front of the column. She relayed the message. Far behind them, the initial pursuit slowed as explosions roared out of the country road. The mines that hadn't gone off when the heavily loaded family wagons rolled over them exploded violently under the treads of the National Guard vehicles. The explosions didn't stop the pursuit, however. Three lightly armed vehicles with their determined and angry crews had gotten through. After reconnaissance specialists realized that the Mormons were heading for Nauvoo, they relayed a message to the three assault vehicles with instructions to eliminate the Mormon lead with all due speed.

"I'm sorry I ever thought this was boring," Lucrezia said aloud, jouncing painfully between the boxes and roof as Tony and the rest of the column shifted into high gear, overloaded engines whining.

Bishop Newstead, realizing that speed, with a healthy dose of divine intervention, was the only thing that could save them now, led the wagon train onto the nearest highway. The shock-punishing bounces stopped, and the race for Nauvoo began.

* * *

From the overhead view of Channel 8's news helicopter, the entire event looked like a caterpillar race in slow motion. The motley-colored Mormon caravan still held a good lead, but the line of khaki military vehicles nudged ever closer. Nauvoo, grown from small-town to small-city with the tide of Church members who had moved in over the years, lay over a slow rise. The helicopter's cameras showed lights glowing invitingly from the city itself, and from the tent and camper community that had sprung up around it. In the center of the lights, the pale, pearlescent walls of the Nauvoo temple shone faintly but fully in the distance, its light refracted slightly through the sprinkle of rain that had begun.

"But the temple's walls are the only walls in sight," Anne O'Neal noted, watching the TV screen from her seat in the Channel 8 news van, which Leon drove in the wake of the National Guard convoy. "They won't offer much protection for the refugees from Lake Creek—or the other Mormon communities around the state, when the word about what happened here gets around."

"Try none at all," Leon corrected.

Anne tried to sort out her own feelings, as the feed from Monk poured through the connection, giving minute-by-minute updates on all official statements about the disaster in Lake Creek. "It's bad enough that Governor Kerr's ordered the National Guard to apprehend every Mormon in Illinois—and now we're getting reports that he's authorized them to shoot any Mormon on sight, whether or not they offer any resistance."

She swallowed hard, remembering the carnage the Guard left behind in Lake Creek—bloody death that Monk was even now receiving orders to spin into Mormon murders. Bad as the bodies had been, the shell-shocked faces of the women and children taken into custody as prisoners of war were worse. *At least they hadn't been shot,* she thought, but it was cold comfort. In the replay coming over her headphones, the governor didn't quite deny giving the annihilation order, but didn't quite disown it either. Monk's instructions flowed across her prompter screen, telling her the official Channel 8 slant on the story, that their viewers were seeing the last stand of a criminal cult whose violent actions had finally pulled off the Church's benign mask, and he wanted an on-air response from her. She plugged her microphone into the van's system while watching the words and visual lineup for the screen, noting that the running banner ads came from Tommy Gibbs's salvation ministry organization. She thought about her own career, the truth, President Rojas, and the bewildered little girl who cried for her daddy while a soldier threw her into a prison van.

Taking a deep breath, she keyed her own response in to the prompter board, sending instructions directly to Kim, Monk's production assistant, telling her she had breaking news and sending the recording to play when Anne signaled her. When Anne got the signal she began, "This is Anne O'Neal, Channel 8 News traveling with the National Guard. I'm sorry we can't get a picture to you now, but we are on the move. Some feel events in Lake Creek reveal the real character of the Church of Jesus Christ. However, the leaders of the Church have issued a statement over a secured transmission to all its members. Channel 8 has obtained a copy of this broadcast from a confidential source." On her cue, Kim projected President Smith's calm face onto the screens of millions of TVs, issuing his message of hope and peace. Fox, Anne's anonymous source, had sent the recording to her at President Nabil's direction—using the power of the ever-present media to get the word to the members who may have missed the broadcast.

As President Smith's message ended, Anne continued, "This official statement gives some evidence of the danger of making judgments about all because of the actions of a few. And, as we watch this drama unfold, it may be wise to remember that the darkest hours in America's history came when our government, in the name of homeland security, disregarded basic civil rights. Live from between Lake Creek and Nauvoo, Illinois, this is Anne O'Neal for Channel 8 News."

Monk, who had lurched nearly out of his chair in surprise when the reclusive Church President's speech began, slowly settled back down as he watched the ratings numbers rise, spike—and hold steady. As much as the general public disliked Mormons, in large part because Channel 8's board wanted them to, most of them were also deeply suspicious of Senator Garlick. "All right, Annie—you pulled a fast one on me, and I'll let it go this time, because it worked. But if you do it again, you'll wish you were only fired."

"What are you going to do? Send me into a war zone?" she muttered, turning off her microphone.

"You keep covering the Mormons with more sympathy than sense, that's where you'll end up," Leon told her, without a trace of his usual twinkle.

"I think that's where we're all going to end up," Anne answered, staring at the transmission from the helicopter's cameras. "Unless we can find somewhere safe."

"Looks like they're the ones who need somewhere safe," Leon said nodding toward the Mormon caravan. In spite of his warning to Anne, a trace of sympathy crept into his own voice as he watched the light military transports bearing down on the fleeing line of almost humorously domestic vehicles.

"I don't think they'll get it," Anne said, her eyes wide as she flicked on the update from Channel 8's military-communications scanners. "Look at this."

"Those poor—" The words on Leon's lips died away as he read the orders scrolling across the screen. Under the governor's orders, another column of National Guard troops had deployed, moving to intercept the Mormon refugees from Lake Creek, easily able to overtake the small column before it reached Nauvoo. The original troops' orders didn't tell them to catch the civilian convoy; they were simply to keep the pressure on the Mormons by closing up the lead to push them into wide-open territory where the larger, more heavily armed contingent could sweep them up easily. "Hounds to the hunters," he said shaking his head.

"Come on!" Anne thumped the dashboard suddenly. "Leon, get around these guys! Don't you realize that the second unit is coming in from the Mormons' front?"

"Do *you* realize that they're coming that way?" Leon stared at her, but gunned the engine as the excitement of the chase hit him. Within moments, he sent the sturdy news vehicle careening off on a side road that cut across the fields. The voices of the commanders of the National Guard units crackled through the cab, as Anne turned the radio to pick up the signal. Crisp military code bounced back and forth, as the ambushing troops sped forward, drawing ever nearer to Nauvoo, preparing to catch the prey their fellows were driving toward them. Two more voices joined the conversation, helicopter pilots reporting successful takeoff from their base despite rising winds and heavy rain.

"Vipers," Leon said, easily picking out the call signals for the heavy gunships amid the rest of the military jargon. "Governor Kerr is serious about this one."

"That looks pretty serious too," Anne observed, holding on to the seat belt with both hands as their wild cross-country scramble finally brought them out of the trees. Nauvoo spread in front of them, well-tended farmland and rolling hills, with the town itself looking innocuous in the center. Above the rural scene, however, a bank of black, swirling clouds towered, walking on legs of lightning toward them. A roar of thunder reached their ears, distant through the heavy air—but frighteningly close through the radio. The echoed explosions fuzzed in a wave of static that almost drowned the suddenly urgent calls from the National Guard officers.

"What did they say?" Anne leaned close to the radio. "What's happening?"

Miles away, the National Guard troops asked themselves the same question, as the sky opened above them. Torrential rain pelted down, blinding their drivers and drowning the roads. Shafts of lightning illuminated the curtains of rain, which veered in horizontal sheets from one compass point to another as gusts of wind shook even the heaviest vehicles. Then, with a noise like a rockslide in a gravel pit, the hail began. Chunks of dirty ice the size of baseballs pelted out of the sky, breaking windshields and denting hoods. The column rumbled to a halt, lightning striking so close that the almond odor of ozone permeated the personnel carriers.

Above and behind the ground troops, the Viper pilots fought with their balky machines as the helicopters swung and struggled against the arms the storm reached out toward them. After one particularly strong gust nearly flipped the leader over, the pilots veered away, reporting the conditions—and their reluctance to continue in the face of what one of the pilots called, accurately, a kamikaze storm.

Furious, the colonel leading the ambush roared revised orders and pungent curses through the curtains of static clouding the radio transmissions.

"It sounds like they're standing down," Leon said, staring at the violence of the distant storm. "Looks like the weathermen bought your Mormons some time."

"Maybe," Anne said tensely, as the colonel ordered the pursuers to move at full speed and to open fire as soon as the Mormons came in range. "Oh, go faster," she whispered, staring away from the storm toward the small column of civilian vehicles, her hands white-knuckled where they still clutched the seat belt across her chest. It never occurred to her to wonder why she thought they would be safe if they could only make it to town.

* * *

As Bishop Newstead's car, its engine howling with effort, reached the turnoff into Nauvoo, they at last came within firing range of the National Guard. The armed vehicles spread onto both lanes of the road behind the refugees, weapons at ready. Crisply acknowledging orders, the lead vehicle opened fire on the end of the Mormon column with its light machine gun.

Lucrezia yipped as a couple of bullets starred the back window, burrowing deep into the boxes of food storage beneath her. Gianni yipped too, and Carmen gasped a prayer. Tony swung the van around the corner as fast as he dared, checking his mirror and unnecessarily telling the drivers of the two cars behind him to hurry. A few seconds later, the smell of pineapple pervaded the van—and, as they reached the outskirts of Nauvoo so did a swelling tide of absolute peace, as if each passenger was suddenly enveloped in a tender, protective embrace.

Not three minutes behind the last car, the lead National Guard armored personnel carrier rounded the corner and rumbled across an invisible line, only to slam to a screeching halt, half blocking the road. The other transports screeched and groaned to a halt also. Inside the vehicles, the soldiers gasped and cried, as their consciences seared their sins into their hearts and minds. Recoiling from the molten onslaught of an unendurable spiritual heat, they turned their vehicles in a quick retreat from Nauvoo, as the protective power of the Prince of Peace descended like a gentle rain over the faithful disciples gathered to His temples and holy places in every corner of the world.

* * *

Dear Chisom,

I can hardly contain my joy! Prophecy has again been fulfilled, and it happened just as John said it would. In Revelation, he looked into the future and saw "a Lamb" that "stood on the mount Sion and with him an hundred forty and four thousand." A Lamb, the Lamb in fact, has now come to Zion, and His glory shines upon His people. The Saints can be, at last, secure. How we have prayed for this time! Now we can enjoy its fruits. The Lord, in Doctrine and Covenants 45, told Joseph Smith that the New Jerusalem would be "a land of peace, a city of refuge, a place of safety for the saints." He went on to say that "the glory of the Lord shall be there, and the terror of the Lord shall also be there, insomuch that the wicked will not come unto it." The Lord has now brought again Zion, but not just here. As he told Joseph Smith in D&C 115, "the gathering together upon the land of Zion, and upon her stakes, [would] be for a defense, and for a refuge from the storm, and from wrath when it shall be poured out without mixture upon the whole earth." That has indeed happened. The glory of God has not only settled upon us here but also in the west and upon the temple communities throughout the world. According to the news, it has created quite a stir. Our enemies stand in fear and other people in consternation. Speculation of what has happened and what it means runs high. It will be interesting to watch how hard those of the world will work to explain it away.

Our faith, my son, has been vindicated. It has been hard, and some have suffered horribly. John accurately described the necessary prelude to this time. "Here is the patience of the saints," he said, "here are they that keep the commandments of God, and the faith of Jesus" (Rev. 14:12). The period of patience gave us time to really express our trust in the Lord by exercising restraint, turning the other cheek, and not giving railing for railing. By doing these things, we demonstrated our faith that God, not the arm of flesh, would be our Savior. As a result, the Lord can now fully bless us for we have proved ourselves. Thus, we can receive His blessed protection. Evil can now move unhindered toward its self-destruction but without taking us with it.

This period also gave the world time to make up its mind. Some have wondered why the Lord waited so long before sending His glory, but the leaders of the earth had to be given a chance to choose God or Babylon. By persecuting the Saints and forcing them out, the world made its irrevocable decision. Now, and only now, can righteous judgment move against it.

Sadly, though the Saints are secure, there are yet many good people—Christians, Jews, Muslims, and others—who are not. They have not contributed to nor do they deserve to suffer the ravages that are upon the world. These we must gather. We will also need to prepare places to receive them. Even as President Smith issues the call for all missionaries to come home, he is organizing a new missionary force—the 144,000 mentioned by John in Revelation. These missionaries will gather out the honest in heart. The rest of us will prepare places to receive them. Empowered as none before and under divine protection for the most part, our missionaries will make one more circle of the earth. Then the end will come.

Between now and then, Satan will unleash his full fury spreading blood and terror into every land. You can bet because he can no longer get to the Church, he will bend his fury on those pockets of good souls who will oppose him. The race is on to see how many we can save before

Satan succeeds in destroying the world. Know this, my son, Armageddon is not far away. Neither is the great moment of cleansing. Then, at last, the earth can rest. I pray for the day.

I rejoice that you are safe with the Chinese Saints where you can continue the work for a bit longer until you come home. Keep us informed and I will do the same,

    With love,
    Your father,
    Chinedu

ABOUT THE AUTHORS

JESSICA DRAPER is unaccustomed to writing about herself in the third person. She is also an avid reader, big sister, trained librarian, amateur needleworker, cat owner, and possessor of a rich fantasy life (obviously). She currently works at the Center for Instructional Design at Brigham Young University, after spending many years writing software documentation (which often qualifies as speculative fiction).

RICHARD D. DRAPER is a professor of ancient scripture at BYU and the director of the Religious Studies Center. He holds a PhD in ancient history. Brother Draper is a best-selling author of several books and talk tapes, and has written numerous articles for the *Ensign* and other publications. He has been a popular lecturer at Know Your Religion and Education Week for many years.

Richard and his wife, Barbara, are the parents of six children and reside in Lindon, Utah. Outside of the fact that he is the only one in his family who dislikes cats, Richard's kids think he's all right.